THE KINGDOM
OF THE
EAST ANGLES

The Complete Series

JAYNE
CASTEL

WINTER MIST
P R E S S

Historical Romances by Jayne Castel

DARK AGES BRITAIN

The Kingdom of the East Angles series
Night Shadows (prequel novella)
Dark Under the Cover of Night (Book One)
Nightfall till Daybreak (Book Two)
The Deepening Night (Book Three)
The Kingdom of the East Angles: The Complete Series

The Kingdom of Mercia series
The Breaking Dawn (Book One)
Darkest before Dawn (Book Two)
Dawn of Wolves (Book Three)
The Kingdom of Mercia: The Complete Series

The Kingdom of Northumbria series
The Whispering Wind (Book One)
Wind Song (Book Two)
Lord of the North Wind (Book Three)
The Kingdom of Northumbria: The Complete Series

DARK AGES SCOTLAND

The Warrior Brothers of Skye series
Blood Feud (Book One)
Barbarian Slave (Book Two)
Battle Eagle (Book Three)
The Warrior Brothers of Skye: The Complete Series

The Pict Wars series
Warrior's Heart (Book One)
Warrior's Secret (Book Two)
Warrior's Wrath (Book Three)
The Pict Wars: The Complete Series

Novellas
Winter's Promise

MEDIEVAL SCOTLAND

The Brides of Skye series
The Beast's Bride (Book One)
The Outlaw's Bride (Book Two)

The Rogue's Bride (Book Three)
The Brides of Skye: The Complete Series

The Sisters of Kilbride series
Unforgotten (Book One)
Awoken (Book Two)
Fallen (Book Three)
Claimed (Epilogue novella)

The Immortal Highland Centurions series
Maximus (Book One)
Cassian (Book Two)
Draco (Book Three)
The Laird's Return (Epilogue festive novella)

Stolen Highland Hearts series
Highlander Deceived (Book One)
Highlander Entangled (Book Two)
Highlander Forbidden (Book Three)

Epic Fantasy Romances by Jayne Castel

Light and Darkness series
Ruled by Shadows (Book One)
The Lost Swallow (Book Two)
Path of the Dark (Book Three)
Light and Darkness: The Complete Series

Visit Jayne's website and blog: **www.jaynecastel.com**

***

For lovers of history – may you enjoy your trip into a forgotten past.

***

Contents

Dark Under the Cover of Night

BOOK ONE
THE KINGDOM OF THE EAST ANGLES

Jayne Castel

Historical Note

Although *Dark Under the Cover of Night* is a work of fiction, the historical figure, King Raedwald of the East Angles, did exist. We have few details about Raedwald's life, but he is thought to have ruled from 593 AD to approximately 625 AD Many historians also believe that Raedwald was the king buried in the famous Sutton Hoo burial. Sutton Hoo sits on the bank of the River Deben near Woodbridge, Suffolk; a Saxon long ship filled with treasures, including the famous Sutton Hoo warrior helmet. Using Raedwald and his family as inspiration, I created a story based around his daughter, Raedwyn. Despite that some historical figures used in the story are based on real figures, and some actual historical events are mentioned, this tale is entirely a work of fiction. I have also used two pieces of famous Anglo-Saxon poetry, written in old English; an excerpt from *The Wanderer* and an excerpt from *Beowulf*. I have used a few words of old English throughout the story, and have provided translations where necessary.

Jayne Castel, August 2012

Hwær cwom mearg? Hwær cwom mago?
Hwær cwom maþþumgyfa?
Hwær cwom symbla gesetu?
Hwær sindon seledreamas?
Eafa beorht bune!
Eafa byrnwiga!
Eafa þeodnes þrym!
Hu seo þrag gewat,
genap under nihthelm,
swa heo no wære.

Where is the horse gone? Where the rider?
Where the giver of treasure?
Where are the seats at the feast?
Where are the revels in the hall?
Alas for the bright cup!
Alas for the mailed warrior!
Alas for the splendour of the prince!
How that time has passed away,
dark under the cover of night,
as if it had never been.

Excerpt from 'The Wanderer'
Translated from Old English

Prologue

Rendlaesham – Kingdom of the East Angles, Britannia

608 AD

"COME, WUFFA. COME!"

The child's voice echoed out across the stableyard. The object of her attention—a tiny puppy with floppy ears, a soft brown coat and mischievous eyes—glanced back at his mistress. Then, willfully ignoring her, he put his head down and barreled towards the gates.

"Wuffa!" The little girl raced down the steps leading from her father's hall and tore across the wide expanse after her puppy. Her blonde curls flew out behind her as she ran, dodging men and horses, over hard-packed earth and through the gates that led out into Rendlaesham. Ahead, she caught sight of a scrap of brown heading straight towards the rear town gates.

"Wuffa, no. Bad puppy—come back here."

The girl picked up her skirts and dashed after her birthday gift. Ahead, the town gates loomed. It was nearing dusk and the gates were still open, allowing in folk returning from the orchards and fields behind the Great Hall. Her parents would be annoyed if she left the confines of the town without an adult present, but the fear of losing Wuffa was greater than that of a growling from her father.

She ran across the wide road that circuited the town walls, and into the apple orchard. The orchard was vast; a wide swath of leafy trees that covered one side of the shallow valley behind Rendlaesham.

Close to tears, for she could no longer see her quarry, the girl called out as she wandered down the narrow lanes between the trees.

"Wuffa, where are you? Wuffa, please come here. Wuffa!"

Eventually, distraught and frightened, the girl began to cry. Wuffa had only been hers a day, but she already loved him so. The thought that she had lost him made the little girl's heart feel as if it were breaking.

"Are you looking for this?"

A boy, a few years older than her, stepped out from behind an apple tree. He was thin and sharp-featured with a mop of dark hair that flopped over his eyes. In one hand, he held an apple with a bite out of it, and in the other, he held her precious puppy.

"Yes!" The girl rushed forward and the boy released Wuffa into her arms. The puppy eagerly licked her tear-streaked face and wriggled excitedly. He liked this game.

"Naughty, naughty Wuffa!" she chastised him as he wriggled into her neck.

"Thank you." She looked across at the boy, who had taken a bite of his apple and was watching her thoughtfully. "He was my birthday present."

"You called him Wuffa?" The boy took another bite of his apple. "Doesn't look much like a wolf to me."

"He will be." The girl lifted her chin haughtily. "When he is grown, he will be ferocious!"

"So today's your birthday," the boy replied with a shrug. "How old are you?"

"I'm four," she announced proudly, her cheeks coloring when he laughed.

"Four! You're a baby. I'm much older than you, I'm nine. I'm Caelin by the way, and you must be Raedwyn."

"How do you know my name?" The girl wiped away any remaining tears with the back of her arm and struggled to keep ahold of Wuffa, who was now trying to wriggle out of her grasp.

"I've seen you about—the king only has one daughter," Caelin replied, watching with amusement as Raedwyn tried to keep hold of her puppy. "If you're not careful you're going to lose him again. Here, I'll hold Wuffa for a while." Caelin threw aside the half-eaten apple and relieved Raedwyn of the wriggling pup. "Come on, I'll take you back to the Great Hall. Your parents will be wondering where you've gone."

"I'm not allowed to stray from the town," Raedwyn informed her new friend, falling in step beside him. "Mōder says I'm too little."

"You are," the boy replied with the air of knowledge that only children possess. "I told you, you're a baby."

"I'm not a baby!" Raedwyn drew herself up, her tiny hands balling into fists. "I'll tell my brothers you said that!"

Caelin laughed at that. "And they'll agree with me. Come now, hurry up a bit. They'll be closing the gates soon."

The two children slipped inside the town gates and made their way along the dusty street that led up to the Great Hall. Dusk was settling over the town and amber streaked the pale sky. It had been a hot day, one of the most beautiful of the summer.

Caelin and Raedwyn entered the stableyard and stopped in their tracks as a tall, handsome man with a mane of golden hair and dark blue eyes strode towards them.

"Raedwyn!" he boomed. "Where have you been?"

"I'm sorry, fæder." Raedwyn rushed forward. "Wuffa ran off and I had to find him. Caelin helped me."

"Did he?" Raedwald, King of the East Angles, scooped his daughter up into his arms and looked down at the boy holding Raedwyn's birthday gift. "Well done Caelin. You're Ceolwulf's boy are you not?"

Caelin nodded, seemingly struck mute in front of his king.

"I thank you for bringing Raedwyn back safely." The king's gaze settled on the puppy in Caelin's arms. "And for rescuing the dog—although I can see I'm going to regret my choice of gift."

"Don't take Wuffa away from me, fæder," Raedwyn squealed, wriggling free of the king's embrace and gently taking the puppy from Caelin. "I promise I won't let him run away again, I promise!"

King Raedwald sighed and smiled down at his young daughter.

"No one is going to take Wuffa away from you my love," he rumbled. "Run along now and see your mother."

Raedwyn clutched her precious puppy to her flat chest and, with a darting glance of thanks to Caelin, took off up the steps towards the Great Hall. Raedwald watched her go before turning back to the boy before him and grinning.

"Only four years old and already able to twist men around her little finger," he observed dryly. "You wait till she grows up."

When Caelin merely stared back at him, uncomprehending, the king shook his head.

"Never mind." He reached down and ruffled the boy's hair. "You'll understand one day. Now off you go, back to your father's hall before he tans your backside for idling!"

Chapter One

Rendlaesham – Kingdom of the East Angles, Britannia

624 AD

THE DRAGON'S HEAD broke through the rolling banks of mist and glided towards the riverbank. A sleek long ship followed in its wake. Silent, despite its great bulk, the Saxon ship emerged from curling tendrils of mist that moved like caressing fingers over its curved bow.

Raedwyn stood next to her mother, on a hill above the river, and watched the long ship approach. Despite that she had been looking forward to this day, nervousness tugged at the pit of Raedwyn's stomach and she glanced sideways at her mother. Sensing her daughter's unease, Queen Seaxwyn reached across and squeezed Raedwyn's hand. Neither of them spoke as they continued to watch the long ship dock.

On the shores of the River Deben, Raedwyn's father, Raedwald, King of the East Angles, stood with his son, Eorpwald, waiting to welcome Cynric the Bold. Nine winters younger than his king, Cynric was one of Raedwald's most trusted ealdormen—one of noble blood. Cynric the Bold would soon become a member of the illustrious Wuffinga Dynasty, for tomorrow at noon he and Princess Raedwyn would wed.

King Raedwald had just passed his fifty-fourth winter but still stood tall and muscular, although silver now threaded his thick, golden hair and his strong face was lined with care and grief. Raedwald had never recovered from the loss of his son, Raegenhere, eight years earlier. Eorpwald, quiet and diffident in comparison to his charismatic older brother, was a poor substitute for Raegenhere.

The gentle splash of oars broke the stillness as the newcomers maneuvered their craft towards the water's edge. Raedwyn's gaze fastened on the group of men on-board, searching for Cynric. Despite the twenty-five years age difference, she had heard the ealdorman was still a striking warrior to behold.

The long ship came to rest in the deep mud at the riverbank and a group of men disembarked. As they heaved the ship closer to the bank through knee-deep mud, Raedwyn caught sight of Cynric at last. He was a big, broad-shouldered man and was dressed more richly than his companions. Gold rings sparkled across his chest and his arms were heavy with silver bracelets and arm rings—all tributes to his heroism in battle. A thick fur cloak hung from his shoulders. Raedwyn was too far away to pick out the details of his face but she could see he had a short blond beard and thick sandy hair flecked through with gray. Raedwyn felt a thrill of excitement. She had hoped he would be handsome.

Satisfied his long ship would not be washed away by the incoming tide, Cynric turned and climbed the river bank. He raised a hand to salute his king when he caught sight of Raedwald awaiting him. Cynric pulled himself out of the mud, strode towards Raedwald, and king and ealdorman clasped each other in a bear hug. Raedwyn could hear them laughing and talking together. She glanced across at her mother and beamed, squeezing Seaxwyn's hand tightly, her earlier trepidation forgotten. Seeing her daughter's obvious excitement, the queen smiled gently back.

The morning was dank and sunless but the mist cast an ethereal beauty over the land. Raedwyn turned from admiring her betrothed and cast her gaze over the mounds of earth behind her. She stood before a row of enormous barrows—burial mounds. Raedwald's forebears were entombed here, as Raedwald himself would be one day. It was a sacred place for her kin but nonetheless the towering barrows made Raedwyn feel uneasy.

A pair of ravens suddenly wheeled through the mist towards the mounds and landed atop one of the barrows with a loud screech. Woden's messengers were afoot. Woden, the father of the gods, had two ravens, Hugin and Munin; one representing thought, and the other memory. The ravens sat on Woden's shoulders and whispered in his ears about the events they saw in their daily flights over the earth. Raedwyn cast a jaundiced eye over the birds before dismissing them.

This morning, nothing could dampen her spirits.

Mother and daughter walked back to where the servants stood with their horses. The men would join them shortly and then they would begin the long ride back to Rendlaesham. The late summer air was sultry, despite the encircling mist. Raedwyn mounted her shaggy bay mare and arranged her long skirts. Glad of the mild weather, she had shrugged off her cloak. She hoped that Cynric would like the forest-green dress she wore. The dress was made of heavy linen, girdled below the bodice and with a wide, embroidered neckline that showed off her neck and shoulders, leaving her arms bare. Raedwyn, although she had her father's coloring, had her mother's build. Queen Seaxwyn was tall with a swelling bosom and rounded rear, both accentuated by a small waist. Over the years, her mother's curves had spread to plumpness but she was still a stunning woman with a thick mane of auburn hair only lightly touched with white, and quick gray eyes.

Male voices carried through the fog and gradually became louder as the king and his companions rode up the incline towards them. Raedwyn's stomach fluttered once more, this time in excitement. She pushed back her long, blonde curls off her shoulders and wished she had not forgotten her comb.

Then her father and brother appeared, followed by Cynric and a knot of horsemen. Raedwyn's gaze fastened on Cynric. The warrior stared back, before his gaze slid down her body and back up to her face. Finding her shape to his liking, Cynric smiled, revealing good teeth for a man his age.

"Cynric, may I present my daughter, Lady Raedwyn." Raedwald made the introductions. The king's voice was hearty, but knowing her father as she did, Raedwyn saw the hint of sadness in his face.

Cynric swung down from his horse and strode across to Raedwyn. Then, taking her hand, he kissed it. "My Lady ..."

"My Lord," Raedwyn replied demurely, even as her heart hammered against her ribcage. He had the bluest eyes she had ever seen.

Cynric released her hand and turned to Raedwald. "My Lord, I will need to leave some men behind to guard the ship. Can you spare four spears?"

The king nodded. "Coenred, Aldfrid, Oswyn and Yffi will stay with your men."

The four warriors Raedwald had nominated reined their horses back and retreated to where the long ship was docked.

"We must make haste." Cynric strode back to his horse. "If we are to make Rendlaesham by this eve—I am eager to wed this fine Anglian beauty!"

The men guffawed loudly at this and Raedwyn blushed. Cynric mounted his horse and winked at her.

"There will be plenty of time to woo my daughter Cynric," King Raedwald grumbled, spurring his horse forward. "Let us ride now."

They rode northwest, across soft folds of feathery heathland, interspersed with clumps of bracken and brambles. Gradually the heath gave way to woodland and, finally, they rode through open terrain interspersed by clumps of coppicing oaks and thickets of lime wood. A crisp wind blew in, chasing away the mist. The sun was dipping beyond the flat western horizon when they reached Rendlaesham at last.

Raedwyn caught sight of the high roof of the king's Great Hall and felt an unexpected pang of sadness. The high-gabled timbered hall towered above the low thatched huts spreading out from the center of the settlement. Her father's hall had been the only home she had ever known and in a day's time, she would be leaving it. Cynric lived far to the south and she doubted they would make many trips here—especially once they had begun a family. Raedwyn chided herself for her sudden melancholy and urged her horse on, through the tangle of timber dwellings and along the winding dirt road that led up to the King's Hall. Crowds of townsfolk gathered at the roadside to welcome them. Everyone was in high spirits, for there was to be a wedding tomorrow. A day when ealdormen, thegns, ceorls and slaves—the four classes under the king—all took a day of rest and made merry.

Travel-weary and hungry, Raedwyn rode past the gatehouse and up the final incline. There, before her, rose Raedwald's Great Hall. Many throughout Britannia knew it as the 'Golden Hall', for its roof was straw thatch, making it appear gilded when seen from far off. Raedwyn dismounted her horse and followed the men up the steps and through the entrance.

The interior of Raedwald's hall was a lofty space and a great hearth burned in its center. A boar roasted on a spit and the mouth-watering aroma permeated the whole hall. Richly woven tapestries and fine furs hung from the walls. Once inside, Raedwyn left the men to down their first cups of mead for the evening while she went to her bower to prepare herself for the evening's feast. Raedwyn's bower nestled in an alcove behind one of the wall hangings. She felt Cynric's eyes on her as she ducked behind it into her small, but private, space.

Raedwyn sighed with pleasure upon seeing a large clay bowl of steaming water awaiting her. Behind her, a young woman dressed in a long brown sleeveless shift belted at the waist, drew back the hanging and stepped inside the bower.

"He's so handsome," the girl whispered as she began unlacing Raedwyn's gown at the back, "even if he is old enough to be your father!"

"Eanfled!" Raedwyn gave her friend a look of mock outrage. "Age matters not in love!"

Eanfled snorted at that but made no response. Raedwyn turned round and let her maid finish undoing her laces. Eanfled was right of course; the age gap between her and Cynric was considerable. However, the king had chosen Cynric the Bold especially for Raedwyn—the ealdorman's honor and valor would make him a worthy husband.

"He certainly does not look like an old man," Raedwyn reminded Eanfled, "and the other servants say that older men make the best husbands!"

Eanfled giggled. "You shouldn't listen to those crones Raedwyn—it's long time since any of them had a man."

"Stop it!" Raedwyn laughed. "Not all of us have your good fortune." She turned to Eanfled then and gave her a wicked look.

"Not all of us are about to marry Alric the Smith."

Eanfled blushed at that. She and Alric's handfast ceremony was in two days—after nearly a year's betrothal. Raedwyn was happy for her maid, and only wished she could attend. However, tomorrow she would leave Rendlaesham and journey south with her new husband.

Raedwyn shrugged off her gown and stepped out of it. Eager to set eyes upon her betrothed again, she washed quickly while Eanfled hung up the dress and retrieved the one that Raedwyn had chosen for this evening; a flowing white dress with a gold embroidered neck and hemline that left her arms bare.

Eanfled helped her into the dress and sighed at the sight of Raedwyn wearing it.

"You look lovely," she breathed. "I feel like such a drab in comparison."

Raedwyn raised an eyebrow and cast her gaze over Eanfled. Even in her simple attire, Eanfled's hazel eyes, creamy skin and long pale brown hair were of a gentle beauty.

"Drab is not a word I, Alric, or anyone in Rendlaesham would use to describe you Eanfled," Raedwyn replied archly.

Eanfled blushed once more and handed Raedwyn two golden arm rings, one for each arm. "I think you should leave your hair loose tonight," she told Raedwyn. "Men love it."

Raedwyn smiled at Eanfled's knowing comment and slipped on the arm rings. The young women were of the same age and had grown up together. They were close friends more than noblewoman and servant.

"Are you excited?" Eanfled asked as she combed Raedwyn's hair. "You will be able to run your own household. I know I'm looking forward to that."

"I am," Raedwyn admitted, "and it's about time. Eni says that if I wait much longer no man will want me!"

At twenty winters, Raedwyn was ripe for handfasting. However, her late marriage was due to the whim of her father rather than lack of suitors. After Raegenhere's death—slain by her father's archenemy, Aethelfrith of Northumbria—Raedwyn had become his only solace. She was Raegenhere's female counterpart, sharing her brother's sharp wit and exuberance. Her uncle, Eni, had pressured Raedwald to find Raedwyn a husband, arguing that there were essential political and military alliances to be made.

Cynric was a good match, for he had a large portion of land to the south, near the Saxon border. Cynric was loyal to the king and an important ally. These days Raedwald did not seem to be interested in extending his kingdom or conquering his enemies. He had become withdrawn and contemplative; even Queen Seaxwyn, whom he loved deeply, had been unable to lift his depression. Only Raedwyn brought a little sunlight into his days.

"It will be a magnificent wedding tomorrow." Eanfled arranged her mistress's hair so that it fell in heavy golden curls down her back. "I cannot believe you will become a wife before me!"

"I'm sorry that I will not be here for your wedding Eanfled," Raedwyn replied. "It's not right that we cannot both wish each other well."

Eanfled made a dismissive sound but Raedwyn knew her friend had been upset to learn that Raedwyn would not be in Rendlaesham for her and Alric's handfast ceremony.

Outside her bower, Raedwyn could hear raucous laughter. The mead was flowing freely now. Taking a deep breath to still the nerves that had dulled her appetite, despite her empty stomach, Raedwyn exchanged an excited grin with Eanfled, drew back the tapestry and re-entered the hall.

Cynric spied her immediately. "Ah, there goes Raedwyn the Fair," he boomed across the hall. His face was florid from the copious mead he had drunk since his arrival. "And I am relieved to see the stories of your beauty were not exaggerated! You are a goddess."

Raedwyn, not shy by nature but not used to such bold statements, felt her face grow hot in embarrassment. Suddenly, all eyes were on her and she felt dozens of male gazes rake her, head to toe.

"Come, Raedwyn." King Raedwald beckoned his daughter over to her place near the head of the table. The king and queen sat at a table on a raised dais. Below the high seats ran two long benches. Raedwyn took a seat in-between her brother Eorpwald and her uncle Eni at the head of one of the tables. Opposite her sat Eni's eldest son, Annan, and Cynric. Raedwald's thegns and most prized warriors sat nearby, closest to the king and queen, while the younger men sat on the other side of the fire pit.

Raedwyn could feel Cynric's stare as she picked at her piece of roast boar. The hall was loud with the crackling and spit of fat in the fire pit and boisterous conversation. Smoke from the cooking tinged the air.

Raedwald was in fine form tonight. The mead had relaxed him and distracted him from the pall of melancholy that hung over him these days. He put an affectionate arm around his wife as he regaled his audience with stories of the adventures he and Eni had shared in their younger days. Raedwyn laughed with the others at the banter that flew between the two brothers. They were good men, her father and uncle, noble men.

Torches, soaked in oil, hung from the walls and their fire illuminated the handsome lines of Cynric's face and glittered off the gold and silver rings he wore on his arms. It was too bold to stare at him but Raedwyn kept her eyes averted with difficulty. She had her mother's strong-willed nature and the role of coy maiden did not sit well with her. She had grown up as the only young female in a household filled with strong, dominant men and with a father who had relished her feisty nature. However, Raedwyn understood instinctively that not all men liked strong-willed women and so she behaved demurely at the table. She nibbled daintily at the meat and bread before her and only took occasional sips of mead.

"You're quiet this eve sister." Eorpwald washed down a mouthful of bread and roast boar with mead and eyed Raedwyn. "You're not usually at a loss for words."

Raedwyn threw her brother a withering look. She and Eorpwald had never understood each other.

"I think I like this new, lady-like sister of mine," Eorpwald teased. "She's much less of a handful."

Raedwyn rolled her eyes and resisted the childish urge to stick out her tongue. "It's not long now dear brother before you shall be rid of me for good," she replied sourly.

"Then our father's hall will become a much sadder and duller place," Eorpwald replied, the teasing tone now absent from his voice.

Raedwyn gave him a sharp look, unsure whether he was still making fun, but Eorpwald was no longer looking at her. He was a small and sinewy young man with mousy hair and heavy-lidded gray eyes; a sharp contrast to the other blond, blue-eyed and physically imposing men of the Wuffinga line.

Eorpwald often irritated Raedwyn. He was observant but indirect and she found him sly compared to her beloved late brother Raegenhere. He would often look on with barely concealed amusement at Raedwyn's exuberant, pragmatic behavior, unfazed by her coolness towards him. Eorpwald's relationship with their mother and father had always bemused Raedwyn. He often appeared ill at ease in his father's hearty company, and relations between Eorpwald and the queen were distant, bordering on cold.

Seaxwyn had always treated Eorpwald like her other children and Raedwyn noticed it was he, rather than she, who was standoffish.

Raedwyn watched her enigmatic brother for a moment longer before turning her attention to her betrothed. Cynric took a gulp of mead from his bronze cup and saluted her. This time Raedwyn held his gaze and smiled back.

The Handfast ceremony took place at noon. Raedwyn stood before Cynric in her father's hall. She felt like a queen, dressed in a magnificent gown threaded through with gold and with flowers woven through her hair. This was not a Christian but an ancestral ceremony that took place on the day sacred to the Goddess Frigg, protector of marriage and childbirth. Raedwald had converted to Christianity and had worshipped at the altar of both religions simultaneously for many years, even if he was not a Christian at heart—much to Seaxwyn's joy, for the queen had always remained loyal to the old gods.

"Do you both enter into this bond with a free will?" King Raedwald's voice echoed in the silent hall. Beside him, Queen Seaxwyn looked on, intently watching her daughter's face.

Both Cynric and Raedwyn nodded their assent.

"Is there anyone present who protests at this union?" Raedwald continued.

A brief silence followed Raedwald's words before the king spoke once more. "Then make your pledges."

Cynric turned to Raedwyn and looked into her eyes. "I, Cynric, pledge to defend my Lady Raedwyn, with my life."

"And I, Raedwyn, pledge to never harm nor bring dishonor on my Lord Cynric," she replied.

Then Cynric knelt and picked up a sword sheathed in a gem-encrusted scabbard. "Take this sword, Dragon Hammer, as a token of my fidelity." He gently placed the sword in Raedwyn's hands.

Raedwyn looked down at the gift. The sword was heavy in her hands, a valuable and exquisitely crafted weapon. Now it was her turn to give him a gift.

"Take this shield as a symbol of my family's protection." She handed Cynric a great lime wood shield studded with an iron boss. He took it reverently, admiring its fine craftsmanship.

Then Cynric reached out and clasped Raedwyn's left hand in his. He had large, blunt hands; rough and coarse compared to his fine physique and handsome face. Queen Seaxwyn stepped forward and wrapped a ribbon around their joined hands.

Cynric and Raedwyn looked into each other's eyes and Raedwyn's heart pounded nervously as they spoke the next words in unison.

"May we be made one."

Seaxwyn unbound the ribbon and passed it to Raedwyn, before they shared a small cup of mead. Cynric sipped from the cup before passing it to Raedwyn. She took a sip and returned it to Cynric who drained the rest in a single draught. Then they shared a piece of honeyed seed cake. It felt oddly intimate for Raedwyn to break off a bit of cake and gently feed it to Cynric while he did the same. An ancient ritual, only the bride and groom were allowed to eat the seed cake. The seeds represented fertility and abundance while the honey symbolized harmony between the new couple. Raedwyn hoped the seed cake would indeed work its magic.

The ceremony ended with Cynric pulling Raedwyn into his arms and kissing her. It was a brief, hard kiss that crushed Raedwyn's lips against her teeth. The crowd cheered exuberantly and Raedwald stepped forward to congratulate his new son-in-law. He then enveloped Raedwyn in a bear hug.

Burying her face in her father's chest, Raedwyn felt like a little girl again. Despite her eagerness to be married, now it had happened she did not want to leave Rendlaesham and her father's protection. Raedwyn fought back tears and stepped back from the king. *You're not his little girl anymore*, she reminded herself as she gave her new husband a bright smile and took his hand in hers, *it's time I grew up.*

Well-wishers swirled around the newly wedded pair and the festivities began.

That eve, nervous despite the mead she had drunk throughout the day, Raedwyn sat on the bed in the bridal chamber, in an annex at the end of the Great Hall, and watched her new husband undress. He was a big man and broad across the shoulders. He deftly removed his clothes, not looking at Raedwyn as he did so. His chain mail vest fell to the floor, clinking like gold coins. Under it, he wore a linen tunic with a silk border and loose breeches that were cross-gartered to the knee. He removed these, still not looking in Raedwyn's direction, until he stood naked before her. He had a virile, mature body that bore the scars of many battles. A curly mat of blond hair covered his chest, and the sun had tanned his face and arms a ruddy gold. The areas of his body where the sun never touched were milk-white. He walked over to where Raedwyn sat, staring at him.

"You're a curious one aren't you?" he said. "Stand up."

Raedwyn did as ordered, only to have him pull the long, ankle length tunic she had changed into over her head in one practiced motion, revealing her nakedness.

"Very nice," Cynric murmured as he took a long look at her body. Strangely, even though he had gazed into her eyes during the Handfast ceremony, he would not look her in the eye now they were alone.

"Nice large ones." He squeezed her breasts hard, making her squeak in protest. His big hands moved down her torso, over the dip of her waist and the curve of her stomach until he gripped her bottom. "I like a girl with a bit of meat on her," he said appreciatively.

Raedwyn felt her face grow hot, as much from annoyance as embarrassment. He was making her feel like a juicy side of pork, rather than a beautiful, desired woman. Despite her irritation, she could feel a curious heat building between her legs. He was naked, big and handsome and he was standing so close she could feel the warmth of his body touching hers.

Cynric pushed Raedwyn back onto the bed and parted her legs wide, staring at what lay between them. Raedwyn saw his face was now flushed with excitement and his erection thrust up, quivering with anticipation, towards her from a nest of blonde curls. Raedwyn's mouth went dry, whether from fear or desire she could not decide.

Cynric's hand slid down her belly and dipped between her legs—the tingle of pleasure it brought made her gasp aloud. That was the only encouragement Cynric needed. With a grunt, he leant over her and kneaded her breasts like bread dough before pushing his hand between Raedwyn's thighs and rubbing so hard she cried out again, this time in pain.

Mistaking her cry for one of pleasure, he shoved her legs so far apart she felt her hip muscles cramp before he thrust his way inside her. Pain knifed through Raedwyn. The urge to scream and rake at his face to get him off her was overwhelming. With a strangled cry, she managed to stop herself and bit down on her bottom lip. Then, Cynric jerked his hips violently and drove himself deeply inside her.

Oblivious to his bride's agony, Cynric bent her legs back and started to pound into her, watching his own performance as he did so. Raedwyn gritted her teeth. He could have been bedding any woman. He had not looked at her face once since they had entered the chamber. She writhed in an attempt to escape the pain; her thigh and hip muscles were held at such an uncomfortable angle the muscles were now burning.

Fortunately, Cynric's passion did not last long. He thrust and grunted for a short while before his face screwed up in an expression more reminiscent of pain than pleasure and he let out a hoarse shout. Then he collapsed on top of Raedwyn and promptly fell into a mead-induced slumber.

Raedwyn lay on the bed, pinned under the heavy body of her new husband, and stared up at the rafters. All was quiet except for the distant barking of a dog. The rest of Raedwald's hall slept peacefully but Raedwyn knew she would not sleep tonight. A single torch burnt on the wall, casting long shadows across the bridal chamber her mother had decorated lavishly for this occasion.

Dry-eyed Raedwyn continued to stare up at the shadows playing across the timbered ceiling. So that was how it was between men and women? Would Eanfled have to endure the same agony with Alric? She had seen animals approach mating with more tenderness than she had just endured. Cynric did not make love; he rutted like a frenzied ram. He had not shown any tenderness towards her. He would rut until he got her with child and then once she gave birth he would rut some more—groping at her body until he tired of it.

The thought made bile creep up into the back of Raedwyn's throat but still she did not cry. She had married Cynric of her own free will and there would be no going back.

Chapter Two

A SHORT WHILE before sunrise, Raedwyn finally drifted off to sleep. What seemed like moments later, she awoke as Cynric rolled off her and belched. The torch had long since burnt out, cloaking the chamber in darkness. Raedwyn feigned sleep as Cynric stumbled across the room to use the privy. Then he threw open the shutters and watery sunlight poured into the chamber. Raedwyn opened her eyes a crack to see gray skies outside, before quickly closing them. Too late, Cynric had seen she was awake.

"Roll over my lovely," he climbed back onto the bed and tweaked her nipples so they stood up hard against her pale skin. When Raedwyn did not respond he pushed her over onto her face and pulled her up onto her hands and knees.

"What a lovely arse!" he exclaimed, slapping her hard across the rear. "It makes a man hard just to look at it!"

Then, as if to prove his point, Cynric gave his new wife a repeat performance of the night before. Raedwyn screeched and tried to claw her way off the bed as he forced himself into her. Cynric ignored her protests, grabbed her hips and lifted them to meet each thrust.

"That's right my lovely, squeal!" he grunted. "I like a bit of noise!"

At his words, Raedwyn promptly bit down on her tongue and endured the ordeal in stubborn silence. Cynric took his pleasure once more, and by the time he collapsed on top of Raedwyn she had curled up in agony.

Raedwyn clamped her eyes shut and felt tears sting behind them—to think she would be forced to endure this repeatedly for her entire married life. How had her mother suffered it?

Cynric eventually rolled off Raedwyn, slapped her naked bottom and, whistling cheerfully, pulled on his clothes. Raedwyn waited until he had left the chamber before she gingerly rolled off the bed. In the privy she examined herself—she was swollen and bruised, and her thighs were smeared with blood. Anger flooded through her as she carefully washed herself.

The pain made it difficult to walk but Raedwyn managed to shuffle across the chamber to where her mother had laid out her clothes for traveling. She dressed in a long, fitted, tight-sleeved tunic with a thick blue woven wool over-dress. Around her waist, she buckled an embroidered leather belt. She pulled her hair back into a bun at the nape of her neck and concealed her hair with a cloth veil.

It was then Raedwyn noticed the brooches. They sat on a stool next to her nightstand. The brooches were beautiful—polished nuggets of amber in a nest of gold. She knew they were from Cynric and her first instinct was to hurl them out the window. However, these were Cynric's *morgen-gifu* or 'morning gift'. As it was customary for a man to give his new wife a present on the morning after they had spent their first night together, she felt obliged to keep them.

Raedwyn's hands trembled as she picked up the brooches. She was using them to fasten her cloak to her shoulders when the tapestry covering the chamber's doorway parted and Seaxwyn hesitantly poked her head into the chamber.

"Raedwyn?"

Upon seeing her mother's face, Raedwyn's self-control dissolved. She burst into noisy tears.

"Raedwyn!" Seaxwyn hurried across the chamber and enfolded her sobbing daughter in a hug. They stood together, unspeaking, until Raedwyn's tears eventually subsided. Seaxwyn stroked her daughter's wet, blotchy cheek and smiled tenderly.

"Was it that bad?"

"Why didn't you tell me?" Raedwyn accused.

"I had hoped you would be one of the lucky ones," Seaxwyn replied. "For that reason, I did not worry you."

"But I thought you and father were happy?"

"We are," Seaxwyn replied firmly, "but that is a rarity amongst the high-born."

Seeing the look of anguish on her daughter's face, Seaxwyn led Raedwyn over to the bed and they sat down on the edge of it.

"I was lucky in Raedwald, for he is a noble and gentle-hearted man," Seaxwyn explained, "but you know he was not my first husband."

Raedwyn nodded. She knew her mother had been married before, to Tondbert, an East Saxon prince. The union lasted only a couple of years, before Tondbert divorced Seaxwyn. Soon afterwards, she had married Raedwald. She had a son from that former union, Sigeberht, who Raedwald had never trusted. As soon as Sigeberht came of age, Raedwald had banished his stepson from his kingdom and now Sigeberht lived in exile in Gaul. Raedwyn knew little of her mother's previous life, or of how having her son in exile affected her. She listened intently as Seaxwyn recounted her tale.

"I was barely sixteen when my father married me to Tondbert. Unlike Cynric who is a decent man, Tondbert was cruel and plagued by dark moods. It took little to irritate him, and when he discovered he had not married a mouse of a woman, he decided to beat any fire out of me."

Seaxwyn looked out of the window at the lightening sky, her finely sculptured face hard with the memory. "He beat me regularly, so badly once that I lost my first baby. When I was with child the second time he left me alone, until Sigeberht was born. Then the beatings became more frequent, until one day he had me cornered and I thought he was going to kill me. I had taken to carrying a knife hidden under my skirts but had lacked the courage to wield it. It was then, cornered and worried for my life, that fear left me and I felt as a man must feel when the lust of battle takes hold. I stabbed him in the leg thrice and left him howling on the floor. I fled immediately with my son for my father's hall, and days later Tondbert divorced me."

Raedwyn was agape at her mother's tale. She had always known her mother was strong but she had never imagined her capable of such anger, or courage.

"After Tondbert, I believed no man would want me—but then, my father discovered the young King of the East Angles sought a wife. I was miserable, imagining that my next husband would be as cruel as my last, but I knew the moment I set eyes on Raedwald that I would love him fiercely. I had hoped it would be the same for you and Cynric."

Raedwyn shook her head and scowled at the thought of her new husband.

"He is a brute," Raedwyn spat. "To think that I will have to endure his touch again and again makes me want to die."

Seaxwyn took Raedwyn's hand and squeezed it. "It's a woman's lot," she said, her tone brooking no argument, "and you could have fared much worse than Cynric. Listen to me Raedwyn!"

Raedwyn felt her mother's grip on her hand tighten with urgency and she looked into her mother's eyes. They were smoky gray and sharp like pieces of flint. "Ours is a world controlled by the warrior and the sword. We women are like seeds scattered by the wind. The wind drops us where it will and there we have the choice to either fight our fate or grow roots and bloom."

"You fought Tondbert," Raedwyn replied, lifting her chin defiantly, "and it brought you to my father!"

"I defended my life from a man who would have murdered me if I had not fought back," Seaxwyn replied, "and I know you would do the same, but you must remember that Cynric, though apparently lacking in the qualities which make him an ideal husband, is not a bad man. You must bloom where you are planted my dear daughter or life will wear you down."

Raedwyn shook her head stubbornly. "The man is a brute!"

"Raedwyn." Seaxwyn gently took hold of her daughter's chin and forced her to meet her gaze. "There is more to a marriage than what happens between man and woman in the marriage bed. You and Cynric are still strangers. Give him some time and you may be pleasantly surprised."

Raedwyn stared back at her mother, disappointed. She could hardly believe that her mother was telling her to accept the touch of a man who had treated her so roughly. She had always thought her mother would protect her from life's sharp edges, but now saw that she had finally entered adulthood and could no longer hide behind her mother's skirts.

Raedwyn's world was not as simple as she had always believed, and nor was her place in it.

Raedwyn left Rendlaesham under leaden skies. A dull gray blanket blocked out the sun and the air was heavy, full of the promise of rain.

Raedwald's eyes glittered with tears when he hugged his daughter tight against him and sent her on her way.

"I will miss you dear girl," he said gruffly. "My hall will appear cheerless without your laughter."

Raedwyn choked back her own tears before hugging her mother and brother. Meanwhile, Cynric mounted his horse, impatient to leave. Raedwald helped his daughter up onto the back of her shaggy bay mare before rejoining Queen Seaxwyn and Eorpwald.

Raedwyn looked back at her family. Her father was stone-faced, struggling to control his emotions, while her mother gave Raedwyn a brave smile, her eyes glittering. Eorpwald watched her solemnly, his quiet countenance giving nothing away.

Raedwyn bit down hard on the inside of her cheek to stop herself from weeping, before she chastised herself for being so ungrateful. Her father had done his best for her and she could not bear to disappoint him. However, despite her mother's advice, Raedwyn could not imagine welcoming Cynric's touch. Just the sight of his self-satisfied face this morning made her want to slap him.

Mounted alongside Raedwyn, Cynric gave his king a hearty salute before urging his horse on, down the incline, and away from Raedwald's Great Hall.

"Raedwyn!" Eanfled appeared at Raedwyn's side, her cheeks flushed with excitement. "Were you going to leave without saying goodbye?"

"Dearest Eanfled!" Raedwyn reached down and clasped her maid's hand in hers. "Of course not, I knew you'd be here to see me off!"

The truth of it was that Raedwyn had avoided seeing Eanfled today. She knew her friend would have asked her about her wedding night, and Raedwyn would have had to tell her the truth. Eanfled had been so excited for her that Raedwyn could not bear to see the pity and worry in her eyes.

"Don't forget me Raedwyn!" Eanfled called after her. "Please visit!"

"Of course I will!" Raedwyn called black, her vision blurring with tears as she waved to her friend and dug her heels into her horse's sides. "I will never forget you Eanfled!"

Moments later, they were riding out of Rendlaesham. Townsfolk lined the streets to farewell the newly-weds. Fifteen warriors rode out behind Cynric and Raedwyn; their escort back to the long ship moored on the banks of the Deben. A few children straggled behind them for a while before the company of seventeen found themselves alone, riding through open country dotted with clumps of woodland.

The farther they rode from Rendlaesham, the better Raedwyn started to feel. Bidding her family farewell had been too raw. Now that she had left them behind, the pain dulled and Raedwyn felt her mood lift.

Cynric did not converse with his new wife during the journey. Instead, he rode ahead with one of his warriors. Raedwyn watched him laugh at something the warrior said and wondered if he would ever be that at ease with her. He was a man who clearly preferred male company; perhaps that was why he had married so late in life.

They retraced their steps from two days earlier, weaving in and out of sheltering woodland. As the day wore on, the sky darkened and the first fat drops of rain fell. Raedwyn watched the drops splash onto her hands and peered up at the ominous sky. Moments later, the heavens opened and rain pelted down on the travelers.

Soon they were all soaked through. Rivulets of cold water ran down Raedwyn's face and down the back of her neck. Miserable, she hunched low in the saddle under her fur cloak.

Gradually the rain lessened to a drizzle and a wet mist settled over the land. The thickets of trees were gradually becoming sparser and would soon give way entirely to wide heathland. The closer they got to the sea, the stronger the wind became, and its icy bite made Raedwyn's fingers and feet numb with cold.

Raedwyn was blowing on her chilled fingers in a futile attempt to warm them when the unmistakable twang of a bowstring cut through the air.

Directly ahead of her, Raedwyn watched a feathered arrow embed itself in Cynric's side with a meaty thud. Cynric grunted and collapsed against his horse's neck as another arrow struck his side.

Cynric the Bold slid off his horse and collapsed on the sodden ground.

Suddenly the air was thick with flying arrows and axes. An axe caught the warrior, who had ridden next to Cynric, in the neck and he toppled off his horse. The warriors behind Raedwyn charged forward to protect her, drawing their swords as they did so.

Terrified, the cold and rain forgotten, Raedwyn crouched down in the saddle. Then, acting on instinct, she turned her mare sharply back in the direction she had come. The mare pivoted on her haunches and bolted. Clinging on as the horse flattened out into a wild gallop, Raedwyn could hear shouts and the sounds of a battle behind her. The clash of swords rang out through the mist and the thunder of horses' hooves gradually grew louder.

They were chasing her.

Panic seized Raedwyn. If she followed the riverbank they would be sure to catch her. She turned her horse into the trees and dug her heels into the mare's slick sides. Wispy shrouds of mist made visibility poor in the thickly wooded copse. Raedwyn grabbed hold of the mare's bristly mane and flattened herself against her neck. The frightened horse stumbled over tree roots, dodged tree trunks and ripped through undergrowth. Raedwyn rode, clinging to her mount and praying the mare would not break a leg on the uneven footing.

Then, Raedwyn chanced a glance over her shoulder—and that was her mistake. For in turning in the saddle to see that she had outrun her pursuers, she failed to spy the low-hanging branch looming before her.

A large, solid object hit the side of her head and ripped her from the saddle.

The hand that slapped her across the face was hard and calloused, bringing Raedwyn violently back to her senses. Her cheek stung from the slap and her head throbbed from the collision with the tree branch. Raedwyn looked up into the leering face of a bearded man with wild dark hair who loomed over her.

Once again acting on instinct, Raedwyn brought her knee sharply up. Her aim was dead-on and her knee connected with his groin. The man gave a strangled yell and fell to one side. Raedwyn scrambled away, her long skirts and cloak catching on brambles. She had barely managed a few yards when a hand fastened around her ankle and pulled her back.

"Little bitch!" the man was no longer leering. "I'll teach you some manners wench!" He hit her hard across the face and threw her on to her back.

It seemed Raedwyn had not kneed the man hard enough to damage him, for he was pulling up his tunic and attempting to free his manhood from his breeches with one hand while pulling up Raedwyn's skirts with the other. She still had a dull ache between her legs after Cynric's attentions. The thought of another man using her, filled Raedwyn with cold fear.

Panicked, Raedwyn kicked and struggled, bit and punched, oblivious to his blows. Eventually her skirts were up around her hips while her attacker was trying, in vain, to rip open the front of her tunic. Her linen tunic fitted her snugly and a thick wool sleeveless overdress covered it. Her mother had designed this outfit for traveling; it was near impossible to rip with bare hands. Finally, realizing he was getting nowhere, the man pulled out a knife and raised it to Raedwyn's face.

"You're almost too much trouble," he hissed, "but I'm going to have you now or I'll cut you up!"

Raedwyn stared up at his maddened face in horror. She was sure he would cut her throat. She had to decide whether letting him use her was better or worse than death.

Fate spared her the decision.

"Hengist!" An angry male voice cut through the close air. Raedwyn's attacker froze in the midst of parting Raedwyn's thighs. His face blanched.

A figure loomed out of the mist and hauled Hengist off her. The knife tumbled into the undergrowth and fists flew. Moments later, Raedwyn's would-be rapist was cringing on the ground, winded. A tall man, wrapped in a dark cloak, stood over him. A large cowl shrouded his face but Raedwyn could feel his gaze burning into her. For a moment, she stared back at him, before remembering she lay in the undergrowth naked from the waist down with her legs spread.

Mortification flooded through her. She yanked her skirts down and dived for the knife that lay an arm's length away. The stranger was too fast for her. He kicked the knife out of reach and pulled her to her feet, pinning her arms to her sides.

"Quiet now, milady," he admonished as Raedwyn attempted to twist free. "I mean you no harm but you will injure yourself if you continue to fight me."

"You mean me no harm?" Raedwyn's voice was shrill with hysteria. "You ambush us and kill my husband, before one of you tries to rape me! You mean me no harm? Someone should cut off your lying tongue!"

The cloaked man did not respond to her scorn. Instead, he turned to the groaning man who was picking himself up off the ground.

"Touch her again Hengist and I'll cut your hands off. My father wants her unharmed and unspoiled."

"Your father is welcome to her," Hengist spat. "Vicious bitch!"

"Come, Lady Raedwyn." The cloaked man pushed her ahead of him, back in the direction of the river. "You have an audience with Ceolwulf the Exiled."

Chapter Three

RAEDWYN EMERGED FROM the copse, accompanied by her captors, into a torrential downpour. Within seconds, she was soaked. Water streamed down her face and bounced off the muddy track. Clutching her cloak tightly around her, Raedwyn struggled through the mud, to where two bedraggled horses stood tied to a tree, patiently awaiting their masters' return. Hengist mounted his beast while his companion hoisted Raedwyn up into his horse's saddle. Now that her anger had worn off, a numb chill settled over Raedwyn. She meekly sat atop the horse, shivering as the rain pelted against her.

Hengist rode ahead while the cloaked man walked next to Raedwyn. They retraced their steps to the site of the ambush. Upon seeing the dead bodies of her husband and escorts, riddled with arrows and sprawled across the path, Raedwyn's stomach roiled. She struggled off the horse and tried to squeeze past her cloaked captor.

"Wait milady." His hand fastened around her forearm like an iron band and halted her.

"I must go to my husband!" Raedwyn ripped her arm free. "Let me be!"

Raedwyn pushed against him and this time he stood back to let her pass. A crowd of bloodied and mud-splattered men stood around and watched Raedwyn pick her way across the mud, to where Cynric the Bold lay face down. Reaching him, she knelt next to his inert body and rolled him over. He was indeed dead. His body had a heaviness that live flesh did not possess. It was an effort to get him onto his back. Two arrows pierced his chest. Cynric's face wore an awful expression. His blue eyes stared sightlessly skyward. Raedwyn had known, as she had watched the arrows hit him, that the shots were mortal. She sat back on her haunches and looked at the men lying scattered around her—not one of them moved. They had killed them all.

"Butchers!" she hissed. Anger rose up in her as she surveyed the carnage. Cynric's men had fought back, but in the end the outlaws outnumbered and overwhelmed them. Raedwyn took a good look at the crowd of men around her. They were dirty and unkempt but well armed. They had used the element of surprise well, for trees surrounded this part of the riverbank. The men gawked at her and Raedwyn stared back, her eyes narrowing into sapphire slits.

Had she the means, she would have slaughtered them all.

"I see you have some of your father's fire m'lady." A rough voice caught

Raedwyn's attention. She struggled to her feet and stood to face the tall bear of a man who limped onto the path. He was a giant, with a long black beard and hair streaked with white. He fixed her with a cold, obsidian gaze. "It's a pity you had not been born a man."

This man scared Raedwyn. Shivering and in shock, the desire to crumble before him was overwhelming but she stood her ground.

"If I had been, you and your toadies would be groveling at my feet now," she ground out between chattering teeth.

To her surprise and indignation, the giant laughed. Around him, his men sniggered, including Hengist, who looked upon Raedwyn with a malicious leer. Only the cloaked man stood silent, like a wraith, at the edge of the group.

"That mother of yours is a hard, shrew of a woman. It appears you are no different."

The giant recovered from his laughter and took a menacing step towards her.

"I see no grief in your eyes for your departed husband. You do not have the guile to feign sadness."

"We knew each other but two days," Raedwyn replied. "I see no point in putting on a show so you and your men can jeer at a woman's tears."

The giant cocked his head to one side and grimaced. "A forked tongue, just like your mother."

"You know nothing of my mother!" Raedwyn spat, stepping back from his menacing presence.

"Don't I?" he was clearly enjoying tormenting Raedwyn. "You are too young to have memories of me but I remember your family well. I was once your father's most trusted ealdormen. I was more of a brother to him than one of his own kin."

Raedwyn stared back at him, disbelieving. Only the fierce expression on his dark face stopped her from declaring him a liar.

"Seaxwyn was a fire-haired Saxon beauty in those days and you were but a young child. However, behind her fairness your mother was devious and sly. She poisoned the king against me. She fed him with lies until Raedwald banished me from his kingdom on pain of death."

The giant reached forward and placed his hands on Raedwyn's shoulders, pinning her to the spot.

"Ceolwulf the Exiled am I—and exiled I was—for many long winters. I have lived in Gaul, awaiting the day I would take revenge on the Wuffingas. That day has now come."

Raedwyn's stomach churned and bile rose into the back of her throat. She thought then of her half-brother whom she had never met, Sigeberht, who Raedwald had also exiled to Gaul. However, her father had never told her of this man.

Ceolwulf was obviously a lunatic; she did not believe a word he uttered but she would not dare contradict him. Her mind scampered about, frantically searching for a way to escape, but there was none. Her false bravado dissolved and she stood there, too frightened to move.

Ceolwulf stepped back from Raedwyn before glancing over to where the cloaked man stood watching.

"Caelin," he said softly, "come."

The man crossed the path, stepping over bodies as he did so, before he stood next to Raedwyn.

"This is my son." Ceolwulf's voice lightened for the first time since their meeting. "He was but a boy when I was exiled, but he remembers your family's treachery well."

Raedwyn turned to the cloaked man. He pushed back his hood and looked directly into Raedwyn's eyes.

"Milady." His voice was low, soothing like the drumming rain.

The impact of their gazes meeting was like a hard punch to the stomach. Raedwyn smothered a gasp and tore her gaze away from his. Gathering control of herself, she looked back at him and tried to fathom what it was about this man that affected her so.

Caelin was dark like his father but the similarity ended there. He was tall, long-limbed but without Ceolwulf's heaviness of stature. Long wavy black hair surrounded a sharply featured face and aquiline nose. He, like a few of the men surrounding them, was clean-shaven. He had piercing dark eyes that were unusual in these parts; more reminiscent of a Roman than a Celt or Saxon. He was a handsome man but there was a quiet, brooding power in him; a sensuality that made Raedwyn's skin prickle. Her reaction to this stranger appalled her. Here she was, her husband not yet cold at her feet, and she was lusting after one of his killers.

Caelin stared back at her, his face giving no hint as to his thoughts.

Raedwyn looked down at the ground and squeezed her eyes shut. It seemed so long ago now since her world had been innocent and light-hearted – just two days and yet a lifetime ago.

She wanted her mother. She wanted to open her eyes and find herself in her father's hall, watching the flames dance in the fire pit while Raedwald and his men sat around drinking mead and swapping stories.

Raedwyn opened her eyes to find the outlaws all staring at her. The rain enveloped them all like a great curtain. Tears leaked down Raedwyn's already wet cheeks. Rendlaesham was lost to her.

The outlaws took her into a dense, dark wood where the trees swallowed all trace of the band. They had bound her wrists, for it was clear Raedwyn would try to escape the moment they turned their backs on her. The ragged group led their horses through the densely packed trees, on and on until the oaks, beeches and elms gave way to a wide clearing. A shabby hamlet filled the glade. A collection of low, thatch roofed timber dwellings; it was a makeshift settlement and there were no women in sight, just lean-faced, hungry-eyed men.

They welcomed Ceolwulf back into the fold like a king. Raedwyn bristled at the sight of them fawning over the gigantic, wild-haired man. The East Angles already had a king—and it was not this bloodthirsty brute. Raedwyn smiled inwardly at the thought of her father's rage when he heard of this treachery. There would be no wood large enough for Ceolwulf and his minions to hide in when Raedwald learned of this.

Ceolwulf's son led Raedwyn through the center of the hamlet, towards the largest of the thatched huts. Ever since she had locked eyes with him back by the river, Raedwyn had avoided looking in Caelin's direction. Even so, she could feel his presence next to her, his hand on her back, steering her through the leering crowd. His hand burned through her sodden clothing and warmed her chilled skin.

Raedwyn's mouth went dry and she walked a little faster. She had to distance herself from this man. She ducked under the low doorway, entering a narrow hall with a small fire pit in the center. Two curtains made of rabbit pelts sewn together, hung either side of the doorway that led through into separate anterooms. Caelin pulled the right hand curtain aside and steered her into a small, sparsely furnished bower. A pile of furs lay in the center of the room and there was a clay washbasin and a privy in the corner. The tiny window was bolted shut. Hanging from the exterior wall, a torch burned steadily. Flickering shadows played across the walls.

"We brought your belongings," Caelin said, dumping four sodden leather bags next to the pile of furs, "so you can change out of your wet clothes."

Raedwyn pushed back her hood and wiped the rain out of her eyes. She looked at Caelin properly then. He met her gaze boldly. Raedwyn scowled at him.

"Leave me," she said coldly.

"When you have made yourself presentable, my father wants you to join us," he replied, his tone equally cold.

Raedwyn watched him turn and duck around the fur partition. In the hall beyond she could hear Ceolwulf laughing and his men congratulating each other. Raedwyn's fists balled in fury. It had been a planned, well-executed attack. They had known King Raedwald's daughter was to wed Cynric the Bold and they had known Cynric had docked his long ship below the Great Barrows of Kings. They had lain in wait and finally the prey had come to them.

Shaking with cold and rage, Raedwyn peeled off her wet clothes and put on a plain woolen tunic. She wrung the water out of her hair and shook her curls out like a dog. Then, she coiled her hair severely at the nape of her neck. Finally, she hung her wet clothes to dry on the wall of her bower before unfastening Cynric's morning gifts from her sodden cloak. She held the amber brooches in the palm of her hand. The amber glowed gold in the torch light. Poor Cynric, she thought. Yet, she could not feel true grief for him. Her only emotion towards him was a vague relief that she would never have to suffer his attentions again.

However, with a shudder Raedwyn realized her husband's unwelcome attentions were preferable to what awaited her.

When Raedwyn finally emerged from behind the curtain, Ceolwulf and his men sat around the fire pit downing jugs of mead. They ogled her as she stood before them, stone-faced. A rabbit stew simmered over the fire pit and the aroma made Raedwyn's stomach rumble, reminding her she had not eaten since the morning.

"Ah, Raedwyn the Fair." Ceolwulf took a swig of mead and wiped his mouth with the back of his hand. "Such a luscious wench you are as well. Cynric must have enjoyed his wedding night."

"One fine memory before death m'lord," one of his men chortled, causing the entire assembly to break into raucous laughter.

Raedwyn stood there with her head down, loathing them. Her father would make them pay for their insolence.

"Come girl, sit next to me." Ceolwulf patted the ground next to him. Raedwyn walked stiffly over and sat down between Ceolwulf and his son. Caelin was the only warrior not laughing and smiling. He drank his mead quietly, listening to the chatter around him with still indifference. He glanced across at Raedwyn, watching her under veiled lids.

Raedwyn sat, feigning submission, hands folded meekly in her lap while the men poured mead down their throats and waited for the stew to cook. Eventually, a trencher bread bowl was passed to her and she ate hungrily. Ignoring the lecherous looks from some of Ceolwulf's warriors, including the vile Hengist, who sat directly opposite her, Raedwyn kept her gaze downcast.

"You don't fool anyone, milady." Caelin's voice, low and teasing, intruded on her reverie. "The role of meek maid does not sit well with you."

Raedwyn looked up sharply and found Caelin watching her.

"I have little choice but to sit here quietly," Raedwyn replied frostily, "since I am not here by my own will."

"Then you can drop the act," Caelin replied. "My father despises simpering women."

"I care not whether I please him," Raedwyn shot back, her spine straightening with indignation, "or you!"

A slow smile crept across Caelin's face, before he spoke again. "That's better."

Raedwyn glared at him upon realizing he had goaded her deliberately.

To Raedwyn's right, Ceolwulf let out a loud belch and wiped his meaty forearm across his mouth. He turned to Raedwyn, his face flushed with mead.

"It was a stroke of good fortune the day I discovered Raedwald's daughter was to finally wed." He winked at her. "Long have I waited for a chance to take my revenge."

Raedwyn stared at him as he continued.

"I knew he would refuse to meet me in battle. After your brother perished, Raedwald no longer enjoyed fighting his enemies. He has grown soft, unmanned by grief and that shrew he married."

Raedwyn ground her teeth at his insults but managed to hold her tongue.

"I also knew if he did meet me in battle, he could summon a huge *fyrd*, a king's army, with too many swords and spears for my men to fight fairly. In order for Raedwald to obey me, I would have to possess something dear and precious to him."

"My father will not let you use me against him." Raedwyn was so angry her voice came out as a hiss.

Ceolwulf was unmoved. "You underestimate your father's affection for you my dear," he rumbled. "With you to bargain with he will do exactly as I ask. He will meet me in battle on Uffid Heath at dawn of the next full moon with no more than two-hundred men. I will return you to him before we do battle but if he breaches our agreement, I slit your throat. Tomorrow a rider goes to Rendlaesham with my terms."

Raedwyn gave a bitter laugh. Silence fell around the fire pit. The men's looks were no longer lecherous, but hostile.

Anger made Raedwyn momentarily fearless.

"It matters not how much my father loves me," Raedwyn spat at Ceolwulf. "You are a fool to think he will be manipulated by the likes of you. You and your filthy rabble will be cut down like the dogs you are and I will spit on your corpse!"

"Insolent wench!"

Ceolwulf's meaty fist sliced through the air and caught Raedwyn across the face. Her head snapped back and she fell against Caelin. Ceolwulf's face was a mask of black rage as he raised his fist to strike her again.

"Father!" Caelin's arm moved in front of Raedwyn's face to protect her. "It won't help our cause if you bring the girl before her father bloodied and bruised!"

Raedwyn sagged against Caelin. Her ears were ringing and her vision swam. He had hit her hard—any harder and he would have dislocated her jaw.

Ceolwulf lowered his arm, breathing heavily as the madness of his rage subsided.

"Insult me again girl and I will give you to my men for sport," he growled, turning away from her and taking the mug of mead one of his men had handed him. "Get her out of my sight."

Caelin got to his feet and pulled Raedwyn up after him. He dragged her back to her bower and pushed her inside before pulling the curtain tightly shut behind them.

"Are you hurt?" he asked.

"Leave me!" Fighting tears, Raedwyn turned her back on him and stumbled over to the far side of the bower. Caelin followed her, taking hold of her shoulders and turning her back to face him.

He took hold of her chin and gently touched her jaw where Ceolwulf had hit her. Raedwyn winced and tried to pull away but his grip on her shoulder held her fast. Once again, the sensation of his nearness was overwhelming. His fingers lightly traced the side of her throbbing face and she closed her eyes to escape the intensity of his gaze.

"When I said my father didn't like simpering women, I didn't mean you should insult him." Caelin admonished her quietly. "Do you realize the danger you put yourself in?"

Raedwyn opened her eyes and stared at him, pulling her face away from his touch.

"I care not," she snapped. "He insults my father and expects me to listen to his lies."

"My father has reason to be so angry," Caelin replied, stepping back from Raedwyn. "You are blinded by love for your father and do not know the injustice mine has had to suffer."

Raedwyn's lip curled. "It appears to me that it is you who is blinded by love for your father. I know Raedwald is a great man, a fair man. I see none of these qualities in Ceolwulf."

Raedwyn watched Caelin's handsome face stiffen and his eyes narrow. He turned from her and walked over to the curtain.

"I am not as easy to anger as my father Raedwyn," his voice was hard, "but I warn you to curb that tongue of yours in future. It will only bring you trouble."

Caelin, son of Ceolwulf the Exiled, returned to his place at the fire pit and stared moodily into the flames.

"Here Caelin." Ceolwulf passed his son a cup of mead. "Drink up, there is plenty to celebrate this eve!"

Wordlessly, Caelin took the cup from his father and took a sip.

"The first stage of your plan has certainly run smoothly father," he admitted. "Now, all we need is Raedwald to agree to your terms."

"Which he will," Ceolwulf replied, his tone supremely confident. "After all, we hold his jewel—his precious daughter."

Caelin glanced at his father's face. All sign of the rage that had caused him to lash out at Raedwyn earlier had disappeared and the Exiled was now in good spirits. In truth, his father's reaction to the girl's anger had surprised Caelin. Women did not usually elicit such a response from Ceolwulf; he treated most of them as if they were beneath his notice.

Not for the first time, Caelin wondered at the deep-seeded hatred behind Ceolwulf's quest for *gnyrnwracu,* revenge. He had always thought that there was more to this whole story than what his father had divulged— but for a long time it had been enough that Raedwald had wronged Ceolwulf, and would have to pay for it.

Now though, the whole affair was making Caelin uneasy.

Caelin took another sip of mead and shifted his gaze back to the dancing flames in the fire pit. Truthfully, he had not enjoyed today. The ambush had been bloodier than he had anticipated and they had treated Lady Raedwyn roughly. Caelin's thoughts focused then on Raedwyn the Fair.

She was a goddess—the kind of woman that men started wars over. He itched to tangle his fingers in her mane of blonde curls. A man could drown in her deep-blue eyes, and her full, sensual lips begged to be kissed. He wondered if she had any idea of the stir she had created amongst his father's men—the camp was alive with talk about their fair captive.

Woden and Thunor save me, she's delicious. The soft swell of her breasts, that narrow waist and those curving hips were a man's dream. She had stood tall and proud before him after the ambush, staring at him with a boldness that had taken Caelin's breath away. Men dreamed of bedding such a fiery beauty—although she had not yet spent a night under his father's roof, Ceolwulf had already lost his temper with her.

She was as dangerous as a siren, Caelin mused. His father would do well to keep her out of sight so that she did not distract his men.

Finishing his mead, Caelin joined the rest of Ceolwulf's warriors as they settled in for the evening. Many stretched out next to the fire pit on their cloaks while Caelin found a space for himself against the wall. He lay there, listening to the rumble of men's voices and tried to get comfortable on the hard dirt floor. His father had gained his first victory, but this one would be his easiest.

Much more blood would be shed before Ceolwulf the Exiled would have his reckoning.

Chapter Four

THE SCENT OF wet earth and vegetation laced the cool morning air. Raedwyn stepped outside Ceolwulf's hall and inhaled deeply. The surrounding woodland glistened after the rain, and water dripped off the thatched roofs. The ground was muddy and all around her Ceolwulf's settlement bustled with activity. A rider had left at dawn, bound for Rendlaesham and Raedwald's Hall, to state Ceolwulf's terms. Raedwyn imagined her father's reaction to the news of his daughter's abduction, and shuddered. The king's wrath would be terrible.

Ceolwulf's men were preparing for battle. Raedwyn watched them sharpening their weapons, mending armor and shields, and sparring with each other. Picking up her skirts to avoid muddying them, Raedwyn threaded her way slowly amongst the huts. Two warriors followed her. She could feel their eyes on her as she walked ahead. Men stopped working and stared at her as she passed.

After many hours cooped up inside her bower, Raedwyn felt relief to finally be outside in the fresh air and stretch her legs. She had dressed in a sky-blue linen dress over a white tunic. Like many of the dresses she had packed, this one left her arms bare, and usually she would have adorned it with a gold chain around her hips and gold arm rings. However, today, she had kept her attire as plain as possible and tied back her blonde curls.

The cool air kissed the skin of her bare arms and, looking skyward, Raedwyn caught sight of the sun rising about the edge of the trees. It would be a hot day, and by rights she should have been sailing south on Cynric's long ship, to her new life. Not for the first time, she regretted her uncharitable thoughts towards her dead husband. She hoped Woden had not read her thoughts and was now punishing her for them.

Raedwyn was so caught up in introspection that she nearly walked into the midst of a group of warriors practicing swordplay.

"M'lady!" One of her guards grasped Raedwyn's arm and pulled her up sharply.

Two warriors wielding heavy swords were fighting directly in front of her. One of them was Caelin.

Raedwyn suppressed a flinch as the sword-blades clashed an arm's length away from her face. Caelin, dressed only in loose breeches, cross-gartered to the knee, was sweating heavily despite the morning's coolness. Raedwyn watched him fight. His long, dark hair was tangled with sweat and his body, though lean, was muscular and broad-shouldered. He moved with fluid grace, concentrating fully on the fight.

It was only when his opponent slipped in the mud and yielded, that Caelin realized he had an audience.

Caelin's eyes widened when he saw Raedwyn staring at him, and his gaze locked with hers.

"Lady Raedwyn." He sheathed his sword and nodded brusquely.

Raedwyn felt a blush bloom on her cheeks and hated herself for it. Why did this man affect her so?

"My Lord Caelin," she said stiffly. "You fight well."

"My Lord?" Caelin's mouth twisted into an ironic half-smile. "My father was an ealdorman but I hold no such rank."

Raedwyn felt her cheeks flame even hotter. She looked down at her clasped hands and wished she was back in her bower. Silence stretched between them then and Raedwyn felt the blush slide down her neck and bloom across her chest. He had just made her look like a fool.

"Did you sleep well milady?" Caelin spoke finally, moving away from where the others continued to practice swordplay. Raedwyn fell into step beside him as he walked through the village, back towards Ceolwulf's hall.

"No, I did not," Raedwyn replied, before she stopped and met his gaze. "What will become of me?"

Caelin held her gaze. For the first time he appeared uncomfortable and unsure of how to answer.

"Your father will not keep his word," Raedwyn continued, her voice low. "I will be raped and murdered here."

Caelin's face stiffened. "We are not savages milady. My father, for all his rough manners is no murderer. Raedwald left him with no choice. He only wants back what your family stole from him."

"And what was that?" Raedwyn asked.

"His pride and dignity," Caelin replied, "and nearly twenty years of life lost in a land he hated."

"I imagine Gaul is not so vile," Raedwyn answered him, and wondered, once again, what had happened to her half-brother, Sigeberht, in Gaul. Raedwald was a fair man and a good king, but he was not to be crossed. His good opinion, once lost was lost forever. She understood him well for she had the same temperament.

Caelin laughed at her comment. "Raedwyn the Fair, you have never left these shores," he teased her. "You know nothing of what lies beyond the flat horizon of this kingdom by the sea."

Raedwyn bit the inside of her cheek to prevent a sharp retort. Caelin treated her like a naïve, foolish maid. His comment stung and she wanted to hit back. However, her temper had gotten her into trouble yesterday, and now she found herself a little afraid of men.

They had reached the main entrance to Ceolwulf's hall and Caelin turned to Raedwyn, his dark gaze ensnaring hers.

"Raedwyn." Caelin's expression had become serious and the teasing tone was gone from his voice. "After last night, I can understand your fears, but you will come to no harm here I promise you that. Upon my honor."

Raedwyn watched his retreating back as he went off with his men to eat.

"Honor?" Raedwyn's mouth twisted. "You do not know the meaning of the word."

The day stretched on and Raedwyn spent most of it enclosed within the walls of her bower. Only at dusk did her guards allow her out once more for a stroll around the village. She had not seen Caelin for the rest of the day and, since he was the only one who bothered speaking to her, Raedwyn spent the day in silence.

That evening, Raedwyn remained in her bower when Ceolwulf and his men entered the hall. The aroma of roasting mutton hung thickly in the air, reminding Raedwyn of how hungry she was. It surprised her that she still had an appetite. She would have thought seeing her husband killed, and her own abduction, would have put her off food, but it had not. After last night's skirmish, she doubted Ceolwulf would demand she ate with them. However, she hoped they would not forget about her—the delicious smell of roast mutton was making her mouth water.

Wondering how long it would take before they remembered she had not yet eaten, Raedwyn perched on her pile of furs and waited.

It was a long while before her curtain twitched and Caelin looked inside.

"I thought you might be hungry."

"Starving." Raedwyn eyed the platter of mutton cuts, a wedge of coarse bread and a pile of small boiled onions he carried in one hand, and the clay cup of mead he carried in the other.

Caelin placed the plate and cup on a low wooden table and turned to leave.

"Enjoy."

"You can keep me company while I eat if you like?" Raedwyn blurted out.

What in Woden's name made me say that?

Caelin turned and looked quizzically at her.

"Milady?"

"It gets tiresome being closeted in here all day," Raedwyn replied hesitantly, regretting her request but too proud to take it back. "I'm used to my father's hall. I miss having someone to talk to."

Deciding that she had humiliated herself enough for one day, Raedwyn sat down on the floor and began her meal. After a moment's hesitation, Caelin sat down opposite her, stretching his long legs out in front of him. Aware of his eyes on her, Raedwyn ate the mutton, onions and bread. It was plain but good fare.

"So you were born at Rendlaesham?" she asked finally, licking grease off her fingers.

"I was, Milady."

"You don't have to keep addressing me as 'Milady'. Call me Raedwyn." She surveyed him over the brim of her cup. "How old were you when you left?"

"Nine winters; a young lad, but old enough to understand that I was no longer welcome in the only home I had ever known."

"Why did you not stay with your mother?"

"She died giving birth to me. My father is the only family I have."

Raedwyn digested this information. That explained his dogged loyalty to Ceolwulf.

"Did you ever see me?"

"Once." Caelin grinned at her. "You probably don't remember. You had just turned four and had lost your puppy, Wuffa. I found him for you."

The memory brought a smile to Raedwyn's face.

"That was you? Of course I remember! It's one of my earliest memories – the boy in the orchard who rescued Wuffa. I looked out for you after that but never saw you again."

"My father was exiled shortly after," Caelin replied, before adding mischievously. "Did Wuffa grow into a ferocious wolf?"

Raedwyn's smile widened. "He did. Wuffa was my father's favorite on the hunt for many years, until he got too old to run with the horses."

Their gazes met once more and air inside the bower suddenly seemed heavier than before. Caelin broke the spell. He rose to his feet to retrieve her empty plate and cup. Raedwyn handed the plate to him, accidentally brushing his hand with hers as she did so. Caelin pulled away as if she had burned him and backed up towards the curtains

"Good night, Raedwyn," he gave her an enigmatic parting smile. "Sleep well."

Raedwyn stirred amongst the furs. She languished in the softness for a moment, rolling onto her back and stretching like a cat. Outside, Ceolwulf's settlement was already awake. Raedwyn could hear the bleating of sheep and goats, as men herded them past her bolted window, and the rumble of voices. The aroma of a stew cooking made her stomach growl. This village may have been makeshift, but it functioned like any other settlement.

She yawned and sat up. Despite everything, she had slept well—better than she had in a long while. Raedwyn could not remember feeling so clear headed. Her senses were as sharp as a sword's edge this morning.

Raedwyn washed and, using a bone comb her brother Raegenhere had carved for her many years before, laboriously untangled her long, blonde hair. Then she broke her fast with a piece of bread and a cup of goat's milk.

When Raedwyn stepped outside for her walk a short while later, the two guards that Ceolwulf had assigned to escort Raedwyn at all times, fell into step behind her. She had dressed in a forest-green dress and tied her hair back with a matching ribbon. All of the clothes in her bags were unsuitable for life as Ceolwulf's captive. They were too showy, and Raedwyn felt the wolfish gazes of Ceolwulf's men follow her as she walked. Nonetheless, Raedwyn walked tall and ignored the attention she was attracting.

Raedwyn was half-way across the village when she spied Ceolwulf. Having not seen the warrior since he had banished her to her bower, Raedwyn felt apprehension flower within her upon catching sight of him. Her confidence wavered. Ceolwulf was over-seeing the sword-smith's work; testing that the blades were sharp and weighted properly.

Ceolwulf looked up, and his eyes narrowed when he saw the attention Raedwyn was attracting. His men were stopping work to gawk at her like pubescent boys.

"Get back to work!" he bellowed. "Have you not seen a fine bit of female flesh before?"

Raedwyn felt her cheeks flame and she bit back a sharp reply.

The huge man was as intimidating and unkempt as usual. His mane of dark hair was tangled and his wild beard obscured most of his face. Ceolwulf wore an intense, almost maniacal expression as he caught Raedwyn's eye.

"As lovely as a rosebud you are Raedwyn the Fair. It's no wonder my men forget themselves when you walk by. Yet, they need no distraction from their work. Go back to your bower now and stay there till I give you leave."

"Are your men so weak willed that a woman amongst them is enough to turn them from their work?" The words were out before Raedwyn could stop them. Despite her flaring temper, Raedwyn's heart thundered against her ribs as she spoke. She had not forgotten the feel of the back of Ceolwulf's hand. He still terrified her.

Much to her chagrin, the giant laughed.

"So fair and yet such a shrew," he rumbled. "You are so like your mother."

Raedwyn clenched her jaw. She was not a shrew—and neither was her mother.

"It seems any woman who does not take a liking to you is named a shrew," Raedwyn replied, watching his brow darken as she spoke but continuing nonetheless. "It's little wonder I see no women among your ranks!"

"My men have sacrificed much to serve me," Ceolwulf replied in a dangerously quiet voice. "Females are a distraction, as your presence here proves. It's your good fortune that I need you alive as a bargaining tool Raedwyn the Fair, or I'd have wrung your neck by now. Get yourself back to your bower."

Raedwyn's temper erupted again. Terrified as she was of Ceolwulf, she was unused to being addressed in such a rude manner. Her father had always spoken to her with respect, as had her brothers. Her fingers clenched tightly at her sides, her nails biting into her palms. Not for the first time she wished she had been born a man.

Raedwyn's next course of action, whether it was to defy Ceolwulf or submit to his will, was interrupted as voices on the far side of the glade reached them.

"Word from Raedwald, M'lord!"

Raedwyn watched as a travel-stained rider atop a stocky dun horse, trotted briskly through the settlement. Defiance forgotten, Raedwyn realized that her father had learnt of her abduction.

Caelin appeared beside his father, his sharp-featured face impassive as he watched the rider approach.

The rider pulled his horse up before Ceolwulf. He was a grizzled warrior covered in battle scars and with a face that seemed hewn from stone.

"What news?" Ceolwulf barked.

"I have given Raedwald your terms, m'lord," the rider replied, "and I made it clear that if I was harmed or if he breaks our agreement in any way, his daughter will have her throat cut."

Raedwyn's hand went instinctively up to her exposed throat. She felt eyes on her and looked across at Caelin. Their gazes met. The enigmatic expression he usually wore had slipped slightly and she saw concern cloud his dark eyes for a moment. Despite his promise she would not come to any harm here, Raedwyn's life was seriously threatened.

Ignoring Raedwyn's reaction to his words, the rider continued. "Raedwald has agreed to meet us in battle on Uffid Heath at dawn of the next full moon with a *fyrd* of two-hundred men—no more—no less."

Ceolwulf's hairy face split into a wide grin. He turned to Raedwyn, giving her a mocking bow.

"In just three nights, your father will meet his maker. Did I not tell you Raedwald would do anything to have his precious daughter returned to him?" Ceolwulf jeered. "Not such a fearless warrior now is he? It seems the great Wuffinga line is nothing but a family of cowards where women rule."

A red haze swept over Raedwyn at Ceolwulf's cruel words. This traitor had slandered her family for the last time. Striking like an adder, Raedwyn leapt forward, grabbed a sword that lay atop a pile of weapons to be sharpened, and plunged it at Ceolwulf. She gripped the hilt with both hands as she had seen men do during swordplay, and the sword would have found its mark if another blade had not blocked hers.

Caelin had stepped in between his father and Raedwyn and stopped her blade a moment before it caught Ceolwulf below his collarbone.

Ceolwulf reeled back and Raedwyn had the momentary satisfaction of seeing the giant caught off guard. Raedwyn was a tall woman and despite her feminine curves, strong enough even to wield a sword with enough power to kill a man.

Caelin twisted his blade and tore Raedwyn's sword from her fingers. Still in a haze of fury, Raedwyn scrambled to retrieve it but Caelin's foot pressed the sword into the mud, foiling her again. He dropped his own sword and grasped her tightly—one arm clamped across her chest, the other around her neck. Raedwyn struggled, kicked and clawed at Caelin. However, his arms were like two iron bands. He held her fast until her struggles ceased.

Panting, Raedwyn looked up and saw Ceolwulf glaring at her, his face swollen and red from the force of his anger. She had humiliated him in front of his men. Her own anger was subsiding now and Raedwyn felt a jolt of alarm as she stared back at Ceolwulf. He would make her pay for attempting to stick him on his own blade.

"I said I'd hand Raedwald's daughter back alive," Ceolwulf growled, "but I did not say what state she'd be in."

He slapped her hard around the face.

"It's time a man disciplined you wench!"

He slapped her again and Raedwyn's head snapped back with the force of the blow. Bright lights exploded in her field of vision as Ceolwulf loomed closer. He grabbed her by the hair and ripped her from Caelin's grasp. Raedwyn fell to her knees, her eyes tearing from pain. Ceolwulf shook her like a dog worrying a rabbit, so hard Raedwyn felt her teeth rattle in her head. He drew back a booted foot to kick her in the stomach. Raedwyn attempted to curl up to protect herself but was unable to do so as Ceolwulf held her in a death grip.

"Father!"

Caelin wedged himself in between Raedwyn and Ceolwulf.

"Come to your senses! You cannot beat her!"

"I can!" Ceolwulf roared back, turning his black rage onto his son. "I can whip and beat this slut black and blue under her dress and leave her face pretty so her father thinks nothing is amiss. Stand aside Caelin!"

"No father." Caelin's voice was low and hard. "Leave her be. It gains us nothing. Do not let the girl enrage you."

"She tried to kill me!" Ceolwulf yelled.

"Then it is because we have all underestimated her," Caelin shot back. "I will ensure she stays confined to her bower from now until we leave for battle. It's better if she is out of your sight."

Ceolwulf locked gazes with his son for a moment. His men looked on tensely, watching, waiting for Ceolwulf's reaction to Caelin's interference. He had killed men for less. Ceolwulf was a terrible foe to cross for he was a warrior to the core – and he had a warrior's pride.

"Father," Caelin softened his voice. "You are right to want retribution. Raedwyn is a stupid, spoiled girl who would make a fool out of you if you let her. Remember that you will have reckoning on the battlefield. Raedwyn will have to watch you slay her father. Surely that will be punishment enough."

Ceolwulf's anger slowly deflated. He let go of Raedwyn and shoved her aside so she fell into the mud.

"Get her inside before I change my mind," he snarled.

Caelin pulled Raedwyn roughly to her feet and manhandled her away through the crowd towards Ceolwulf's hall.

His fingers dug painfully into Raedwyn's arms as he propelled her through the main entrance. Caelin pushed aside the rabbit-skin partition and hurled Raedwyn inside. Immediately, she flew at him, nails raking at his face.

"Cur! How dare you call me stupid and spoiled!"

Caelin's patience finally snapped. He grabbed hold of Raedwyn and threw her down onto her pile of furs.

"Do you realize the danger you put yourself in?" he shouted.

Raedwyn looked up at his face and saw Caelin was white. In contrast, his eyes were black and his brows drew together above the bridge of his nose, giving him a hawkish appearance.

"You *are* stupid and spoiled." Caelin stood over her, daring her to get to her feet and attack him again. "And you have a temper to rival my father's. It's not a good combination Raedwyn and it will be the end of you if you continue to bait men like my father."

Raedwyn sat up and glared at him, aware as she did so that she was covered in mud and that her hair had come loose of its ribbon and now hung in her face like a madwoman's.

"You have no idea what it's like," she hissed, "to be a woman in a man's world – to be married off in order to strengthen political alliances and then to be used to bargain with. If I were a man, I would have at least had the chance to die valiantly in battle like my brother Raegenhere. Instead, I have to listen while Ceolwulf insults my family and publicly humiliates me. It was not to be borne Caelin! I had to react, even if your father killed me!"

Hot tears slid down Raedwyn's face and she buried her face in her hands as the shock of her ordeal hit her. They were also tears of impotent rage for she knew that if Caelin had not intervened, she would have fought Ceolwulf even while he beat her, until pride dictated that he killed her.

"Raedwyn." Caelin's voice was gentler now as he hunkered down before her. "I've never met such a proud, foolhardy woman. Under different circumstances, I would admire your fire but here as my father's captive, I counsel you to restrain yourself. Ceolwulf has been pushed to his limit. One more folly and he will slay you."

Raedwyn did not respond to his words. She only cried harder. Caelin watched her with growing dismay. Like most men, he could not bear a woman's tears.

"Raedwyn, please," he impulsively reached out and pulled her gently into his arms.

The shock of Caelin's arms around her stilled Raedwyn's tears. He smelled of fresh sweat, leather, horse and an underlying male musk that made her instinctively relax against him. She remained motionless for a while, enjoying the closeness, the warmth of Caelin's body and the sound of his heart through the linen tunic he wore. As he held her, Raedwyn felt the tempo of his heart quicken and knew that having her in such proximity was affecting him.

Raedwyn's own heart raced as she lifted her tear-stained face to his. She kissed him gently on the lips.

Caelin drew back in surprise; confusion and longing played across his face. Then, he gave into the need that the touch of her lips on his had aroused. His mouth came down fiercely over hers.

He pulled her hard against him and tangled his fingers in her hair, forcing her head back so that she was trapped in his embrace. The feel of his body against hers and the urgency of his kiss unlocked something primal within Raedwyn. Before she knew what she was doing, her hands slid over Caelin's torso and she pressed the length of her body against his.

This kiss was nothing like her wedding night with Cynric. That experience had been cold and violent—while this made her senses reel, and released a hunger from inside of Raedwyn that she had never known existed.

Suddenly, Raedwyn had never wanted anything so badly in her life than she wanted Caelin to lay her back on the furs, lift her skirts and take her.

It was Caelin who broke away first. He grabbed Raedwyn's shoulders and held her back at arm's length, breathing heavily. His face had flushed about the cheekbones, and his eyes had glazed with lust. Raedwyn imagined she looked the same. As she gazed at him, she saw the expression he usually wore slip back into place as he regained self-control.

"A dangerous wench you are, Raedwyn the Fair," he said thickly. He let go of her shoulders and got to his feet. "One moment you seek to enrage and humiliate my father in front of his warriors, while the next you play the role of helpless maiden, followed by that of seductress."

Raedwyn stared at Caelin dumbfounded, before a tide of shame flooded through her. He thought she had been trying to manipulate him. The realization horrified her—how could he think her reaction to him was feigned? Watching her, Caelin gave a bitter smile.

"You are a sensual, beautiful woman I'll grant you that," he spoke coldly so that the compliment stung like a rebuke, "but a woman who uses her charms like weapons cannot be trusted. It will be a relief to hand you back to your kin."

If he had slapped her hard across the face, as Ceolwulf had done earlier, it would have been less painful. For once, Raedwyn was lost for a response; he had just succeeded in humiliating her totally.

Caelin halted in the doorway as he drew back the curtain and looked at her once more. His expression was unreadable but she saw the contempt in his eyes.

"Caelin ..." Raedwyn managed, her voice unnaturally high, "I—"

Caelin put up a hand to silence her. "No more, Raedwyn. Our 'friendship' is at an end. From now on if you speak with me you will do it before my father."

Raedwyn watched as he turned and left her bower, the curtain swishing shut behind him. Alone in the tiny, drab bower, Raedwyn felt her chest constrict as if an iron band was tightening against her ribs. Her eyes burned with unshed tears and she fought back a growing nausea. She could not believe what had just transpired.

Fool, she berated herself, *you should never have kissed him.*

Caelin had not been her friend, but he had been the only person here who had shown her any kindness. Now, she had made him an enemy.

Caelin wandered away from his father's hall and, avoiding the men who were working in the center of the glade, made his way into the shadowy green of the woods behind the settlement. The cool, peaty scent of earth and vegetation calmed him somewhat but his heart still hammered against his ribs.

Damn her. Why had he not heeded his own advice and kept away from her?

She was a witch; a seductress who had nearly entangled him in her snare. Even now, he ached for her, but seeing the shock and hurt on her face just moments earlier had forced him to be even harsher than he intended. He could not let Raedwyn see how much he wanted her.

Raedwyn the Fair was so different from the cowed, work-worn women who had toiled in the villages in northern Gaul where he had grown up. She was the daughter of a king, proud and strong-willed. She was a golden-haired goddess, but her beauty paled against her spirit. Raedwyn indeed should have been born a man for she wielded her beauty like a weapon, and no man who met her was immune to it.

Caelin leaned up against the trunk of an ash tree and rested his forehead against the rough, cool bark. He had not led an easy life, and it had tested him more times than he cared to remember. The injustice Raedwald had committed against Ceolwulf had long become his own and he lived for the day when this quest for revenge would be sated, when he and the others who followed Ceolwulf would be free to live their lives as they saw fit.

This life made him weary to his soul. Alone in the woods, with only the trees as witness, Caelin made a silent promise: if he lived through the looming battle, Caelin would bid his father and his life as a mercenary goodbye and travel this wild, green land until he found a quiet corner—far from war, blood lust and feuding.

Far from the bewitching presence of Raedwyn the Fair.

Chapter Five

DUSK SETTLED SLOWLY over the woods; a long amber-hued twilight, as day released its grip and night's shadow beckoned. The late summer days were long but the slight chill that came as the sun slipped beyond the treetops warned the autumn was not far off and that soon the days would shorten and the leaves would turn.

Ceolwulf's settlement was subdued as the light faded. The low rumble of men's voices, the crackling of meat cooking on spits, and the gentle noises of horses as they munched their evening meal, all filled the wide glade. Now that Raedwald had accepted Ceolwulf's challenge, they had little to do but wait. The anticipation was far worse than battle itself—every warrior knew that—for in waiting a man's imagination could torture him. In the heat of battle, blood lust took over and obliterated all other thoughts. It was an oblivion Ceolwulf's men would welcome, but for now they were forced to bide their time and await the next full moon.

Inside her bower, Raedwyn had come to a decision.

Listening to the sounds of men talking in the hall next door, she dressed in a plain tunic and overdress she used for traveling. She belted it securely around her waist and pulled on her thick woolen cloak, fastening it with a brooch. All her other belongings she would leave behind. They would just slow her down and since she carried neither food, nor weapons, it was better to be unencumbered.

After Caelin had left her, Raedwyn had sat numbly on her furs, pondering her predicament. She had wanted to cry, but the situation was too serious for tears. She could not remain here—it was time to take action.

Raedwyn finished dressing and stood silently in the center of her bower, listening to the sounds within the hall.

They were roasting another side of mutton above Ceolwulf's fire pit. The smell was mouthwatering, reminding Raedwyn that no one had brought her food that evening, and she doubted anyone would. The fat from the mutton had dripped into the fire pit and created a greasy smoke that hung over the entire building, including Raedwyn's annex.

The smoke had given Raedwyn her idea.

Unlike Rendlaesham, Ceolwulf had built his settlement hastily. As such, the buildings were flimsier than those Raedwyn was familiar with. The walls of Ceolwulf's hall were made of thatched bundles of willow twigs, rather than more durable timber planks.

Raedwyn opened her leather bag and retrieved a small clay pot. She pulled out the wooden plug, revealing a solid white substance beneath—pig's lard. Her mother swore by lard as a beauty aid. For years, Seaxwyn had smeared it on her face before going to bed, much to Raedwald's disgust. She had insisted Raedwyn took some with her—but Raedwyn did not intend to use it on her face.

Raedwyn scooped out a chunk of lard and smeared it on the wall, at a place where two bundles of long twigs were bound together. She emptied her pot of the remaining lard and wiped her hands on an undershirt that she had twisted into a makeshift rope. Raedwyn held the end of the greasy rope into the flame of the torch chained to the wall. Then, she waited until the end caught alight. The flames licked hungrily at the grease and Raedwyn deftly tucked the shirt into the crack between the bundles of twigs.

Then she stood back and watched.

The lard worked better than she had imagined. In a short time, smoke filled her small bower and she had to cover her mouth with her cloak to prevent herself from coughing. Soon Ceolwulf and his cohorts would notice the smoke, but for now, the smoke from their roast mutton would camouflage it. The flames spread over the area Raedwyn had spread with lard and soon ignited the dry twig bundles.

Raedwyn waited until the flames had almost burned right through the wall. Then she picked up one of the heavy furs she had slept on. Draping it against the burning wall, she shoved her hand through it at the burning wood until she felt the wall give. Raedwyn smothered the flames with the fur, her eyes streaming from the smoke as she worked. She was relieved to see that her idea had worked perfectly—for now there was a smoking gap in the wall and the evening air filtered into her bower. It was not a large hole but with a bit of a squeeze Raedwyn was sure she would be able to wedge herself through it.

Quickly now, for Raedwyn knew if she hesitated someone would catch her, she poked her head through the hole and glanced from side to side. Fortune was indeed with her for she spied no one guarding this wall of Ceolwulf's hall. Another, lower dwelling sat a few feet away, obscuring Raedwyn from the rest of the settlement. Taking her chance, Raedwyn pulled herself through the narrow gap. It was a tight fit and Raedwyn was afraid the still smoldering wood would cause her clothes to catch alight, but after a few moments of struggle, Raedwyn toppled, face-first onto the dew-laden grass.

Night had almost fallen; the sky was a dark indigo against the black silhouette of the treetops. Raedwyn was glad of the darkness as she crouched in the deep shadow between the buildings and pondered her next move.

She had not thought any further ahead than breaking free of her bower, but now that she was outside, Raedwyn's heart raced. Freedom was so close she could taste it. If they caught her now, Ceolwulf would murder her.

Creeping to the back of Ceolwulf's hall, Raedwyn peeked out, judging the distance to the edge of the woods. There were a few huts with thatched roofs between her and the dark line of trees. She could see the glow of fires and the shadows of men moving about indoors. Nearby, she saw the outline of one or two of them patrolling the area. Raedwyn's heart was now thundering in her ears. She could either run like a hare for the trees or sneak quietly, flitting in and out of shadows until she reached safety.

She chose the second option.

Raedwyn moved from her hiding place and, with the hood of her cloak pulled up around her head, crept in-between the huts towards the woods. She was but yards from the trees, and passing the last hut, when she heard the sound of footfalls. A man emerged from the doorway behind her. Raedwyn dove behind the hut and cowered in the shadows as he wandered over to the trees. The man unfastened his breeches and relieved himself in the undergrowth. Raedwyn flattened herself against the damp ground, praying her dark cloak would camouflage her in the darkness. The man took his time relieving himself and farted loudly before making his way back to his hut. Raedwyn guessed from the unsteady way he was walking that the man was drunk. He staggered past Raedwyn and ducked back into his hut.

Raedwyn lay there, frozen with fright for a moment or two before she slowly got up and dove for the sheltering boughs of the woods. Inside the protective shadow of the trees, Raedwyn grinned in the darkness.

I've escaped—I'm free.

Wrapping her cloak tightly around her, Raedwyn attempted to orientate herself. She had no idea which way was north, east, south or west. She had no idea in what direction Rendlaesham was, but she was free and she intended to remain so. She decided that the best route was a straight one, as far from Ceolwulf and his minions as possible. She cared not if she became lost in the forest, for then nobody would find her.

Raedwyn moved through the trees away from the sounds and smells of civilization, into a dark, primeval world where the only sounds were those of night creatures, rustling in the undergrowth or screeching overhead; and the only smells were forest scents. In truth, Raedwyn was terrified of being in the woods alone at night. She tried not to think of the wild boars or wolves that inhabited the forest.

Darkness cloaked the woods. The moon had not yet risen, and so Raedwyn fled blindly, away from her captors.

The half-moon was rising into the night sky when Raedwyn heard the far off shouts of men behind her and knew they had discovered her absence. Drenched with sweat, her heart now hammering from exertion rather than fear, Raedwyn halted for a moment, listening to the sounds of her hunters. Every muscle in her body tensed, like a deer sensing a predator nearby.

The hoary light of the moon turned the forest into an ethereal landscape. Raedwyn had reached a small stream. It burbled gently and twinkled in the moonlight. Raedwyn stepped into the cool water and felt it soak through her boots. She waded upstream in an attempt to mask her trail from her stalkers.

Raedwyn knew not how long or far she fled. She thought of nothing but escape. Finally, scratched, aching and almost collapsing from exhaustion, Raedwyn realized she no longer heard those who hunted her. She knew it was still not safe to tarry but she could go no farther. She had to rest, and she needed to find a safe place to do so.

The stream had widened to a lazy river and the bank rose up steeply on one side. A narrow cleft cut into the bank, obscured by a fringe of thick undergrowth. Raedwyn wriggled under the cloaking underbrush, ducking her head to avoid catching her hair in the brambles. It was a snug fit and in normal circumstances Raedwyn would have worried her hiding place was some unfriendly forest creature's home, but such was her exhaustion that the damp, mossy ground felt like the softest fur bed and she did not care if she had to share it.

Trembling, Raedwyn pulled her hood up over her face, curled up into a ball and pulled her cloak tightly about her. Sleep swallowed her and she sank into an exhausted, dreamless oblivion.

Hunger pains awoke Raedwyn from a deep sleep. Her stomach gurgled loudly, reminding her she had not eaten since the morning of the day before. Damp and aching, Raedwyn wriggled out from the undergrowth and blinked like a sleepy owl. She rubbed her gritty eyes and looked up, surprised to see the sun already high in a cloudless, blue sky. She had slept for a lot longer than she had intended. She only hoped her hunters had overtaken her by now.

Raedwyn knelt over the river's edge and splashed water over her face. The shock of the cold water cleared the last vestiges of sleep and sharpened her senses. She took a long drink from the river and felt her stomach pangs ease somewhat. However, it was no substitute for food.

After a brisk wash in the river, her skin now tingling from cold, Raedwyn broke her fast with a few handfuls of juicy blackberries. Then she set off again, following last night's route upstream. For some reason, she felt safer following the river. Since she was now completely lost within the woods, the river represented the only landmark she could steer by.

The day grew steadily warmer and sweat soon trickled down between Raedwyn's breasts and shoulder blades. The woods grew denser and this worried Raedwyn. If she had been traveling in the right direction, surely the woods would have given way to open country by now. Raedwyn had the niggling feeling she had made a mistake, but she was so intent on escaping Ceolwulf that she decided it was better to continue this way rather than turn back and risk capture. As she journeyed on, Raedwyn kept her senses sharp for any sign that Ceolwulf's men had picked up her trail. However, apart from the chatter of birds, the forest was silent and Raedwyn began to hope that she really had escaped.

Hunger gnawed at Raedwyn's belly as she walked. Apart from the odd handful of blackberries, she had not eaten in a day and a half. Lack of food sharpened her senses and made the sights, sounds and smells of the woods even more vivid. Raedwyn's skirts were now mud stained and ripped from where she had pushed through brambles and undergrowth. Burrs matted her travel cloak and mud caked her boots. She longed to stop by the river and bathe in the cool water but instead she pushed on. This forest had to end before too long, she told herself.

At times, the trees formed a canopy overhead but despite the warm shafts of sunlight that filtered down onto the forest floor, Raedwyn could not see what direction the sun was traveling in. She still journeyed blind, hoping she was heading towards her father.

Finally, the heat of the day waned and dusk approached. So weary that she felt on the edge of tears, Raedwyn collapsed on the riverbank and pulled off her boots. She removed her cloak and hitched her skirts high around her hips. Then, with a sigh of relief, she sank into the cool water and waded into the river. The water was a soothing balm to her aching feet and tired legs. The river eddied gently around her legs; the water was brilliantly clear so she could see her pale feet standing on the pebbly bottom. She splashed water between her legs and over her face and neck, letting it run down her chest and back under her scratchy clothing. She longed to undress completely and loll in the river like an otter but she decided against such recklessness. Ceolwulf's men were still pursuing her.

Dusk cast a golden hue over the woodland and Raedwyn thought to herself that she had never been in a place so peaceful and lovely. She straightened up from washing and listened to the evening chorus of birdcalls. She could live in a place such as this.

Then, all at once, Raedwyn knew she was no longer alone. The sense that she was being watched caused the fine hairs on the back of her neck to prickle. Raedwyn's empty stomach twisted itself into a hard ball. She had relaxed too soon. Slowly, Raedwyn turned back towards the riverbank. Her heart jumped into her throat when she saw the tall figure of a man swathed in a dark hooded cloak. He was standing on the riverbank next to her discarded boots and cloak, watching her. As she stared at him, paralyzed, the man pushed back his hood.

It was Caelin.

What a fool she had been to think she could outrun them. His face was unreadable, although she could see dark circles under his eyes.

"You are a difficult prey to track Raedwyn the Fair," Caelin said finally, "but luckily for me I realized what the others did not."

Raedwyn stared at him, unable to speak.

"You have no sense of direction," Caelin continued, raising a dark eyebrow as he spoke. "While the rest of the trackers have gone north or west, the direction they assumed you'd go if you were searching for your father, I knew you'd blindly flee without much regard for direction.

Raedwyn felt her stomach sink earthwards at this news.

"Where am I then?" she whispered.

"Quite a considerable distance southeast."

Raedwyn stared at Caelin, not sure whether she wanted to believe him.

"Are you coming out of the water Raedwyn," Caelin said after a lengthy silence, "or must I come in and get you?"

Raedwyn glared at him. He was so smug in the knowledge he had caught her. She could not stand him smirking at her as if she was a naughty maid who had run away from home after a scolding from a parent. With a snarl, Raedwyn picked up her skirts and dove for the far riverbank. She slipped on a mossy stone and stubbed her toe, but scrambled on nonetheless. The water deepened and her wet skirts dragged her down but Raedwyn was determined. She reached the far side, and was just grappling her way up the steep bank when strong arms gripped her around the waist and yanked her back into the water.

Raedwyn screamed, drove her elbow back into Caelin's stomach and kicked him in the shin. She heard Caelin swear as he released her and she scrabbled, once more, for the bank. This time Caelin grabbed her by the hair and pulled her back into the water. Raedwyn went under and came up spluttering and kicking, but Caelin held her fast. She glared up at his face, expecting to see Caelin furious as well, only to find him grinning at her.

"That was a decent enough attempt at escape." He towed her back towards the opposite river bank. "I would have thought less of you if you hadn't tried to get away, but we both know I'd catch you eventually."

"Dog!" Raedwyn hissed at him as he pulled her up from the water. "My father will dismember you for this!"

They faced each other, both dripping wet, on the riverbank.

Despite her slowly subsiding anger, Raedwyn was suddenly aware of how close Caelin was standing to her—so close that she could feel the heat of his body touching hers.

Caelin was watching her closely and Raedwyn felt her skin prickle under his surveillance. She was aware that her dress was now plastered against her skin and hugged every curve of her body. She looked down and was horrified to see her breasts were clearly visible and, worse still, her nipples were hard, straining against the wet fabric. She looked up and saw the state of her breasts had not been lost on Caelin. He was staring at them, his lips slightly parted. Then, his gaze moved upward and seized hers.

Caelin swore softy, stepped forward and brought his mouth down on Raedwyn's. Their bodies, with only wet layers of clothing separating them, pressed together. Raedwyn's head swam as his lips parted hers and the heat of his tongue filled her mouth. His hands moved across her shoulders, down the length of her back, and cupped her buttocks; bringing her hard against him so that she could feel his arousal.

Despite herself, Raedwyn groaned, and the sound brought Caelin to his senses. He tore his mouth from Raedwyn's and released her. Caelin stepped back and Raedwyn saw the conflict on his face before he mastered his lust and took a deep breath.

"It seems that now we are even, Raedwyn the Fair," he said before he reached down and picked up her cloak, tossing it to her. "Dry yourself off, or you'll catch cold."

Raedwyn clutched her cloak to her and dried her face on the scratchy woolen material before throwing Caelin a venomous look. Did he really think this was a game?

Meanwhile Caelin picked up his own cloak that he had discarded before going after Raedwyn and dried himself. He wore a thin linen tunic that hung to mid-thigh, belted at the waist; leggings and soft leather hunting boots. Wet, the clothes clung to his tall, lithe frame and Raedwyn allowed herself a moment of silent admiration, before she sat down and pulled on her boots.

"So what now?" she asked, her voice flat. "Are you taking me back to Ceolwulf?"

"Not today," Caelin replied, still not looking at her. "We are both exhausted. We rest here this eve and travel at dawn tomorrow."

Raedwyn felt a surge of wordless relief at this news; if she had to travel anymore today she would collapse. It was then she saw the two dead rabbits that hung from a nearby tree. Caelin saw the direction of her gaze and smiled.

"I thought you might be hungry," he said lightly. "Help me gather wood for a fire and we can get these two roasting."

A soft blanket of darkness settled over the trees as another night crept across the woodland. It was a still, warm night with a slightly clouded sky. They made camp by the river and Raedwyn sat before the fire, watching the rabbits roasting while she listened to the gently burbling river. The aroma of roasting meat was almost unbearably appetizing and Raedwyn stared at the bubbling rabbit skin, willing it to cook faster. Finally the rabbits were cooked. Caelin removed them from the spit and wordlessly the two of them fell upon their supper.

The rabbits were plump and juicy, and by the time Raedwyn had eaten her fill, nothing but a spare skeleton remained. After supper she went down to the water's edge to drink and wash her greasy hands and chin before returning to the fire. Caelin had also finished eating and was poking the dying embers of the fire with a stick. The glowing embers lit Caelin's face from below, casting his eye sockets into deep shadow and making him appear even more aloof than usual. Raedwyn sat down opposite him, placing the fire between them. She tucked her legs under her and watched him surreptitiously under lowered lids.

Silence had stretched between them for hours now, and Raedwyn was grateful for it. Her body ached and the rage and frustration of being caught had drained away, leaving her strangely numb. She had tried to fight them, and she had tried to escape. She had failed. Just one more night remained before Ceolwulf and Raedwald would meet in battle at dawn on Uffid Heath.

"You've succeeded in enraging my father once again." Caelin spoke finally. "I thought he was going to swallow his own tongue when we discovered you were gone."

Despite herself, Raedwyn smiled at the thought of Ceolwulf, purple-faced, choking on his tongue in a fit of apoplexy, before her smile faded and she met Caelin's eye.

"He'll murder me this time."

Caelin shook his head. "He will have calmed down by the time we return."

Silence hung between them for a moment before Raedwyn spoke.

"You don't appear afraid of him. All the other men are."

Caelin raised an eyebrow. "And with good reason."

"So why aren't you?"

Now it was Caelin's turn to give a bitter smile. "Who says I'm not? My father and I have had our moments. I've had a lifetime to get used to him and his ways."

"He appears to listen to you," Raedwyn ventured. "No one else would stand up to him."

"It was not always the case," Caelin's replied. "I have clear memories of our life at Rendlaesham before my father's banishment. He was a proud and strong-willed young warrior who did not have much time for a young son. During my early years, I ran free in the King's Hall and was raised by a collection of servants. After his exile, he was a wrathful and harsh father for many years. I was a constant reminder of the life he had left behind."

Raedwyn pondered on his words for a moment before she asked. "Did he love your mother?"

Caelin chuckled then, his dark gaze pinning her.

"Love? Raedwyn, I don't think love ever came into his feelings for my mother. If he ever pined for her, he'd recovered well enough by the time I was old enough to notice such things." He paused then, observing her for a moment, before he sighed and stretched his long legs out in front of the fire. "Surely, you of all people know that most men and women come together, not out of love but necessity."

"What's that supposed to mean?" Raedwyn tensed.

"You didn't marry Cynric for love, anyone could see that."

"Of course I didn't!" Raedwyn replied frostily. "It was an arranged marriage, like all royal marriages. It doesn't mean I don't believe in love. My parents love each other. I married Cynric as a duty to my father."

"You are loyal Raedwyn," Caelin said with a smile but there was no teasing in his voice. "We are both loyal."

"Is that why you do your father's bidding so readily," Raedwyn asked, "out of loyalty?"

Caelin did not reply for a moment. He paused, as if measuring his words before answering her. "I am loyal to him yes, but I would not follow my father if I thought he was misguided. He was wronged and I gave him my word that I would fight by his side to regain his honor."

Raedwyn could sense another argument brewing if she pursued the topic any further. Whereas a day earlier she would have lashed out at Caelin for his misguided loyalty to a brute like Ceolwulf, tonight she did not have the energy. She was tired of fighting him. She felt uncharacteristically fragile.

An owl hooted overhead and Raedwyn caught a glimpse of the night predator as it swooped soundlessly towards some unseen prey on the forest floor. The moon was rising above the treetops now and Raedwyn felt a pang of despair. This time tomorrow the moon would be full and they would be on the eve of battle.

Raedwyn yawned and rubbed her tired, gritty eyes.

"I think, if you don't mind, I'll sleep now," she said, wrapping her cloak about her and stretching out on the ground next to the fire.

Caelin got to his feet and stretched before coming over to her side of the fire, wrapping himself in his cloak and lying down behind her. He reached across and pulled her against him so her back pressed up against his chest.

Raedwyn squirmed away from him. "What do you think you're doing?"

Caelin laughed. "Don't worry princess, I shall try and keep my hands to myself this time. Sorry, but I'm not letting you out of my sight again. We're going to have to sleep together so I'll wake up if you try to sneak off."

"I won't be able to sleep with you snoring in my ear!" Raedwyn protested, feeling her face grow hot. She had been so tired and dejected the thought of escape had not crossed her mind. Now though, she realized it would be easy to slip away into the darkness while Caelin slept.

"Who says I snore?" Raedwyn could hear the laughter in his voice. He was enjoying this. Caelin had always appeared so cool and aloof around his father and the other men. This light, more playful side to him surprised Raedwyn.

"And I won't be able to sleep with you gripping me in a bear hug either!" Raedwyn struggled against his arm that lay across her waist and stomach, which only caused him to tighten his hold on her.

"Bad luck then," Caelin replied, "because I won't have any trouble sleeping myself."

Raedwyn lay there, her body as rigid as a drawn bow-string while acutely aware of the warmth of Caelin's body pressing against her. If she had not been so affronted, the feel of his arms around her would have been pleasant but Raedwyn felt worn out. She did not want to be touched tonight. Tears stung her eyes but she did not bother to argue any more.

Time passed slowly in the dark woodland and presently Raedwyn heard Caelin's breathing deepen. The arm he had wrapped around her relaxed and gradually Raedwyn felt the tension ebb out of her own body. Despite everything, she found Caelin's presence oddly protective and reassuring. Yet, the things he had said to her back in Ceolwulf's camp still stung—and she would not forget them in a hurry.

Tomorrow he would drag her back to Ceolwulf, and despite Caelin's assertion that his father would control his temper, Raedwyn was not inclined to believe him. She had seen the madness light in Ceolwulf's eyes when he looked upon her. He hated her. Raedwyn doubted her father would get her back alive.

Chapter Six

RAEDWYN AWOKE FROM a deep slumber and had a few moments of reprieve, before reality came crashing back and emptied over her. She stifled a groan and wished the oblivion of sleep could have continued indefinitely.

"Sleep well?"

The voice in her ear made her stiffen.

"Excellently, thank you," she replied coldly.

Ignoring how warm and safe Caelin's body felt curled around hers, Raedwyn pushed away from him and sat up. A misty dawn greeted her; the new day had brought with it gray skies and a light drizzle. Raedwyn's cloak was damp and her limbs had stiffened during the night. She stood awkwardly and flexed her stiff knees and ankles.

"I feel like an old woman," she complained.

"A night sleeping rough will do that to you," Caelin replied. He got to his feet and brushed himself off. Then he reached into the leather pack he carried and pulled out a loaf of coarse, unleavened bread. He ripped it in two and tossed half to Raedwyn.

"It isn't much as I didn't have much time to gather provisions."

Raedwyn took a hungry bite of the bread. It was stale and heavy as a brick but it tasted heavenly. She chewed wordlessly as Caelin doused their campfire with water. Finishing their breakfast, they took a drink from the river before Caelin filled two bladders with water and passed one to Raedwyn.

"Try to ration it," he warned her, "as we'll be leaving the river now and I don't think we'll cross another before we reach our destination."

Raedwyn nodded wordlessly. Caelin was distant this morning; his dark eyes were unreadable as they brushed hers.

The lack of sun and the persistent drizzle made them both ill tempered and so they started their journey without much conversation. Caelin instructed Raedwyn to walk in front of him so he could keep an eye on her. They turned back on themselves, not taking the river but striking out into the middle of the woodland instead.

Raedwyn pushed her way through wet, spiky undergrowth, and as they travelled she felt her spirits sink lower and lower. She could only blame herself for this. Perhaps, she should have been biddable and done as Ceolwulf ordered her. She had been proud, had thought that since she was of Wuffinga stock she would defy him as one of her brothers surely would have.

They rested briefly when the sun was high in the sky; a pallid orb barely visible through the thick cloud cover. There was no food for a midday meal so they sat in silence for a short while, sipped some water and rested their legs. The silence between them was beginning to oppress Raedwyn. She was not a chatterer but she did like to have a little conversation. Caelin avoided speaking with her, except when necessary.

"I know you must think me a stupid woman," Raedwyn said finally. "My father did overprotect me and my mother taught me to have an independent spirit. I am unused to being told what to do and I'm afraid it's made me foolhardy."

Caelin turned to face her and a pained expression passed across his features before he shook his head.

"We both know you're not stupid Raedwyn," he said softly. "I only said that in anger. You're foolhardy perhaps, but certainly not stupid."

He sighed then and ran a hand over his face. Raedwyn could feel the tension emanating from him. "You're a survivor Raedwyn. Your father would be proud. I'm just sorry you had to be involved in this bloody feud."

Caelin got abruptly to his feet and stretched, shattering the fragile connection between them.

"Come, the day wanes and we still have a distance to travel." He reached down and grasped her hand, pulling her up next to him. The feel of Caelin's hand in hers made Raedwyn's stomach arch upwards as if she had just jumped off a cliff. She let go of him, her palm still tingling from his touch and strode off ahead.

"Raedwyn!" Caelin called after her.

Composing herself, Raedwyn turned coolly back towards him.

"What?"

"You're going the wrong way."

Caelin smiled then, his aquiline features softening as he did so. He pointed to the right of where Raedwyn stood. "We are traveling in that direction."

The weather worsened as the day progressed. The drizzle increased to a steady, drumming rain. It had been a wet summer, and with each hour that passed Raedwyn cursed the rotten weather that plagued her homeland. Her cloak and skirts were sodden, dragging her down as she walked. Finally, she was so wet it did not matter if she got any more soaked, so she pushed back her hood and let the rain sluice down over her face and hair. She turned her face up to it and found the steady tattoo of raindrops on her skin oddly relaxing. Raedwyn glanced over her shoulder at Caelin and saw he too had pushed his hood back. The rain had plastered his long dark hair against his skull. He blinked water out of his eyes and gave her a half-smile.

"Enjoying yourself?"

Raedwyn threw Caelin a sour look and turned her back on him. She had never felt so uncomfortable. She was completely soaked. The coarse material chafed against her skin and her boots squelched with each step.

The light began to fade in late afternoon, earlier than usual owing to the bad weather, and Raedwyn wondered how much farther they would have to travel before Ceolwulf's camp hove into sight. Then, so suddenly that it made Raedwyn squint and shield her eyes against the glare, the rain stopped and shafts of sunlight pierced through the cloud, warming her face. Raedwyn realized then that it was not as late in the day as she had supposed. The bad weather had cast a shadow over the world. The surrounding trees sparkled in the late afternoon sun and steam rose off the ground, creating an ethereal mist that curled like witch's hair through the trees.

Moments later, the trees fell back and Raedwyn walked out onto the edge of wide, flat, open land. Clumps of brambles and black thorn punctuated the featureless heath that eventually stretched to a flat horizon.

Raedwyn turned to Caelin with a frown.

"Where are we?"

Caelin stopped beside her and looked around, making sure they were alone.

"The woodland ends here. To the north stretches open country. Uffid Heath is directly north-west. Your father should be making camp at the far northern edge of the Heath as we speak."

Raedwyn stared at him, her frown deepening. "Why have you brought me here?"

Caelin took a deep breath before answering. "You are free to go Raedwyn. You must hurry for my father's men will still be searching this area for you."

"You're letting me go?" Raedwyn breathed, scarcely believing him. "But why?"

Caelin smiled. It was an expression tinged with many emotions, all of them bittersweet.

"I have tried to fight against it Raedwyn," he said, his smile slipping slightly, "but in the end you got the best of me. I cannot take you back to my father for I know it would be signing your death warrant to do so, and I cannot have your death on my conscience."

Raedwyn stared at him, stunned, before speaking.

"Your father will kill you for setting me free."

"Only if he knows I found you," Caelin replied, impatience creeping into his voice. "If I come back empty handed he will be none the wiser. Now go Raedwyn, before I change my mind. Travel swiftly towards the horizon."

He pointed towards to the north-west. "It will be nightfall in a couple of hours. Hopefully you should reach your father before then."

Raedwyn continued to watch Caelin before she stepped forward and gently kissed him on the lips. Her mouth tingled as she pulled away from him.

"Thank you, Caelin," she said softly.

He nodded curtly and backed away from her, his gaze shuttered. "Go!"

Raedwyn clumsily pulled her sodden hood up over her head while Caelin moved back inside the trees; a shadowy, cloaked figure watching her.

Raedwyn turned, not daring to look back at him. She wrapped her cloak around her and struck out northeast across the heath.

Under the sheltering boughs of the forest, Caelin watched until Raedwyn's cloaked form was nothing but a speck in the distance. When Raedwyn had vanished from sight, Caelin tore his gaze away from the far horizon and pulled up his hood. With one last glance at the now empty heathland stretching behind him, Caelin disappeared into the trees.

It was almost dark when Raedwyn spotted the tents in the distance. Her legs ached and her feet dragged heavily, but she managed to break into a run. Two warriors guarding the far edge of the encampment saw her approaching and strode out to meet her, weapons at the ready. As she drew closer, Raedwyn pushed back her hood and they gasped in recognition.

"Raedwyn!"

A surge of relief flooded over Raedwyn—Ceolwulf could no longer reach her. She still could not believe that Caelin had released her. Raedwyn gave the guards an exhausted smile and let them lead her towards the encampment.

"Raedwyn!" Raedwald, King of the East Angles, enfolded his daughter in a bear hug that nearly suffocated her. Raedwyn finally extricated herself from his embrace and saw tears brimming in her father's eyes. Watching him, Raedwyn found she could not speak for a moment, and when she did, her own eyes overflowed with tears as she hugged her father again, burying her face in his chest.

"Yes father, I escaped them."

"Did they hurt you?" Raedwald's voice hardened. "Did any of Ceolwulf's thugs defile you, Raedwyn?"

Shocked by the brutality of the question, Raedwyn drew back and met Raedwald's suddenly cold, hard gaze without flinching. "No father."

Naked relief flooded across the king's face.

"How did you manage to escape?" Eorpwald, his face shining, stepped forward to greet his sister. Raedwyn awkwardly hugged her older brother, realizing as she did so that she had not embraced Eorpwald since they were children. Eorpwald seemed genuinely pleased to see her and Raedwyn realized with a pang that she had always been overly hard on him. Since childhood, she had made unfavorable comparisons between her two brothers, and that had been unfair to Eorpwald.

Raedwyn took a deep breath before answering her brother. Then she told them of her capture, of Cynric's death, of Ceolwulf's settlement deep within the woodland, and of her escape from Ceolwulf's hall. The only elements of the story she left out were Caelin, and her wandering off, lost, in the wrong direction. In her story she made it appear that she had lost her way before finding it again, slipped past those tracking her and made her way to where her father camped.

She did not mention Caelin once.

Raedwald's chest puffed out in pride at the conclusion of her tale.

"You are indeed of Wuffinga descent, dear Raedwyn." He grinned at her, the lines of care and grief on his face smoothing out a little. Since her abduction, he had aged a decade in just a handful of days. His once blond hair was now nearly completely gray and there were deep grooves either side of his nose and pouches under his eyes. "You have made your father a proud man this day."

A fire pit roared inside her father's tent and Raedwyn seated herself next to it. She removed her wet cloak and hung it up to dry. Her gown was sodden, dirty, and ripped about the hem from trudging through brambles and spiky undergrowth. However, she had no other clothing to change into. She took off her boots and put them to dry by the fire. Plump wood pigeons were roasting on a spit and Raedwyn slowly felt days of accumulated tension fade from her as she sat quietly sipping a clay mug of mead and listening to her father, brother, uncle Eni and cousins Annan, Aethelhere and Aethelwold.

They spoke of the upcoming battle, of tactics and of Ceolwulf's most likely method of attack. Raedwyn realized, listening to the Wuffinga men, that Ceolwulf and his rabble would be hard pushed to defeat her father and his *fyrd*. Raedwyn focused on her father as he concluded their discussion.

"I want Raedwyn well away from here long before the battle begins," Raedwald instructed the others. "Let her rest a little here and then I want an escort of warriors to take her back to Rendlaesham."

"What of the reinforcements?" Annan spoke up. "Should they still await your orders?"

"Now that there is no risk to Raedwyn, send word they are to join us at the rear just after sunrise," Raedwald ordered.

"You have more warriors waiting father?" Raedwyn asked, remembering Ceolwulf's demand that Raedwald bring two-hundred spears and no more, otherwise her life would be forfeit.

"Ceolwulf should know better than to dictate to me," Raedwald replied, his blue eyes like two chips of ice. "Another two hundred spears await two leagues north of here. They have my order to attack after the battle is underway."

Raedwyn was secretly aghast at this news. Her father had risked her life in defying Ceolwulf. He had taken a dangerous gamble, for Ceolwulf would have scouts out making sure Raedwald was sticking to the terms they had agreed upon. Raedwyn's escape would have distracted them but, had she not created a diversion, it was likely they would have discovered the king's deceit.

Did Raedwald not realize that Ceolwulf would have then slit her throat without compunction? Raedwyn looked upon her own father with new eyes, aware for the first time of what a formidable opponent he was. Ceolwulf was a man not easily crossed but then neither was Raedwald. As all those bred to rule, he would crush those who opposed him without hesitation or remorse. Raedwald was older now and tired of war but life's hardships had not worn him down as Ceolwulf supposed. Raedwald had an inner core of iron and Ceolwulf had vastly underestimated his ruthlessness.

If the men had noticed Raedwyn's discomfort, they showed no sign, so absorbed were they in talk of tomorrow's battle. Raedwyn took a sip of mead and forced it down her now constricted throat.

Two hundred outlaws would not withstand Raedwald's *fyrd* of double that. Four hundred men was only a small part of the *fyrd* of warriors Raedwald could have called to fight for him. Raedwald's kingdom was now vast and, knowing this, Ceolwulf had been strict with his terms. So sure was he of Raedwald's word, he would not suspect a trick.

Raedwyn was not sorry for Ceolwulf. He was an arrogant, callous brute who had selfishly involved others in his blood feud. However, Caelin—quiet, enigmatic Caelin with dark eyes and the patrician features of a Roman centurion—whose whole life had been dedicated to his father's grudge, would die on Uffid Heath the following morning.

When the wood pigeons were roasted, Eni plucked them from the spit and distributed them with chunks of bread, and boiled wild onions. Raedwyn was faint from hunger but her thoughts had given her a nervous stomach.

She forced herself to eat the meal placed before her. It was delicious food but it felt dry and tasteless in Raedwyn's mouth.

Raedwyn was in a deep, exhausted sleep when Eorpwald gently shook her awake. Raedwyn groaned and swiped at him before turning over and burying herself under a nest of furs.

Eorpwald smiled and pulled back the furs.

"Some things never change dear sister. Come Raedwyn, it's but a short while before dawn. You must leave now."

Raedwyn sat up and blinked like a sleepy, angry owl.

"It's almost dawn already?"

Moving stiffly, Raedwyn pulled on her still damp boots and cloak and followed Eorpwald out of the tent. The rain of the day before had completely cleared, leaving a wide, star dusted sky above. The ground was still spongy from the rain, and the damp, chill air penetrated through Raedwyn's clothing. She shivered and squelched across to where her father stood waiting with her horse. An escort of warriors was mounted nearby, heavily armored and armed.

Raedwyn looked into her father's face, shadowed in the darkness and felt a sudden jolt of fear for him and Eorpwald.

"May Woden protect you tomorrow father." She threw herself into Raedwald's arms and hugged him tightly.

"*Wyrd* will dictate who lives and dies when the sun rises," Raedwald replied bluntly, "although it's not us that'll need Woden's protection. Ceolwulf abducted my daughter and murdered my son-in-law. May it be Woden's ravens that peck out that traitor's eyes as he lies dead on the field of battle!"

Raedwyn did not answer her father. Raedwald's view of the world, like most Anglo-Saxon warriors, was fatalistic. Death was a way of life. In a world dominated by blood feuds and wars, death in battle was the best end a man could hope for. Even Woden, father of all gods, could not protect a man from *wyrd* – fate. Raedwald lived by the motto: *wyrd bið ful ãræd—* fate is all.

Raedwyn gave Eorpwald a hurried hug. Never a garrulous man at most times, Eorpwald was silent and reflective as he embraced his sister. Despite her worry for the fate of her father and brother, Raedwyn was eager to get away from the encampment.

War was indeed a man's domain. Raedwyn did not like to see the hardness in her father's demeanor. Battle brought out an entirely different side in Raedwald, and it was a side that she feared. She preferred the laughing, kind man; a loving husband and father, adored by all who knew him, to this cold, fatalistic warrior, who was now as bent on retribution as Ceolwulf.

The dun mare waited patiently as Eorpwald cupped his hands under Raedwyn's foot and boosted her up into the saddle. Impulsively, Raedwyn reached down and squeezed her brother's hand before he stepped away. Eorpwald gave a quick, hard squeeze back and a moment of silent understanding passed between them. Then Eorpwald moved back to stand next to his father. Eni, Annan, Aethelhere and Aethelwold looked on from behind the king, and Raedwyn waved good-bye to them before her escort closed in on her. A ring of shields now surrounded Raedwyn, obscuring her from view.

The knot of riders trotted out of the encampment and joined the darkness. Raedwyn's escort was silent and watchful. From under heavy helms, the warriors' eyes scanned the shadowed heath for any sign of ambush.

Raedwyn settled deep into the saddle as the mare broke into a canter. As she rode, Raedwyn looked east where the first blush of dawn stained the sky, and tried not to think of what she had left behind.

Chapter Seven

CEOLWULF'S ARMY RODE out onto Uffid Heath a short while before dawn broke across the land. Under the veil of darkness, horses emerged from the edge of the woodland and moved across the damp heath to where the battle would take place. The horses were impatient, sensing their riders' tension. They snorted and stamped their feet; their bits jangling and nostrils flaring. Their hooves sunk into the soft earth, making soft sucking noises as they walked.

Caelin rode out front, next to his father. He could still feel Ceolwulf's fury, radiating out from him like heat from a roaring fire. The girl had eluded them. Ceolwulf's only bargaining tool had gone.

Morale had dropped among the men; without Raedwyn they knew Raedwald would not fight fair. If the girl had reached him already, Raedwald would have sent for reinforcements. If the king was not greeted by his daughter the following morning he would suspect foul play and his rage would be blistering. Either way, Ceolwulf's tightly woven plan was unraveling rapidly.

Caelin would have wagered that Raedwyn had reached her father's encampment safely, but he would not share this information with Ceolwulf. When Caelin and the other trackers had returned empty-handed after two days searching in the woods, Ceolwulf had railed at their incompetence. How could a cosseted young woman with no weapons, provisions or survival skills, manage to elude some of the most skilled huntsmen in Britannia? Ceolwulf had been particularly vicious with his son who was an expert tracker and yet had still failed him.

Glancing across at his father's profile, as hard as granite in his iron helm, Caelin remembered the vicious rebuke his father had given him upon his return. He had not risen to his father's anger, despite the provocation. He had not wanted the last words between them to be angry before battle. He had stood silently before his father while Ceolwulf raged. No one dared try to calm him. Finally, Ceolwulf's anger had spent itself, but instead of dissolving, the icy rage had burned inwards. This morning, Ceolwulf had barked orders at his men and refused to talk with any of them of the looming battle. He had not spoken a word to Caelin since losing his temper with him.

A pale morning mist snaked across the damp ground as the sun rose to their right. Shafts of light peeked over the eastern horizon and suddenly the sky was streaked with amber, orange and gold against the washed out blue of the coming day. Caelin watched the sunrise, knowing it was likely to be his last. The knowledge made this spectacular dawn all the more poignant. Caelin thought of Raedwyn briefly then. She had indeed bewitched him for he could hardly believe that he had let her go free. He had nothing in return, besides a parting kiss—but knowing his father as he did, Caelin was sure Raedwyn would not have survived Ceolwulf's vengeance. She was too beautiful, too proud and too vibrantly alive to die at the whim of a man driven mad by a world he could not control.

Finally, Caelin glanced back at Ceolwulf. Caelin knew he would not be able to go to his death without at least trying to make amends with his father.

"Father, I am sorry we lost Raedwyn. I'm sorry I failed you." Caelin spoke quietly but in the silence of the early dawn, he knew Ceolwulf had heard him.

"I have always followed you willingly," Caelin continued. "I have never questioned your choice to seek retribution. I still do not question it. Raedwyn is gone but you have forced Raedwald's hand. You can still fight to regain your honor. Your warriors and I will follow you to whatever end."

Caelin was unused to speaking so frankly before his father. He knew Ceolwulf had always found him to be an enigma. He had a different character to his father; less intense and mercurial, more reflective and private. Despite that Ceolwulf had disappointed him numerous times since his boyhood, he had still done his best to make his father proud of him. It appeared that he had failed, for Ceolwulf did not answer him now. He only stared fixedly ahead at the evaporating mist where a line of riders, a phalanx of shields and spears bristling against the sky, appeared.

Raedwald had come.

Ceolwulf's warriors fanned out either side of their leader and watched the approaching army. From here, it was difficult to guess their number. Raedwald's army drew nearer, halting when the two war parties were about thirty yards apart.

Caelin's heart started to beat faster then. He could hear it steadily thumping in his ears. He had fought battles many times, but never with such an awareness of his own mortality. He was aware of the warmth of his skin, the pulsing of blood through his veins, the brightness of the world around him.

The heavy yoke of duty to Ceolwulf and the lack of joy in his daily life pulled back like a curtain and, for the first time since he was a boy, Caelin saw the miracle of his existence that he had taken for granted for so long. Dogged loyalty to an unyielding father had made living such an effort of late. It had caused him to withdraw, to cloak himself in a mask of indifference. Now, as the last moments of his life played themselves out, Caelin understood how much he had wasted.

Caelin's gaze moved along the line of mounted warriors, and there, emerging from their midst, he spied the king himself. An awesome sight in the parting mist, Raedwald of the East Angles was impossible to miss. He rode a magnificent gray stallion fitted with a silver and gold studded bridle and chest harness.

A great shield hung at his side, as did a sword. In his right hand, he carried a spear. A royal blue cape rippled from Raedwald's shoulders, held in place by Romanesque silver-plated clasps. Heavy chain mail covered his chest and stout gloves protected his hands. A heavy scarlet tunic, hemmed in gold, hung down to his knees and he wore thick blue leggings cross-gartered to the knee. Bronze plated armor protected his neck below a splendid helmet. Silver-plated, the helmet completely covered the king's head and face, obliterating his identity, save for the cold blue eyes that stared out from two eye slits. The front of the helmet had been beaten into a stern warrior's visage. It made Raedwald appear inhuman, like one of the old gods bent on reckoning. The effect was chilling, as Raedwald had known it would be.

Ceolwulf's composure had been momentarily affected by the sight of this warrior king before them, who was—and was not—the man he had spent so much of the last twenty years hating. Recovering his wits, the big man spurred his horse forward and rode to meet the king. The two men stopped a short distance apart, their gazes meeting in cold complicity.

"You hide your face from me Raedwald," Ceolwulf growled. "Have you grown so decrepit you are loath to ride into battle bare-faced?"

Raedwald's gaze glittered with wintry disdain but he did not rise to Ceolwulf's provocation.

"Greetings, Ceolwulf the Exiled," he rumbled, his voice void of emotion, "Raedwyn returned to us last night. You are without an innocent life to bargain with but still you come to do battle."

"The girl is nothing," Ceolwulf spat. "She squeals like a stuck pig while being bedded. After my men and I each took a turn with her, the harlot slunk off into the forest. It matters not that the whore returned to you, for you have met us to do battle, have you not?"

Ceolwulf watched Raedwald's eyes and cursed the impassive silver mask that covered his features. He felt at a disadvantage and the king knew it.

Unbeknown to Ceolwulf, Raedwald's mouth twisted at his enemy's vicious words. How he would enjoy twisting a blade in Ceolwulf's gut. Raedwyn had sworn that none of her captors had defiled her but upon hearing Ceolwulf's gloating, Raedwald was not so sure she had been truthful. He would rather see his daughter dead than carrying the seed of one of these barbarians. The killing rage Raedwald had felt upon seeing Aethelfrith, his enemy, cut down his son Raegenhere during the Battle of the River Idle eight years earlier, rekindled in the pit of his stomach. In that terrible battle, he had breached Aethelfrith's lines and butchered his enemy in a great slaughter of the Northumbrians that had led to Raedwald's victory.

His kin were untouchable. Ceolwulf had committed a grave error in ruining his daughter.

"We have indeed met you to do battle," Raedwald said finally, "but do not expect me to keep to your terms. You have done more than just insult me this day. I will not leave Uffid Heath till you lie dead upon it."

With that, Raedwald reined his horse back and rejoined his warriors.

Caught off-guard by Raedwald's abruptness, Ceolwulf stared after him before his mouth twisted in a snarl. He turned his horse and galloped back to his men.

"Father?" Caelin brought his horse up close to Ceolwulf. Like the others, he had not heard what had passed between the two men.

"Silence!" Ceolwulf roared. "Ready yourself to do battle and do not disappoint me!"

The rhythmic clang of spears beating against shields reverberated around the battlefield as both sides advanced. Then, blood-curdling yells split the air as the thundering of hooves shook the earth. The two armies rushed at each other and met with a hollow, dull crunch of flesh, armor and metal colliding.

Raedwyn and her escort reached Rendlaesham mid-afternoon. The chill, misty morning had given way to one of the last hot days of a rainy summer. Raedwyn was sweating under her heavy cloak. Her skin was itchy and she longed to shed her filthy clothes and wash away the dust, dirt and sweat of the last few days.

Townsfolk clustered at the roadside to watch as the knot of warriors rode briskly through their midst and up to the Great Hall that commanded over the wattle and daub huts of the township. Raedwyn's eyes brimmed with tears as she saw her father's Great Hall once more. Its thatched straw roof glowed gold in the afternoon sun and at the entrance she could see the figure of a woman, framed in the doorway, watching their approach.

Raedwyn saw Seaxwyn scan the approaching group. Then, recognizing her daughter, the queen picked up her skirts and rushed down the incline to the stables where Raedwyn was dismounting.

"*Mōdor!*" Raedwyn suddenly lost the brittle composure she had maintained since returning to her father. Tears coursed down her face as she threw herself into her mother's arms.

Raedwyn sighed as she squeezed out the cloth and let hot water run down between her breasts. Servants had manhandled a large, cast-iron tub into her bower and filled it with hot water. Rosemary and lavender scented the water, and it smelled as heavenly as it felt on her scratched and aching limbs.

A bath was a singular treat. Like her mother, Raedwyn usually washed before a steaming basin. It was only on special occasions that she bathed in a cast-iron tub. The tub was not large and Raedwyn had to fold her long legs up to fit in properly. She washed her hair with a strong lavender infusion before relaxing against the edge of the tub.

Running an objective eye over her body, Raedwyn realized how rare it was for her to see herself naked. There was little privacy in her father's hall and only now with all the virile men away at battle could she remain naked without worrying about being walked in on. Her skin was milk white and her body strong. Her long legs and arms were finely muscled although scratched from struggling through the undergrowth.

As she glanced down at her pale, pink- tipped breasts, there came the memory, unbidden, of Caelin standing next her after he had dragged her out of the river. The smell of him, his nearness, had made her feel oddly light-headed. Her body had betrayed her, even while she berated him. Her breasts had been all too evident through the wet material. They had swelled under his gaze, her nipples budding hard through the linen. Then he had kissed her, and driven away thoughts of anything else. If he had not broken their embrace, who knew what would have happened.

Raedwyn's mouth went dry at the memory and her breathing quickened. She looked down at her breasts to find them responding the same way they had by the river. The base of her throat ached now, as it had then, for his touch.

Raedwyn abruptly sat up, sloshing water over the side of the tub. The pleasure of languishing in a hot bath had dissolved.

Outside, the day was ending. Raedwyn could see the sky had turned dusky rose and she knew the battle would be long since over. Raedwyn thought of the blood that would now be soaking into the peaty earth on Uffid Heath and shuddered. She prayed to Woden that her kin were safe.

Plagued with such morbid thoughts and with her bath water turning cold, Raedwyn climbed out of the tub and dried herself off. She dressed in a simple wool tunic with a linen over-dress, cinched around her waist with a tie-belt. Then, she combed her wet hair back and let it dry in curls down her back.

Joining her mother in the main hall, she helped the servants prepare the evening meal: roast pike, pottage and griddle bread. As Raedwyn kneaded the dough for the bread, her ears strained for any sound of approaching horsemen. Catching herself listening for her father's return for the hundredth time since the sun had started to set, Raedwyn forced herself to focus on the task at hand. Her mother had said they would not return before the next morning.

Raedwyn set the pummeled wheel of dough on the griddle hanging above the fire pit and soon the aroma of baking bread filled the hall. She turned the bread over and allowed the other side to cook until golden. Raedwyn's stomach growled as she placed the bread on the table to cool, reminding her of how hungry she was.

That evening, the atmosphere was subdued. There were few at dinner, as most of the warriors were away with Raedwald. Eanfled had not appeared, for which Raedwyn was grateful. She wanted to see her friend, but did not feel up to answering the barrage of questions that Eanfled would inevitably fire at her. Tomorrow, she would seek her out. Seaxwyn picked at her food, her face pinched with worry. Raedwyn chewed on a piece of fragrant griddle bread and took a sip of mead, watching her mother over the rim of her cup. She could not tell Seaxwyn not to worry, as she too was troubled about how the battle had gone. Instead, she decided to tell her mother about Ceolwulf.

"He is an ill-mannered bear of a man," Raedwyn said ripping her bread into two pieces with vehemence, "and a bully!"

"That he is Raedwyn." Seaxwyn nodded distractedly before taking a small mouthful of pottage. "He was once as close to Raedwald as Eni. They grew up together, became men together and fought alongside each other, but things changed after Raedwald married me."

"How so?" Raedwyn asked.

"Ceolwulf was ever a dissatisfied and unsettled man," Seaxwyn replied. "He had a woman, Hilda. She was a quiet, dark-haired girl, who it was rumored had been sired by a Roman, but he was not satisfied with her. She bore him a son, I forget his name, but she died in childbirth."

"Caelin," Raedwyn said without thinking, immediately regretting it when her mother's gaze rested shrewdly on her.

"Yes, that was his name. How did you know?"

Raedwyn took a large gulp of mead and feigned disinterest.

"Caelin follows his father," she said in what she hoped was a matter-of-fact tone.

"He was two winters younger than Raegenhere," Seaxwyn continued, "but Ceolwulf ignored him most of the time and allowed the boy to run wild. Ceolwulf could have remarried, and there were plenty of fine young women to choose from – but it was me he wanted."

"What!" Raedwyn spluttered, almost choking on her mead.

Now it was Seaxwyn's turn to look discomforted. "I did not encourage him!" she retorted. "But soon after I became Raedwald's wife I realized that Ceolwulf was insanely jealous of his king. Ceolwulf wanted a high-born woman, not some Roman spawn."

Raedwyn noted the acidity in her mother's voice as she finished her sentence. Seaxwyn's dislike of the Romans was no surprise. She associated them with the encroachment of Christianity. Even Raedwald had converted to the new religion, although Seaxwyn made sure that her husband always honored the old gods.

"Slowly, insidiously, Ceolwulf began to show me more attention." Seaxwyn continued her tale. "He made excuses to seek me out, flattered me and flattered Raedwald even more so. His attention worried me, and I even mentioned my fears to Raedwald but he brushed them off, saying that Ceolwulf was just behaving like any strong virile male and there was no harm in it."

Seaxwyn stopped here and Raedwyn noticed her mother's cheeks were flushed. Seaxwyn poured herself some more mead before continuing. "To cut a long story short, one day Ceolwulf cornered me and tried to force himself upon me. Raedwald had been away hunting and came back in time to find me fighting Ceolwulf off. He banished him from Rendlaesham that very day."

"That explains it," Raedwyn murmured.

"Explains what?" Seaxwyn frowned.

"He was very bitter about you. He said you poisoned father against him."

"Now you know why he would say such a thing," Seaxwyn replied. "He could never accept that his feelings weren't reciprocated."

Raedwyn finished her mead and stood up, feeling the effect of the drink as the walls around her swayed slightly. She was exhausted and the mead had only exacerbated her fatigue.

"Let us hope then, that it is father who returns to us in victory tomorrow." Raedwyn kissed her mother on the cheek. "I just want this nightmare to be over. The waiting is the hardest part."

"Goodnight Raedwyn."

Seaxwyn remained seated at the empty table while her daughter disappeared into her bower. The queen pushed away her bowl of pottage, largely untouched, and massaged her temples.

She had thought it had all finished, but even all these years later the past would not be forgotten. Her gray eyes fixed unseeingly on the low flames in the fire pit before her as the years rolled back and suddenly it was as if no time had passed at all.

Chapter Eight

RAEDWYN PULLED HER hair back into a braid, wrapped a shawl about her shoulders and stepped outside her father's hall into the morning light. She turned her face up to the sky and let the sun warm it before casting her gaze over Rendlaesham below. She knew this place so well. Life at Rendlaesham always followed a steady, unchanging pattern, year after year and Raedwyn found comfort in that.

It was now harvest-time and the arable fields that spread out around the town were full of ceorls—the *folcfry*—free folk who farmed the land around Rendlaesham. Also about were kotsetlas and geburs, higher and lower ranks of peasant bound to their lord Raedwald. This morning they were harvesting the summer barley and owing to the mild weather, the task was a pleasant one.

Raedwyn walked down into Rendlaesham and made her way to Eanfled's new home. Eanfled would be a married woman now, as her wedding had been organized for two days after Raedwyn's. Despite everything, Raedwyn was eager to see her friend in her new life as Alric the iron smith's wife.

The smithy sat in a narrow street just behind Rendlaesham's main thoroughfare. It was a long, low-slung dwelling with the forge at one end and the living quarters at the other. Alric was at his forge. He waved to Raedwyn, put down his hammer and stepped out onto the street to greet her.

"M'lady!" Alric was a stocky young man with dark brown hair, a short beard and kind blue eyes. As always, he was a little shy in her presence. "I'm glad to see you safe."

"Thank you, Alric," Raedwyn replied gently. "I never thought to return to Rendlaesham so soon, and certainly not in these circumstances."

Alric nodded, his brow crinkling in concern. "It's terrible news about your husband m'lady, and the whole town awaits word about the Battle of Uffid Heath," he continued, "although I can see that mention of this pains you. Come, Eanfled is baking. She will be pleased to see you."

Pleased was an understatement. Eanfled dropped the rolling pin she had been using to flatten a sheet of pastry and flew across the kitchen to give Raedwyn a floury embrace. Alric left them with a smile, knowing his presence would not be missed.

"I heard you returned yesterday, but I wanted to let you rest." Eanfled dragged Raedwyn into the kitchen and pushed her into a chair. "I shall make us some hot spiced cider."

Raedwyn was glad of Eanfled's industrious, boisterous energy. She had been afraid that she would burst into tears at the sight of her friend, but Eanfled's fussing galvanized her.

"I could not believe it." Eanfled poured some cider into a cast iron pot and hung it above the kitchen's fire pit. "I feared I would never see you again—and your poor husband! I heard that Cynric did not even have the chance to defend himself. The outlaw who brought Ceolwulf's terms bragged about it after his audience with the king. Was it indeed an ambush?"

"It was," Raedwyn replied. "They lay in wait for, and killed them all."

Eanfled glanced across at Raedwyn, her pretty brow furrowing, before she added some spices and honey to the cider and stirred it with a wooden spoon.

"You are not yourself, Raedwyn," she observed. "I'm sorry for my prattle. It's the last thing you want."

"It's not that," Raedwyn replied with a tired smile, "I feel as if years have passed and it has only been a few days."

"It's cruel to take your husband from you." Eanfled used a ladle to pour two generous cups of spiced cider, before passing one to Raedwyn. "You were so beautiful and happy at your handfast ceremony Raedwyn—you look so sad now."

Raedwyn sighed and took a sip of her cider. It was delicious and soothing. She would have to tell Eanfled the truth or their friendship would never be the same. Raedwyn wanted to confide in someone, and she trusted no one else as she did Eanfled.

"Things are never what they appear," Raedwyn replied, "and although I was happy at my wedding, it did not last long. Sit down Eanfled for I have many things to tell you."

Eanfled did as she was bid. She sat opposite Raedwyn at the scrubbed wood table and listened without interrupting as her friend told her everything that had happened to her since the handfast ceremony. Raedwyn left nothing out—Cynric's rough taking of her maidenhead, Ceolwulf's vengeance, her hopeless attraction for Caelin, and Caelin setting her free—she told Eanfled everything.

By the time Raedwyn had finished her tale, Eanfled's eyes were like two huge moons.

"Woden!" Eanfled breathed, her fingers curled around the cup of cider that she had barely touched, and had now gone cold. "For once, I am at a loss for words!"

Despite everything, Raedwyn laughed. "I never thought I'd see the day when you would be struck dumb by something I said!" she teased her friend.

Eanfled shook her head, her gaze still fixed upon Raedwyn's face.

"I cannot believe that you survived," she replied, "and if it had not been for this man, Caelin, it sounds as if Ceolwulf would have killed you."

"He surely would have," Raedwyn agreed, remembering the maddened look on the Exiled's face as he stood over her and drew his foot back to kick her in the stomach.

Raedwyn could see that this tale had upset her friend, and the worry on Eanfled's face was more than Raedwyn could bear.

"Come now, Eanfled." Raedwyn reached across the table and took hold of her friend's hands. "I did survive and my father will make sure Ceolwulf pays for his treachery. But what of you? What is it like being married to Alric and living here under his roof?"

Eanfled's face broke into a wide smile and despite herself Raedwyn felt a small needle of envy pierce her. It was the smile of a woman in love.

"He is a wonderful man," Eanfled breathed. "I can't believe we are finally together. We were betrothed for so long that I had started to worry that he would change his mind. However, Alric insisted that he had wanted to establish his trade in Rendlaesham first before marrying and starting a family."

"He just wanted to make sure he could take care of you," Raedwyn agreed, pushing aside her envy. What right had she to be jealous of Eanfled's happiness, especially when it was so hard earned? "I've never seen a man look so pleased with himself!"

Eanfled threw back her head and laughed. A moment later, Alric appeared at the kitchen door. His bemused gaze rested on his young wife.

"Have I been missing out on a great tale?" he asked. "There has been a lot of laughter coming from this kitchen."

Eanfled smothered her laugher and gave Raedwyn a conspiratorial wink.

"No, my love, we were just prattling, as usual!"

Seaxwyn was at her loom, weaving a tapestry, when Raedwyn entered the Great Hall. Her afternoon with Eanfled had relaxed her immensely, and it had taken her mind off this morning's battle and her worry about the outcome.

The tapestry Seaxwyn wove was a detailed one, and when finished it would be one of the queen's best. It depicted a rearing white horse with a warrior astride it, a royal blue cape rippling from his shoulders. It was Raedwald—victorious on the field of battle.

Like her mother, Raedwyn was a talented weaver. She had passed many a dark winter's day at the loom learning her mother's craft. Raedwyn sat down next to her mother now while Seaxwyn worked and chatted to her about Eanfled's new life with Alric.

Seaxwyn listened to her daughter but said little. Raedwyn had inherited her father's uncomplicated and open nature rather than her mother's quieter more introspective ways. Both strong women, they dealt with the tense wait in their own manner.

The shadows were lengthening and the birds were starting to roost, when the horses appeared at last. Moving as one entity of bristling shields and spears, they crested the last hill to the south and headed towards Rendlaesham.

"Mother!" Raedwyn was standing outside the hall with her eyes fixed on the southern horizon and was the first to see the riders. Moments later, Seaxwyn appeared beside her daughter and together they watched the *fyrd* enter Rendlaesham. Dust boiled up from under pounding hooves and spears bristled above bobbing heads. The horses streamed into the town.

Raedwyn's heart lurched when she saw the standard held by the first riders bearing her father's crest. She glanced at her mother, who had also seen the standard. Relief bloomed in Seaxwyn's face and the tension melted from her features, giving her the countenance of a woman half her age. Despite her obvious relief, tears streamed down the queen's face.

Seaxwyn picked up her skirts and rushed down to the stables. The path, leading down from the Great Hall, widened out into a spacious yard. Raedwyn followed her mother, running to keep up with her.

Raedwald's *fyrd* thundered into the yard, filling it. Many warriors were forced to draw their horses up outside as there was not enough space for all of their number within. The king himself was out front with Eorpwald by his side. Raedwald no longer rode his white stallion but an ill-tempered bay that snorted and rolled its eyes as Raedwald drew up.

He rode with his helmet tucked under one arm and his hair tumbling over his shoulders like a lion's mane. Despite that he was no longer a young man, Raedwald was virile and regal in his victory. The king swung down from the saddle and Raedwyn saw, for the first time, that he was injured. His right arm, his sword arm, carried a deep sword wound. Someone had bound the injury but Raedwyn could see the blood seeping through the bandages. Eorpwald dismounted next to his father. Lithe and physically smaller than his father, Eorpwald landed lightly on his feet, despite the heavy armor he wore. Sweat tangled his shoulder length brown hair and he had suffered a graze to his left brow. Apart from that, he appeared uninjured, although exhaustion made his face pinched and sharp.

Raedwyn watched as townsfolk helped the injured and dying from their horses and carried them away to healers.

Seaxwyn rushed into her husband's arms. They clung together for a moment before Raedwyn saw her father mumble into his wife's hair.

"It's over at last. He is dead."

Raedwyn glanced over at her brother. Feeling his sister's eyes on him, Eorpwald's gaze met Raedwyn's before he winked at her.

"Thought you had got rid of me, eh?"

Raedwyn punched Eorpwald on the arm in response before hugging him tightly.

"I've already lost one brother to battle," she told him, "and I am relieved you came home safe, as you well know!"

Once Seaxwyn had released Raedwald and moved to greet her son,

Raedwyn went to her father. Raedwald hugged his daughter stiffly. Raedwyn felt the discomfort in his embrace and drew back, confused.

"Father?"

Raedwald turned aside to shout an order to his men.

"Bring up the prisoners!"

Raedwald smiled then, a cold vindictive smile of someone who had savored revenge and enjoyed the taste—then his gaze met Raedwyn's.

"I fought Ceolwulf the Exiled, and slew him before taking this ill-tempered steed of his," he explained. "We thought all were dead but upon combing the battlefield we discovered two survivors."

The crowd parted and a horse appeared with two men slung across its back—one was unconscious while the other stared defiantly at the watching crowd.

Raedwyn went cold.

The survivors were Caelin and Hengist.

Caelin lay immobile, his arms trailing earthwards, his dark hair falling about his shoulders while Hengist had twisted to scrutinize his captors.

"One of them was playing dead," Raedwald said, motioning to Hengist, "while the other one was near death and has not awoken since we captured him."

Raedwald turned to his daughter then, and held her gaze fast in his.

"Do you know either of these men, Raedwyn?"

Raedwyn nodded. She sensed a trap and knew it would be better for her if she spoke the truth.

"What are their names?" Raedwald pressed.

Raedwyn licked her suddenly parched lips and looked at the two prisoners. Hengist stared defiantly at her, his gaze as cold as her father's, and suddenly Raedwyn felt as she had in Ceolwulf's encampment—a deer cornered by hunters with nowhere to turn.

"The one who is awake is Hengist." She returned Hengist's stare unflinchingly. "While the other is Caelin."

"This Caelin is more finely armored than the others, save Ceolwulf, and rode at the Exiled's side. Who is he?"

Raedwyn met her father's gaze again and had the sensation that Raedwald already knew the answer to his question. She was right, he was testing her.

"Ceolwulf's son." she replied without hesitation, "but I think you already know that father."

Raedwald turned to the warrior leading the horse. "Untie them."

Raedwyn watched as her father's men unbound Hengist and Caelin and pulled them from the horse's back. They lowered Caelin to the ground, where he lay, unmoving. His chest moved shallowly; he was still breathing, but two arrows protruded from his side and he was deathly pale. Hengist could not walk. An axe had shattered his left leg, and the limb dragged behind him uselessly. Two warriors held Hengist up so that he could face Raedwald.

"Hengist and I had an interesting talk this morning," Raedwald explained. His voice was gentle and quiet; the tone he used when he was the most furious. Raedwyn sensed danger, but her father's hostility towards her was confusing. The fact she had done nothing to warrant it did not quiet her instincts.

"Hengist is as disloyal as he is a coward." Raedwald stared at his captive, who had the good sense to look away from the king's hard gaze. "He told me of Caelin's identity. He also told me that upon your capture you begged Ceolwulf and his men to free you and offered your body to them."

"No!" choked Raedwyn, "Never!"

"He also said," Raedwald continued, cutting his daughter off, "you were only too eager to share your body with him and that Ceolwulf and his whelp took turns with you. His men were most appreciative of your willingness to accommodate them. I met with the Exiled, moments before battle and he said the same. Do you deny their words, daughter?"

Raedwyn's world shrank as she listened to her father's accusation. She stopped breathing for a moment, her surroundings blurred and she came the closest she had ever felt to fainting. She knew, as she opened her mouth to defend herself, that her father had believed the words of his enemies rather than those of his own kin—and without solid proof she could not convince him otherwise.

"I deny their words!" Raedwyn choked out eventually. Hard, accusing stares surrounded her, cutting into her flesh like knives. It was like wading through thick mud that pulled her under with each step forward she managed. Raedwyn took a deep breath and the world expanded once again as the panic subsided somewhat.

"Ceolwulf lied to, father," Raedwyn's voice was low and vehement. "Surely you know I would never do as Hengist and Ceolwulf have said. Ceolwulf never laid a finger on me. He said it only to bait you, and as for Hengist." Raedwyn watched Hengist now, amazed at how brazenly he stared at her. "When I was captured he tried to rape me but was prevented by the man who lies dying next to him."

A chilling silence fell on the knot of warriors surrounding the two injured men.

Hengist spat on the ground and lurched towards Raedwyn, held back by his broken leg and the two men who held him fast.

"Lying, filthy little slut!" he bawled. "You behaved like a bitch in heat, as you well know!"

These were the last words Hengist ever uttered for Raedwald unsheathed his sword and, unhindered even by his injured arm, ran Hengist through with the blade. Hengist fell gurgling and twitching to the ground and died as blood pooled on the dusty earth beneath him.

"He was beginning to vex me." Raedwald calmly cleaned his blade on the dead man's clothes before re-sheathing his sword. "The cur had a loose tongue."

Unconcerned by the sudden, violent death in their midst, two warriors picked up Hengist's carcass and dragged it from the scene.

Shaken and feeling as if she would be violently ill, Raedwyn stood before her father. She stared at the bloodstain on the ground, not daring to meet her mother or brother's gaze for she could not stand to see the blame in their eyes. It broke her heart to see her own father disbelieving her—and she could not bear the rest of them to think her a liar as well.

"Hengist lied," Raedwyn said finally.

The king ignored her and Raedwyn watched him walk over to where Caelin lay. Ceolwulf's son lay on his back, his face chalk-white but still breathing, despite his grave injuries.

Raedwald looked down at the unconscious man and frowned. "The last time I saw Caelin he was a child," he mused. "There is little of his father in his looks; more of that ill-fated wench who bore him. It's ill for him that he survived the battle. He has lost all honor."

"We should let him die." Eni, his entire left side bandaged, limped up beside his brother. "There is nothing to be gained in keeping your enemy's spawn alive."

Raedwyn's chest ached as she looked upon Caelin's unconscious face, but she was inclined to agree with her uncle. Caelin had lost everything.

"If he has no honor then it is all the more reason for keeping him alive," Raedwald replied with a vindictiveness that made Eni draw back in surprise. "We will tend his injuries and if he lives he will reside here as my slave, more lowly even than a theow. Ceolwulf's debasement will live on, even after his death."

Raedwyn looked at the others: Eni, his sons, Seaxwyn and Eorpwald, and saw her own shock reflected in various degrees on their faces. Her father's hatred for Ceolwulf had driven him to the edge of madness, so much so that he would even inflict his revenge further upon Ceolwulf's son.

Tears coursed down the queen's face as she gazed upon her husband. Raedwald's face was hard and devoid of mercy. No one dared question him.

Raedwyn stood, unable to move lest her legs gave way from shock, while Raedwald brushed past her and took his wife's arm.

Watching her father walk away, Raedwyn felt a crushing sense of betrayal. Her own father had humiliated her in front of his *fyrd* and her own kin. He had accused her of behaving like a whore and, even though he had slain Hengist for insulting her, he had not cleared her name before the crowd.

No one spoke to her.

The battle-weary warriors turned from her and moved off to tend to their horses and see to their own wounds. They were treating her as if she was a *nithing*—forfeiting all honor and respect; an individual dead to their eyes.

Raedwyn stood looking down at her bloodless hands. She clasped them in front of her and wished the ground would open up and swallow her whole. When she looked up, she found that Eni, Annan, Aethelhere, Aethelwold and Eorpwald were still standing watching her.

It was an effort to meet their gazes, but when she did, Raedwyn was surprised to see compassion on their faces. She had thought they would share her father's scorn; that they too would believe her to be a whore.

"It's truly a man's world," Raedwyn whispered brokenly, "when a father believes the words of his enemy over those of his own daughter."

In unison, her brother and uncle stepped forward and pulled her into their collective embrace. They smelled of sweat, horse, blood and leather. Raedwyn hugged them tightly to her, their strength and vitality seeping into her like a healing balm.

Finally, she let the tears come.

Chapter Nine

A CHILL WIND battered against the timber framing of Raedwald's Great Hall and howled around the eaves. Night had long since fallen across Rendlaesham, but the feasting and celebrations had only just died away.

Once inside his hall, the king's mood had seemed vastly improved. Mead flowed, music echoed amongst the rafters and the weary but triumphant warriors feasted on roast mutton and pottage, followed by slabs of bread and honey. Tales of the Battle of Uffid Heath echoed from side to side of the hall and Raedwald handed out silver and gold neck and arm rings to those warriors who had fought the most bravely during the battle. Eorpwald, who carried only a few arm rings, received a beautiful golden arm ring from his father.

"You fought well son." Raedwald's eyes had brimmed with tears from mead-induced sentimentality. "You have made your father proud."

Eorpwald had blushed deeply as, beside him, Annan slapped him on the back. Raedwyn watched her brother and was glad for him. Long had he lived in Raegenhere's shadow; now it seemed his dead brother's shade had moved on.

Little was said to Raedwyn during the celebrations and, unlike other feasts in the past where she had happily been the center of attention, Raedwyn was content to watch and listen to the tales which swirled around her. Their victory had been hard won and Ceolwulf's army had slain many of the king's *fyrd* before succumbing to its sheer size. Raedwald did not speak to, or look at, his daughter all evening. Despite Eorpwald and Eni's kindness, Raedwyn still stung from her public shaming.

Hours after the feasting finished, Raedwyn lay in darkness within her bower and listened to the wind. She wondered how long it would take for her relationship with her father to recover from this. She had never seen him so angry with her and the injustice of it should have made her respond in kind. In the aftermath of her father's accusations, Raedwyn wished she had defended herself more strongly. She should have been the one to run Hengist through with a sword for his vicious, lying words. However, shock had rendered her wooden. She could not understand the depth of her father's hatred towards Ceolwulf, and she knew to be wary of him while it held him in its thrall.

Sleep would not come and so, finally, Raedwyn rolled off her bed and wrapped a fur cloak around her shoulders. She pulled aside the tapestry that shielded her bower from the rest of the hall and stepped outside.

Slumbering bodies carpeted the floor and darkness shrouded the hall, save for the embers still glowing in the fire pit and the odd torch flickering gently on the wall.

Padding across the floor barefoot, Raedwyn stepped over sleeping men and made her way to the annex at the end of the hall, where she and Cynric had spent their wedding night. Memories of that unpleasant episode flooded back as Raedwyn pulled back the curtain and stepped inside the chamber.

Two torches burned within, illuminating the figure stretched upon the bed. They had stripped Caelin of his armor and mail shirt. He wore nothing but a pair of loose breeches. Raedwald's healer had removed the arrows, with great difficulty, and the bleeding had been profuse. The healer had bound Caelin's chest with linen, and blood now stained the pale material. Raedwyn wondered if the arrows had pierced anything vital, although she supposed if that had been the case, he would be dead already.

Caelin's skin was pale in the torch light and when Raedwyn put out a hand and touched his forehead, she found his skin clammy and waxy to touch. It should have been a great honor, to be tended under Raedwald's roof and by his personal healer – but Raedwyn knew it was not kindness that had prompted her father's concern. He wished for Caelin to live, but not out of mercy.

Raedwyn perched on the side of the bed and, taking an earthen bowl of water infused with herbs, wet a cloth before mopping Caelin's brow. The dark shadow of a new beard covered his chin and bristled under Raedwyn's fingertips. Not knowing why she did so, Raedwyn gently traced her fingers over his patrician features that were beautiful in repose. She re-wet the cloth and wrung it out before running it over the areas of his chest and stomach not covered by the bandages. He had a lean, strong body; his chest sprinkled with dark curly hair that tapered down to a thin line of down over his stomach before it disappeared under the drawstring waistband of his breeches. Noticing the direction of her gaze, Raedwyn deftly placed the cloth back over the rim of the bowl.

It was idiocy to be here, alone, with him, even if he posed no danger to her in this state. Her father needed no further reason to disbelieve her. Yet, ignoring good sense, Raedwyn lingered a while longer at Caelin's side. She folded her hands on her lap and looked into Caelin's face.

"I'm sorry Caelin," Raedwyn whispered. "This should not have been your end."

Raedwyn rose from the bed. Then, she bent over and placed a gentle kiss on Caelin's forehead, before walking over to the doorway. She pulled aside the curtain and looked back over her shoulder at his still form. His chest still rose and fell, albeit shallowly, but he looked like a corpse. Raedwyn turned away and let the curtain fall, wondering whether she would find him alive in the morning.

Autumn arrived in a sudden bluster of icy gales and shorter evenings. The leaves on the trees surrounding Rendlaesham changed from green, to gold and then brown before falling from their host and carpeting the ground. The harvest was over and, despite a wet summer, there was ample food for the coming winter. Wood smoke laced the air around Rendlaesham in the evenings and the townsfolk took to wearing stouter clothing and cloaks.

As memory of the summer faded and winter beckoned, life in Raedwald's hall settled back into its old routine, save for one element—for the hall now had a new resident.

Caelin, son of Ceolwulf the Exiled, did not die.

Much to the surprise of all, after many days of fever and insensibility, Caelin awoke and, owing to the healer's ministrations and cunning use of herbs, his wounds slowly healed.

"As soon as he's well enough I want him out working," Raedwald ordered the healer. "Let it be known he is not here as my guest—he is my slave!"

"Yes M'lord," the healer replied before venturing. "He is yet too weak to stand. His wounds were great and 'tis a miracle he survived them. "It will be mid-winter before he is well enough to work."

This news had not pleased Raedwald and it seemed to his kin that he now regretted his decision to keep Ceolwulf's whelp alive.

Raedwyn had secretly visited Caelin a few times while he was still unconscious but once she heard he had awoken, she hesitated, fearing his reaction. Her father's attitude towards her had thawed a little; now he treated her with mere indifference rather than disdain. No one ever brought up Hengist and Ceolwulf's claims against her again, but Raedwyn knew they had not forgotten. The issue still festered and Raedwyn longed to sit before her father and argue her innocence. In the past, she had never been afraid of her father, but now she hesitated to cross him.

Seaxwyn made up for her husband's coolness by mothering her daughter and fussing over her in a way that irritated both Raedwyn and Raedwald. The king's hall had always been a happy, relaxed home, but now Raedwyn found her bower stifling and the underlying tension between her and Raedwald needled her.

During the day, she was careful to show no interest whatsoever in her father's new slave. She did not ask after his progress, nor venture near the annex at the back of the hall. Instead, she assisted her mother with her tapestries and helped bake bread every morning. She spent her afternoons visiting Eanfled or riding her horse, Blackberry, in the folds of land around Rendlaesham.

Life slowly returned to its old rhythm and, despite her father's continuing coolness towards her, Raedwyn started to feel her old self once more. In the evenings, she insisted that Eorpwald taught her how to play

Hnefatafl, 'King's Table'; a board game she had watched her brother and cousins play for years.

One evening, as rain drummed against the thatched roof of the Great Hall, Raedwyn sat opposite Eorpwald at one of the long tables next to the fire pit playing *Hnefatafl*. Between them lay a beautiful board, marked out into twenty-six squares. Raedwyn picked up her king and grinned at Eorpwald as she moved the piece three spaces to the edge of the board.

"Ha brother, I win!"

"Not again!" Annan called out from where he sat nursing a cup of hot mead farther up the table.

Eorpwald shook his head and glared down at the board, unable to believe she had beaten him.

"Ruthless wench!" he muttered.

"Admit it," Eni, who had also been watching the game, chimed in, "after beating four men in one evening, Raedwyn's a better strategist than you all!"

"It's only a game father," Annan protested, while his two brothers whom Raedwyn had bested earlier that evening, Aethelhere and Aethelwold, also looked disgruntled at their father's rebuke.

Raedwyn beamed at her uncle. It was not often Eni admitted a woman could beat at man at anything.

"What say you, Eorpwald?" Raedwyn turned back to her brother. "Another game?"

Eorpwald threw up his hands. "Sorry dear sister but I don't think my pride could withstand another defeat!" His grey eyes twinkled as the chagrin of losing faded from his face. "What I need now is a large cup of mead!"

"Cousins?" Raedwyn looked hopefully towards Annan, Aethelhere and Aethelwold but they only shook their heads, while Annan muttered something about bad winners under his breath.

"Suit yourselves then," Raedwyn replied cheerfully, "but tomorrow eve shall we play again Eorpwald?"

"Of course," Eorpwald sighed. "I shall ready myself to take another beating."

Still smiling from her victory, Raedwyn bid her menfolk goodnight and retired to her bower. Despite that her father still sat apart from her every evening, and only spoke to her when absolutely necessary, Raedwyn had grown closer to the rest of her family of late. Their games of *Hnefatafl* had forged a bond between Raedwyn and Eorpwald. No longer offended by her brother's sharp wit, Raedwyn found herself looking forward to spending time with Eorpwald, and she often sought out his company.

Raedwyn lay awake listening to the rain and waited for sleep to claim her. Eventually the Great Hall quietened as everyone else retired for the night. Still wide-awake, Raedwyn decided that it was time to face Caelin.

Raedwyn slipped out of bed, wrapped herself in a fur cloak and silently made her way to Caelin's annex. She pulled back the curtain and saw he was sleeping under a heavy blanket. Someone had shaved his chin, and cut his dark hair short to denote his new slave status. His face was thin and strained. Around his neck, he wore an iron slave collar. Raedwyn padded over to his bedside and tweaked at his blanket.

"Caelin," she said softly, shaking him gently when he did not respond.

A hand suddenly fastened around Raedwyn's forearm and she had to bite down on her tongue not to cry out in alarm.

"Raedwyn." Caelin's dark eyes were open and he stared up into her face. "I was wondering when I would see you."

He kept hold of her arm but his grip was not so strong that she could not have escaped it if she had wished. Raedwyn perched on the edge of the bed and without thinking placed her free hand over the hand gripping her arm.

She saw Caelin's eyes widen at that, but she kept her hand over his nonetheless.

"You look at me with such pity in your eyes," Caelin said finally. "Am I so diminished now I am your father's theow?"

Raedwyn shook her head, suppressing the urge to weep.

"You know why my father has kept you alive then?"

Caelin nodded. "It was my misfortune not have died on Uffid Heath," he replied. "The feud between Ceolwulf and Raedwald continues, even after my father's death."

"It's not right." Raedwyn shook her head. "To rid you of your honor."

Caelin looked at her and Raedwyn saw emotion flare in his eyes, before a dark veil slid across them.

"You still haven't learned, have you?" he said finally, his voice though weak, had a flinty edge to it.

Taken aback, Raedwyn stared at him. When she did not reply, Caelin continued.

"Have not the events of late taught you that it matters not in this world what is right and not right?"

"It matters to me!" Raedwyn shot back.

"Why?"

"Because you did something selfless and kind for me—and this is how we repay you?"

"Did you tell Raedwald I set you free?" Caelin's eyebrows lifted.

Raedwyn jerked her arm from Caelin's grip and stood up.

"No, I have not," she replied, meeting Caelin's gaze with difficulty. "I thought he would use it against you."

Caelin laughed softly and shook his head. "I think you're more concerned he could use it against you."

Anger erupted in Raedwyn then, and it was a strain to keep her voice hushed, lest the sleeping hall hear her.

"Why do you deliberately assume the worst of me?"

"No, Raedwyn," Caelin replied softly. "I am just reminding you that despite knowing what is 'right' you have chosen to look after yourself first. And that is how it should be if you wish to survive."

Raedwyn clenched her fists at her sides, and suppressed the urge to hit his sanctimonious face. He was behaving like one of those pious Christian martyrs she had heard about from the priest who had baptized her father. She knew that *wyrd* determined the course of their lives, but she could not believe that even fate was not to be argued with when life had dealt you unfairly.

"So you will be my father's toadying theow for the rest of your days and just accept life isn't meant to be fair?" she snapped.

Caelin stared back at her, his eyes dark and bleak.

"The rest of my days?" he replied slowly. "Raedwyn, I should have perished on Uffid Heath, as fate wished. As far as I'm concerned, I died there, alongside my father and all those who fought with me. The man who gave you your freedom and disappointed his father is dead."

"So you regret letting me go free?" Raedwyn's whisper was almost inaudible.

"Regret would mean I feel something. I feel nothing."

Raedwyn stared at him for a moment, searching his face for a sign he was lying, but the face that returned her stare was a cold mask. Caelin's eyes were that of a stranger's.

Raedwyn opened her mouth to apologize—but the words would not come. Even in her head, they sounded hollow. She could not change events. An apology could not even begin to heal the wounds that festered within the man before her.

Saying no more, Raedwyn turned and made her way to the door. She felt Caelin's eyes upon her as she slipped beyond the curtain and left him alone with the void that filled him.

Caelin watched Raedwyn disappear behind the curtain. He lay still on the bed and listened to the gentle sounds of the sleeping hall outside. His arm still burned where she had touched him and there was still an indentation on the bed next to him, where she had sat.

Caelin took a deep breath and relaxed his hands. He had balled them up into fists so tight his nails had bitten into his palms. He had lied when he told Raedwyn he felt nothing—the truth of it was that he felt too much. A squall of rain hit the hall then; icy fingers drumming against the shutters. Caelin closed his eyes. The life of a free man was lost to him.

Chapter Ten

SOME RENDLAESHAM WINTERS could be mild, with only light frosts carpeting the ground in the mornings, brief snowfalls, and enough clear days to allow the sun to show its face. Other winters were bitter from the first to the last, with vicious hoar frosts, days of snow that froze on the ground, and day after day of impenetrable gray skies. This winter was the latter. Raedwyn remembered such icy weather when she had been around twelve winters old. A number of elderly and infants had perished and she, like all at Rendlaesham, had forgotten what warmth felt like. This winter brought back memories of that experience: constantly numb toes and fingers, cramped muscles from the chill, and being wrapped up to the nose in furs.

The snows came early, before winter solstice, and a pristine, white crust covered the world. Unable to bear being cooped up inside the hall mindlessly working at her distaff or weaving, Raedwyn took to riding often. Her father had never encouraged his daughter to ride, as women did not go hunting or ride with men to war, but Raedwyn had always enjoyed the freedom of it. Now it offered her respite from the cramped confines of her father's hall. She rode Blackberry; a shaggy, bay mare of advancing years. The mare was not an attractive beast, but a safe ride and not a horse her father's servants worried about her taking out.

One morning, wrapped up warmly in leggings and furs, Raedwyn rode Blackberry out of the stables and down through the township. She passed low-slung wattle and daub houses, and saw smoke rising from holes in their roofs, staining the pallid sky. She rode by a group of children playing in the snow and lopping snowballs at each other. They called out to her and she waved as she passed them. Raedwyn had become a common sight of late, riding alone around Rendlaesham. A little farther out from the town, she passed peasants collecting firewood, before she rode into a copse of skeleton trees and urged her mare into a slow canter.

The snow lay a foot deep, but deeper in places where the land dipped, and Raedwyn was careful to keep to the terrain she knew so Blackberry would not stumble. Despite her heavy clothing and the rabbit-skin gloves covering her hands, the chill bit into her skin and burned her face. Even with the cold, Raedwyn felt peace settle over her as she rode alone through the silent countryside. She never had a moment to herself cooped up inside the Great Hall, and as much as Raedwyn enjoyed the company of her brother and cousins, there were times when she needed freedom.

Raedwyn looked forward at where the mare's furry ears pricked forward as she plodded through the snow, and her thoughts returned to her conversation with Eanfled that morning. She had visited early with a small batch of hot apple pies, to find her friend wan and sickly. A moon-cycle after her wedding, Eanfled had discovered that she was with child. She was finding the early stage of her pregnancy a trial but managed to nibble at one of the pies that Raedwyn had brought, before pouring her friend a cup of hot milk with honey.

"I saw Ceolwulf the Exiled's son yesterday for the first time," Eanfled had announced. "You did not tell me he was so handsome! Even with his hair cropped and that awful iron collar, he's striking!"

Raedwyn had felt her face heat up at Eanfled's frank appraisal. Mention of Caelin was off-limits under the king's roof but in the safety of her own home, Eanfled spoke openly. Although Raedwyn had known Eanfled would keep her secret, she now wished she had not been so frank with her.

"I can see why you were taken with him," Eanfled continued. "If I were not with Alric he'd be just the man to tempt me!"

"Eanfled!" Raedwyn glared at her friend. "You're a married woman!"

Eanfled had given her a sly look before taking another small bite of her pie.

"Don't play the prude. I'm still able to appreciate a good-looking man am I not?" she replied. "He might be a theow but he doesn't carry himself like one."

"He's a warrior," Raedwyn admitted, "although nothing like his father."

"I imagine he's a good kisser." Eanfled gave Raedwyn a wicked look. "No need to say anything, you've gone as red as the sun!"

"For the love of Freya," Raedwyn had thrown up her hands. "You're really not helping—now pass me one of those pies and let's change the subject!"

Deep in thought about her conversation with Eanfled, Raedwyn pushed her horse into a faster canter. Eanfled's pragmatism was refreshing, but then she had been born into a more straightforward world than Raedwyn.

Blackberry suddenly stumbled and went down on her knees, tearing Raedwyn from her introspection. Her attempt to cling on was futile. She sailed over the mare's neck and landed on her stomach in the snow with a crunch.

For a moment, Raedwyn could not breathe. Luckily, the powdered snow had broken her fall. Gasping for breath, Raedwyn rolled onto her back and wiped the snow off her face. Blackberry stood nearby, watching her reproachfully. Raedwyn was relieved to see the horse was not favoring a foot. Such a stumble could have broken Blackberry's leg. Berating herself, Raedwyn attempted to get to her feet, only to gasp in pain and sink back down onto her haunches. She had twisted her ankle badly, despite the fur ankle boots she wore.

"Raedwyn the Stupid," she muttered as she reached down and gingerly touched her ankle. It felt hot, although she was able to move it a little. Raedwyn hissed through her teeth when she flexed it too far. She hoped it was just a bad sprain, and not broken.

Raedwyn finally managed to get to her feet by rolling onto her knees and using her good ankle to lever herself up. She hopped over to where Blackberry still stood, eyeing her patiently. Raedwyn reached out and stroked the velvety muzzle.

"You're a loyal one, aren't you?" She ruffled the horse's fluffy forelock and looked into its kind eyes. "That was my fault, not yours."

She tried to mount but the pain in her ankle was excruciating. After clinging to Blackberry's furry neck until the pain subsided, Raedwyn limped back the way they had come, using her horse as a crutch. As if sensing her rider needed assistance, the mare plodded sedately alongside Raedwyn, allowing Raedwyn to clutch onto her mane to keep her balance. Raedwyn had ridden quite a distance from Rendlaesham and her progress back was slow. It was bitterly cold and soon Raedwyn's fingers and toes were numb. The air stung her lungs as she breathed.

She was still some way from Rendlaesham when it began to snow. One moment the sky had been clear; the next, a soft white shroud settled around Raedwyn, obliterating her surroundings. The snow fell silently, gently, but its innocuous appearance did not deceive Raedwyn. She knew how quickly someone could die in a blizzard. Almost immediately, she lost her sense of direction. The snow covered the tracks she had made earlier and she could not see more than a yard in front of her. Certain that Rendlaesham must be ahead if she continued in the same direction, Raedwyn hobbled on while the snow fell ever thicker.

A while later, Raedwyn stopped and wiped snow from her numb face. Blackberry halted next to her. Snow frosted the mare's mane, forelock and eyelashes. Blackberry's thick winter coat protected her from the weather but Raedwyn could feel herself weakening. For the first time she felt a tickle of fear but she pushed it aside angrily.

Rendlaesham must be close by. She had the disconcerting sensation she was hobbling round in circles with the town just out of reach. She cursed her poor sense of direction. Memories of getting lost in the forest after her escape from Ceolwulf's encampment flooded back—a deranged bat could navigate better than her.

Deciding that her current path was not leading her home, Raedwyn turned Blackberry left and they continued their sluggish journey.

Time passed slowly in a silent, white world and Raedwyn could feel tears of panic pricking at her burning eyelids when the figure of a man appeared in the distance. He materialized like a shade from a cloud of swirling snowflakes. He was shabbily, if warmly, dressed and dragging an enormous basket of firewood. A fur-lined hood was pulled up over his head and it was only when he was close by that Raedwyn recognized him.

She abruptly brought Blackberry to a slithering halt.

Caelin stopped a few feet from her and pushed his hood back, looking upon her with surprise.

"Raedwyn?"

When she did not reply he came closer, frowning in concern. "What are you doing out here?"

"I went out for a ride, fell off, hurt my ankle and now I'm lost," Raedwyn replied stonily, hating herself with a passion at that moment.

Raedwyn looked into Caelin's face and saw he looked considerably healthier than the last time she had spoken to him. She had not sought his company after their conversation in his sickroom. After his first, relatively slow, period of convalescence, Caelin's body had healed itself quickly. As soon as he had been able to walk, Raedwald had set him to work. Raedwyn had rarely glimpsed Caelin inside the Great Hall after that, for Raedwald grew vile tempered whenever Ceolwulf's son crossed his path. A theow could own property, such as a cow or a couple of sheep and had some rights, but the king gave Caelin nothing. He spent his days doing the chores everyone else despised: shoveling muck, cleaning privies, collecting wood, washing clothes, dying wool and tanning leather. They fed him the leftover food that was usually thrown to the dogs and he slept with the horses in the stables.

Despite his ragged, dirty appearance, Caelin's face had filled out and lost the haggardness of near death. Still, his eyes were tired and haunted.

"What are you doing out in this weather?" she asked, immediately regretting asking such a foolish question—as he was towing a bag of firewood behind him it was obvious what he had been doing.

"There isn't enough wood for the Yule bonfire," Caelin explained, "so I've been sent to collect some pine cones and oak branches."

"In a blizzard?" Raedwyn arched an eyebrow.

"Well they don't want to make things too easy for me do they?" Caelin replied, and Raedwyn saw a glimmer of his wry sense of humor return for an instant.

"Come," Caelin said, stroking Blackberry's neck. "We'll both freeze if we stay out here much longer. Let me help you up into the saddle."

He cupped his hands under Raedwyn's knee and boosted her up onto Blackberry's back. When she had mounted, Caelin took hold of the mare's reins and turned her left.

"How far are we from Rendlaesham?" Raedwyn asked.

"We're closer than you'd think," Caelin replied. "Your father's hall lies just through that copse of trees and over the next rise."

"But your firewood?"

"I'll come back for it," Caelin answered, unbothered by the basket he was leaving behind, "I think your father would judge your safety more important that a load of dead wood."

Raedwyn's response was out before she could censor it. "I don't know about that. I think he might prefer it if I were dead."

Caelin turned to her frowning. "Why would you say such a thing?"

Raedwyn stared at him, wishing she had not spoken, but knowing that, now the words were out she would have to tell him the truth.

"Ceolwulf and Hengist both told my father that I offered myself to your father, and that you and his men all took great sport with me."

Caelin's face darkened further. "What?"

"You were not the only survivor – Hengist also lived and tried to escape the battle before they caught him. After he called me a lying slut in front of my family, my father slew him."

"You told them it was a lie?"

Raedwyn nodded. "Most of my kin believed me, except for my father. Since that moment, he no longer bothers himself with me." Although Raedwyn tried to keep her voice matter-of-fact, she felt tears sting her eyes at her admission.

Caelin shut his eyes for a moment and rested his forehead against Blackberry's neck.

"I can go to him," he said finally. "I can tell him you were not touched."

"It will make no difference," Raedwyn replied, panic rising inside her, "and my father will believe I have seduced you into defending me. He will only think worse of us both and you'll be whipped. It's better to let it lie."

Caelin straightened up and his eyes met Raedwyn's for a moment. He opened his mouth as if to argue with her, but then thought better of it. His shoulders rigid, he turned and led Blackberry through a thick copse of young skeleton oaks. They emerged the far side and climbed up an incline. The snow was falling so heavily now, they could hardly see a yard ahead. They struggled down a slope and suddenly squat wattle and daub huts appeared. They had reached the outskirts of Rendlaesham.

Raedwyn's face burned with embarrassment at how close she had been to home – she had indeed been riding around in circles.

There was no one about as they trudged through the settlement towards the Great Hall. The townsfolk were all safely indoors now, sheltering from the blizzard. Wood smoke and the smell of roasting mutton tinged the gelid air. A tall wooden fence ringed Raedwald's hall and the stables below it. Two sentries, huddled within heavy cloaks, guarded the gate. They looked upon Caelin with hostility as he led Blackberry past. Only Raedwyn's challenging stare prevented the guards from blocking their path.

The stable yard was deserted. Caelin led Blackberry into one of the stables reserved for the royal family's horses and helped Raedwyn dismount. Raedwyn's teeth were chattering and her ankle was now a dull throb.

"I should get back to the hall," she said between clenched jaws. "Mother will be worrying."

Caelin took off his cloak and wrapped it around Raedwyn's shoulders. Then he helped her over to a pile of clean straw so she could sit down.

"I will take you up," he said, turning from her to where Blackberry stood looking dejected, "as soon as I see to your horse."

Raedwyn watched as Caelin removed Blackberry's saddle and bridle before he rubbed the mare down with a twist of hay. Caelin worked with the ease of someone reared around horses, although when he lifted off the saddle, Raedwyn saw him wince.

"You are not yet healed," Raedwyn observed.

"I'm well enough," Caelin replied. "Time will take care of the rest."

Caelin fed and watered Blackberry before going to Raedwyn and kneeling down before her.

"How is that ankle of yours faring?"

Raedwyn grimaced. "I should go, Caelin."

"Let's take a look at it," Caelin ignored her protest, gently took hold of her ankle and rested her foot on his knee. He then outbound the leather lacing which bound the fur boot to her foot and ankle before removing the boot itself.

"It's very swollen." His cool finger tips softly traced the line of her ankle and prodded around the bone. "But I think it is not broken, just bruised."

He looked up at her and Raedwyn felt a lump settle into the back of her throat. His face was impassive, almost cold, but his eyes were not. He was so close, all she had to do was reach out and touch him.

The moment shattered as the stable door crashed open, bringing with it a gust of icy, snow-laced wind. Raedwyn brought her hand up to shield her face from the flurry, but saw, too late, the unmistakable outline of her father's tall, broad shouldered frame filling the doorway. With him, was one of the sentries they had passed at the gate.

Raedwyn knew that it looked incriminating—her sitting on the straw, wrapped in Caelin's cloak while he knelt before her, holding her bare ankle. There was an intimacy in their manner that implicated them both. Caelin went very still as he returned Raedwald's stare, a dangerous and unwise thing for a slave to do.

"*Fæder*," Raedwyn managed finally, feeling her father's glare shift to her. "I fell off my horse while riding and got lost in the snow. Caelin found me and brought me home."

Even to her ears, the words sounded trite. They may have been the truth but her father, it seemed, was ever ready to think the worst of her.

Raedwald's face darkened. "Caelin?" he spat out the name as if it were something foul. "He lost the right to a name when he became my slave—yet you use it easily as if it were familiar to you."

This was the sign Raedwald had been waiting for; the proof his daughter had made herself his enemy's whore.

Anger erupted within Raedwyn. She pushed Caelin aside and stood up, ignoring the pain that lanced up her leg from her injured ankle.

"Why, father?" Her voice lashed across the stable, causing Blackberry to start nervously. "I have never given you cause to think me a slut! All you have is the words of two men who hated you, who sought to wound you. Have you ever asked Caelin what happened while I was Ceolwulf's captive? Perhaps you should! I am innocent of all you accuse me of!"

"Silence!" Raedwald roared. His face was florid and Raedwyn realized he had been drinking. He towered over Raedwyn menacingly and, for a moment, she was afraid he would hit her. Instead, he turned to Caelin, who had risen to his feet and was observing the altercation between father and daughter.

"Dog! Don't you dare look in my daughter's direction again! The next time you touch her, I will cut off your fingers and feed them to you!"

"Your daughter is innocent," Caelin replied, ignoring the king's threats.

"Not I, nor my father, nor any of his men took sport with her."

Raedwald's fist shot out and hit Caelin in the mouth.

Caelin had not expected the king to strike him. Caught off-guard, he staggered backwards and fell against the wall. He slumped forward as blood gushed from his mouth.

Raedwyn watched her father approach his slave, towering over him so that when Caelin looked up, wiping the blood off his chin, the King of the East Angles filled his vision.

"Your death will be long and painful if you ever defy me again slave," he warned, his voice soft. "One who has lost all honor does not have the right to speak either to me or any member of my family. If you wish to survive you must be as invisible as a wraith and slink around like the cur you are."

Caelin looked up at the king and held his gaze defiantly.

"You do not want to test me slave," Raedwald said finally. "For I do not make threats lightly."

Then, letting his words hang in the chilled air, Raedwald turned and left the stable – dragging Raedwyn after him.

Alone in the stable, Caelin climbed to his feet and checked to see if the king had broken any of his teeth. The inside of his upper lip had split open; smashed against his teeth by Raedwald's fist. One of his top teeth was loose but he had suffered no further injury.

Caelin mopped up the last of the blood and, with a suddenness, which caused Blackberry to start for the second time, smashed his fist against the wall. Wood splintered but even the pain that lanced through his fist did not lessen the stomach clenching rage which consumed him. It was his first strong emotion since he had awoken to find himself Raedwald's captive.

His anger had been long suppressed. He had tried to ignore the part of him that 'felt'; the part of him that wanted freedom and would not accept this was this fate. However, it would not be ignored. He would have to leave this place, or he would die before the next winter. He could not be subservient. It was not in him to grovel at another man's feet.

Raedwald was vastly different to the man Caelin remembered from all those years ago. Then, Raedwald had been loud, good-natured and, although severe when crossed, he had always been fair. That man was gone. It would not be long before Raedwald lashed out again—and next time Caelin would hit back. After that it would be finished for him.

Caelin went outside and picked up a handful of clean snow, pressing it against his swollen mouth. A few servants moved by in the shadows, struggling through the ever-deepening snow with heavy baskets and buckets. All of them ignored Caelin. It was as if he were a ghost here. Caelin watched them trudge by, huddled within their furs, and realized the fact that everyone disregarded him here might prove advantageous one day.

He would wait out the winter, until the spring had begun to settle into early summer and then he would make his escape. Even if he died trying it would be preferable to this half-life.

Caelin thought of Raedwyn then. It was not deliberate, for an image of her came to his mind unbidden. Nonetheless, he did not like to dwell too long on Raedwyn. When she was in his presence she overwhelmed his senses, which was dangerous. She brought out a protective, fool-hardy streak in him which could easily get him killed.

Pushing away thoughts of Raedwyn, he re-entered the stable and retrieved his cloak. Caelin then wrapped the cloak around his shoulders and pulled up his hood, before making his way back out into the snow.

He had a basket of sticks to retrieve before nightfall.

Chapter Eleven

"I DON'T WANT you going near that piece of maggot ridden dog spawn!" King Raedwald of the East Angles roared out across the hall, causing his daughter who stood before him to cringe as if he had slapped her. "He and his kin are *nithing*, without honor and accursed. Have you not shamed your family enough without disgracing yourself further?"

"Why won't you believe me father?" Tears streamed down Raedwyn's face as she stood shivering before the king.

Father and daughter had a considerable audience. Seaxwyn sat upon the raised dais, reserved for the king and queen, embroidering. Eorpwald sat at one of the long tables nearby, where he had been playing knucklebones with his cousin, Annan. Eni had been drinking with some of the king's thegns, emptying mead from a huge barrel into clay mugs. Servants were roasting a deer over the fire pit, boiling vegetables and baking bread on a griddle. Despite the Great Hall's cavernous interior and high gabled roof, the air was close and rank with the smell of too many people cooped up together in an enclosed space – a smell not even the cloying smoke and appetizing aroma of roasting venison could mask.

Seaxwyn had gone pale and put down her embroidery when her husband had entered, dragging a disheveled and limping Raedwyn behind him.

"Raedwald?" Seaxwyn stood up and stepped down off the dais, coming to Raedwyn's side. She gathered her daughter's sobbing form in her arms. "What have you done to her?"

"What have I done to her?" Raedwald roared as if his wife stood on the other-side of Rendlaesham rather than two feet from him. "She had the stupidity to go out riding in a snow-storm and fell off her horse. Then this slut enlisted the help of the Exiled's whelp to bring her back to Rendlaesham. I found them alone together in the stables."

Raedwald let the incriminating words hang in the air while the others gaped at Raedwyn as if she had been caught cavorting naked on the snow with the king's theow.

Swallowing her sobs, Raedwyn straightened up and pushed her hair off her face.

"You know it was innocent! You know I am blameless! He was only making sure my ankle was not broken. It's only *you* father that makes it sound sordid. It's only you who twists things to seem foul and wrong!"

"You lie!" Raedwald bellowed. "I saw it in your face when Hengist accused you!"

"I don't know what you saw," Raedwyn parried, "but you are wrong! You have never been more wrong!"

The ringing sound of the slap, as the flat of Raedwald's hand connected with Raedwyn's face, echoed around the hall. The force of the blow caused Raedwyn to stagger backwards. She would have fallen if her mother had not grabbed hold of her.

"Father!" Eorpwald jumped to his feet.

Raedwald ignored his son. He glared at Raedwyn, as if there was only her and him in the Great Hall.

"You are a disrespectful, lying slut of a girl who I should have married off years ago. I tried to forgive you. I let you stay on here despite your shame but you could not mend your ways. As soon as spring comes I will wed you to the first man who'll have you."

"Raedwald!" Seaxwyn cut in, her face pinched. "How dare you talk to our daughter thus! If she says she is innocent then you should believe her, not continue to humiliate and berate her."

The king turned on his wife then, and the force of his venom caused all in the hall to grow still in shock.

"You would say that dear wife, wouldn't you? It's mother like daughter I fear. I was foolish enough to forgive you, but now my own daughter has proven to be a deceitful whore and it will not be borne!"

Seaxwyn stared at Raedwald as if he had not struck Raedwyn but her.

Her look of horror caused Raedwald to check any more angry words that he might have let forth. A dreadful hush fell across the Great Hall then, as if the king had uttered a terrible curse.

Raedwyn forgot her own misery and stared from her father to her mother. This had nothing to do with her. Instead, it was some history between the king and queen that had been long buried—one that they had kept secret from her.

Seaxwyn did not speak. Her face was set like a stone sculpture of an ancient, wrathful goddess. Without uttering another word, the queen turned and left the hall.

Raedwyn's left cheek still stung from her father's hand, but she ignored it. She swept her gaze across the hall, to see the reaction of the others present. Her cousins looked as horrified as her, and so did many others.

Only Eni and Eorpwald showed something other than shock. Eni looked immeasurably sad and careworn. He was Raedwald's younger brother but at that moment, they seemed the same age. There were pouches under Eni's eyes, and he looked like a weary old wolf that had lived long and had to hunt one time too many. He looked upon his brother with sorrow in his eyes.

Eorpwald had gone almost as pale as his mother; his thin face drawn. When Raedwyn looked into his eyes, she understood that he and Eni had carried this secret for as long as her parents.

Her world had suddenly shifted. One moment, Raedwyn had been defending herself from a raging father, and the next, years of smothered tensions and resentment had exploded between her parents, uncovering something best kept hidden.

Everything Raedwyn had ever known seemed unreal. During her infancy and girlhood, her family had protected her from more than just the outside world – all those years they had been protecting her from themselves.

Raedwald still stood, staring into the mid-distance at something only he could see. Raedwyn left him to his demons. Limping on her sore ankle, Raedwyn made her way to her bower, pushed the tapestry aside and let it fall behind her.

Once away from the stares, Raedwyn collapsed onto her furs and curled up into a ball. As she lay shivering, she realized that she had felt safer as a prisoner in Ceolwulf's encampment than within the embrace of her family. They were her kin; the people who were supposed to love and protect each other from the bloodshed and violence of the world, not savage each other like wolves.

Eorpwald pushed aside the tapestry and padded softly into his sister's bower; his thin fingers clasped around a steaming mug. Raedwyn was huddled within her furs, sleeping. Many hours had passed since he had witnessed the altercation between Raedwyn and her parents. Eorpwald had decided to let his sister sleep for a while before he went to her. He sat on the edge of the furs and watched Raedwyn for a moment. She looked far younger than her twenty-one winters in sleep, even if awake she had long lost any vestiges of girlishness. Her pale hair was spread out like a bird's wing across the furs; the same color as their father's when he had been young.

"Raedwyn." Eorpwald gently shook her awake. "I've brought you spiced mead."

Raedwyn's blue eyes flicked open and focused on Eorpwald. Her face lost its relaxed cast and he saw her muscles tense, as if ready for yet another fight. Unsmiling, Raedwyn sat up and rested her back against the wooden partition. She took the cup of hot mead and wrapped her chilled fingers around it, sighing with relief as the warmth seeped into her hands. Neither of them spoke for a moment or two. Raedwyn then took a sip of mead before fixing her gaze on her brother.

"Why didn't you tell me?"

"How would that have aided you Raedwyn?" Eorpwald replied, returning her stare. "It would have been better if you had never known."

"I agree, but since there was never any guarantee of that, I'd appreciate it if you would stop trying to protect me. I need to know the truth. Tell me what happened."

Eorpwald sighed and massaged a tense muscle in his shoulder, almost as if to distract himself.

"I knew it would fall upon me to explain this to you, if discovered."

Raedwyn said nothing. She waited in silence as Eorpwald gathered his thoughts, choosing his words carefully before continuing.

"I will tell it plainly for I cannot sweeten the truth with honeyed words," Eorpwald began. "I don't know if you have already drawn your own conclusions but this has everything to do with Ceolwulf. Father loathed that man with a passion that will go with him to his grave. He hates him for he once seduced our mother."

Seeing the shock, followed by the confusion that clouded Raedwyn's face, Eorpwald began his story at the beginning.

"It was late summer and you had just had your fourth birthday. Father decided to take Raegenhere and myself out hunting with his men. We were still boys but father wanted us to feel the blood lust of the hunt and prepare us for the warriors we were one day to become. We set out not long after sunrise, but we were only a few leagues away from Rendlaesham when one of my father's servants reached us. His horse foamed at the mouth. He had galloped all the way from the Great Hall. He approached father and whispered something into his ear. The king's reaction was terrible. I've never seen father like that—he looked as if he might collapse. Then he roared like a wounded beast and turned his horse back in a wild gallop for Rendlaesham. Thinking something terrible had befallen you or our mother, Eni, Raegenhere and I followed him.

Father was already pounding up the steps towards the hall when I reached the stable yard. Although I was thin and small for my age, I could run like a rabbit, faster than my brother and uncle. I took the steps two at a time and rushed into the Great Hall ahead of them. I saw father yank back the tapestry to his bower. Then he froze and so did I. Eni and Raegenhere who were close behind, nearly collided with me—but all four of us were witness to what lay within that bower." Eorpwald paused then, his face pained. "They were naked: mother and Ceolwulf. They were rutting on the floor."

Raedwyn winced at the crudeness of her brother's statement but Eorpwald did not notice. He took a deep breath, as if forcing himself to continue. "To a boy's eyes it appeared he was attacking her, for his torso was covered in scratches and bite-marks and she was making sounds as if she was in pain. Of course as soon as I got older I realized the opposite was true."

"Why didn't father kill Ceolwulf?" Raedwyn finally found her voice. She was gripping the mug of cooling mead so tightly she was surprised it did not crumble in her hands. She felt ill, and Eorpwald had gone very pale and kept swallowing hard.

"He tried," Eorpwald replied simply, before leaning forward and resting his face in his hands. "It was an ugly scene Raedwyn. You are fortunate you did not bear witness to it. Your mother had sent you into Rendlaesham to play with your new puppy. One moment Ceolwulf was rutting, and the next he and father were fighting on the floor. Mother screamed, jumped into the furs and covered herself up. Her screams went on and on, echoing throughout the hall in a terrible wail. She cried that Ceolwulf had forced her and that she had fought him.

Ceolwulf roared at her, calling her a lying whore. He said she had pursued him like a bitch on heat. Father went mad—he hammered at Ceolwulf with the intent of killing him. However, The Exiled was a warrior of father's equal and he fought to kill. Ceolwulf was ambitious. He wanted Raedwald's queen and his place as King of the East Angles.

It was our father's rage that won him the fight. He was relentless. Generally, it's easier to fight naked for clothes can hamper you, but Raedwald finally gained the advantage and throttled Ceolwulf until he passed out.

Father should have slain Ceolwulf then, while he had the chance. Instead, he wanted vengeance—he wanted Ceolwulf to grovel at his feet and beg forgiveness before he died. He told his warriors to take Ceolwulf to the market square and truss him up ready for a public beheading; the king would wield the axe himself.

Father's warriors left him to deal with mother and dragged Ceolwulf, unconscious, from the hall. Unbeknown to father, some of the warriors were loyal to Ceolwulf. Instead of taking him to the market square as ordered, they slung him over the back of a horse and galloped from Rendlaesham. They took Ceolwulf's son and a small band of men loyal to the ealdorman with them."

Eorpwald broke off his tale to take note of his sister's reaction. Raedwyn was pale and very still. Her face was taut and her eyes huge, but she was taking it all in. She would hear more.

"Ignorant of his warriors' betrayal, father unleashed his rage on mother. He seemed to forget that Raegenhere and I were standing witness as he pulled mother up from the furs by her hair and threw her out of the bower. He was crying as he shouted at her. He told her to tell him the truth or he would kill her. There are women who may have become hysterical in such a situation, but it was mother's calm head that saved her life that day.

I watched her plead and reason with father. I saw her swear upon Woden and Frigg that she was innocent. She swore that she had been working at her distaff when Ceolwulf had entered the hall and dragged her into the bower. She showed him the welts, which would purple into small bruises over her breasts and arms. She talked and talked until father's rage subsided."

Eorpwald paused and looked into his sister's eyes then. "Even as boys, Raegenhere and I knew our mother was lying, burying her deceit with clever words—but father wanted so badly to believe her he would not hear otherwise. He nearly broke Eni's jaw days later when he suggested Seaxwyn had deliberately deceived him. Unlike Raedwald, who had been blind to the growing attraction between Ceolwulf and Seaxwyn, Eni had noticed their stolen glances during the months leading up to the incident. A wet spring had fuelled their frustration, cooped up inside the Great Hall without a moment alone together. They had been waiting for the opportunity to consummate their lust.

Deep within himself, father knew the truth but it would have destroyed him to admit it. When he discovered that Ceolwulf had gone, he sent warriors after him. However, when they returned empty-handed, he had no choice but to banish Ceolwulf instead, to strip him of his title of ealdorman and to proclaim him *nithing*. Henceforth he was known as Ceolwulf the Exiled." Eorpwald let out a deep sigh as he finished his tale. "And then we buried it. We hid it deep and forgot it ever existed. However, when Ceolwulf reappeared and abducted you, father was forced to face the whole ordeal again. The thought Ceolwulf and his men may have defiled you has nearly driven him mad. He was wrong to keep Caelin alive for it just adds to his bitterness and suspicion. When mother defended you today, it tore the scab off a wound which has festered for too long."

Raedwyn watched her brother's face, saw the naked grief there, and understood his coldness towards Seaxwyn over the years. He still resented her, blamed her for what happened.

"Just after my marriage to Cynric," Raedwyn began in a low voice. "I was upset and mother came to me. She told me about her violent marriage to Tondbert, of how she came to be married to father."

There was a pause while Eorpwald digested her words. "Our mother is strong Raedwyn. Over the years she has done whatever necessary in order to survive."

"I thought she loved father."

Eorpwald smiled sadly at that. "I believe she does."

"Then why would she do something so despicable to him?"

"I know not," Eorpwald replied gently. "Mother is the only one who could answer that question."

Night was falling when Raedwyn emerged from her bower. The Great Hall was strangely silent for this time of day. Eorpwald had gone to carouse with friends at the mead hall in town; a place often frequented by ealdormen and thegns, and Raedwald had retired to his bower. Dinner had long since cooked and congealed over the hearth.

The servants had all gratefully retired for the evening, happy to be free of the turmoil within the King's Hall. A couple of men sat dozing near the fire pit. They watched her lazily as Raedwyn seated herself at the long table. She cut herself some strips of cold venison, poured a jug of mead and helped herself to a hunk of overcooked griddle bread. Despite the day's trauma, Raedwyn felt hunger stirring in her belly. She ignored the thegns' stares as she ate, although when she had finished her meal she forced herself to meet their gazes. Before her shaming, neither of them would have dared to stare at her like that.

"Where is my mother?"

"Not here M'lady," one of the thegns replied, feigning disinterest when Raedwyn sensed he burned to know what was behind the altercation between the king and queen earlier. "Perhaps she's in the store or the workshop?"

Raedwyn went back to her bower and pulled on a dry cloak before returning to the fire pit. Ignoring the thegns, who were still watching her, she collected some more dinner scraps and a jug of mead and, pulling up her hood to protect her head from the chill, left the Hall.

Outside it was snowing gently. Night had come even earlier than usual. It was silent outdoors and the air, although cold, was wonderfully fresh after the fetid air within the Hall. Raedwyn intended to seek out her mother, but first she had something else she felt compelled to do.

Still limping, she crunched through the snow, down the steps, and into the empty stable yard. This time she made sure no one saw her, keeping to the shadows. Grateful for the swirling snow, she crept past the individual stables that housed Blackberry and the other horses ridden by Raedwyn's kin, and into the main stable. The air was warm with the smell of hay, dung and horses. She moved past the lines of shuffling horses to the stall at the far end.

A light flickered at the end of the stalls and she found him there, asleep on the hay. A small torch, chained to the wall above him, guttered on the verge of extinguishing itself.

Caelin lay on his side. Upon creeping closer, Raedwyn saw he held a heavy piece of wood against his stomach while he slept. Wise, she thought, since he was not safe here. The torchlight and shadows played across his features as he slept. Raedwyn watched her father's slave with interest.

Caelin's mouth had swollen. Raedwald could have killed him for daring to defend her honor. Careful not to wake him, Raedwyn knelt and placed the meat, bread and jug of mead on the hay near Caelin, so he would have food to break his fast tomorrow morning. Then, extinguishing the torch, Raedwyn left Caelin to sleep and crept back the way she had come.

Once again out in the snow, Raedwyn intently surveyed her surroundings. Her instincts were sharp, as they had been the evening she had escaped from Ceolwulf. With her family in turmoil, Caelin was not the only one in danger here. Certain there was no one peering at her from the shadows she made her way back up towards the Great Hall. Half way up, the stairs forked and Raedwyn took the right path.

Ahead, loomed the shadow of the three buildings that housed the barracks, store and workshop. Raedwyn rarely ventured here. Her father's warriors slept in the barracks and as such it was not a place she had ever visited—Raedwald would have had her whipped if she had dared. She had played in the store house and workshop as a child but had been discouraged from continuing to do so once her girlhood ended.

Raedwyn checked the workshop first but found it ice-cold and empty. Next door, the store house was a considerably larger building. Just after harvest, their winter store of food packed it to bursting, although now with Yule nearly upon them, it had emptied slightly. Raedwyn pushed back her hood as she stepped inside.

Clay cressets filled with oil burnt near the entrance and cast a dim light over the interior. It was considerably warmer than the workshop. Peering beyond the stacks of barrels and sacks, Raedwyn caught sight, in the shadowy recesses of the building, of a figure seated upon a pile of sacks of grain.

"*Mōder?*"

There was a lengthy silence before a woman answered.

"Leave me Raedwyn." Seaxwyn's voice struck Raedwyn as if her mother had just slapped her.

For a moment, Raedwyn just stood there. The force in Seaxwyn's voice almost made her obey, but a resolve not to let more things remain unsaid, forced her to stand her ground.

"Leave me!" Seaxwyn's voice caught and Raedwyn realized her mother was crying.

"Eorpwald told me everything mother," Raedwyn said and waited for Seaxwyn's reply. When none was forthcoming, she continued. "I just want you to know I understand why you couldn't say anything. You and father hid the truth from me so well that if Ceolwulf hadn't resurfaced I would never have known what had happened. You managed to be happy together despite everything. Some things are best buried and I'm sorry that when you defended me father threw the past in your face."

Raedwyn broke off, near to tears, and waited for Seaxwyn to reply. When the queen did not, she understood her mother had meant her words. She did not want company tonight. Raedwyn did not blame her. She doubted things between the king and queen would ever be quite right again—and it was partly her fault. She opened her mouth to say more but no suitable words would come. Feeling sadness wrap around her like a heavy cloak, Raedwyn turned and left the storehouse.

Outside, it had stopped snowing and the clouds parted revealing an inky, star strewn sky. From here, Raedwyn could see the fires of the rest of the town huddled in the shallow valley below the Great Hall. She stood there awhile watching the sleeping town, until her feet ached with cold, before she crunched through pristine snow back to her father's hall.

Chapter Twelve

YULE ARRIVED WITH yet another wintry blast of snow and ice. Raedwyn had always loved Yule, especially in milder winters when she and her kin would join the people of Rendlaesham outdoors in the celebrations. However, this mid-winter solstice she could not dredge up much enthusiasm. The winter's chill had crept into her father's hall since that fateful evening. Despite the roaring hearth in the center of the Great Hall, the atmosphere within the timber walls was frosty. The queen spent most of her time weaving in her bower while the king sulked. Everyone, including the servants, was unsmiling and on-edge, as if they expected hostilities to re-erupt at any time.

Raedwyn remembered happy occasions on past years. Apart from the special food they would prepare and enjoy, one of Raedwyn's favorite traditions at Yuletide was placing cakes in the boughs of the oldest apple trees in the orchards outside Rendlaesham. They would sacrifice animals under the trees and let their blood soak into the earth to give thanks for the fruit. The sacrifice also ensured that the trees produced abundant fruit in the future.

Boughs of mistletoe and holly festooned the town and, in the center of Rendlaesham, a great bonfire burned on Yule Eve. The Yule bonfire gave renewed life and power to the sun, ensuring its rebirth so that the darkest part of the winter would be over and they could all look forward to gradually lengthening days and the approach of spring. The townsfolk began building the Yule bonfire with oak and pine branches two moon-cycles before the mid-winter solstice.

As Yule approached, Raedwyn helped the servants prepare the Yule delicacies. Most of the cakes they prepared were round and golden, like the sun, and served warm. Raedwyn helped the other women bake huge batches of hot scedcakes, spiced buns, and sour plum or apple cakes sweetened with honey. Chestnuts popped and snapped in the hearth, filling the frosty air with their sweet aroma. Big pots of mulled, spiced mead simmered over fires before servants ladled it into earthen mugs; a welcome remedy for numb lips and fingers.

On the morning of Yule Eve, Raedwyn awoke early, as was her habit, and dressed in her best winter dress; an embroidered blue gown with a heavy, floor length woolen tunic and long, tight sleeves underneath. She pulled fur-lined boots onto her feet and fastened her finest rabbit fur cloak to her shoulders with the two matching amber brooches Cynric had given her as her 'morning gift'. Raedwyn had not touched the brooches since the day of the ambush but they were so beautiful it had seemed a pity never to wear them.

Raedwyn pulled on gold bracelets and clasped a gold, jewel-encrusted circlet around her neck. She left her hair loose and emerged from her bower to find her mother at her distaff, seated on the raised dais at the end of the hall, while her father and two of his ealdormen chatted with Eni and her cousins near the fire pit. Eorpwald was playing Hnefatafl with one of his father's thegns while, around them, servants scurried like squirrels late stocking their winter store.

The smell of roasting chestnuts and honeyed seed cake mingled with that of the enormous boar roasting on a spit. Raedwald had selected the boar especially for Yule. They had sacrificed it that morning. The scent was heavenly and Raedwyn's mouth watered. She took a drink of water, feeling as she did so, someone's gaze upon her. The thegn who played Hnefatafl with Eorpwald was staring brazenly at her. He was the same one who had stared at her on the night she had learned of her mother's deceit. Like then, Raedwyn chose to ignore him.

Raedwyn was helping herself to a seed cake when Caelin appeared, swathed in furs and weighed down by a load of logs for the fire pit. Raedwyn felt an unexpected jolt at seeing him. She had deliberately not sought Caelin out, even if she had found him in her thoughts more often than she wished. The king and his men ignored Caelin as he made his way over to the stack of logs against one wall. Raedwyn's gaze tracked him, like a moth irresistibly drawn to a flame, even at its own peril. Should her father see her watching his most reviled slave, she knew he would punish them both, but even this knowledge could not prevent her.

Feeling her gaze upon him, Caelin returned Raedwyn's gaze for a moment. He gave her a fleeting, slightly mocking smile, before he started to stack the logs.

Someone else had noticed their exchange. The thegn excused himself from playing Hnefatafl with Eorpwald and let another take his place, before sauntering over to the fire pit. There, he retrieved some roast chestnuts and placed them in a small basket.

"Here, M'lady," he said solicitously, placing himself in front of Raedwyn and blocking her view of Caelin. "Would it please you if I peeled these?"

"No thank you," Raedwyn replied icily, taking the basket from him with ill-grace. "I shall peel them myself."

The thegn smiled, as if her rudeness had no effect on him. "You look especially fair today, M'lady." His gaze dropped to the circlet she wore around her neck, then to the swell of her bosom under her dress, before his voice softened to almost a whisper. "I look forward to the celebrations this eve, I hope to dance with you."

Scowling, Raedwyn picked up a chestnut and peeled off the blackened skin. The chestnut was still red hot; she could not eat it yet. She felt like stuffing one into this man's mouth – anything to prevent him from irritating her further. By the time the thegn had finished whispering compliments and trying to gaze longingly into her eyes, Caelin had finished stacking wood and had left the hall. The thegn then strolled back to rejoin Eorpwald for another game of Hnefatafl, a triumphant smile lingering on his lips.

Irritated, Raedwyn ate her chestnuts and let her gaze travel around the interior of the Great Hall. Its lushly decorated interior was even more splendid with the mid-winter solstice festivities. Boughs of holly and mistletoe hung from the rafters. Oil infused with rosemary and pine burned in clay cressets. Raedwyn's kin were all dressed as richly as she was. Seaxwyn was dripping in gold and gemstones. She had piled her hair onto her head, revealing her long, shapely neck. Raedwald too looked handsome in his finery, although Raedwyn noted that her father's hair was now nearly completely gray and his skin had lost the ruddy bloom he had possessed as a younger man.

Relations between the king and queen were still frosty and they both remained cool and detached towards their only daughter. If it had not been for Eorpwald, Eni and her cousins, Raedwyn might have felt as if she were living in a house full of strangers.

Finishing her chestnuts, Raedwyn made her way outside. She had been so used to seeing low cloud and either driving sleet or snow, that the bright sunlight that greeted Raedwyn made her squint. The snow still lay thick on the ground but the sky beyond the horizon was limpid blue and unmarred by even a single cloud.

Raedwyn sighed in pleasure at the feel of the sun on her skin. She turned her face up to its warmth and closed her eyes. If the weather remained like this it would be pleasant to venture outside after dark to watch the Yule Bonfire burn and celebrate Mother Night; the first eve of the twelve days of Yule.

Ealdormen, thegns, ceorls, and the king and his kin filled the Great Hall for the Yule feast. They banqueted on roast boar and onions followed by sour plum cakes. The feasters downed the rich food with copious quantities of warmed mead. Once night fell, the revelers left Raedwald's Hall. They crunched through the snow, down into the center of Rendlaesham and lit the vast bonfire that the townsfolk had spent the last two months building. There the music and dancing began. Someone began playing a bone whistle, and its haunting notes carried far across Rendlaesham.

Raedwald and Seaxwyn made an appearance, as was customary on Mother Night, and made a show of togetherness. They stood side-by-side and even held hands at one stage, but Raedwyn saw that they barely spoke to each other. The bonfire crackled, sending tongues of flame licking up into the night sky, before the king finally took up his lyre and began to sing.

Raedwald was a gifted musician and singer. Raedwyn recalled many a winter's eve when she would curl up like a puppy at her father's feet near the fire pit and listen to the soothing lilt of his baritone as he sung heroic lays and sad songs of lost love. Despite his bluff exterior, Raedwald was a man of hidden depths that he rarely revealed, except to those closest to him. However, when he sang, Raedwald exposed his soul for all to see. As it was this eve.

The king drew a bow sweetly across the strings of the small wooden lyre and began to sing. He sang of battle, he sang of bloodshed and loss, of brotherhood and valor, and finally, of treachery and reckoning. Raedwyn listened, feeling the fine hairs on the back of her neck prickle. Raedwald's voice and that of the lyre rose in harmony while around him, some people sang, while others danced.

Eanfled and Alric had attended the Yule bonfire. Raedwyn thought her friend had never looked more beautiful or serene as she danced with her beloved. Eanfled's pregnancy was now starting to show but she moved with the same grace as ever. Finally, breathless, Eanfled sought out Raedwyn while Alric went to find himself a cup of mead.

"Your father's voice is so beautiful!" Eanfled exclaimed. "I love to hear him sing!"

"So do I," Raedwyn admitted, "although his choice of theme these days is a bit repetitive for my liking."

Eanfled nodded. Raedwyn had told her of the secret her family had kept for the past sixteen years. For the second time in only a few months, Eanfled had been struck dumb by Raedwyn's news—only this time they could find no humor in it.

"Are they still not speaking then?" Eanfled asked, glancing over at where Seaxwyn was conversing with the wife of one of the king's ealdormen. "They seem happy enough this eve."

"Yes, at least they are not still at war," Raedwyn admitted. "He forgave her once—perhaps he will again and things will go back to the way they were, in time."

At that moment, Raedwyn's admirer—the amorous thegn—appeared in front of them.

"I promised you we would have our dance Raedwyn the Fair." The man's teeth flashed against his tawny beard. "And I am a man of my word!"

Raedwyn's heart sank, and she would have refused him if Eanfled, completely misreading Raedwyn's pained expression as one of shyness, had not pushed her into his arms.

"Go on Raedwyn—you have not yet danced!"

Needing no further encouragement, the thegn grasped hold of Raedwyn's arm and swung her round into the whirling dancers.

"My name is Osric," the thegn introduced himself, before he crushed her foot under his, "and I have long awaited this day."

Raedwyn grimaced and tried to keep her feet clear of him. She was relieved when the dance forced him to fling her away from him and twirl her around him.

"I must confess," he breathed into her ear when he pulled her close once more. "I was disappointed when Raedwald married you off to Cynric. I wanted you for my own."

There was a lull in the music, as the king finished his epic lay and took a long draught of mead. Raedwyn stepped back from Osric who was eyeing her like a hungry wolf.

"I must accompany my mother back to the hall," she said, hurriedly glancing over at Seaxwyn. The queen looked tired and drained at the conclusion of the king's song. Raedwald's lay of treachery and retribution had exhausted her.

"Do not tarry." Osric let his gaze trail down Raedwyn's body. "I want plenty more dances before this night ends." As if to make his point all the clearer, he squeezed her bottom as she turned away.

Seaxwyn was visibly relieved when Raedwyn offered to take her back to the Great Hall. The king had begun another song, this one even angrier and more heart-wrenching than the last. The strains of his voice died away as the two women made their way through the snowy streets. It was a clear night and the full moon lit their way. They walked in silence for a spell, each immersed in their own thoughts before Seaxwyn spoke.

"You must hate me as your brother does."

Raedwyn was taken aback.

"You are wrong, mother," she replied when she had recovered. "Neither I nor Eorpwald hate you."

The silence drew out between them for a short while before Seaxwyn spoke again. "I thought your father would never forgive me all those years ago, and I was so grateful when he did. I realized how blessed I was. Ironically, we were even happier together after that, for we no longer took the other for granted."

"If Ceolwulf had not returned you would have remained happy together," Raedwyn replied sadly. "Father seems so altered. He has no proof against me but he continues to believe I gave myself to Ceolwulf and his men. He is so bitter, so angry. Nothing I say will make any difference."

Seaxwyn nodded and Raedwyn saw in the cold, silver light of the moon, that her mother's cheeks were wet with tears. Raedwyn put her arm around her mother's waist and hugged her tightly as they walked. Before them loomed the Great Hall and soon they were swallowed within its shadow.

Inside the hall it was deserted. The hearth still burned, and after putting some logs on the fire, Raedwyn began to remove her cloak.

"What are you doing Raedwyn?" Seaxwyn, who had removed her own cloak and sat by the fire pit warming her hands, raised her eyebrows at her daughter. "Mother Night has only just begun and you are young. Don't stay here with your old mother. Dance, enjoy yourself!"

"You sound like Eanfled," Raedwyn replied sourly. "Frankly, it was a relief to get away from that annoying Osric!"

Seaxwyn laughed then and upon hearing her, Raedwyn realized it was the first time she had heard her mother laugh in a while.

"He won't be able to get up to much mischief in a crowd." Seaxwyn reminded her daughter, "and besides I so rarely have solitude that I wish just to sit here by the fire and enjoy the silence."

"I can see I'm not wanted," Raedwyn grumbled. She placed a kiss on her mother's cold cheek and refastened her cloak. "I shall leave you in peace."

Raedwyn left the Great Hall and realized, as she stepped outside into the crisp night air, that she felt a little lighter of heart. Her conversation with Seaxwyn had reforged the link between them that Raedwyn had thought lost, and she felt less alone after speaking to her mother.

Raedwyn walked slowly down the steps, away from the hall, taking care not to slip and hurt her ankle again. It had just healed, although it could be tender at the end of the day. Raedwyn was in no hurry to return to the bonfire, to Osric's pawing and her father's heart-wrenching songs. She walked slowly across the stable-yard towards the gates and hesitated.

There were no guards at the gate. All were at the Yule bonfire. Raedwyn wondered if Caelin had also gone to the bonfire, to watch from the shadows while the townsfolk reveled, but not able to join in. On instinct, Raedwyn turned away from the gate and ducked inside the stables. She did not question her decision, but rather followed a nameless impulse. If her father caught her here he would be livid—but she would hazard the risk.

She found Caelin grooming one of the king's prized stallions in a stall at the far end of the stables. Caelin had not noticed her approach. He was talking to the horse gently as he worked. It was warm inside the stables and Caelin was dressed lightly in leggings, boots and a loose, sleeveless tunic belted at the waist. His clothing was simple and of poor cloth but it molded his tall, muscular frame. The skin of his arms was still slightly tanned, despite the long, cold winter they were enduring.

"Caelin."

He turned with a suddenness that made the stallion start. The horse rolled its eyes nervously and stomped, narrowly missing Caelin's foot.

Caelin stared at Raedwyn. "You shouldn't be here."

His reaction surprised Raedwyn. She had expected a warmer reception. Moments of silence passed before Raedwyn spoke.

"You weren't at the bonfire."

"I didn't think I'd be welcome." There was no mistaking the bitterness in Caelin's voice.

Raedwyn could feel a creeping embarrassment steal over her and realized that she had made a fool of herself by coming here.

"It is a beautiful night out," she said lightly. "It has stopped snowing."

Caelin gave her an incredulous look. "Have you come here to inform me of the weather?"

Raedwyn felt herself go hot from growing mortification.

"N ... no," Raedwyn stuttered, watching as he put the brush aside and ducked out of the stable, so that he stood before her in the straw-strewn corridor between the stalls.

"Do you realize the danger you've put us both in coming here?" Caelin was frowning and did not look at all happy about her surprise visit. "Do you want to see me killed? Is that your game?"

"No!" Raedwyn choked out. "I only ..."

"You are a spoiled child. Your father forbids something and you must test him. You're not used to being told what to do Raedwyn—and it shows."

"Why are you being so nasty?" Embarrassment faded and anger surfaced in its place. "Nobody knows I'm here. Everyone is at the bonfire. I only wanted to make sure you were well. There is no need to insult me!"

"Well as you can see I am well. Thank you for your concern."

Raedwyn's eyes narrowed into slits.

"Why do you insist on treating me like a child? You have no right!"

"Because that's what you are." Caelin's face darkened. "You come here because it suits you, because you're bored. Did you really think I'd be pleased to see you?"

Under Raedwyn's anger, hurt stung her to the quick. Perhaps she should not have come here but there was no need for him to be so rude. She stepped back from Caelin, forcing down the ridiculous urge to cry— then he really would think her a child.

"You are wrong about me," she whispered, staring into his eyes for a moment before she turned and fled down the aisle between the stalls.

Raedwyn had almost reached the door when Caelin caught up with her. Before Raedwyn even had time to react, he had pulled her up short, pushed her against one of wooden supports that held up the stable roof, and covered her mouth with his.

Outraged, Raedwyn pushed against Caelin's chest, but instantly lost any will to fight him when his tongue plunged into her mouth. Raedwyn groaned and let her own tongue dart forward to tangle with his. Her hands moved across his chest to his broad shoulders and the finely chiseled muscles of his upper arms. She pressed herself up against him and ran her hands down his back as Caelin slid his thigh between her legs and tangled his hands in her hair.

Raedwyn's head swam and she drank him in. She did not care that anyone could walk in on them. He could have taken her right there against the wall and she would have let him. All good sense left her and the world shrank till only the two of them existed.

It was Caelin who stopped it. He tore his mouth from hers and, gasping for breath, stepped back from her.

"Caelin ..." Raedwyn reached for him but Caelin shook his head and took another step back.

"Please," Caelin's voice was hoarse with longing, "I shouldn't have done that. This is madness Raedwyn. Just go."

Raedwyn took a shuddering breath and the haze of lust that had momentarily consumed her began to ebb. Without another word, she turned and fled from the stables.

Caelin watched Raedwyn's retreating back and suppressed the urge to drag her back into his arms.

Raedwyn intoxicated him, as she had from the first time he had kissed her. Caelin could still feel her hair entangled in his fingers, the heat and taste of her mouth as it opened under his and the feel of her soft body against him. She had nearly unraveled his self-control. On one level Raedwyn had no idea what she did to him, and on another she was only too aware of the power she wielded. For that she was dangerous.

Caelin leaned up against the beam and stared up at the thatched ceiling. He had been harsh with Raedwyn in an attempt to distance himself from her. Plans for escaping Rendlaesham occupied his thoughts of late. Once the snow thawed, he would start to lay provisions on the edge of the apple orchard near the town.

Caelin planned to leave his past at his back and travel to a corner of Britannia where Raedwald would never find him. He had never been a free man – first a servant to his father's quest for revenge and now Raedwald's slave. His life had never been his own.

He would not allow his lust for this beautiful woman sabotage his plans.

Caelin returned to the stall, picked up the brush he had abandoned upon seeing Raedwyn, and resumed grooming the stallion. He had to forget Raedwyn the Fair for she was part of the existence he would soon leave behind.

Chapter Thirteen

"RAEDWYN, I HAVE found you a husband."

Raedwald's announcement caused all seated at the long table below the king and queen, to cease eating and stare at the king. Then, collectively, they turned their attention to his daughter. It was nearly a moon's cycle since Yuletide and winter's chill still held Rendlaesham within its grip. Raedwyn had dressed warmly this eve; a fur cloak around her shoulders, and her thick hair pulled back from her face. She paled at Raedwald's words. Then, she swallowed the mouthful of pottage she had been chewing and met her father's gaze.

"Who's the lucky man then?" Eni boomed, pretending not to notice the tension between father and daughter.

Beside Raedwald, Seaxwyn glanced nervously at her husband. Despite that relations between them had improved, Raedwald had not shared his plans with his queen. Opposite Raedwyn, Eorpwald took a sip of mead and watched his sister over the rim of his cup.

"Yes, father?" Raedwyn finally spoke up. "Who am I to marry?"

Raedwald leaned back in his ornately carved wooden throne and took a draught of mead.

"Come spring you will be married to Eafa the Merciful of Mercia."

Raedwyn's eyes grew huge on her pale face. Seaxwyn's sharply indrawn breath and Eni's hiss of shock accompanied the sound of Eorpwald choking on his mead.

"You cannot marry Raedwyn to Eafa, father!" Eorpwald managed after Annan had belted him across the back a few times, expelling the mead from his windpipe. "He's an animal!"

Raedwald brought his tankard down on the table with a thump, his eyes flashing at his son. "We need to strengthen our alliances in Mercia. It's newly conquered territory. Raedwyn will serve her family well by marrying Eafa. I sent word to him before Yuletide and a rider arrived with tidings of his acceptance yesterday. Upon my word they will marry!"

Raedwyn breathed in deeply to quell the panic rising within her. Folk had named Eafa 'the Merciful' in irony, for he was among one of the cruelest, most terrifying men in Britannia. He had fought against Raedwald in his younger days before making peace with the East Anglian King. Of late, relations had been good between the East Angles and the Mercians but, ever an able politician, Raedwald would not miss an opportunity to strengthen his alliances—or to punish Raedwyn.

Raedwyn looked down at her hands and struggled to keep her composure. She had met Eafa once, three summers ago. Eafa had visited Raedwald, bringing gifts and pledging loyalty to his king. Raedwyn remembered him as a tall, raw-boned man with a cruel face, long thick pale hair and eyes colder than a frozen lake. He had watched her often during that visit and Raedwyn had squirmed under his gaze. She could not bear the thought of marrying Eafa. Raedwald was not a fool. He knew what sort of man he had betrothed his daughter to.

"How can you be so cruel father?" Raedwyn finally replied. "Eorpwald is right. The man is not human. Why would you consign me to such a life?"

Raedwald's eyes narrowed but his face revealed no emotion. "As a daughter of the Wuffinga line you have a duty to your king. You will marry whoever I deem suitable.

"But father ..."

"Silence!" Raedwald's temper boiled over. "You are turning into a nagging shrew Raedwyn. My word is law here. You will obey me!"

Raedwyn fixed her gaze on her trencher, still half filled with food, and remained silent, fighting back tears. Everyone's gaze was upon her. She could feel the hall charged with unvoiced emotion; some in favor of the king's decision, some pitying her. She avoided their eyes and got to her feet.

"Raedwyn." The king's voice was rough with anger. "You will stay here and finish your meal."

Unspeaking, Raedwyn fled to her bower.

"Raedwyn!" Raedwald bellowed after her but she ignored his command. She disappeared within her bower, the heavy tapestry swinging shut behind her.

Within her bower, Raedwyn stood at her small window and looked down at the thatched roof of the barracks below. She heard her father shout her name once more, before soothing words from Seaxwyn and protests from Eorpwald silenced him. Raedwyn almost expected him to come in after her and drag her back out by the hair, but he did not. He had never been a violent, domineering father—before now that was. She did not know him these days; she was afraid of him, but more than that she was furious.

Tears of rage wet Raedwyn's face and she curled her hands into painful fists. *If only I had been born a man!* She was not like other royal women; she could not bear being treated like a fattened pig to be sold at market. She hated that her fate was in the hands of her father.

I cannot believe he will marry me off to that monster!

Raedwyn stayed still, facing the window for a long time, her eyes fixed on a horizon that she could not see. Gradually, the serpent of rage within her stopped writhing and coiled itself into an iron core. If her father thought he could turn her into a cowed, fawning drab he was wrong.

An icy wind howled through Rendlaesham, rattling and pummeling the wattle and daub buildings; its cruel fingers probing under doorways and tearing at the clothes of those unfortunate enough to be outside.

Caelin was one such unlucky individual. He was warmly dressed—slaves were no use if they died from the cold—in thick leather breeches cross-gartered to the knee, two wool tunics and a heavy fur cloak, but still the cold penetrated to the bone. Using a crudely constructed shovel, Caelin scooped muck onto a cart while the wind buffeted him. The manure pile he stood before was nearly shoulder high, as they kept many of the animals confined for weeks due to the bad weather. The snow was slowly melting, turning the stable yard into a stinking sea of mud and dung, but the manure had to be moved. The stench made Caelin's eyes water.

Once the cart was full, Caelin then pulled it through the mud, out of the gates and down to the outskirts of Rendlaesham. There, he unloaded the manure around some of the fruit trees. Caelin worked methodically, but without hurrying. He welcomed the hard, physical labor for when he worked he was warm. Work also allowed him respite from his thoughts. He was by nature a patient man but this winter was dragging on interminably and he longed for some sign of approaching spring.

Spring would herald his escape from this place.

Unfortunately, the apple trees in the orchard were still bare of leaves. Nature was still in hibernation. He would wait a while longer.

Returning to the muckheap, Caelin set about reloading the cart before dragging it back down to the orchard once more. A gray dusk was approaching as he pulled the empty cart back up towards the Great Hall. The wind had not lessened. It slapped him around the face and stung his cheeks. Back at the stable yard, Caelin deposited the stinking cart under a lean-to and made his way, not back to his freezing stall, but into the main stable building.

Inside, three other slaves, Alchfrid, Immin and Sebbi, were standing around a small fire warming their hands. A pot simmered over the embers. Caelin liked these men; they were Northumbrian, taken after Raedwald bested the Northumbrian ruler, Aethelfrith, nine years earlier. Then, they would have been boys on the edge of manhood. Now they were tall, gruff men who, a few summers younger than Caelin, looked to him as their unofficial leader. Caelin's life here was harder than theirs; his duties the heaviest and most unpleasant, but this only increased his standing with his three new friends. Their common bondage united the four of them. They were at best ignored, or at worst, reviled by Raedwald's other servants.

"Whew, you reek of the dung heap." Sebbi made space for Caelin by the fire.

Caelin shrugged and placed his hands before the flames, sighing as the fire's warmth seeped into his numb fingers.

"Who would have thought a horse could shit so much!" Immin, who was looking pale and pinched, grumbled. He wrinkled his nose as the stench reached him. "Bloody beasts!"

Caelin grinned, despite his tiredness, at Immin's outburst. Alchfrid caught his eye and winked. "Someone got kicked in the cods today."

Caelin scrunched up his face in sympathy. "Not Raven?"

"He's a demon," Immin exploded. Relations between Immin and Raedwald's prize young stallion were not friendly. The yearling chaffed at being cooped up indoors and regularly took his vile temper out on Immin who was charged with his care. "A vicious beast only fit for the dogs!"

Caelin shook his head, suppressing laughter. "You and Raven would tolerate each other better if you stayed clear of his rear end."

"Believe me, I try to." Immin shifted his weight and winced. "But he twists like a snake. The bastard nearly gelded me!"

"There is a pail of hot water in the stall at the back Caelin," Alchfrid interrupted Immin's lament. "We thought you might need it."

Caelin nodded, tiredness creeping over him now that he no longer had to fight with the howling wind. He could still hear it, hammering against the walls.

"I thank you Alchfrid," Caelin replied. "What's this foul thing you've got boiling here?" Caelin peered into the pot. "Looks like innards. Immin—you didn't gut Raven did you?"

"If I didn't fear having my head parted from my shoulders by Raedwald's blade I would have," Immin replied looking glum.

"It's a stew I made with pork scraps," Sebbi interjected with an injured tone. "It will be better than an empty belly."

"When will it be ready?" Immin complained. "A man could starve to death waiting to be fed."

"Stop bleating," Sebbi snapped before giving the stew a cautious stir. "It will be ready soon Caelin if you want to wash up."

Caelin removed his stinking self from the fireside and left his friends to breathe sweeter air. Reaching the stall where he slept, he found a steaming pail of water, clean clothes and a rag to wash with. Caelin stripped off and hung his filthy clothes over the partition between the stalls. There was no use in washing them, as there was still muck to shovel tomorrow. He hurriedly sluiced himself down with hot water, scrubbing at his skin until it glowed a dull red, before dunking his head into the cooling water and scrubbing at his scalp. It was cold inside the stables now that he was away from the fire. Caelin quickly dressed in the only semi-clean clothes he had: woolen leggings and a long wool tunic. He then pulled on some fur-lined boots before re-joining his friends.

They were gossiping about the goings on within the King's Hall when Caelin inserted himself between Immin and Sebbi. He took the stale trencher Alchfrid handed him, while Sebbi filled it with steaming stew. Breaking off their conversation to eat, the four men sat cross-legged on straw around the fire and attacked their food. Despite its vile appearance, Sebbi's pork stew was tasty. He had somehow managed to purloin a few onions and carrots from the servants to add flavor to the meal. The stale bread trenchers softened with the stew and the hungry men ripped them into bits and ate them too once the stew was finished.

Once their bellies were full, the men continued their earlier conversation.

"I overheard the servants today." Immin, ever eager to spread a good rumor, leaned forward over the fire as he began his tale. "They say the king's betrothed his daughter to Eafa of Mercia."

Alchfrid shrugged. "It was bound to happen sooner or later. Her husband's been dead since summer."

"Yes, but do any of you know who this Eafa is?" Immin continued.

Sebbi and Alchfrid shook their heads while Caelin remained still. Pleased he could finish his tale unhindered, Immin belched, before continuing. "The servants spoke of him as a great Mercian ealdorman. He is known as 'the Merciful'."

"Eafa the Merciful," Sebbi nodded. "Indeed, I have heard of him."

"So have I," Alchfrid added before shaking his head. "I pity Raedwyn."

"What do you mean?" Caelin turned to Alchfrid, his voice sharper than he had intended. None of them knew of the connection he had with Raedwyn, and now Caelin cursed himself for showing too much interest. They were intelligent men and it would take little for them to suspect something.

However, Alchfrid was so involved in the tale, that he did not appear to notice. "You've never heard of Eafa the Merciful? Raedwald did well to make him an ally. He is a great warrior but famed for his cruelty."

"I thought he was married," Sebbi added. "His wife must have died."

Sebbi's words hung in the air between them. Caelin sat quietly and tried to keep his face expressionless. In reality, this news hit him like a blow to his gut. Sudden, stomach-knotting jealousy that another man would be able to touch the woman he could not have, consumed him. Then, a chill that had nothing to do with the icy wind outside, crept over Caelin.

"It is sad." Alchfrid's young face creased into a frown. "For Eafa will ruin a lovely wench like Raedwyn."

Alchfrid, like many young men in Rendlaesham, had lusted after Raedwyn from afar. Her ill-fate since the death of her husband had been the topic of many a conversation over the long winter months.

"She's too headstrong," Immin replied, shaking his head. "A woman like her needs a firm hand. Maybe that's why the king's chosen Eafa for her."

Caelin sat listening to them discussing Raedwyn's fate. His dinner sat heavily in his stomach like a lump of clay. Bitterness soured Caelin's mouth then, and he tasted what his father must have felt. For the first time, he understood Ceolwulf's rage and hatred. Fate had always ridden against Ceolwulf the Exiled. It had soured his mind and poisoned his soul— Raedwald of the East Angles had been its instrument then, as it was now.

Chapter Fourteen

SHORT DAYS AND long, cold nights passed before winter relaxed its grip. The days gradually lengthened and the wind lost its raw edge. The snow had long since melted and life at Rendlaesham continued in a steady rhythm, as it had for many a year.

Raedwyn the Fair tried to forget what the spring held in store for her.

Eni and Eorpwald had argued with Raedwald about the king's decision to marry Raedwyn to Eafa, but their protests had done no good. It only made Raedwald even more stubborn. Still, Raedwyn appreciated the efforts her uncle and brother had made on her behalf. It was a far cry from Eni's earlier insistence that the king find his daughter a husband. These days Eni had become protective of his niece. It seemed that the further Raedwald withdrew from Raedwyn, the closer she became to her uncle.

Embracing the warmer weather, Raedwyn took to walking. After the incident with Caelin, the king had forbidden Raedwyn to go riding. Instead, she enjoyed walks through Rendlaesham and into the fields beyond. Some days she did not stray far, visiting the weekly produce market near the main gates, or Eanfled, who was now heavily pregnant; while on others she would walk all afternoon through the gentle folds of land around Rendlaesham.

One afternoon, Raedwyn decided to take one of her longer walks. She had spent the day winding wool onto her distaff, which would later be used for spinning clothes. It was mundane work and Raedwyn longed to stretch her legs. She wrapped herself in a thick blue wool cloak and slipped out of the Great Hall.

It was a fresh, sunny day; the first that heralded the coming spring, with a limpid sky overhead. The Wuffinga menfolk were all out hunting so there was no one except her mother who would notice her departure from the hall. Raedwyn left Rendlaesham through the rear gate and set off down the narrow dirt road that bisected the apple orchards. Signs of spring were everywhere; bright green shoots pushing up by the roadside and splashes of white and pink as the first spring blossom appeared.

Usually, Raedwyn adored the spring but today the first signs of it unnerved her. It heralded Eafa's coming. She followed the road through the shallow valley and up another hill before descending into thickets of ash and beech. Here, scrubby undergrowth framed the road on both sides. Although Raedwyn was enjoying the beautiful day, the fresh air and the sun on her face, her mind returned to the tale she had heard that morning about Eafa the Merciful.

Two female servants had been whispering, not far from where Raedwyn sat at her distaff, about how Eafa's last wife had died of mysterious injuries. His young wife had once been a sweet, gentle girl, one of the women had explained in a grave voice, but Eafa had enjoyed turning her into a broken, miserable creature. Raedwyn had listened with growing concern, before she had realized that the women had deliberately positioned themselves within earshot of her. They had wanted Raedwyn to hear.

"Take your poison elsewhere!" she had instructed them, enjoying the shock on their faces at being spoken to thus. However, ever since that moment, Raedwyn's thoughts kept returning to their words.

"Raedwyn!"

Lost in her musings, Raedwyn did not hear someone approach from behind. She turned swiftly to see Caelin standing behind her. He was dressed in leggings and a patched but clean shirt, belted around his waist. His hair was slightly damp, as if he had just bathed.

"Did you follow me?" Raedwyn had not seen Caelin since their encounter on Mother Night. Her surprise at seeing him now made her voice harsher than she intended.

Caelin nodded, unfazed by her coldness.

"I thought you wanted us to keep away from each other?"

Caelin did not respond, instead he stood there before her, his gaze fixed upon her face.

"I hear you are to be married," he said eventually.

"Have you come to congratulate me?" Raedwyn could not keep the bitterness from her voice.

"I have heard of this Eafa the Merciful." Caelin's voice was quiet, measured, as if he was testing each word. "And I do not like the sound of him."

"His cruelty is legendary," she replied flatly, "but he is an important ally who must be kept happy. It is my father's will."

Silence stretched between them then. The air was heavy with so many things unsaid.

"You father is a proud, conceited fool." Caelin's voice was hard and bitter when he eventually spoke. "You deserve so much better than this Raedwyn."

Raedwyn studied him for a moment and was opening her mouth to reply, when the tattoo of approaching hoof beats intruded. Birds flew up from nearby trees and the tranquility shattered.

Horses were approaching fast from beyond the bend in the road.

"My father!" Panic seized Raedwyn by the throat.

Caelin grasped Raedwyn by the arm and propelled her into the thickets on the roadside. Branches and brambles tore at their clothes. They dove into the undergrowth and rolled to the ground, hidden from sight. Moments later, a group of horses thundered past. Raedwyn risked a peek over the edge of the brambles and caught a glimpse of her father out front, with his long, gray-threaded hair, flying behind him. Eorpwald rode close behind the king, followed by the rest of the Wuffinga men and a small group of warriors. Some had deer slung over their saddles; the Great Hall would dine well on roast venison.

When the riders had disappeared towards Rendlaesham, Raedwyn sank back against the ground, her heart hammering against her ribs. She could feel the cool damp against her back, even through layers of clothing. Looking around her, she realized that the brambles hid her and Caelin from view on all sides – they were alone together in a damp, bramble-enclosed bower. Caelin must have realized this too, for he remained on his side, next to Raedwyn, and in no hurry to move on.

Caelin propped himself up on one elbow and gazed down at Raedwyn. His face was unreadable, and she longed to know what he was thinking. Suddenly, it was airless and overly warm in their bramble hiding-place, and Raedwyn was aware of the rise and fall of her chest, and of Caelin's nearness.

Raedwyn felt her face heat up under the scrutiny of his stare and, attempting to distance herself from him, she tried to push herself up into a sitting position. In doing so, she merely launched herself into his arms.

One moment, they were laying side-by-side, and the next, they were in each others arms.

Caelin's mouth sought hers with a hunger that bordered on violence. He pulled her hard against him so that Raedwyn straddled his lap. Unfastening her hair, he tangled his fingers in it.

All thought, fled Raedwyn's mind. All sense, all caution, all fear disappeared. Her hands tore at his clothes, seeking the warm skin beneath, and she drank him in like a hot cup of mead at the end of a bitter winter day.

They shed their clothes with fumbling, desperate fingers—their cloaks pooling on the ground next to them. Caelin shrugged off his shirt and pulled Raedwyn's linen shift over her head with one movement. Naked, her hands trembling, Raedwyn undid the laces of his breeches and pulled them down. His manhood greeted her, hard and proud against his flat belly. She whimpered and, reaching out, stroked the long, silky length of it.

He growled her name and pulled her back onto his lap, kissing her deeply, his tongue exploring her mouth and lips. Pleasure pulsed through Raedwyn's body as his hot mouth moved down her neck, and she bit her lip to stop herself from screaming when he took one of her nipples into his mouth and suckled her.

It all became a wild, ecstasy-filled blur from that moment on. Raedwyn was vaguely aware of her own voice, sobbing, pleading and begging as Caelin kissed, sucked and stroked his way down her body.

Finally, his eyes glazed with desire, Caelin sat back. Raedwyn could feel him trembling as he pulled her on to his lap so that she straddled him.

"Caelin," Raedwyn whispered, tracing his lower lip with the tip of her tongue.

"Sweet goddess!" he gasped. "Raedwyn!"

She laughed, enjoying the feeling of power she had over him.

Caelin's next act stilled Raedwyn's laughter and drove all thought from her mind. He lifted her hips and slowly lowered her on to him, impaling her on his hard shaft. Now it was Raedwyn's turn to gasp. Heat vibrated up the core of her body and she shuddered. Raedwyn cried out and a feeling of throbbing torpor filled her; she clung to Caelin as the pleasure crested once more.

Caelin pushed her back onto his cloak and, spreading her legs wide, took her hard. Then he withdrew and thrust deep into her once again. Raedwyn wrapped her legs about him, pulling him in deeper with each thrust, until she could bear it no longer. Her body arched and shuddered, and pleasure pushed her over the brink. She could hear Caelin crying her name before he too lost control. Then he cried out, spilling his seed deep within her.

They lay there for a while, limbs entangled and hearts pounding. Then, Caelin gently cupped her face with his hands and kissed her deeply, tenderly. When they broke apart, Raedwyn buried her face in his neck. She did not want this moment to end, but already reality was stealing back in, robbing her of these wonderful moments of freedom. For a short while, the world had existed only of her, Caelin and their bramble bower—everything else had ceased to be.

"Raedwyn," Caelin said, gently cupping her chin and forcing her to look at him, "I will never be sorry for this."

Raedwyn stared into his dark eyes and felt emotion choke her.

"Neither will I," she whispered, "but I am sorry that we can never be together again." Tears suddenly split down her cheeks then, despite Raedwyn's attempt to keep her composure. "*Wyrd* is so cruel."

Caelin nodded, his own eyes glittering with tears, before he pulled her into his arms and held her fast.

"You are mine Raedwyn," he whispered fiercely into her ear, "and I am yours. Whatever happens, never forget that."

Chapter Fifteen

HEAVY SPRING RAIN sluiced across the flat landscape as Eafa the Merciful rode east towards Rendlaesham. The rain, though not cold, was a deluge that blinded man and beast alike. It was a five-day ride from Eafa's Hall at Tamworth in Mercia—home of Ceorl, the ailing Mercian King—to Rendlaesham. However, Eafa did not mind the long journey. It made his anticipation all the sweeter. Rivulets of water ran down his face. He was soaked through. His wet clothes chafed him and he knew by the time he reached Rendlaesham he would be stiff and sore. Nonetheless, Eafa was the closest to happy he had ever been, or was capable of.

Life was good for Eafa the Merciful. The king, his uncle, was getting sicker by the day of an unnamed illness that gnawed at his innards and caused him terrible pain. The old king had no surviving sons while his brother Pybba, who had once been King of the Mercians, had produced two sons—Eafa, the elder, and Penda. Eafa was next in line to the throne, and judging from the king's rapidly declining health, Eafa would take the crown within a year at most. The other boon was that Aedilhild, his wife of five years and a constant source of irritation to him, had died, leaving him free to marry again.

Aedilhild had been a disappointment of a wife; too eager to please, too easily subdued. In the beginning, she had even seemed to enjoy his attempts to dominate and humiliate her, both within the walls of their bower and without, in front of his family and servants. It had not taken her long to fear his touch. Then, just after the harvest last autumn, after he had beaten her viciously before bedding her, as was his habit, Aedilhild's health had deteriorated. Her bruises never healed and she started to lose weight and get severe nosebleeds. Within a moon's cycle, she was dead. Eafa had not mourned her passing.

Through the curtains of rain, Eafa spied the banks of a river ahead. The river was at its narrowest at this spot and spanned by a crudely built wooden bridge. However, the heavy rain had caused the river to swell to a muddy torrent that almost touched the belly of the bridge. Eafa and his men dismounted and led their nervous horses across on foot. The bridge creaked and whined under their weight and the company was relieved to reach the other-side without one of their number toppling into the water. None of them could swim.

Eafa remounted his stallion and spurred it along a muddy track leading southeast. They would reach Rendlaesham before nightfall. Now that the treacherous river was behind them, Eafa's thoughts shifted to his betrothed and he felt his loins tightening in response. Raedwyn the Fair was a maid he had long coveted. Golden haired and lusciously built with a fiery temperament to match, Raedwyn was the type of girl who would fight him. He imagined her spitting and clawing like a cat, naked and trapped within their bower while he used his fists on her until she was barely conscious. Then he would use her as he pleased. Such a daydream caused his manhood to strain uncomfortably against his wet clothes. Eafa shifted in the saddle to ease his aching groin and reluctantly pushed aside his favorite fantasy.

Soon Raedwyn would become a delightful reality, a dream no more. Eafa cared not that she was a widow, no longer a virgin. By all accounts, Cynric the Bold had only spent a night with his new bride. Then there were the rumors that while Ceolwulf had held her captive, he had handed her around like a plaything to be used by the Exiled and his men. Eafa cared not for the rumors either. Raedwyn would fare far worse in his hands than theirs; he would make sure of it. And if she had given herself to them willingly he would discover the truth—and take pleasure in punishing her for it.

Shifting his thoughts from Raedwyn, Eafa took note of his surroundings as he rode. They had entered the Kingdom of the East Angles, Raedwald's territory, and already Eafa was beginning to tire of the flat, marshy landscape. He loved the wooded hills of Mercia and the king's fortress at Tamworth, rising like a stone sentinel above the trees. Raedwald had long been a thorn in his side. He was a formidable leader and a warrior, whom it was unwise to anger. The Northumbrian's defeat was still fresh in everyone's minds. The Mercians did not want a dispute with the East Anglians.

Eafa would have preferred to arrive at Rendlaesham, wed Raedwyn and depart the next morning, but Raedwald had insisted that Eafa turn up seven days before the handfast ceremony and enjoy some East Anglian hospitality. They would feast, hunt and down copious quantities of mead in the days leading up to the wedding.

Eafa was no fool; he understood Raedwald wanted information about the state of the Mercian Kingdom, the king's health and the likelihood of Eafa's succession. Raedwald wanted to build an alliance between them that would benefit them both. Eafa had a grudging respect for the East Anglian King; he was a shrewd politician who understood leadership was more than being able to lead a *fyrd* into battle.

Eafa's company rode on through the day. The pouring rain finally lessened to a drizzle and they rode across a gently undulating, marshy landscape dotted with thickets of coppicing trees. Signs of civilization appeared; small clusters of thatched wattle and daub buildings rose in the distance. These were satellite settlements around Rendlaesham, which grew ever more common as they approached the heart of the East Anglian Kingdom.

Finally, Rendlaesham itself appeared; a carpet of thatched huts encircled by a high wooden wall. On a hill in the center of the town, surrounded by another fortified wall, was the famed Great Hall. Today, rather than gold, it was a dirty yellow. Nevertheless, Eafa had to admit it was an impressive building of considerable workmanship and grace.

Eafa rode through the town gates and up the muddy street towards the Great Hall. Townsfolk came out to gaze at the infamous Eafa the Merciful. He rode like Thor himself through their midst without once looking in their direction. He was a magnificent man to behold; tall with a mane of ice-blonde hair. However, to gaze upon him was to look upon one of the cold, marble statues the Romans had left behind—devoid of mercy, empty of warmth.

Eafa left the people of Rendlaesham chilled and subdued in his wake.

The banquet was one of the finest Raedwald had ever held. It was the end of a long, hard winter but the king had recklessly emptied out his store to impress his prospective son-in-law. Pies, stews, spit-roasted meats and sweet apple cakes covered the table in the Great Hall. A servant poured Raedwald's best mead into the large mug at Eafa's elbow.

Whereas Eafa drank slowly, the king threw back his mead with abandon. As the meal progressed, his face grew ever more florid. His gestures were increasingly enthusiastic, and his voice roared like a stag's across the table. He regaled Eafa with every hilarious anecdote he had ever recited and often broke into song. At one stage, he called for his lyre to be brought to the table. Then, he sung a rousing song of victorious battle and of brotherhood among warriors.

At the table, the mood amongst the diners varied. Seaxwyn was pleasant and conversational, although there were lines around her eyes that had not been present before the winter and her face had a strained look. Eni and his sons were loud, encouraging the king to recount tales of his youth.

Eorpwald was an enigma as usual, his cool manner giving nothing away—although his keen gaze missed nothing. He observed Eafa the Merciful, noticing that he ate and drank leisurely, savoring the quality of the meal. An aura of self-contained power surrounded the Mercian. Eafa largely ignored the woman who would be his wife in just six nights. Only occasionally did his pale gaze flick in her direction, but his expression revealed nothing of his emotion towards her. Raedwyn was beautiful. She had spring flowers braided into her hair and wore a blue wool gown that revealed the pale curves of her shoulders.

Eorpwald was secretly impressed by his sister. Despite everything that had befallen her of late, she radiated strength and calm. She had matured greatly in the past year; gone was the indulged girl who was the apple of her father's eye and the center of attention at every meal, and a poised young woman had replaced her. Although he had never resented his sister,

Eorpwald had not been close to Raedwyn before now. He had always come a poor second to their dead brother, Raegenhere. Now, the two of them were friends but soon, Eorpwald reminded himself, he would lose his sister to this cold stranger.

Eorpwald looked down at his half-eaten pie. He did not have an appetite for the events of late.

He turned his attention to the king, watching his father down yet another mug of mead and sway drunkenly across the table. Where was the man who had led his people to victory in Northumbria? Where was the king of temperance and mercy? Eorpwald doubted he would ever respect his father again.

The feast dragged on late into the night. It was a long while before Raedwyn was able to excuse herself from the table. If the king had not been so drunk, music and dancing would have followed the feast. However, Raedwald was in no state to either sing or dance. He slumped over the table upon the dais and his snores filled the hall, signaling the evening had ended. Eni and Annan, both barely able to stand, dragged Raedwald to his feet and maneuvered him towards his bower. The queen bid the rest of the revelers goodnight and followed in their wake.

Raedwyn tentatively drew back her chair and got to her feet. She threw Eafa a sidelong glance and his gaze snared her. He had the eyes of a lizard, holding her fast.

"Milady." His voice was as cold as his eyes. He rose from the table, took hold of her hand and made a show of leading her away from the others.

Raedwyn's skin prickled as if she had just dived into an icy pond. She sensed danger in every pore. She did not want to be alone with this man— ever. His grip on her hand was light but Raedwyn could feel the power he held in check.

"I bid you goodnight, milord." Raedwyn halted and found her voice.

"Goodnight, Raedwyn." Eafa fixed her with his gimlet stare and, raising her hand to his lips, kissed it. His lips burned her skin like salt and Raedwyn barely resisted the urge to yank her hand away.

"Till the morrow." The innocuous words sounded like a threat.

With as much good grace as she could manage, Raedwyn extracted her hand from his and fled to her bower. Once inside, she sat down on a stool next to her furs and was surprised to note she was trembling.

Raedwyn poured herself a mug of water from a pitcher beside her furs and drained it. Outside it was a still night. She imagined Eafa sleeping just a few feet away from her, near the fire pit, and suppressed a shudder.

Putting down her empty mug, Raedwyn began to undress, readying herself for bed.

Perhaps I am overreacting, she told herself, as she combed out her hair, *still the man makes my skin crawl. Even in my father's hall I do not feel safe from him.*

Tomorrow she would take a knife, one of the wicked-looking implements the servants used to gut animals, and find a way to hide it on her person. What would she do when she was Eafa's wife though?

Raedwyn slipped into the nest of furs. She enjoyed this time of day—but the solace of being alone in the darkness, able to think her own thoughts, was bittersweet. Now, was the only time she allowed herself to think of Caelin. She had not seen him since their tryst in the brambles.

She had actively gone out of her way to avoid him.

Raedwyn could not bring herself to regret what had happened, but it was painful to see her father's slave, knowing she could never again touch him. She imagined he felt the same, for there had been no sign of him around the Great Hall for days. Their union had been the most beautiful moment of her life—and she longed to repeat it. Tears stung Raedwyn's eyes as they did every night when she thought upon Caelin. Memories of him rushed back—the warmth of his skin, the timbre of his voice, and the wildness of his passion. It was him she should have been marrying—not this cold, cruel Mercian.

Chapter Sixteen

CAELIN DUNKED HIS head into a bucket of icy water and came up gasping. The water was colder than he had expected. It had been a chill night and although it would warm during the day, a thin crust of frost lay upon the ground. Caelin sat back on his haunches and splashed water over his naked neck, shoulders and chest. He shivered as he pulled a sleeveless tunic over his head before belting it around his waist. The freezing water dissolved the fog of fatigue that hung over him most mornings. They worked him from sunrise until after dark, and the precious hours that he spent sleeping never seemed long enough.

Each morning he had the task of emptying the privies in the barracks. It had to be done first thing and Raedwald had already had him whipped for failing to work fast enough. Caelin pulled on his boots over his leggings and walked across the deserted yard, towards the barracks. He did not wish to draw attention to himself today; he wanted to be as a wraith, beneath the notice of all. It would make it easier to slip away tomorrow while the handfast ceremony was taking place.

Today would be his last in Rendlaesham.

The sun was rising; golden light spilling over the treetops to the east as Caelin climbed the steps to the barracks. Tomorrow he would see the sunset as a free man – but the prospect, which had kept him going over the long, hard winter, no longer thrilled him. The reality was that Eafa and Raedwyn would marry on the morrow, and no amount of freedom could remove the bitterness that had taken residence in Caelin's gut. He could not bear the thought of proud, brave and beautiful Raedwyn being wed to Eafa the Merciful—but short of killing the man, and being slain for the act himself, Caelin had no choice but to follow through with his plans. He had considered taking her with him, but they would never be safe from Raedwald and his desire for vengeance.

Caelin reached the barracks and found them empty. The warriors had risen early to go hunting. Beginning his task of emptying the stinking privies, Caelin reminded himself that escape was the only option he had left—he had been a privy-emptying lackey for too long, and he missed the feel of a sword in his hand. Raedwald had confiscated his sword, Shadow Catcher, upon his capture. He had seen it since then, hanging from the wall inside the Great Hall—a trophy for the king to gloat over. When he was free, he would have another sword made. The only way Raedwald would take it from him would be from his cold, dead hands.

When he had emptied the last privy, Caelin returned to the stable complex, stopping at the trough outside to scrub his hands. Inside the stables, Alchfrid tossed him a hunk of stale bread to break his fast. Sebbi and Immin had already eaten and were outside harnessing the horses that would plough the fields outside Rendlaesham once the frost thawed. Today, the four of them had the back-breaking chore of walking behind the plough and clearing the stones from the turned earth.

"It will be warm today," Alchfrid said after swallowing his final mouthful of bread. "The sweet smell of spring is in the air."

Caelin raised a dark eyebrow in response.

"What have you got to be pleased about? None of us will be able to walk upright by sunset."

Alchfrid shrugged and took a gulp of water to wash down the dry bread.

"There's to be a wedding tomorrow," the Northumbrian replied, "which means it will be a day of rest for us for once."

"It's not a day to celebrate," Caelin answered, unable to mask the bitterness in his voice, "Eafa will send his new wife to an early grave, like the last one."

Alchfrid frowned, his blue eyes gleaming in the half-light inside the stables.

"Aye, that's true enough," he admitted, watching his friend shrewdly, "but there's nothing you or I can do about it Caelin. Don't take it so hard."

Caelin opened his mouth to reply but the arrival of one of Raedwald's thegns interrupted him. The man loomed in the doorway, took one look at Alchfrid and Caelin, and shook his fist.

"You two—stop yapping like crones and get your arses outside!" he roared. "Anymore slacking and I'll have you both whipped!"

Bowing their heads as the cowed slaves they had learnt to be, Caelin and Alchfrid followed the thegn outside and helped harness the rest of the horses to the ploughs. Then, as the sun rose into the heavens, Caelin, Alchfrid, Sebbi and Immin followed the other theow through the town and out into the fields to begin a long day of work.

Raedwyn awoke early and sat at the window of her bower, watching the sky lighten. She had slept fitfully during the night; a regular occurrence these days, and when she had slept she had dreamt that Eafa was chasing her through a dark forest, his cold voice calling her as she ran. The nightmare still lingered as Raedwyn dressed slowly and strapped a knife to her right thigh. She hoped she would not have to use it, but the feel of the cool metal against her skin made her feel a little safer.

Finally, Raedwyn smelled the aroma of freshly cooked griddle bread and knew she could linger no longer in her bower. She joined her mother at the table and was thankful to see the men were all absent.

"Raedwald has taken Eafa hunting," Seaxwyn informed her with a tired smile. Masking the relief that flooded through her at the welcome news, Raedwyn nodded and took a seat at the long table. She broke off a piece of griddle bread and dipped it in the gruel.

"There is much preparation that still needs to be done for tomorrow," Seaxwyn said, pouring herself a cup of water. "I will need you here with me today to help with the decorations and your dress needs some finishing touches."

On the eve of the handfast ceremony, Raedwald's hall pulsed with industry. The decorations were to be even more lavish than for Raedwyn's wedding to Cynric, with feasting and reveling long into the night. Ever since Eafa's arrival, Raedwald had been in high spirits. He had even become affectionate towards Seaxwyn again, although he still treated his daughter coolly.

After servants cleared the remnants of food away, Seaxwyn got to work. She ordered the servants to open the two doorways at either end of the hall to let in the fresh morning air and had them scour the interior of the building clean. They removed the old rush matting; filthy after the long winter, and replaced them with clean mats.

Raedwyn sat outside the main entrance, on the narrow terrace above the steps leading down to the stable complex, and painstakingly embroidered the finishing touches on the gown she and her mother had made for her wedding. The dress was the most beautiful Raedwyn had ever seen—what a pity she was not looking forward to wearing it. It was pale blue, like the morning sky in summer, with a delicately embroidered hemline and sleeves.

The breeze was cool but the sun warmed Raedwyn's face as she worked. Now and then she would glance down over Rendlaesham. Despite her decision to put him out of her thoughts in daylight, Raedwyn found herself scanning the town, hoping to catch a glimpse of Caelin. However, he was nowhere to be seen.

The men returned in the early afternoon with their horses laden with spoils from their hunt; deer and boar carcasses slung across their saddles. Raedwald and Eafa traveled together at the head of the column and rode into Rendlaesham like brothers. Eafa was in a good mood as he entered the Great Hall. Raedwyn had been helping the servants prepare seed-cakes. She had her back to him, bent over slightly as she rolled the dough into rounds and flattened them with the palm of her hand.

Eafa's gaze devoured her, taking in her long hair that flowed down her back, the dip of her waist and the curve of her hips and rounded buttocks. The woolen dress she wore hugged her form deliciously and made his mouth water; he could barely wait for his wedding night.

Every day here was slow torture. Raedwald and Eni's loudness got on his nerves, while Eorpwald's quiet appraisal irked him. The king's whelp had nothing to be supercilious about. Raedwald's firstborn, Raegenhere, had been a much finer specimen of a man, muscular and virile like his father. Eafa did not like the shrewdness in Eorpwald's gray eyes, nor the way he was quietly amused by everything. Like Eorpwald, Eafa was a man who gave little away and as such knew what a dangerous trait that was.

"Milady." Eafa stepped beside Raedwyn and placed a hand on her arm. She jumped like a startled rabbit before looking up at him. She met Eafa's gaze boldly and that pleased him. No one had broken her spirit yet. He had observed her often during the last four days and her lack of fire had irritated him. He had begun to think she was not the girl he remembered. Now he saw some of her spark return. She did not like him touching her. Her arm under his hand tensed as if it took all her will not to wrench it away. A lazy, calculating smile crept across Eafa's face and he reached out and stroked her cheek.

"Soon Raedwyn you will be mine," he whispered, "and then you will have to suffer my touch."

Raedwyn's jaw set and anger kindled in her eyes. She stepped back abruptly and Eafa dropped his hand. If they had been alone he would have struck her across the face for her defiance. Anticipation burned within him and he cursed the night that still lay between him and his prize.

Her encounter with Eafa left Raedwyn unsettled for the remainder of the afternoon. She busied herself in the hall but kept a watchful eye on her betrothed, careful not to let him catch her unawares again. The afternoon passed quickly, while outside the sky clouded and a cool wind sprang up. Finally, the sun sank towards the western horizon.

Raedwyn removed the last batch of seed cakes from the griddle and brushed crumbs off her hands.

"Mother, I'll be back soon. I need some fresh air." Raedwyn fastened her cloak about her shoulders and gave Seaxwyn a tired smile.

The queen nodded, weariness etching her own face. "You've worked hard today Raedwyn. Take a stroll, not too long mind for rain clouds approach."

"I have my cloak, I will not stray far," Raedwyn promised before she left the hall and took a deep breath of the cooling air as she stepped outside. Slowly, she descended the steps outside the hall, relishing the peace of solitude. Raedwyn had almost reached the bottom of the steps when a voice behind her chilled her blood.

"Milady, may I join you on your stroll?"

Although he had phrased it as a request, Eafa the Merciful's tone of voice brooked no argument. He appeared at Raedwyn's side and solicitously took her arm.

"I saw you leave the hall and thought it would be a good moment for us to spend some time together."

Raedwyn schooled her features into a passive mask and nodded, not trusting herself to speak lest Eafa hear the dread in her voice. Unspeaking, they resumed their walk. Eafa hooked his arm protectively around Raedwyn's and once they had passed through the gates in the wall encircling the Golden Hall, Eafa steered her through the township, towards the back gates.

"Tell me, Milord," Raedwyn made an attempt at conversation. "I have never been to Mercia. Is it as beautiful as these lands?"

"More beautiful," Eafa replied, his voice dispassionate, "Green and wooded. Your father's hall appears a thatched barn in comparison to the stone walls of Tamworth."

Raedwyn sucked in her breath. "It must be distasteful to you to sojourn in such foul accommodation." She could not keep the ice from her voice. Even if she was no longer welcome here, Rendlaesham had forever been her home. The beauty of Raedwald's 'Golden Hall' had become common knowledge throughout Britannia.

Eafa laughed and the sound chilled Raedwyn.

"I am willing to put up with such discomfort in order to marry you dear Raedwyn." He slid his hand up the inside of her arm. "I grow weary of waiting. I must have you." He stroked the soft skin under her arm sensuously. "Your virtue matters not anymore, does it?"

Raedwyn's heart started to race. Was he intending to take her to a secluded place so he could rape her?

She considered screaming and drawing attention to them, but Eafa's grasp on her arm was an iron band. No one would prevent the Mercian lord from escorting his betrothed for an evening walk. Raedwald would be furious if she offended her betrothed.

"Tomorrow you shall be mine," Eafa continued, "but I think I deserve a taste of the honey that I will soon own."

Fear closed Raedwyn's throat—then she felt drops splatter against her face and looked up. Dark clouds had rolled in overhead from the east, blotting out the remnants of the dusk and throwing the landscape into shadow. Overhead, the sky rumbled. *Thunor* was on the move. Raedwyn imagined Thunor, the god of thunder, careening across the sky in a chariot drawn by his two male goats, 'Tooth-gnasher' and 'Gap-tooth', bringing with him the rain. Her fear blossomed into panic; Eafa would use the approaching storm to his advantage. Everyone would be sheltering from the rain and there would be no one about to see him drag her away.

"Lord Eafa!" A man's voice hailed them from behind.

Eafa cursed under his breath and turned, still holding Raedwyn fast at his side. Raedwyn's cousin, Annan, approached. As usual, Annan was in good spirits. He walked with a jaunty stride, seemingly oblivious to Raedwyn's terror or Eafa's irritation at his interruption.

"What is it?" Eafa growled. "Why do you disturb us?"

"A messenger has arrived from Tamworth with urgent news for you, Milord."

Eafa dropped Raedwyn's arm. "Where is the messenger?"

"He awaits you in the hall with the king," Annan replied.

Raedwyn forgotten, Eafa pushed past Annan and stalked back up the street between rows of thatched huts. Annan watched him go before turning to Raedwyn.

"Is all well with you Raedwyn?" Annan's face clouded. "You are deathly pale."

Raedwyn forced a smile. "I'm just a bit tired after being inside all day. I think I'll take a stroll around the walls."

"I'll see you back at the hall then," Annan replied. "You'd better hurry that walk or you'll get drenched. A rain squall's on its way."

Raedwyn watched Annan turn and follow Eafa back up the street, before she took a slow, shuddering breath.

Her marriage to Eafa would only end in death—but would it be his or hers? Her hand trembled as she felt beneath her tunic, her fingers clasping around the blade she had secreted.

Would she have the stomach to use it? Raedwyn's grip tightened on the knife. *Courage Raedwyn*, she told herself, *you are of Wuffinga blood. None of your male kin would allow themselves to be brutalized, and neither will you. You will fight him, even if he kills you for it.*

Night fell over Rendlaesham in a thick rain-swept shroud. The storm had cut short the slaves' work in the fields, and so Caelin, Alchfrid, Immin and Sebbi had returned before dusk. Muddy and shivering, they had seen to the horses and cleaned the plough, before retreating inside the stable to dry off.

They had depleted their stock of half-rotten and rancid food—left-overs from Raedwald's hall—and their bellies were hollow and aching. Hunched over a pitiful fire, Sebbi's face was a picture of misery.

"How do they expect us to work," he growled, "if they don't feed us!"

"It's the boon of having slaves," Alchfrid replied through chattering teeth. "If one drops dead while polishing his lord's arse, there are plenty more to put to work."

"Sebbi's right," Caelin spoke up. "We must eat. Yesterday I saw Eafa's men cooking a stew in the western wing of the stables. I'd wager they have supplies there still. Even if its stale bread and moldy onions, we need something to fill our stomachs. Shall I go and see?"

Alchfrid gave a low whistle at that, while the other two merely gazed at Caelin, their eyes huge on their drawn faces.

"You've got bollocks, I'll give you that." Alchfrid shook his head. "But if Eafa or his men find you there, you'll be given much worse than a whipping."

Caelin grinned, his teeth flashing white in the dimly lit stable. "It just makes the challenge all the sweeter!" He replied recklessly.

Alchfrid, Sebbi and Immin watched Caelin slip away into the shadows before they exchanged glances.

"I can't decide whether he's brave or mad." Immin shook his head. "You wouldn't catch me going anywhere near the west wing tonight."

Alchfrid's gaze flicked back at where Caelin had disappeared before he replied, "A bit of both I'd say. Have you not noticed? Since the king announced Raedwyn's marriage to Eafa, Caelin has changed. He's careless, angry and bitter."

His companions' eyes widened at that. Obviously they had not observed any change in him.

"You mean ..." Sebbi began, as the full implication of Alchfrid's words hit him, "that the fool is lovesick?"

"The man is miserable with longing for her. Can't you see it?" Alchfrid replied.

Immin nodded slowly. "Now that you mention it ... he always goes quiet and serious whenever anyone mentions Raedwyn."

"He has hidden it well though," Sebbi added, "and I'd wager he wouldn't thank any of us for mentioning it. I've never met such a proud fool."

Alchfrid nodded, his face thoughtful. He warmed his hands over the embers of their fire and decided to let the matter drop. "Let us hope that our proud fool comes back from his forage," he replied, "or it will be a hungry night for us all."

Thunder boomed overhead and the thick veil of rain aided Caelin as he moved around the edge of the stable complex, towards the western wing where Eafa's men stabled their horses. His boots squelched in the mud but there was no one about to hear him. Water sluiced down his face and ran into his eyes. Caelin blinked it away and slowly edged his way around the building. The first entrance he came to was too busy to risk entering. Behind the wattle door, Caelin could hear the rumble of men's voices and the smell of cooking meat. His mouth filled with saliva; he had not eaten since his stale bread at breakfast and his stomach growled in protest.

Passing the door, Caelin edged farther up the building and came to a narrow door at the far end. Carefully, Caelin pulled the door ajar. Beyond he could see nothing but darkness. The smell of horse filled his nostrils. Slipping inside, Caelin pulled the door closed and crouched low, letting his eyes adjust to the darkness.

Eventually, Caelin could make out the edges of the stalls and the outlines of the horses. Some munched on hay, while others fidgeted in their stalls. Caelin was sure they smelled him but, fortunately, his presence did not startle any of them. Moving quietly, Caelin crept down the aisle between the horses. He reached a partition between the horses and the men, and it was here that Caelin discovered the food store.

He could hear men's voices just beyond the thin partition and firelight shone through the thin wall in fine shafts, illuminating the shadowy corner where Eafa's men kept their food supplies. Caelin felt around inside the store, discovering sacks of onions, carrots and cabbages. He moved quickly, filling a small sack that he had brought with him, before he discovered a side of salted pork. Grinning at his stroke of luck, Caelin took out a small knife that he used for boning fish, to cut a thick slice off. He now had the ingredients for a half-decent stew.

Caelin was about to continue searching through the store, just to see if he had missed any other delicacies, when he heard someone approaching on the other side of the partition. He had just enough time to fling himself into the next stall and crouch down next to its occupant, when the door opened and light flooded into the stables. The horse snorted nervously and shifted away from Caelin as the silhouette of a tall man appeared in the doorway.

"Where did you put the onions?" the man called back over his shoulder.

"At the front," came the answer, "and find us some carrots for this stew while you're at it."

Caelin held his breath as the man foraged around in the store, and the odor of mead reached him. The men had been drinking – and Caelin hoped that in the man's inebriated state, he would fail to notice the horse pawing and snorting next door.

"Milord!" the voice that had asked for the carrots, rang out across the stable, followed by the respectful chorus of "good evening, M'lord!" from the other men present.

Caelin froze, his hands clutched around his sack of food. There was only one man that made others that nervous.

Eafa the Merciful had paid his men a visit.

The man searching for onions and carrots, hurriedly exited the store with a handful of vegetables, and pulled the thin wattle door closed behind him.

"My Lord Eafa," he greeted the newcomer, "will you join us for boiled mutton and pottage?"

"I have already eaten," came Eafa's cool reply. "I did not come here to break bread with you Yffi—instead, I bring news that will affect you all. My uncle, the King of Mercia is dead."

Silence followed Eafa's words. They had all been expecting this, for King Cearl had been ailing for a long while. His twenty-year rule, a time of relative peace for Mercia, was now at an end. They now stood before their new leader—for it was Eafa who was in line to succeed him.

"My father died while I and my brother Penda were babes," Eafa continued, "and Cearl stepped in, taking the throne for himself. He should have handed it over to me when I came of age but no, the old goat hung on to it like it was his birthright. Now he is dead and I finally have the lands I was born to rule. Kneel before your king!"

Caelin heard shuffling as the men hurried to do their lord's bidding. Even from behind the partition, he could taste their fear of this man. Just his voice made Caelin's blood run cold.

"That's better." Eafa's voice was quieter now. "Rise and listen to me now. There is no time to waste. The greatness of Mercia depends on the actions of us all now. Tomorrow, I will wed Raedwyn the Fair, daughter of Raedwald, King of the East Angles—and after the ceremony, while Raedwald feasts and drinks to my health, I will kill him in his own hall."

Caelin heard the sucked-in breaths of Eafa's men, and a shocked silence followed before Eafa continued speaking.

"It is time that Mercia took her rightful place, as Britannia's leader. We cannot lead if we are mice. I have brought fifty spears with me; enough men to justify my protection on the road to Rendlaesham, but not enough to arouse suspicion. If we take the Great Hall and kill Raedwald and all his male heirs, and take the women as hostages—the Kingdom of the East Angles will be ours!"

"My Lord," Yffi ventured, his voice brittle. "The hall will be full of Raedwald's ealdormen, thegns and those loyal to him."

"Then we will have to kill them all," Eafa replied decisively. "My spears will encircle the hall. Nobody will be let out alive, unless they swear their allegiance to me, and forswear all loyalty to Raedwald."

The silence in the stables lay heavily after Eafa the Merciful had spoken. Eventually, Yffi, obviously the leader here for the others had lost their voices, answered his king.

"My Lord Eafa, we have little time to prepare. Have you planned the deed? If we are to do this, nothing can go ill or Raedwald will have us all butchered like pigs."

"I knew there was a reason I brought you with me Yffi." Eafa's dry wit did not elicit any laughter among his men—for he had not meant it to. "Of course I have a plan. Once the handfast ceremony is completed, we will sit down to a feast. There will be honey seed cakes served for the bride and groom, as is customary, at the end of the meal. At that point, I will rise from my seat and go to Raedwald with my cup raised, as if to toast him. Instead, I will slit his throat and I expect all my men in position to act the instant I kill Raedwald. Eorpwald, Eni, and his whelps—all must die."

"Yes My Lord," Yffi replied. "I will gather your spears now and explain your orders to them."

"Just one more thing Yffi," Eafa said, his voice dispassionate, as if he were arranging a hunting expedition rather than a massacre. "Raedwyn must not be touched. Spread the word that all male Wuffingas must die but I will disembowel any man who lays a finger on my bride."

Caelin slipped out of the stables, back into the wet night, clutching his sack with numb hands. The rain fell heavier than before, and Caelin was soaked within moments. Moving quickly, for Eafa's men were now moving about, passing word of their new orders, Caelin made his way back to his fellow slaves.

Sebbi's face split into a delighted grin when he saw Caelin emerge, dripping, from the darkness carrying a sackful of food.

"Woden, you did it!" He rushed forward and took the sack from Caelin, emptying the contents onto the pitted wooden board that he used for preparing food.

"Salted pork!" he exclaimed. "Caelin found us salted pork boys!"

"Well done!" The fatigue lifted from Immin's face. "Let's get started on a stew then, I'm so hungry I could eat it raw!"

Only Alchfrid saw the drawn expression on Caelin's face.

"What is it?" he asked as Caelin stepped up next to him in front of the fire and warmed his chilled hands. "You look like you've just seen your father's ghost!"

"Worse than that," Caelin replied quietly, "I have just overheard Eafa the Merciful planning to kill Raedwald after the handfast ceremony tomorrow."

Caelin looked up from the dancing fire into the shocked faces of his friends. Sebbi and Immin had abandoned their preparations for the stew. Their faces had gone slack as they struggled to comprehend what Caelin had just told them.

"It cannot be the truth," Alchfrid hissed. "Even Eafa could not murder a king in his own hall in cold blood. There is no honor in it!"

"He is a king now too," Caelin replied. "Cearl of Mercia is dead, and Eafa will be crowned upon his return to Tamworth."

"And what glory, to return home with the head of the King of the East Angles," Immin added bitterly. "Alchfrid is right. The man has the honor of a carrion crow!"

Sebbi spat on the ground, his face twisted in disgust. "You insult crows!" he growled. "We are slaves, and have more reason than most to loathe Raedwald of the East Angles, but to murder a king at his own table, after you have just wed his daughter, is detestable!"

"That it is," Caelin agreed. "If Eafa succeeds it will be a dark day, not just for East Anglia, but for all Britannia."

His gaze swept over their faces: Alchfrid, Immin and Sebbi—three of the best men he had ever met.

He was about to find out if they were also the bravest.

Chapter Seventeen

RAEDWYN AND EAFA'S wedding day dawned, gray and cool. A veil of misty rain shrouded the world from view, enveloping Rendlaesham and Raedwald's Great Hall in an iron curtain. Standing at her bower window, Raedwyn looked out into the murk and thought that there was no weather more fit for the ceremony that would take place today.

Tired from a sleepless night, Raedwyn turned from the window and cast her gaze over her wedding dress, which lay spread over her bed. It was so beautiful—yet she loathed the touch of it against her skin. Once the dress was on, Raedwyn stood patiently while Seaxwyn tied the intricate laces at her back. The two women did not speak. Seaxwyn had no words of advice for her daughter this time, and Raedwyn had no words at all.

Raedwyn looked down at the delicately embroidered sleeves of her gown; needlework that she had done herself, and felt a pang. It was hard to believe that she had once dreamed of this day.

Seaxwyn finished tying up her laces, and left her daughter alone to finish dressing. Raedwyn retrieved the knife from its hiding place under her furs and strapped it to her right thigh—as she had done each morning since Eafa the Merciful arrived in Rendlaesham.

What are you doing Raedwyn? A small voice warned at the back of her mind. *What will your new husband do when he beds you this evening— and finds you armed? Are you planning to kill him before he takes you away from here?*

Raedwyn had no answer to give. Strapping on the knife was instinct. She was not sure what would happen when she and Eafa were alone tonight. She imagined Eafa would be clever enough to keep his fists to himself while they were still under her father's roof. Still, a bleak fatalism now gripped Raedwyn. If she was doomed, she did not intend to become an object of pity.

Raedwyn emerged from her bower to find the Great Hall a glorious sight to behold. Wreaths of spring flowers hung from the walls and garlanded the ceiling. The interior of the hall sparkled after the thorough cleaning the day before.

Feeling everyone's eyes upon her, although Eafa was thankfully nowhere to be seen, Raedwyn walked across to where Eorpwald was breaking his fast, and took a seat opposite her brother.

"Good morning, Eorpwald," Raedwyn took the plate of bread smeared with butter and honey. "Could you pass me a cup of mead?"

Eorpwald nodded, making no comment about the fact that Raedwyn never usually drank mead at this time of day. They both knew she needed something to take the edge off what was to come. Raedwyn's gaze met his, and she was relieved to see no pity in her brother's eyes—just sadness. Usually, bread, butter and honey was Raedwyn's favorite way to break her fast, but this morning it merely choked her. She took a couple of mouthfuls and washed it down with a second cup of strong mead.

"Eorpwald," Raedwyn said finally, her voice low so that they were not overheard. "Brother, I know that you have fought father on this, and I thank you. We were never close as children, and that was my fault not yours. I have realized your true worth too late."

Eorpwald's face went still for a moment and the enigmatic mask he wore slipped. His eyes glittered with sudden tears and he reached across the table and covered Raedwyn's hand with his.

"You talk as if we shall never see each other again," he replied quietly.

Raedwyn smiled, realizing as she did so, that her expression must have appeared forced.

"You know the truth Eorpwald," she replied gently. "We need not speak of it."

Eorpwald's face had gone pale. He squeezed Raedwyn's hand and she could see the effort he was making not to say more.

"Raedwyn," he whispered. "I wish things were different."

"So do we all." Raedwyn removed her hand from his and took a deep draught of mead.

Caelin was shoveling muck next to the stables when he saw Eorpwald make his way down the steps beneath the Great Hall. The king's surviving son looked serious, his eyes downcast, as he strode across the stable yard towards the gates.

It was the moment Caelin had been waiting for. It was the only chance he would get.

Caelin casually put aside his pitchfork and followed Eorpwald through the gates into the street beyond. It appeared that Eorpwald had decided to take a short walk before the handfast ceremony. He paid no heed to his surroundings as he walked towards the orchards. Eorpwald had almost reached the gates when Caelin reached him.

"My Lord Eorpwald!"

Eorpwald came out of his reverie and turned. His gray eyes widened in surprise at seeing his father's theow before him—not only that, but the slave was addressing him direct. Eorpwald's gaze narrowed and Caelin saw his face harden. He only had moments to make Eorpwald listen to him and he could not waste any of them.

"I apologize for approaching you," Caelin said, "but this is urgent, it cannot wait!"

"What is it?" Eorpwald's voice was clipped when he replied. "State your matter and be gone."

Caelin took a deep breath and held Eorpwald's gaze fast in his.

Everything depended on how he worded this. If he spoke rashly or unclearly, Eorpwald would not believe him—or even worse—would haul him up in front of the king.

"My Lord," Caelin began. He measured each word carefully, hoping to impress his seriousness upon the man before him. "Eafa plans to kill the king."

The handfast ceremony passed in a blur. Raedwyn looked on, feeling more an observer than a participant, as Eafa presented the Wuffingas with a gorgeous golden cup. It was a king's cup, studded with precious stones and exquisitely worked. On behalf of her kin, Raedwyn presented him with a two handed battle-axe with a crescent-shaped iron head. A magnificent, deadly weapon it was, and Eafa smiled as he received it. It was the first real smile Raedwyn had ever seen him give. He admired the sharp edge of its blade and the long hardwood handle, reinforced with engraved metal bands.

"A worthy gift," he murmured, and Raedwyn saw her father beam at the compliment.

Raedwyn and Eafa shared a cup of mead and a honey seedcake, as the ceremony dictated, before Eafa kissed her briefly. His lips were cold and hard. There was no raucous applause, as when she had wed Cynric. There was no backslapping, or ribald comments, just a subdued rumble of approval that came from her father and Eafa's men.

Once the ceremony was over, Raedwyn sat down next to Eafa, at the head of the banquet table. The king, queen and Eorpwald sat to their right and Eni and his sons to their left. There was enough food before them to feed three times the number seated at the table. Men carried in spit roasts of wild boar, venison, and suckling pig that had been stuffed with the last of the winter store apples. More servants followed, carrying trays of baked eel and clay pots of rich rabbit stew. They set these dishes down alongside mountains of griddle bread, boiled carrots glistening with butter and honey, braised leeks, and cabbage fried with slivers of salted pork.

Raedwyn was surprised to see Caelin amongst the servants who carried in the spit roasts. Her throat closed at the sight of him but he did not once look her way. She belonged to Eafa now—and Caelin knew it. If her marriage had made him unhappy, there was no sign on Caelin's face. His expression was neutral, his eyes downcast.

For the first time all day, Raedwyn struggled to maintain her composure. The sight of Caelin brought everything rushing back. His bravery, tenderness and passion, the way he had protected and defended her when no one else would—she had never met a man like him, and knew she never would again. Raedwyn took a deep breath and blinked furiously as her vision blurred. She could not cry now—Eafa would be furious and she would pay for it later.

Once Caelin had completed this task, he returned bearing an enormous jug of wine, and took his place at the end of the table next to the other slaves, waiting while the rest of the food was brought out. Seaxwyn gave the signal, and he and the other slaves began filling everyone's cups with potent apple wine.

Musicians, one playing a lyre and the other a bone whistle, took their places on the podium behind the newly-weds. They began to play, and the strains of a jaunty tune suddenly filled Raedwald's hall.

Recovering her self-possession, Raedwyn's gaze tracked Caelin as he moved down the table. It was odd to see him and her father's Northumbrian slaves here, serving at the wedding banquet—but she knew why her father had done it. Having these men, warriors stripped of everything, serve at the wedding feast was a show of the king's power. They had all bathed and dressed in clean clothes, but the iron bands around their throats and their closely cropped hair marked them clearly as Raedwald's slaves.

Raedwyn took a sip of apple wine, and felt it burn down her throat. It was much stronger than mead, and she decided to drink sparingly. Although she had downed a few cups of mead this morning to fortify herself for the handfast ceremony, she now decided that, with her wedding night fast approaching, she would keep her head clear. Her father had no such hesitation. After declaring a toast to the bride and groom, he gulped down his first two cups of apple wine as if it was water.

The food was delicious but Raedwyn did not enjoy a mouthful of it. Beside her, Eafa also ate and drank lightly. He was so different to the men in her family. Raedwald, Eorpwald, Eni and her cousins all had great appetites; although Raedwyn could not help but notice that her father was the only one with a voracious appetite at the table today. Even Eni, usually the loudest and drunkest at any celebration, was subdued. Still, the wine flowed and the table gradually emptied of food.

"More wine, M'lord?" One of the slaves appeared at Eafa's elbow with a jug of apple wine. The Mercian shook his head and pointedly moved his cup away into the center of the table. The slave moved on and promptly refilled Raedwald's cup instead.

"Give me the lyre!" Raedwald shouted. "I will sing!"

The music halted and the lyrist hastily handed over his instrument to the king. Raedwald sat back in his chair and began to play, his fingers moving with agility and skill over the strings. When he began to sing, his rich baritone filled the hall.

Raedwald sang of brothers, of loyalty, and of honor between men. He sang of peace, of a great green isle blessed by Woden. It was a beautiful song, and not one Raedwyn had ever heard him sing before. Despite the king's mood, the song had a melancholic edge to it. Raedwyn stared down at her plate and felt her eyes fill with tears once more.

Despite everything he had done, she still loved her father.

The slaves eventually brought out the final dishes of the banquet:

platters of cheeses, apple tarts, spice bread, and honey seed cakes for the bride and groom. At this point, Eafa held his cup out to one of the slaves to fill.

"A toast is in order." He smiled then, his gaze meeting Raedwald's. "A toast to my King!"

Out of the corner of her eye, Raedwyn saw Caelin approach and discreetly pour wine into Eafa's cup, before he then stepped back from the table. Eafa got to his feet and raised his cup. Then, he stepped down from the dais and approached Raedwald.

"To Raedwald," Eafa continued, still smiling. "The king who brought East Anglia and Mercia together, and offered his fair daughter as a sign of his love!"

Raedwald turned in his chair and raised his own cup. His face was florid with drink and he was swaying slightly in his seat.

As Raedwyn watched her new husband stop before her father, a flash of silver suddenly caught her eye.

Raedwyn's breathing stopped as she realized what Eafa was about to do.

"No!" her scream echoed throughout the hall and brought the festivities to an abrupt halt.

The music stopped and Raedwald's Great Hall erupted into chaos.

Eafa lunged at the king, a knife gripped in his right hand. Raedwald's eyes widened as he realized, too late, that Eafa meant to kill him.

Eafa would have slashed the king's throat open then, if Eorpwald and Caelin had not flung themselves upon Eafa. Nonetheless, the tip of the knife nicked Raedwald's throat. The king dropped his cup and grasped his neck as blood trickled over his fingers.

"Traitor!" Raedwald roared and lunged for a weapon. Grabbing a carving knife, the king went after Eafa.

Raedwyn looked around frantically and spied the three Northumbrian slaves at the doors. They had just pulled the heavy oak doors closed and bolted them. Raedwyn could hear angry shouts coming from outside, followed by the pummeling of fists against the wood as men sought entrance to the Great Hall.

Wine and food went flying as guests leapt to their feet.

Eni, Annan, Aethelhere and Aethelwold grabbed what weapons they could and made their way around the table towards where Eafa struggled to free himself of Eorpwald and Caelin.

Raedwyn watched, heart in her mouth, as Eafa drove his elbow into Eorpwald's stomach and twisted free. He then smashed his fist into her brother's face and Eorpwald crumpled to the ground. Writhing like an eel, Eafa smashed a jug of wine over Caelin's head and sent him reeling, before turning to face the enraged king.

"Filthy whoreson!" Raedwald shouted, his face puce with rage. "Treacherous dog!"

Seaxwyn's screams filled the hall as Eafa and Raedwald grappled like lovers. The blades of the weapons they wielded flashed as they slashed viciously at each other. Dripping with wine, Caelin picked himself up off the floor, shook his head to clear it, and edged towards the pair. However, it was difficult to get close to them and Caelin was forced to hang back.

Raedwyn reached under her dress and slid the knife free of its sheath.

Suddenly, the king grunted and his face went slack. The carving knife slid from his fingers and fell onto the rush matting floor.

A moment later, Eafa screamed. The Mercian let Raedwald crumple to the ground, before he staggered away, clawing at the knife protruding from between his shoulder blades. Eafa could not reach the blade to pull it free.

Raedwyn stood behind him. She had sunk the knife in to its hilt.

Eafa turned, his face twisted in agony. His gaze fixed upon his new bride. In his right hand he still held his knife—only now the blade was coated with blood.

"Wuffinga bitch!" he snarled, staggering towards her. "I'll cut your throat!"

Eafa never reached Raedwyn. Moving swiftly, Caelin retrieved Raedwald's carving knife from the floor, stepped up behind Eafa and, grabbing the Mercian's hair with one hand, drew the knife across Eafa's throat with the other.

Eafa fell, choking, to the floor.

Raedwyn stepped over her dying husband and fell to her knees beside her father.

Raedwald, King of the East Angles lay, white-faced, gazing sightlessly up at the smoke stained rafters of his own Great Hall. Raedwyn stared down at the wound that had killed him—watching in horror as blood flowered across the sleeveless linen shirt he wore. Eafa had stabbed him, once, in the heart.

Raedwyn was vaguely aware of her mother kneeling opposite her. She looked up at Seaxwyn's stricken face.

"My love." Seaxwyn's voice was a broken whisper. She picked up his limp hand and squeezed as tears coursed down her face.

The Great Hall had suddenly gone silent, save for muted sounds of fighting outside. Shaking, Raedwyn got to her feet and looked down at Eafa's body. The Mercian's face had frozen in a terrifying grimace. Even in death, he was frightening. Raedwyn looked upon his cold face and wished his end had been slower. She had stabbed him between the shoulder blades but she had wanted to twist it and listen to his screams for mercy.

No mercy for the man who had none.

Raedwyn looked across at Caelin. Like the other slaves, he had thrown down his weapon, just in case he was mistaken for one of Eafa's men. Blood, Eafa's blood, stained his face. Caelin was pale but his face was resolute, with that same strength she had seen in him upon their first meeting over a year earlier.

Caelin's gaze met Raedwyn's for an instant before he knelt down and helped Eorpwald to his feet. One side of her brother's face was so swollen that he could not see out of one eye. The blow had knocked Eorpwald out and although he was now conscious, her brother staggered as Caelin supported him.

Seeing his father dead on the floor before him, Eorpwald's battered face crumpled. His body sagged and he would have fallen if Caelin had not been holding him upright.

"Father," he whispered, "I failed you."

Once more, Raedwyn's gaze locked with Caelin's.

"You tried to save my father's life. After everything he did to you. Why?"

Caelin opened his mouth to speak before his gaze focused upon Eni, who was watching him. Caelin closed his mouth and dipped his head, stepping aside as the king's brother approached.

"Eorpwald." Eni's voice was rough with grief. "Did you know Eafa was planning this?"

Eorpwald nodded, his eyes glittering. "Caelin warned me this morning. He overheard Eafa planning to murder us all. I should have gone straight to father, but I thought I could stop Eafa. I wanted father to be proud of me, like he was of Raegenhere. Now, because of me, he is dead."

Silence echoed around the Great Hall then and all eyes fixed upon the king's son.

"No Eorpwald," Eni replied gently. It is not you that killed Raedwald. Everyone here saw you try to save him."

Seaxwyn was sobbing as she rose from her husband's side and let Eni enfold her in his arms. Eni held Seaxwyn close and looked down at Raedwald, his eyes burning.

Raedwyn felt tears scald her face as she stepped close to Eorpwald and placed a kiss on her brother's uninjured cheek.

"Eni speaks the truth. The only man responsible for this lies dead at your feet."

Raedwyn turned from Eorpwald and knelt next to her father. Gently, she placed her hands over Raedwald's staring eyes. When she removed her hand, the king's eyes were closed.

"*Slæp fæder*," Raedwyn murmured. *Sleep father.*

Chapter Eighteen

THE ANCIENT BARROWS of Kings loomed out of the mist. Their great shadows guarded the eastern shore of the river Deben. Riding upon Blackberry, Raedwyn caught sight of the barrows and remembered the last time she had been here, waiting for Cynric the Bold. Thinking back to that day, Raedwyn recalled the pair of ravens that had landed atop one of the barrows. It had been an omen, Raedwyn saw it now; Woden's messengers Hugin and Munin had come to warn her. She had known it at the time, but filled with girlish thoughts of romance, she had dismissed their warning.

So much had happened since then—had it really been less than a year since she had waited here for Cynric?

Behind her, Raedwyn could hear the creaking of the wagon that carried the carved wooden coffin. Her father lay within, slain by a man he had foolishly trusted.

Raedwald's burial was to be the most elaborate in the history of his people.

Wrapped in a cloak, her eyes stinging from all the tears she had shed over the past day, Raedwyn watched as a team of men; Eorpwald, Eni, her cousins and the king's thegns and ealdormen, dragged a long ship up from the river to the top of the high bluff. They placed it in a trench that they had dug at the end of the row of barrows. It was Cynric's long- ship, with the carved dragon's head on its prow. Since its owner's death, the ship had remained on the bank of the Deben—now it was taking its last journey.

The men erected a gabled hut amidships with Raedwald's coffin inside. Around him, the women placed their king's treasures—personal ornaments inlaid with gold and garnets, weapons, silverware, cooking equipment and coins. There were two objects that Raedwald prized the most—his helmet, with its warrior face, and his ceremonial whetstone, which he had always used to sharpen his sword before battle. Seaxwyn and Raedwyn laid these treasures amongst the other items before they climbed out of the ship, and left their menfolk to complete the burial.

The men worked tirelessly, filling in the trench and raising a mound over the ship, as a thick mist snaked around the barrows. Raedwyn stood beside her mother, watching. Neither woman spoke—they had barely exchanged any words since Raedwald's murder. For the first time ever, Seaxwyn appeared old. Grief had etched deep lines on her face, and her hair, once a fiery red, hung lank and gray-threaded in a plait down her back. Raedwyn worried for her, but was reluctant to attempt to comfort her mother. Seaxwyn was proud and unpredictable, and Raedwyn suspected that a deep rage lurked beneath her grief.

In truth, Raedwyn feared her mother would blame her for Raedwald's death.

Caelin was among the men assisting with the burial. He no longer wore his slave collar and was dressed in a clean shirt, leather jacket and leggings of good cloth. Alchfrid, Immin and Sebbi—the Northumbrian slaves who had helped defend the Great Hall, also worked alongside Caelin. Eorpwald had given them all their freedom, and when his father's former slaves had asked if they could assist with the burial, he had agreed.

As they smoothed and shaped the surface of Raedwald's barrow, Seaxwyn began to sing. Her voice was beautiful and clear. The mournful funeral lament soared above the barrows and through the stillness, chilling all who heard it.

Then dark comes,
night-shadows deepen,
from the north there comes
a rough hailstorm
in malice against men.
All is troublesome
in this earthly kingdom,
the turn of events changes
the world under the heavens.
Here money is fleeting
here friend is fleeting
here man is fleeting
here kinsman is fleeting.

þonne won cymeð,
nipeð nihtscua,
norþan onsendeð
hreo hæglfare
hæleþum on andan.
Eall is earfoðlic
eorþan rice,
onwendeð wyrda gesceaft
weoruld under heofonum.
Her bið feoh læne,
her bið freond læne,
her bið mon læne,
her bið mæg læne,
eal þis eorþan gesteal
idel weorþeð!

Raedwyn blinked as her vision blurred with tears. Her father, the man she had loved best in the world, but who had betrayed her, was dead.

Buried under the earth, surrounded by his treasures, he would now set sail for the afterlife. Never again would she hear the timbre of his voice, or the rumble of his laughter. Worst of all, she would never be able to tell him that despite everything she still loved him, and always would.

Seaxwyn's voice faded and she let her daughter embrace her as the tears returned. Holding her mother's shaking body, Raedwyn was reminded, not for the first time, that her mother had truly loved her husband. It was a love that had endured, even through betrayal.

A wave of sorrow descended upon Raedwyn, and she bowed her head as the tears streamed down her face. Then, the feel of a woman's hand, slender and cool, taking hold of her own hand roused Raedwyn from her grief. She raised her head to see Eanfled standing beside her. Her friend, who had attended the funeral despite her advanced stage of pregnancy, gave Raedwyn a brave smile and squeezed her hand. Alric stood beside Eanfled and he nodded to Raedwyn. Sadness lined his face. Raedwyn gave them both a tremulous smile and squared her shoulders. She had cried enough – tears would not bring her father back.

It was then that Raedwyn saw Caelin. He was standing on the far side of the group of men who had toiled all day to build Raedwald's barrow. His gaze was riveted on her face and, longing to go to him, Raedwyn stared back.

Eorpwald stepped forward and faced the group of mourners. A livid bruise now covered the left side of his face and his left eye had now completely swollen shut.

Despite his injuries, Eorpwald's face was resolute. His good eye glittered with emotion.

"Today we mourn the greatest of kings," he began, his gaze sweeping the assembly that had gathered around the base of the barrow. "Let not the manner of his death diminish all that Raedwald of the East Angles achieved, or the prosperity that this kingdom has known during his rule. I can only hope to be half the leader he was."

Eorpwald's gaze rested on Caelin then. The crowd grew still and all eyes fixed upon Raedwald's former slave—the man who had risked his life for the man who had killed his father.

"Caelin, son of Ceolwulf the Exiled—I recognize your valor," Eorpwald said. "Despite all that has befallen you since your father's death, you warned me of Eafa's treachery and attempted to save my father's life. There are few men who would have done such a thing. Please come forward."

Caelin did as Eorpwald bid, kneeling before the man who would soon be crowned King of the East Angles.

"I give you back *Shadow Catcher*," Eorpwald took a cloth-wrapped object from one of his thegns and unwrapped it. The sword's blade glinted, despite the dull day.

Caelin smiled as he took back his sword. "Thank you, milord."

"I have given you your freedom and returned your sword," Eorpwald continued, "but name a gift and, if it is in within my power, I will give it."

Caelin's face froze for a moment; such was his shock at Eorpwald's declaration. Until then, Caelin had carefully kept his emotions locked inside, but when he looked back at Eorpwald, all could see the naked gratitude on his face.

"My Lord Eorpwald," Caelin began, "there is nothing I would ask, except the hand of your sister, Raedwyn—and that is only hers to give."

There was a collective gasp from the crowd. Some faces blackened in anger that a former slave would dare ask for such a thing. Seaxwyn's face pinched and her gray eyes turned hard as she glared at Caelin. She shrugged off her daughter's arm and stepped away from Raedwyn, as if she had instigated this act.

Only Eorpwald appeared unmoved by this announcement. He even smiled, although the expression was more of a grimace on his swollen face, as if he had been expecting it.

"Then, I give you permission to wed my sister, Raedwyn, daughter of Raedwald, should she be in agreement." Eorpwald turned to Raedwyn and his face was serious. "Gone are the days my brave sister when your future is decided by others. Now, I give you the choice to make."

Raedwyn ignored her mother's hard stare and exchanged a look with her brother that needed no explanation.

"Thank you Eorpwald." She smiled, stepping forward. "And I accept."

"What!" Seaxwyn could not hold in her vitriol any longer. She grabbed Raedwyn's arm and yanked her to a halt. "Your father is barely buried and you plan to take up with a *nithing!* Raedwald would turn in his grave to know his daughter betrayed him so!"

Raedwyn turned to her mother, her expression sad.

"Mother," she said softly, "the hate has to end now. I never betrayed my father in the past, and I'm not doing so now. Father had his revenge against Ceolwulf, and if he had left it there then he would still be alive."

"To marry Ceolwulf's son is to betray Raedwald!" Seaxwyn shouted, her voice hoarse.

"Why?" Raedwyn replied. "Both men are dead—the feud has ended. Neither Caelin, nor I were responsible for the hate between them. We are finished paying for it."

Raedwyn left the words both women knew to be the truth, unsaid. Instead, their gazes locked and Raedwyn let her response sink in. She understood her mother's grief, her loss, but she was finished with taking the blame for something that had nothing to do with her.

"Mother," Eorpwald said gently, "Caelin risked his own life in trying to save father. Raedwyn has since told me that he also saved her life. It is time to let the past go. I know better than most, the effect that Ceolwulf's treachery had on our family. Hating his son will not bring your husband back."

"Time to let the past lie, Seaxwyn." Eni stepped up beside the queen and put an arm around her trembling shoulders. "Raedwald had his reckoning with Ceolwulf and he should have left it there. Don't make the same error."

Seaxwyn's face crumpled and she sagged against Eni.

"I miss him," she wailed. "I want him back. Give me my husband back!"

Sadness etched Eni's face as he held Seaxwyn close and let her cry against his chest. He looked across at Caelin then and nodded. It was a wordless gesture but all there knew what it meant.

Eni was giving Caelin and Raedwyn his blessing.

"There has been too much bloodshed, too much death of late," he said gruffly. "What Rendlaesham needs is a real wedding, not that mockery of one." Eni paused there, his gaze meeting Caelin's. "Now, why don't you kiss the girl and brighten up this dreary day!"

Eorpwald laughed, Caelin looked stunned and Raedwyn blushed.

"Go on then," Eorpwald encouraged, his good eye twinkling. "My uncle has spoken, and you had better do as you're told!"

Caelin smiled then, and the expression lit up his face. Needing no further encouragement, Caelin walked across to where Raedwyn stood, her face flaming.

"Raedwyn the Fair." He stopped before her and inclined his head. "May I?"

Raedwyn did not answer. Instead, she threw herself into his arms. Caelin's mouth came down upon hers, and he kissed her there for all to see.

The crowd of mourners cheered. Raedwyn's cousins Annan, Aethelhere, and Aethelwold made the loudest noise, and the pall of grief and sadness that had weighed upon the crowd lifted. Even Seaxwyn lifted her tear-stained face from Eni's chest to watch the lovers embrace.

Raedwyn pulled back from Caelin, gasping for air, and her gaze locked with his. She could not believe this moment was real. She had thought she would never be able to see, let alone touch, Caelin again. Now, *wyrd* had finally turned in her favor.

Her brother had given her the freedom to love as she chose and she grabbed this chance with both hands. She thought then of the lament her mother had sung as Raedwald's burial was completed. Their lives, friendship, kin, love and happiness were all indeed fleeting—and for that reason she would not waste a moment more.

"*Ic þe lufu*," she whispered into Caelin's ear as the crowd cheered. *I love you.*

Epilogue

THE SUN SET slowly behind the ancient Barrows of Kings. The mist had cleared and pink ribbons laced the dusk sky, promising good weather for the coming day. All of King Raedwald's mourners had now returned to Rendlaesham—save two.

Raedwyn knelt before her father's barrow and placed a wreath of spring flowers she had just made on the fresh earth. Behind her, standing at a respectful distance while his beloved paid her last respects to her father, Caelin waited.

Dry-eyed, Raedwyn sat back and let her gaze shift, from her wreath, up over the dark mound of earth that shadowed her. It was spring and within days, grass and weeds would appear in the soft earth. By mid-summer Raedwald's barrow would be part of the landscape, like the others beside it. After an emotional day, Raedwyn now felt a great peace settle upon her. Seaxwyn had returned to Rendlaesham and taken with her any lingering disapproval.

Finally, Raedwyn and Caelin were alone together. They had tethered their horses nearby – Blackberry, and Mist, a stocky gray gelding that Eorpwald had gifted Caelin. In a short while, she and Caelin would ride off to their new life together. They would be married on the morrow and the thought of the adventure that lay before them—as man and wife—made Raedwyn's belly flutter with excitement.

"Goodbye father," Raedwyn whispered. "I wish you a safe journey."

Raedwyn got to her feet and brushed earth off her cloak. Then, she turned and walked back to where Caelin waited for her.

"Are you ready?" he asked softly, his dark gaze riveted on her face.

Raedwyn nodded. "Thank you for waiting. I wanted to have some time alone with him, after the others had gone."

"I understand," Caelin's expression was wistful. "I would have liked to have given my father a proper burial."

Raedwyn stepped close to Caelin and kissed him softly on the lips. "I know," she replied.

In response, Caelin pulled her close and kissed her back. His kiss was initially gentle, but quickly grew urgent. Raedwyn felt one of his hands rest on the small of her back, pressing her against him, while the other hand cupped the base of her neck. It was a possessive gesture and Raedwyn melted into his arms. Her mouth opened under his and the world disappeared.

When the kiss finally ended, Caelin's eyes were glazed with longing.

"We should go," he urged her. "I've no wish to desecrate a burial ground but if I keep this up for much longer I cannot be answerable for my actions."

Raedwyn laughed and the warm sound shattered the day's somber tone.

"Very well my love." She linked her arm in his and steered Caelin towards their horses. "Take me to a place where you can kiss me to your heart's content."

"I plan to do much more than that," Caelin replied with a wolfish grin. "Lead the way sweet Raedwyn."

The End

Nightfall till Daybreak

BOOK TWO
THE KINGDOM OF THE EAST ANGLES

JAYNE
CASTEL

***

For Tim, with love.

***

Wyrd oft nereð unfaégne eorl þonne his ellen déah.

Fate often saves an undoomed man when his courage is good.

Excerpt from Beowulf

Prologue

North coast of Gaul—Kingdom of the Franks

Spring, 629 AD

THE WAVES CRASHED against the rocks, sending foam into the salty air. Gulls shrieked overhead and a cold wind whipped off the churning sea. The wind stung Aidan's face as he walked towards the four longships.

His men had dragged them up to the waterline and were readying the large boats for their journey to Britannia. Sigeberht was already there waiting, his tall spare frame wrapped in thick furs. He spied Aidan's approach and walked forward to meet him. Sigeberht's grey eyes were steely; his long, wind-burnt face set in determination when he stopped before his thegn.

"Are we ready?"

"Yes, milord."

"Will four ships be enough?"

The wind whipped Aidan's dark hair in his eyes. He pushed it aside before answering.

"You have one hundred and twenty-two spears. I could find you more but there is no time."

Sigeberht's mouth thinned at Aidan's response. He looked out across the churning grey sea. It was not ideal weather to journey in but they could not delay.

"Britannia." Sigeberht savored the word as his gaze focused on the northern horizon. "I've spent so many years in exile that I can barely remember my homeland."

Aidan did not reply, knowing that his lord's decision to leave Gaul and return to the Kingdom of the East Angles had not been easy. News of the murder of Eorpwald—Sigeberht's half-brother—at the hands of Ricbehrt the Usurper had forced him to leave his life dedicated to the study of Christianity and learning, and go to war.

"I must have reckoning for Eorpwald's death," Sigeberht repeated the vow that had spurred him on this journey. "The Usurper cannot wear the East Anglian crown. I may not be of true Wuffinga blood but I am the rightful heir to the throne. I must take it back for my family."

Aidan nodded. "You will have your reckoning, milord."

Sigeberht smiled and clasped his arm around Aidan's shoulders. Together the two men walked to the nearest longship, where warriors were starting to push it into the water; it took nearly forty men to heave the heavy craft into the waves.

"I thank thee Aidan. I could not do this without you."

"You gave a lost Irish boy his freedom." Aidan grinned back at Sigeberht. His lord's thanks brightened the chill spring day. "I told you I would never forget that. I would lead this army against the northmen if you asked it!"

"Let us pray to our Lord that it never comes to that!" Sigeberht gave a rare laugh. "I will have enough heathens to deal with back in Rendlaesham!"

With that, Sigeberht climbed onto the longship and took his place at the stern. He pulled his fur cloak close around him and nodded to Aidan.

"Gāð!" Aidan shouted, "go!"

Aidan ran to the next ship and helped haul the massive craft into the rolling surf. He waded into the water, feeling its chill bite through his breeches and fur-lined boots. Then, he swung up onto the boat and settled himself at the stern.

Before him, forty warriors jostled into place, each taking hold of a heavy oak oar. Moving as one, they propelled the longship through the choppy waves and out into the open sea. Aidan glanced behind him and saw the final two boats were also afloat and cutting their way through the surf. Ahead, Sigeberht's longship moved swiftly northeast. Aidan could see them unfurling the sail from the ship's central mast, and he called to his men to do the same.

The longship, loaded with warriors, weapons and supplies, sat low in the water. Yet, its shallow-draft hull allowed it to move swiftly through the waves like a fleet sea creature. The biting wind whipped away the shouts of his men as they heaved their oars through the heavy swells.

At the front of the boat, his strong face creased in concentration, sat Lothar. Like most of the men in Sigeberht's army, Lothar was a Frank. The same age, Aidan and Lothar had grown from boys to men under Sigeberht's roof. Blond and built like an ox, Lothar was just the sort of man Aidan wanted at his side when they attacked Rendlaesham. Besides Sigeberht, there was no one he trusted more.

"Enjoying the ride?" Lothar shouted at his friend over the wind, and pulled back on the oars once again. "I wouldn't want you to feel useless, perched there like a maid at her distaff!"

Aidan snorted. "I'll take my turn soon enough Lothar. Just keep rowing!"

Lothar grinned, his teeth flashing white against his tawny beard.

An arc of sea-spray cascaded over the boat, drenching them all and cutting Lothar and Aidan's conversation short.

Blinking the water out of his eyes, Aidan looked about—a grey, cold world surrounded him. The sea was the color of beaten iron and the sky that of smoke. It was not long before the coastline of northern Gaul, Aidan's home for the past seventeen years, receded to a green and brown strip on the southern horizon.

Aidan looked towards their destination and, although they were still some way off, he caught a glimpse of white cliffs on the horizon.

Britannia.

A thrill of excitement went through Aidan at the thought of what lay ahead. At twenty-seven winters, he longed for a challenge. Aidan had been only ten when he was taken from his village in Connacht, West Ireland. Saxon raiders had attacked, pillaged and set fire to his village and Aidan had been among the handful of slaves those blond savages had taken away. Once they reached Gaul, the raiders sold Aidan to a long-faced young man with fierce grey eyes: Sigeberht, the exiled stepson of King Raedwald of the East Angles.

Woden, father of the gods, had favored Aidan, for his new master treated him kindly and upon Aidan's sixteenth summer, he gave his slave freedom. Aidan could have left Sigeberht's hall then, but he had chosen to stay on as a retainer. His loyalty had paid off, for now he commanded this small but fiercely loyal army.

If Sigeberht's attack succeeded, his lord would soon be King of East Angles—a massive step up in the world from the exiled man who lived like one of the monks he admired so much. In truth, there were times when Aidan found Sigeberht a bit dry and humorless; his devotion to Christianity influenced all who lived under his roof. Aidan, like all the others, had converted to his lord's religion. Yet, in secret, Aidan still prayed to the old gods—Woden and Thor meant more to him than this new god who appeared to praise abstinence and piousness above all else.

Aidan kept his gaze on those white cliffs. He urged Lothar and his men on; his throat straining with the effort it took to be heard over the roar of the wind. Soon he would be standing on Britannia's fair soil and breathing in her fine air. A new life awaited him, and Aidan was impatient to embark upon it.

.

Chapter One

Kingdom of the East Angles, Britannia

Spring, 629 AD

Three days later ...

FREYA GENTLY PEELED a piece of lichen off a rock and placed it in her basket. Straightening her aching back, she inhaled the briny air deep into her lungs and gazed out to sea. A cold breeze whipped her long dark-red hair around her face and snagged at her shawl.

Despite the chill, it was a beautiful day to be gathering lichen for her mother's herbal remedies; clear and bright with white billowy clouds scudding across the sky. She stood on the edge of a flat landscape dominated by a huge sky. The North Sea glittered like beaten bronze this morning and waves foamed against the pebbly beach. To the north, stretched an endless shingle shore, and although a low bluff blocked her view to the south, Freya knew that the mouth to the Woodbridge Haven estuary lay beyond.

Freya's bare feet sank into the shingle as she continued her way along the shoreline. Humming gently to herself, Freya went about collecting the lichen; carefully peeling it off rocks with a small bone handled knife and placing each precious piece in her basket.

Eventually, her basket was a third full but despite her aching back, Freya was reluctant to return home just yet. An afternoon of weaving awaited her; Freya's most hated chore. She had time for a short dip in the sea.

During the summer, Freya often stripped and swam naked here, even though the sea's chill took her breath away. Today it was far too cold for such things but she still wanted to feel the salt-water on her skin. Putting her basket aside, Freya hiked her sleeveless shift and woolen over-dress up around her hips and slid down the steep shingle bank to where the water sucked against the shore.

Freya let out a shriek as the cold bit into her flesh. Gritting her teeth, she forced herself to wade forward till the surf foamed against her thighs. The power of the North Sea awed her, as always. It was rarely a tranquil sea, and hardly ever blue. Yet, it was all that divided Britannia from the barbaric lands beyond.

Freya was gazing at the horizon, lost in her thoughts, when a man's voice shattered her peace.

"Wes hāl!"

Freya turned, nearly falling in her haste; her gaze fixing upon a dark haired man standing upon the shingle bank.

He was possibly the most attractive male she had ever seen in her twenty winters. Dressed in well-fitting breeches cross-gartered to the knee and a loose shirt, the man had a lithe, athletic frame. He wore a heavy belt buckled at his waist and his black hair fell in waves about his shoulders. His face was beautiful—piercing blue eyes, a slight cleft in his chin, a straight nose and high cheekbones—marred only by an arrogant smirk. His gaze raked her from head to toe.

It was then that Freya noticed the stranger was holding her basket of lichen.

"Hello!" he repeated his greeting. "It's rare I go walking and find a red-haired nymph cavorting in the sea. What a pleasure!"

Freya's shock at having her peace intruded upon was replaced by anger. Where had he come from? He did not look or sound like men from any of the villages nearby. His eye-color and raven hair marked him as a Celt rather than an Angle and he had a pleasant, lilting accent. Aware that she was standing with her naked legs uncovered, she waded to the shoreline and let her skirts fall about her ankles.

"That basket belongs to me." She struggled up the bank towards him, the soft shingle making her movement ungainly. "And I'd thank you to give it back and spy elsewhere!"

To her irritation the man laughed. As she neared him she saw he was young, under thirty winters, and even more attractive than she had previously noted—his smooth skin and long eyelashes were enough to make any woman envious.

"I wasn't spying." He grinned, backing away from her and holding out the basket teasingly just out of her reach. "Can a weary traveler be blamed if he comes upon a fair wench bathing? I'm a leather merchant traveling to Gipeswic to sell my wares. I thought I'd take a stroll along the shore before catching the evening tide up the Deben—and I'm glad I did. I was hoping you were about to disrobe completely. What a disappointment!"

"Churl! Give me back my basket!"

"Not till this pretty siren gives me a kiss!" he taunted, flicking the basket once again just out of reach.

"Dog!" Freya lost her patience and lunged for him. The man took a couple of rapid steps backwards to avoid a collision but slipped in the quicksand-like pebbles.

The basket of lichen went flying and the pair of them sprawled to the ground.

Freya found herself lying atop this arrogant stranger, her body pressed along the length of his. Her face flamed and she was struggling to get off him when, quick as a striking adder, he rolled over so that she was under him.

166

A moment later, his mouth came down on hers, smothering Freya's rage. The touch of his lips against hers, soft yet insistent, momentarily drove all thought from Freya's mind. His fingers tangled in her curls. She gasped at the unbidden heat that suddenly pulsed between them.

"Get off me!" Freya shoved at his chest and knocked him backwards. Then she drew back her right hand and slapped his face, hard. Her sanity had returned.

Laughing, the stranger quickly rolled off her, and held his hands up in surrender.

"Such a fiery wench! Fire to match your flame hair. Have no fear, I only wanted a kiss, nothing more!"

"Come near me again and I'll kick you in the cods!" Freya scrambled to her feet and retrieved her basket.

"You would too," the stranger replied, not bothering to get up, but sitting back and admiring her. His blue eyes twinkled. "I like a girl with spirit!"

Freya ground her teeth together and swallowed her next insult. The dog was clearly enjoying this and she would not give him the satisfaction by engaging him further. She could feel his gaze upon her as she gathered the scattered lichen. Beneath her rage, she felt all hot and confused. She was anxious to get away from this man. He had ruined her peaceful afternoon. She hated the way he found her so amusing.

Retrieving the last piece of lichen, Freya turned and bolted for the bank.

"Wait," he called after her, "Hwæt is þīn nama?"

If he thought she would ever tell him her name then he was stupid as well as arrogant.

Freya fled into the woods and did not look back.

Aidan watched the pretty flame-haired maid storm off and raised a hand to where she had slapped him. The skin still stung but Aidan did not mind; he had deserved it.

What a girl, he smiled at her retreating back and got to his feet. *It's a pity I'll never see her again.*

She was a beauty, with creamy skin and long, shapely limbs. Her hair was like red fire tumbling down her back. It was not the first time he had seen a redhead, but he had never met a girl with as much presence as this one. The memory of her flashing green eyes and the feel of that beautiful mouth under his, suddenly made his breeches feel uncomfortably tight.

Aidan regretfully turned and began walking south. Now was not the time to be distracted by winsome wenches. Sigeberht would be wondering what had become of him. After two days on the longship, journeying across the water between Gaul and Britannia, and then north along the coast, Aidan had been eager to stretch his legs; never imagining what he might find during his walk.

Aidan left the shingle shore and climbed up onto the low bluff. It was a windswept outcrop of land with a flat top. He crossed it and made his way down a grassy slope towards the waiting longships. Before him glittered the wide estuary known as Woodbridge Haven. The estuary was the mouth to the river Deben. On the muddy bank rested Sigeberht's four longships. It was a remote and largely uninhabited area. Sigeberht had assured them there would be few locals to notice their presence here.

Joining the others, Aidan hoped his story about being a leather merchant on his way to Gipeswic had convinced the girl. He knew he should tell Sigeberht about her. Yet, something stopped him. Sigeberht would be angry on two counts: that he had let himself be seen, and that he had let the girl go. She could raise the alarm and destroy their whole campaign. Still, Aidan decided to keep quiet. Trusting his instincts, Aidan doubted the redhead would cause problems for them.

Aidan made his way over to Sigeberht, who was taking a drink from a water bladder. His lord took a few gulps and offered the bladder to his thegn. Aidan took it and quenched his thirst on the lukewarm, stale water, before stoppering it.

"Must we wait till nightfall?" Aidan asked. "It's exposed here."

"It's too risky to sail up the river in daylight," Sigeberht replied. "The Deben is wide but, if my memory serves me, there are scattered villages on its banks. Someone could see us and send word to Ricberht."

"How far can we travel upriver?"

"As far as the Great Barrows of Kings." Sigeberht's face grew even sterner than usual as he named the place where East Anglia's rulers were entombed. "From there it's a two-day journey on foot. It will take us longer for we must travel at night and hide ourselves during the day. We must reach Rendlaesham unseen."

Aidan nodded. As much as he wished to move swiftly now that they had entered the Kingdom of the East Angles, he knew that Sigeberht spoke sense. None of them, save Sigeberht, had ever set foot in Britannia before, and they relied upon their lord's memory to ensure they reached the King's Hall unnoticed. Their greatest advantage was the element of surprise. If the Usurper discovered their plans, he would gather a fyrd, a King's army, and make it difficult, if not impossible, for them to defeat him.

"How does it feel to be home, milord?" Aidan asked Sigeberht and was rewarded with a rare, unguarded smile.

"Better than I can describe." Sigeberht's grey eyes were alight as he spoke. "I had no wish to leave these shores and was but a callow youth when Raedwald banished me. My exile has made me the man I am. I will have my vengeance and take back what is rightfully mine—or I will die trying."

With that, Sigeberht called to his men and instructed them to hide the longships as best they could and find a place to take cover till nightfall. Sigeberht had told them that this estuary was often used by merchants travelling up-river to Gipeswic and Rendlaesham. As such, it was not wise to remain out in the open.

Freya strode through the lime-wood copse, her cheeks still burning. It had been a surreal but humiliating encounter and Freya's lips still tingled from the stranger's kiss. Boys had kissed her before; eager fumbles on Mother Night at Yule or at the Eostre spring celebrations, but she had never been kissed by a man.

An insolent man with no manners or honor.

Freya glanced over her shoulder, relieved that the churl had not followed her, before she quickened her pace towards home.

Wild flowers scattered the woods and iridescent swaths of bluebells carpeted either-side of the narrow path. Despite the flush of green and new life around her, spring had been late arriving this year. Even inside the sheltered copse, the wind had an icy bite and Freya pulled her woolen shawl close about her.

Ahead, Freya glimpsed the low-slung outline of her home through the trees and felt her heart lift. She shared the squat, thatched-roof, wattle and daub cottage with her mother, Cwen. The cottage sat alone in the woods, at the center of a small clearing. They had lived an isolated life here over the past four years. The nearest settlement, Bawdsey, was a morning's journey on foot, but it was a life they loved.

Freya reached the cottage and pushed open its wattle door. Inside, she found her mother winding wool onto a distaff; one of Freya's most hated chores. It reminded her of the afternoon of weaving that awaited her.

"There you are." Cwen looked up from her distaff. A small woman with thick brown hair, Cwen's hazel eyes twinkled as they settled on her daughter. "Surely it doesn't take that long to collect half a basket of lichen?"

Freya ignored her mother's jibe and placed the basket on the work-worn table that sat against one wall. In the center of the cottage, a fire pit glowed welcomingly. Freya hastened over to it and warmed her chilled fingers over the flames.

"It's cold by the water but I found plenty of lichen."

"I thank you, love," Cwen smiled at her daughter. "I've almost run out."

"I don't know what the folk of Bawdsey would do without you. They've come to depend on your skills as a healer."

"Flattery won't get you out of your afternoon chores," Cwen reminded her daughter with an arch smile. "That cloak won't weave itself."

"Yes, mōder," Freya sighed, "just let me get some feeling back into my fingers first."

Freya closed her eyes as heat seeped into her hands. Then, her thoughts returned to her encounter on the shore. She thought about telling her mother about the arrogant man who had accosted her, but decided against it. Cwen was suspicious by nature and would be overly alarmed. Two women living alone in the woods had to be careful and Cwen was forever warning Freya about men and how they could not be trusted. Her mother would pepper her with questions and Freya felt an odd reluctance to tell her about the stranger with black hair and piercing blue eyes.

Opening her own eyes, Freya glanced around the interior of the cottage. Her surroundings were as familiar to her as the back of her hand. It was small and, at times, cramped, but this cottage kept them warm, dry and safe. Freya's gaze then settled on the small loom that awaited her on the other-side of the fire pit. Feeling that she had delayed long enough, Freya reluctantly stepped away from the fire and went to retrieve it.

She was just settling herself onto a stool when a man's voice intruded upon the afternoon's peace.

"Wes hāl!"

Freya went as rigid as a rabbit poised to flee a fox.

He followed me, she thought in numb disbelief. *What in Woden's name does he want?*

"Open your door in the name of the king!"

Freya felt a surge of relief, tinged with alarm, when the man's voice rang out once again. It was not the voice of the stranger she had met on the shore; he had not been a king's emissary.

A moment passed before Cwen set aside her distaff and stood up. Wordlessly, Freya also rose to her feet and followed her mother to the door.

Two men waited outside. They were dressed in leather with bronze and silver arm-rings—warriors. Her father, dead four years now, had been a man such as these. Tall and muscular with a mane of red hair, Aelli of Gipeswic's arms had sparkled with arm-rings, all tributes to his valor. Yet courage had not saved his life.

Cwen greeted the newcomers coldly.

"What do you want?"

The men stared back at her, before their gazes slid across to Freya. They were only a couple of years older than her, and they eyed Freya with interest as she stepped up beside her mother.

"Cwen of Shottisham?"

Cwen nodded reluctantly.

"The king commands your presence." The warrior's gaze lingered on Freya before he fixed Cwen in a hard stare. "He requires a healer urgently."

"If you could tell me what ails him, it would help me know what to bring." Cwen's voice had an acerbic edge that made Freya suppress a smile. She loved the way her mother spoke to men. Cwen was so different to some of the fawning women they had known in Rendlaesham.

"It's a matter between you and the king," the warrior replied stubbornly. "Now gather what you need and let us depart."

Cwen glared at the man before turning to her daughter.

"Freya—fill a bag with food while I put some grain out for the hens."

Freya nodded and went back inside. She filled a cloth bag with whatever she could find: a loaf of bread baked that morning, a wedge of hard cheese and the remains of a rabbit pie they had planned to eat for supper. Then, Freya pulled on her fur-lined boots, slung the bag across her chest and exchanged her woolen shawl for a thick rabbit-skin cloak.

When Freya emerged from the house, ready to travel, Cwen was waiting for her with a heavy shawl about her shoulders. In front of her, she grasped a large, deep basket containing her cures. The warriors bristled with impatience. Freya could sense the irritation emanating from them in waves.

They were not used to waiting for women.

Following the warriors and Cwen out of the clearing, Freya glanced back at the home she shared with her mother. Like Cwen, she did not like leaving it unattended but, hopefully, they would not be away for more than a few days.

Chapter Two

THE WARRIORS LED the women away from the coast, southwest through the trees, until they reached a narrow forest path. The woods sheltered them from the chill wind but Freya was glad for the comforting weight of her cloak nonetheless; she would need it after nightfall.

The sun hung low in the sky when they reached the banks of the Deben. A boat, just big enough to hold four people, awaited them in the mud. The incoming tide lapped gently at the stern, guaranteeing the travelers a swift journey up-river.

Cwen and Freya climbed onboard while the warriors pushed the boat into the swirling water. Moments later, they were away and paddling with the creeping tide inland. Freya sat quietly and watched the bramble clad riverbank slide by. This close to the estuary, the Deben was so wide that the far bank was difficult to make out. A cold wind whipped across the water and made Freya draw her cloak even tighter about herself.

The two warriors chatted amongst themselves but did not engage the women in conversation. Freya attempted to talk to her mother, only to receive short, terse responses. Cwen appeared distracted and Freya wondered if it had anything to do with the fact that the last time they had travelled upon the Deben, her father had only been dead a matter of days. Freya had been nearing the end of her sixteenth summer when her father went into battle alongside King Raedwald on Uffid Heath. The king won the battle that day but Aelli of Gipeswic died upon the Heath.

Freya felt her eyes sting with tears at the memory of the last time she had seen her father, smiling and full of brash self-confidence as he kissed his wife goodbye. Her mother's grief had been almost as difficult to bear as the loss of her beloved father—and for a time Freya had worried her mother would never recover from it. With Aelli dead, their life in Rendlaesham had ended. While King Raedwald celebrated his victory, Cwen had packed up their belongings and moved herself and her daughter far from Rendlaesham and its memories.

"*Mōdor.*" Freya reached out and placed her hand on her mother's arm. "I miss him too."

Cwen glanced across at Freya, her eyes shining with tears. "Damn that man." She attempted a brave smile. "Why is it that even years on I can't forget him?"

"Because you loved him." Freya struggled not to cry as she answered. "And the gods cruelly took him from us."

Cwen wiped her eyes, her face hardening as she did so. Freya, without meaning to, had just touched a raw nerve. "The gods are not to blame for Aelli's death." Cwen's voice was laced with iron. "Raedwald was."

Dusk had settled and the last vestiges of light were fading from the sky, when the small party arrived at the Great Barrows of Kings.

The silhouettes of the giant mounds stood out against the indigo sky. Freya felt the skin on the back of her neck prickle at the sight of their majesty. All of the East Anglian kings lay here, including King Raedwald himself.

The king had died less than a year after her father. Freya remembered catching glimpses of him during her childhood. Tall, blond and imposing, Raedwald had been a leader of men. Indeed, he had led her father to his death. Although she held no anger towards the dead king herself, Freya could understand her mother's bitterness. Raedwald had led his men into battle in order to settle an old score. If Aelli had died defending the kingdom from an invading army, Cwen might have understood. Aelli had died so that Raedwald could have his reckoning—Cwen had never been able to forgive that.

On the riverbank, two more warriors stood awaiting them, torches aloft. The men exchanged brusque greetings, as they heaved the boat in to shore. Then, they helped Cwen and Freya disembark. Horses waited nearby, under the shadow of the barrows. The warriors led the women over to them without preamble.

"The king wants us back by daybreak," one of the warriors reminded his companions. "We will have to ride through the night."

Freya caught the edge of irritation in the man's voice and wondered what concern of the king's could be so urgent that they were expected to travel without rest to see him. Due to their isolated life, Freya had heard little of Ricberht; besides that he had killed Raedwald's son to gain the throne. Judging from the behavior of these warriors, Ricberht the Usurper was not a man to be crossed.

It had been a long while since Freya had been on a horse and, after a short time, her posterior was aching. It was a chill, windy night and the riders travelled in a tight knot. Freya watched the torches of the two warriors in front of her gutter in the wind. Around them, the darkness was impenetrable—making the journey slow and difficult. The moon had reached the end of its cycle and did not show its friendly face to guide them. The men obviously knew this road well or it would have been perilous to travel on it. Freya could not help but worry about outlaws, and her imagination ran wild as she rode.

The night crept by slowly. Freya and Cwen did not converse, save the odd word, as they both struggled to keep awake. Fatigue pulled down at Freya and her eyelids grew heavy. Many times she felt sleep almost claim her, before she pulled back from the brink and jolted into wakefulness.

They rode in silence. No one spoke but Freya wished the men would. The rumble of conversation would have made it easier to stay awake. Eventually, Freya had to keep pinching herself to keep sleep at bay. She was terrified that she would topple off her horse and be trampled by the two following close behind.

Eventually, a faint glow appeared in the east, heralding the approaching dawn. Freya's eyes burned; they felt as if they were full of grit. She yawned, rubbed her eyes, and wished they could rest a short while before seeing the king.

The party rode through flat, green landscape, interspersed with clumps of woodland. It was gentle, lush countryside dominated by a wide sky. The spring had been wet and the bright green of new growth was everywhere. Gradually, the land became more undulating until, nestled in a shallow valley ahead and framed by arable fields to the south and vast orchards to the north, lay Rendlaesham.

The morning sun warmed Freya's face as they neared the town. From a distance, Rendlaesham—the seat of the King of the East Angles—looked no different to how she remembered it; a carpet of thatched roofs with the golden roof of the Great Hall rising above it all.

The morning was clear and still. Freya could see smoke rising from the roofs, blending with the silver blue of the lightening sky. Freya's memories of their life at Rendlaesham were mostly pleasant but, still, she felt a stab of misgiving at the sight of the town's wattle and daub houses and sturdy wooden perimeter fence. It was a reminder of another life—one that was lost to her.

It was only when they rode down the last incline towards Rendlaesham that Freya noticed a great change in the town from four years earlier. The patchwork of fields surrounding the town should have been brimming with produce and freshly tilled earth. Yet, the fields that greeted Freya were neglected, rife with weeds and overgrown in places. There were occasional signs of industry, and a few haphazard plots grew spring vegetables, but the general sense of desolation shocked Freya. She glanced across at her mother and saw her own surprise reflected on Cwen's face. Rendlaesham had prospered under King Raedwald's rule. They had heard that his son, Eorpwald, had also ruled well.

Ricberht had only had the throne since mid-winter. How had things deteriorated so quickly?

As they approached the main gates, Freya's gaze rested upon a grisly spectacle. A man hung from a gibbet to the right of the gates. He did not look long dead, yet when they neared him Freya caught the putrid odor of decay. She slapped a hand over her mouth as her bile rose. Ravens had picked out his eyes. The man's purpled face grimaced at the party as they rode by. Freya averted her gaze and wondered what the man had done to merit such punishment.

Through the gates they went, and the neglect that Freya had witnessed in the fields was mirrored within. Refuse littered the dirt streets and the reek of sewage and rotting food hung in the air. Freya swallowed as her stomach roiled, and looked up at the Great Hall. The magnificent timbered building was as beautiful as ever. The morning sun gleamed off its straw-thatch roof, making it appear gilded.

They rode up to the high fence that ringed the Great Hall and Freya felt apprehension flutter up inside her ribcage. Not for the first time, she wondered what they would find there.

The small party passed through the gates and into a wide stable yard. Like the town outside, there were signs of neglect here also; piles of stinking dung, buzzing flies and rotting food scraps.

Freya winced as she slid off her horse. She was so stiff that she wondered, for a moment, if she would be able to climb the stairs up to the Great Hall. Cwen's face was also taut with pain as she followed two of the warriors towards the stairs; her gait stiff and labored. Freya hobbled after her mother. The stairs seemed to stretch upward for an eternity and she gritted her teeth with each step. She drew in a deep breath of relief on reaching the top step.

Two guards flanked the great oak doors upon a wide wooden ledge that ran the width of the hall. Upon seeing the two warriors who escorted the women, the guards stepped aside and pulled the doors open.

Freya stepped inside. Her gaze traveled around the Great Hall's interior, and she blinked rapidly as her eyes adjusted to the dimness. All the years she had lived in Rendlaesham, she had never before set foot inside the King's Hall. It was a magnificent building with high rafters, stained black from years of smoke. Unlike the neglect and filth outside, the Great Hall appeared clean and well maintained. Clean rushes covered the floor and heavy tapestries and finely crafted weaponry that gleamed in the firelight—axes, swords and shields—hung from the walls. A huge fire pit dominated the space and a carcass of mutton spit-roasted above it, causing a pall of greasy smoke to hang in the air. The aroma of roasting meat was a welcome relief after the stench of Rendlaesham. Yet, like her mother, Freya's gaze did not linger on the mutton. Instead, it shifted to the man lounging on the throne at the far end of the cavernous space.

The king noticed the two women immediately. His gaze gave nothing away as it moved over them and settled upon Freya.

The nervous fluttering in Freya's chest tightened into a hard knot of apprehension. This man was as different to King Raedwald, as night to day. He was tall and lean with an angular face and eyes so dark they almost appeared black. Unlike Raedwald, who had been a proud but good-natured man, King Ricberht exuded danger.

Chapter Three

RICBERHT, KING OF the East Angles, watched the two women he had summoned enter his hall. The four warriors he had sent to fetch the healer followed at their heels. They had done well to fetch the women so quickly, although he had demanded nothing less.

Ricberht's gaze swept across the healer, and the woman he presumed to be her daughter. Unlike many peasant women who lost their looks early due to a hard life, these two were quite lovely. The older woman was still a beauty, despite her melancholy air, but her daughter was ravishing. An exotic red-haired wench with milky skin, full and beautifully molded lips; she had a sultry emerald gaze that intrigued Ricberht. What a pity that none of the women he was currently considering for marriage were as winsome as this one. Yet the fact that this girl was lowborn would not prevent him from enjoying her.

"Greetings." Ricberht stood up and only just prevented himself from wincing as pain lanced up his right leg. "Cwen of Shottisham—your skills as a healer have reached my ears. I have need of your ministrations. Come."

Limping heavily, and cursing himself for no longer being able to hide his injury, Ricberht gingerly stepped down off the dais and made his way to the far end of the hall. He led them to a private area separated from the rest of the Great Hall by heavy tapestries.

Ricberht pushed aside the tapestry and ducked inside his bower. It was a simply furnished area; rush matting covered the floor and a nest of furs dominated the center of the space. A small window was open, letting in the sounds of the morning; the crow of a rooster and the plaintive bleat of a goat waiting for milking. Ricberht limped across to the furs and sat down heavily. He was only beginning his twenty-eighth summer but this ailment made him feel twice his age.

This woman must heal me.

Two of his most trusted warriors followed the women into the king's bower. Mother and daughter both looked uncomfortable at entering the king's private chambers but Ricberht did not want the rest of his household, his ealdormen and thegns, to see his weakness, or hear what he was about to say to the healer.

"It's my right leg," he told the healer when she approached him. "Take a look and let me hear your judgment."

Freya followed her mother into the king's bower. Her hands that grasped the handle of her mother's remedy basket were slick with sweat.

177

The moment the King of the East Angles had looked upon her, Freya had wanted to turn and run from his hall. His hawkish gaze had fastened upon her and his lust was palpable.

She never wanted to be alone with this man.

Freya hung back as Ricberht lowered himself onto his furs. Her mother approached him and gently undid the garters that laced his breeches around his right calf. Yet, when Cwen attempted to roll up the leg of his breeches, he let out a strangled cry.

"Careful woman!" The king hissed between clenched teeth.

Cwen frowned. "I'm afraid sire that I *was* being gentle. If you don't wish me to hurt you further I will have to cut open your breeches."

Ricberht had gone pale and Freya noticed a faint sheen of sweat now covering his face. He glared at Cwen but eventually nodded.

Cwen unsheathed a small boning knife from the belt at her waist and carefully cut down the length of material covering the king's calf. She then peeled it back to find a thick wad of linen bandages beneath. Freya could see a dark, yellowed stain on the bandage and when her mother removed them, the stench that filled the bower made the king's men take a few hasty steps backwards. Freya clamped a hand over her mouth to stop herself from retching. It was the sweet, putrid odor of festering flesh, and Freya had aided her mother enough times over the years to know that a stench like this boded ill.

Cwen was the only person in the bower, save the king himself, who did not shrink away from the sight of the swollen wound that oozed pus. Not for the first time, her mother's strength impressed Freya.

"What caused this sire?" Cwen asked gently.

"I had kicked that craven, Eorpwald, to the ground when he stabbed me. Don't worry, I slit his throat for that," Ricberht replied between gritted teeth. "It was over three moons ago but the wound has never healed."

Cwen's mouth compressed at this news before she replied. "I will need to clean the wound to see the extent of the festering," she said finally, "although it may hurt you."

"Do it then," Ricberht snapped, "but be quick about it woman."

"Freya." Cwen turned to her daughter. "Can you bring me my basket?"

Freya did as asked, before passing her mother some clean linen and a bowl of scalding water that one of the warriors had brought with him into the bower. Working deftly, Cwen opened one of her precious drawstring pouches of herbs and sprinkled a couple of pinches into the water. Then, she wet one of the cloths, wrung it out and proceeded to clean Ricberht's wound.

The king howled and writhed as Cwen worked; so much so that his men had to hold him down. The fuss he was making surprised Freya. She had helped her mother at births where women made less noise than this man. Cwen's face was grim when she had washed away the pus and examined the wound properly.

Cwen straightened up and fixed the king with a level gaze. Sweating copiously now, his eyes glassy with pain, Ricberht glared up at her.

"So what's your judgment healer?" he panted.

"I'm afraid it's serious sire," Cwen replied. "I can cut away the worst of it and make a poultice, but those livid red streaks running down your shin from the wound tell me that you have waited too long before calling upon my help. I advise that we remove your leg below the knee rather than risk the infection spreading."

"Bloodthirsty bitch!" Ricberht roared. "You'll not take my leg off!"

Cwen stepped back, her face blanching at the king's rage.

"Listen to me woman." Ricberht lifted himself up on his elbows and fixed Cwen in a cold, hard stare. "The last person who suggested that 'cure' is now swinging from the gibbet outside the town gates. That bungling fool failed to heal me and then wanted to saw my leg off. I'll not have it, you hear me?"

Cwen let his threat hang in the air before she replied. The paleness in her face was the only sign that the king had scared her.

"Sire," she ventured, her voice low and calm as if she were speaking to a frightened child. "You speak the truth. He should not have left your leg to fester so. But if I do not remove your leg, and the festering spreads, you will die."

"Silence bitch!" Richberht snarled; his eyes were glazed with pain. "I'll not suffer any more of your flapping tongue. Now heal me!"

Freya watched her mother's mouth compress into a thin, angry line.

"I will need a clean knife to cut away the damaged flesh before I can apply a poultice," she replied coldly before turning to one of the warriors. She handed him the knife she had used to cut open the leg of the king's breeches. "Put this blade in the fire until it glows red," she instructed the man.

With a wary glance at his king, the warrior took the knife and ducked through the hanging, back into the hall. While the knife was being cleaned, Cwen set about making a poultice. Freya stood at her mother's elbow, as she always did when Cwen worked, passing her the herbs and powders she asked for. Cwen's face was tense with concentration as she bashed up the dried herbs with a little water using the small pestle and mortar she carried in her basket.

When the warrior returned with the knife, Cwen carefully took it from him.

"You will both need to hold the king down," she instructed the warriors. "This will hurt him."

Freya stepped back from the bed and watched as her mother leaned over Ricberht's festering leg.

Moments later the king started to scream. It was a terrible, blood-chilling sound and Freya backed up as far as she could away from it, until her back was pressed up against the tapestry dividing the bower from the rest of the hall. Ricberht writhed, as if having a fit, and the two warriors were barely able to hold him down. They called for assistance and it took four men, pinning Ricberht against the furs, to hold him still while Cwen cut away the putrid flesh. All the while, Ricberht screamed and howled. It took all of Freya's will just to make herself stay inside that bower.

"Freya," Cwen instructed her eventually. "Help me apply the poultice."

The king's leg was crimson with blood, but at least the pus was now gone. Freya passed her mother the mortar and watched as Cwen gently spread it across the gaping wound. She helped her mother wind clean bandages tightly around Ricberht's calf. When they had finished, the warriors released their king and stepped back from him.

Ricberht's face was murderous. Tears streaked his cheeks and his gaze burned into Cwen as she stood before him.

"Vile witch," he croaked, his voice hoarse from screaming. "You enjoyed maiming your king. I should have you hung for hurting me so."

"No, sire," Cwen replied, meeting his gaze boldly. "I did not want to hurt you. I only did what you instructed."

Ricberht's face twisted as he gazed upon the healer. A tense silence hung in the cramped bower before he spoke again.

"I'll not suffer a woman with a forked tongue under my roof." Ricberht's voice was low and malevolent. "Gather your belongings and go!"

"But sire," Cwen frowned. "You have instructed me to heal you. The poultice and bandages must be changed every two days or you will most certainly die."

"Your daughter shall stay behind and tend me," Ricberht replied with a cruel smile, "and if I die, so shall she."

The gasp escaped Freya at this news. Cwen stepped back abruptly from the king's bedside.

"No m'lord!" Cwen's boldness disappeared, and desperation rose in its place. "Please. I can stay and tend your wounds. Let my daughter return home. I beg you!"

Ricberht smiled; the expression a grimace. "It's too late for toadying. Leave behind your basket of herbs and your daughter will make the poultices. If she serves me well, and heals me then I may consider returning her to you—but not before."

"But m'lord ..."

"Silence!" Ricberht shouted before turning to his warriors who had been silently watching the scene unfold. "Drag this woman from Rendlaesham and if she tries to re-enter the town slay her!"

Two warriors seized Cwen and dragged her towards the doorway.

"No, mōdor!" Freya flew at the warriors, fists flying, but they swatted her aside. The remaining two warriors grabbed Freya and held her fast. On the edge of hysteria, Freya writhed in their iron grip and kicked uselessly at their shins. Yet, nothing made them loosen their hold on her.

Freya and her mother locked gazes as the warriors dragged Cwen from the bower. Cwen struggled viciously, and dug her heels into the rushes to slow her departure.

"Freya!" Cwen's face crumpled and tears streaked her face. "My darling Freya!"

That was Freya's last glimpse of her mother before the warriors towed her from sight.

Freya fought her captors—attempting to bite, claw and kick—while Cwen's sobs and pleas echoed through the Great Hall. The sound of her mother's grief-stricken cries echoed in Freya's ears, long after the warriors had dragged her out of earshot.

Eventually, Freya sagged in her captors' arms and squeezed her eyes shut against the hot tears that scalded her eyelids.

I will not let this monster see me cry!

She took deep, steadying breaths until she had regained control. When she opened her eyes, she saw Ricberht was watching her.

"You have your mother's fire," he observed with a cool smile that did not reach his eyes. "Let us hope that you do not have her forked tongue as well. I do not tolerate shrews."

Chapter Four

FREYA CROUCHED NEXT to the fire pit and removed a disc of bread from the searing hot griddle hanging above the embers. Working quickly, so as not to burn her fingers, she flipped the bread into a wide basket and retrieved more slabs of griddle bread from the fire.

Freya's vision swam as she worked and she blinked furiously in an effort to stem her tears. She had not had a moment alone since her capture. What good would crying do now anyway?

Retrieving the last disc of griddle bread, Freya straightened up and brushed flour off her hands. It was early evening and the hall was starting to fill with rowdy, hungry men, clamoring for their evening meal. A great cauldron of simmering leek and bean pottage sat at the center of the fire pit. Servants were ladling it into large clay tureens. A boy was now slicing the side of mutton that he had been laboriously spit-roasting all afternoon over the pit. He placed the meat on large wooden platters, which other servants carried to the table.

Freya was aware of the men's stares as she carried her basket of griddle bread the length of the hall, distributing it along the long tables that ran either side of the fire pit. They were hungry, wolfish stares and, despite she had never been afraid of men, Freya felt her stomach knot under their scrutiny. Some of them tried to gain her attention, and some men even attempted to fondle her as she passed by. Freya's heart was pounding in her chest by the time her basket was empty. Glad to have a chore to keep her busy, she returned to the fire pit and tended to the next batch of griddle bread.

Around her, mead flowed and wooden cups were filled and emptied. The smoke from the fire hung over the tables and stung Freya's eyes. As she stood over the bread, Freya was aware of Ricberht's presence, and of his gaze, which often settled upon her.

The king sat at the head of one of the tables, lounging in an ornately carved oak chair. As the rest of the diners fell upon the pottage, bread and mutton ravenously, Ricberht ate sparingly and with a listless appetite. Yet he drank copiously.

Her mother had been right, Freya reflected as she started turning the bread—that wound had made Ricberht ill. Even though Cwen had cut away the putrid flesh, cleaned away the pus and dressed the wound, Freya knew enough of her mother's craft to realize that Ricberht was doomed.

If that was the case then so was she.

The evening drew in and the men lingered over the remaining scraps of dinner and last cups of mead. Eventually, the tables were pulled to one side and everyone bedded down on the floor for the night. The king's highest-ranking thegns took the best spots, close to the fire, while the others slept where they could find a space on the crowded floor. Freya was picking her way across to a small space next to the far wall when the sound of Ricberht's voice made her freeze mid-step.

"Girl!" he shouted from where he had unsteadily risen from his throne. "You will be keeping me company tonight. Come!"

Freya's face burned at his tone; he addressed her like she was a dog. She turned and warily met the king's gaze. She could hear the sniggers of his men around her. She hesitated to obey Ricberht's command.

Upon seeing her reluctance, Ricberht's face turned thunderous. The copious amount of mead he had drunk had not improved his temper.

"If I have to repeat myself you will pay for it." His voice, slurring slightly, echoed across the room, silencing the laughter.

Head downcast, her heart hammering in her ears, Freya did as he bid. She reached the king's side, avoiding his gaze when he put a hand on her shoulder. His fingers dug into her skin and Freya winced.

"Help me to my bower," he whispered in her ear, his breath ripe with mead. "You will pleasure your lord tonight."

It took all of Freya's will not to rip herself free of his grip and bolt from the Great Hall. She knew that such an action would be folly. They would catch her easily and it would only anger Ricberht, who might then give her to his men.

The king leaned heavily on Freya's shoulder as she led him to the far end of the hall. Together, they climbed the raised dais and stepped behind the heavy tapestries that screened the king's bower from the rest of his hall.

It was a chill evening. Servants had shuttered the small window and replaced the furs on Ricberht's bed, as the old ones had been ruined when Cwen lanced his leg. This far from the fire pit, it was so cold that Freya's breath steamed in the air. Her bare feet sunk into the soft sheepskin on the floor and she noticed that servants had adorned the bower with sprigs of rosemary and lavender, presumably to freshen the room. Yet, the faint odor of putrefaction still tainted the air.

Ricberht swayed drunkenly against Freya, his hands roughly fondling her as he did so.

"Help me disrobe," he ordered.

Freya unclipped the brooches fastening the king's rabbit-skin cloak to his shoulders and removed the cloak itself. She then undid the belt that girdled a long-sleeved tunic around his waist. It was made of fine linen and had a red silk border. Under it, he wore a thin, sleeveless tunic.

Ricberht sat down heavily on the furs and stretched his legs out in front of him.

"Ungarter me."

Freya knelt before him and started untying the laces.

"Such a luscious maid," Ricberht slurred, staring down at her as she worked. "I will enjoy having your pretty mouth pleasure me!"

Horrified, Freya glanced up at Ricberht and saw that the king's gaze was bright with fever. She knew little of men and their needs; her isolated life had protected her from such things, yet she could see the king was not in a fit state. Freya's hands trembled as she began unlacing the second leg of his breeches. She could not bear the thought of touching him—or of letting him maul her.

I'll die if he rapes me.

All of a sudden, Ricberht slumped back on the furs and lay there, unmoving.

Freya stopped unlacing his breeches and stood up. The king lay so still that, for a moment, she thought he was dead. Yet, she could see the shallow rise and fall of his chest. A moment later, he began to snore gently.

Freya let out the breath she had been holding.

Thanking the gods, who surely must have been watching over her this evening, Freya stepped back from the furs. She could not leave the bower, for she risked harassment from the king's men if she did so. Instead, she would have to sleep here. She glanced once more at Ricberht. He was already sleeping deeply and Freya decided that it would be unlikely that he would stir before daybreak. For the moment, she was safer inside the king's bower.

Freya lay down on the sheepskin at the foot of the furs, as far as possible from the sleeping king, and curled up into a ball. Outside the bower, she could hear muffled conversation from those who had not yet gone to bed. Freya could not sleep. Instead, she waited, staring out at the darkness, until the Great Hall finally quietened.

Now that she had a moment of privacy, the tears would not come. Instead of grief, Freya felt hollow and chilled. She had won but a short reprieve tonight. Upon the dawn, she would not be able to escape Ricberht's attentions.

What if I kill him in his sleep? She thought. *I could smother him with this sheepskin. I'm strong enough and he is weakened …*

Freya did not entertain such thoughts for long. Once the king's men discovered Ricberht was dead, they would know she was to blame. She shuddered to think what they would do to her.

The night wore on and Freya felt her eyelids begin to droop. After a night and day without sleep, she could not hold back the tide of fatigue any longer. Eventually, Freya fell into a fitful, restless slumber, filled with dark dreams.

Shouts tore Freya from her sleep. Disoriented and, forgetting for the moment where she was, Freya sat up.

What am I doing here?

Then, the events of the last two days rushed back and Freya froze.

The shouts were coming from inside the Great Hall; from behind the tapestries that shielded the king's bower from the rest of the space. Shortly after, screams, the clash of iron and thud of shields and axes echoed through the hall. Freya scrambled to her feet.

Woden, save me!

Freya went to Ricberht, who still lay sleeping. Oblivious to the chaos inside his hall, the king's slumber was deep. Freya shook him.

"M'lord!"

Ricberht groaned and pushed her away. "Leave me be," he slurred. "Let me sleep!"

"M'lord please!" Freya's voice was shrill with panic. "The Great Hall is under attack. Your men are dying. Sire!"

Her words finally reached Ricberht. He struggled into a sitting position. The single candle that burnt in the corner of the bower highlighted the gaunt angles of his face and the fury in his dark eyes.

"Pass me my sword!" he growled at Freya. "It's over there. *Now,* slut!"

Spying the weapon leaning up against the wall near the window, Freya hurried to obey. The iron sword was heavy in her grasp and her hands were shaking when she handed it to Ricberht.

The king had managed to struggle to his feet, although the effort had caused sweat to bead on his forehead. He snatched the sword from Freya and drew the blade from its leather scabbard in one practiced movement. Then, ignoring his slave, he limped across the bower. Shoving the tapestry aside, Ricberht joined the fray.

Freya had just one glimpse of the mayhem beyond, before the curtain swung closed.

The interior of the Great Hall was a sea of fighting, writhing men, blood, gore and swinging axes. Some faces gleamed with the glory of battle, while others were ashen with fear.

One glance was all Freya needed.

Shaking, she sank back on the edge of the furs. She was trapped in here, and soon they would come for her. What she needed was a weapon, but it did not appear as if there were any within the king's bower. Freya frantically searched the furs, hoping to find a knife hidden there, but her search was in vain. The rest of the bower was empty—there was not even a cup or spoon she could use to defend herself.

The din of battle beyond the tapestry had reached its peak. The screams of the dying and the war cries of the living echoed amongst the rafters.

Freya crawled into a corner. With her back up against the wall, she drew her knees up to her chest and waited.

The fighting had died away—moving outside the hall—when the tapestry was ripped aside. Leather-clad men carrying spears, axes and shields burst into the king's bower. Still held in the thrall of battle—their eyes wild, their faces splattered with blood —the warriors were terrifying.

Freya hunched back against the wall and prayed that the gods would make her invisible.

"Nothing, just the king's whore." One of the men spat out a tooth and a gob of blood on the rushes.

One of the men grabbed Freya by the arm and hauled her to her feet. "Aye, and a fair one at that!"

"Let me be!" Freya snarled, outrage suddenly overcoming terror. She kicked the warrior in the shin, twisted free of him and sprinted for the open hall beyond.

Freya had only taken a few steps when she collided with a man who strode up the steps to the bower. It was like hitting an iron wall. Freya bounced off his breastplate and staggered backwards, into the arms of the warriors she had been running from.

"Who's this?" a deep male voice boomed.

Freya looked up into the face that belonged to the voice and shrank back. It was a cold, hard face; long with austere angles. The man had flint grey eyes and a wintry expression. Instinctively, she knew he was this rabble's leader.

"Just a girl we found in the king's bower." One of the men hauled Freya upright and placed a possessive arm around her waist. "A fine prize she is too!"

Their leader's face twisted and he stepped up onto the platform. He was tall; towering over the man who held Freya.

"There'll be no rape here," he rumbled. "We may have shed a lake of blood to take back Rendlaesham, but I'll not have my men rape and pillage like northmen!"

The warrior reluctantly let go of Freya and stepped back from her, his face sullen.

"Milord." Another man climbed the steps behind their leader. "We've taken the outer buildings as well and secured the gates. Rendlaesham is ours."

"Thank you, Aidan." The leader turned to the warrior, his expression softening slightly. "You and your men have done well."

The warrior stepped up onto the dais.

"Woden!" The man's gaze swept over Freya, his eyes widening. "What are you doing here?"

Through her fear and shock, Freya realized that she had seen this warrior before. Indeed, it would have been impossible to forget him. The blue eyes, the cleft chin and the wavy black hair—even splattered in blood, carrying a spear and dressed in leather armor, with a deep slash across one cheek, he was handsome.

The churl who had accosted her while she had been out collecting lichen stood before her. He was certainly no merchant.

Chapter Five

"HAVE THE PAIR of you met?" The tall grey-eyed man frowned.

The man he had named Aidan grinned.

"Yes, three days ago. We met on the shore near Woodbridge Haven." He paused and met Freya's gaze, "and I stole a kiss."

The leader's gaze narrowed. He gave Aidan a look of stern disapproval before he turned back to Freya. "What's your name girl? What are you doing so far from home?"

All eyes turned to Freya. She took a steadying breath and realized that this was her one chance to explain herself.

"My mother is a healer. I accompanied her to Rendlaesham two days ago," she began. "The king had called her to attend him as he had a wound that would not heal. When my mother told him that he would have to lose his leg, he demanded that I remain here as his theow and attend him. I would not go free unless his wound healed."

"Did he use you?" The man's voice was hard, his iron gaze fixed upon Freya.

Feeling her face flame at the bold question, Freya struggled to hold his gaze.

Men are beasts, she thought angrily. *How dare he ask me that!*

"No, he did not. He was too ill."

"Then you are still a maid?"

Freya felt humiliation burn down her neck and across her chest. She clenched her fists at her side. "Yes," she replied quietly, staring down at her feet. At that moment she hated them all.

"My Lord Sigeberht. Why all these questions?" Aidan interrupted; the grin had disappeared from his face. "Surely, we should let her go now that Ricberht is dead."

"All the possessions of Ricberht the Usurper are now mine," Sigeberht replied coldly. "I will not tolerate having his whore under my roof, but since she's untouched, the woman can stay. I have need of slaves."

"But he kept me here against my will," Freya burst out. She knew it was foolish to speak up to this cold, hard stranger, but with freedom slipping away from her once again, Freya felt a chill needle of fear pierce her breast. "Please let me return home. My mother will be worrying for my safety!"

"You're staying here as my theow," Sigeberht replied, his tone brooking no argument. "You are a woman grown. Your mother doesn't need your assistance—but your king does."

With that, Sigeberht turned his back on her. He walked back down the steps to the floor of the Great Hall. Bodies littered the wide space, tables and benches were overturned and blood stained the rushes dark.

At the foot of the steps lay Ricberht.

Sigeberht stopped before the dead king and rolled him over with his foot. Ricberht's eyes stared sightlessly up at the rafters. A hand-axe protruded from his chest.

"That was for my brother," Sigeberht said softly. "May you burn in hell."

Sigeberht then turned and stalked from the hall, his blood-stained cloak billowing behind him.

A bloody sunrise stained the eastern sky. It was as if the gods knew how much blood had flowed that night in Rendlaesham.

Aidan of Connacht wandered across the stable yard, overseeing his men cart dead bodies from the hall and out of the gate. The dead would be burned on a pyre outside the town's walls at dusk.

Now that the fire of battle had left him, Aidan felt hollow and numb. His body ached and the cut across his cheek throbbed. He had not felt it during the battle, but now that the fighting was over, weariness clubbed him across the back of the shoulders. Still, it had been necessary. Blood had to flow if Sigeberht was to claim the throne. Ricberht would never have abdicated without a struggle.

Despite the element of surprise it had been a difficult assault. They had used grappling hooks to scale Rendlaesham's walls and had lost a few men before they even reached the Great Hall. Fortunately, Ricberht's garrison was disorderly, drunken and unprepared, for even then it had taken Sigeberht's men most of the night to subdue them. They had fought like cornered wolves, with the reckless courage of those who knew they were doomed.

Aidan massaged a tender muscle in his shoulder and halted in the middle of the stable yard. He glanced back at the steps leading up to the Great Hall; his gaze taking in the mighty timbered building and its golden thatched roof. He had never seen a building like it. As he admired the Great Hall, a young woman emerged from the doorway, carrying two large wooden pails.

She was a beauty, with milky skin, long limbs and a mane of flame hair. Unfortunately, the girl looked miserable. The woolen shift she wore was stained with blood and grime, as were her hands. Sigeberht had insisted Freya help clean the interior of the hall—and that meant scrubbing down the blood and replacing the soiled rushes.

The girl spotted Aidan watching her, and the unhappiness on her face deepened to dislike. Her green eyes narrowed. She marched down the stairs and, ignoring him, made her way to a stone well at the far end of the stable yard. There, she began refilling the buckets.

Aidan watched her go before turning back to his men. He was sorry that the lovely Freya had been involved in this. He had tried to convince Sigeberht to release her, but Sigeberht had been obstinate. What was Ricberht's was now his, and Aidan would not push it any further.

Aidan walked over to where warriors were struggling to lift corpses into a cart, and moved to help them. There would be a lot of work to get through today—in the aftermath of the battle for Rendlaesham – and much of it unpleasant. Still, it was far better than being on the losing side of battle.

Despite his injuries, Aidan knew there would be no rest until sundown.

Later that day, as the sun sank towards the west, Sigeberht rode out into the streets of Rendlaesham to greet his people. He rode a grey stallion that had belonged to Ricberht, and cut a dramatic figure in dark leather with a heavy black cloak rippling out behind him. He was flanked by Aidan to his left and Lothar to his right. The rest of his men paraded behind him, battle-weary but proud.

Rendlaesham's townsfolk clustered along the edge of the street: men, women and children, all straining for a glimpse of the man who had taken back the Golden Hall for the Wuffingas.

Sigeberht reached the market square and a great roar went up amongst the crowd. Seeing the joy on their faces, Aidan felt a surge of elation.

This was why Sigeberht had returned to Britannia.

These people had prospered under Raedwald and Eorpwald, but had suffered under the cruel hand of the Usurper. Sigeberht had given them back hope. The remnants of Ricberht's garrison had either surrendered to Sigeberht or fled.

Finally, Rendlaesham had been washed free of the Usurper's stain.

Freya carried the last pile of filthy rushes from the Great Hall. Gingerly, she picked her way down the steps to the stable yard and dumped the rushes on a cart, before retracing her way back up the steps.

Her feet dragged as she mounted the last steps and re-entered the hall. It had been an exhausting day. Freya's back and shoulders ached from being bent over for hours, scrubbing. Initially, she had let fury propel her forward, until the rage at her imprisonment eventually left her. Now, her mind was blank, and her senses numb.

Around her neck, she now wore a slave collar; an uncomfortable iron band that chaffed when she sweated. It would be a constant reminder of her enslavement.

The interior of the Great Hall shone from the hard labor of Freya, and the others, who had scrubbed it clean. A fire crackled in the fire pit in the hall's center, smoke was escaping through a slit in the roof, and servants prepared a celebratory feast: roast boar, griddle bread and a thick onion and carrot stew. Freya inhaled the aroma and felt her stomach growl in response. She had not eaten since the night before and felt light-headed and sick with hunger. She stepped onto the fresh-matting, feeling it crunch under her bare-feet, and went to help the other theow who were setting up the long tables for the feast.

By the time, Sigeberht and his men entered, shortly after dusk, the interior of the Great Hall was unrecognizable from the scenes of carnage at dawn.

Sigeberht looked pleased, although it was difficult to gauge such an expression on a face so severe. Only the lifting of the corners of his mouth and a brusque nod to his servants, told them that he was satisfied with their labor. At least he did not appear a cruel man, Freya noted. He would be difficult to warm to, but he did not make her instincts scream danger, as Ricberht had.

A short while later, warriors took their seats at the long tables. Despite being battered and bruised, they were in high spirits as they filled their cups and fell upon the feast. Sigeberht sat at the head of the table closest to the fire pit.

Freya filled his cup with mead before joining the other servants below the salt; at the farthest end of the hall. She sank down on the hard bench, with a sigh of exhaustion, between two other slaves: Hereric and Hilda. Hereric was an elfin-faced boy with a quick gaze that missed nothing, whereas Hilda was a wiry young woman with fine light brown hair and protruding eyes that gave her a nervous look. Like Freya, both Hereric and Hilda wore iron slave collars about their necks.

Hilda had dished her up a bowl of stew and cut a slab of bread for Freya. Rewarding Hilda with a grateful smile, Freya fell upon her meal, ravenous.

Sigeberht waited until his men had taken the edge off their hunger, before he stood up and raised his cup.

The rumble of conversation died away as Sigeberht's warriors waited for their leader to speak.

Freya saw the fierce loyalty on their faces.

"My warriors!" Sigeberht called out, silencing the last few men who had not ceased their chatter. "Today was a day of victory! My thanks go to every last one of you, and to those who fell so that we may take Rendlaesham!"

Sigeberht's words brought a roar of approval from his warriors. Their voices echoed up amongst the rafters and they slammed their cups on the table tops as they cheered.

"Sigeberht the Righteous! Sigeberht the Righteous!"

When the din had died down, Sigeberht continued. "Much blood was lost so that we could take Rendlaesham—blood that we must make penance for."

Sigeberht's words caused a tremor of uneasiness among his men, but heedless, their leader pressed on. "Vengeance is mine but our Lord will expect payment for such sacrifice!"

Freya listened with interest, her exhaustion momentarily forgotten. It appeared that Sigeberht was one of those who had shunned the old gods; still a novelty here in the Kingdom of the East Angles. She had heard that King Raedwald had converted, but there had been no sign of it in the daily life of Rendlaesham. This man seemed deathly serious about his beliefs. His words had cast a pall of discomfort over the hall. Many were visibly relieved when their leader changed the subject, although Sigeberht did not appear to notice.

"Aidan!" Sigeberht turned to the man seated to his right, at the head of the table. "Stand up so that I may thank you before our warriors!"

Freya watched as Aidan put his cup down and stood up. Unlike the day Freya had met him, Aidan's face was serious this evening. The cut across his cheek had crusted, and she imagined it would leave a deep scar. He was still dressed in grime-encrusted leather armor. Looking upon him, Freya admitted to herself that he was, indeed, the kind of man that drew a woman's eye.

He may be pleasing to look upon, but he has the manners of a goat!

"Aidan of Connacht, you are like a son to me!" Sigeberht clasped the younger man around the shoulders and held his cup high. "You have shown loyalty and valor. Now, you will be at my side while I make Rendlaesham truly ours. I honor you!"

The warriors cheered and held their cups high. Aidan smiled and bowed his head in thanks.

Once the cheering abated, Aidan sank back down on the bench. He helped himself to another slice of roast boar and raised his cup to Sigeberht.

Then, as if sensing her gaze upon him, Aidan glanced up and looked straight at Freya.

For a moment, their gazes met and held.

His eyes were a dark blue; of a shade she had never seen before. The intensity of his gaze made goose pimples prickle Freya's skin.

Then he smiled, and the moment shattered. It was the same arrogant smirk he had given her on the shore at Woodbridge Haven. Freya tore her gaze away from his and turned her attention back to her meal, although her appetite had now dulled.

Swine.

Freya tore off a piece of griddle bread and took a bite, before swallowing with difficulty. She hated it here. She longed for the simple life she had shared with her mother in Woodbridge Haven; away from Rendlaesham and this hall full of loud, boorish males. She hoped Cwen had managed to return home safely. Thinking about her mother, made her heart ache.

I will not stay here, she vowed, *I am no slave!*

Freya would bide her time, but as soon as the opportunity arose, she made herself a silent promise. She would escape.

Chapter Six

FREYA WAS BEATING dust out of a pile of furs when she heard horses approach.

She straightened up from her chore and turned her head towards the sound. She did not recall any visitors being due at the Great Hall today. A group of warriors had gone hunting this morning, but they were not due back for another two days.

Freya turned back to the furs and rubbed her itching nose. She had carried the bedding from Sigeberht's bower for cleaning; a task that her master demanded she undertake every three days. Sigeberht was a fastidious man who liked his sleeping area scrubbed clean on a daily basis. He did not adorn his bower and, unlike Ricberht, did not keep any weapons there. The only decoration was an iron cross that hung from the wall.

Before the sound of hoof-beats had distracted her, Freya had just been thanking her namesake, the goddess Freya, for the fact that Sigeberht had not insisted she shared his bed. Six days had passed since Sigeberht had taken Rendlaesham, and he had not shown any interest in her, beyond that of a slave. Instead of joining him in his bower, she slept against the wall, near the rear of the Great Hall. It was an uncomfortable spot, cold and draughty, but Freya cared not. She was merely relieved that Sigeberht appeared not to want her in his bed.

A knot of riders appeared in the stable yard below, kicking up a cloud of dust behind them. Freya put down the stick she had been using to beat the furs, and regarded the newcomers.

Three upstanding men with blond hair, and a woman, dismounted their horses. An escort of around a dozen warriors accompanied them. The three men were all handsome and carried themselves with warrior arrogance. The woman wore a long, blue hooded cloak that shadowed her face.

Behind Freya, Aidan of Connacht stepped from the Great Hall and swept his gaze over the group below. He glanced across at Freya and raised a dark eyebrow. She gave him a chill look in response and shrugged.

"Why do you look at me for answers?" she snapped. "I know not who they are."

Unbothered by her viperish tongue, Aidan turned his attention back to the newcomers.

"Welcome to Sigeberht's hall," he called down. "To whom do we owe the pleasure?"

The eldest of the three men, a warrior of around five and thirty winters, stepped forward.

"I am Annan," he introduced himself. "Son of Eni of the Wuffingas. These are my brothers, Aethelhere and Aethelwold. We are Raedwald and Eorpwald's kin—and the kin of Sigeberht."

Annan turned then to the woman, who stepped forward and lowered the hood obscuring her identity. She was an older woman, although still handsome, with a mane of red hair, threaded with white. She regarded Aidan with cool grey eyes.

"I am Seaxwyn." Her voice, although quiet, held the power of one who was used to commanding others. "And I wish to see my son. Take us to Sigeberht."

Freya placed a ewer of apple wine on the table, Hilda laid out cups for the guests, and Hereric brought out a platter laden with cheese and fruit.

The quiet inside the hall was unnerving and Freya was grateful to move away from the table. She and Hilda went to the fire pit and continued the chore that Hilda had been busy with before the party's arrival—kneading bread. Freya would have to finish cleaning the furs later. Now, with guests that evening, they had extra food to prepare.

Sigeberht, after greeting the party, had seated himself at the end of the table. Aidan stood a few steps behind him, while the guests sat at the other end of the table.

Freya had never witnessed such a cold reunion between mother and son. There had been no hugs, no tears and very few smiles; just strained greetings and an awkward moment when Sigeberht had knelt to kiss his mother's hand.

It was as if they were strangers—which, in fact, they were.

Freya kneaded a lump of dough and flattened it into a disc with the heel of her hand, watching the conversation at the other end of the hall surreptitiously as she did so.

"'It has been a long while, mōder," Sigeberht rumbled, steepling his fingers in front of him and regarding Seaxwyn with an iron-grey gaze. They had the same eyes, Freya realized; the color of storm clouds.

"I've lost count," Seaxwyn admitted. "You were hardly out of boyhood when Raedwald banished you."

"Old enough to be a threat." Sigeberht's mouth curled.

Freya noticed that the three warriors: Annan, Aethelhere and Aethelwold, all stirred uneasily at this comment. King Raedwald had been their uncle, and they did not appreciate anyone speaking ill of him.

"I have often thought of you Sigeberht," Seaxwyn continued softly, leaving the cup of wine untouched at her elbow. "I have wondered how you fared in Gaul."

Sigeberht's mouth pursed. "And is that why you are here? To hear tales of my life in exile?"

196

Seaxwyn smiled, ignoring her son's frosty sarcasm.
"No Sigeberht. I have come here for your crowning."

Warriors jostled elbow-to-elbow within the Great Hall, the rumble of their voices filling the air. Two sides of venison roasted over the fire pit and the aroma of roasting meat and root vegetables drifted across the wide space. The long tables had been pulled back, allowing the crowd to fill the center of the hall.

On the high seat, at the far end, stood Seaxwyn. She was widow to the late King Raedwyn and mother to the late King Eorpwald—and also mother to the man who stood in the doorway to the hall, waiting for the ceremony to begin. At the front of the crowd were Sigeberht's three step-cousins. In high spirits, after a few cups of strong ale, Annan was deep in boisterous conversation with Aidan.

Hilda and Freya stood before the fire pit, slowly turning the spits.

"According to folk, Seaxwyn was wed before marrying King Raedwald," Hilda whispered conspiratorially to Freya. "To a Saxon lord. The tale is that she stabbed him for beating her so he divorced her and sent her back to her father. Seaxwyn took their son, Sigeberht, with her."

Freya glanced across at Seaxwyn with interest. The woman did possess a certain strength. She was tall and curvaceous, and wore a fine green gown that complemented her pale skin. Even though she was now in her sixtieth year, she was still an attractive woman. Freya imagined she must have been a beauty in her youth—and since Sigeberht had just passed his forty-fifth winter, she would have had him young.

"Raedwald was looking for a wife and 'tis said that when he saw Seaxwyn he fell in love with her instantly," Hilda continued, her voice tense with excitement. "But, the king did not love her boy. He wanted sons of his own blood. Sigeberht was a threat to the Wuffinga bloodline. Once Sigeberht reached manhood, Raedwald sent him from Rendaelsham, banishing him to Gaul."

Freya nodded, captivated by the story. With such excitement within the Great Hall over the past day, she had almost forgotten her misery. She still missed her mother, especially at night when she would stare up into the dark and think of home, but Sigeberht worked her so hard that she had barely a moment to herself during the day.

Inside the hall, the din died away and pipes began to trill, announcing that the coronation was about to start.

The crowd parted as Sigeberht, dressed in black, with a fine fur cloak swinging from his shoulders, strode towards the dais. Two amber brooches, gleaming in the torchlight, fastened his cloak to the heavy black tunic he wore. His face, even at such a moment, was severe, as if hewn from stone.

Had such a man ever been young and light of heart?

The pipes died away as Sigeberht reached the dais and knelt before his mother.

"Sigeberht, rightful heir to the throne of the East Angles, I welcome you," Seaxwyn's voice echoed across the empty hall. "May Woden protect you and Thunor guide your hand in battle. May wyrd favor you always."

Freya saw Sigeberht's jaw clench at his mother's words, but he held his tongue. She wondered if Seaxwyn knew that her son had cast aside the old gods. Sigeberht no longer believed that fate ruled one's life.

Oblivious to her son's glowering, Seaxwyn lifted the simple iron crown; the one her husband had worn during the long years of his reign.

"I crown you, Sigeberht King of the East Angles."

She placed the crown gently on Sigeberht's head, and the hall erupted with cheers and applause.

The feasting went on, long into the night. By the time the last revelers staggered from the hall, Freya's body ached. She longed to stretch out on the rush matting and rest her weary limbs. Like Freya, Hilda's face was gaunt with fatigue as she cleared away the food scraps and wiped the tables down.

An area at the far end of the hall had been curtained off for the guests, opposite the king's bower. Seaxwyn had retired earlier than the men-folk, and Annan, Aethelhere and Aethelwold had all consumed so much ale that they had to be led to their beds.

Freya looked up from her industry to see Aidan returning from making sure the king's step-cousins had all made it to their beds. He paused in front of where Freya was collecting the last cups from the tables.

"Goodnight, sweet Freya."

"Goodnight," she replied coldly, not bothering to look his way. She wished he would leave her be.

Freya collected up two handfuls of empty cups and turned to make her way up to where Hilda was washing plates and cups in a large pail of soapy water.

She collided with the wall of a man's chest.

Aidan had been standing closer to her than she had realized. She had walked straight into him. With a strangled cry, Freya stumbled backwards and nearly dropped the cups.

To her horror, he laughed and put his arms around her waist—an action which both prevented her from falling and also imprisoned her in his embrace.

"Careful now," he whispered in her ear. Freya could hear the smile in his voice and fought the urge to slap him; although such an act would have been difficult with her hands full.

His nearness was overwhelming. His warmth, the hardness of his chest, the strength of his arms, and the gentle way his arms encircled her, made Freya dizzy. She glanced up at him and instantly regretted it.

His dark blue gaze snared hers. As they stared at each other, the smile faded from his lips. Freya wrenched free of Aidan's embrace and stepped back from him. She could feel her cheeks heating up from the intensity of his gaze.

"Goodnight." She mustered as much cool dismissal as she could in that word, but it merely brought that conceited smirk back to his face.

Freya joined Hilda at the pail of soapy water and began to wash the cups. She felt Aidan's gaze on her for a moment or two, but when she finally risked a glance in his direction, she saw him making his way over to the fire pit. Piles of furs, for Sigeberht's highest ranking thegns, had been laid out around the edge of the pit. Aidan chose one of them and sat down, pulling off his boots.

Freya hurriedly looked away before he caught her staring.

Sigeberht's hall broke their fast with griddle bread, cheese and small, sweet onions. It was simple fare but Sigeberht had straightforward tastes when it came to all things, including food.

Freya blinked sleepily as she ladled a thin broth into earthen bowls and placed them on a wooden tray. Once she had filled the bowls, she carried the tray to the long table where Sigeberht was breaking his fast with his mother and step-cousins. Aidan was seated to Sigeberht's right; Freya made a point of looking through him when he tried to catch her gaze.

"Thank you, Freya," Aidan said when she passed him a bowl of broth. The others all looked up from their meals and Freya silently cursed him. It was unseemly to address a theow by name. Doing so, made it appear as if she and Aidan were intimate.

Annan grinned at Aidan, broke off a piece of griddle bread and dipped it in his broth.
"I wish the serving wenches in our hall at Snape were as comely as this one." He winked at Aidan.

Her face burning, Freya hastily moved down the table.

Fortunately, Sigeberht ignored the younger men's comments and continued the conversation that Freya's arrival had interrupted.

"I am sorry to hear of your father," Sigeberht addressed Annan, Aethelhere and Aethelwold. "Eni was always good to me as a boy."

Annan smiled, sadness briefly lighting in his blue eyes. "There will never be another man like my father," he said quietly; his brothers nodded their agreement.

Seaxwyn cast her nephew a sympathetic look across the table. "They were inseparable: Raedwald and Eni. Your father was never the same after Raedwald's death."

Their words cast a somber mood across the table.

"Still," Seaxwyn said before taking a sip of broth, "they are with Woden now, watching over us all."

"Perhaps." Sigeberht's mouth twisted. "If you believe in the old gods. Some of us beg to differ."

"They are the only gods," Seaxwyn replied coolly, her gaze resting on the iron cross that her son wore around his neck.

Sigeberht's expression darkened. "I had heard that you had a closed mind to the teachings of Christ." His voice was harsh. "But even Raedwald saw the truth in his later years. Was he not baptized?"

Seaxwyn regarded Sigeberht with thinly veiled contempt; the fragile reconnection between mother and son had dissolved.

"He was baptized to appease that meddling monk who nagged him, day-in, day-out. I was relieved when that fool left Rendlaesham."

Freya watched the brewing argument with fascination. She had never come across a woman as outspoken as Seaxwyn. Even her mother, who was in no way meek, would not have dared openly criticize one of her male kin in front of other men. Frankly, Freya was in awe of this woman—and a little frightened for her.

"I do hope you are not going to become a bore Sigeberht the Righteous," Seaxwyn continued, oblivious to her son's thunderous expression. "Be warned that I have no patience for it. I have lost my husband and both my sons cruelly. I will not have you tell me it was *your* god's will!"

Sigeberht slammed down his cup on the table, splashing milk over its surface. His eyes burned with fury and for a moment Freya worried he would leap across the table and strike his mother. Instead, he took a deep breath and struggled to rein in his temper.

"There is only one God," he ground out, "and we are all his servants. You ignore his existence at your own peril. We are not prisoners of fate, bound by pagan beliefs and outdated fears. You speak with the vehemence of ignorance!"

"Ignorance?" Two red spots appeared on Seaxwyn's cheeks. "It's not I who is ignorant Sigeberht. Only a lost soul clings to his religion like a drowning man. I did not travel here for a sermon. There's no sign of the son I remember before me."

It was as if Seaxwyn had slapped him. Sigeberht bolted to his feet, upending his bowl of gruel on the floor as he did so.

"You never knew me," he snarled. "I was a reminder of a life, and a man, you hated. I saw the relief on your face the day Raedwald sent me away. It's too late to act the loving mother now. I know you for the cold, hard bitch that you are!"

With that, Sigeberht kicked his stool aside and stormed from the hall. He left a chill silence in his wake.

Chapter Seven

AIDAN SLOWED HIS horse to a trot and caught sight of the straw-thatched roof of the Great Hall glinting in the distance. From his vantage point on the brow of a hill, Aidan could see Rendlaesham's walls rising from the trees in the shallow valley below. It was late afternoon and smoke wreathed into the pale sky as townsfolk lit their fires for the evening. Around Rendlasham spread a patchwork of fields and orchards, nestled in soft folds of land.

A moon's cycle had passed since Sigeberht had taken the throne; spring deepened towards the fullness of summer and life in his new home had settled into a routine. Aidan liked Britannia. He appreciated the gentle beauty of this land. Rendlaesham had welcomed him and his men, despite that many of them, Aidan included, were foreign.

Aidan glanced across at Lothar. His friend rode at his side, leading a pony with a boar slung over its back. The Frank had settled into Rendlaesham so quickly that it had felt like a homecoming rather than an arrival. He already had learned a few words of the local tongue, a language Aidan had learned from Sigeberht as a boy, and had wasted no time in finding a pretty wench to woo. Aedilhild was the winsome daughter of the town's baker. She had many men interested in her, yet Aedilhild appeared taken with Lothar. Aidan wondered how long it would be before the Frank wedded her and set up his own household in Rendlaesham.

For himself, Aidan had no such plans.

I rallied a force of loyal warriors for Sigeberht. I brought his army across the water and led them to victory against Ricberht, Aidan thought with a stab of impatience. *He promised to reward me— so why hasn't he?*

He wanted Sigeberht to give him the title of ealdorman; an elevated position indeed if he remembered his beginnings as Sigeberht's theow. Becoming an ealdorman would mean leaving Rendlaesham, and setting up his own hall elsewhere in the kingdom. It would mean leaving Sigeberht's side. Yet it appeared that the king was not yet ready to relinquish him.

"It will be a pleasant eve for a feast." Aidan pushed thoughts of his future aside, and gestured to the boar they had skewered with the help of the group of men and dogs that trailed behind them. Their hunting expedition, which had kept them away from Rendlaesham for the past three days, had not been as successful as Aidan had hoped; they only had a boar and two deer for their efforts.

"Hopefully our lord is in the mood for one," Lothar replied, raising a fair eyebrow. "His humor has been dark of late."

Aidan nodded and the two men shared a look. Ever since Seaxwyn and his step-cousins' return to their hall in Snape, the king had brooded. Rather than enjoying his newfound kingdom, Sigeberht behaved as if he had just bitten into a rotten fruit. Aidan was at a loss to understand why. He could only think that his argument with his mother had soured his return to Rendlaesham, for they had not parted well.

Instead of taking the road that led to Rendlaesham's main gates, the hunting party followed the path that skirted the western walls of the town and cut through apple orchards to the back gates. This route was easier than making their way through the town's crowded thoroughfares. They rode through the orchard; the apple trees were in blossom, a sea of fluttering white that spread out down the hillside.

"It's a glorious spot this," Lothar said, gazing upon the view. "I would be a happy man if I grew old here."

Aidan gave him a wicked smile. "Thinking of asking Aedilhild if she'll have you, eh?"

Lothar grinned back. "Just you wait, come Eostre she'll be mine."

The hunting party rode into Rendlaesham and down the wide street that led up to the king's hall. They clattered into the stable-yard and dismounted. A few of Aidan's men carried their kill up to the Great Hall while the rest of the men saw to the horses. Aidan unsaddled his stallion, rubbed him down and led the horse over to the water trough for a drink.

Hot and sweaty as he was, the sight of the cool water was too tempting. Aidan stripped off his sleeveless tunic and bent over the deep trough. He dunked his head under and came up with a gasp—the water was freezing. Still, the feel of it running down his neck, back and chest was a relief. He felt like diving into the water, although he doubted the horses would have appreciated it.

Aidan wiped water out of his eyes and straightened up, stilling when he saw a young woman standing nearby watching him.

Freya carried a huge basket of loaves, and she was staring at him brazenly.

Bold wench. As the initial surprise faded, Aidan watched her gaze slide up his torso till their eyes met. Her cheeks were flushed and her green eyes were dark pools. Looking upon her, Aidan felt a blade of lust stab him.

Usually, Sigeberht's fair slave treated him as if he was a piece of dung; yet now he realized her disdain was merely a mask. That look said it all.

She wanted him.

"Wes hāl, sweet Freya," he said with a grin. "Can I help you?"

"I'd wager you can," one of the warriors, who was watering his horse next to Aidan, chortled. "The wench looks like she wants to feast on you!"

"Swine!" Freya jumped as if someone had just slapped her. Her face flamed. "Never!"

With that the girl stormed past them and rushed up the steps to the Great Hall, nearly dropping her basket in her haste.

Once inside the hall, Freya struggled not to burst into tears. Clasping the basket to her breast, she hurried across to the tables where Hilda and the other theow were preparing food for the evening meal.

She cursed herself for suggesting that it was she, rather than Hilda, who collected the loaves from the baker this afternoon. Usually it was Hilda's chore, but the day had been so bright. Freya was tired of being cooped up inside the gloomy hall and had welcomed the chance to get some fresh air. She had enjoyed the stroll through Rendlaesham's streets, and the chat with the baker's wife as she filled her basket.

Even now, she did not know what had possessed her, upon returning to the hall, to stop and watch Aidan of Connacht bathe.

She had merely glanced his way as she passed, but the sight of his lithe, strong body had rooted her to the spot. She had stood, mesmerized, watching as water glittered off his skin and ran down his naked chest.

Fool. Tears flooded her vision. *Behaving like that will make him start pestering you again.*

Her coldness had made Aidan keep his distance over the past moon's cycle. Although she had welcomed being left alone, Freya had still been acutely aware of this man's presence. It was irritating, but whenever he was in the Great Hall, she had to force herself not to look in his direction. There was something about him that drew her gaze, like a moth to an open flame.

She had just been burned.

"Freya?" Hilda frowned as she took the basket. "Are you unwell? You're flushed."

Freya shook her head and forced a smile. "I'm fine. I'll get started on the pottage."

As Freya chopped turnips, leeks, beans and cabbage for the stew, she slowly composed herself. She would just ignore him and pretend she had never embarrassed herself.

Freya finished chopping the turnips into cubes and reached for the leeks. Her back ached and she arched it in an effort to ease the muscles. Her life here was an endless grind—from dawn to dusk she toiled for her master. Although Sigeberht was not a cruel man, he was harsh. Just the day before, he had caught her taking a moment's rest on a stool near the fire pit. She had just finished cleaning out the embers and was catching her breath before beginning her next task, which was to sweep out the hall.

"What are you doing girl?" Sigeberht had boomed, striding towards her across the hall. "I will not have sloth in my hall!"

"Sorry, m'lord." Freya had bolted to her feet, bracing herself for punishment.

Sigeberht, whose mood had been vile ever since his mother had departed, stood over Freya menacingly.

"You rest," he growled, glaring down at her, "from nightfall till daybreak. During the day you work. You only stop when I say so, is that understood?"

Freya had nodded, fear rendering her mute.

I cannot stay here, she thought as she kneaded her aching back. *This hall will never be my home. Sigeberht will never be my master. This life will wear me down to dust.*

Supper consisted of pottage in bread trenchers, not the roast boar Aidan had hoped for. He took a mouthful of the vegetable stew and was reminded why this was not his favorite dish. Unlike Gaul, where even vegetable stews were seasoned with herbs, here a pottage was stewed in a cauldron over the fire pit, until it was a watery, tasteless mush.

Aidan swallowed his mouthful of pottage and took a sip of ale to wash it down. He glanced to his right, to where Sigeberht sat at the head of the table. As usual, the king looked as if he had just swallowed a mouthful of vinegar, an expression that had nothing to do with the unappealing fare.

"Gluttony is sin," Sigeberht had reproved Aidan earlier that day when he had suggested they roast the boar and invite the king's men in for a feast that evening. "We only feast on special occasions. This is not such a day."

Aidan had not made any further suggestions. On some things, Sigeberht could be inordinately stubborn. Watching the king's glum face, Aidan decided it was time Sigeberht spoke of what galled him.

"Milord, something has been amiss since your crowning. May I ask what it is?"

Sigeberht frowned and took a sip of water from his cup. "Why do you ask?"

"You are now King of the East Angles," Aidan pointed out. "You had the reckoning you came for and your kin have recognized you, but you have appeared unhappy of late. Why?"

Aidan knew it was risky to speak so frankly with Sigeberht. Due to their long years of acquaintance, the king trusted him. Yet Sigeberht was a solitary figure, who did not confide in many. He had never married, nor shown any interest in doing so. In all the years Aidan had known him, Sigeberht had not shown lust for any woman—or man. He was a singular, austere individual who Aidan struggled at times to understand.

"So much blood was spilt," Sigeberht told him finally. "I know it had to be done, but I feel as if Ricberht's gore is still on my hands. I must—we must—atone for it."

Aidan frowned. This was not the first time Sigeberht had raised this subject. Aidan did not share the king's views on this, yet he knew it would be unwise to contradict him.

"Milord," he ventured cautiously. "If it had to be done, why does it pain you so?"

"Because I learned differently. My studies in Gaul taught me that there are other ways, besides battle, to gain victory. I knew this and yet I chose the easy path, that of violence and bloodshed."

Silence stretched between the two men for a few moments. Frankly, Aidan was at a loss for words. It was too late now to regret a course of action that, at the time, Sigeberht had been fixed upon. Ironically Sigeberht was a talented commander in battle. To Aidan, it seemed as if the king was making himself miserable for no cause.

"So what will you do?" Aidan asked finally.

"I have thought long upon it," Sigeberht replied, pushing aside his half-eaten pottage, "I need to find a way to appease the Lord. My words with Seaxwyn reminded me of what a heathen land this is. If I can bring God's word to my people then maybe he will pardon me for my actions."

Aidan remained silent. The king's words made him uneasy.

"While you were away hunting I sent word to Gaul, to the monks I knew there, asking them to send me a missionary," Sigeberht continued, "but even here there are pockets of Christianity. I've heard that there is a new monastery at Iken—an island of faith in a sea of the faithless. I wish to travel there."

"Then you should, milord," Aidan replied, heartily wishing they could now change the subject.

Sigeberht took another sip of water and regarded Aidan with that uncompromising, iron-grey gaze his thegn knew so well.

"Aidan, I wish you to come with me," Sigeberht replied.

Chapter Eight

FREYA WATCHED THE king and an entourage of warriors—with Aidan among them—ride out of the stable yard. She stood on the steps, listening to sound of their fading hoof-beats as they rode towards the town's rear gates. When they had gone, Freya turned back to the Great Hall.

A smile crept across her face.

Sigeberht had decided to visit Iken, a newly founded monastery that lay just under a day's ride away from Rendlaesham. He had informed Freya and the other slaves that he would be away at least three days, before leaving them a back-breaking list of chores to complete during his absence.

Excitement formed a hard fist in Freya's stomach when she re-entered the hall. This was her chance. She would be a fool not to grasp it with both hands.

She made her way towards the king's bower, to begin her task of carrying the furs outdoors for beating, but her mind was elsewhere. She would hide some food later in the day. With Sigeberht's hawk-like eye removed from the hall it would be easy to put some food aside, with a bladder of water. She would need to slip unnoticed from the hall after midnight. Fortunately the privy was outside, beside the stables, so it was usual for people to come and go from the hall during the night. She would also have to find a way to slip past the guards at the Great Hall's gate. This task was trickier; the town's gates would also be closed till dawn—and guarded.

Freya picked up an armful of furs and pushed the heavy tapestry aside. She made her way through the hall, past where a group of women worked at their distaffs. The women wound wool onto wooden spindles that would later be woven into fabric. They gossiped as they worked, ignoring Freya and the handful of other slaves who moved about the interior of the hall. Since Sigeberht's arrival at Rendlaesham, a number of ealdormen and thegns had flocked to him from throughout the kingdom. Now that Ricberht the Usurper was dead, they pledged their loyalty to a king who had reclaimed the throne for the Wuffingas.

These women were wives of high ranking men. Observing them, Freya could not prevent a stab of envy at the sight of their fine clothes, jeweled brooches and arm rings. She felt like a drab in their presence. They spoke with high, musical voices and laughed often.

In contrast, Freya had not laughed since her arrival here.

A cool sea breeze feathered across Aidan's face. He inhaled the salty tang and was reminded, for the first time in years, of the air in the tiny village where he had lived as a boy on the west coast of Ireland. He had only vague memories of his homeland, but the smell of the air had always stayed with him. Despite that he had not wanted to accompany the king on this visit, Aidan felt himself looking forward to seeing the coast again.

The monastery sat on the southern banks of the River Alde, at the edge of marshland. At this point the river snaked its way through mud flats, reed beds and islands. It was late afternoon when the party made their way, single file, along a narrow path. The trees drew back and the travelers rode out onto a mound that jutted out into the wide estuary.

There, ahead of them, sat a sturdy wooden hall with a thatch roof. A sparse vegetable garden surrounded the hall. It was a lonely spot. The sun glittered off the water of the incoming tide and birds dived low over the mud flats. On to the northwest, Aidan could see a wall of reeds waving in the breeze against the low horizon.

"M'lord," one of Sigeberht's thegns, a local man who had served both King Raedwald and his son, Eorpwald, called out. "We are but a short ride from Snape. On the other side of the marsh lies Annan's hall, where your mother lives. Perhaps you would like to pay your kin a visit when we finish our business here?"

Sigeberht cast a dark glance in the warrior's direction before turning his attention to the monastery before them. "I did not come here to see them," he replied, his face twisting. "We have nothing to say to each other."

Aidan rode in silence behind his king. In his mind, Sigeberht's foul mood was due to more than a burning conscience. Although the king would not admit it, his mother had sorely disappointed him. It was more than her stubborn refusal of his god. Perhaps during all those years in exile, Sigeberht had formed an image of his mother that could never stand up to the reality. Even though she had appeared pleased to see him, it had been clear to all that she had more affection for her nephews than her lost son. The harsh words they had exchanged could never be taken back.

As the riders approached the monastery, a man emerged from a doorway. He was lean and dressed in an ankle-length, un-dyed, woolen tunic that was belted at the waist with a girdle. A small, drawstring pouch hung from the girdle and swung against his hip as the man approached the newcomers. When the man neared them, Aidan could see he was at least five and forty winters. He was balding, and had a weathered, gentle face.

"Wes hāl!" he greeted them, his face splitting into a smile when his gaze rested upon Sigeberht. "We are indeed blessed if this is King Sigeberht, the Righteous, before me?"

"It is," Sigeberht replied gruffly, his face softening for the first time in days. "I thank thee for your welcome."

"I am Botulf," the man smiled. From behind him, Aidan saw another two monks, younger than their leader and dressed in the same woolen tunics, emerge from the hall. They lacked their leader's charisma and both looked a bit worried. Aidan realized that living in such an isolated spot made the monks vulnerable to raids. Sigeberht had not advised the monks of his coming.

The king swung down from his horse and extended a hand to Botulf. "I have sorely missed the company of men such as yourself." Sigeberht bent and kissed the monk's hand. "I have much to discuss with you. I hope your hall can accommodate us for a day or two."

"Of course, sire." Botulf bowed his head. "You are our honored guests."

They sat on mats around the fire pit, and ate pottage and freshly baked griddle bread. Botulf's hall was simply furnished, with little in the way of furniture. A heavy curtain made of rabbit fur divided the long space, creating a separate prayer room at the back of the hall.

"I fear our food may not be to your men's taste." Botulf passed Sigeberht an earthen bowl of pottage. "We do not consume meat and our fare is very humble."

"They will not complain. I do not encourage overindulgence in my hall," Sigeberht replied.

Aidan received his bowl of pottage. After a mouthful, he decided this was even worse than the muck they served in the king's hall. No wonder the monks were so thin. He broke off a piece of griddle bread and ate that instead; it was still warm and although made of coarse flour, it was tasty enough. Chewing slowly he listened to Sigeberht and Botulf's conversation. They were speaking quietly, and only Aidan sat close enough to make out their words.

"I find myself in a difficult position Botulf," the king began, staring down at his pottage. "When I heard that Ricberht had killed my half-brother and taken the crown of the East Angles, I was filled with rage. A need for vengeance fuelled me. It drove me across the water and, blind with it, I struck Ricberht down and took back Rendlaesham for my family. Now that the throne is mine, I feel empty, lost."

"Why is that?" Botulf replied gently. "Surely the throne was your right?"

"It was, but we butchered many to take it. I feel that I have sinned greatly, and that our Lord will never forgive me."

"Sigeberht." The monk leaned towards his king, his face solemn. "May I say that you are most severe with yourself; far more so than I believe our Lord would be."

The king shrugged and stared moodily into the fire pit's flickering flames.

"You are right to feel sorrow for the lives you and your men have taken. But there are ways to atone for it."

"How?" The king looked up and seized the monk's gaze in his.

Botulf smiled and took another mouthful of pottage.

"Tomorrow we shall talk of this. For now fill your belly my king, enjoy our hospitality and rest."

In Rendlaesham, a solitary figure picked her way towards the door of the Great Hall. The only light within the hall came from the glowing embers of the fire pit; just enough light for Freya to make out the shapes of slumbering men and women that carpeted the floor.

It took an age to cross the hall and Freya's heart was pounding when she reached the doorway. Slipping out into the night, Freya welcomed the cool air on her heated face. She paused on the steps outside, steeling her nerves, before she descended into the stable yard below. In the shadow of one of the buildings, under a pile of straw, she fished out the bag she had hidden just after dusk. She had filled a small jute sack with two loaves of bread, a large slab of cheese and a water bladder.

Slinging the sack over her shoulder, Freya crept towards the gatehouse. She hugged the shadows and crept silently towards the gates. She could see that they were open. Then, she spied the outline of a guard, leaning up against the wall.

Freya shrank back into the shadows.

Woden save me.

Had he seen her?

It appeared not, for a moment later Freya heard the rumble of snoring. The Father of the Gods appeared to be watching over her. The guard was asleep. Freya tip-toed past the slumbering guard, holding her breath as she did so.

On the empty street beyond, she made her way up to the back gates, only to find them locked. Heart thumping, she retraced her steps and walked through the streets of Rendlaesham towards the main gates. The town slept, and apart from two drunken warriors leaving the mead hall, she saw no one. The men were so drunk that they paid Freya no mind. They staggered across the street in front of her, barely able to walk, let alone take note of their surroundings. Nonetheless, Freya froze to the spot and held her breath till they disappeared down a narrow lane.

Upon her arrival at the main gates, Freya also found them locked for the night. It was as she had feared. She had no choice now but to wait until daybreak. The guards usually opened the gates at first light, to allow out the peasants, who worked the fields around Rendlaesham. It was risky to wait until then before leaving, but with no other choice, Freya slipped into the shadows and looked for a hiding place.

Crouching under the eaves of a nearby house, she began the long wait till dawn.

Aidan awoke at daybreak and, bleary-eyed, accompanied Sigeberht to the altar on the other side of the partition.

He would have preferred to sleep a little longer. Yet the king had insisted that Aidan, who had been baptized over five winters earlier, join him for morning prayers. Like the rest of the monastic structure, the prayer room was starkly furnished; a large wooden cross stood upon a carved table at one end and sheepskins lay on the dirt floor before it. Stubby tallow candles burned around the edge of the space. The delicate flames guttered as the two men made their way before the altar and knelt on the sheepskin.

Aidan bent his head, listening as Sigeberht murmured the prayer in Latin. Aidan had no idea as to the meaning of the words, and frankly he did not care. He had only allowed himself to be baptized to appease Sigeberht. If the king knew just how little this interested Aidan, it would have upset him. Still, Aidan told himself that it was the price he'd had to pay for Sigeberht's love. Yet, there were times, such as now, when Aiden wondered if the cost had been too high.

As they prayed, Aidan's thoughts drifted to Freya. Her sensual face swam into his mind. He remembered the look in her eyes when she had gazed upon him at the water trough. It surprised Aidan that he had started to think of her so much of late. Although he enjoyed women, he took a practical approach to them. He viewed Lothar's longing for Aedilhild with slight derision; his friend risked mockery if the girl chose another at Eostre.

Freya was lovely, with enough fire to keep a man on his toes. Yet Aidan had not intended to take his interest in her past a bit of mild flirting. She was Sigeberht's slave, and Aidan needed his king's favor if he was ever to rise to ealdorman. It would be so easy to get the slave girl alone and take his pleasure. He had not been with a woman since Yule and his body craved release. Unfortunately getting his way with her would anger the king.

They knelt for a while, and Sigeberht's voice droned on. Aidan's knees were beginning to ache when the king finally straightened up. Gazing upon the cross, he crossed himself and got to his feet.

Unspeaking, the two men made their way outside.

The sun was rising to the east, its golden rays glistening over the mud flats. They circled the hall, along a dirt path that led through beds of cabbages, leeks and turnips, and found Botulf standing at the edge of the bluff. He held an iron cross high and was whispering under his breath. Sigeberht and Aidan halted and watched the monk. A short time later, when he had finished, Botulf turned to them and smiled. Aidan saw that the monk's lean face was etched with fatigue.

"Unfortunately, many evil spirits reside in this place," he explained. "I must admit that expelling them exhausts me."

"Perhaps you would be happier basing yourself elsewhere?" Sigeberht replied with a frown. "We could build a monastery together nearer

Rendlaesham, away from these evil marshes."

Botulf shook his head. "I thank you, milord, but these marshes, although a difficult place for a man of god, have called me to them. I intend to grow my community here and travel up the River Alde to visit your kingdom and help those in need."

Sigeberht shrugged, although Aidan could see from his expression that the monk's refusal had displeased him.

"I wish to aid you," he told the monk as they wandered back towards the hall. "Tell me how and it shall be done."

Botulf looked a little surprised at the king's offer. He studied Sigeberht's face a moment before replying.

"We have everything we need here. The only assistance you could give us is to spread the word about this monastery, and encourage those who have felt god's call to join us."

"I could leave one of my men here?" Sigeberht suggested, turning to where Aidan trailed behind them. "Aidan. You aided me in my quest for vengeance—your men slaughtered Ricberht's at my request. It's now time to atone for it. You shall remain here, and take your vows."

Panic tore through Aidan at Sigeberht's words. "Sire, I will do no such thing!"

Sigeberht's face darkened. "What, do you defy your king?"

"Sigeberht." Botulf stepped between them and placed a calming hand on the king's arm. "You cannot demand a man join us. It's a calling, not an obligation. This man is a warrior; he is not made for serving god. Leave him be."

Ignoring the monk, Sigeberht glowered at Aidan. "I gave you this life," he growled. "I elevated you from a slave to the commander of my army and this is how you repay me?"

"Milord, the price is too high," Aidan replied through gritted teeth. "I will obey you in most things. But not in this."

The two men stared at each other. Although he stood upon the brink, Aidan did not back down. If this was all the future offered him, he would have willingly stayed in Gaul. Sigeberht owned his body; he would not have his soul as well.

"Send me those suited to this life," Botulf repeated. He eventually managed to gain Sigeberht's attention. The king dragged his gaze away from Aidan's and nodded brusquely at the monk. Then he turned, his cloak billowing in the morning breeze, and stalked off.

Aidan and Botulf watched him go, before the monk turned to Aidan.

"Do not trouble yourself. He will see it our way eventually," Botulf assured him.

"I thank you." Aidan gave the monk a strained smile. "He would have not let the matter go so easily if you had not objected."

Aidan glanced in the direction that Sigeberht had disappeared with a sinking heart. He may have got his way, but in doing so he had just damaged a relationship that had taken years to build. He hoped that the king would not take his defiance as a sign of disloyalty. If that was the case,

Aidan's dreams would never be realized.

The gates to Rendlaesham rumbled open with the sunrise. Head bent low, and grateful for the mist that curled through the streets, Freya joined the crowd of peasants waiting to start a day's toil in the fields. The mist had turned them into ghostly shapes and Freya fell in behind them. She kept her head down as she passed through the gates, looking neither left nor right.

Fortunately, no one paid her any mind. Not even the peasants who stumbled forward in the half-light, barely awake.

Freya walked briskly along the lane that led out through the fields. She did not even risk a glance behind her, lest one of the guards spy her slave collar and realize who she was. Once again, the wreathing mist was her ally.

Around twenty feet from the gates, Freya disappeared into the murk.

She broke into a run and did not slow her pace until Rendlaesham lay far behind her.

Chapter Nine

FREYA TRAVELED SOUTH, making for the River Deben and the Great Barrows of Kings; from there she would be able to follow the river south-east to Woodbridge Haven. On foot, she guessed that the journey would take at least four days.

Of course they would send out men after her. Hiding from them would slow her down.

The morning wore on, and the mist burned away to reveal a bright, windy day. The farther she walked, the more nervous Freya became. Her ears strained for the sound of hoof-beats, the baying of hounds and the shouts of men. She was beginning to tire. Her coarse shift clung to her sweaty back and her feet ached. Eventually she veered off the road and walked parallel to it, under a canopy of trees. Through the coppicing lime-wood, she caught glimpses of the shadowy figures of travelers on the road between the Great Barrows of Kings and Rendlaesham.

As yet there was no sign of her pursuers.

Perhaps they were waiting till Sigeberht returned. She was a slave, after all. His men may have thought the king cared not if he lost one female theow. Perhaps the king would not want to waste men and horses on her. In any case, Sigeberht was not due back from Iken for another day at least. This thought filled Freya with hope. She would be able to put considerable distance between herself and Rendlaesham by then.

By mid-afternoon, Freya was too weary to continue. Her breathing came in ragged gasps and her legs dragged. Her tiredness was made worse by the fact that she had not slept the night before. Freya had not dared close her eyes while she crouched in the shadows near Rendlaesham's gates, for she had feared that if she fell asleep she might miss her chance to escape.

She decided to rest for the remainder of the day and travel by night. It would be safer to continue her journey after dark, when there would be fewer travelers on the road. Climbing a mighty oak, she found a spot on a wide branch and leaned against the trunk. She ate some bread and cheese, before washing it down with a gulp of stale water. Then, she gingerly stretched out on the branch, laying face down against its rough surface.

Freya wondered how she would ever fall asleep in such an uncomfortable spot. She worried that she might fall out of the tree and hurt herself – but moments later, the dark abyss of sleep took her.

When Freya awoke, night shrouded the world. The cold had woken her. She sat up, shivering, and stiffly climbed down from the oak, pulling her bag of provisions with her. At the foot of the tree she hiked up her skirts and relieved her bladder. She peered around her, waiting until her eyes fully adjusted to the darkness before she stood up.

Fortunately, there was a full moon out. It cast a silver light over the copse of trees, making them appear as if they were frosted. The moon would light her way, but Freya hesitated before moving off. The forest, which appeared friendly by day, was a cold, frightening place at night. It was full of strange sounds and deep shadows.

For the first time since fleeing Rendlaesham, Freya felt fear seize her. There would be wild animals about: wolves and boars. She had heard that outlaws patrolled the forests around Rendlaesham. Perhaps it had not been wise to wait until dark to continue her journey.

Freya took a few deep, steadying breaths before she slipped through the trees towards the road.

When she stepped out onto the hard-packed earth, she was amazed at how bright the moon shone; it illuminated the world in an ethereal light. Ignoring her pounding heart and sweaty palms, she strode out along the road, jumping and twitching at every movement in the bushes, and every shadow that moved in the trees.

Ahead, Freya watched a white owl plummet to the earth and seize a door-mouse that had been scurrying across the road. She stopped a moment, her heart hammering, and watched the bird fly off with its prey. Nearby, the lonely cry of a wolf echoed through the night. Freya broke out in a cold sweat and resumed her journey, increasing her pace as she did so.

Fool—you never thought about the dangers you might encounter on the road, did you? She berated herself. *If you had you might never have had the courage to run away.*

It was too late now for such regrets. Freya had to keep moving, although she prayed for the dawn to arrive swiftly.

She walked and walked, until her legs ached with fatigue and her senses numbed. Finally, just as the eastern sky lightened, Freya reached the shores of the river Deben. Here, close to the river's upper reaches, the river was narrow, but as Freya followed it south-east, the Deben's banks gradually drew wider apart. The tide was out and the mud near the banks glistened when the first rays of sun peeked over the horizon.

After a brief rest on the river bank, and another nibble of her provisions, Freya resumed her journey. It was mid-morning when she spied the silhouettes of the Great Barrows of Kings ahead. It was hard to believe that just a moon's cycle earlier, she and her mother had alighted here on their journey to Rendlaesham. So much had happened since then.

Freya approached the burial ground warily. The barrow nearest her was the largest of them all – the burial mound of King Raedwald, who they had entombed with all his treasures inside a longship.

Looking upon it, Freya remembered her father's funeral—it had been a very different affair to the king's. Outside the walls of Rendlaesham, they had laid Aelli of Gipeswic upon a pyre. After dark, those who had known and loved the red-haired warrior formed a circle around the pyre. Cwen, her eyes haunted, and her voice strained, had sung a lament for her dead husband, before she stepped forward and lit the fire. The memory of the sadness in her mother's voice as she sang made Freya's heart ache, even now.

What good was loving when all it brought you was pain?

Freya was so caught up in her thoughts and memories that she did not notice the group of men that stood, resting their horses, in the shadow of trees nearby. Her gaze had been fastened upon King Raedwald's barrow; she had not thought to glance at the copse of trees beyond.

She had stopped before the barrow, and was gazing up at it, when a chill feathered up her spine and made the fine hair on the back of her neck prickle. A moment later, a man's shout caused her to swivel towards the trees.

"Cuman hēr wlitignes!" one of the men called.

Come here beautiful!

Freya turned on her heel and sprinted back the way she came.

Shouts echoed behind her as the men gave chase. Exhausted and frightened, Freya knew she could not outrun them. Her tired legs would not move fast enough. She abandoned her bundle of provisions and sprinted towards the cover of the woodland.

The trees were too far away. She would not reach them in time.

Suddenly, Freya's ankle rolled. She collapsed with a scream, and toppled into the reeds on the river bank.

Within moments, they were on her.

Rough hands pulled her out of the reeds. Coarse laughter followed as one of the men pulled her against him and fondled her.

"Let me go!" Freya kicked at the man's shins. "Lout!"

"She's got fire this one!" the man laughed. Then he shook her, so hard that Freya's teeth rattled. The man who groped her was young and sinewy, with a pox-scarred complexion. He leered at her. The other men surrounding him were similarly dressed in muddy breeches—cross-gartered to the knee—rough-spun woolen tunics and tattered cloaks. They grinned at Freya, as if they could not believe their luck.

A man, more finely dressed than the rest, pushed his way through the gawking mob and approached Freya. He was tall, with the same brooding dark looks of Ricberht; although unlike the dead king, who had been clean-shaven, this man wore a short, neatly trimmed beard. He carried himself with warrior arrogance, displaying a number of bronze, silver and gold arm rings upon his bare arms. Incongruous with the rest of his appearance, he also wore a small iron cross around his neck.

"Let her go, Oeric. I wish to see our prize."

Oeric reluctantly obliged. Freya shook herself free of him and turned to face her captor.

"Now, what do we have here?" he mused, stopping before her. He reached out and touched the slave collar about Freya's neck.

"What is your name, wench?"

"Freya," she replied reluctantly.

"And the collar you wear? To whom do you belong?"

Freya raised her chin and glared at the warrior. She belonged to no man. Yet, she was not bold enough to state that here, surrounded by a group of thugs. "King Sigeberht," came her cold reply.

The stranger raised a dark eyebrow. "Really? Am I right in guessing that you have run away?"

Freya looked down at her feet. Her vision swam with tears.

"I thought as much." The warrior reached out, took hold of her chin and forced her to meet his gaze. "What luck, for we are headed to Rendlaesham. We shall take you with us—and I shall hand you over to the king personally."

"Lord Ecgric," Oeric whined. "I thought me and the lads could have some fun with the girl. The king never has to know that we found her."

Freya's breathing stopped. She glanced up at their leader—Ecgric—to see his reaction.

"Jolthead," Ecgric sneered at the younger man. "This is just the opportunity we need to find favor with the new king. Such a fair slave will be sorely missed, I'd wager. You can find yourself a whore in Rendlaesham. Touch the girl and I will cut off your cods."

Oeric glowered at his leader but remained silent.

Freya slowly let out the breath she had been holding. While she had this rabble's attention, she wanted to make sure that rape was indeed out of the question.

"I thank you. The king is a pious man like yourself," she motioned to the cross about Ecgric's neck. "He keeps me as a theow for I am a maid still. It would anger him most foully if you handed me back to him spoiled."

Ecgric's mouth pursed, his eyes narrowing. "You are a maid with much to say for herself," he observed. "Something I would beat out of a woman. Your mouth is much prettier when closed; I suggest you hold your tongue for the remainder of your time with us. When I return you to the king, I will see to it that he has you flogged."

When the king's Great Hall appeared in the distance, Freya's heart started to race. Her spirits, already flagging from a day's travel with Ecgric and his band, were at the lowest ebb of her life. A wave of self-pity crashed over her as they trotted down the hill towards the town gates.

Escape had seemed like such a valiant idea. She had not allowed herself to think of the consequences if she was recaptured.

Freya rode in front of Ecgric. She had endured hours with his arms about her, his breath hot on her neck. He may have not allowed himself or his men to rape her, but that did not stop him from pushing himself lewdly against her as they rode. The only positive aspect of her return to Rendlaesham was that she would escape this man's foul attentions.

They clattered into the town and up the main thoroughfare towards the Great Hall. It was early evening and the sun cast a golden hue over the rooftops. Townsfolk thronged the streets, gawking at the band that rode through their midst.

Miserable, Freya kept her eyes fixed straight ahead. When they rode in through the gates, into the Great Hall's stable yard, her vision had blurred with tears.

Sigeberht's rage would be blistering. She could only hope that he had not yet returned from Iken.

Ecgric drew up his horse and dismounted, pulling Freya down after him. She looked about, her fragile hopes dissolving. The king's grey stallion was being rubbed down outside the stable complex. It appeared that their arrival had coincided with Sigeberht's after all.

Aidan followed the king outside. Together they descended the steps into the stable yard. A dark-haired warrior with a neat beard, accompanied by a roughly-dressed rabble, awaited them.

Aidan's gaze swiftly moved to where Freya, her gaze fixed upon the ground, stood before the newcomers.

Foolish girl, he thought with exasperation. *What have you done?*

Sigeberht had only just learned that one of his theow had run off. They had just entered the hall after seeing to their horses when the arrival of this group of strangers was announced. It appeared that Freya had not gotten far.

"My king." The stranger knelt and inclined his head. "I heard that Sigeberht the Righteous had reclaimed the throne for the Wuffingas. I am here to offer you my service, and that of my men. I am Ecgric of Exning— and I pledge you my allegiance."

Sigeberht walked towards the newcomer; yet his gaze was fixed upon Freya. "I thank you, Ecgric of Exning. Your allegiance is most welcome. However, I see you have something that belongs to me."

"Yes, sire." Ecgric pushed Freya towards the king. "We found your slave at the Great Barrows of Kings this morning. I have brought her back to you."

Aidan watched Freya lift her tear-streaked face to Sigeberht. He could see the fear in her eyes. Not for the first time, Aidan cursed the girl for her rashness.

"The Great Barrows of Kings?" Sigeberht's gaze snared Freya's. "I would like to think you were visiting the tomb of Raedwald in a show of loyalty to the Wuffingas—but of course we both know you were running home to your mother."

Freya did not reply. Aidan saw that her face had gone the color of milk.

"Milord." The newcomer, Ecgric spoke up with an obsequious bow. "Such behavior in a theow is unacceptable. If you wish it, I will have her flogged in front of the townsfolk."

Sigeberht's gaze narrowed as he shifted his attention to Ecgric. This stranger's presumption made Aidan's hackles rise. Yet Sigeberht merely

219

shrugged the suggestion off.

"I think not," he replied before turning back to Freya. "I will punish her myself. Aidan, take the girl to my bower. I will deal with her later."

Aidan stepped forward, took Freya by the arm and led her away from the king. They did not speak during their journey up the steps and through the Great Hall. Aidan kept a firm grip on her arm.

"Freya!" Hilda gasped when they passed by. The girl was kneading a bowl of dough and was dusted up to her elbows in flour. Beside her, the boy Hereric stared at Freya, his eyes huge on his fox-like face. Like Hilda, he had thought he had seen the last of Sigeberht's flame-haired slave.

Aidan saw Freya cast her friend a beseeching look that stopped Hilda from saying anything more. He steered Freya up on to the dais and across to the heavy tapestry that screened the king's bower from the rest of the hall.

Once inside, he let go of her arm and watched Freya turn away from him.

Aidan stood in silence for a moment, observing the girl bow her head forward and struggle to control herself, before he finally spoke.

"Pretending I am not here will not make me go away," he said gently.

"Leave me be," she whispered.

"Freya." Aidan placed his hands on her shoulders and pulled her round to face him. "I am not your enemy, so stop treating me as such." His gaze met hers, and Aidan saw tears glittering on her eyelashes. "I will not ask you why you did it—that question will be for the king—but could you have not planned it better? You must have realized what would befall you if you were caught?"

Freya shook her head and dipped it so that her hair fell in a rippling red curtain over her face. "I did not have time," she whispered. "I knew the king would only be away for a couple of days. I thought if I ran far enough away, he would not bother to come after me ..."

"It was too great a risk," Aidan chided her gently.

Silence stretched between them and the muffled sounds of Sigeberht and his men entering the hall could be heard beyond. Aidan glanced towards the noise before focusing once more on Freya. She still refused to look at him. Despite that few civil words had passed between them since their first meeting, and that she had consistently shunned him, Aidan felt a surge of protectiveness. He owed her nothing but was still sorry she would be punished for her foolishness.

Pushing the sensation aside, Aidan stepped back from Freya and attempted to distance himself emotionally from her plight.

"I cannot protect you from what is to come Freya." He turned towards the curtain and pulled it aside. "But I will ask Sigeberht to be merciful."

With that, Aidan stepped outside and let the tapestry fall behind him.

Damn her. He was already unpopular with the king at present, and had no wish to anger Sigeberht further. He was beginning to rue the day Freya, winsome and captivating as she was, had appeared in his life.

Chapter Ten

FREYA PERCHED ON the edge of the furs and listened to the sounds of Sigeberht's warriors dining in the Great Hall. Their voices caused a great din, momentarily distracting Freya's thoughts from her fate.

In truth, she was terrified. Aidan's unexpectedly kind words had just made her more frightened. For the king's thegn to lose his bumptious manner with her had to mean she was in for a flogging.

Aidan had been right, of course; she had not thought her plan through. Once she made the decision to run away there was no turning back. She would now have to take her punishment.

The smell of roast goat and baking bread wafted into the bower but, despite that Ecgric had not fed her much during the journey back to Rendlaesham, Freya's stomach knotted itself into a tight ball. In her current state, she could not have forced down a mouthful.

Freya sat, listening to the jovial sounds of men eating and drinking, and waited for the king to come for her.

Aidan chewed on a piece of roast goat meat, his gaze fixed upon Sigeberht. The king helped himself to a ladle of boiled cabbage. Then he glanced up at his thegn.

"What is it Aidan? You have been staring at me since we sat down."

Aidan raised his cup to his lips and took a mouthful of mead. When he lowered it, his gaze met Sigeberht's.

"The girl is very sorry sire..."

Sigeberht frowned. "I'm sure she is," he replied, scooping up a pile of cabbage on a piece of bread, "but a slave should not cause me such trouble."

"I agree milord." Across the table Ecgric leaned forward eagerly. "The wench does not show proper subservience. She is a *nithing* and should behave as such."

Once again, Aidan felt a surge of annoyance at this newcomer's freedom with his opinions.

"I trust you and your men did not touch her on the journey here," Aidan addressed Ecgric directly.

Ecgric's cheeks flushed and he drew himself up, indignant. "We did not. Although I find it hard to believe no man here has had her," he sneered insinuatingly back at Aidan.

"She is untouched," Sigeberht replied coolly. He leaned back in his chair and watched Ecgric over the rim of his cup, "and will remain so while she is my slave."

Ecgric's expression soured, but he wisely remained silent.

The king, Aidan and Ecgric focused on their meals then, listening to the drunken voices and rough laughter of the other men dining at the long tables framing the fire pit.

When he had finished eating, Sigeberht turned to Aidan.

"Fetch me a stick—a willow wand will do."

"But sire, the girl ..."

"Aidan—I tire of you crossing me," Sigeberht snapped. "Do as I bid!"

Aidan drained the last of his mead, slammed his cup down on the table and got up from the bench. When he turned to leave, he could not help but notice Ecgric's gloating expression.

That man's face makes me want to smash my fist into it.

Aidan stalked outside and made his way away across the stable yard. Outside the wooden gates and fence which encircled the hall, he turned right and left Rendlaesham by the town's rear entrance. Dusk was settling, and the guards advised Aidan that he would not have long before they closed the gates. He promised them that he would return shortly, and set off at a jog down the hill. At the bottom of the shallow valley outside Rendlaesham, where the apple trees ended, a small brook babbled over a stony bed. Weeping willows, their foliage creating a vivid green curtain, bowed their heads over the water. Breaking off a long wand of a coppicing willow, Aidan made his way back up the hill, through the rows of apple trees to the gates; slipping inside just as the guards began to heave them shut.

Keep a hold of your temper, Aiden counseled himself as he made his way back into the hall. *'Twill not help the wench if you enrage the king.*

Wordlessly, he handed the willow wand to Sigeberht. The king's long face was stern as he took the wand and stood up. Aidan sat back down and poured himself a large cup of mead. His gaze tracked Sigeberht's journey across the hall, towards his bower. He ground his teeth before tearing his gaze away from the king.

A short while later, a high-pitched cry echoed from the bower.

The interior of the Great Hall fell into a sudden hush. Warriors and servants turned their faces towards the sound.

The crack of the wand hitting flesh cut through the silence, followed by another wail of agony.

Aidan stared down at his cup of mead. He was filled with the sudden, dangerous urge to storm into the king's bower and break that willow wand over Sigeberht's head.

What's come over me? Aidan took a deep, steadying breath and listened to the crack of the wand and the screams that followed—again and again.

You've killed men in battle, and witnessed far more brutality than this beating, Aiden chided himself. *Has this wench unmanned you? She would not care if you were flogged to death in front of her.*

It was only this sobering thought that prevented Aidan from leaping from the table and doing something he would sorely regret.

Mercifully, the sounds stopped a short while later. They were followed by the muffled sounds of Sigeberht's voice and a woman's quiet sobbing.

Aidan let out a slow breath and uncurled his fingers from around his cup. He had been gripping it so hard that his fingers ached. Then, he took a deep draught of mead, in an attempt to drown the conflict that warred within him.

When he lowered the cup, Aidan's gaze met Ecgric's. The newcomer was watching him. Aidan did not care for the sly look on his face.

Aidan may have had to control his temper with Sigeberht, but he owed Ecgric of Exning nothing. He put his cup down and leaned across the table, until his face was just a hand's span from Ecgric's.

"Mind yourself Ecgric the Eager," he hissed. "You may have fooled the king, but I see right through you. Keep out of my way."

Freya gingerly made her way down the steps to the stable yard, pressing against the wind that buffeted her. She had plaited her hair into two long braids but the wind caught wayward strands and whipped them across her face.

It was a bright, crisp spring day; billowy clouds scudded across a cerulean sky. Freya was carrying the last of the wicker baskets down the steps to the cart. Bent like a crone, the task had taken her far longer than usual.

Remember to keep bent, she reminded herself. *You must remember to look as if you're in pain.*

She placed the baskets in the cart and carefully picked up the handles at the front of the cart, feigning a wince as she did so. Ecgric was standing near the steps, talking in a low voice with his toady, Oeric; the callow youth appeared to shadow Ecgric everywhere.

Aware that their lecherous gazes were upon her, Freya ignored them both and towed the cart through the stable yard, towards the gates.

Halfway across, she looked up to see Aidan, and his companion, the blond Frank, watching her. Their faces were serious.

As always, the sight of Aidan set butterflies dancing in her stomach. He was even more beautiful to gaze upon when solemn. Aidan was dressed in light breeches, cross-gartered to the knee and a loose, sleeveless tunic. Around his waist, he wore a heavy, studded belt. Even standing there, casually talking to the Frank, Aidan exuded confidence—a subtle arrogance that drew a woman's gaze. Most of the women in the Great Hall, high and low born alike, noticed the aura of sensuality he radiated; Hilda had whispered to Freya a number of times that Aidan of Connacht was a common subject amongst the gossiping wives of the ealdormen.

Like everyone within the Great Hall, Aidan and Lothar had observed

Freya this morning as she crept from the king's bower. Hilda had been on the edge of tears, fussing over Freya and watching her with worried eyes. She had wanted to take a look at Freya's back and rub some salve into the wounds. Freya had refused, with the excuse that doing so would only enrage the king further.

This morning, it was Freya's task to collect provisions for the Great Hall from the miller. She would also visit the peasants who were bringing in cartloads of freshly picked produce from the fields this morning.

Relieved to be leaving prying eyes behind for a short while, Freya pulled the cart out through the gate and down the wide street leading into the center of Rendlaesham. She had only gone a few yards when a man's voice hailed her.

"Freya, wait. Let me help you with that."

Aidan appeared at her side and took one of the handles.

"I thank you," Freya murmured, embarrassed, "but there's no need."

"Are you in pain?" Aidan asked, frowning.

His concern only caused Freya further embarrassment. Despite that she had sworn to Sigeberht that she would tell no one, Freya realized that the truth was likely to remain safe with Aidan.

"No, I'm not," she replied softly, avoiding his gaze as they continued their way towards Rendlaesham's market square. "The king did not beat me – but you mustn't tell anyone."

"Hwæt!" Aidan stopped in his tracks, causing the small cart to buck and slew sideways. "What?"

Freya met Aidan's dark blue gaze and saw his confusion.

"He used the cane on the furs instead of on my back, and told me to scream, to feign agony. When he'd finished, he made me swear to tell no one—indeed, I don't know why I've just told you. Please keep this a secret."

Silence fell between them for a moment. Then, Aidan turned his gaze from her and they continued on their way.

"You mean it was all mummery?" he murmured, incredulous. "Sigeberht had us all fooled."

"He told me that although he abhors violence, he would have to play the part. His thegns and ealdormen expect such behavior from a king. To not punish me would have been seen as weakness."

Aidan nodded, his face gradually relaxing. Their gazes met once more and Freya was surprised to see relief there.

"Don't worry, the king's secret is safe with me," he assured her.

They had almost reached the market square. Aidan brought the cart to a halt and stepped aside so that Freya could take hold of both handles.

"Since you have not had the skin flayed from your back, you have no need of my assistance, sweet Freya," he said, winking at her. "I shall leave you to your errand."

Freya watched, bemused, as Aidan turned and strolled back up the street towards the Great Hall. Watching him go, her gaze traced the breadth of his shoulders and the length of his back, down to his narrow waist and hips. He walked with the stalking, loose-limbed gait of a cat.

Her eyes lingered on Aidan until he disappeared at the top of the hill, and when Freya turned back towards the market square, she was irritated to find her heart beating quickly.

Dusk was settling over Rendlaesham when a cloaked man on horseback rode up the hill towards the Great Hall. The cloaked figure rode a shaggy bay pony; both beast and rider were travel worn and weary. The pony carried its head low and the man sagged in the saddle.

Clip-clopping up the last incline, they reached the guard house outside the Great Hall. Here, two warriors barred the stranger's path with their spears.

"Who goes there!" one of the men demanded.

The cloaked man pushed back his cowl and fixed the guard with an imperious stare.

"I am here to see your king," he replied, his words heavily accented. "Tell him that the missionary he sent for has come."

"What name shall we give him?"

"I am Felix of Burgundy," the newcomer snapped. "I have not travelled days to bandy words with the likes of you. Take word of my arrival to the king!"

"Felix!"

Sigeberht leaped up from his chair and rushed to greet the travel-stained figure who had just stepped through the threshold.

Aidan watched the reunion, mystified. In all the long years he had known Sigeberht, he had never witnessed him greet anyone with such warmth. He had heard of this monk, Felix, for Sigeberht had often mentioned him in Gaul. Yet, this was the first time he had seen the monk.

The king clasped Felix in a hug and smiled warmly. The newcomer was a slight man no older than thirty winters.

"Felix of Burgundy, I am pleased that it was you they sent to aid me!"

Felix smiled back at Sigeberht. He had a finely sculpted, almost womanish face with large, deep-set eyes, a slightly upturned nose and a neatly pursed mouth. His sandy hair was cut short against his scalp. Around his neck, in contrast to his dusty and stained robes, a golden cross gleamed on his chest.

"I am pleased to be here milord," Felix replied, his smile becoming somewhat strained, "although I must admit that the journey has wearied me."

"Come!" Sigeberht ushered Felix towards his table. "Dine with us!"

The assembly of warriors, thegns, ealdormen and their wives, who had been consuming their evening meal of roast marsh hen and pottage before Felix's arrival, all turned back to their food and conversation now that the moment had passed.

"Aidan, move down so that Felix may take your place," Sigeberht ordered, before he caught Freya's attention. "Theow, bring our guest a large trencher and some meat."

225

Freya, who had been refilling some of the cups with mead, nodded and hurried over to the fire pit to fetch the food.

Aidan moved down the bench, allowing Felix to take the honored position at Sigeberht's right hand. He did not mind shifting for the king's guest, but noticed the pleasure on Ecgric's face when Sigeberht gave the order. Ecgric sat directly to the king's left but Sigeberht had not suggested he move.

Aidan ignored Ecgric's gloating. He had little patience for the jostling for position and power that went on within the Great Hall. Ecgric was not alone in his attempts to ingratiate himself with the king; many others sought his favor. Back in Gaul, Sigeberht had worked hard for the love and respect of his retainers and warriors. These days, these came without Sigeberht making the slightest effort. Aidan and Sigeberht may have had their differences of late but he was sure his lord would not forget his years of loyalty, or the fact that he had travelled northern Gaul in search of men who would join Sigeberht's cause.

"You're looking pensive this eve." Lothar, who was seated to Aidan's right, pushed a fresh cup of mead towards him. "Is something the matter?"

Aidan shook his head and raised his cup to his friend; some things at least never changed. He knew he could always rely upon Lothar.

"No, it has been a strange past few days that's all," he replied. "And we are surrounded by all too many boot-lickers for my liking."

Chapter Eleven

EOSTRE APPROACHED AND the balmy spring weather turned suddenly chill and grey. Wood smoke wreathed Rendlaesham for days on end. Curtains of rain swept over the town. For once, Freya was glad of her constant activity, which at least kept her warm.

Despite the foul weather, the townsfolk doggedly went about preparations for the yearly fertility festival. They collected birch branches and twigs for the bonfire, and fashioned a may pole out of birch. Other folk set to work on the Wicker Man—a giant effigy made from wicker and straw that would burn upon the Eostre fire.

Within the Great Hall, the king showed little interest in the upcoming festival. Now that Ecgric and Felix resided within the Great Hall, there had been a subtle shift of atmosphere; a formality that had not been there before. Freya could not help but notice that both men exerted a subtle influence on the king.

For her part, she disliked both the newcomers.

Ecgric made her skin crawl; the fact that he had fondled her on their journey from the Great Barrows to Rendlaesham, had made him bold with Freya at any opportunity. She often found Ecgric's gaze lingering upon her while she worked within the Great Hall and he wasted no chance to surreptitiously rub himself up against her. Felix on the other hand, was a cold, stifling presence within the hall, with his pursed mouth and haughty manner. He was always ordering her and Hilda about, although he shrank from any physical contact with females. Felix avoided the ealdormen's wives and when Freya's hand had accidently brushed his while she was passing him a trencher one evening, Felix had screwed his face up and yanked his hand away as if he had just touched a leper.

The day before Eostre, the rain clouds cleared and the sun showed its face for the first time in days. The ground steamed in the sudden heat, drying the muddy streets and evaporating the puddles that covered the stable yard in front of the Great Hall.

Townsfolk brought armfuls of bright spring flowers into the Great Hall and festooned the walls with garlands. Felix of Burgundy looked upon this industry with a curled lip. He muttered under his breath about pagan rites being the work of the devil. Fortunately, most of the Great Hall's inhabitants ignored him, although Sigeberht and Ecgric nodded piously at the monk's more strident comments. Freya was aware of the widening gulf between Sigeberht and his men. Of late, she had heard a few of them muttering darkly about the unwelcome change in the king's manner. The king's close friendship with Felix, and his alliance with Ecgric, had made them suspicious.

Freya saw very little of Aidan in the days leading up to Eostre. He had been away hunting with a band of warriors, and returned on the morning before Eostre with two deer and three wild boar; all of which would be spit-roasted for the fertility festival.

Since her bungled escape, life within the king's hall had become a dreary grind. Now that her one hope had been extinguished, Freya's future had become a routine of endless servitude to the king.

She feared she would wear her slave collar forever.

On the morning of Eostre, Freya served the king and his retainers a simple gruel and freshly baked griddle bread to break their fast. Aidan took his seat at the long table, and Freya noted his thunderous expression. In Aidan's absence, Felix had taken his spot at the king's right hand and appeared to have no intention of giving it up.

'Ecgric the Eager'—as many among the hall had started calling him— wore the expression of a well-fed cat this morning. He fondled Freya's bottom as she placed a clay bowl of gruel on the table in front of him. Freya jerked away from his touch and glared at him. If she had been a free woman, she would have upended the bowl over his head. Ecgric merely laughed in response, his gaze devouring her as she moved on.

While Freya continued to serve the gruel, Sigeberht turned to Ecgric. "I heard news yesterday that the Mercians have been bothering our western borders. You come from the west Ecgric. Is it true?"

In response, Ecgric turned and spat on the rushes. "It's true milord. That pagan warmonger who leads them itches to extend the Kingdom of Mercia east."

Sigeberht frowned at this news and Freya felt a pang of misgiving. Ever since he had taken the throne four years earlier, Penda of Mercia had given the kings of the East Angles plenty of cause to worry. Unlike the king before him, Cearl, who had suffered from ill health for the last years of his reign, the young king appeared hungry for war.

"If this is the case, we will need to strengthen my fyrd," Sigeberht replied.

"We are already doing so milord," Aidan spoke up. "I have sent word across your kingdom to call warriors to us."

"That was many days ago. Where are these warriors?" Ecgric sneered. "I see them not."

Sigeberht's frown deepened. "Perhaps we need to increase our efforts."

"Milord, I think ..." Aidan began, only to be cut off, mid-sentence, by Felix. The monk had been listening in on the conversation with interest and was eager to add his opinion.

"I believe we need a man who believes in god's word, a pious man, to gather a mighty fyrd on your behalf. We need to do more than merely 'call' men to join you. A god-fearing man would be better suited to this task."

Felix's gaze rested upon Ecgric as he spoke. Ever since the monk's arrival, Ecgric had taken to praying with Felix every morning. They made unlikely allies, but friends they appeared to be. Ecgric's devotion would not have gone unnoticed by the king.

Sigeberht listened to Felix before his gaze flicked from Aidan to Ecgric.

Aidan of Connacht's face was taut with fury. Freya could see the muscle working in his jaw as he sought to restrain himself.

"I am the leader of your fyrd, milord," Aidan ground out finally, ignoring Felix.

"You have been," Sigeberht replied before lifting the bowl of gruel to his lips and taking a sip. "However, you have been tarnished by the blood we spilt to put me on the throne, and you have made no attempt to help me atone for it."

"There can be no war without blood," Aidan replied, his voice barely above a growl. "It was the reckoning you sought! Why should I atone for it?"

"Reckoning we must pay penance for," Sigeberht answered Aidan swiftly. "Felix speaks true, I require a pious man to gather my fyrd. Ecgric of Exning will command my army from now on. You shall take orders from him."

"Hwæt!" Aidan exploded.

"My word is law here." Sigeberht put a hand up to silence him. "If you defy me, you defy the king. The penalty is exile."

A deathly silence fell at the table then.

Freya, who was about to fill a bowl of gruel, froze and looked across at Aidan's face.

His skin had drained of color, except for the smudges of red across his cheekbones. His eyes had turned black with the force of his anger. He shoved his bowl of gruel aside, splashing it over Felix, who yelped like a scalded dog, and leaped to his feet.

Then, without a word, he turned and stalked from the Great Hall.

Tongues of flame licked the night sky. The Eostre fire roared and sent sparks shooting up into the darkness.

The townsfolk had cleared a space in the apple orchards for Rendlaesham's fire and, in the distance, the glow of other fires illuminated the night. The strains of the lyre and the rhythmic pounding of drums echoed across the orchard and through Rendlaesham's empty streets.

From her vantage point, before the doors of the Great Hall, Freya watched the crackling fire. She could see figures, the silhouettes of men and women, dancing around it, laughing and singing. Later, many couples would go 'green gowning' – running off into various corners of the orchard and the bushes beyond to make love. It was the eve of life, fertility and joining.

Freya had attended Eostre celebrations before, but had always rebuffed the advances of boys who tried to drag her off into the bushes. Her mother, rightly so, had warned her that one night of passion would see her shackled to the man in question for life. If she was to go 'green gowning' then she needed to choose wisely.

Freya sighed and stretched her aching back. She need not worry these days. As Sigeberht's theow, she was not permitted to join the celebrations.

Returning inside the hall, Freya knelt next to where Hilda crouched on the rushes, mending the king's clothes. Hilda sat close to the wall, under the glow of a burning torch, so that she did not strain her eyes.

Hilda threw Freya a tired smile. She passed her a tunic that needed mending, along with a bone needle.

"Are the fires bright?" Hilda asked with a wistful smile.

"Yes. The dancing has begun." Freya felt a stab of sadness for the girl. Hilda appeared so resigned to her fate that there were times when it appeared as if any joy had long drained out of her.

Will that be me soon? Freya thought with a chill. *Will this life wear me down to a husk?*

"Hilda," Freya began quietly. "How did you come to be the king's theow?"

"My father gave me to Ricberht, the day after the Usurper took Rendlaesham," Hilda replied. "My father was one of Eorpwald's thegns. He helped Ricberht gain entrance to the Great Hall and gifted me to the new king. In thanks, Ricberht had him murdered. He said that if my father could betray one king so easily, he could betray another."

Aghast at Hilda's tale, Freya stared at the girl. Hilda's eyes shone with unshed tears, a sign at least that this life had not robbed her completely of emotion.

"I cannot believe a father would treat his daughter so. Although I can believe that Ricberht could be so vicious," Freya eventually gasped.

Hilda nodded, wiping away a tear that ran down her cheek with the back of her wrist.

"Father knew the king would rape me, but he only cared about finding favor with him."

Freya shuddered and placed her hand over Hilda's. "At least Ricberht is gone now. Sigeberht leaves us alone," she murmured.

Hilda nodded and gave Freya a tremulous smile. "In that we are truly fortunate. I know he is stern, but I believe we are lucky to have Sigeberht as our master."

It was quiet in the hall this evening. Only a few of the hall's older residents sat about the fire pit, conversing in low voices. The younger warriors, Aidan and Ecgric among them, were not present this eve. The king and Felix sat on the dais, deep in discussion. Above the crackle of the fire pit, Freya could make out their conversation.

"I remember the schools you showed me in Gaul." Sigeberht leaned close to the monk, his eyes alive with rare excitement. "I wish to open such a school here. It's my dream to teach boys how to read and write in Latin."

"Then you should," Felix replied eagerly, "and I would be honored to help you."

"I shall begin looking for a suitable position then. What do you think about the Lark Valley? Would it not make an ideal site?"

Freya, bored of eavesdropping on what she found to be a dull conversation, focused instead on her mending. Outside, she could hear the faint rhythm of drums, as the night's festivities continued. She sighed and blinked her tired eyes. With a pile of clothing to mend, it would be a long evening.

Aidan took a gulp of mead and watched the flames dance. He had thought that joining the revelers this eve would improve his mood but he had been wrong. If anything, the revelry and laughter just grated upon his nerves and made him feel even angrier.

His dreams were in tatters.

With just a few words, Sigeberht had cast him aside like a soiled garment. It mattered not that he had served Sigeberht loyally for years, or that he had risked his life for him numerous times. These days, the king preferred to agonize over the fact that they had fought their way into Rendlaesham, before slaying Ricberht and all others who opposed them. It had been a bloody, vicious battle; but without it, Sigeberht would not be king.

Ecgric and Felix now had his ear. Seeing how readily Sigeberht hung on their every word, Aidan realized how important their shared faith was to him. Aidan had refused to take his vows and remain at Iken to salve the king's conscience. As a result, Sigeberht had turned to others for support; those who were not a constant reminder of his past.

Aidan spotted Ecgric on the opposite side of the fire; as usual he was accompanied by Oeric. They were ogling a group of giggling young women. Aidan found Oeric only marginally less unpleasant than Ecgric, although the boy's lack of cunning and utter spinelessness meant that he would forever be a follower rather than a leader. Not a bad thing in Aidan's opinion, for the youth was odious.

To Aidan's right, he spotted Lothar and Aedilhild deep in conversation. Oblivious to the other revelers whirling around them, they shared a cup of mead while they talked, their heads bowed together. He had to admit they made a striking couple: Lothar hulking and blond, Aedilhild slender and dark haired. As he watched, Lothar took hold of Aedilhild's hand and whispered something in her ear. She looked up at him, her face flushed, before nodding. Then, without a backwards glance, the lovers stepped away from the fire and disappeared into the darkness.

Lothar had got his wish tonight then; come daybreak Aedilhild would be his.

Watching them go, Aidan felt an odd pang, a constriction in his chest that cut through his resentment at Sigeberht.

He felt alone.

A girl approached him. She was blonde and winsome, with flowers in her hair. She beckoned for him to join the dance around the fire. On other occasions, on other nights, Aidan would have been only too pleased to join her, but tonight he felt so wearied by life that he could not dredge up the slightest enthusiasm.

Aidan shook his head and turned away from the girl. He drained the last of his mead, before tossing his cup aside. He was in no mood for celebrating.

"I'm thirsty," Freya declared, putting down her sewing and climbing to her feet. She glanced down at Hilda. "I'm going to fetch a cup of water. Do you want one as well?"

Hilda nodded, not bothering to look up from her mending. "Thank you, Freya."

Stretching her cramped limbs, Freya made her way over to the large wooden water butt in the corner of the hall. She picked up a long handled ladle and dipped it into the barrel, only to find it empty.

Freya cursed under her breath. Hereric should have refilled the water butt this afternoon. She swept her gaze across the interior of the Great Hall, but the lad was nowhere to be seen. If Freya wanted some water, she would have to fetch some from the well in the stable yard.

Freya took two empty pails and made her way outside. The air was fresh and laced with wood-smoke. The strains of a lute and the chorus of voices in the orchard beyond echoed through the still night. Freya carefully picked her way down the steps. The torches that burned in brackets either side of the doors only illuminated the first few steps, casting the rest into shadow. Only the silvery light of the moon lit Freya's path as she reached the bottom of the steps and turned right, towards the well.

There were two wells in Rendlaesham: one in the center of market square, used by townsfolk, and one outside the Great Hall, for the king and his household. Carrying water was a regular and tiring chore for Freya. She had been pleased when another theow had been given the task today. She would clip Hereric's ears when she saw him next—if she was not allowed to shirk her duties then neither should he.

Reaching the well, Freya lowered a bucket into the black pit before her. A rope had been tied around the bucket's iron handle. Freya leaned up against the cool stone and listened for the splash of the bucket hitting the water. She filled the first bucket and had just hoisted it up over the edge of the well when she caught sight of a man's silhouette crossing the stable yard towards her.

Freya's eyes had now adjusted to the darkness; the full moon illuminated her surroundings well enough to recognize the man when he drew closer.

It was Aidan.

"Freya." He stopped before her. "It's late to be collecting water. Will the king not let you go out and join the revelers?"

Freya let out a snort and poured the water from the bucket into one of the pails she had brought with her. "The king will not let me out of his sight for long," she snapped. "Unlike Hereric, who should have refilled the water butt, I cannot leave the hall. The shirker decided to run off and enjoy himself instead."

Freya cringed at the tone of her voice.

I sound like a harridan.

Yet her abrasive reply was merely a response to this man's presence; Aidan made her nervous, although she was determined not to let him see just how much.

"How old are you Freya?" Aidan asked, stepping closer. She could now see his face. The smooth planes of his cheeks glowed palely in the moonlight, while his eyes gleamed out of shadowed sockets. His nearness made her mouth go dry.

"Twenty winters," Freya replied, stepping backwards against the well. "Why?"

"Too young to sound so bitter."

Freya stiffened and felt the heat of embarrassment creep up her chest towards her neck. She was grateful that the darkness hid it. Yet at the same time, Aidan's words goaded her.

"Do I not have reason to be bitter?" she replied, her voice sharp. "I'm a *nithing* now. I had a life before coming here. It was a simple one but it was mine."

Aidan did not reply immediately. He appeared to be thinking upon her words. When he finally answered, his voice was tinged with sadness.

"I tried to convince Sigeberht to release you but in some things he is bull-headed. I know this is not the life you deserve but at least you grew up free; I would like to have such memories. I know what it is like to live as a theow, for I was Sigeberht's slave for many years."

"You were?" Freya stared at him, incredulous. She found it hard to imagine Aidan as anyone's slave.

"I grew up in Connacht, on the western coast of Ireland. I had just passed my tenth winter when a Saxon raiding party attacked my village. They raped and killed my mother and slit my father's throat—but they spared my life, and the lives of a handful of children they took as slaves," Aidan paused here. The brutality of his story had made Freya's breath still in her chest. She would never have thought he had lived through something so awful. It was true that she had lost her own father, but not in such cruel circumstances.

"What happened to you then?" she whispered.

"After they had finished with my village they travelled down the coast, burning, raping and killing as they went. Eventually, they had nearly thirty slaves, all children. We sailed to northern Gaul and there, at a slaver's market, Sigeberht bought me. He kept me as his slave for six years before giving me my freedom."

"And you stayed with him afterwards?"

Aidan's shrug was barely discernible in the shadows.

"He treated me well. Once I was free I could have returned to Ireland, but there was nothing left for me there. With Sigeberht I had a chance to make something of myself. It took me another decade, but I eventually became his most favored retainer and the leader of his army."

Aidan's voice trailed off here. Freya had caught the bitterness in his voice. He had seen her witness his humiliation that morning. Aidan was a proud man, she reflected, and one who revealed very little of his true self to others; even in telling the harrowing story of his past.

"So I should bow to wyrd then?" Freya said. "As you did, and be grateful for it."

Aidan stepped closer still, so that they stood just a hand's span apart. Freya pressed herself up against the well, cornered. She could feel the heat emanating from him, the whisper of his breath on her cheek. His nearness made her feel dizzy and weak. She looked down and tried to ignore her rapidly beating heart. He was too close. She needed to put distance between them. Yet she did not move away.

"Wyrd bith ful araed," he whispered.

Fate is everything.

Aidan gently took hold of her chin and brought her face up towards him. A moment later, his lips touched hers.

Just like on the shore at Woodbridge Haven, she was powerless to resist him. The feel of his mouth on hers, the gentle pressure and softness of his lips, caught her in an invisible vice. She sighed and a moment later, his arms wrapped around her. He drew her against him.

Desire exploded inside Freya—wild and overwhelming. Her lips parted under his, and she was lost. She heard Aidan groan, deep in his throat, and his mouth moved hungrily over hers. His hands slid up the length of her back and tangled in her hair. Unthinking, Freya pressed herself up against him, her own hands moving up over the hard planes of his chest to the breadth of his shoulders. Her heart pounded in her ears as he pushed her back against the well and pressed his hips against hers.

She gasped, feeling the hardness of his arousal against her. Aidan kissed her deeply in response, cupping one of her breasts with one hand and sliding his other hand up her thigh. She felt his hand stroke her naked skin and shuddered with the pleasure that even this simple touch provoked in her.

"Freya," he groaned, tearing his mouth from hers and kissing the column of her neck.

The sound of his voice made Freya ache to be even closer to him. She felt boneless and without a will of her own in his arms. His mouth sought hers once more and she kissed him back, reckless to the consequences.

The sound of male voices, raised in drunken song, intruded upon their intimacy.

With a muffled curse, Aidan stepped away from the well and moved back into the shadows, pulling Freya with him. Hidden under the low eave of one of the stables, they watched the silhouettes of men stumble and sway across the stable yard.

Freya recognized Ecgric's voice, raised above the others. Thank the gods she had not been out here on her own when he returned from the celebrations. Sober, Ecgric the Eager was a lecherous pest, drunk she wagered he would try to rape her without compunction. She and Aidan remained silent and still in the shadows while the party climbed the steps and disappeared inside the Great Hall.

Aidan stood behind Freya; his body pressed the length of hers. He ran his hands up, over her belly, to her breasts, where he cupped them. He trailed gentle kisses up her neck and Freya's body trembled in response.

"I cannot stop touching you Freya," he whispered, his voice strained. "If you do not leave now, I will take you here—whatever the consequences."

His words reached Freya through the haze of passion that had addled her senses like strong mead. His meaning was sobering. Part of her did not care; there was a wild side to her that longed for him to kiss her till she no longer cared. Yet, another part of her, the cold voice of reason that had taken care of her till now, warned Freya that she should heed his words. Abandoning herself to a tryst against the stable wall would seem folly in the cold light of day. If Sigeberht discovered she was a maid no longer, he would not treat her as mercifully as he had when she had escaped.

Worse still, if it resulted in her carrying Aidan's child she would be ruined.

Freya gathered what little will remained and wrenched herself from Aidan's arms. Then, she turned towards him and backed towards the well. She could not see his face, for he stood in the shadows, and was grateful for it.

"Then I shall leave." Her voice was tremulous and she hated herself for it. It took all her strength not to fling herself back into his arms. He had woven an enchantment about her and she had not yet broken free of it.

He said nothing but she could feel his gaze upon her. Gathering her wits, Freya picked up the one pail of water she had managed to fill and fled across the stable yard. The water sloshed over the edge of the pail and soaked her shift but she paid it no heed. Reaching the steps she began to climb, her legs weak and shaking.

Behind her, the drums continued their rhythmic tattoo.

Chapter Twelve

FREYA LEANED HER broom against the wall and straightened her aching back. She had almost finished one of her most hated chores: sweeping out the Great Hall. Once a month, Sigeberht insisted that the old rushes were taken out, the floors swept and fresh ones brought in. It was a task that took her and three other slaves an entire afternoon.

The day was hot and sweat slid down Freya's back. Her homespun shift clung uncomfortably to her skin and was beginning to chafe her under the arms.

"Here Freya, let me sweep for a while." Hilda approached her and took hold of the broom before Freya could argue. "There are still soiled rushes to go outside. The cart's in the stable yard."

"Very well." Freya was grateful to take a break from sweeping. Being tall, the task made her back ache terribly after a while. She made her way over to the water butt in the corner of the hall and helped herself to a ladle of cool water.

Meanwhile, Hilda started vigorously sweeping where Freya had left off. Freya watched the girl with awe. They had become close friends over the two moon cycles she had been here. Despite everything that had happened to her, Hilda was a cheerful, straightforward companion, who dealt with her servitude by keeping herself focused on the endless stream of tasks she was saddled with. The only time that Freya caught a glimpse of Hilda's sadness was when they sat together at the day's end, in a rare moment of quiet before going to sleep. Some mornings Hilda would greet her with red and puffy eyes, and Freya knew the girl had cried for most of the night. Yet for most of their time together, it was Hilda's strength that kept Freya going.

Freya made her way over to the soiled rushes and picked them up, wrinkling her nose as she did so. Although she despised this chore, she could see why Sigeberht had this matting removed once a moon cycle. The hall's inhabitants tracked mud inside and threw remains of food and drink at their feet after every meal. Dogs slunk around the tables during the main meal at midday and sometimes relieved themselves inside the hall—although they were beaten if caught.

Freya carried the armful of rushes out of the hall and carefully made her way down the steps. Bright afternoon light greeted her, making Freya squint after the dimness inside.

In the stable yard, Ecgric was leading a group of men through sword practice. He strutted about, shouting orders and waving his sword as if he were king himself. The weapon was magnificent; its long blade beaten iron overlaid with steel, with a fine leather pommel.

Ecgric had often boasted about the sword over a few meads in the evenings. The sword was called *Æthelfrith's Bane*, so named after the Northumbrian ruler that King Raedwald had slain in battle many years earlier. The sword had belonged to Ecgric's father. Ecgric's favorite boast was that the sword had cut down so many of Æthelfrith's warriors that by the time the Northumbrian king met Raedwald face-to-face, he was floundering in a lake of blood.

What have you done to earn that sword? Freya thought, ignoring the lustful glance that Ecgric cast her way before he turned his back to bellow instructions at his warriors. Ecgric's attentions had been steadily growing more annoying over the past few days. He never missed the chance to leer at her or grab her bottom when the king's back was turned.

You've fooled the king with your honeyed words about your god and piety, she thought sourly, *but I know what you really are.*

Freya dumped the rushes into the cart and was about to turn and make her way back up the steps when the sound of approaching horses made her pause. A moment later, horsemen thundered into the stable yard.

The king had returned.

A band of warriors carrying shields encircled King Sigeberht and Felix of Burgundy. They drew their horses to a halt, kicking up dust as they did so. Sigeberht swung down from his horse before tossing the reins to Aidan. As always, the king was dressed in black, and a heavy fur cloak swung from his shoulders.

"Milord." Ecgric approached the king. "Was your trip successful?"

"Very. We have found the site for our school," the king announced with a rare smile.

"The upper reaches of the Lark Valley," Felix spoke up, his narrow face flushed with excitement, "at Beodricesworth. It's an excellent location."

"I have left some men there to begin work. I expect it to be ready by midsummer," Sigeberht added. His gaze then swept over the men who Ecgric had been training. "Are these the new warriors you spoke of?"

Ecgric nodded. "And more will come."

"You have done well," Sigeberht replied, falling into step with Ecgric as they crossed the stable yard together. They passed Freya but neither man acknowledged her.

"While we camped at Beodricesworth, word reached me that Penda of Mercia plans to extend his border east within a year," Sigeberht continued. "Will the fyrd be ready for him?"

"A year is plenty, milord," Ecgric replied smoothly. "We will be ready for the Mercians when they come."

Freya watched Felix join the king and Ecgric, and together the three men talked in low voices for a few moments. Then, the king took his leave and, with Felix trailing behind him, mounted the steps to the Great Hall. Ecgric sauntered back to his warriors, whispering an obscenity in Freya's ear as he passed her. She shrank back from him, resisting the urge to spit at his feet.

"Come lads." Ecgric sheathed his sword. "That's enough for today—the mead hall awaits!"

The rabble of warriors, many of them new to Rendlaesham, gave shouts of agreement at this suggestion. They piled out of the stable yard, their voices echoing in the road beyond as they made their way down to Rendlaesham's mead hall.

Freya watched them go, relieved that Ecgric had removed himself from her presence, before her gaze swiveled to Aidan. Many days had passed since Eostre, and Aidan had barely glanced her way ever since. He ignored her now, as he instructed his men to look after the horses. Having ignored Ecgric and his warriors, he then led his and the king's horse away to the stables without a backward glance.

Freya's gaze tracked him, willing him to turn around, to meet to her gaze. She knew that such wishes were folly. He had given her a choice and she had made it. If he kept his distance from her now, it was for good reason.

Memories of that stolen moment by the well, of his mouth on hers, his arms about her, his hands stroking her, flooded through Freya. She tried not to think about it, but at unguarded moments the memories came flooding back – and with them a strange emptiness. In Aidan's arms she had felt alive. Nothing had mattered; nothing in the world had existed but him. She had briefly been given the taste of another life. One she could never have now.

Smoke settled over the thatched roofs of Rendlaesham. It was a balmy evening and the scent of wood smoke, along with the less savory aroma of cabbage and turnip pottage, wafted through the air. Glancing up at the sky, Freya realized it was far later in the day than she had thought. She had dragged the cart laden with soiled rushes, out of Rendlaesham, and down to the dust-heap. The heap lay just beyond the orchard, not far from the road that snaked its way through the fields. Once every few moon cycles, when the heap reached a certain size, the townsfolk set fire to it.

Freya off-loaded the rushes and frowned up at the pink and gold sunset that blazed overhead. She should have completed this chore earlier, instead of returning to the hall to help Hilda. It was foolish to linger outside the town's walls at this hour.

She had initially left Rendlaesham by the top gates, but there would be no time to return that way. At this rate, she risked being shut out for the night. Freya shook her head as the irony of her situation hit her. Not too long ago she would have welcomed such a chance for escape. Yet after her disastrous attempt, she worried about angering the king further. He had shown her mercy once, she doubted he would do so a second time.

Deciding that she would make for Rendlaesham's main gates, which were closer than the top gates, Freya picked up the handles of her cart and towed it along the bumpy track. Ahead of her, she could see the last of the peasants who worked the fields, filing inside. The guards were starting to close the gates. Freya picked up her pace, heedless to the rattling cart.

"Wait!" she called, breaking into a run.

Freya slipped inside the gates, just as the guards were closing them.

"That was close girl." One of the guards glowered at her. "Next time we'll lock you out."

Freya ducked her head in apology and towed her cart across the dusty square. Leaving the guards behind, she made her way towards the thoroughfare that led up to the Great Hall. She passed closely packed houses and noted that there were few people about. At this hour, everyone was indoors eating their evening meal before bedding down for the night.

Deep shadows stretched across the road. Freya could hear the sounds of muffled voices inside the wattle and daub dwellings she passed.

Halfway up the street, she reached Rendlaesham's mead hall. The focal point of the town, the mead hall was a long, bow-sided, windowless structure with a thatched roof. Light blazed from its open door and the rowdy sound of men's voices and singing echoed out onto the deserted street. The sound made Freya's heart quicken; this was the other reason she would have preferred to use Rendlaesham's top gates this evening. It was not safe for unescorted women to walk the streets after dark.

Freya was just passing the entrance when a handful of drunken men staggered out onto the street.

Her heart sank when she saw that Ecgric, and his hanger-on, Oeric, were among them.

In the light emanating from the mead hall, Ecgric spied her immediately. Despite his swarthy complexion, she could see that his cheeks were flushed with drink. He staggered towards her, and grabbed hold of the side of the cart to steady himself.

"*Hōre,*" he leered at her. "Slut. So the king has let you out of his sight at last has he?"

"*Lūtan!*" Freya snarled back without thinking. "Lout, leave me be!"

"Go on lads." Ecgric waved his drinking companions away. "I'll take great pleasure in escorting this whore back to the hall."

"Let us all have some fun with her," Oeric protested. "Go on, she's had it coming for weeks!"

"Push off!" Ecgric slurred, shoving Oeric in the direction of the departing warriors. "Find your own girl to play with."

The other warriors departed with crude laughter and ribald comments, while Oeric trailed sullenly behind them. Freya watched them go with rising panic; she did not want to be left with this man. She stared at the warriors' retreating backs and attempted to follow them.

Ecgric grabbed her arm and pulled her up short.

"Why the haste?"

"Let go of me!"

"Not so fiery now are you?" Ecgric yanked Freya away from the cart and pulled her towards an alleyway a few yards up the street. "Not when I've finally got you alone."

Fear clawed at Freya, momentarily suffocating her. He was much stronger than her; his grip was an iron clamp around her upper arm. Nevertheless, she began to struggle. Once he pulled her into the shadows, she knew what he intended to do.

"The king will be furious if you touch me." She dug her heels into the dirt and shoved at him with her free hand. "Loose me!"

Ecgric turned and slapped her hard across the face.

"Shut your mouth! What do I care if the king discovers you are no longer a virgin. With any luck he'll give you to my men afterwards."

Despite his command, fear gave Freya courage. The pain from his slap merely galvanized her. If he was to rape her, it would not be without a fight.

She screamed and, closing her hand into a fist, punched him as hard as she could in the jaw.

Ecgric staggered back, his face black with rage. Recovering swiftly, he grabbed Freya by the hair and propelled her towards the alleyway. Freya fell forward on to her knees and was scrambling to her feet when Ecgric leaped on her. His breath was hot and stank of mead. With one hand he grasped her around the neck, cutting off her breathing, and any chance that she might scream again; while with the other hand he yanked at her clothing, struggling to pull up her skirts.

His nearness only caused Freya to fight harder. She twisted in his grip, panic coursing through her as his hand pressed down on her windpipe. She brought her knee up hard, into his cods.

Ecgric released her with a strangled wail. Freya wriggled free of his grasp, knowing she had but moments before he grabbed hold of her again, and bolted up the street.

"You won't outrun me!" he yelled after her, his voice raw.

Freya's bruised throat constricted in terror. It was still a distance up to the gates of the Great Hall. He would surely catch up with her before she reached them. She could hear him gaining on her with every stride. That blow to the cods should have felled him, but still he came after her.

His ragged breathing, and gasped curses drew ever closer. Freya stifled a sob. He would catch her.

Ahead, she spied the outlines of two men. They were walking downhill, presumably making their way to the mead hall. It was possible they were brutes like Ecgric, but Freya had no choice but to hurl herself in their direction.

"Please!" she gasped. "Help me!"

She hurtled into the arms of the man closest to her, almost knocking him off his feet. He recovered swiftly and reached out to steady her.

Freya looked up into Aidan's face. He stared back at her, his eyes widening in surprise. "Freya?"

"She's mine!" Ecgric loomed through the shadows towards them. "We have unfinished business. Give her to me."

Aidan put his arm around Freya's shoulders, squeezing firmly as he did so, and turned to face Ecgric. Beside him, Freya recognized Lothar. The Frank's blond hair gleamed in the half-light. Ecgric halted before them, his hands balled into fists.

"What's this?" Lothar's mouth twisted. "The king's favorite stalking the streets of Rendlaesham after dark, molesting maids?"

"Shut your mouth Frank," Ecgric sneered, turning to Aidan. "Give the whore to me."

Silence followed Ecgric's words before Aidan eventually spoke.

"Call her a whore again and I will kill you."

Ecgric stared at Aidan, his eyes bulging with the force of his rage. There was a calmness in Aidan's tone, a coolness, which convinced Freya he would do exactly as he promised if Ecgric did not heed his words.

"Filthy foreign dogs!" Ecgric spat at their feet. "The girl is mine."

"Freya is the property of the king," Aidan replied, with the same calm voice as earlier, "and you will not touch her again."

Freya's legs trembled as she watched the anger boil in Ecgric's face. He looked at Aidan with pure loathing. In aiding her, Aidan had just made an enemy for life.

"You may have the king's ear, but we know you for what you really are," Lothar growled, his hands straying towards the knife he wore strapped to his thigh.

"Turn around and walk away," Aidan added, his voice like cloaked steel. "I won't warn you again."

Moments passed, and Freya was sure that Ecgric would attack them. Aidan and Lothar had just grievously wounded his pride; he could not let that pass.

"You just want to put your cock in her," Ecgric growled. "You want her for yourself!"

Without bothering to warn Ecgric again, Aidan leaped forward and hit him hard.

Ecgric's head snapped back and he staggered. Clutching his eye, he swore foully.

"Do you have anything else to say?" Aidan asked.

"I will not forget this." Ecgric backed away. "You'll pay."

With that, Ecgric turned and staggered away. Moments later, the shadows swallowed him whole.

Aidan released Freya and turned to face her.

"Did he hurt you?"

Freya shook her head. Now that the ordeal had passed, she felt on the edge of tears. "He hit me a few times but I managed to escape before he raped me."

"What in Woden's name are you doing out on the streets alone at this hour?"

"I had taken a load of rush-matting to the dust-heap," Freya replied, her voice quivering, "but I didn't realize it was so late. I only just made it inside the main gates before they closed them."

Aidan slowly let out the breath he had been holding. Even in the half light, Freya could see the concern, warring with anger, which played across his features.

"Wyrd has been kind to you this eve," Lothar spoke up. "He would not have been gentle. You must be more careful in future, girl."

Freya shuddered at the reminder. "I know. I am grateful to you both. Now, please escort me back to the hall; my absence will soon be noticed."

Aidan turned to Lothar. "You go on ahead. I'll take Freya up."

"Very well." Lothar's gaze settled on Freya's face, before moving to Aidan's. He paused a moment, as if considering something. When his gaze met Freya's once more, it was thoughtful. A moment later, Lothar turned and strode off down the hill towards the mead hall.

"Come, Freya." Aidan gently took hold of her arm. "Let's get you inside."

They walked in silence. The only sounds were the muffled voices inside the dwellings they passed, the barking of a dog in the distance, and the wail of a babe. As they walked, Freya started to feel increasingly uncomfortable. This was their first contact since Eostre; a terrible parody of what they had shared in the darkness on the night of the fire, the drums and the dancing.

"Lothar speaks true," Aidan spoke up finally. "You must be wary around Ecgric in future. He has watched you since his arrival here, waiting for his chance. He will not be foiled again. Next time, I may not be around to help you."

There was something in his tone that stung Freya. She almost preferred the old Aidan, the arrogant warrior with the honeyed words. Of late, he had become serious and withdrawn. This evening, there was a bitter edge to his words.

"I will watch him," she replied stiffly.

Ahead, the gates to the Great Hall loomed. They would not be alone for much longer. Freya turned to Aidan, attempting to catch his gaze, although it was now almost dark.

"I thank you, again, Aidan."

"Good eve." One of the guards at the gate eyed their approach.

"One of the king's sheep lost its flock." Aidan flashed the guard one of his cocky smiles, his teeth white in the darkness. "I found her wandering the streets alone after setting out too late on an errand. Make sure she gets back inside the Great Hall safely will you? I've got a stool at the mead hall being kept warm for me."

The guard laughed at that and took hold of Freya's arm. "Consider it done."

Freya watched as Aidan turned, without so much as a glance in her direction, and walked off down the hill. His behavior was a slap across the face after what she had just endured. His dismissive manner made her anger rise for the first time since Ecgric had accosted her. Her mother had been right to choose a life alone in the forest, with only her daughter and animals for company. The world of men was a callous, brutish place.

Aidan ducked his head as he stepped inside the mead hall. His gaze swept over the rowdy interior until he spied Lothar. Rendlaesham's mead hall was a long and narrow structure with tapered ends. A fire pit glowed in the center with two narrow tables stretching from one end of the hall to the other either-side. Two boys were roasting a row of spitted rabbits over the embers and, as ever, the mead flowed.

Pushing his way through the throng, Aidan reached Lothar's side and sat down on the low bench. Lothar pushed a cup of frothy mead across the table and raised an eyebrow.

"Is the maid safely indoors?"

Aidan nodded and took a deep draught of mead. "Have you seen Ecgric?" he asked the Frank, casting his gaze around the hall as he spoke.

Lothar shook his head. "The Eager is off somewhere licking his wounds. He won't show his face, or that black-eye you gave him, in here again tonight."

"I'd like to take an axe to that man's head," Aidan replied, his gaze meeting Lothar's. "He's had it coming for a while."

Lothar chuckled at that. "You'd have no protest from me; although the king might not be pleased."

"Before that worm wriggled his way into our lives, I had a purpose and a place at Sigeberht's side. I don't know how he's managed it, but he has won the king's loyalty and praise without having to prove himself. I've been left with nothing."

Lothar listened to Aidan, his face creasing into a frown.

"It's not just Ecgric," he reminded Aidan. "Sigeberht was looking for a way to dispose of you after you refused to stay on at Iken. Ecgric soothes his conscience; whereas you are a constant reminder of what he had to do to claim the throne."

"If this isn't the life he wanted, then why did he go after it?" Aidan replied, bitterness making his voice harsh.

Lothar did not reply. His face was troubled and Aidan realized that his explosion of vitriol had worried his friend. He had not meant to unleash his bitterness on Lothar but he could not keep his anger hidden any longer.

Unlike Aidan, Lothar was happy. His life had improved greatly upon his arrival in Britannia. He and Aedilhild had now wed; their handfasting had taken place shortly after Eostre. Lothar now spent his nights in Aedilhild's father's hall; a modest dwelling after living so long under Sigeberht's roof. Yet Aidan envied him his autonomy. In truth, he envied Lothar most things these days, and this realization galled him even more. He would never have imagined he would become one of those individuals who ruminated on the wrongs done them, while envying others their good fortune.

Aidan and Lothar sipped their mead in silence, while around them drunken voices roared like waves breaking on a shingle shore. Eventually, Lothar spoke up.

"You are changed Aidan. And I think it is more than just Sigeberht's favor for Ecgric. I saw the way you looked at that girl earlier. Are you in love with her?"

Lothar's words made Aidan choke on his mead.

"Hwæt?"

"You heard me. I don't know why I hadn't noticed before. In my defense, I've been a bit preoccupied recently. You want the girl. It's as plain as the nose on your face."

"Lusting after a wench and being in love with one are two different things, as you well know," Aidan responded when he had finished spluttering. "Freya is fair, but I'm not the first to have noticed that."

Lothar gave Aidan a penetrating look in response.

"There's no shame in admitting it Aidan," he said quietly. "There's no weakness in love."

"Soft-headed cuckold!" Aidan snarled at his friend before shoving his cup of mead to one side and getting to his feet. "If this is what wedded bliss does to a man, I'd gladly do without!"

Lothar watched his friend stalk off, shouldering his way through the group of men who were standing near the door. The Frank then turned back to his mead with a sly smile and a nod.

"It's true then," he said to no one in particular. "The man is most definitely in love."

Chapter Thirteen

"I HAVE DECIDED." Sigeberht surveyed his retainers over the rim of his cup. "I cannot stay on in Rendlaesham any longer. My hall at Beodricesworth is ready, and my heart lies there."

It was a warm, late summer's eve. The doors to the Great Hall were open, allowing a sultry breeze to waft through the stuffy interior. Freya sat on the matting, next to Hilda, topping and tailing blackcurrants. They had spent the afternoon collecting the berries from where they grew wild next to the brook behind the orchards. Tomorrow, they would make the berries into a pie, and some into jelly.

Nearby, the king lounged at the head of one of the long tables. He sipped a cup of mead, flanked either side by his constant companions: Felix and Ecgric. At the other end of the table, a group of warriors, Aidan among them, had been playing a game of knuckle bones.

"Milord." Ecgric sat up in surprise at this news. "Is that wise? You are needed in Rendlaesham."

Sigeberht waved him away. "I decide where I am needed. Over the summer I have watched my new hall being built. Each departure from Beodricesworth has been more difficult. It has been a wrench for me to leave such a place of tranquility. I will go there for a time, and you, Ecgric, shall rule in my stead."

Silence fell in the Great Hall.

The men who had been playing knuckle bones all froze, their gazes swiveling first to the king, and then to the man he had just named his co-ruler: Ecgric of Exning. None of them, save Oeric, looked pleased by this news.

Freya stared at the king, as shocked as his warriors by this announcement. At Sigeberht's left, Felix appeared unruffled. In fact, he was having trouble hiding a smile.

To his credit, Ecgric looked slightly panicked by this news. Ever since he had tried to rape her, Freya had kept as far as possible from the king's right hand; a task made easier by the fact that he now ignored her. For the first time since his arrival at Rendlaesham, she was free of his leering and crude comments. It had been a blessed relief, but she was still weary of Ecgric and made sure she kept her distance from him.

"But milord," he stammered, "with the growing Mercian threat, are you not needed here? Your men serve *you*, not me."

His words brought rumbles of agreement from the other warriors seated around the table. Ecgric was either a consummate liar or genuinely discomforted by the responsibility the king had just thrust upon him. Either way, the other warriors approved of his reluctance.

"They will serve whomever they are told." Sigeberht's face hardened. "You will rule in my place and I will do god's work at my new hall. It is decided."

"The king will bring a small group of warriors and slaves with him," Felix spoke up, allowing himself a thin smile. Watching him, Freya decided she almost disliked Felix more than Ecgric. She would not have been surprised if Felix was behind Sigeberht's decision.

The king nodded. "We will bring only enough servants to run the hall. The rest will stay behind in Rendlaesham."

Sigeberht's gaze settled upon Aidan then. The thegn, who had once been his most trusted retainer, stared back at the king coldly. Over the summer, Freya had hardly seen Sigeberht and Aidan exchange more than a handful of words. Aidan looked upon his king with barely concealed resentment now. Sigeberht ignored his hostility.

"Aidan. You shall be joining me in Beodricesworth. Gather twenty spears to join us."

"Twenty?" Aidan frowned. "Surely that is not enough ... milord."

"Twenty will suffice. We leave the day after tomorrow so you have a little time to organize yourself."

Sigeberht then swiveled around in his seat and cast his gaze over at where his slaves were working near the fire pit.

"Freya and Hereric; you will also join me in Beodricesworth. At dawn tomorrow, we will begin preparations for our departure."

At this news, Freya glanced over at Hilda. Her friend gave her a small smile in response but Freya saw the panic in her eyes. Their friendship had blossomed over the summer; Hilda had made life here bearable and Freya had given Hilda the companionship she craved. It would be a lonely existence in the Great Hall for Hilda once Freya had gone.

A grey veil of rain cloaked the world on the morning of their departure. It was not cold but the damp was clammy against Freya's skin. It made the strands of hair that had escaped from her braid, curl against her cheeks. She pulled the rough woolen cloak about her shoulders and picked her way across the slippery stable yard with the last basket of provisions to be loaded onto the cart.

The rain fell silent and still, beading on the eyelashes of the horses like tiny sparkling gems. The air smelt rich with the smell of wet earth. Freya wedged in the last basket and tied down the sacking that would protect the provisions from the rain. Then, she perched on the edge of the cart, finding herself a small though uncomfortable seat for the journey. Hereric, who would drive the cart, climbed up front. Harnessed to the cart, a shaggy bay pony waited patiently for the party to move off.

Sigeberht emerged from the Great Hall and made his way down the steps, his dark cloak billowing behind him. He reached the party waiting for him in the stable yard. Taking his stallion from one of the slaves, the king swung up into the saddle. Nearby, Aidan and the twenty warriors he had been ordered to gather, had already mounted and were awaiting orders from their king.

Ecgric stepped forward to address the king. The rain ran in rivulets down his face and through his neatly trimmed beard.

"Milord." He blinked the rain out of his eyes. "I promise you I will rule with a just hand in your stead. I will send word regularly and will consult you on all matters."

"No need to go overboard Ecgric," Sigeberht replied as he adjusted his stirrups. "Only bother me on matters of great importance. The rest I trust you to deal with as you see fit."

"Keep up your morning prayers," Felix addressed Ecgric from where he sat on a dun pony, "and remember the Lord's toil is the most important work. See to it that your warriors follow your example."

Felix had pulled up his cowl, hiding his face, but his silky voice made Freya's hackles rise.

That man is as slippery as an eel, she thought, *and it amazes me that the king cannot see it.*

The small party eventually moved out of the stable yard, and into the thoroughfare beyond. The cart bearing the provisions, Hereric and Freya was the last to leave. Gripping on to the sides of the cart, Freya glanced back at the group of warriors and servants watching them go. Hilda was at the back; her pale face was drawn and sad. The others wore a variety of expressions, from mutiny to worry.

Yet it was Ecgric who drew Freya's attention. Pride, ambition and fear warred across his features as he fingered the hilt of his sword. Next to him, stood Oeric, his pock-marked face flushed with excitement; it was not every day one became hand to the king.

Sensing someone's gaze upon him, Ecgric looked straight at Freya. Too late she snatched her gaze away.

Ecgric's expression darkened, his gaze simmering with hate. Then, he drew his lips back in a snarl and spat on the ground.

They left Rendlaesham by the top gates and made their way down through the orchards. The trees were heavy with apples. Most of the fruit wore a red blush on their skin, signaling that they were ready to be picked. Freya's stomach growled at the sight of the fruit, reminding her that she had barely managed a few gulps of gruel this morning before the king had started barking orders at her.

The way was bumpy and by the time they reached the bottom of the hill, Freya's back was aching. It would be a long, uncomfortable ride to Beodricesworth at this rate.

The party rode onwards, skirting the edge of the town and reaching the road that cut south through a patchwork of fields. Unlike the day that Freya had arrived in Rendlaesham with her mother, the fields were now well tended and brimming with produce. It had been a good summer and one look at the bounty growing in the fields—cabbage, turnips, leeks and carrots—told Freya that it would be an excellent harvest. It felt odd to be leaving Rendlaesham again. She had lived two lives here: the first when her father had been alive—the carefree existence of a girl—and the second as a slave. Despite the circumstances of her second stay here, Freya felt a little discomforted about leaving Rendlaesham. She may not be happy under the king's roof but it was a known quantity. Beodricesworth, and the life awaiting her there, was not.

Freya's last glimpse of Rendlaesham was of the golden roof of the Great Hall, disappearing into the grey mist.

They left the town behind. Then, a short while later, the party turned north-west and left the road. From here, they cut across country. Freya had heard that the journey would take them two entire days and another morning. It was slow going, what with the cumbersome cart bringing up the rear, but they gradually made their way across a flat landscape made up of wide meadows, open heath and clumps of woodland.

Their journey meant that they had to cross a number of waterways; some were little more than muddy channels, while others were shallow rivers with muddy bottoms. At one point the cart got stuck and it took the entire party, including Freya, to free it from the clinging mud.

Reaching the bank, Freya had clambered back onto the cart, dripping river mud. She watched as Aidan strode past her towards his horse. He was also covered up to the knees in mud. His face flushed from the effort it had taken them to free the cart.

He did not glance in her direction.

The party resumed their journey and Freya sat on the edge of the cart, shifting from time to time to relieve her cramped legs and buttocks. After a while, her muscles too stiff and sore to bear sitting any longer, Freya jumped down from the cart and followed for a spell on foot.

She walked barefoot, over the soft, wet grass, enjoying the feel of it through her toes. Once the weather grew colder she would wear fur boots laced to her ankles, but this time of year she was used to going barefoot, and the soles of her feet had grown tough to withstand it.

The weather did not improve during their journey. It was too overcast to track the sun's journey across the sky, and as such Freya soon lost track of time. After a while, the king eventually called them all to a halt. They ate their midday meal under a stand of old oaks, with water dripping on their heads.

Freya and Hereric doled out rounds of griddle bread, hard cheese and apples, which the hungry warriors washed down with cups of milk. Freya approached Aidan and handed him his provisions, receiving a curt nod in response.

It's a far cry from the Aidan I met on the shore of the North Sea, Freya thought wryly. *To think I used to hate his flirting and teasing, and now I am sad because he ignores me. If only women were not so fickle and men were not so cruel.*

Taking some food for herself, Freya retreated to the wagon and fell hungrily upon it. As she ate, she listened to the rumble of the men's voices. The air smelt of wet man, horse and earth. The gentle patter of the rain on the leaves of the great oak she sat under had a soothing effect on her. Freya finished her meal and, reaching up, fingered the slave collar about her neck. Even if she was never in any doubt that she was Sigeberht's theow, she often forgot that she wore the collar these days.

It was an odd thing, but the fog of misery that had consumed Freya since Ricberht enslaved her, had lifted. Despite the rain, her wet and muddy clothes, and her tired, aching limbs, Freya felt alive. She was not a free woman, and she had neither husband nor children. Her life consisted of hard labor—and yet Freya was suddenly overwhelmed by a feeling of relief, of gratitude. Sigeberht was a humorless, dry man but he was a kind one. While she served him, he would treat her well. She was now away from Ecgric's cruel, sneering face and rough hands. The king was taking them to a place of tranquility and beauty.

There were worse lives than this one. She would have preferred to have been in Woodbridge Haven with her mother, but that was not to be her fate. Thinking about her mother made Freya's chest ache. Even though she knew Cwen was strong, she often worried how her mother was faring in the woods on her own. Yet, the thought of remaining in the king's service did not make Freya miserable as it once had. Instead, she almost found herself looking forward to the future.

This realization shocked Freya, and she was still reeling from it when they packed up and continued on their journey. She followed the cart, her gaze sweeping over the rain shrouded landscape, with a sudden lightness in her heart.

It's true that my body is shackled to the king, she thought with a smile, *but my mind and my soul are my own. In many ways I am freer than these warriors who follow Sigeberht with such blind loyalty.*

Freya's gaze rested on Aidan then. He was riding a short distance ahead of her. Whenever she looked upon Aidan these days she could see the unhappiness that bubbled within him. Sigeberht had given Aidan his freedom and in return, the young warrior had given him his loyalty. Yet, Aidan had expected much from his service to the king. He had come to the Kingdom of the East Angles with dreams, that was clear enough to see, but his relationship with Sigeberht had turned sour, and with it his hopes of becoming an ealdorman. Now, as an added insult, Sigeberht had named Ecgric—a man he barely knew—as co-ruler. That must have stuck in Aidan's craw like a piece of dry bread, Freya thought sympathetically. Most would have felt the same in his place.

Aidan was indeed driven, but it appeared to Freya that beyond his ambitions, he had nothing else. Beneath his easy smiles and cocky manner, Aidan of Connacht was lost. Inside the warrior still lived the boy who had been sold into slavery in Gaul.

A boy with no home.

They made camp for the night on the edge of a thicket, shrouded in a wet mist that showed no signs of receding. The men lit a fire and soon the bitter perfume of wood-smoke laced the air. The evening meal was similar to the one they had eaten earlier: more griddle bread, this time accompanied by salted pork and small, sweet onions. One of the warriors unstoppered a barrel of wine and poured cups for all present, except the two slaves who drank water.

Aidan ate his meal in silence, staring into the crackling, hissing fire. Despite that it was not raining heavily, the damp had sunk through all his layers of clothing. His skin felt clammy and itchy, and he longed to take a swim in one of the waterways they had passed on the journey here. They still had another day and a half's journey before they would make the upper reaches of the Lark Valley. Beodricesworth lay close to the banks of the Lark River, where Aidan would be able to bathe.

Upon their arrival it would be a relief to get away from Sigeberht for a short while. Unlike the old Aidan, the thegn who rarely left his lord's side, he craved solitude these days.

Don't tell me I'm turning into a monk, Aidan thought wryly. *After everything that would be an irony.*

Truthfully, Aidan was still reeling after the king's decision. To hand your kingdom over to a man who had neither proved his worth nor earned your loyalty, so that you could hide away from the world and contemplate your god was pure self-indulgence. Even thinking on it made Aidan's stomach cramp with anger. There was a kingdom to rule. Sigeberht's people needed him. Their borders were not safe. Whispers of a growing Mercian threat grew daily and yet Sigeberht paid them no heed. He lived increasingly in his own world; one where only the praise of Felix of Burgundy mattered.

Frankly, Aidan was not sure how much more of this he could take. He knew that he had sworn his loyalty to Sigeberht, but that was in different circumstances. It did not mean he would follow him blindly forever—especially if it meant his own ruin.

Aidan's thoughts were giving him an acid stomach. He took a sip of wine, which only worsened it, and glanced over at where Freya sat well back from the fire, under the eaves of an ash. She had wrapped a coarse blanket around her shoulders to stave off the night's damp and chill. Her fingers wrapped around a cup of milk; her green eyes were riveted on the dancing flames.

Watching her, Aidan felt a constriction in his chest that made his breathing quicken. She was a beautiful girl; her fine features relaxed in repose, her damp red curls framing her face. Had his life not been unraveling before his eyes, he would have enjoyed teasing her, flirting with her. Yet after Eostre he had realized that Freya had a way of stripping him of self-control. He did not trust himself alone with her. She made him feel desperate, and in his present circumstances he did not enjoy such a sensation. He preferred being able to take or leave women.

You're wrong Lothar, you Frankish oaf, he thought as he tore his gaze away from Freya and took a deep draught of mead. *I'm not in love with her. I'd love to bed her—but that isn't the same thing.*

Chapter Fourteen

BEODRICESWORTH LAY IN a shallow valley, surrounded by copses of trees. When she set eyes upon it for the first time, Freya could see why Sigeberht had chosen this location for his new hall. It was a lovely spot.

They rode into the valley, the sound of birdsong and the babbling waters of the River Lark, which flowed between two gently sloping hills, echoing in their ears. Yesterday's rain had disappeared with the sunrise, and the sun shone once more.

Ahead, the thatched roof of Freya's new home peeked out of the trees. According to Hereric, who had eavesdropped on the warriors' conversations long after Freya had gone to sleep the night before, there were two villages nearby: Saxham and Barrow. The first was a short enough walk on foot, whereas the second was around thrice the distance; they would not be greatly isolated here.

The riders approached the hall, and Freya could see it was very different to the king's magnificent residence in Rendlaesham. In comparison, Beodricesworth appeared a thatched barn: a long, low-slung structure with a collection of huts scattered around it. Ahead, Freya could hear Felix proudly explaining the state of affairs here to the king.

"I have arranged for a number of peasants to move here from Saxham and Barrow," he announced. "They wish to aid you to grow a settlement. The peasants have brought goats, sheep, pigs and chickens with them and, already, they have started growing vegetables on the land behind the hall. There should be enough food by harvest to see us through the winter."

"Very good," Sigeberht replied. "You've done well Felix."

The party drew to a halt in the open space in front of the hall. Freya climbed down from the cart and stretched her limbs. It was a relief to have finally arrived at their destination. Hereric climbed down from the front of the cart and, together, they began unloading baskets of provisions. The king and his men entered the hall, while the two slaves brought up the rear, carrying a wicker basket each.

Inside was quite different to what Freya had expected. The interior appeared austere compared to the wall hangings, furs and weaponry that graced the walls in the Great Hall. It was very clean and the fresh rushes crunched underfoot. A fire pit, crackling gently, sat towards the front of the hall and in the center of the space hung a heavy curtain, blocking the other half of the space from view. Freya imagined that the king's quarters lay beyond the curtain, but when she later brought a basket of the king's clothing into the hall, she discovered that his bower was but a small,

255

curtained-off alcove, set against the wall. The rest of the space was dedicated to an austerely furnished prayer chamber behind it.

The prayer chamber was impressive. Although the walls of the hall were made of wood, stone had also been used as decoration here. Much labor and skill had obviously gone into it. Smooth, round river stones covered the floor, having been pressed into the soft earth to form a layer of pavers. Stone plinths skirted the edges of the chamber, on which burned tallow candles, and a great stone altar rose at the far end. An ornately carved wooden cross perched atop it.

This was what Sigeberht had given up the magnificence of the Golden Hall for; this was his dream.

Once Freya and Hereric had finished unloading the cart, the king sent the boy out to light the clay and turf oven while Freya set about preparing the evening meal. It was a special occasion and so Sigeberht had wavered from his usual request for pottage and griddle bread, instead requesting a rabbit pie.

A brace of rabbits sat on one of the tables, ready to be gutted and skinned, and Freya got to work without delay. The warriors left the hall to see to the horses and explore the surrounding area, while Sigeberht and Felix disappeared behind the curtain to devote themselves to prayer.

For the first time ever, Freya found herself alone inside the hall of her lord. Glancing about, she reveled in the sudden privacy. Unlike Rendlaesham's Great Hall, which always had groups of women sewing, weaving or at their distaffs, or warriors playing knucklebones by the fire, Sigeberht's new home was quiet and still. The responsibility for cooking and cleaning here would be hers, and no one else's. Used to hard work, the thought did not worry Freya overly much. In fact, she found herself enjoying the peace as she made bread dough, skinned the rabbits and made a suet pastry for the pie. She flavored the pie's filling, as her mother used to, with herbs, onions and wild garlic, before covering it with the crust.

When the pie was ready to be baked, Freya carried it outside, her arm-muscles protesting from the weight of it. To the left of the hall, she found the small clay and turf oven. Smoke drifted from the oven's entrance, making it resemble a dragon's lair. Hereric had been toiling over it for a while, his eyes streaming from the smoke. Freya left the pie with the boy, warning him that she would do more than clip his ear if he let it burn. She then returned to the hall, where she kneaded the loaves of bread that would go in to bake later.

The men would need some vegetables to go with their rabbit pie, so Freya took a large basket and made her way back outside. The aroma of baking pastry greeted her when she ducked out of the doorway. Hereric waved to Freya, assuring her that the precious pie was cooking nicely.

"I'm going to collect some vegetables from the fields," Freya called to him. "I shall be back shortly if anyone needs me."

Humming softly to herself, Freya walked around the edge of the hall and down a slope to where two neatly tended fields ran down to a row of willow trees and the banks of the Lark River. There were few people about, just an elderly man and women who were weeding at the end closest to the hall.

"Wes hāl!" Freya called to them. "I need some vegetables for the king's dinner. What's ready to be picked?"

"There are some cabbages that need eating." The elderly man straightened up and motioned to the end nearest the river. "And a few sweet carrots too."

Thanking them, Freya set off down the field. She enjoyed the feel of the sun on her face; although there was a slight crispness to the air that warned that autumn was approaching. She reached the end of the garden, put down her basket and set about choosing two cabbages for the evening meal. Freya pulled up a large bunch of purple and red carrots and was dusting the soil off her hands, when she heard the splash of water in the river behind her.

She turned and peered through the curtain of draping willow. Where had that noise come from?

At first she saw nothing, but when she stepped closer to the bank and pulled aside a branch so that she could see better, Freya realized what it was that had been splashing about in the river.

Her breath caught in her throat and she froze, staring through the gap in the foliage.

A strikingly beautiful man was bathing in the river.

She watched, transfixed, as the man stood up. He had a warrior's body. His back was to her and the water streamed down the muscular planes of his shoulders, back and buttocks. He was naked save for his arm rings, one on his left arm and two on his right, bronze and gold – gifts from his lord for his valor. Then, oblivious to his audience, the man dove into the water once more, disappearing under its eddying surface for some time.

Freya swallowed and let out the breath she had been holding. She should move away before he saw her but still she lingered, waiting for him to resurface.

When he did, he was facing her this time. Freya sucked her breath in once more as her gaze raked down the hard, masculine lines of his body.

It was Aidan. The sight of him, his skin glistening in the afternoon sun, made Freya's limbs melt. She felt breathless, as if she had been running.

Unaware that he was being watched, Aidan flicked his wet, dark hair off his face and began to wade towards the bank.

It was then that he saw her. He stopped, mid-step, their gazes meeting.

Unlike if their positions had been reversed, there was no embarrassment in his eyes. Aidan returned her stare; his face unreadable. Moments passed before he slowly smiled. It was a sensual, knowing smile—a dangerous smile. The same one he had given her when he had caught her staring at him by the water trough.

Mortified, Freya ripped her gaze away and stumbled back from the river bank. Would she ever learn? Woden save her, he was beautiful to look upon. Just the sight of his nakedness made her senses reel- made her itch to touch him. The worst of it was that the arrogant churl knew it.

Freya hurried back to her basket, scooped it up and strode back up to the hall.

Aidan watched Freya flee back up the narrow strip of grass between the vegetable beds. Her back was rigid and her shoulders hunched in her mortification. Aidan's smile faded and he sighed.

He was tired of this game.

The naked lust on her face as she had watched him told him everything he needed to know. Despite her rejection of him at Eostre—one that he had invited—Freya wanted him as badly as he did her. He had tried to keep his distance, to pretend she did not matter but the truth of it was that she was never far from his thoughts. He knew that his distant manner and coldness, after his charm and smiles, had confused her. Initially, he had thought she would welcome it but the look on her face just now told an altogether different story.

Aidan waded to the bank and retrieved a scratchy blanket that he had hung over a willow branch.

She is the only beacon of light in your life since you set foot in Britannia, he reminded himself as he climbed out of the water and began to dry himself off. *Perhaps it's time you treated her with the respect she deserves.*

That evening, Sigeberht, Felix and the king's men dined on rabbit pie accompanied by boiled cabbage and carrots that had been tossed in butter and sweetened with a little honey.

Freya nervously cut wedges of pie and served them to the king and his companions on wooden plates. Hereric filled the men's cups with mead before the two slaves stepped back and allowed the men to enjoy their meal.

"It smells good," Hereric whispered to Freya, his eyes huge on his thin face. "Will there be enough for us?"

Hereric's impish expression made Freya smile.

"We'll have to see. It depends on how hungry the men are."

Sigeberht took a mouthful of pie, before giving a grunt and a nod that the food was to his liking. He did not look in Freya's direction, or acknowledge her in any way; nevertheless Sigeberht's reaction pleased her. He usually paid little attention to food. This was the most noticeable reaction her cooking had ever roused in him.

Aidan, on the other hand, took his first bite and chewed carefully, pleasure suffusing his face. Freya had noticed how the unrelenting diet of pottage, gruel and boiled vegetables at Rendlaesham had made him screw his face up on more than one occasion. This fare was far more to his liking and the delight on his face was evident. He took another mouthful. Then, he straightened up and looked straight at Freya.

Once again, he had caught her watching him.

He smiled then—not the smile when she had caught him bathing in the river—that had made her body go both hot and cold, and had caused her mind to whirl in confusion. This was a warm smile, one of thanks.

Then, Aidan winked at her before returning to his meal.

Freya looked down at the floor. Aidan knocked her off balance. First his flirting, then his dismissal, followed by warmth; it was impossible to know how he would react. He may not be the king's slave but the events of the past summer were changing him.

Freya wondered what kind of man he would be by the time Yule arrived.

Chapter Fifteen

TWO DAYS AFTER his arrival at Beodricesworth, Sigeberht rode with Felix and a handful of warriors to Barrow.

On horseback, it was a short enough ride from the king's new hall. Aidan and another warrior named Aldwulf led the way into Barrow, through a scattering of wattle and daub houses. Smoke drifted up from holes in the thatched roofs. It was a crisp morning with a bright blue sky and gently scudding clouds. Villagers came out to greet the king and his entourage. Children called out in sing-song voices and ran behind the horses.

They rode into the center of the village; a narrow green surrounded by houses. A structure, larger than the surrounding dwellings, sat at one end of the green: the hall of Bercthun, one of Sigeberht's ealdormen. It was Bercthun the king had come to see.

The small party drew to a halt and dismounted their horses.

Bercthun of Barrow stepped out of his hall to greet them. He was a stocky, muscular warrior with a grizzled blond beard and piercing blue eyes. He wore a ring vest and a collection of arm rings that glinted in the morning light. A rabbit fur cloak hung from his shoulders and he wore fur boots and lambskin breeches, cross-gartered to the knee.

"My King." Bercthun knelt before the king and kissed his hand. "We received word of your visit, and are honored to receive you."

"Thank you, Bercthun." Sigeberht nodded to his ealdorman, waiting till the warrior had risen to his feet before continuing. "Did you also receive my request?"

Bercthun nodded, his weathered face giving nothing away.

"I did, milord, and I have four boys for you to take away with you today—one of which is my son.

Bercthun turned and shouted over his shoulder. "Edwin. Bring the others out to greet your king."

Moments passed before a boy of around eight winters stepped out of the hall, followed by three other, younger lads. The boy had his father's coloring but any similarity finished there. He was thin and pale, his blue eyes huge on a frightened face. The three other boys were similarly cowed. They were all wan and weedy. One of them was sniffing, and wiping his eyes.

A buxom woman with long curly brown hair, wearing a sleeveless green shift of good cloth and bronze arm rings, followed the boys. She had a pugnacious face that was set in anger.

Aidan imagined this was the ealdorman's wife. Judging from the way she put a protective arm around Edwin's thin shoulders and threw her husband a look of pure venom, the ealdorman's decision to gift his son to the king had not been well-received.

Ignoring his wife's glare, Bercthun motioned to the boys. "The tallest of the four is my son, Edwin. The others are Osfrid, Paeda and Sebbi. Like Edwin, these boys are all the youngest sons of some of my retainers. They all have a number of sons and are happy to gift their youngest to the king. I have five sons and Edwin is not cut of a warrior's cloth. He would be better suited to the life you can offer him."

"Edwin's place is here with his kin!" Bercthun's wife exploded, unable to hold her tongue any longer.

"Silence woman," Bercthun roared, turning on her, his face coloring. "Get yourself indoors before I raise a hand to you!"

Shooting her husband a vicious look, but nevertheless obeying him, Bercthun's wife gave her son a brief, violent hug, before she turned and went back inside the hall.

Bercthun turned back to Sigeberht with a sigh.

"Apologies, milord. At times, Aedilthryd forgets her place."

"No apology is necessary," Sigeberht replied, his iron gaze fastening on Edwin, before it shifted to the other three boys. "She need not worry. Under my care, Edwin will be clothed and fed, and will learn to read and write in Latin. When he comes of age, he will take his vows and live on at Beodricesworth as a monk."

"It's a great opportunity for the lad," Bercthun rumbled, ruffling his son's hair. "And one he is grateful for. Is it not lad?"

"Yes, fæder," Edwin replied, his voice quavering slightly.

Watching the boy, Aidan felt a stab of pity for him. The youngest of five sons, scrawny and gentle-natured, Edwin had been born into a harsh world where brawn ruled. Men like Bercthun had no use for the weak; Sigeberht had offered him the perfect solution for ridding himself of a son he did not want.

"I shall take the boys," Sigeberht said, with a rare smile. "Aidan, give him the gold."

Aidan reached under his cloak and drew out a heavy drawstring bag. The gold pieces inside clinked as he handed it to Bercthun. The ealdorman took it with a nod.

"Each of you, take a boy with you," Sigeberht ordered his warriors. "Edwin, you will ride with Aidan."

Without looking at his father, his blue eyes glistening with unshed tears, the boy walked over to Aidan and lightly sprang up onto the front of his horse. He may have been thin and sickly-looking, but he was as nimble as a goat.

The smallest boy, Osfrid, was crying openly now. Aldwulf led him over to his horse and lifted him up front. The two remaining warriors accompanying Sigeberht, beckoned Paeda and Sebbi over. Both boys were sniffing as they approached the warriors, but were just managing to hold back the tears.

"May God bless you and your kin." Felix of Burgundy spoke for the first time. "I will ask the Lord to watch over Barrow and its folk and keep you all safe."

"Thank you," Bercthun replied, his expression hooded. "That is most kind."

The ealdorman turned his attention back to the king then.

"Milord. You have heard of Penda's warmongering?"

Sigeberht nodded, his lips pursing slightly as if he did not wish to speak of this subject. When he did not offer a comment, Bercthun continued.

"I can offer you at least fifty spears, strong fearsome warriors who will strike fear into the hearts of those Mercian dogs."

Sigeberht nodded once more. "I thank you, Bercthun. Ecgric now rules in Rendlaesham in my place. If the time comes when our kingdom must defend itself, he will do what is necessary."

Bercthun frowned at that. Looking on, Aidan felt embarrassment at Sigeberht's lack of honor. A king's duty was to protect his people; he should have no other allegiance. Sigeberht's people loved him. They wanted to see him behave with the same defiance he had demonstrated when he stormed Rendlaesham and killed Ricberht.

The man before Bercthun was not behaving like a king.

"Surely, you will not leave the kingdom's defenses to a man who has no claim to the throne? Ecgric the Eager is not my king!" Bercthun's face colored once more. "I and my men want to fight for the Wuffingas. Surely, you will lead your fyrd into battle when the time comes?"

"The king serves his people in far greater ways than merely with a sword or an axe," Felix sniffed, looking down his long nose at the ealdorman. "And it is not your place to question him."

"Good day Bercthun." Sigeberht spoke up before Felix could continue. Bercthun's face had gone thunderous and Aidan could sense conflict brewing. It would be best if they moved off.

Aidan turned his horse and followed Sigeberht out of Barrow. Behind them, the ealdorman's gaze burned into their backs until they rode out of sight.

They rode in silence across a flat landscape dotted with trees. The long grass whispered in the breeze and the sun was warm on Aidan's face. In front of him, he could feel the thin body of the boy, Edwin, trembling. He was crying.

Aidan struggled for something to say that would soothe the boy's suffering but could think of nothing. Edwin's father had just handed his son over, without a glimmer of sadness or regret, for a pouch of gold in return. Despite the hardships that Aidan had endured in his childhood, he had never known the desolation of not being wanted. His father had died defending his wife and son; he would never have sold Aidan into a life of servitude.

Edwin, son of Bercthun, had lost more than his family this day. He had lost his innocence and his trust. He had lost his childhood.

Freya was retrieving eggs from the hen house when the riders returned to Beodricesworth. Upon hearing the thud of hooves and the rumble of men's voices, she placed the last egg, still warm, in her basket and made her way across the yard beside the hall. There, she spied the king, Felix and a handful of men dismounting their horses.

They had four boys with them.

Freya's heart sank when she saw the stricken, tear-stained faces of the lads. The thin, blond boy with Aidan wore such an expression of raw grief that it almost brought Freya to tears to look upon him.

These were the boys she had heard Sigeberht and Felix discuss the night before; the sons of warriors who would learn to read and write here at Beodricesworth before going on to become monks.

She supposed there were worse lives. But if that were so, why did all four boys look miserable?

Oblivious to his new charges' unhappiness, Sigeberht strode ahead into the hall, while Felix brought up the rear, ushering the boys ahead of him. Freya watched them go before glancing at Aidan and Aldwulf. The latter shook his head in disgust and spat on the ground; his gaze was still fixed upon the door the king had disappeared through. Aldwulf was a muscular young warrior with a mane of light brown hair and a heavy-featured face. He was a man of few words, although when he did speak, he usually had something of note to say.

"Those boys belong with their families," he muttered, "and the king belongs back in Rendlaesham with his people!"

Aldwulf then turned on his heel and stalked off. Aidan watched him go before turning back to Freya.

"Sigeberht is starting to make himself unpopular," he said in a low voice, taking care not to be overheard. "He cares not who he offends with his words about how Ecgric will protect the kingdom from the Mercians, and how his god will save us all. He offended one of his ealdormen this morning, Bercthun of Barrow, when he told him that Ecgric would be leading his fyrd, should the Mercians attack."

Freya felt a sting of misgiving at Aidan's words.

"I can't believe he would let Ecgric lead his army into battle," she gasped. "Why would he go to all the trouble of taking back the throne for the Wuffingas, if he is willing to give it to a man he hardly knows?"

"He's conflicted," Aidan replied softly, his gaze meeting hers. "Sigeberht cannot reconcile his loyalty to his family with his allegiance to his god. He expected his mother and cousins to welcome him back to the kingdom with open arms. When that didn't happen, his victory soured. He shed a lake of blood and murdered a king for a cold, lonely throne."

"He blames you too, doesn't he?"

Aidan gave a lopsided smile at that. Freya was aware that he was standing close, so close that she could feel the heat of his body. The sensation made it difficult to concentrate.

"I remind him of his quest for vengeance," Aidan replied. "He's angry because I won't pay penance. He wanted me to take my vows and become a monk but I refused. He'll never stop punishing me for that."

"He wanted you to become a monk?" Freya raised her eyebrows and struggled to keep the incredulity out of her voice. "What good would that do?"

"It would ease his conscience." Aidan's gaze shifted to where the king had disappeared into the hall. "That's why those boys are here. Sigeberht doesn't need a kingdom to rule—just a group of young minds to bend to his will."

The evening meal was a somber affair. The meal was simple; no rabbit pie this evening but vegetable pottage, boiled eggs and griddle bread. The new additions to Sigeberht's hall: Edwin, Osfrid, Paeda and Sebbi sat below the salt, at the far end of the table, whey-faced and red-eyed.

All four boys picked at their food and kept their gazes downcast. Freya felt a pang as she placed cups of water at their elbows. They looked so lost.

"Tomorrow will be an important day," Felix announced to the table once Freya and Hereric had finished serving them. The monk's gaze was riveted on the king's four young charges. "On the morrow our king will take his vows. Sigeberht will become a monk and will aid me in your instruction."

The hiss of indrawn breaths from Sigeberht's warriors punctured the silence. Aldwulf's eyes bulged and he nearly choked on his mouthful of griddle bread.

Aidan blanched, his gaze narrowing. "What is this?" he asked quietly. "Milord! You cannot take your vows without giving up the throne."

"I'm aware of that," Sigeberht responded, his voice chill, "and I tire of hearing this subject repeated as if I am an imbecile. I will say it once more, and it will be the last time. Ecgric of Exning now rules the Kingdom of the East Angles. I took back the throne for my family and I avenged Eorpwald's death – but received little gratitude from my own kin in return. I wish to have my life back. I have found a far greater purpose and I wish to fulfill it. I wish to serve the Lord and no one else."

Next to Sigeberht, Felix struggled to contain the smile that was slowly creeping across his face. There—the king had finally admitted it. He did not want his crown. Yet, Aidan was not about to let the matter rest.

"You made a promise to the people of this land when you were crowned king," Aidan ground out, barely able to restrain his temper. "They will not accept your decision. They will expect you to lead them, to protect them. The Mercians are gathering at our borders. Ecgric is amassing a fyrd, but they will be *your* men, *your* spears. They will fight for you and no one else."

"Enough!" Sigeberht slammed his cup down on the table, sloshing mead over the rim. His face was taut with fury, his grey eyes hard flecks of iron. "That is the last time you speak of this Aidan of Connacht—ever. You forget your place. I gave you the rank of thegn and I can take it away from you just as easily. Never forget it!"

Chapter Sixteen

THE SUMMER, ONE of the fairest that folk could remember, slowly drew to a close and autumn gathered Beodricesworth in its chill embrace. Crisp frosts carpeted the ground in the mornings and the trees were ablaze with shades of red, orange and gold. Leaves softly fell to the ground like molten snowflakes and an ever-present tang of wood-smoke laced the air.

It was a time of great industry for Freya. The store house had to be filled before Winterfylleth: the celebration that marked the first full-moon of winter. She had to salt and dry the meat, make cheeses and oversee the stocking of the larder. Sacks of barley and rye had arrived from Rendlaesham, along with bunches of onions and sacks of apples. The fields behind Beodricesworth yielded many carrots and turnips, and Freya hoped there would be enough produce to see them through the long winter.

Freya and Hereric worked tirelessly, preparing the winter store. Sigeberht's warriors also assisted with filling the store house. Aidan led his men out every day to hunt for rabbits, boar and deer. Upon their return, they did much of the skinning, gutting and hanging of the meat. Freya often saw Aldwulf hard at work out in the fields, helping the peasants harvest the vegetables and tend to the soil.

During all this industry, Sigeberht dedicated himself wholly to his new charges. Dressed in an ankle-length, un-dyed, woolen tunic, girded at the waist, Sigeberht no longer cut a kingly figure. Freya had been used to the king striding about, wearing black leather breeches, silk-edged tunics and gleaming brooches, with a fine fur cloak billowing out behind him. Like Felix, he had cut his hair in a tonsure; shaving the hair from the crown of his head while the rest remained uncut. According to Felix, the tonsure was a way for a new monk to demonstrate his renunciation of all his worldly possessions and needs. Freya could not get used to the sight of her king, in his long tunic, crudely sewn leather boots and shaved crown.

Strangely, Sigeberht had never appeared happier.

The four lads: Edwin, Osfrid, Paeda and Sebbi had settled into their new life well enough. They rose at daybreak and accompanied Sigeberht and Felix into the back of the hall. There they pored over heavy books that had been bound on boards. The books had parchment pages and had been clamped with brass clasps and leather straps. The boys were also learning their Latin letters; a process that appeared to test Felix's patience.

One morning, Freya had entered the monastic section of the hall to replace some candles, and found the boys bent over scraps of parchment with quills clasped in their fists. The look of intense concentration on their faces made Freya smile. Sigeberht and Felix looked on over the boys' shoulders as they wrote. Felix's face was twisted in a perpetual scowl as he barked instructions. In contrast, Sigeberht spoke in soft tones with the boys.

Upon hearing Freya's approach, Felix looked up from checking Edwin's writing. His scowl deepened and his cheeks flushed. "What are you doing in here girl?"

"I've brought the candles that Lord Sigeberht asked for," Freya replied with a tight smile. "Shall I light them?"

Felix grunted and turned his attention back to Edwin's letters. "Make sure you take the stubs of the old candles away with you," he snapped.

Freya moved around the room, replacing the old candles with the new and lighting them. Candles were a novelty for Freya; most folk could not afford them. She finished her task and was making her way towards the curtain that shielded the monastic space from the rest of the hall, when Felix's sharp voice lashed across the room.

"You took your time girl! This is not a place for women—your presence here sullies sacred ground. From now on, send Hereric here in your place. If I see you inside this space again I will have you whipped!"

A hot rush of anger swept over Freya. She bit her cheek to stop herself from snarling at the monk. She would like to see the weasel try and whip her. She would rip the whip from his hands and use it on him instead— whatever the consequences. Without deigning to look his way, Freya shoved her way through the curtain and strode back into the hall.

Hereric, who was turning a row of spit-roasting rabbits over the fire pit, watched Freya storm across the hall towards him.

"What's the matter Freya?"

"It's Felix," she replied, attempting to keep her voice low despite the anger boiling within her. "He treats me as if I were some turd he has to step around. I'd love to shove that cross he wears right up his arse!"

Hereric sniggered at that; like Freya he had no love for Felix of Burgundy, although the monk treated him with slightly less disdain due to the fact he was a male.

"I'd like to see that," Hereric replied with a grin. "And I'd wager most of those living under this roof would pay gold to see it too."

That afternoon, Freya was sitting outside the hall mending one of the boy's tunics, when Edwin, son of Bercthun, approached her.

The boys were assigned chores every afternoon, and Edwin had just returned from the fields with an armful of cabbages. He stopped before Freya, his clear blue-eyed gaze meeting hers. The boy had been withdrawn in the first days after his arrival at Beodricesworth, but as the summer slipped into autumn he had become more forthcoming. He appeared to enjoy his studies a little more than his companions and was proving to be a quick and able student. Freya recognized the intelligence in his eyes as her gaze met his.

"Where do you want these Freya?"

"Freya, eh?" She smiled in return. "Not many here call you by my given name, I'm surprised you do."

"Hereric does," Edwin replied. The boys had become fast friends since Edwin's arrival here. "And Aidan does too."

Freya felt her cheeks heat up at the mention of Aidan. It was true that he made a point of addressing her by her given name, even though it infuriated Felix. Yet, Freya was glad that Aidan paid the monk no mind. It pleased her to hear him say her name; in more ways than she could express or admit.

"Yes, but the others don't," she reminded him.

Edwin was silent a moment before he stepped forward and lightly touched the iron collar around Freya's neck.

"Do you wear this because you are a theow?"

Freya nodded. "Doesn't your father have slaves?"

Edwin shook his head. "He doesn't need them. I have four sisters. They and my mother do all the work."

Freya smiled gently in response; it was indeed a woman's lot. Before becoming the king's slave, she had never appreciated the freedom she and her mother had enjoyed alone in the woods at Woodbridge Haven. There, they had been their own masters. In the hall of an ealdorman or thegn, the women lived to serve their men. It was a different kind of slavery, but slavery nonetheless.

"You can put the cabbages in the store house Edwin," she said finally.

Edwin went off to the store and had just disappeared inside when a knot of horsemen appeared over the hill to the east. Aidan led a group of warriors with the carcasses of two boar hung over one of their horses. He pulled up before Freya and rewarded her with a wide smile. For the first time in months, Freya was reminded of the old Aidan; the cocky man with melting eyes that she had met on the shore.

"Afternoon, sweet Freya," he announced, swinging down from the saddle and leading his horse up towards the hall while the other warriors led their horses towards the stable.

"Greetings, Aidan." Freya's gaze went to the carcasses of the two boar that hung over the back of the horse he led behind his. The boars' blood dripped onto the earth, staining it dark. "I see this hunting trip was more successful than the last."

Aidan stopped before Freya, so close that his shadow fell over her. Freya looked up into his dark blue eyes. As always, his nearness mesmerized her.

"Yes, it was," he said softly. The intensity of his gaze made Freya light-headed. He had not looked at her like this since spring—not since Eostre. "Does it please you?"

Freya stared back at him, aware that he was deliberately teasing her; he was enjoying the blush that had crept into her cheeks.

"Aidan," Freya replied when she had found her voice. "You knew it would please me. However, we both know it's not my favor you need."

Aidan's smile faded slightly although his gaze still burned into hers. "Of late, your opinion is the only one that matters to me. The others can hang for all I care." He stepped closer to her then.

"Winterfylleth is but three nights away. I was wondering if you would accompany me to the bonfire in Saxham?"

The heat that had been kindling in Freya's cheeks burst into flame. She tore her gaze away and stared down at her hands. It was a bold question, too bold.

"I would like that," she stammered, "but it's not my... it's not my decision."

Aidan stepped forward and gently took hold of her chin; drawing her face up to look at him. He was smiling, but it was not a smile designed to seduce her. Instead, it was warm and tinged with mischief. "I'm sure we can find a way around that."

"Aidan!" Edwin emerged from the store house and ran across the yard towards the warrior, his face alight. "I was wondering when you would be back! Did you kill both those boar yourself?"

"One of them I did," Aidan replied stepping back from Freya and ruffling Aidan's blond hair as the boy skidded to a halt before him. "Do you want to help me string these boar up? They'll need to be skinned and gutted before nightfall."

Edwin nodded eagerly.

"Come on then, let us leave Freya to her work."

Aidan winked at Freya and turned to lead the horses away. Freya saw Edwin's gaze flick from Aidan to her and back again. Woden, that boy was sharp. He missed nothing.

Aidan led the horses to where a row of birches grew tall and strong to the right of the hall. There, he showed Edwin how to tie ropes to the hindquarters of each boar and winch them up onto the tree. Like most lads his age, Edwin had taken part in skinning and gutting beasts before, so Aidan got him to bleed the boars from the neck into a wooden pail. Pig blood was precious and Freya would be able to make blood sausage with it later.

Freya. What spell had the girl woven upon him? He could not stop thinking about her of late. They lived in much closer quarters here at Beodricesworth than they had at Rendlaesham; here they were far more part of each other's life. She slept just yards from him every night on the floor. He had chosen to sleep away from the warmth of the fire pit, just to lie closer to her. It had become a sweet torture; one that had awakened his senses and slowly drawn him out of the misery of the past summer.

Aidan had just cut down the belly of the boar and was preparing to skin it, when the ground began to tremble. Horses, and many of them, were riding fast towards the hall. Aidan whipped around and saw a dark wave of men and horses, with spears bristling against the horizon, crest the brow of the hill.

"Edwin, stay here," he ordered the boy. "Keep out of sight."

With that, Aidan strode back to the hall, his hunting knife in hand, to greet the warriors.

The riders thundered into the yard and pulled up sharply. Aidan saw Freya cast her sewing aside and stand up to greet them. Not for the first time, he was struck by her presence, her proud stance. Unarmed she stood firm and raised her chin to look the warriors in the eye. As Aidan reached her, he saw the color drain from her face and her expression harden. He followed her gaze to its source and knew why she had reacted so.

The man leading these warriors was Ecgric of Exning. Aidan recognized many of the faces, one of which was Oeric. The youth looked far less cocky than the last time he had seen him.

"Milord," Freya greeted him coldly. "Why are you—"

"Silence!" Ecgric snarled. "Speak another word to me and I'll take my fist to you. Go and get the king!"

Freya's gaze narrowed and Aidan could see her fury at being spoken to thus. Nonetheless, she wisely decided to do as she was bid. Anyone could see that Ecgric was in a vile temper.

When Freya disappeared inside the hall, to interrupt Sigeberht from his afternoon prayers, Ecgric's gimlet gaze moved to Aidan.

"Enjoying it here are you?" Aidan felt Ecgric's gaze slide over him. "I always thought you were far more suited to the life of a peasant than retainer to a king."

"And I always thought you more suited to emptying privies than leading armies," Aidan replied. "A man who lives outside his limitations is a fool indeed."

Ecgric's face darkened. His brows drew together and his neat beard seemed to grow to a point—giving him a vaguely demonic appearance.

"Foreign cur," he growled. "I'll cut your tongue out by the roots one day."

"Why not now?" Aidan felt a red haze settle upon him as he casually raised the blood-stained hunting knife he carried. "Go on and try."

Ecgric's hand strayed to the pommel of his sword, but froze there when a figure emerged from the hall.

The Eager's gaze fastened on Sigeberht. In the two moon cycles since he had left Rendlaesham, the king had undergone a huge transformation. Gone were the kingly robes, jeweled brooches and iron crown; the man before him truly was Sigeberht the Righteous: a clean-shaven man with a gentle face, barefoot and wearing a long wool tunic.

"Milord?" Ecgric queried. "Is that you?"

"It is," Sigeberht replied with a smile. "Do you find me so altered Ecgric?"

Ecgric nodded wordlessly, his gaze riveted upon the man who had elevated him to the position of ruler, and then abandoned him in the role. Looking upon Ecgric the Eager, Aidan could see signs of strain. He had lost weight and looked gaunt. His eyes were hollowed from stress and there were deep grooves either side of his mouth that had not been there mid-summer.

"What is the reason for your visit?" Sigeberht continued when Ecgric did not speak. "You know I left the kingdom entirely your responsibility. I am content to let you rule without my counsel."

"And I would have been glad to continue doing so," Ecgric replied, eventually finding his voice. "However, war is now upon us milord."

Silence fell in the yard. Moments passed and Aidan could hear the sounds of the late afternoon around him: the bleating of a goat in the distance, the cluck of chickens, the babbling of the Lark River and the laughter of children helping their parents in the fields behind the hall. It was a peaceful, autumn afternoon; it seemed absurd that war was upon them.

"Penda has gathered a sizeable fyrd at our western border. He will make for Rendlaesham and his path will take him straight through this valley. I have called as many men as I could. You now have a fyrd of three thousand spears. Yet I fear that Penda's army is nearly double that."

Ecgric paused and the silence stretched on. When Sigeberht made no comment, Ecgric continued.

"We will meet the Mercians on the fields just outside Barrow. Bercthun of Barrow has joined us, as has your cousin, Annan. Penda's army is rumored to begin its march tomorrow at daybreak. It will take them four days to reach Barrow Fields. We must be ready for them when they arrive."

Again, Sigeberht did not respond. Two patches of red appeared on Ecgric's cheeks. He had expected some comment from the king by now, not a vacant expression.

"Milord," he began again, his voice rising slightly. "Your army awaits you. They will not fight without their king. You must come with me now to Barrow and plan for war."

"I think not," Sigeberht replied mildly. "When I handed my crown to you, I renounced all my kingly responsibilities. If war must come to this kingdom, you must lead the East Angles into battle. I am a man of peace now. I will never raise a sword against another man again."

Hearing Sigeberht's words, Aidan felt ill. Sigeberht did not seem to understand. Ecgric had not come here to ask him to lead his fyrd, he had come here to *tell* him.

"You are our king," Ecgric ground out, his face now the color of raw meat. "I have ruled in your stead; I have done all you asked but your spears, swords, axes, and the shield wall—they will only fight for you. You were crowned King of the East Angles, not me."

Sigeberht shook his head, his expression closed and stubborn. "I will not fight, that is my final word."

Ecgric leaned forward in the saddle. Aidan could almost taste his rage and his desire to draw *Æthelfrith's Bane* and strike Sigeberht down with it. Despite that he found Ecgric despicable, Aidan felt a stab of pity for him. He had been burdened with a terrible responsibility. No wonder Oeric looked pained. Following a king was one thing; following him to war was another. The kingdom was on the verge of falling and Sigeberht thought praying to his god was of greater importance. Aidan's palm itched to slap some sense into the king.

"So be it, but hear my final word," Ecgric hissed. "You will fight. You will lead your army. When the Mercians approach I will come for you and I will drag you kicking and screaming onto the battlefield if I have to. You shall lead your men."

With that, Ecgric gathered his reins and prepared to ride off.

"Ecgric!" Aidan stepped forward into Ecgric's line of sight. The warrior's gaze was still riveted on Sigeberht so it was the only way to gain his attention.

"There are twenty of us here who will fight," Aidan told him. "Send word and we will come."

Ecgric nodded curtly, the closest Aidan would ever receive to thanks, before he wheeled his horse away and led his warriors away from Beodricesworth. The ground shook and it was a while before the thundering of hooves faded.

Aidan turned back to Sigeberht and attempted to meet his gaze. Yet the king ignored him; his thoughts having turned inward. Without another word, Sigeberht turned and went back inside the hall to resume his prayers, leaving Aidan to wonder if the king had lost both his wits and his courage.

Chapter Seventeen

THE EVE OF Winterfylleth arrived. It had been a crisp, bright day and the sun was setting to the west in a blaze of red and gold when Freya hurried into the hall to dish up the evening meal of pottage and griddle bread.

As usual, the evening meal was a subdued affair. Ever since news of the approaching Mercian army had spread through Beodricesworth like wildfire, folk wore startled, frightened expressions and jumped at shadows. If Ecgric's warning was true, then the army would arrive within a day.

Freya ladled pottage into wooden bowls and passed them to Hereric who served SIgeberht and Felix first. As she worked, Freya cast a watchful eye over Sigeberht. Unlike Felix, who had looked a bit pale and tense ever since the news of Penda and his great fyrd, Sigeberht appeared calm, verging on serene.

"Let us pray this eve," Sigeberht said to Felix. "For the souls of Penda and his blood-thirsty horde. May the lord show them the right path; the path of peace."

Felix nodded, although Freya noticed his mouth had pursed, as if he was chewing on something unpleasant.

Freya passed Edwin a bowl of pottage and upon seeing his worried face she cast a warm smile in his direction. Of course, Edwin and the other boys had been distraught at the news of the approaching army. Barrow was their home and all their male kin would join the East Anglian army. Barrow Fields were just a short distance from Edwin's home. Freya knew he worried for his mother and his sisters should the battle go ill.

You should worry for us all if the battle goes ill, Freya thought with a chill. *For once he burns Barrow, Penda will march straight here and do the same.*

After everyone had finished eating, Freya began clearing away the wooden bowls and clay cups. Sigeberht and Felix disappeared behind the curtain to spend the evening at prayers while Edwin and the other boys sat near the fire pit and practiced their spoken Latin together, as they did every evening. Some warriors remained indoors, playing at knucklebones or drinking, while others drifted off. Aidan was one of these.

Freya's stomach knotted when she saw him make for the door. It was Winterfylleth, Winter Full Moon, and Aidan had promised to take her to Saxham to see the fires.

Maybe he has forgotten. She could not blame him; the news of coming war had thrown them all into upheaval.

Yet Aidan paused in the doorway and glanced back at Freya. His gaze met hers and he smiled. Freya's stomach leaped. He had remembered; he would wait outside for her until she managed to slip away.

Freya busied herself with washing the bowls and cups in a pail of waiter before she wiped down the tables. Then, she picked up the pail as if she intended to take it outside to empty it, and made her way casually towards the door.

No one stirred or looked her way as she stepped outside.

Night had fallen. Freya's breath steamed before her in the cool air and she glanced up at the blanket of stars overhead. The night was still young; the full moon had not yet risen.

"Freya." A man's voice hailed her as she walked across the yard. She stopped and peered into the darkness. She could just make out the outline of a man on horseback standing in the shadow of the store room.

"I was worried you'd not be able to get away," Aidan said as she approached. "Here, I brought you a woolen shawl. It's cold this eve."

"Thank you," Freya murmured, wrapping the shawl about her shoulders. She wore a sleeveless shift and the night air had a bite to it.

"Here, climb up in front of me." Aidan reached down to her. Freya took his hand; it was cool and strong in her grasp. She placed her foot on top of his and vaulted up so that she sat side-saddle in front of him. Her balance was precarious in this position, but she could not sit astride without hitching up her skirts. Considering the strong attraction between them, Freya thought such an act would be unwise.

Unspeaking, Aidan put one arm around Freya's waist, to steady her, while keeping hold of the reins with his opposite hand. He urged his horse forward and they slipped away from the hall.

Freya waited until Beodricesworth lay behind them before she spoke again. She turned her head towards Aidan, but like the night of Eostre, his face was cast in shadow.

"I hope the others don't notice my absence."

"Even if they do, what does it matter?" Aidan replied. "Sigeberht has more to worry about these days than the whereabouts of his theow. You have had a hard year Freya; I wanted to give you an evening away from it all. Once the Mercians arrive I won't have another chance."

"It's true then that his fyrd is much bigger than ours?"

"That's what I've heard."

"And Sigeberht won't fight?"

"He will. He doesn't want to, but he will."

"Will you fight?" Freya cursed the darkness for she wanted to see Aidan's face then; she wanted to see the expression in his eyes and know the truth of matters.

"I will," he replied quietly. "I must."

Saxham was a short ride from Beodricesworth but Aidan did not hurry. By the time they reached the edge of the village, a huge glowing moon was rising over the treetops. It flooded the world in silver light and Freya could now see the outline of Aidan's face.

They dismounted at the edge of the village and Aidan tied his horse to a tree. Then, unspeaking, they made their way towards the heart of Saxham: the village green.

Saxham was a small hamlet—around half the size of Barrow—but it glowed brightly in the darkness on this, the first full moon of winter. Fires and torches burned everywhere, inside and outside the squat wattle and daub hovels that filled a wide clearing. As she walked, Freya peered inside open doorways and saw jugs of milk, mead and wine placed on the edge of the fire pits, alongside a spread of food: pies, cakes and breads. On this night, the villagers left their doors unlocked to allow the dead to enter. Torches had been placed at many open doorways guiding in the good spirits and deterring the evil ones.

A great bonfire burned in the center of Saxham; hungry tongues of flame licking up at the darkness. It was a time of declining sun, and the villagers had lit a bonfire to encourage it back. Blotmonath, Blood month, was almost upon them. Tomorrow the villagers would perform rites for Hela – the Underworld Goddess who raised the dead – and the day after that Woden – father of the gods – would ride his eight-legged horse through the mortal world.

Freya and Aidan joined the folk who clustered around the edge of the bonfire and gratefully received wooden cups of hot, spiced wine. Wrapping her chilled fingers around the cup, Freya enjoyed the warmth of the fire caressing her face and was reminded that Winterfylleth was a time when everyone moved indoors, into the relative warmth, and outdoor activities ceased for the long winter. Darkness was about to return and nature would soon go to ground. Despite this, Freya loved Winterfylleth. Joining this celebration reminded Freya of other, happier times.

"You look deep in thought," Aidan observed, passing Freya a slice of hot apple tart, sweetened with honey.

Freya smiled and took a bite of the tart. Its sweet tang made her sigh with pleasure. She rarely ate food like this these days.

"I was just remembering other Winterfylleth eves," she said wistfully. "When my father was alive."

"When did he die?" Aidan asked gently, the firelight dancing in his eyes as he watched her.

"Only five years ago – at the Battle of Uffid Heath – and yet it seems much longer than that."

"He would have fought with King Raedwald." Aidan's voice was tinged with awe. "The greatest king this land has ever known. I would have liked to have met him."

Freya nodded, breaking eye contact with him and looking into the flames. "He was a great king," she admitted. "My father would have followed him anywhere."

Freya did not add that her mother had nursed resentment against Raedwald ever since her husband's death, or that she had shared her mother's feelings. It all seemed so petty now. Since her freedom had been taken away from her, Freya now understood that Raedwald had not compelled her father to fight and die for him on Uffid Heath. Aelli of Gipeswic had lived and died a free man. These days she understood how precious that was.

"I remember well the year my father died," Freya replied as memories of the past flooded over her. "The king's daughter, Raedwyn, fell out of favor when she fell in love with her father's slave—the son of his sworn enemy."

"That must have been Caelin, son of Ceolwulf the Exiled. Raedwald killed Ceolwulf upon Uffid Heath and enslaved his son. I have heard the story. It has become legend in Rendlaesham. I hear it ended well for the lovers though."

Freya cast Aidan a sidelong glance, not sure whether he was teasing her or not.

"Yes it did. Raedwald tried to marry his daughter, Raedwyn, to Eafa of Mercia. It was a terrible mistake, for after the wedding, Eafa sought to slay Raedwald in the Golden Hall and take the kingdom for the Mercians. He stabbed the king and would have slit his throat if Caelin had not stopped him. It was Raedwyn who slew Eafa, but the king died of his injuries anyway. The new king, Eorpwald, gave Caelin his freedom and his sister the right to choose her future. She chose love."

"See, sometimes things do end well," Aidan replied with a smile. "Slaves do gain their freedom. Surely I am proof of that also."

Freya took a sip of mulled wine and felt its warmth seep down through her body. "Truthfully, I've made peace with my enslavement for the moment." Freya reached up with her free hand and touched the iron collar about her neck. "There are worse lives than this one. My lot improved the moment we left Rendlaesham and Ecgric behind. Beneath his stern exterior, Sigeberht is a kind man; and Edwin and the others are sweet boys. My daily toil is not as back-breaking as it was. My fate would have been a lot worse if Ricberht still ruled."

Aidan held her gaze, respect glittering in his eyes. "You are quite a woman Freya," he murmured. "I only wish I could keep you safe from what is to come."

Silence fell between them then as their thoughts returned to the approaching Mercian fyrd.

"Eafa the Merciful was Penda's elder brother," Aidan mused, "and by all accounts the Mercian King is as cold and ruthless as his dead sibling. I hear that he wishes to make this kingdom bow to his. Without a charismatic leader like Raedwald, I fear it might happen."

"Why do you stay?" Freya asked suddenly. "You owe this land nothing. Why not return to Gaul and go back to your old life. I'd rather you did that than died for us."

Aidan smiled then, a sad smile with a trace of bitterness around the edges.

"Ah, if only there was something to go back to. Sigeberht was my life in Gaul—it's no more my home that anywhere else. I wanted to make a life for myself here Freya. I wanted Sigeberht to grant me land so that I could have my own hall, farm the land and raise a family. Unfortunately Sigeberht was not cut out to be a king. He does not reward loyalty and he does not want the responsibility of ruling a kingdom. If he had given me some land I would have asked for nothing else save to meet a woman like you, sweet Freya, and make her my wife."

Freya stared back at Aidan. His admission felt as if someone had just punched her in the stomach. There was no teasing in his gaze, just a quiet, sure intensity.

She realized with a jolt that he was telling the truth. If she had been free, he would have chosen her for his own.

Tears stung Freya's eyes and she hurriedly looked away so that Aidan could not see them. The fire's heat scalded her face and helped her collect herself. When she looked back at Aidan, she took a deep, trembling breath and fought the mountain's weight of regret and sadness that threatened to crush her.

"I would have liked that," she said quietly, meeting his gaze.

The night stretched on and the moon rose high into the heavens. Eventually, their bellies full of sweet treats and spiced wine, Aidan and Freya reluctantly moved away from the dying bonfire and made their way towards the horse that awaited them on the outskirts of Saxham.

"Let us walk rather than ride," Freya suggested. "I am in no hurry to return to Beodricesworth. I'd like to feel like a free woman for a while longer."

"Very well," Aidan replied, leading his horse forward as Freya fell into step beside him. "I too am not in a hurry to go back."

The full moon shone so bright that the woodland around them was clearly visible. Silver light bathed the ground, which crunched slightly underfoot; a frost was forming. They walked in silence for a short while before Aidan wordlessly reached out and took Freya's hand. Her breath stopped as he gently entwined his fingers with hers. Her heart started to pound when he stroked the center of her palm with his thumb. She suddenly felt both shivery and hot at the same time. Who would have thought her hand could contain such sensation.

"If I could stop a moment in time and make it last forever, it would be this one," Aidan said softly. "If I wasn't so bound to honor and duty I would ride away with you from this place and never look back."

They stopped then and stared at each other.

"I wish you were not so bound by honor and duty then." The words burst from Freya before she could stop them. "I wish you'd throw aside that yoke and live selfishly just once. Where has loyalty gotten you?"

Aidan stared at her in shock for a moment.

Then, he stepped forward and pulled her roughly into his arms. His mouth came down hard on Freya's and all words, all thought, disappeared from her mind.

His kiss was hot and urgent. Freya's mouth opened under his with a gasp. Her legs went weak as his tongue slid against hers. His hands cupped the back of her head and he deepened the kiss. Freya's hands clutched at his chest, looking for a way through the barrier of his clothing. Her fingers ached to touch his naked skin. She pressed herself up against him and drank in his taste and smell.

Despite the chill night, she felt as if she were on fire, burning with need for a man she had wanted from the first moment she had seen him.

Yes, she admitted it now, at the end when it was almost too late.

They were in a small glade, surrounded by elms. It was a secluded spot, away from the prying eyes of Sigeberht's hall; away from anyone who could stop what was about to happen.

Freya stepped away from Aidan, threw aside her shawl and kicked off her boots. Then, she untied the girdle about her waist and, in one smooth movement, pulled her tunic over her head so that she stood naked before him. She had never done anything so bold, and had never had the inclination to do so—until now. Life was so fleeting; they had to live this moment before it was taken away from them.

She could feel Aidan's gaze upon her. It slid over her body, and lingered on her breasts before he looked back at her face.

"You are beautiful," he whispered. "You are so lovely it hurts to look upon you."

With that, Aidan unbuckled the heavy belt he wore across his hips, shrugged off his cloak and pulled his tunic over his head. The moonlight glistened on the muscular planes of his chest as he undid his breeches and the garters that tied his boots to his calves.

Watching him, Freya felt a heat grow between her legs and spread through the pit of her belly. His arousal was obvious and the sight of it made her breath come in sharp gasps.

When he stepped towards her once more she remained motionless. Her body felt boneless and weak. She could not have run from him, even if she had wanted to.

Aidan's mouth claimed hers once more—hungry and insistent. He pushed her up against the trunk of one of the sheltering elms and pressed the length of his naked body against hers. Freya could feel the cold roughness of bark against her back but cared not. Her whole will was focused, instead, on the heat of his mouth and the warmth of his hands as they slid over her body. When he tore his mouth from hers and began to suckle one of her breasts, Freya cried out. Her hands tangled in his hair while he suckled one nipple and then the other. Then he straightened up and, once more, covered her mouth with his.

Freya, all restraint a faint memory, ran her hands down the length of his torso, before her fingers traced the hard length of him. Aidan's breathing was ragged now and he groaned when she began to stroke him.

"Freya," he groaned in her ear. "You will drive me insane if you continue to do that."

In response, Freya gave a husky, breathless laugh. "So be it."

She stroked him again, this time gently biting his neck as she did so.

Aidan gave a strangled cry and, cupping her bottom with his hands, lifted her up against the trunk. Her legs parted and she felt him, hard and trembling against her.

"I don't want to hurt you," he murmured between gritted teeth, "but I don't know if I can do this slowly."

Freya angled her hips towards him in response and the pressure increased. She kissed him deeply and slid her tongue into his mouth, mimicking the act she wanted from him. That was all the encouragement Aidan required. With a groan of pleasure he pressed against her.

Freya felt him slide into her before a stab of pain knifed through her. She gasped and went rigid. Aidan froze. Freya clung to him a moment, breathless, before she wrapped her legs about his hips and drew him closer.

Aidan sank deep into Freya until he filled her completely; a glorious sensation that sent tremors of pleasure through her. Then, Aidan began to move his hips as he drove deeper still.

Freya whimpered and buried her face in his neck. The pleasure was almost unbearable. Then, when he began to move more forcefully within her she cried out, digging her nails into his back.

"Freya," Aidan gasped, pushing her higher against the tree trunk so that he could penetrate deeper into her. "I can't stop, I can't ..."

"Don't stop!" Freya cried out as he thrust into her once again. She could feel a pressure inside her mounting and she raised her hips to meet him, again and again.

Despite the chill night, sweat slicked their bodies. Freya cried out as her body sang with pleasure; then she collapsed against Aidan, her limbs trembling. He only lasted a moment longer before his cries mingled with hers in the silent glade.

Freya leaned into his chest, their hearts hammering in time like the drums of Eostre . Aidan's fingers were entwined in her hair that had come loose from its long braid.

They stayed like that for a while, each savoring the pleasure that slowly ebbed from their bodies, and resisting the reality which their lovemaking had momentarily kept at bay.

Freya's mind felt like a gently rippling pool; a cool, wide, peaceful lake, far from the hard edges of the world. She clung to that peace, as she clung to Aidan—in the hope that wishing would make it so.

Chapter Eighteen

MOONLIGHT POURED ACROSS the glade, outlining the shapes of the trees and the horse that patiently stood at one end, awaiting its master.

Aidan raised himself up on an elbow and looked down at Freya. His throat closed as he gazed upon her; taking in the pale, smoothness of her skin and the mane of dark red hair that spread out around her.

They lay upon a mattress of their discarded clothes, with Aidan's cloak covering their nakedness from the chill night air. Gazing upon her, Aidan was aware that Freya too was studying him; her eyes two dark pools in the moonlight.

"I don't want to go back," she murmured, her soft voice breaking the silence. "Let's just remain in this glade forever."

Aidan smiled down at her, and felt a weight settle upon the center of his chest.

"If only we could," he whispered.

Freya reached up and stroked his face. "So handsome," she sighed. "I've never seen a man so fair."

Aidan chuckled at that, gently taking hold of her hand and kissing her palm. "Why thank you, sweet Freya. Although I was prettier before life took its toll."

He felt Freya's cool fingertips trace the scar on his cheek; the one from the battle for Rendlaesham. It had healed well but had left a silver line down the length of his cheek.

"Life only adds to it," she said softly. "You needed a few scars or you'd have women resenting your beauty."

Aidan snorted at that. "Now you go too far!" He looked down and saw that she was grinning up at him—enjoying the opportunity to tease him. This playful side to Freya was new, and delightful. He was pleased to see that life as the king's theow had not crushed her spirit.

"I will never forget tonight." He smiled down at her. "Never. We will stay here till dawn. This night, from nightfall till daybreak, you are mine."

"Well then Aidan of Connacht," Freya ran her hands down over his torso and stroked his manhood, which was beginning to rise again in response to her caresses. "We had better not waste a moment of it."

Aidan leaned down and laid the length of his body against hers. He stroked the milky skin of her breasts. He heard her gasp when he gently pinched her nipples. She groaned against him when he started to kiss her neck.

Moments later, there was no more time for words, or worries of what the future held—only loving.

The eastern sky was lightening when the lovers eventually rose from their makeshift bower and dressed. It was a chill morning and a frost twinkled around them. Freya's breath steamed in the air as she walked across the frosty ground towards where Aidan had already mounted. She wrapped her shawl tightly about her shoulders and vaulted up in front of him. Strangely, she did not feel the cold this morning, even after a night out in the open. Unspeaking, she leaned against Aidan's chest and relaxed against the gentle thud of his heart.

Then, still without a word spoken, Aidan urged his horse forward and they rode out of the glade.

It was a short ride back to Beodriceworth—too short. Freya was dozing against Aidan's chest when the trees drew back and they rode out into the Lark Valley. They made their way up a shallow rise and down the hill towards Sigeberht's hall.

As they approached, Freya could see a cloaked figure standing in front of the entrance to the hall.

Freya's stomach clenched. Although he wore a cowl over his face, she recognized the figure's height and bearing. Sigeberht was waiting for them.

Aidan had also noticed the silent, cloaked figure, for Freya felt his body tense against hers. Freya sat up straighter and squared her shoulders. Whatever came next, she knew it would be unpleasant. There was no way they could have hidden this from Sigeberht long-term. Perhaps it was better they confronted him about this now.

Aidan drew up his horse and Freya slid to the ground. Aidan dismounted and stepped up beside her. The figure before the entrance to the hall pushed back his hood and stepped forward to meet them.

In the soft light of dawn, Freya could see the anger, but also the lines of fatigue, on Sigeberht's face. He had not slept.

"You will come no closer." Sigeberht stopped a few feet away. He was wearing short, leather boots and carried a long wooden staff, which he used to bar their path. "Neither of you are welcome in my hall."

"Sigeberht ... milord," Aidan began cautiously. "This was not done to spite you. We—"

"Enough!" Sigeberht boomed, his voice lashing across the yard and causing a stir behind him. Freya glanced over Sigeberht's shoulder and saw Felix emerge from the hall. Behind him, Freya caught a glimpse of four young faces in the doorway: Edwin, Osfrid, Paeda and Sebbi. The boys looked pale and worried.

"I know what you've done. You know the rules of my hall. I will not tolerate a theow under my roof that is not chaste, and I will not suffer a thegn who defies me. You are both banished!"

"My Lord Sigeberht." Felix rushed forward, his face pinched in rage. "These two have done more than defy you. They have sinned! Your punishment must be greater than banishment. Put him in the stocks for a week and have the girl whipped. They must serve as a warning to others!"

"Hold your tongue monk!" Aidan's temper snapped. He stepped towards Felix and raised his fist. "Take your poison elsewhere. We have not sinned—we have only done something that is as natural as living and breathing. It is you who twists such things into sin."

"Silence!" Sigeberht roared, stepping between the two men. "My word is law here. Felix, I will not compound their sin by adding to it with our own. Aidan and Freya, I want you both gone. You may take nothing but the clothes on your backs. I wish never to..."

Sigeberht's last words were drowned out by the sudden tattoo of hoof-beats, approaching at a gallop from the north-west.

Freya, who had not uttered a word since Sigeberht had barred their path, swiveled round and gasped at the sight of horses, approaching over the brow of the hill. Aidan put his arm around her shoulder and pulled her to one side. The horsemen thundered into the yard. The horses skidded to a halt; their breaths steaming as they tossed their heads and jangled their bridles. They had been ridden hard.

Ecgric the Eager rode forward and stopped before Sigeberht. The co-ruler of the East Angles was dressed for battle, in boiled leather and iron, and his face was set in hard, dark lines.

"The Mercians approach Barrow Fields," he barked, his gaze riveted upon Sigeberht. "What say you, *milord*? Will you come willingly, or will we have to drag you?"

"I will not fight," Sigeberht growled. "I am a man of god now. You cannot compel me to kill!"

"It is kill or be killed in this world," Ecgric snarled before he glanced over his shoulder at the men he had brought with him. "Bind his hands and put him on a horse. He is coming with us."

What followed was an ugly, harrowing scene. Aidan and Freya looked on as four warriors wrestled Sigeberht to the ground and bound his wrists behind his back. Felix, seized by a sudden hysteria, ran flailing and clawing at the warriors, only to be felled with one punch. He crawled, whimpering back to the doorway, where Sigeberht's four charges watched in horror.

Yet even unarmed, Sigeberht was a strong, muscular man, still very much in his prime. In the end, it took six warriors to subdue him, and manhandle him onto a horse.

Freya watched her master, bleeding from the lip, one eye already beginning to swell, slump in the saddle, defeated. She fought back the urge to cry. Despite everything, Sigeberht had been good to her. He did not deserve to be treated thus.

Satisfied that Sigeberht was subdued and bound securely, Ecgric turned to Aidan. His gaze rested on him a moment before flicking to Freya. Aidan's arm about her shoulders told him all, and his lip curled.

"So your little slut likes foreign cock does she?"

Aidan stared back at him coldly, refusing to be baited. Seeing that this was neither the time nor the place to trade insults, Ecgric returned to the task at hand. Behind him, his men were coldly silent; Ecgric's outburst had lowered him in the eyes of all present.

"You said you had twenty spears to add to my fyrd," he bit out each word resentfully. "Gather them now and follow us to Barrow Fields."

Aidan nodded curtly. "We will come."

With that, Ecgric wheeled his horse away and dug his heels into its sweat-slicked flanks. Freya watched the group of horsemen, with Sigeberht riding in their midst, gallop away, and disappear over the brow of the hill.

The sun had risen over the eastern horizon, rays of golden light warming the frosty ground. Freya turned back to Aidan, her heart in her throat.

"We almost had our freedom," she managed, her vision blurring with tears. "Sigeberht banished us. We could ride out of here and never look back ... but you can't."

Aidan met her gaze. His face taut as he struggled to control himself; his gaze conflicted.

"You know I can't," he replied huskily. "I made a promise and I must keep it. I'm sorry Freya but I must go."

"Aidan!" Aldwulf emerged from the hall, hurriedly doing up the cross-garters on his legs. "Is it true? Does the enemy approach?"

"They do," Aidan turned from Freya, the warrior's mask slipping into place. Gone was last night's lover. She did not know this man before her. "Ready the men, Aldwulf. We ride for Barrow Fields."

Chapter Nineteen

AIDAN SHRUGGED THE chain vest over his head and felt its weight settle against his chest; a sensation that he would always associate with battle. Standing before the smoldering fire pit in the hall, he placed leather arm guards over his forearms and upper arms and waited while Edwin laced them up for him. Felix was nowhere to be seen, and nor were the three other students.

This was the warriors ritual, one that meant war was coming and blood was about to be shed. Aidan's weapon of choice was not a sword—for only ealdormen and their kin carried these—but a spear. Aidan's spear had always meant a lot to him; it symbolized his freedom from slavery. Only a free man could wield one. This spear was around eight feet in length and made out of ash, with a lethal iron point. When fighting, Aidan always carried a spear in his right hand and a shield in his left.

As Edwin finished tightening his arm guards, Aidan's thoughts momentarily strayed from the approaching battle to Freya.

A hard knot of sorrow tightened in the center of his chest. The memories of last night broke over him, like water bursting from a dam. Last night he had known a joy he had never thought existed. He had been with plenty of women since reaching manhood, but none had made him feel like Freya did. Even now, he ached to rush to her, to touch and kiss her; to hear the sound of her voice and breathe in the scent of her skin. She made him feel truly alive. Wryd, fate, had cruelly cheated him. He had been given too little, too late.

Aidan took a deep breath and forced his thoughts on to what lay ahead. Edwin finished tightening the last arm guard and stepped back, his blue eyes huge on his thin face.

"Thank you lad." Aidan forced a smile. "Look out for the others. If the battle goes ill, the Mercians will come here. You may want to consider hiding in the woods until everything's done."

Edwin nodded wordlessly, although Aidan could see that his words had given the boy no solace. As young as Edwin was, he understood that there was no honor in hiding in the woods while the rest of his male kin went into battle.

"Listen to me Edwin." Aidan hunkered down so that their gazes were at the same level. "There is nothing pretty about war. I know you want to be with your father and your brothers, but it is best you stay here. The other boys are not as strong as you; they need you to look after them."

Edwin's eyes filled with tears.

"Why would I want to be with my father when he sold me for a pouch of gold?"

Aidan felt sadness stab him through the guts at the anguish on the boy's face.

"It's true," he admitted gently. "You owe such a man nothing. All the same, you are needed here. Felix will not protect you when they come."

With that he gave Edwin a fierce, brief hug and got to his feet. He felt the boy's gaze burning into him and forced himself to turn away. Aidan strode out of the hall and, not for the first time, wished that things were different.

Freya stood in the yard and watched Aidan, and the twenty spears who had followed him and Sigeberht to Beodricesworth, gather with their horses in front of the hall. They were all heavily armed and armored, and carried heavy wooden shields and lethal-tipped spears. Aidan stood in their midst. His face was unreadable as he waited for the last spear to join him.

A strange numbness spread over Freya. She did not want him to go but she knew he must. She was helpless to stop the course of events now. Yet she would not have changed last night for anything. It would be her dearest memory, till death.

Stop it! She berated herself. *You're telling yourself he's never coming back. You're acting as if this will be the last time you'll ever see him.*

Aidan approached her now. All twenty warriors waited behind him; some were tightening their horses' girths, while others were mounting. He stopped before her and Freya looked down at her feet, unable to meet his gaze. Her vision swam with tears and she cursed herself as she struggled to keep control. He did not need to see a woman's tears before he went into battle.

"Freya." His voice was soft but rough with pain.

Freya inhaled deeply and raised her face so that their eyes met.

"You know why I must go, don't you?"

Freya nodded, blinking furiously. She could not stop the hot tears that streamed down her face.

"Yes," she managed. And it was true, she did know. When her father had gone to war she had not understood; his loyalty to a king who was going into battle to settle old scores seemed foolhardy. At the time, she and her mother had grieved for the fact that Aelli had thrown his life away for a reckoning that was not even his. Yet, this was different. This was a threat to the safety of the kingdom and of all that lived within it. She did understand why he was going—only it did not make it any easier to bear.

"Come back safe," she whispered. "Please don't throw your life away."

Aidan's face twisted as if she had just slapped him. Then, he gave a pained smile.

"I am not a reckless man, Freya. How do you think I've lived this long?"

"Wyrd has been good to you perhaps."

"Fate shines on a man who shows courage—*wyrd oft nereð unfaégne eorl þonne his ellen déah*," Aidan replied with a grin. The expression was

288

that of the man who had stolen her heart, and not of the stern warrior of just moments earlier.

Freya smiled back at him through her tears. "I hope you are right."

Aidan pulled her into his arms and kissed her softly on the lips. It was a sad kiss, full of longing and unspoken words. Freya entwined her arms about his neck and kissed him back, before stepping back and putting some distance between them. Part of her did not believe he was going; that she may never see him again.

Aidan took a deep breath and Freya saw the warrior's mask slide down over his features.

"You need to go from here. As soon as we leave, take as many provisions as you can carry, and steal a horse if you have to. Travel back to Woodbridge Haven, to your mother's house. You will be safe there. I will find you."

Freya nodded, not trusting herself to say another word.

"I promise you this," he said fiercely, seeing the doubt on her face. "If I live through this battle, I will find you."

With that, Aidan turned on his heel and strode over to his horse. He swung up onto the saddle and slid his feet into the stirrups. He then gathered the reins and exchanged one last glance with Freya before he wheeled his horse away.

"We ride to Barrow," he shouted, "and to battle!"

Freya stood alone in the yard and watched the warriors ride over the brow of the hill. When they disappeared, she turned back to the hall with a hollow feeling in her stomach. Hereric was standing before the door, his elfin face pale and strained. He approached Freya, fingering the slave collar about his neck as if it were strangling him.

"Are you leaving too?" he asked, and Freya realized that he was struggling not to cry.

Freya nodded.

Hereric's face started to tremble and his eyes filled with tears. "What will happen to me? I have nowhere to go."

"Hereric." Freya took the boy's hand and squeezed hard. "I'm not leaving you here. If you wish to, you can come with me."

The boy's face brightened, as if the sun had just come out from behind a cloud. "You would?" he asked, his voice quavering.

Freya nodded. "Now listen," she said, lowering her voice. "Once the battle's over we'll travel to my mother at Woodbridge Haven, but first there is something that must be done. Will you help me?"

Hereric nodded mutely, not knowing what Freya was about to suggest but so relieved to have a purpose that he did not appear to care.

"Help me gather some food to take with us," she urged him. "Take any bread you can find, even if it's stale, from the hall and meet me shortly in front of the store room."

Freya placed a wheel of cheese, eight crisp red apples and a few handfuls of carrots and onions into a jute sack. The sack was of the same kind she had used during her foiled escape in early summer- it seemed like a lifetime ago now. Then, she added a large piece of salted pork and tied the top of the sack with a piece of string.

In the murky light inside the store, where the only light came from the open door, she caught sight of a knife protruding from another wheel of cheese. She needed a knife. It would come in handy for preparing food, and it would be the only weapon she had. Freya pulled the knife out of the cheese and slipped it into the leather pouch that hung from her girdle.

Freya stepped outside to find Hereric waiting for her. He wore a coarse sacking cloak, which would at least keep the rain off, and carried a sack similar to hers. At the sight of him Freya felt a pang. She would have liked to have brought the other boys away with her as well. Yet she knew they would not want to leave the Lark Valley and their families in Barrow.

"I took three loaves of yesterday's bread," he announced proudly.

"Is that so!" A voice boomed out behind them.

Felix of Burgundy stepped out of the shadows.

Freya's stomach plummeted. Not now—not when she and Hereric were so close to freedom.

"Thieving theows!" Felix snarled, his eyes bulging with the force of his outrage. "How dare you steal from your master!"

He made a grab for Hereric, who dodged him easily and scampered backwards.

"Conniving bitch!" Felix advanced on Freya. "Sigeberht treated you better than you deserved and this is how you repay him?"

Freya sidled around, so that the store house was no longer at her back. "Sigeberht is not here to give the orders any longer," she snarled at Felix. "You aren't, nor will you ever be my master."

Felix lunged at her.

Freya was ready for him. After Ecgric's attack she had vowed to fight any man who attacked her, even if it led to her death. She was tired to the depths of her soul of being downtrodden. Last night with Aidan had freed her from her life as a slave; she was now free and intended to stay that way.

Felix grasped her around the throat, with the intent of throttling her. But striking with ruthless determination, Freya drove her knee up into his cods; like she had with Ecgric, only harder.

The monk's howl cleaved the morning air like an axe. He dropped Freya as if he grasped a hot coal and crumpled to the ground wailing.

Freya did not waste a moment more. She picked up her sack, darted around Felix and sprinted away from the hall.

"Follow me, Hereric!" she called over her shoulder, "Run!"

They ran like hares pursued by hounds, their feet barely skimming the ground. Out of the valley and into the woodland beyond, still carrying their sacks of food, they sprinted. On and on they ran, until their breathing grew ragged and the blood roared in their ears. They fled until the stitches in their sides forced them to slow their pace.

Eventually, just short of Saxham, Freya stumbled to a halt. Bent double, she took great, gasping breaths of air into her burning lungs. Beside her,

Hereric flopped on to his back, his thin ribcage heaving up and down like forge bellows.

"Freya!" Hereric eventually gasped, rolling over on to his side and fixing her with a desperate stare. "We've been running in the wrong direction. Woodbridge Haven lies many leagues to the east!"

"I know," Freya eventually managed. She straightened up and wiped the sweat from her eyes. "We are not going to Woodbridge Haven just yet. First, we travel to Barrow Fields."

Chapter Twenty

AIDAN WALKED ONTO the edge of Barrow Fields; a huge grassy expanse bordered by Barrow Woods to the south, and stopped for a moment. The fields lay just beyond the village of Barrow itself. The East Anglian army had gathered on the eastern end of the field. The Mercians would come from the west.

Like the other warriors who had joined him from Beodricesworth, Aidan had left his horse at Barrow. Unlike Gaul, where Aidan had been used to wielding a spear on horseback, it appeared that here in Britannia, only the king and certain ealdormen rode horses into battle. Everyone else fought on foot.

Aidan's gaze scanned the sea of swords, spears and axes before him. He was looking for a familiar face in the crowd; the face of a friend.

He eventually found him.

"Aidan!" Lothar shouldered his way through the throng and clasped his friend in a bear-hug. "I was beginning to think you would not come."

"You knew I would." Aidan forced a smile. "Someone has to watch your back."

Lothar snorted before stepping back and casting a shrewd eye over Aidan. "Something has happened," he noted with a frown. "What is it?"

"Have you seen the king?"

"Which one?"

"Sigeberht."

"He is here?" Lothar's frown deepened. "I thought the coward refused to come."

"He did," Aidan replied, his gaze sweeping over the army, "but Ecgric brought him anyway."

At that moment, the milling crowd of spearmen before them parted and Ecgric, astride a heavy-set black stallion, rode through their midst towards the front line. At his side, carrying a spear, his face ashen with fear, walked Oeric. Behind him, Ecgric towed Sigeberht.

Even brought low, Sigeberht the Righteous walked tall and proud. Conspicuous in his monk's habit, he carried his staff in one hand. A rope had been fitted about his neck, so that if he struggled or tried to run away, he would strangle himself. One of his eyes had now swollen shut and dry blood covered his chin; yet Sigeberht appeared oblivious to his injuries.

"Woden," Lothar hissed. "He's not armed."

"He refuses to bear a weapon," Aidan replied, his gaze never leaving Sigeberht. "He will go into battle as you see him, bearing only a staff."

Lothar shook his head and swore under his breath. Aidan tore his gaze from Sigeberht and regarded his friend squarely once more. He could see that the Frank's face was dark with anger.

"Most of these men are here for Sigeberht, not that ferret Ecgric," Lothar growled. "News of Sigeberht's taking of Rendlaesham, of his valor and skill as a leader of warriors, spread throughout the kingdom. They would not have come here if they thought Ecgric had called them."

"How big is our army?"

"Five-hundred."

"And the Mercian army?"

"From what we've heard, at least eight-hundred. The difference is big enough to matter if morale is low."

As he finished speaking, Lothar hefted his axe. Only a warrior of Lothar's strength and build could wield one of these weapons effectively. It was a long-shafted, double-headed 'bearded' battle-axe; a lethal weapon in the style of the northmen. It was a weapon that could shatter shields and slide through flesh like butter. It was an axe made for battle, rather than for felling trees or working timber, with a long ash shaft inlaid with langets; metal bands that protected the wood from enemy blades.

"How long will Sigeberht live if someone attacks him with one of these?" Lothar asked grimly.

"You've seen him fight," Aidan replied, adjusting his lime-wood shield so that it hung from his back. "Even with a staff Sigeberht is dangerous."

Lothar rolled his eyes. "Listen to you. Even now you're still loyal to him. Even after how he's treated you. He's elevated that son of a pox-ridden whore to king while he treats you like something he has just scraped off his boot. Yet you still treat him like he is Woden himself!"

"Is there any point in me raging against him now Lothar?" Aidan shot back, his anger finally surfacing. "If you and I want to survive this, we need to drive our rage against the Mercians, not each other."

Lothar's mouth compressed in a thin line at this, but he eventually nodded.

Aidan stepped forward and placed his hands on his friend's shoulders. Their faces were just inches apart.

"We have much to live for," he said quietly. "You want to return home to Aedilhild and I want to be with Freya. You were right Lothar—I am in love with her. I should have told her before I left Beodricesworth. Now it's too late."

Lothar's expression softened. "You should have told her." His voice roughened then as he struggled to compose himself. "Aedilhild is with child. I must return to her."

Aidan nodded. "Then we must focus on that, and nothing else."

It was then that Aidan spotted another, familiar figure, making his way through the army towards the front. It was Sigeberht's cousin—Annan. He was a striking sight; his leather armor creaking and the ring vest he wore across his chest clinking. His long, blond hair had been tied back for battle and his handsome face was set in hard lines. At his side was a heavy sword while on his back he carried a lime-wood shield.

Judging from the grim expression on Annan's face, he had already seen Sigeberht and was on his way to confront him. Aidan and Lothar fell in behind Annan and followed him to the front.

They found Sigeberht, standing alone on the edge of the fyrd, with the rope still tied around his neck. Nearby, Ecgric spoke in intense tones with a group of his ealdormen; Bercthun of Barrow was among them.

Aidan and Lothar hung back as Annan approached Sigeberht.

"Cousin." Annan stopped before Sigeberht and dropped to one knee. "My King. What evil has befallen you?"

Sigeberht smiled down at his cousin and winced at his split lip. "There's little use in kneeling before me now Annan," he said gently. "I have renounced my worldly kingdom and now live only for the heavenly kingdom. I refuse to fight—but it remains my choice."

"Please reconsider," Annan replied, his voice urgent. "You know that you will die if you go into battle unarmed."

"We all must die cousin," Sigeberht replied with the same gentle smile. "Sooner or later it comes to us all."

Sigeberht's gaze then shifted over Annan's shoulder and came to rest on Aidan. His good eye widened slightly.

"You're here Aidan—why?"

Aidan stepped forward. He felt a surge of relief at having the chance to speak with Sigeberht before they went into battle. He had thought Sigeberht would have refused to acknowledge him after the final words between them back at Beodricesworth.

"I gave my word I would come, and I have," Aidan replied gently. "I'm sorry I disappointed you, but most of all I'm sorry it has come to this."

Sigeberht gave a sad smile at that. "I too wish things were different Aidan. There were so many things I wanted to do at Beodricesworth and now I'll never get the chance."

"You would," Annan cut in, his voice urgent. "If you'd agree to carry a sword you might live through this."

"I'd not waste your breath trying to convince him." Ecgric turned from consulting with his ealdormen. His face twisted when he looked upon Sigeberht. "He has clearly lost his mind. Speak with us instead Annan. We are discussing tactics. You are more use to us than to that craven."

Annan's face darkened. He was about to reply when the sound of a horn echoed over Barrow Fields. It was a mournful, lonely sound that caused the fine hair on the back of the men's necks to prickle.

Aidan, who stood a few paces back from Annan, turned and looked west. There, emerging over the brow of a low hill, at the far end of the fields, was a long bristling line of spears.

The Mercians had come.

Panic rippled through the army. Aidan felt a cold sense of foreboding clench at his chest; he could taste their fear. This was not how an army should approach war. They needed a leader who could inspire them, set fire to their blood and turn them into fell, dangerous warriors. Ecgric had failed to do this, and they were all too aware of their mortality. A larger army approached them – an army hungry for war.

Ecgric appeared oblivious to this. Upon setting eye on the approaching army he sprang onto his horse and rode up his lines.

"Form the shield-wall!" he shouted, brandishing *Æthelfrith's Bane* high. "Do it now!"

Then, Ecgric reined his stallion around and galloped back down his lines to where Sigeberht, Annan, Aidan and Lothar awaited his orders.

"Aidan of Connacht," Ecgric sneered. "Do you know what a shield-wall is?"

"Yes," Aidan replied coldly. Shield-walls were only used here in Britannia, and as such he had never fought in a battle that used them. Nevertheless, he knew what a shield-wall was. All warriors did.

"Then it's time you showed that fighting skill I've heard so much about. You will join the first line of this shield-wall. Let's see how much fire you've got in your belly now!"

Aidan felt the chill that had settled in his chest, slide down to his guts.

Of course, he should have expected this.

Ecgric wanted revenge for his humiliation on the evening he had tried to rape Freya. Aidan had sorely wounded his pride, and he had made the mistake of thinking Ecgric had forgotten about it.

A man like Ecgric never forgot about such things.

Aidan nodded to Ecgric and schooled his features into an impassive mask. He glanced across at Lothar and the two friends exchanged one last look. Then, Aidan un-slung his shield from over his back and strode across to where a line of spearmen were forming the shield-wall.

Even though he had never fought in one, Aidan knew the odds of surviving the first line of a shield-wall were slim—especially against a significantly bigger army. Still, he would rather have been boiled alive than see the satisfaction on Ecgric's face if he had showed even a glimmer of fear.

Jostling himself into place between two warriors who looked barely out of boyhood, Aidan saw the naked terror on their faces.

This would not do.

"Are you ready to send those Mercian dogs running with their tails between their legs?" he grinned, showing his teeth. "I hope so, because this kingdom—your kingdom—is depending on us keeping this shield-wall from breaking. Imagine one of them raping your woman, or your mother or sister. Imagine them burning your village and taking your brothers as slaves. They will do it. If you show them a shred of mercy they will stick you like a pig."

Watching the faces of the young men, Aidan saw the anger kindle in their eyes. "The men of the East Angles are made of iron," he pressed on, noticing that his speech had gained the attention of other spearmen who were jostling for position around them. "Remember who you are fighting for. Your courage cannot fail. Send these men into the afterlife so that they may face eternity in torment. Let them wade through wild, poisonous rivers. Let Nithhogg suck their blood and wolves rip them limb from limb!"

That was all the warriors needed. Aidan had just spoken of the otherworld those who committed evil deeds would be consigned to—and of the dragon residing there who would torment their enemies. He had reminded them that they had every right to stand firm and defend their home. They, not Penda and his invading army, were in the right.

A roar went up along the shield-wall and Aidan allowed himself a grim smile.

That's better. Let Penda hear that and pause. Even if we all fall on the battlefield, this will be no easy victory.

Freya heard the armies before she saw them: the shouts of men rising and falling in waves, and the rhythmic beating of spears against shields. With Hereric at her side, Freya crept through the undergrowth, while attempting not to get snagged by black thorn and bramble, and made her way to Barrow Wood's edge. Hiding behind the trunk of an old elm, she peeked out and looked for the first time upon Barrow Fields.

The sight of the two armies—still some way apart while they made preliminary preparations for war—made her breath catch. She had never seen so many men in one place. Spears bristled against the skyline like a carpet of nails. They were too far off for her to make out the faces, but the din echoed across Barrow Fields. It was a bloodthirsty, raw sound.

Freya shuddered. This was no place for a woman. She wanted no part in this slaughter; she was loath to stand here and look on while men butchered each other senselessly. Yet she found herself rooted to the spot. Somewhere in that heaving sea of men was Aidan. She would not leave this spot until she knew his fate.

Tearing her gaze from the battle lines, Freya glanced over at Hereric.

I shouldn't have brought him here. He's too young to watch this.

And yet Hereric's face was composed. His eyes looked as if they belonged to someone much older. Freya knew little of Hereric's life before he became the king's theow. Only that his mother had also been a slave, who had been raped by one of the king's thegns. She had died of a fever when her son was tiny. Hereric had grown up in slavery and had been kicked like a dog far too many times in his short life. He would handle this much better than her, Freya realized.

Freya looked back at the two armies, in time to see a huge man atop a shaggy bay warhorse ride up and down the Mercian lines. He stood up on his stirrups and bellowed at his army, the great sword he wielded flashing in the sunlight. He wore an iron helmet that obscured his face. This must be the infamous Penda: the Mercian warmonger. Even from this distance he looked terrifying and Freya crouched lower against the tree trunk in response, despite that she knew he could not see her. In front of the East

Anglian line, Ecgric rode his black stallion along his lines, employing the same tactic; only his lack of charisma and commanding presence were woefully evident. Penda's warriors roared as their leader galloped past. Ecgric's men were painfully silent.

After a while, both kings retreated behind the lines and the armies advanced to close quarters. Each army appeared a living entity, rather than a crowd of men, as they edged closer like two giant caterpillars.

The start of the battle, when it came, was almost a relief after the breathless waiting. It fell swiftly in a hammer blow. One moment the two shield walls were facing each other, the next a battle cry echoed across Barrow Fields. Penda's shield-wall advanced. Arrows, javelins, axes and rocks flew.

The two shield-walls collided with a terrific crunch.

Chapter Twenty-one

SHIELD TO SHIELD, the Mercian and East Anglian armies pushed against each other in an attempt to break the enemy line. Aidan kept his head tucked in and down as arrows flew overhead and peppered the shields behind him. A rock glanced off his shoulder and he narrowly missed being gored when a spear found a gap between his shield and that belonging to the warrior beside him, and jabbed viciously.

The roar of men's voices was almost deafening; the air was rank with the smell of blood, sweat and fear. Somewhere in the midst of it, the fire of battle caught alight in his veins. He slammed his foot down on the protruding spear and rammed his shield against his attacker. Then he thrust his own spear through the gap. A strangled cry reached him. When he twisted his spear and pulled it back, it was coated in blood.

The shield-wall buckled and strained; it was a vain attempt to hold back the tide but the warriors who made up that first line made a valiant and prolonged effort to keep the Mercians at bay. Sweat streamed down Aidan's face; the muscles in his upper arms and shoulders burned from the effort it was taking to keep his shield up.

When the East Anglian shield-wall finally broke, all hell broke loose. The warrior on Aidan's right fell with a spear through the chest, as did the man to his left.

The shield-wall shattered like leaves in the wind.

The Mercians fell upon them, howling. Aidan slammed his shield against a warrior who was coming straight for him and gored him with his spear. The warrior crumpled screaming, but Aidan barely had time to draw breath before another man replaced him. As he fought, Aidan caught glimpses of his surroundings. To his left, he saw Sigeberht. Incredibly, he was still alive, although his staff was about half the length it had been before the battle. Further on, again to his left, he saw Annan, howling the Wuffinga battle cry as he swung his sword with deadly precision. To his right, Aidan caught a glimpse of Lothar. The Frank fought like a berserker. He howled as he cut down Mercians like barley stalks.

There was no sign of Ecgric; Aidan imagined he was cowering somewhere at the back of the army – whereas Penda was right out front. He was a fell, terrifying sight in his blood-splattered iron helmet and gleaming breastplate. He had either left his horse behind, or had lost it in the battle. On foot, he moved with surprising grace for such a big man. He roared like a stag with each stroke of his sword.

Aidan saw the moment Penda spotted Sigeberht and came for him in great strides—cutting down man after man who tried to block his path. In the meantime, Aidan was forced to turn his attention fully to defending himself from a crazed axeman. Only his nimbleness and skill with a spear saved his life. He had just driven his spear through his opponent's neck and was ripping it free when he saw Penda drive his sword through Sigeberht's chest.

The king fell to his knees before he crumpled to one side. Penda withdrew his sword, kicked Sigeberht aside, and headed towards Annan.

Aidan felt pain lance through his side as a spear sliced through his leather armor and nicked his ribs. In response, he smashed his shield into his assailant's face, reducing it to a bloody pulp before he finished him off.

Then, to his right, he saw Lothar fall.

His friend had looked invincible, as formidable a warrior as Penda himself. Then a hand-axe hurtled through the air and caught him in the throat. Lothar dropped his axe and fell clutching his bleeding neck.

Raw grief ripped through Aidan. It was a lance of pure agony, as if he had just been stabbed.

Not Lothar.

Aidan had never doubted that Lothar would survive this, even if the rest of them fell.

Lothar had so much to live for.

Grief turned Aidan savage. He threw aside his spear, retrieved a fallen sword from beside one of the dead East Anglian ealdormen, and unleashed himself on the enemy in a killing rage.

The only thing that stopped him was the dull, meaty thud of an arrow piercing his left shoulder. He staggered back and another arrow hit him, just below the first. Then a sharp, blinding pain to the back of his head obliterated everything else. Aidan fell forward and knew no more.

Shortly after the battle started, Freya could bear to look upon it no more. She left Hereric to gape, wide-eyed and ashen, while she turned from the carnage and sat with her back against the old elm. She stared out at the woodland and covered her ears with her hands. Yet it barely muffled the din. The sound of iron, pain and death echoed inside her skull.

Somewhere, Aidan was in the midst of it, fighting to stay alive. Before the battle, Freya had felt hope that he may survive but now, as the chilling screams of dying men seeped past her fingers and stabbed at her ears, she felt increasing waves of hopelessness wash over her.

How could Aidan survive this? How could anyone? Freya rested her forehead on her knees and eventually let the tears come.

Eventually, the sounds of battle dimmed. It was gradual, but when Hereric began to pluck at Freya's skirt, the roar had been replaced with the muffled sounds of the dying.

"It's over," Hereric told her, his cheeks streaked with tears. "The Mercians have won."

Freya turned numbly and braced herself to look out onto the devastation.

It was worse than she had expected—a blanket of bodies strewn, broken and impaled over the field. The light was starting to fade. It was late afternoon; the battle had begun just after noon. The East Angles had defended themselves well, but in the end the Mercians had been too many.

"Look!" Hereric hissed, pointing to where a handful of injured men were being dragged west towards the Mercian encampment. "There are some survivors. They're taking them prisoner."

Freya craned her neck and struggled to make out the features of the survivors. There was one man, tall and blond, who stood out from the rest but he was not close enough for her to recognize his face. It was impossible to make out the faces of the others. Could Aidan be among them? Despite their injuries, the men fought their captors as they were dragged from the battlefield. One of the men received a spear through his belly for the trouble and was left to die while the others were taken away.

"We need to go and search the field," Hereric refused to take his gaze off the dead. "Maybe Sigeberht or Aidan are alive?"

"We need to wait till the Mercians have gone," Freya replied, trying to prevent her voice from trembling. She was not sure she could go out there and walk amongst that carnage; although if she wanted to know Aidan's fate she would have to. "It's not long till nightfall and they are exhausted. I'd wager that they'll be back tomorrow morning to loot the dead. We should have some time before it gets dark."

Hereric nodded and was just about to suggest something when a rustling in the undergrowth behind them, made both woman and boy start.

"Get behind me Hereric," Freya hissed, drawing the knife she had taken from the store. Silently, the boy obeyed.

There was another sound, the cracking of someone stepping on a dry twig, before a tussled blond head appeared from the bushes.

"Edwin!" Freya's heart thudded painfully against her ribs with relief. "You nearly frightened us both to death!"

The boy slowly got to his feet, wincing as a bramble snagged his arm. He moved forward, his gaze widening when he caught a glimpse of the battlefield behind Freya and Hereric.

"Why are you here?" Freya asked, although she regretted the words as soon as she had said them. What a foolish question—it was obvious why he was here.

"I couldn't stay behind," he said quietly, his eyes brimming with tears. "I had to see if my father and brothers have lived. I must know what happened to them."

Dusk settled across Barrow Fields in a grey haze and tendrils of white mist snaked across the ground, forming a welcome veil for the three figures that crept out of the woods and hurried across to where the dead lay.

Freya glanced nervously over her left shoulder to where the fires from the Mercian encampment glowed in the distance—pale orange through the fog. They would not be able to linger here or they would be spotted.

The three companions fanned out and began to comb the center of the field, with the intention of moving gradually east. Nausea rose in Freya. The ground was slippery with gore; the earth stained dark with blood. The smell of death was metallic and ripe. It was the smell of a slaughterhouse.

Hereric found Sigeberht. He lay on his side, his eyes sightless, his chest covered in blood. The boy began to sniff as Freya and Edwin approached him; Sigeberht had always treated the young slave kindly and Hereric had worshipped him.

Forcing themselves on, stumbling as they reeled at the horror of it all, Freya, Hereric and Edwin continued combing the battlefield. During the course of their search they found Aldwulf, Lothar and many others—all dead.

Edwin found his father, Bercthun, and his four brothers—all slain. Edwin crouched over his father, weeping, while Hereric sat by his side in silent solace. Meanwhile, Freya continued to search the dead, moving gradually east. Aidan was nowhere to be found. Eventually, she found Ecgric. He was far from the front lines, next to the corpse of his regal black stallion and his ever-faithful Oeric. Ecgric lay on his front with an axe embedded between his shoulder blades—almost as if he had been fleeing when the end came.

Freya reached the end of the field, but there was still no sign of Aidan. Maybe he had been among the survivors after all. Or perhaps she had missed him. Visibility was poor and getting worse by the moment. The mist wreathed like probing fingers. She returned to the boys and helped Edwin to his feet.

"Come," she whispered. "We must go now."

They were crossing the center of the field, making their way back towards the woods, when Freya spied a man pinned under the corpse of a huge warrior. Intuition needled at her. She left the boys and sidled round to get a closer look. There, she saw a shock of shaggy jet black hair.

Freya's stomach clenched.

She had only ever seen one man with hair that shade.

"Help me." She motioned to the boys. "I think Aidan is under here."

Hereric and Edwin hurried back and, together, the three of them heaved the corpse of the Mercian axeman off the man beneath.

It was Aidan. Freya's first thought was that he was dead.

He lay on his front. The back of his head was a matt of hair and blood and she could see the points of two arrows sticking out of his left shoulder. They gently rolled him over and Freya knelt at his side, fearing the worst.

"He's alive," Hereric hissed. "Look, his chest is moving!"

All three of them stared at Aidan's ribs. There, they saw the shallow rise and fall. Hardly daring to believe her eyes, Freya reached down and felt for his pulse. His skin was warm and his pulse was easy to find, although not strong as he had obviously lost a lot of blood.

Freya glanced over her shoulder at the Mercian encampment and saw the lights of torches slowly approaching. The enemy was not going to wait till daybreak to search for spoils after all.

"Help me carry him," Freya urged. "We must get off this field now."

Unspeaking, the boys nodded and, together, they lifted Aidan's prostrate form off the ground. Stumbling over the dead in their haste, they carried him into the woods.

Chapter Twenty-two

IT WAS A still night. Smoke from the fire pit at the heart of Penda's tent drifted lazily towards the opening above. Outside, torches that had been staked into the ground, framed either-side of the entrance. They burned gently; their flames licking up at the moths dancing around them. Mist snaked through the Mercian encampment in the aftermath of battle.

There was little movement in the encampment. The muffled cries and groans of the wounded was one of the few sounds, apart from the low timbre of men's voices inside the tents.

Inside the king's tent, Penda of Mercia poured himself a cup of mead and stood watching the glowing embers of his fire pit. The tent was a cavernous space, with the king's sleeping area curtained off at one end. Heavy tapestries hung from the walls and rush-matting had been rolled out over the floor. Although temporary, it was a comfortable and kingly abode. A magnificent, blood-stained sword hung from one of the tapestries: *Æthelfrith's Bane*. The axeman who had slain Ecgric of Exning had pried the sword from his victim's dead hands and brought it to his king as a trophy.

Penda paid little attention to his surroundings. He was deep in thought as he sipped meditatively at his mead. He drank from a golden cup, studded with jewels; his victory cup he liked to call it. Even dressed in a linen tunic and leggings, cross-gartered to the knee, with little finery or armor, Penda of Mercia cut a formidable figure. He stood at well over six feet and was heavily muscled. A shock of white blond hair ran down his back, and his face—belonging to a man who looked no older than his early-thirties—was carved of stone. He may have been handsome as a boy, but as a man his face was cruel and austere. Pale blue eyes flickered in the firelight.

There was much on Penda's mind tonight. For the first time in years, he thought of his older brother—Eafa. They had never been close. Eafa had been too wary of Penda as a possible threat to the throne to ever befriend him. He had always known that Penda was cleverer than him, and a far better strategist. In fact, Eafa's attempt to butcher the East Anglian royal family nearly five years earlier—an attack that was as badly planned as it was executed—had resulted in Eafa's death and had cast shame upon the Mercians. Penda had stepped directly into the breach left by his foolhardy brother and had barely thought of him since. Yet now, after defeating the East Anglians in battle, memories of Eafa resurfaced. Not particularly pleasant ones, since Eafa had been cold and bullying towards his younger brother.

"I succeeded where you failed dear brother." Penda murmured, raising his cup to the firelight. "I've taken back dignity and pride for our family."

"Milord." A voice behind Penda caused him to turn sharply from the fire. His instincts were still battle-honed, and had he been carrying his sword he would have raised it. He relaxed slightly when he saw it was one of his ealdormen. "We have brought the prisoners, as you asked."

Penda nodded, before finishing his mead in one gulp. "Thank you, Aldric. Bring them in."

Five men, bruised, bloodied and battered, were herded into the tent. A tall, blond man with sea-blue eyes led the group.

"Annan of the Wuffingas," Penda acknowledged their leader. "Wyrd did shine upon us today. I never thought to catch the nephew of the great King Raedwald himself alive."

Annan's face darkened at this observation. It was a terrible insult to a warrior not to let him die a warrior's death on the battlefield.

"We fought and you bested me," Annan ground out roughly. "You could have killed me then but chose not to. If I stand here before you it's because you chose to let me live. We both know it was not mercy that stayed your hand. What do you want Penda?"

The King of Mercia smiled. He was sharp this one; far cleverer than that oaf Sigeberht had handed his kingdom over to. Yet despite his brave words, Penda could see that Annan was in pain from his injuries. Penda's blade had sliced him across the ribs and cut deeply into one shoulder. The wounds had been tended to and bandaged but Annan's skin was ashen in the firelight and covered with a faint sheen of sweat. The other East Angles who had survived the battle, looked on, hollow eyed. They could see that Penda was playing with Annan.

"What do I want?" Penda sighed, warming his hands in front of the fire and pretending to ponder the matter. "I think you know exactly why you're still alive Annan. I want you to take the East Anglian throne and, in gratitude for keeping your life, you are to bend the knee to Mercia."

A cold silence followed Penda's words. There was no surprise on Annan's face. He had known this was coming. Yet his face twisted savagely. "No."

Penda's smile broadened. "I don't remember phrasing that as a question. It's not a request, but an order."

"And if I refuse?"

"Then I kill each of these men, one by one in front of you."

"Nithhogg take you!" Annan snarled. "I will not rule as your puppet!"

Penda turned calmly to his ealdorman and inclined his head. "Aldric—if you please."

The warrior struck so quickly that none present had the chance to react. One minute, the young, injured warrior beside Annan was alive, the next his throat was cut and he writhed on the ground, clutching his neck as his blood flowed out onto the rush matting.

"We have all night," Penda said quietly. "And I assure you that they will not all die as easily as this one. We will kill each man slower than the last. I'll make sure the last one begs for his mother before I kill him. Now what is your answer?"

Penda had seen anger in many forms—but never had he seen such pure, killing rage as that in Annan's eyes. For a moment he paused, on the brink of reconsidering his decision to place Annan as ruler of the East Angles; a king who would do his bidding. Perhaps it would have been wiser to have killed him on the battlefield after all. Yet Annan was the right choice. He was of Wuffinga blood and that mattered to the East Angles. The people would be suspicious of a ruler they did not know. They would not suspect that Annan was Mercia's puppet.

"I'm still waiting Annan," Penda's smile grew thin. "What is your answer?"

Annan's gaze dropped to the body of the warrior who was still twitching at his feet. Penda felt a thrill of victory as he did so. He had known that Annan would not want these men's death on his conscience.

"Very well," Annan ground out finally, his voice barely above a whisper. "I will be king."

The small campfire crackled as Hereric added some more twigs to it. Edwin edged closer to the flames and warmed his hands. Although the wreathing fog meant that there would be no frost, it was a cold night and the damp seemed to drive straight into their bones. After the horror they had witnessed that afternoon, shock settled over the companions in a chill shroud, making their limbs shake and their teeth chatter.

They had managed to carry Aidan some distance from Barrow Fields, and were now in the heart of the strip of woodland between the village of Barrow and the Fields. They would not be safe in Barrow Woods long, but Freya guessed that for tonight at least, they could linger.

While the boys lit a fire, Freya took a close look at Aidan's wounds. They were serious, although not immediately life-threatening: a nasty gash to the ribs, two arrows piercing his left shoulder and a wound to the back of his head. The years Freya had spent tending the sick and wounded at her mother's side, meant that she knew exactly what to do now.

With the boys' assistance, she removed Aidan's leather armor and cut away the linen tunic underneath. Using water from the bladder she carried, she gently washed the wound on his ribs. It needed stitching but she had left her bone needle back in Beodricesworth. She left his head wound for now. The matt of bloodied hair was at least providing some protection and she decided to leave off her inspection until she had better light. With Hereric's help, Freya snipped off the ends of the two arrows and slowly drew them out of Aidan's flesh. She then instructed Edwin to boil a little water in the small iron pot Hereric had stolen from the hall. Once the water was bubbling, she poured a little over Aidan's shoulder and chest wounds to cleanse them properly and stave off infection.

Freya's eyes stung with fatigue as she ripped Aidan's tunic into bandages. She would use them to bind his wounds tomorrow morning. For now, they lay Aidan as comfortably as they could near the fire and covered him with the blood stained cloak they had used as a makeshift stretcher to remove him from the battlefield. Bone-weary, Freya sat next to Aidan and gratefully took the hunk of bread and cheese that Hereric passed her. All three companions ate in silence; the only sound was the crackling of the fire and the rustling of night creatures in the undergrowth nearby.

Aidan's breath was a little deeper than earlier and his pulse stronger. After her supper, Freya gently dripped some water into his mouth and took a sip herself. Her water bladder was now empty.

"We'll need to find a stream tomorrow morning," she told the boys. "We won't be able to travel far without water."

"There's a brook outside Barrow," Edwin replied, speaking for the first time since he had found his father and brothers dead on the battlefield. "We can fill up our bladders there." Edwin paused for a moment, his face, hollowed and gaunt with grief. "I can also get us a cart for Aidan. We won't be able to travel far, or fast, if we have to carry him."

Freya nodded, giving Edwin a tired smile. Bercthun of Barrow had under-estimated his youngest son. Edwin may have been small for his age, and not as rough and ready as his brothers, but he had a quiet, sure strength and maturity, rarely seen in a boy his age.

"Freya." Hereric poked the fire with a stick and fixed her with an earnest gaze. "How far is it to Woodbridge Haven? Will Aidan make it?"

Freya sighed and tried to force her tired mind to calculate how long the journey would take. "Seven days at the least," she said finally, "although with Aidan it may take us longer. We're still wearing our slave collars, which might draw unwelcome attention. As such, it's best we keep off the roads unless absolutely necessary."

Hereric nodded, taking it all in. "I have my slingshot," he told them. "I can hunt birds and rabbits on the journey, once our food runs out."

Freya smiled at the boy's eagerness. This was his first taste of freedom and he did not intend to waste it. Despite her misgivings earlier, she was glad Hereric was with her.

They packed up at daybreak. Freya bound Aidan's wounds and replaced his leather vest over the bandages on his chest and shoulder; it would give him a little extra protection. She bound his head carefully, wary of winding the bandage too tight as she did not yet know the extent of his injury. Then, carrying their unconscious patient between them, they made their way towards Barrow.

The sun was just beginning to rise over the treetops to the east when they reached the fringes of Barrow Woods. As promised, a small brook babbled its way past them. Smoke wreathed from the thatched roofs of Barrow and a rooster crowed. Freya wondered if the villagers knew what had happened on Barrow Fields. Surely they would have sent someone to scout for them.

"Wait here," Edwin whispered. "I'll be back soon."

Neither Freya nor Hereric had a chance to say anything before Edwin slipped away, his thin figure wraithlike in his long woolen tunic and ankle boots. They filled their water bladders and waited in breathless silence.

Freya was beginning to worry that someone had seen him, when Edwin returned pulling a small wooden cart. It was a similar cart to the one Freya had used to collect supplies at Rendlaesham. It was light and well-made, and would make transporting Aidan much easier.

Carefully, they lifted Aidan onto the cart, and made a pillow for his injured head with some sacking. Then they covered him with the blood-stained cloak.

"I must leave you now." Edwin turned to Freya and Hereric, his thin face set in determination. "I'm staying here."

Freya stared back at Edwin for a moment, confused. Then, realizing that this had been his plan all along, she nodded. She had not really expected Edwin to accompany them to Woodbridge Haven. His family was here.

"So you won't go back to Beodricesworth? You know you'd be safer there."

Edwin shook his head. "I didn't mind my time there; Sigeberht was good to me and I enjoyed learning. Yet, life with Felix will not be the same. I might be safer in a monastery but my mother and sisters have lost all their men. I am all they have left. Soon the Mercians will come. Whatever happens, my kin need me."

"You're right, they do." Freya embraced Edwin and kissed the top of his head. "Keep them safe, Edwin. Keep yourself safe."

Hereric looked on the verge of tears as he hugged his friend. Life as a king's theow was a lonely existence. To most within the Great Hall he had been invisible. Most highborn children had either ignored or bullied him. His friendship with Edwin had been the first of his life.

"Live well, Hereric," Edwin told his friend, his eyes brimming with tears. "I will never forget you."

Wiping away tears of her own, Freya turned and picked up the cart's handles. Hereric fell in next to her and took one of the handles. Together, they lifted the cart and towed it forward.

Edwin stood at the edge of the woods, with the shadowy outline of Barrow behind him. When Freya had gone a few paces, she glanced back over her shoulder and looked upon the boy one last time. Edwin rewarded her with that fey, wistful smile that she had come to know so well. Then he raised his hand and waved farewell.

Chapter Twenty-three

THE FIRST DAY of their journey was a nerve-wracking game of cat and mouse. They were within easy reach of the Mercian army. Freya hoped that Penda would spend the next day celebrating his victory, rather than sending his warriors out to raid villages and hunt down any stragglers. Yet she had a gut feeling that their escape from the area would not be so easy.

As soon as Freya and Hereric left Barrow Woods behind, they were able to move quicker through sloping meadows, towing the cart behind them. Freya did not like being out in the open. It made her nervous. She kept getting an odd, tickling sensation between her shoulder blades, but when she turned to look over her shoulder, she could see nothing but grass and trees. Still, her intuition warned her that they were not safe here.

Despite her hopes, she knew the Mercians would be combing the land around Barrow Fields.

They were not far from Saxham now, and the surrounding woodland that stretched down to the upper reaches of the Lark Valley and Beodriceworth. Freya intended to cut behind Saxham and bypass the valley before heading south-east. Her plan was to make for the upper reaches of the River Deben. It was an ambitious and slightly foolhardy choice. Unlike the land around Woodbridge Haven, which she knew intimately, this stretch between Beodricesworth and the Deben was unknown to Freya. It would have been a safer, albeit slower, option to retrace their journey towards Rendlaesham and then veer south, but Freya decided against this. If the Mercians decided to ride to Rendlaesham, they would be taking the same route. It was too risky.

They had almost reached the line of trees behind Saxham when Freya skidded to a halt, causing the cart to buck behind her.

"What's wrong?" Hereric looked on in concern as Freya dropped to her knees and placed her palms on the ground.

"Feel the ground," Freya urged, her heart starting to pound. "It's shaking!"

Hereric followed her lead. His eyes widened. "Horses!"

"Run!" Freya leaped to her feet, grabbed the cart and took off towards the woodland. They crashed into the trees like hunted deer. Hereric had just finished helping Freya pull the cart into a thick matt of bracken, when the sound of thundering hoofs reached them.

Freya peered cautiously through the bracken and saw a band of warriors galloping towards the woods.

"Saxham," Freya whispered. Her voice caught as she remembered that friendly village and the Winterfylleth bonfire.

"But if they've come this far that means they've already sacked Barrow," Hereric whispered back. "What about Edwin?"

Freya shook her head. "I know not. We can only hope that Edwin was spared."

"Will they sack Beodricesworth too?"

Freya glanced over at the boy and realized he was terrified. She placed a reassuring hand on his shoulder, even if her bowels felt as if they were turning to water.

"Perhaps not," she ventured. "Even if Penda is pagan, he may still respect a holy place. He may spare Beodricesworth."

Once the warriors had crashed through the woods, making no attempt at stealth, Freya got to her feet and yanked the cart out of the bracken.

"Come. We need to move quickly while they're in Saxham. If we delay they may cut off our escape."

They skirted the woods close to Saxham; too close for soon the screams of the villagers reached them. Shortly after, smoke wafted through the woods.

The Mercians had set fire to the village.

Freya and Hereric fled, pulling the cart behind them and trying not to think about what the Mercian warriors were doing to the folk of Saxham. Aidan, still in a deep, injured sleep, was being jostled about during the bumpy journey. Yet they could not risk slowing their pace.

A short distance from Saxham, they passed through a leafy glade. Freya's breath stilled when she realized where they were. This was the place where she and Aidan had stopped on their way back from Saxham; where they had stripped naked in the moonlight and made love. The memories of that night rushed back. The memories warmed Freya's soul but brought with it a sweet pain. It had only been one night ago, but it felt as if weeks had passed.

Still, things could have turned out much worse. Aidan could have died like all the others. *He may only be half-alive, but at least he has a chance!*

The sight of the glade, and all it represented, galvanized Freya's resolve. It also helped her get their bearings. Instead of heading south, towards Beodricesworth, like she and Aidan had done just a day earlier, Freya angled the cart east.

She and Hereric fled through the woodland and out into open grassland. On and on they raced, with the cart bumping behind them, until their chests burned. By the time they could run no more, the sun hung high in the sky, signaling that it was about noon. They had been on the move, almost entirely without rest, since daybreak.

Freya unstoppered a water bladder and took a couple of gulps before gently giving some water to Aidan. While Hereric took his turn, she leant against the cart and looked up at the sky. She had been so intent on fleeing that she had paid little heed to the weather. It was a grey, damp day; a colorless sky stretched from horizon to horizon. All color appeared to have leached from the world.

Hereric had sunk down into a sitting position, his back braced against the wheel of the cart. He was still gasping, and looked about to collapse. Freya sat down next to him and they remained there for a while, unspeaking, until they caught their breaths and rested their limbs. They sat in the middle of wide, flat grasslands that appeared to stretch away into eternity in all directions.

"Which way are we travelling now?" Hereric asked when he had recovered sufficiently to speak.

"East, roughly," Freya replied. "Watch the sun as the afternoon passes. We should be travelling in the opposite direction to it."

Hereric nodded. "Do you think we've outrun the Mercians?"

Freya smiled at that. "I don't think we've outrun them Hereric. If they'd been chasing us, they would have caught us a long time ago. We're just travelling in a different direction to them at present. We must keep moving if we don't want to cross paths again."

By the time night fell, Freya and Hereric were so exhausted they had begun to stagger. They rested for the night near a water course filled with murky water that did not look fit to drink. Freya noticed the ground was getting damper and spongier, and wondered if they were wandering into marshland. She hoped not. Trekking across marshes would be slow, unpleasant and potentially fatal.

Hereric was too exhausted to go rabbiting with his slingshot, so they ate stale bread, salted pork and a crisp red apple each. Too exhausted to even speak, they sat either side of the campfire and listened to the night. Once she had recovered sufficiently, Freya hobbled over to the cart and checked on Aidan. His brow was warm, rather than feverish, which was a good sign; although once again the light was too poor for her to check his head wound. Still, she reflected, their priority today had been to get as far from the Mercians as possible. They would be able to travel at a more moderate pace tomorrow.

Like the night before, Freya got Hereric to boil some water for washing Aidan's wounds. As he had still not woken, they could feed him nothing. Instead, Freya sat, with his head on her lap and dribbled water into his mouth.

It would have to be enough to sustain him for now.

The next morning, Freya awoke to find the sun shining on her face. She sat up, groggy and with a faint sense of panic that she had overslept. In contrast to the day before, today was breezy and cold. Scudding clouds moved across the sky, playing hide-and-seek with a pale sun.

"Hereric," Freya croaked. She clambered to her feet and winced as her limbs protested. She ached all over. Muscles hurt that she did not even know she possessed. Today, she would have to take things slower, whether she wanted to or not. Nearby, her young companion rolled over onto his side and rubbed his eyes. Leaving him to wake up, and prepare something to break their fast, Freya hobbled over to the cart to check on Aidan.

There did not appear to be much change from the night before. Aidan still slept deeply, and showed no sign of waking. Carefully, Freya rolled him onto his front so that she could check the injury on the back of his head. It was difficult to see the extent of it as his hair had dried into a thick, bloodied mat. It was with regret that Freya was forced to use her knife to cut away his beautiful hair so that she could see his scalp. When she finally saw the injury, Freya winced. It looked as if something blunt and heavy had hit him very hard. The flesh was swollen and scabbed but when Freya probed gently with her fingers she could find no fractures or breaks in his skull. Her mother needed to see this wound. It was beyond her skill to heal.

Stay with me Aidan, she stroked his brow and gazed down at his face. *You've made it this far, just a bit farther.*

A short time later, they set out once more. Yesterday's fears were realized when Freya saw they were travelling further into marshland. The ground became wet underfoot and they soon had to navigate their way around stagnant pools and reed beds. Yet, this was the way east, and Freya was determined that they should continue in this direction. She was afraid that if they changed direction, they would never find their way back to Woodbridge Haven.

"At least the Mercians won't bother riding in here," Hereric commented, swatting at a cloud of midges that were attempting to eat him alive.

"That's true enough," Freya replied sourly, heaving the cart through a deep puddle. "Only a fool would lead you through the middle of a bog!"

Four days later, they finally reached the upper reaches of the Deben. When Freya saw the unmistakable outline of the Great Barrows of Kings rising before her, she nearly wept for joy. Unlike the Freya's last visit to the Barrows, this spot appeared deserted.

There had been times over the past few days when she had been sure she had got them well and truly lost. The marshland had nearly been their undoing. She had lost count of the times she and Hereric had struggled to pull the cart free of a sucking bog. They had spent two nights in the marshland, and had slept huddled in the back of the cart with no fire to warm them; there had been no spot dry enough to make camp in.

Through it all, Hereric had not complained once. He was a cheerful companion, even when the skies opened and pelted them with stinging hail, or when they ran out of food in the marshland and had nothing but an onion each for supper. Freya knew she would never have reached the Great Barrows of Kings without him.

That night they camped in a lime-tree copse, not far from the barrows. Hereric went out with his slingshot and brought back four fat rabbits.

While he was away hunting, Aidan awoke.

Freya had been tending the fire, coaxing it with damp sticks and cursing the two days of rain since they had left the marshes, which made finding any dry wood a challenge, when she heard a faint groan.

She dropped the wood and rushed over to where Aidan lay on his right, facing the fire. His eyelids were flickering. As Freya reached him, he groaned again.

"For the love of Woden I'm thirsty." Aidan's voice was so hoarse he could barely speak.

"Here." Freya unstoppered the water bladder and placed it to his lips. "Take a few sips, gently now."

"Has a horse ridden over my head?" His eyes flickered open, unfocused for a moment before he fixed upon Freya. She could see the confusion in his gaze but waited for him to adjust to his surroundings before she explained anything.

"I should be dead," he rasped. "Are you my prize in the afterlife?"

Freya laughed at that. "I doubt you'll be as fortunate as that Aidan of Connacht. No you are very much alive—and so am I. Hereric and I found you on the battlefield and we're taking you back to Woodbridge Haven."

Aidan stared at her, taking it all in, before his eyes closed once more. Freya saw the naked pain on his face—not the pain from his wounds—but from the memories of what he had seen and lived through on Barrow Fields.

"The Mercians won." It was a statement rather than a question but Freya answered it anyway.

"Yes—they took a small group of warriors hostage; the rest they left on the battlefield."

"Do you know who survived?"

"No, it was too far away to see, but when we searched the dead I saw Ecgric, Sigeberht, Aldwulf and Lothar. Edwin helped us search for you, but he found the bodies of his father and brothers on the field. Not one of his kin survived."

"I told him to stay in Beodricesworth," Aidan growled, reopening his eyes, "and I told you to go straight home."

Freya had to smile at that. "Since when do boys do what they're told, or women?"

Pain clouded Aidan's face then, a sensation that was more than physical.

"I saw Lothar fall," he said hoarsely, tears running down his cheeks. "My friend—with a pregnant wife waiting for him at home. Life is a cruel bitch. I would have given my life for that man. It's not right that I should live and he not."

Hereric returned with the rabbits and was delighted to find Aidan awake. He sat, chattering to Aidan, regaling him of their adventures since the battle, until Freya told him to leave Aidan be and help her skin and gut the rabbits.

Once the rabbits had spit-roasted over the fire, the three companions devoured them. Freya was worried that, since he had just awoken, Aidan would lack appetite. The opposite was true. They propped him up against a tree trunk so that he could eat his rabbit without choking. Like Hereric and Freya, he gnawed at the bones, even when he had picked them clean.

"How are you feeling?" Freya threw the rabbit bones on the fire and sat down next to Aidan. "How's your head?"

"I've felt better." Aidan managed a weak smile. "Although that rabbit has made all the difference. My head still feels about twice the size though. It hurts me badly."

"You took a massive blow to the back of the head. It looks like you were hit by a rock or the blunt edge of an axe," Freya replied. "We found you pinned under a Mercian axeman."

Freya paused then as another thought suddenly occurred to her. "Of course, there may have been others who were still alive amongst the dead, but there was no time to search for them."

Aidan nodded, his dark-blue eyes filled with pain. "What you did was very brave, and very foolhardy, sweet Freya." He reached out and placed a hand over hers. "But I am pleased you did it."

Freya looked down and fought back tears. "I had to look for you. I couldn't go on with my life wondering what had happened to you. If you were dead then I needed to see it with my own eyes."

"You are unlike any woman I have ever met," Aidan replied quietly, his voice catching. "Brave, proud and beautiful. I love you. I should have told you before I left for Barrow Fields but I foolishly thought I'd wait."

Freya stared at Aidan, tears running down her face. She was unable to speak, and when she finally managed, the words were barely above a whisper.

"And I love you."

Aidan squeezed her hand tightly, his gaze holding hers fast. "You are worth living for, and you are worth dying for. You are the only woman I will ever love."

Chapter Twenty-four

IT WAS A cold, misty morning when Freya rose from beside the fire and poked at the dying embers with a stick. Hereric sat opposite her, owl-eyed from taking the last watch. Behind them, Aidan slept fitfully. His head was paining him terribly, and this worried Freya. He needed Cwen's care.

"Are we going soon?" Hereric asked.

Freya shook her head. "It will take us at least another day if we continue on foot. I was hoping to find a way to travel down-river."

"But we don't have a boat."

"I know that," Freya sighed as fatigue weighed down upon her, "but maybe I can find one. Wait here and keep the fire burning. I'll be back in a bit."

Freya wrapped the shawl that Aidan had given her back in Beodricesworth about her shoulders. The shawl was a little worse for wear now, but it still provided some protection from the damp, chilly day. Taking care to move quietly, Freya made her way out of the copse and peered out at where the shadows of the Great Barrows of Kings loomed over the river.

The tide was coming in. At its lowest point, the water was just over two feet, too shallow for any boats to sail in. At high tide, the river rose to at least eleven feet; more than deep enough for most barges and longboats. There were no boats laying on the bank this morning, but Freya knew that most travelers on their way to Rendlaesham docked here. There were a number of villages on the banks of the Deben and it was a busy waterway. As such, Freya guessed that if she waited a while, a boat would come.

She sat down at the edge of the copse, hidden from view by undergrowth, and waited.

The tide rose quickly and a misty rain began to fall, coating the world in tiny, sparkling droplets. Freya's hands and feet felt numb with cold and her nose was starting to run, but still she waited.

Mid-morning, a small boat appeared down-river. It moved quickly, its single oarsman paddling with the tide. There were two men on-board but the boat sat low in the water as it was bearing heavy sacks.

Freya watched, her pulse racing, as the boat angled towards the muddy bank. The men climbed out and waded through the water, pulling the boat up through the mud. Once they reached the bank, they hefted the two jute sacks out of the boat.

"How far till Orford?" one of the men asked his companion.

"We should reach it just after noon," his companion replied, "but the tide will have turned by then. Once we off-load these, I suggest we spend the rest of the day in the mead hall. It's just the weather for it. We'll sail back to Ramsholt with tomorrow's tide."

"You've got no argument from me there," his companion agreed, "but let's hide the boat if we're going to leave it overnight."

Freya held her breath and watched as the men placed the oars inside the boat and carried it into the copse. A moment later, she realized they were coming straight towards her. She flattened herself on the ground and had just wedged herself under some prickly undergrowth, when she heard the men stop just feet away.

"Cover it up with some ferns," one of the men instructed. "It should be safe here, especially in this weather."

Freya lay still and silent while the men moved off. She waited until their voices had completely faded before she wriggled out from the undergrowth and ran to get the others.

Soon the tide would turn, and they would be on their way to Woodbridge Haven.

The rain fell in a soft veil over the world. Freya heaved back on the oars and raised her face to it. Either-side of her the waters of the River Deben stippled slightly in the rain. They had been travelling down river ever since noon, but it was impossible to know how much time had actually passed for the sun had not once shown its face.

Hereric sat behind Freya, perched at the bow, while Aidan sat at the stern. The paleness of Aidan's face worried Freya, as did the deep grooves of pain that appeared either side of his mouth. He slumped against the side of the boat and did not pay much attention to his surroundings.

The farther they travelled down-river, the wider the Deben became. Once they reached the estuary, the river would become so wide that it would be impossible to see from one bank to the other. Freya had instructed Hereric to keep a watchful eye out for a stand of trees close to the north bank once they passed a few tiny islands in the center of the estuary. Those trees signaled the edge of the woodland where her mother lived.

"Look, Freya!" Hereric eventually called out. "Are those the trees you spoke of?"

Freya glanced over her shoulder. Her heart soared when she saw the dark line of trees that almost reached the water's edge, followed by a steep bank with steps leading down to the mud.

"That's it!" she called back, her voice tight with excitement. "We're home!"

Freya and Hereric clambered off the boat and waded in through the clinging mud, pulling the boat in as close to the bank as they were able.

It was an effort to get Aidan off the boat. His movements were slow and sluggish, and he was finding it difficult to coordinate his limbs properly. Eventually, they managed to help him to the bank, and up the narrow steps that had been cut into it.

Reaching the top, Freya felt a rush of joy as the smell of wet vegetation hit her. There had been times over the past few months that she had thought never to see these woods again.

With Hereric supporting Aidan's right side, and Freya his left, they made their way down the leaf-strewn path that cut through the forest. Eventually the path would lead to the other-side of the woods, and the hamlet of Bawdsey—but they would not need to travel that far.

After a while, Freya instructed Hereric to veer right, off the path. They had walked some distance farther when the trees drew back and they stepped into a small clearing.

A small wattle and daub cottage, with a thatch roof in need of repair sat in the heart of the clearing. A large vegetable plot stretched behind the structure, as did a small fenced enclosure where Cwen of Woodbridge Haven kept her chickens.

"Mōder!" Freya shouted as they approached the cottage. "Mōder, are you there!"

Freya saw smoke rising from the thatched roof and her eyes filled with tears. Her mother was home. They were safe.

The door flew open and Cwen rushed out, her hands dusty with flour. They had interrupted her in the midst of making bread. "Freya!"

Cwen sprinted over the wet ground, her long brown hair flying behind her like a flag. Freya stepped forward and embraced her mother fiercely, unable to stop the tears that suddenly flowed over her cheeks. Great sobs rose within her. The relief was so great she felt as if her legs might give out under her.

"You're home!" Cwen cried, hugging Freya so hard her ribs hurt. "But how? How did you ..." Cwen reached out and touched the iron collar around Freya's neck, her eyes narrowing.

"It's a long story; one that needs us all sitting in front of a warm fire with food in our bellies." Freya stepped back and wiped her eyes. "For now let me introduce you to Hereric and Aidan. Mōder, Aidan has been wounded in battle. His wounds are seven days old. Can you help him?"

Cwen's gaze shifted to Aidan, her practiced healer's gaze taking him in with a single sweep. Looking upon her mother's face, Freya saw there were lines that had not been there a year ago. There were more strands of grey in Cwen of Shottisham's brown mane than Freya remembered. The grief of losing her daughter to Ricberht had taken its toll. Yet her hazel eyes were as bright as ever.

"We need to get him inside," she said quietly. "Follow me."

It was warm and dry inside the cottage, with a roaring fire in the hearth. Hereric sank down onto a sheepskin with a sigh of pleasure and gratefully took the earthen bowl of pottage that Cwen passed him. Meanwhile, Freya had taken Aidan over to the pile of furs, where Cwen slept in the far corner of the dwelling.

"Boil me some water Freya while I get my herbs," Cwen ordered.

Freya smiled as she went to do her mother's bidding; she had missed

Cwen's bossiness.

Aidan was sitting groggily on the furs, watching the industry of the two women. "She's quite a woman your mother," he commented when Freya helped him out of his leather vest. She began to unwind the bandages around his chest, shoulder and head so Cwen could take a look at his injuries.

"She most certainly is," Freya smiled. "She'll take good care of you."

"I wouldn't be here now if you hadn't already done that," Aidan gave Freya a smile that made her insides melt.

"Let's take a look at you," Cwen bustled up and handed Freya her basket of herbs and potions. "Even battered and bruised you're a handsome one. No wonder my daughter cannot take her eyes off you."

"Mōder!"

"What?" Cwen replied without a hint of embarrassment. "I may be getting old, but I'm not blind."

Cwen examined Aidan's chest and shoulder wounds while Freya looked on intensely. "These are healing well," Cwen reported, "although the cut on his chest should have been stitched."

"There was no time for that," Freya replied quietly.

Cwen cast her daughter a questioning glance before checking the arrow wounds. "You cleaned these well. There is no festering."

Aidan caught Freya's glance then and winked.

"It seems you're well enough to flirt with my daughter. You can't be in too bad a shape after all," Cwen observed tartly.

"It's my head that hurts the most," Aidan admitted.

Cwen examined the wound and frowned when she gently probed the scabbed wound with her fingertips and Aidan yelped in pain.

"This came close to splitting your head open," she told him. "The wound needs a poultice. I'm afraid you're going to have sore head for a while yet, but it should come right eventually."

Freya felt giddy with relief at this news. "Really? He will heal?"

Cwen glanced from Aidan to Freya and gave a knowing smile. "Yes he will."

Epilogue

Six months later ...

"FREYA, IT'S DONE! He's finished it. Go and see!"

Freya straightened up from retrieving the last warm egg from the hen house and glanced over at where Hereric was almost hopping up and down with excitement at the foot of the garden.

"He can't have finished it yet. He still had the door to put on and a wall to finish this morning."

"He has. Go and see!"

"Very well." Freya approached the boy, ruffled his hair and handed him the basket of eggs. "Here, take these to Cwen. If you help her with the baking, she might cook you some eggs."

Freya made her way out from behind her mother's cottage and down the path to the edge of the clearing. There, another, newer, dwelling stood basking in the noon sun. Aidan had forbidden her from visiting him during the final stages of building, having insisted that it should be a surprise.

This was their new home. Tomorrow they would have their handfast ceremony in nearby Bawdsey. From tomorrow, they would live in this cottage as man and wife.

As Freya approached the cottage, Aidan stepped out of the entrance.

The sight of him never failed to make Freya's heart race. His short hair was starting to grow out, and it flopped in a black wave over one eye. He was dressed lightly today, as it was one of the first warm days of spring, in light breeches and a sleeveless tunic belted at the waist. Upon catching sight of her approaching, Aidan leaned lazily against the doorframe and greeted her with a smile.

"I hear from Hereric that you're done here." Freya stopped a few yards away and regarded him skeptically. "Was that one of his exaggerations, or another one of your boasts?"

Aidan laughed. "Neither. It's done. Would you like me to carry you across the threshold milady?"

Freya regarded him archly. "I'm no lady. I think I'm capable of walking through a doorway myself."

Aidan approached her, a wicked gleam in his eye. "What if I insist on carrying you?"

Freya tried to dart past him, but Aidan was too quick. He grabbed her and scooped her up in his arms. Then, ignoring her protests, he carried her down the path and across the threshold.

Freya's half-hearted objections died on her lips when she saw inside.

A fire burned in the fire pit at the heart of the dwelling, illuminating the clean and tidy space. He had already furnished it for her, with clean rushes upon the floor, a small work table near the door, and hand-carved stools around the fire. There was a mountain of furs at the far end of the room, partially shielded from view by a curtain of rabbit-skins sewn together. It was a cozy, homely space. Freya could scarcely believe that it was hers.

"It's beautiful," she whispered, her eyes brimming with tears. "You've worked so hard Aidan—it's perfect."

Wordlessly, Aidan set her down on the floor and pulled her into his arms. His kiss was urgent and Freya responded in kind, twining her arms about his neck and pressing her body along the length of his. Their time together since coming to live with Cwen had always been stolen. Aidan's head had taken a long time to heal, and they had been confined to the cottage for long periods over a bitter winter that had seemed to drag endlessly. Once spring arrived they had been able to make love for the first time in the woods, but there was never any time to linger over it, or to lie naked for hours afterwards.

Breaking away from his kiss and gasping for breath, Freya glanced over at the furs and felt heat seep through her body. It was their bed and they would be able to spend every night there from tomorrow on.

As if reading her thoughts, Aidan chuckled. "I'm tempted to try out those furs now," he whispered in her ear, "just to make sure they're comfortable for our wedding night."

"You'll have to wait till then," Freya replied with a grin. "I've got honey-seed cakes to bake for tomorrow and mōder wants to make the final touches to my dress."

"I prefer you naked," Aidan replied, his eyes dark with passion. "The cakes and the dress can wait." He pulled the door shut and bolted it. "But this can't."

With that, Aidan scooped Freya back into his arms and carried her over to the furs.

This time she did not protest.

The End

Historical note from the author

Although the lovers in *Nightfall till Daybreak*, Freya and Aidan, are purely figments of my imagination (even if I'd like to think they really did exist), many characters within this novel are based on real historical figures. All of the following 'real people' play an important role in the novel: King Sigeberht; his co-ruler, Ecgric; the monks, Felix of Burgundy and Botulf of Iken; Sigeberht's step-cousin Annan; and the bloodthirsty Mercian King, Penda.

Of course, in the name of telling a good story I have stretched a few facts, embellished events and shortened timelines. Botulf set up his monastery at Iken a few decades later than in this story and Sigeberht actually ruled from 629-634 AD; but for the purposes of my tale I pack his six-year reign into one eventful year.

Nightfall till Daybreak is based around Sigeberht's actual life; in fact it was his story that gave me my first inspiration for this novel. The lovers came later – it was Sigeberht who initially caught my attention.

Sigeberht gets a mention in *Dark Under the Cover of Night,* the first novel in my Kingdom of the East Angles series. He was King Raedwald's stepson, who the king had exiled to Gaul when Sigeberht was still a youth, fearing that the young man might try to claim the throne over one of Raedwald's own sons. Sigeberht lived in Gaul for many years. *Nightfall till Daybreak* begins after the murder of Sigeberht's step-brother, Eorpwald, the current King of the East Angles. The 'usurper', Ricberht, had taken the throne and Sigeberht sailed across the water to Britannia, to take it back for his family.

Sigeberht killed Ricberht, took back Rendlaesham and was crowned. However, Sigeberht's new life did not sit well with him. In Gaul, he had dedicated himself to religious studies and he eventually left Rendlaesham to set up a monastery and Beodricesworth (now Bury St. Edmunds). He left a relatively unknown individual – Ecgric – to rule in his stead. Sigeberht eventually abdicated, took his vows and dedicated himself to teaching young boys how to read and write Latin – but, unfortunately, he could not throw aside his responsibilities so easily. When the Mercians, led by King Penda, attacked East Anglia, Sigeberht was dragged from his monastery and onto the battlefield. He refused to bear arms and went into battle carrying only a staff. The rest, as they say, is history...

Many years later, Sigeberht was sainted. His feast day is on 29 October.

In all my novels set in the Anglo-Saxon period, I enjoy using actual historical events and figures to drive the story forward. Although these are romances, with the love story as the enduring theme, there is something exciting about reliving (or rewriting) history. This period of British history is shadowy and not particularly well documented. The main source for this period came from *Bede's Ecclesiastical History of the English People*, which was not completed until the 730s, and was written from a religious perspective—however, I found this lack of detail freeing rather than constricting. It allowed me to really bring Anglo-Saxon England to life using my own knowledge of how people actually lived, and the beliefs that drove their lives forward.

The Deepening Night

BOOK THREE
THE KINGDOM OF THE EAST ANGLES

JAYNE
CASTEL

***

For Tim.
Ic þe lufu.

***

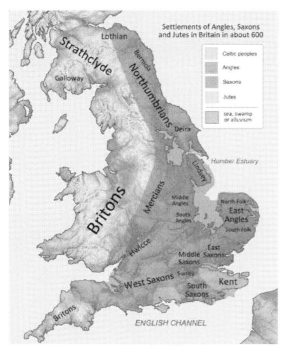

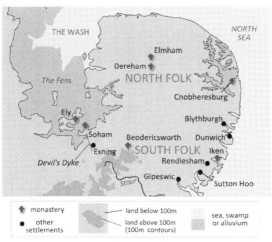

Character list for 'The Deepening Night'

Annan – King of the East Angles.
Saewara (pronounced: *Sewara*) – sister of Penda, the King of Mercia.
Aethelhere (pronounced *Aythilhair*) – Annan's brother.
Hereswith – niece of the Northumbrian King – promised to Annan.
Eldwyn – Hereswith's handmaid.
Penda – King of Mercia.
Cyneswide (pronounced: *Sinswid*) – Penda's wife.
Aldfrid (pronounced *Oldfrid*) – one of Penda's most trusted ealdormen.
Sabert (Saba) – Ealdorman and Annan's best friend.
Hilda – slave in Annan's hall.

Family Tree: Kingdom of the East Angles

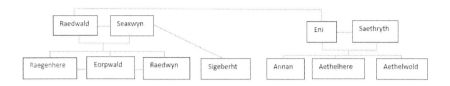

Wuffinga family tree (adapted for the purposes of fiction)

Family Tree: Kingdom of Mercia

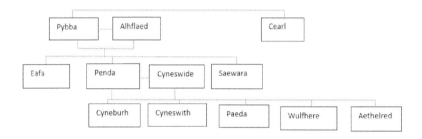

Mercian family tree (adapted for the purposes of fiction)

"Better to die on your feet than live on your knees."
- Emiliano Zapata

Prologue

The Funeral

Tamworth, the Kingdom of Mercia—Britannia

Spring 630 AD

THE CROAK OF ravens echoed through the morning air. Their cries followed Saewara through the curling mist, mocking her. There was not a breath of wind this morning; the shrouded hillside sat in a world of its own, a lonely island in a milky sea.

Head hung low, so that others could not see her face, Saewara followed the mourners up to the barrow where Egfrid would be entombed alongside his forefathers. Behind her, she could hear the quiet sobbing of his mother, who had been inconsolable ever since hearing the news of her eldest son's death.

Egfrid had been one of the king's bravest and most formidable warriors. His death, in a border skirmish against a band of Cymri—the people inhabiting the land to the west of Mercia—just three days earlier, had shocked them all.

The dead man lay upon a litter; his face chalk-white, his arms folded over his chest. They had dressed him in his finest clothes: a fur cloak, a fine royal blue tunic and an embossed leather breastplate. Gold rings crowded his muscular biceps, each one won for his valor and presented after battle. His long brown hair had been brushed and tied back against his nape.

Egfrid's wounds had been terrible; he had been slit open from sternum to bowel. It had taken the women most of the night to prepare him for burial, binding up his wounds so that he could be dressed in his finery. In the end, they had succeeded in creating the illusion that the warrior had come to a peaceful end. To look at him now, no one would have guessed at the deep lacerations beneath his clothing.

The mourners climbed the last stretch before the barrow. Egfrid's burial place marked the end of a line of mounds where Mercian kings and nobility lay. The last king to be buried here had been Cearl, nearly five years earlier. The last peaceful King of Mercia, he had ruled without incident for nearly two decades, before finally succumbing to illness.

Saewara halted before the entrance to the barrow, watching as her husband's litter was lowered before it. Beyond, the shadows loomed.

Darkness stretched out toward Egfrid the Strong, beckoning him toward the afterlife.

As his wife, Saewara was expected to sing the lament for his death. Steeling herself, she squared her shoulders and lifted her head, filling her lungs with cool, damp air. Then she sang, her voice lifting above the mourners and drifting through the encircling mist.

> *Egfrid the Strong*
> *What great loss we suffer*
> *A warrior, a husband, a son*
> *That went away, this also may*
>
> *Sorry and longing are ours*
> *Exile in the cold winter*
> *For he no longer serves his lord*
> *That went away, this also may*
>
> *It is the will of fate*
> *That shapes all our lives*
> *Grief, loss and suffering*
> *That went away, this also may*

Saewara's voice trailed off, while around her the eyes of many present brimmed with tears at the lament's haunting beauty. Saewara cast her eyes down once more as Egfrid's brothers slid his body inside the barrow and sealed the entrance.

The mourners drifted away from the barrow, and retraced their steps down the slope. Saewara lingered on the knoll for a few moments longer, before following them. The mist was even thicker now. It created a milky shroud around the mourners, blocking the outline of the Great Tower that rose from a grassy hill to the south. Saewara walked slowly, lost in her thoughts.

She did not notice a tall figure fall into step next to her.

"You played your part beautifully, Saewara—ever the actress."

Saewara started, and looked up at her brother's cruelly handsome face in surprise.

He knew her grief was feigned. She had thought Penda had gone ahead. Yet instead he had lingered behind to speak to her.

In the pale morning light, Penda was a striking sight. He wore a magnificent black fur cloak, clasped to his broad shoulders with gleaming amber brooches. Despite the iron crown on his head—a plain circlet with a garnet at its center— he dressed like the warrior he was. His heavy sword swung at his side as he walked, and his tall, muscular frame was encased in leather armor. His blond hair, so pale it was almost white, hung in a smooth curtain over his shoulders.

Not for the first time, Saewara wondered at how different they were. Her brother was as tall, cold and pale as a mountain summit; in contrast to

Saewara's dark hair, small frame and fiery disposition. She was so short that the crown of her head barely reached the center of his chest. Their eldest brother, Eafa, who had died in East Anglia a few years earlier, had spent years taunting Saewara about her looks—even going as far as to say that their mother must have lain with a Cymru savage to beget her, for she could not be of the same blood as Penda and him.

"You enjoyed the lament then, brother?" she asked coolly, preferring to respond to Penda's barbed comment with a question.

"Yes, you have an enchanting voice."

Saewara did not reply. She and Penda rarely spoke these days, and he did not usually seek her out unless he had some purpose. She guessed that this was also the case now. As such, she waited for him to speak again.

"You do not mourn him."

It was a statement rather than a question.

"No," she replied quietly. "Do you blame me?"

Penda shrugged. "I care not what goes on between man and wife. It was a good match—or it would have been if you had given him a son."

Saewara looked away, slowing her step so that the mourners before her drew ahead. She did not want her mother by marriage eavesdropping on their conversation.

"We tried, but my womb never quickened."

"You are barren."

Saewara bristled. "He had other women, you know that. None of the others bore his child either."

"If a marriage does not produce children it's the woman's fault, not the man's," Penda replied with a snarl in his voice.

Saewara clenched her jaw and bit back an angry reply. She knew she should mind her tongue. Many thought her husband's ready fists would have taught her meekness over the past few years. Indeed it had made her wary of men; yet Egfrid's violence only served to make the rage within her grow.

Soon, all of this will not matter, she consoled herself. *Soon you will be free of this place and all the vile, scheming people who live here.*

"Yes, brother," she managed finally. "You are right. I am barren and no good as a wife. In a few days, I will leave here and go to Bonehill, where I will take my vows. There, I will be out of your life, and no longer a thorn in your side."

"Bonehill?" Penda queried coolly. "I think not, dear sister. Barren or not, it would be a waste to send you off to a nunnery for the rest of your days."

"Hwaet?" Saewara lost her tightly won control for a moment. She stopped and swiveled toward her brother, her gaze sweeping up to meet his. "But there's no point in marrying me to anyone else!"

"You are of royal blood," Penda reminded her with a cruel smile, locking her arm in his and forcing her to continue walking. "And too valuable to cast aside so young. I have plans for you."

Saewara walked on, her heart thumping against her ribs. She could not believe she was hearing this from Penda. After the sacrifice she had made for him – marrying a man all knew to be a brute—and suffering greatly as a result, this was the ultimate betrayal. She knew that Penda held no love for her—she imagined him incapable of truly loving anyone—but now he appeared to be exacting some kind of twisted vengeance upon her.

"Who is it?" she gasped finally. "What animal will you marry me to this time?"

"Use that tone with me again Saewara and I will strike you to the ground," Penda replied, flatly, "sister or not."

Saewara shivered. Having seen what her brother was capable of, she knew he would do as he threatened.

They walked in silence for a short distance before the king spoke once more.

"You will marry Annan of the East Angles," Penda informed her dispassionately. "Annan has 'bent the knee' to Mercia and I need to ensure that he will continue to do as he is told. You will play a role in uniting our two kingdoms in readiness for the day I take East Anglia for our own."

Saewara was shocked into silence.

This was worse than she had ever anticipated. Her brief glimpse at freedom, at a life away from being a pawn in a man's world, dissolved like smoke before her eyes. Not only would her brother barter her like a fattened sow at market, but he would give her to his enemy to further his political ambitions, without a thought to her wishes.

She dipped her head, letting her cowl fall over her face and block out the world.

Tears flowed, hot and bitter, down her cheeks.

Chapter One

A King's Sacrifice

Rendlaesham, the Kingdom of the East Angles—Britannia

Ten days later ...

THE SUN WAS sinking beyond the western horizon when Annan led his men back into Rendlaesham. An ash longbow hung on his back, and his quiver was empty. A feeling of well-being suffused his exhausted limbs. A knot of warriors followed the king, their kill slung over the backs of their horses: three boar and two deer.

The hunt had been one of the most enjoyable of Annan's life. It had been a joy to use a bow and arrow again after a bitter winter that had kept everyone indoors; to feel the tension of the hemp bow-string as he drew it back and hear the whisper of the arrow loosing.

The men were in high spirits, singing loudly as they rode through Rendlaesham's gates and up through the town. Yet Annan was in a reflective, pensive mood this afternoon. He did not join in the singing, but instead let his gaze wander over his surroundings.

Riding back into Rendlaesham never failed to make his pulse quicken. All of this was his.

Despite the battle that had brought the Kingdom of the East Angles to its knees, just months earlier, the folk living here still looked to him for guidance and protection. He was one of the Wuffingas, the family that had ruled this kingdom for centuries; a family born to rule.

Above the low-slung wattle and daub dwellings of Rendlaesham, rose the fabled 'Golden Hall'. It was a massive wooden structure, and its thatched straw roof gleamed in the sunlight. Even now, nearly six months after taking the throne, Annan found it hard to believe that he actually lived here.

Young boys ran out to greet the king and his men, their faces beaming when they saw the boar and deer carcasses. Annan grinned down at them, remembering how he too had run behind his father and his men, impatient for the day he would be able to join them on a hunt, and in battle.

Annan's grin faded at that last thought.

Battle. It was a fact of life in the world they inhabited, and yet the reality of it was cruel. He, like those boys, had been brought up to believe that war

335

was valor and glory. Instead, it was blood, fear and death, grieving widows and shattered lives. You could not tell a boy that though; he would never believe it.

The king and his men clattered into the stable yard under the shadow of the Great Hall. A steep set of steps climbed up to its huge oaken doors, which were flanked by two spear-wielding warriors.

Casting aside his gloomy thoughts about war and it consequences, Annan swung down from the saddle and glanced up at the majestic outline of his hall silhouetted against the darkening sky.

"Saba—get those beasts skinned, gutted and hung," Annan called to one of the warriors, "and I'll have a cup of mead waiting for you by the fire when you're done."

Sabert, a big, broad shouldered ealdorman with wavy, brown hair, grey eyes and a long nose that had been broken years earlier and never set properly, gave a snort in response.

"Typical—leaving all the work to me."

"A king shouldn't need to get his hands dirty," Annan grinned, enjoying the banter that he and Saba had shared since they were boys.

He was glad Saba had finally agreed to join him here at Rendlaesham. It had been an effort to convince him to leave Snape, where his kin resided, and Annan knew that his friend preferred the freedom of his old life. Still, in a king's hall, surrounded by toadies, and those whose loyalty was as fickle as the wind, Annan was pleased to know he had someone he could trust by his side.

Leaving his friend still good-naturedly grumbling, Annan rubbed down his horse, before watering and feeding it. He was making his way across toward the steps, when the doors to the Great Hall above him drew open and a tall, blond man stepped out into the golden rays of the setting sun.

"Wes hāl, Annan!" Aethelhere shouted with a cocky grin.

Annan waved back and watched as his younger brother approached. He descended the steps with loose-limbed grace; and as Aethelhere drew closer, Annan saw he had a mischievous glint in his eye. A look that Annan knew well.

"You have visitors," his brother boomed, his grin widening, before he slapped Annan on the shoulder. "It appears Edwin of Northumbria is a man of his word."

Annan inclined his head, his eyes widening. "What? He has sent me a woman to wed?"

Aethelhere's grin turned wolfish. "He has. Just wait till you see her."

The brothers exchanged a look and, without another word, mounted the steps to the 'Golden Hall' together.

Annan was not sure how he felt about this news. He had known that the Northumbrian King was sending him a bride, as they had agreed at Yule. Now that the moment had arrived, he suddenly felt reluctant to meet her—despite Aethelhere's evident approval of Edwin's choice.

Inside the Great Hall, the smell of simmering pottage assaulted Annan's nostrils. It was a pungent aroma; that of carrots, onions and cabbage cooked for so long that it became a mushy, sulfurous stew. It was not Annan's favorite, but at least they would soon have some spit-roasted meat to vary the meals over the coming days. Hilda, the slave that Annan had inherited with the Rendlaesham's 'Golden Hall', was a good-hearted young woman, but a poor cook. She stood now, pummeling griddle bread into rounds with the heel of her hand, and instructing two other, younger, girls on how to do the same.

Despite that Annan had never ill-treated her, Hilda was a nervous girl, with large light blue eyes that regarded the world with trepidation. Her thin body was strong from years of hard physical labor, and her fine light brown hair fell in a long, thin braid down her back. About her slender neck she wore a pitted iron slave collar.

"Evening, m'lord Annan." Hilda glanced up as a draft of air from the opening doors, alerted her to the king's arrival. She dropped into a low curtsey.

"Evening, Hilda," Annan acknowledged her with a smile. His gaze then travelled across the interior of his hall. Even after months of living here, he still was not used to the size of his home.

The blackened timbers of the ceiling rose high above his head, like the ribcage of a great dragon. Luxurious tapestries—works of art that often took decades to fully complete—hung from the walls, alongside ornamental shields, axes and swords. A massive fire pit dominated the space and long tables ran either side of it. Dogs skulked around the margins of the hall, gnawing on bones; or waiting under the tables for scraps during the approaching evening meal. This eve, ealdormen, thegns, and their wives filled the Great Hall—it was always a hive of activity. Many got to their feet upon seeing the king's arrival.

Yet Annan's gaze sought out the face of the young woman who was to become his wife.

Two women sat at one end of the long tables, flanked by four travel-weary warriors.

Annan's gaze rested upon the face of a slender, blonde beauty at the center of the group. Then, he glanced across at Aethelhere with a grin.

"For once, you weren't exaggerating, brother."

"When it comes to pretty women I never exaggerate," Aethelhere replied, feigning offence, before stepping forward to make the introductions.

"Lady Hereswith of Bebbanburg, niece to King Edwin of Northumbria, may I introduce you to our king, Annan of the East Angles."

"Milord." The blonde girl rose to her feet, blushing prettily, before she curtsied deeply.

"Milady," Annan replied, his gaze devouring her. She was even lovelier up close than from a distance, with flawless, milky skin, huge blue eyes and hair the color of sea-foam.

Marriage to such a woman might not be such a trial after all.

At thirty-three winters, Annan was well past the age when most men married. Given the chance, he would have preferred to remain unwed. Out of the three brothers—Annan, Aethelhere and Aethelwold—only Aethelwold had married; to a sweet woman who had given him two sons. Like his elder brother, Aethelhere also remained unattached. However, with kingship came certain responsibilities—bproducing an heir among them. As much as Annan liked his freedom, and preferred taking a woman for a night or two, rather than saddling himself with a wife, the time had come for him to be handfasted.

Still, Annan reflected, not taking his gaze off the beauty before him, some sacrifices were easier to make than others.

"Welcome to Rendlaesham." Annan stopped before her and smiled into her eyes; he was aware that although slender as a reed, she was taller than most women. She barely had to lift her chin to meet his gaze.

"I trust you had a safe journey south?" Annan's gaze shifted to the mousy-haired woman next to Hereswith who wore a pinched expression.

"The journey was uneventful enough," the woman replied, her gaze meeting the king's boldly, "although the weather was bitter. I am Eldwyn, hand-maid to Lady Hereswith."

"I welcome you all to my hall," Annan replied before glancing over at where the unappetizing pottage bubbled away in a huge cast-iron pot. "And if I'd realized you were arriving today, I would have had a feast prepared in your honor. However, I can offer you all a hot meal and mead this eve, and tomorrow we shall dine on roast venison."

A pall of smoke, as always, hung over the hall, making Annan's eyes sting. Yet, he paid it no heed. His attention was focused upon the lovely girl who delicately supped at her bowl of pottage to his left. She noticed his gaze upon her and cast him a flirtatious look from under long lashes.

Despite himself, Annan grinned foolishly. Hereswith was bolder than she first appeared, a trait he liked in a woman.

Annan chewed on a piece of griddle bread and leaned back in the carved wooden seat reserved for the East Anglian king, at the head of one of the tables. The noise in the hall was deafening; the volume increasing as his men consumed more than their fair share of mead and ale.

"More pottage, sire?" Hilda appeared at Annan's elbow, with an iron pot filled to the brim with steaming vegetable stew. She had such a hopeful expression that Annan felt a pang as he shook his head.

"I thank you, but no," his gaze then flicked over at where Saba had just started on another cup of mead. "However, Sabert here has a mighty appetite. Fill up his bowl!"

Saba glowered over the rim of his cup as Hilda eagerly moved around to the right of the table and filled up the warrior's bowl, using a long-stemmed wooden ladle. Saba leaned back, to give her space to move, and glanced up at her face.

"What's your name, girl?"

"Hilda, m'lord," she replied timidly, casting a nervous glance in the king's direction. Annan pretended not to notice her discomfort; it was obvious the girl had been ill-treated in the past. Not likely by the previous king, Sigeberht, who although severe was not a cruel man, but by his predecessor, Ricberht, and, perhaps her own father. Her eyes were wide and frightened. She regarded Saba as if he were about to cuff her around the head.

"It's a pretty name." Saba smiled up at her, with uncharacteristic gentleness. "For a pretty wench."

Hilda turned deep red and, clutching her pot to her breast, fled to the other end of the table.

Annan watched her go before winking at Saba. "Still charming the women I see."

Saba shrugged before dipping a piece of bread into his pottage. "The girl is comely."

A disapproving, unladylike snort interrupted the men. The woman who accompanied Hereswith as her chaperone and maid, Eldwyn, clicked her tongue loudly and shook her head.

"Slaves should not be addressed by name," she reprimanded Saba imperiously, looking down her nose at him. "The girl must know her place."

Saba's gaze narrowed. "Yes—but you do not appear to know yours."

Eldwyn sniffed and looked away from him, not in the least chastised by his baleful glare.

"Hilda is a sweet-natured wench." Aethelhere, who was seated to Saba's left, helped himself to another piece of bread and winked at Eldwyn. "Yet certainly not worth arguing over."

"Very well, Aethelhere," Saba replied, his gaze never leaving Eldwyn's face; daring her to make eye-contact with him once more. "Although, some should remember they are guests in another king's hall before they open their mouths."

Eldwyn ignored him. Her mouth pursed as she looked down at her bowl of half-eaten pottage.

Annan had remained silent during the exchange, but now he regarded Eldwyn coolly. Her bitterness and austerity stood in contrast to the fresh beauty of the girl beside her. Hereswith gave her maid a quelling look and whispered something to her. Eldwyn nodded stiffly but said nothing— although her expression had turned sour.

"Hereswith." Annan raised his cup to the girl beside him, deciding that women like Eldwyn were best ignored. "I will send word back to Edwin that I am very pleased with the match."

Hereswith flushed with obvious pleasure. "I thank you, sire. I would be honored to become your bride."

Annan smiled at her, unable to stop himself from imagining what Hereswith looked like naked. If that clinging woolen tunic she wore was any indication, he guessed she had a body like a nymph.

"Then we shall be handfasted," he announced, the mead loosening his tongue and making him reckless. "Tomorrow I will ..."

At that moment, the doors to the Great Hall flew open, bringing with them a gust of cold, damp air that made the coals in the fire pit glow and the flames in the clay cressets along the walls gutter.

A man, wrapped in a thick fur cloak, his cheeks ruddy with cold, stepped into the hall. He was broad and stocky, with a thick, grey-streaked beard and hair. He carried himself with arrogance, and noble bearing.

The Great Hall grew still as the gazes of all present shifted to the newcomer. Conversation died away and the only sound, save the growl of one of the dogs under the tables, was that of the crackling fire pit.

Aware that he was the subject of hostile stares, the man's iron-grey gaze swept across the hall's interior. A little of his earlier confidence had dimmed as his gaze came to rest upon Annan. The king returned the newcomer's gaze and felt himself go cold. The good cheer and anticipation of wedding, and bedding, his winsome bride, dissolved.

He recognized this warrior, and knew who had sent him.

"Aldfrid of Tamworth." Annan slowly rose to his feet, never taking his gaze off the newcomer's face. "What brings you to my kingdom?"

Aldfrid stared back at him, insolence in his eyes.

"*Your* kingdom? I suppose it still is ..." he mused. "Penda sends his regards."

The name, hated amongst all the East Angles, had an explosive effect on the hall. Some men slammed their cups down on the table before them with a thud, some spat out curses, while others jumped to their feet.

"You are a brave man," Annan remarked, feeling the tension grow around him with each passing moment, "or a very foolish one to speak that name under this roof. Say your piece and be off. You aren't welcome here."

Aldfrid's face darkened at that, although, aware that some of the warriors were now unsheathing their knives, he held his tongue. When he did speak, his voice was rough from suppressed anger.

"You made a pact with Mercia," he replied, choosing his words carefully, "and the time has come to keep your end of the agreement."

Annan was having difficulty controlling himself. It was all he could do not to launch himself across the hall and slam his first into Aldfrid's face. Everyone present knew what the Mercian ealdorman really meant.

You 'bent the knee' to Mercia. You sacrificed your honor for your people. Now you must pay the price.

When Annan did not reply, Aldfrid continued, his gaze flicking to where Hereswith sat silently next to Annan.

"The king's sister—Saewara—is recently widowed. Penda has decided she will make an excellent match for you."

His words caused the silence inside the hall to deepen. Sensing the atmosphere in the hall was on a knife-edge, another dog, this one sitting on the rushes only a few yards from Aldfrid, began to growl.

"The marriage between you will bring our kingdoms even closer together." Aldfrid kept his gaze averted from the dog and delivered the rest of his message. "Penda commands it."

Annan stared back at Penda of Mercia's messenger in shock. He had not expected this move. "He cannot command me to marry his sister," he finally ground out. "I refuse."

"You 'bent the knee' to Mercia," Aldfrid spat out the words, sweat now beading on his heavy brow. "Or do you forget? The bodies of the East Angles lay scattered over Barrow Fields and you stood before Penda in his tent. You swore, on the lives of your men that you would do as Penda bid. You swore an oath—upon your own honor. Do you retract it now?"

Annan glared back at him; those were inflammatory words. Men had been killed for less. Helpless rage almost blinded him, but with it a cold, sickening dread seeped through his gut. Indeed, he had made that oath; he had been given no choice. At the time, Penda had already had one of Annan's men killed before him, for refusing. Penda had threatened to slay each one, until he got the promise he wanted.

Annan had paid for their lives with his own honor—and now bitterly regretted it. He should have let Penda kill them all, him included, rather than suffer this humiliation. Although none present would ever have voiced such a sentiment, he felt as if he had failed his people; the only king of the East Angles to submit to Mercia. Raedwald, the great Wuffinga king his father had served, would turn in his grave to see that it had come to this.

"I already have a betrothed," Annan rasped. "I will marry Hereswith of Bebbanburg, ward of Edwin of Northumbria."

"Betrothals are not written in blood," Aldfrid replied before spitting on the rush-matting at his feet. "You have not yet wed—you are free to marry whom Penda sees fit. You know what will happen if you refuse him. Make your choice."

Annan stood, motionless, in a sea of his ealdormen, thegns, warriors and their kin. Many, Saba and his brother amongst them, had risen to their feet in support of their king. The Mercian ealdorman, to his credit, stood firm. His iron gaze never left Annan's face.

They both knew the truth of it.

Annan, as formidable a warrior as he was, lacked the ruthlessness of the Wuffingas who had ruled before him.

They both knew that despite Annan's show of defiance and anger, he would submit. He had the lives of everyone under this roof—all those who resided in Rendlaesham and the settlements beyond—in his hands. He could not sacrifice them.

Annan was trapped, and Aldfrid knew it.

Chapter Two

The Widow's Escape

Tamworth, the Kingdom of Mercia

On the same eve ...

NIGHT CAST A dark, chill blanket over the Great Tower of Tamworth, throwing it into shadow. Darkness veiled the gently rolling hills around the stone tower, and the stars stood out in sharp relief against the deep black of the sky.

Inside the Great Tower, the evening meal had come and gone. Women sat around the fire in the hall, gossiping at their distaffs. Dogs stretched out at their feet, enjoying the lingering warmth from the two great hearths that warmed the stronghold. Men sipped ale and lounged at one of the main long tables around the cavernous space, playing knuckle bones or *Cyningtaefl*, 'King's Table'—exchanging ribald comments as they moved pieces about a large board. On the floor above, a wooden platform with a ladder leading down to the main hall, Penda had retired early with his wife, Cyneswide.

At her seat by one of the hearths, Saewara laid aside her embroidery and rubbed her stinging eyes. Nearby, her two nieces played with a puppy on the rushes. The girls, just four and three winters respectively, had their father's ice-blond coloring but their mother's sweet, trusting disposition. Saewara watched the girls for a moment, filled with a hollow sadness.

I wish I could protect you from the world, she thought. *From all that it means to be a woman.*

All of a sudden, the sound of Cyneswide's muffled shrieks above, as her husband serviced her, reached those on the floor below. Seeing her nieces questioning gazes directed upwards, Saewara hastily looked away, lest they ask—as they had before—whether fæder was hurting mōder.

Nearby two women, wives of Penda's thegns, sniggered knowingly.

Saewara gazed into the glowing embers of the fire pit and wondered if it was still too early to make her move. She had planned this evening so carefully, she could not risk making a mistake now. She had not expected her brother and his wife to retire so early, but now that the opportunity had presented itself, she would be a fool to let it go.

Saewara knew she had but days left. Her brother had sent word to the

343

King of the East Angles, informing him of his impending nuptials to a woman he had never met. Just the thought of marrying this Annan of the Wuffingas made her stomach twist. She had not intention of marrying anyone. She wanted to spend the rest of her life in peace; in the gentle seclusion of a cloistered life, away from the Great Tower of Tamworth. Tonight would be her last chance—she would get no other.

Above, Cyneswide gave a loud groan.

Saewara's cheeks flamed. Not for the first time, she failed to understand why such a sweet-tempered woman like Cyneswide could find such pleasure in her brother's bed. He was a cold, brutal man with all that knew him; yet it was well known that he had not been able to keep his hands off his wife since the day of their handfasting five years earlier. He and Cyneswide said little to each other with the others present, but often retired early to their platform above the great hall; a bower that afforded them far more privacy than most. Penda's marriage had always perplexed Saewara. Perhaps he showed his wife a gentler side—one that the rest of the world had yet to see.

Although she had planned to slip away later, when fewer folk would be about, Saewara decided that she would make her move now, while her brother was otherwise occupied. She casually rose to her feet and made a show of stretching.

"I'm stepping outside for a breath of fresh air," she told the two women who she had barely spoken to all evening. "I need to stretch my legs."

They nodded coolly, before turning back to the conversation she had interrupted. Of late, Saewara had not been a chatty companion at the fireside. As such, they would not miss her company. Taking a fur cloak, for although spring had arrived the night air still had a bite to it, Saewara made her way across the wide floor. She left the hall through oak doors; rushes crunched underfoot. She passed two guards, who stood chatting together next to where a row of torches flamed against the damp, stone wall.

"Where are you off to, M'lady?" one of them queried.

"Just getting some air," Saewara replied demurely, "I'm cramped from sitting for too long."

"Don't go far," the guard called after her.

"I won't." Saewara threw a timid smile over her shoulder. "Just a short stroll."

Heart hammering, she made her way down the stone steps and across a wide courtyard that was lined with low, thatched buildings. These were where most of Penda's warriors slept, next to the stables. The cold air stung Saewara's face as she walked past. The sound of laughter and drunken male voices reached her and, aware that she was still in sight of the guards at the doors, she forced herself to slow her pace.

She had to make this look like an evening stroll, not an escape.

Moments later, she had passed under the stone archway and into the narrow streets of Tamworth itself. The town, a tangle of thatched wattle and daub houses, spread around the base of the hill, and the stone edifice that rose above it. The Great Tower of Tamworth was famed across the land—the only one of its kind in Britannia—where most lords resided in great wooden halls. Penda, like his predecessors, was very proud of his tower, despite that it could be bitterly cold in winter. He boasted that, unlike the halls of other kings, his was built to last.

The dirt-packed streets of Tamworth were largely empty. It was a moonless night but the glow from inside the low buildings cast a dim light, allowing Saewara to navigate her way easily through the rabbit warren of narrow lanes toward the town walls.

As she approached the main gates, her heart began to slam wildly against her ribs.

What if he had lied?

Saewara wiped her sweating palms against the thick woolen shift she wore.

What if there is another on duty at this hour—and I am caught?

There was no time for second thoughts. She knew she had but a tiny window of opportunity before she was missed. She had to leave now.

A high wall circled Tamworth; a solid construction made of stone and wood. The gates themselves were heavy oak and studded with iron spikes. A single guard stood before the gates.

Saewara, quick and silent, and blending with the shadows in her dark fur cloak, crept close to the guard.

"Oswald," she whispered. "It's me."

The man started, before turning quickly to her, his face panicked. "Saewara, you're early," he hissed. "I thought you would come later. There are still too many guards around—someone might see you."

"I had to come now," she replied. "There wouldn't have been a better chance later."

Oswald, a young man with a thin, sensitive face, glanced nervously around him before pulling Saewara into the shadows. "M'lady—are you sure this is wise?"

"Of course it isn't," Saewara replied, irritation surfacing in her voice, "but my brother has left me with no choice."

"But Penda is not lightly crossed."

"It won't matter. Once we reach Bonehill, we will gain sanctuary. We will *both* be safe there."

Oswald frowned, still not convinced, although his body appeared to relax slightly. "But the king worships the old gods," he whispered.

Sweat shone on his skin in the flickering torch light. For the first time, Saewara regretted involving him. Oswald had seemed so keen when she had presented the idea to him. He chafed at the life of warrior here in Tamworth. He longed to become a monk and worship the one god—the true god. She had convinced him it was possible; all he had to do was help her get away from Tamworth.

Now it appeared he was losing his nerve.

"Listen to me, Oswald." Saewara placed her hand on his arm and squeezed firmly. "There is no time for second thoughts. If you wish to serve

God, you must take risks. You will never be able to carry out the Lord's work here. We must go—before the king's men come looking for me. We need to get a head-start on them. Have you hidden the horses?"

Oswald nodded, his eyes gleaming.

"Let's go then," Saewara urged. "No more talk. I will follow you."

Oswald gazed at her, as if awed by one small woman's resolve. Yet Saewara knew the danger she was placing them both in. For her, the alternative was worse than the penalty if she was caught. He paused a moment longer, and even opened his mouth to protest once more, but one fierce look quelled him. He swallowed, gave one more, nervous glance about them, and turned toward the gates.

Casting his gaze nervously into the shadows, lest anyone was around to see them, Oswald pushed the gates apart, just enough for them to slip through. Then, one at a time, they squeezed between the gates and into the shadowed world beyond. Just a few yards from the gates, darkness swallowed them.

Despite that Saewara could not even see her hand before her face, she was grateful for the moonless night. Oswald had done well, to insist he would take the first watch alone this evening, while his friends went to drink in the mead hall. Now, he had to keep his courage and they would soon be far from here.

Saewara stumbled over a tree root and reached forward, grasping Oswald's arm for support. He knew the land outside the walls far better than she, and despite that he could see nothing in the pitch black, made his way confidently toward a copse of trees to the east of the walls. Behind them, the muted sounds of Tamworth broke the night's stillness: the occasional bark of a dog, men's voices raised in drunken laughter – and somewhere, so faint that Saewara almost could not make it out—a woman's voice, singing.

A short while later, they reached the horses. Oswald had tethered them under a large, spreading oak in the heart of the woods. Working by feel, Saewara sprang up on to the saddle and fumbled for the reins.

Moments later, they were off. Oswald led the way, guiding his horse through the darkness, away from Tamworth. He knew these woods well, and rode as if he had the eyesight of an owl. Saewara followed blindly behind, letting her horse follow by instinct. Bonehill was some distance to the south; it would take them the entire night to reach it.

They had been riding a short while when the trees drew back and they rode under an ink-black, star-sprinkled sky. The air was cold but there was not a breath of wind. The night was eerily quiet, and Saewara's nerves, already on edge, stretched taut. Her ears strained for any sign that they were being pursued. Yet apart from the rustling of animals in the undergrowth, and the far off hoot of an owl, they now rode through an empty land.

"Can't we ride faster?" Saewara brought her horse level with Oswald, who was nothing more than a dark silhouette against the starlit landscape.

"No," he replied, his voice sharper than she had expected. "It's too dark.

If one of our horses stumbles into a rabbit burrow or over a tree root, they could break a leg."

Saewara lapsed back into silence and reined her horse back slightly so that she followed behind Oswald once more. Although she chafed at their slow pace, she knew he spoke the truth. Fleeing in a panic, could end up ruining everything.

They rode south through the night, over a rolling landscape of fields, streams and wooded valleys. Saewara and Oswald spoke little, their senses tuned for any sign that they were being pursued. No sign came.

Eventually, the first glow of the approaching dawn stained the eastern sky. Saewara blinked tiredly; her eyes stung from fatigue. They had been riding all night without rest. She could feel exhaustion dragging at her but knew they could not afford to rest – even now when they were so close to Bonehill. Her eyes had long adjusted to the darkness, and as the first rays of light illuminated the eastern horizon, she found herself straining her eyes to see what lay ahead. They were riding up a hill now, and Saewara was sure that the monastery, where they would find sanctuary and peace, lay just beyond the horizon. Hope lifted her flagging spirits. Just a little longer and she would be free.

Then, the ground began to shake.

Saewara's horse, a shaggy dun mare, snorted nervously and side-stepped, nearly dislodging its rider.

"Oswald?" Saewara called out. "What's that noise?"

Her companion turned in the saddle, his gaze taking in his surroundings, before focusing on something beyond Saewara's left shoulder. His face blanched.

"Horses!" he croaked. "Coming fast from the north."

Saewara's breathing stilled. She swiveled in the saddle, and gazed back at the way they had come. There, drawing closer with every moment that passed, was a galloping group of horses. She saw the outlines of spears, bristling against the lightening sky, and felt her body go cold.

Penda had caught up with her.

"Ride!" Oswald shouted at her. "Bonehill lies but a short distance to the south. We may outrun them yet!"

Without waiting for her response, the young man dug his heels into his horse's flanks and took off up the hill. Saewara tore her gaze from the approaching riders and followed suit. Crouching low over the dun mare's prickly mane, she focused on the top of the rise. Her horse was tired, but she urged it on. They had to outrun those warriors. She could not return to Tamworth. She would rather die.

As if sensing its rider's desperation, the horse gathered its last reserves of energy and thundered up the slope. It was an exposed spot; there were no thickets of trees to hide in. They would have to outrun their pursuers or be captured.

Saewara crested the top of the hill and saw that Oswald was already half-way down the slope. He was fleeing now, with no thought to her safety. Although she could hardly blame him, for she too feared Penda's wrath,

Saewara felt a stab of outrage at his cowardice.

She cursed under her breath and clung on as her horse raced down the hill. Beyond, lay a wooded valley, and a stream that twinkled in the dawn. There, in the heart of the valley lay the thatched roof of a long timbered hall, surrounded by a high perimeter fence constructed of sharp wooden palings: the monastery of Bonehill.

Saewara nearly sobbed in relief at the sight of her destination. She had come so far. She could not bear to be thwarted now. The thundering of horses' hooves shook the ground around her. They were close; so close that she could hear the grunts of their horses and the curses of the men who pursued her.

Her horse squealed in panic then, took the bit between its teeth and bolted.

Saewara had no choice but to cling on with her knees. Her surroundings passed in a blur and she quickly gained on Oswald.

Then, she heard the unmistakable twang of a bow-string releasing, and cursed.

She should have realized that her brother would send his bowmen after her. This was no battle—a place for spears, axes and swords—but a hunt.

A moment later, Oswald fell. An arrow hit him square between the shoulder blades, and he pitched from his horse with a strangled scream. A moment after that, Saewara's horse went down from under as an arrow caught its hind-quarters.

Suddenly, Saewara was airborne, hurtling through the air like a pebble from a slingshot. She curled herself up into a ball, as she had been taught when learning how to ride, and braced herself for impact.

Saewara hit the dew-laden grass and felt the air gush from her lungs. She rolled down the hill and came to a halt at the bottom, face-down on her stomach.

She lay there for a few moments, the sound of laughter and approaching hooves, ringing in her ears. Gingerly, she drew her knees in to her chest and rolled over onto her side, wincing as she did so. Her entire left side felt as if it were on fire. Oswald lay nearby, face-down, unmoving.

A group of warriors, riding lathered horses, drew to a halt around her. She recognized many of the faces. Penda's loyal warriors and thegns—men as ruthless and cold as the man they served. One of the men, Thrydwulf, a warrior that Saewara had always feared, swung down from his horse and strode over to Oswald.

He turned him over with his foot before spitting on him.

"Pity." He cast a cold glance over his shoulder. "He's dead. Penda was planning to make sport of your lover."

"He wasn't my lover," Saewara wheezed, struggling to regain the breath that had been knocked out of her. "He was only helping me."

"No man risks his life for a woman unless he thinks she's his," Thrydwulf walked toward her. "Slut."

"You're wrong," Saewara gasped, knowing she should hold her tongue, but finding herself unable. The disdainful gazes of the men surrounding her was more than she could take. "Oswald was going to take his vows at Bonehill. He wanted to become a monk—to serve god!"

The warriors laughed then, mocking her.

"A monk, eh?" Thrydwulf looked back at where Oswald gazed sightlessly into the heavens. "Then a quick death was the best thing for him."

"Hōre!" The flat of Penda's hand connected with Saewara's cheek with a crack, sending her sprawling back across the floor. She landed on her back and sat up, clutching her stinging cheek. Tears blurred her vision. The faces of those around her distorted, as if she was looking at them from the bottom of a clear, deep pond.

Saewara bit the inside of her cheek and tried to stop the tears. She had promised herself on the ride back that she would not cry—that she would exhibit the same coldness as Penda himself. Yet when faced with his icy rage, it had been too much.

Cyneswide stood at the edge of the room, near the fire pit, her face white and taut, while her two daughters clutched at her skirts, crying.

Penda ignored them.

He walked over to Saewara and pulled her up by her braid. The pain was excruciating and it took all of Saewara's will not to cry out. She stared up into her brother's pale blue eyes and felt her skin prickle with terror.

"You bring shame upon your kin," he hissed in her face. "You must obey me in all things but you and your lover thought better."

"Oswald was not my lover," Saewara whispered, her voice breaking slightly. "I want nothing more to do with men. I've already told you that he wanted to take his vows. Like me, he planned to live at Bonehill as one of god's servants."

"You serve no one but me, hōre," Penda shook her hard. His face was white with rage. She had never seen him so angry. Usually Penda's temper was like a wintry blast—but this anger pulsed like the hot core of a furnace. "You will marry who I say—even if I have to drag you into his bed myself!"

Saewara's tears flowed, uninterrupted. Her one chance, her only hope, had gone. Nothing but a bleak, empty future faced her now.

"Why don't you just kill me," she sobbed. "I don't want to be another man's wife. If I can't be free I'd rather be dead. Just kill me!"

"Silence!" Penda roared, shaking her so hard that her teeth rattled. Her scalp burned where he gripped it. "I *would* kill you, if this marriage wasn't so important to Mercia. Don't think I wouldn't."

"Then why don't you? I've brought shame on our family. I'm not fit to marry!"

Penda slapped her again with his free hand, snapping her head back. This time, Saewara screamed, the sound mingling with the wails of her young nieces.

"Look at me!" Penda ordered.

Saewara opened her eyes to find his face just inches from hers.

"You are indeed a disgrace to the Mercian line," he snarled. "But you will still do as you're told. You will do what you were bred for. Annan of the East Angles will be here in days and you will marry him without a whimper of complaint. Is that clear?"

Saewara stared back at him, gasping in agony. He shook her again and her head swam as her vision began to speckle.

"I didn't hear you?" he hissed.

Saewara closed her eyes, blocking everything out, before she gave a barely perceptible nod. "Yes, Milord," she whispered.

Chapter Three

Between Brothers

"HWÆT!" ANNAN STARED at his brother in shock. "What did you just say?"

Aethelhere returned Annan's gaze without faltering, his face uncharacteristically serious.

"Hereswith. I want your permission to marry her."

Annan stepped back from Aethelhere, just in case he was seized by the urge to strike him down. No, he had heard correctly; as if things were not bad enough, even his own kin were turning against him.

He could not believe the injustice of it all. It was not that he was in love with Hereswith—he hardly knew the girl. Yet she was comely with a gaze that promised much; if he was to marry anyone, he wanted it to be her. Why should his brother be happy when he was miserable? Was wyrd, fate, trying to punish him?

"Don't look at me like that," Aethelhere was resolute. He appeared to have no intention of retracting his request. "I would never have asked, had it not been clear that you will do as Penda bids. As you're about to leave, I knew I had to ask you—otherwise Hereswith will be gone by the time you return and I will have missed my chance."

"I was to marry her," Annan ground out. "Do you think I want you rubbing that in my face?"

"I don't ask this to spite you," Aethelhere countered. "It's time I took a wife—and if you will not have Hereswith, I will."

"She's not a ewe you can barter at market," Annan snarled, turning on his heel and stalking to the other end of his bower, where he had been packing away the last few items he would take with him to Tamworth. "She may have something to say on the matter!"

He stuffed a heavy woolen tunic into his saddlebag and glanced back over at where Aethelhere stood, immobile, beside the curtain that screened them from the rest of the hall.

To Annan's fury, his brother now wore a cocky smile. "I'm sure I can convince her to marry me, instead of you," he said confidently, "after all, if she returns to Bebbanburg, the Northumbrian King may marry her to some ageing ealdorman. I'm a much better choice."

"You astound me." Annan shook his head, still choking down rage.

"Since when did you get so full of yourself?"

"So do you give your permission?"

"Thunor's hammer—you're like a dog with a bone!"

"I need to know."

Annan cursed and kicked the helmet he had been about to pick up across the bower. It bounced off the tapestry-covered wall with a dull thud.

"Nithhogg take you! She was mine. Now I'm going to be saddled with some Mercian bitch."

"You're marrying this widow anyway," Aethelhere responded stubbornly. "What does it matter?"

"It matters because if I can't have her, I don't see why you should!" Annan roared.

Aethelhere stared back, waiting for his answer.

"Very well," Annan snarled, "you can have he—if she'll have you!"

"Thank you, Annan."

The relief in Aethelhere's voice made jealousy twist Annan's stomach. Hereswith was a woman that men, even brothers, could easily become enemies over.

"I wouldn't be so smug," Annan continued, unable to stop himself from ruining his brother's victory. "The King of Northumbria might have something to say about your match—he wanted his niece wedded to the King of the East Angles, not his brother."

"Then I won't give him the chance to interfere," Aethelhere countered, as cocksure as ever, "If Hereswith says 'yes', I'll wed her before he has time to protest."

"Do what you want, you will anyway." Annan turned his back on Aethelhere then. Just when he thought his life could not get any bleaker, his brother had to go and kick him in the guts. "Only, make sure you're wedded by the time I return, I won't be attending your handfasting."

Annan made his way down the steps from his bower and across the Great Hall toward the entrance. Outside, a group of his most loyal warriors, Saba among them, would be waiting patiently for their king. They should have departed Rendlaesham at dawn but Annan had delayed as much as he was able. Now, Aethelhere's announcement made him want to get away from the 'Golden Hall' as quickly as possible.

It made him never want to return.

Hereswith was there, sitting beside the fire pit at her distaff. He caught a glimpse of her out of the corner of his eye. Even pale and strained, her eyes red-rimmed from weeping, she was beautiful. Her hair flowed in a golden curtain down her slender back as she sat, ramrod straight at her distaff.

Aethelhere would not have had time to approach her as yet.

Annan wondered if she would refuse him; she did seem very upset at the prospect of losing Annan. Part of him, the part that did not see why his brother should be happy when he was not, hoped that she would shun Aethelhere and return north. Annan was not sure he could bear to return here and see Hereswith wed to his brother; although with a long journey ahead of him, he preferred not to dwell on it.

Annan acknowledged Hereswith with a curt nod. The gazes of those who served him, tracked the king as he crossed the floor. It was a relief when he reached the oak doors and stepped outside into the crisp morning air. He was half-way down the steps to the stable yard when a woman's voice hailed him.

"Milord!"

Annan recognized the voice instantly. He turned, and found himself but a yard away from Hereswith of Bebbanburg.

"Hereswith," he said gently. "You should not follow me. There is nothing to say."

"But I would say 'goodbye'." Her voice trembled and her eyes filled with tears. "Were you going to leave without speaking to me?"

"I thought it would be easier this way. I am sorry we cannot be wed," he replied.

"Can you not refuse Penda?" she asked. The hope in her voice cut him like a freshly sharpened blade.

Annan shook his head.

"It has gone too far for that. I swore an oath to Penda, and I must uphold it. If it were for myself I might not—but I'm responsible for the well-being of this kingdom's folk. Penda is not a man lightly crossed."

Anger flared in Hereswith's blue eyes. "But neither are you. Tell him 'no'."

Annan shook his head and gave a wry smile. "Penda and I are very different men. He seeks to rule whereas I had this responsibility thrust upon me. I know how to lead an army and inspire man's loyalty—but Penda knows how to conquer. As lovely as you are Hereswith, I would not risk my people's lives for you. Do not ask me to."

Hereswith's mouth thinned slightly at that. Suddenly, for an instant, Annan had a glimpse of a woman who was nothing like the sweet maid she appeared to be. There was a core of iron hidden under that beautiful façade. Yet this did not make Annan want her any less; if anything, her fire stirred him.

In this case, however, this woman was not destined to be his.

"Goodbye, Hereswith," he said gently. "I wish you well."

With that, he turned, the heavy cape he wore about his shoulders swinging, and descended the rest of the wooden stairs. In the stable yard below, Saba stood waiting, with a party of twenty warriors and their horses. They were all grim-faced; Penda might not be marching on the kingdom, but this latest development had made them all uneasy. Annan did not blame them. Penda was too ambitious to leave them alone for long. This was but a sign of things to come.

Wordlessly, for both men knew there was nothing more to be said until they were far from Rendlaesham, Saba nodded to his king. Annan gave him a curt nod in response before strapping on his bags behind the saddle. Then, taking the reins from Saba, Annan swung up onto the back of his horse. The heavy-set black stallion shifted under him, impatient to be on its way.

A crowd had now gathered to see off the king. Ignoring them, especially the stricken face of one woman in particular, Annan slung his heavy lime shield over his back and adjusted his sword—*Night Bringer*—so that it sat within easy reach should they be attacked during the journey. Close to Rendlaesham it would be relatively safe, but Annan had seen enough of the world to know that it was in the moments when a man let his guard down that he came to grief. Next, he put on his iron helmet. It was heavy and uncomfortable, and would cause him to sweat if he wore it for too long. Yet, it shielded his face, from his nose up, from view—something that Annan was grateful for as he took his leave of Rendlaesham.

Annan turned his stallion and urged it into a brisk trot. He led his men out of the shadow of the Great Hall, and through the gates into Rendlaesham. They rode through the town toward the main gates, along a wide, unpaved street. Crowds of townsfolk came out to see the king.

They were all there: the peasants who worked the fields and orchards outside Rendlaesham, the iron smith, the carpenter, the baker, and the brewer. Even the keeper of the town's mead hall had made an appearance; a florid-faced man who appeared as if he consumed as much mead as he served. Crowds of women and children gathered at the roadside. Some waved, some called out to him—while others watched on silently— their faces strained.

Their expressions pained Annan. Although he had temporarily saved them from the axes and spears of the Mercians, most folk knew that it was but a stay of execution. He had given away his own, and the Kingdom's, pride for a fragile peace.

Annan shared their worries, for there were many nights when he lay awake thinking of the choice he had made. Now, more than ever, he was coming to regret it.

A golden dusk settled over the flat meadows of the East Anglian countryside, bringing a long day's journey to an end. The king's party made camp next to a stand of lime trees and a small, clear brook. After a cold start, the day had warmed considerably. Even as the sun slid behind the western horizon, the air had a warmth to it; soft with the promise of summer.

They erected a tent for the king, and another for his thegns. The remaining men would sleep before the fire outside or keep watch over the camp. Annan stayed outside for a while, watching as the last of the sunset faded from the sky and night stole over the world. He shared a cup of ale with his men around the fire and together they ate rabbits that they had roasted over the embers.

Once he had eaten, Annan retired to his tent. There, he sat before the small fire pit in the center, on the edge of the mound of furs. Outside, he could hear the muted sounds of his men's voices, punctuated by the distant hooting of an owl. It was peaceful out here, far from those who made demands on him, and Annan relished the quiet.

I'm but thirty-three winters, yet I feel as if I carry the weight of the world upon my shoulders, he thought, feeding the fire with some dry sticks. *Just a year ago, I spent my days hunting, chasing women and drinking. How things change.*

Once he had organized the first watches around the camp's perimeters, Saba joined Annan for a cup of mead in front of the fire.

"Still brooding?" his friend observed as he sat down on a pile of furs opposite the king and took the cup Annan passed him.

"No," Annan replied, stretching his long legs out before him, "just reflecting."

"Sounds like brooding to me."

Annan shrugged. "Call it what you will. And wipe that smirk off your face—just because you're lovesick for Hilda doesn't mean the rest of us have to go around grinning like idiots."

Saba roared with laughter at that, nearly spilling his mead into the fire. When he recovered, his eyes sparkled with mirth.

"You've developed a forked tongue of late," he observed, "although you're not wrong. That slave girl is a pretty wench. I'd willingly take her to my bed."

"She might have something to say about that," Annan replied. "Every time you look her way the girl wilts in terror."

"She's been treated cruelly, that much is clear." Saba frowned then. "But given time I will teach her we are not all beasts."

Annan returned his friend's gaze before nodding. "May fate favor you both, if you wish to pursue her upon our return to Rendlaesham I will allow it."

"Wyrd has been kind to me so far," Saba replied, "and I hope my good fortune will continue. Thank you—I would like to pursue her."

The men lapsed into silence then, each lost in their own thoughts for a few moments. It was Annan who spoke first, his gaze fixed upon the dancing flames.

"Aethelhere has asked me for permission to wed Hereswith."

Saba's eyebrows shot up at this. "Truly?"

Annan nodded. "He asked me just before we departed the Great Hall. He couldn't risk her returning to the north while we are in Mercia."

"You gave him permission?"

"I did—I wanted to smash my fist into his face but in the end I agreed."

Saba took a deep draught from his cup before responding. "Was that wise?"

Annan shrugged. "Probably not, but since I can't have her it seemed petty to deny my brother."

Saba shook his head at that. "You are a fair man Annan—sometimes too much so. Did you not think about how it will be when Hereswith bears your brother's children while you're saddled with your Mercian bride? It will eat you up inside."

Annan did not respond, and so Saba continued. "It will not be easy, what is coming. Are you ready to face Penda again?"

Annan scowled. "I don't fear that bastard—it's only the threat he poses to my kingdom that makes me do his bidding."

"I know that," Saba replied, "but you need to prepare yourself for meeting his sister. Are you ready to take her home? She will be hated in Rendlaesham, and marrying her will not make you popular either."

"You speak the truth," Annan admitted grimly, before draining the rest of his cup and pouring himself another. "Although I am not in the humor to hear it."

"I'm not trying to blacken your mood," Saba countered with a wry smile. "I just think it's important you reconcile yourself to your fate, *before* we enter Tamworth."

Annan nodded before staring moodily into the fire.

"Saewara of Tamworth," he said her name for the first time, although it left a bitter taste on his tongue. "My doom."

Chapter Four

The Betrothal

"SAEWARA, THE EAST Angles have come."

The words that Saewara dreaded had been spoken.

Five long, miserable days had passed since her disastrous escape attempt, and during that time Saewara had barely left the Great Tower of Tamworth. Penda had assigned two of his ealdormen's wives to watch over her at all times; even escorting her when she went to the privy or standing over her while she bathed. She was allowed not a moment on her own, and it appeared all in the Great Tower, but her sister by marriage and nieces, now shunned her.

Not that Saewara was good company. She sat, eyes downcast, and shut out the world. Not even the playful antics of her nieces, or Cyneswide's gentle concern, could draw her out of her misery.

And now the day of execution had arrived.

"Saewara?"

Cyneswide's voice roused Saewara from where she sat unthinkingly winding wool onto a distaff. For the first time in days, she looked directly at her sister-in-law, and saw the worry etched on her lovely face.

"So they have come?" Saewara's voice was husky from the hours she had spent crying every night since her recapture. "The waiting is over—I should be grateful for that at least."

"Come." Cyneswide beckoned to her. "We must get you ready for your betrothal. The king has gone out to greet them but they will enter the tower soon."

Saewara rose to her feet and followed the queen without complaint; they both knew the time for resistance had long passed.

The two women entered an alcove at the back of the hall, screened by a heavy tapestry. For the first time in days, Saewara had a moment of relative privacy. Moving woodenly, as if in a trance, she pulled her heavy woolen over-dress and linen under-tunic over her head and stood naked on the rushes while Cyneswide placed a basin of hot water before her to wash with. Saewara bathed quickly, in deft movements. Despite that it was not cold in the hall, she stood shivering while Cyneswide handed her a freshly laundered linen under-tunic followed by a thick green woolen *wealca*; a tubular dress clasped at the shoulders by two bronze brooches. Around her waist, she clasped a heavy leather belt, studded with gold, and she adorned her bare arms with gold and silver rings. Then, she donned a dark green cloak, embroidered with gold around the borders. On her feet, she strapped on light leather sandals.

Cyneswide then brushed out Saewara's long hair, letting it fall down her back in a dark curtain. She had just finished fussing over Saewara's cloak, and was stepping back to admire her handiwork, when the rumble of men's voices entering the Great Tower, reached them from beyond the tapestry.

Saewara's legs began to tremble. Suddenly, the numbness that had protected her over the past days lifted, and she was acutely aware of her surroundings.

"I can't go to them," she whispered, clutching at Cyneswide. "Please don't make me!"

"Saewara!" Cyneswide gave her a fierce hug. Then she stood back and took hold of Saewara by the shoulders, her face uncharacteristically resolute. "You must do this. If I could, I would help you—but there is no choice. Only this."

Saewara stared at her sister by marriage, frozen to the spot.

"You look beautiful." Cyneswide gave her a tremulous smile, in an effort to bolster Saewara's courage. "Your new husband-to-be will be enchanted."

Saewara choked back hysteria at that. "Beautiful?" she gulped, glancing around like a hare cornered by hounds. "I am nothing more than a pawn, as well you know, Cyneswide."

Her gaze met Cyneswide's and she saw the tears brimming in the queen's eyes.

"I'm sorry," Saewara gasped, "but I was not made for a life such as this—it will kill me."

"Saewara!" Penda's voice sounded on the other side of the curtain. "Annan of the East Angles is about to enter this hall. Come out now or I will drag you out by your hair."

The two women exchanged glances; looks full of unsaid words that could never, and would never, be uttered. They knew their lot—and it was time for Saewara to bow before the life she had been given.

Saewara closed her eyes, clutching the crucifix she wore around her neck to her breast and saying a silent prayer. Then, opening her eyes, she squared her shoulders and stepped toward the tapestry.

Annan walked up the stone steps to the great oaken doors of Penda's hall, with as much enthusiasm as if he were walking to his own hanging. His warriors flanked him, with Saba at his right side. Their presence did little to alleviate the dread which increased with every step.

Above him, reared the Great Tower of Tamworth; a magnificent, if somber, sight against a colorless sky. Annan had heard many a tale of this fortress, but even so was awed by its size and solidity.

At the doors, Aldfrid of Tamworth, the ealdorman who had brought tidings of Annan's impending nuptials, stood waiting. He had lost none of his arrogance since the last time they had met; if anything the heavy-set warrior looked even fuller of himself. Of course, he was on home ground now, surrounded by his own people.

They did not speak. Instead, Aldfrid led the way, across an antechamber and into the Great Hall of Tamworth.

A vast circular chamber greeted Annan. There were two great fire pits at one end and a high wooden platform at the other, with stairs leading up to it. Heavy tapestries lined the damp stone walls and flames flickered from clay cressets, illuminating the cavernous space in soft, golden light. A row of narrow windows, high up, let out the smoke from the fire pits.

At the far end, upon the high seat stood King Penda of Mercia, with his radiant blonde wife at his side. At the foot of the wooden platform, her gaze fixed upon his face stood another, very different, woman.

Saewara of Tamworth— his betrothed.

Ealdormen, thegns and their families packed the Great Hall. Each gaze bored into Annan as he walked the distance between the doors and the high seat. The crowd parted before him. His boots crunched on the fresh rushes and he felt the heat emanating from the fire pit closest to him.

The time had come for him to meet his betrothed—and there she was before him.

Frankly, she was not what he had expected.

He had expected a tall, pale, ice-blonde woman; hard-featured and cold like her brother. However, the woman before him bore no resemblance to King Penda of Mercia. She was small with long dark hair. Her figure was hidden under a voluminous green cape but her face was heart-shaped and her skin milky. She had a full mouth, delicate features and eyes that were the color of the sky before a thunderstorm.

Her gaze was riveted upon Annan but her expression was one of barely concealed terror, as if she watched a demon approach.

Annan had never seen a woman quite like her, and he could not help but compare her to the woman he had left behind in Rendlaesham. Hereswith was willowy and fair-haired, a beauty of Germanic stock like many on the eastern coast of Britannia; yet the woman before him looked like one of the Cymri. That was not to say she was unattractive, it was just that Annan had always preferred tall, slender blondes.

Saewara's pulse throbbed in her temples and she clenched her fists against her skirts in an effort to control her panic. She watched as a tall, blond man stepped through the archway into the main hall and crossed the wide space toward her. Behind him trailed a group of East Angle warriors. One of them, a tall man with dark hair and a forbidding expression, carried something large covered by a linen cloth.

Despite her fear, she could not help but observe the man who approached. Annan was far more handsome, and younger, than she had expected. His mane of golden hair was tied back in a thong at the nape of his neck. He was clean shaven and dressed in a fine linen tunic, a black leather vest, and calf-skin breaches. A thick, rabbit fur cloak hung from his broad shoulders. Like many of the men here, his arms were bare, and his muscular biceps wore numerous gold and bronze arm rings—all tributes to his valor in battle. He moved with a loose-limbed, confident stride, with his back ramrod straight. When he drew closer, Saewara saw that his eyes were a deep blue.

Annan, King of the East Angles, stopped before the high seat and, for the first time, made eye-contact with Saewara.

She stared back at him, and for a moment time stilled.

Here was a man, very different to any she had known; she could sense it. But whether that boded ill or well for her, she did not know. His gaze held hers for a few moments and when he looked away, Saewara slowly released the breath that she had been holding.

Penda stepped down from the high seat to greet Annan, and Saewara was struck by how different the two kings were. They were both tall and blond, but any similarity ended there. Penda's looks were ice-cold, chiseled and hard; whereas Annan's golden hair and rugged good-looks gave him a warmth that made her brother look even colder.

"Wes hāl." Penda greeted Annan coolly.

The King of the East Angles gave a curt nod in response and kept his gaze fixed upon the Mercian King as he returned to his wife's side on the dais. Saewara knew Annan was deliberately avoiding looking at her; and she did not blame him. He seemed as unwilling as she to be wed.

"Let us pledge these two individuals, Annan, King of the East Angles, and Saewara of Tamworth." Penda paused then before his gaze met Annan's.

"Annan, are you ready to make a contract between our two families—to make the handa sellan and pay the handgeld in order to wed my fair sister?"

Annan nodded curtly. Penda spoke of the 'hand-shake' in which he would formally promise to marry Saewara, and the payment, which would seal the marriage pledge. Annan would also have to make another 'payment'—the morgengifu, or 'morning gift', on the morning after their wedding night—but, for now, the handgeld was sufficient to seal the promise.

"Annan, take Saewara's hand," Penda continued, "and tell us of the handgeld you bring in exchange for this woman."

Annan turned to Saewara, his gaze still avoiding hers, and took hold of her hand. His hand was warm and strong, and his touch made Saewara's pulse quicken.

"Sabert." Annan turned his head to where the dark-haired warrior stood behind them, acknowledging him for the first time. "Show him the shield."

The warrior nodded and removed the covering from the large object he carried; revealing a huge lime wood shield, covered with leather and studded with an iron boss. It was mighty, well-made and heavy.

"This shield was made for my father, Eni of the Wuffingas," Annan said, his voice toneless and flat, his face a mask. "He passed away before he was able to wield it, so I give this shield as handgeld, in payment for this woman. As morgengifu, your sister will receive two gold arm rings."

360

Penda nodded. "Your handgeld is accepted. Say then, the words that will seal your betrothal."

Annan turned back to Saewara. His gaze met hers, but it appeared that he was looking through, rather than at her. His hand that enclosed hers did not move but Saewara saw the despair in his eyes. This was even worse than she had thought; they both despised this union.

"I, Annan of the East Angles, declare myself witness that you, Saewara of Tamworth, bond me in lawful betrothal," Annan began, his voice low and emotionless, "and with this handshake you pledge me marriage in exchange for the handgeld I have given and the morgengifu I have promised. You are henceforth betrothed to me and will fulfill and observe the whole of the oath between us, which has been said in the hearing of witnesses without wiles or cunning, as a true and honest oath."

A silence followed his words and Saewara closed her eyes as he released her hand.

It was done.

"Very well." Penda broke the silence. "Now, all that remains is to fix the date of your handfast ceremony. I will make the arrangements."

"No," Annan replied, his tone firm. "We will marry in the 'Golden Hall' of the Wuffingas, surrounded by my folk, not here under your roof."

Penda regarded Annan, his pale eyes clouding. "I don't think you should be so hasty to make demands while you are 'under my roof'. If I insist you are hardly in the position to deny me."

"If my people are to accept your sister as queen, it is better that we wed in Rendlaesham," Annan replied, his tone brooking no argument. "That way, they would witness the joining of our two kingdoms."

A tense silence now filled the hall. Annan held the Mercian King's gaze, refusing to back down. Eventually, Penda gave a low, mocking laugh.

"It seems you are resolute. Very well, marry her in Rendlaesham if you must. However, I will send one of my men with your party to ensure the handfasting actually takes place."

Annan's gaze narrowed. "Do you doubt my word?"

Penda's mouth curved into a cold smile. "Naturally."

Another uncomfortable silence stretched between them, before Penda stepped back and gave another smile, this one considerably warmer.

"Enough with the formalities Annan. You are, after all, a guest in my hall and welcome to enjoy my hospitality. If you insist on waiting until you return to your kingdom before marrying Saewara, at least indulge me by staying on in Tamworth another day. Tomorrow, I have organized games to take place outside the walls: archery, axe-throwing, wrestling, sword-fighting. It will be a fine contest. What say you?"

Annan hesitated a moment before he nodded curtly. "Very well, I can wait a day."

"Excellent." Penda stepped back onto the high seat, his smile widening. "Until then, let us break bread and drink together as brothers—for soon we shall be family."

Annan's expression darkened at that, although he wisely held his tongue.

Saewara watched her brother with growing concern. Knowing him as she did, she did not trust his sudden friendliness toward the King of the East Angles. The forced joviality in his tone, and the wolfish edge to his smile, made her wary.

What was he plotting?

Chapter Five

Penda's Game

SAEWARA STEPPED OUT into bright sunlight and blinked rapidly while her eyes adjusted. After a long, dark winter, she was unused to seeing the sun's friendly face. A warm breeze laced with many smells, some pleasant, others less so, caressed her face. The wind brought with it the smell of grass, wildflowers and warm earth; overlaid with the stench of human and animal waste from the cesspit on the eastern outskirts of Tamworth. All it took was for the breeze to blow from a certain direction and the air became foul; now, was one such occasion.

Flanked by the two ealdormen's wives, Saewara picked up her skirts and made her way out of the yard that ringed the Great Tower, and into the streets beyond. They followed the crowd of townsfolk toward the meadows west of Tamworth, not far from where the barrows of the Mercian kings and nobility formed a silhouette against the sky.

Leaving the stench of decomposing waste behind, Saewara breathed deeply once more. She was dressed for the mild weather, in a long linen sleeveless tunic with a green woolen over-dress, belted at the waist.

Enjoying the feel of the sun on her skin, Saewara stepped out onto the meadow. Despite her unhappiness, she could not help but look about her with interest. She always enjoyed the spring games. They were a celebration of winter's end, and the meadows around Tamworth were bright with spring flowers and lush with new growth.

A festive air had brought smiles to the faces of the folk who crowded around the perimeter of the cordoned off area. A wrestling and sword fighting ring had been erected, and two bare-chested warriors were in the middle of a wrestling match in the center of it. Saewara recognized the dark-haired East Angle warrior with the broken nose, who had accompanied Annan, as one of the contestants. Even from this distance, he was clearly winning. A cheering crowd ringed the wrestlers, urging and heckling in turns. At the other end of the area, burly warriors were lining up to throw axes, while archers were taking their place in front of where lads were setting up a row of ten targets. The targets were round, and stained in five rings: yellow at the center, followed by red, blue, black and white.

Saewara recognized the targets. They were the same ones she had spent many an afternoon practicing on as girl, back when life had been so much simpler. Those days, it had not mattered that she was female; and with no mother to keep her in check, Saewara had run wild. She had dressed like a boy, and had followed her two elder brothers around like a lost puppy, much to Eafa and Penda's chagrin.

However, once childhood ended, so did her freedom. From that point on, she had become a pawn to trade at will. Archery was not a sport for high-born ladies to partake in.

A roar went up to Saewara's left as the East Angle warrior bested his wrestling opponent. The warrior grinned maniacally as he ground the loser into the dirt. Saewara watched with interest, before spying Annan on the opposite side of the wrestling ring.

Her betrothed had not yet seen her. Annan stood watching his countryman beat his opponent. He was dressed simply, in a sleeveless tunic; a heavy, iron-studded belt; and breeches that were cross-gartered to the knee. His face was unreadable this morning. He watched the festivities dispassionately and not once glanced in Saewara's direction.

Out of the corner of her eye, Saewara saw a flash of white blond hair and black fur and leather, as Penda of Mercia took his place amongst the crowd. She hoped that he had not yet seen her, and was about to drift away, with the intention of finding a spot to watch the archery competition, when the Mercian King's voice boomed out across the crowd.

"A fine display of East Angle prowess!" Penda stepped forward and clapped his hands, applauding the dark-haired warrior for his victory, although his gaze was mocking. The warrior in question straightened up, his expression darkening.

Penda's gaze, however, was not on the wrestler, but on the King of the East Angles. Annan stared back at him, his face giving nothing away.

"Come, Annan," Penda continued with a smile that did not reach his eyes. "Join your men in a bit friendly competition. I hear you are highly skilled with a longbow. Why not accept a challenge against my champion in archery?"

"Archery?" Annan frowned. Archery was not a 'kingly' sport. While it was common for most warriors to learn how to wield a bow and arrow, and use them while hunting, these weapons were not used by ealdormen and nobility in other circumstances, especially in battle. Saewara's gaze flicked between her brother and Annan. She could see from Penda's face that he had not yet finished.

"Yes—we Mercians are fine bowmen," Penda continued smoothly, "although I've heard it said that the East Angles are better. Come now, prove your skills against my champion."

Penda's words drew some sniggers from the crowd, although the faces of the East Angle warriors present grew thunderous. To his credit, Annan had managed to keep his expression impassive.

"So be it," he replied, his voice quiet. "And who is your champion?"

Penda grinned then, and swiveled round to face Saewara, his gaze snaring hers. Saewara's stomach twisted – she knew that smile.

"One of the finest archers in my family," Penda drawled. "My sister."

Saewara took the ash longbow and quiver full of yew, feather-fletched arrows that one of the lads assisting with the archery competition handed to her. Despite her shock at being forced into a competition she had not prepared for, she felt an unexpected rush of pleasure at the feel of the longbow in her hands.

It had been a while, but some things were never forgotten.

At that moment, Annan strode by. He walked right by Saewara, without acknowledging her, carrying his bow at his side and a quiver of arrows over one shoulder. His face was thunderous.

Saewara watched him go, nonplussed. She had been about to greet her betrothed, but seeing his deliberate refusal to acknowledge her, she felt an unexpected, hot rush of anger.

It did not matter what she did, where she went, or what she said – men were determined to treat her as if she was a *nithing*—a creature not even worth greeting. The rage that coursed through her, now overcame the misery and the self-absorption that had immobilized her for so long. The force of it galvanized Saewara's resolve. She watched the men, all individuals who worked the fields around Tamworth, take their places.

I'll show you all, she thought bitterly before her gaze settled upon Annan, who had taken his place at the far end. *I will beat you this day.*

Saewara took her place at the end of the row; the position nearest the noisy crowd – and the place all the other contestants had avoided.

Ignoring her surroundings, Saewara busied herself with checking the tension of her hemp bow string, and selecting the six arrows she would use for the first round.

The Range Master for the competition was a huge man, with handsome, chiseled features and cruel eyes. His gaze settled on Saewara for a moment, his mouth twisting in derision, before he began to shout out the rules of the competitions.

"Archers—there will be three rounds," he shouted. "After the first round, your scores will be counted and the five top scoring archers will pass to the next round. Only the top two scoring archers will go through to the third, and final round. The points are as follows: one for the white, two for the black, three for the blue, four for the red – and five for those who hit the yellow."

The rules were simple enough; Saewara had watched plenty of archery competitions although she had never taken part in one. She could hear the sniggers and ribald comments from the crowd, and could feel the hot stares of the men. Ignoring them all, Saewara squared her shoulders and breathed deeply, fixing her gaze on the target.

"Archers, ready your bows!" the Range Master ordered. "On the count of three—loose your arrows! One, two, three!"

Saewara's arrows flew straight and true. She hit the yellow twice, the red once and the blue thrice. When she had loosed the sixth arrow, the Range Master's voice boomed across the meadow.

"Archers—lay down your bows. Your scores will be counted."

Saewara did as she was told, resisting the urge to glance along the line to see how the others had fared, especially Annan. She was pleased with her score, although she knew she could do better. When her name was called as one of the five to go ahead to the second round, she felt a thrill surge through her. It did not matter that to the world she was worth nothing—she was good at something at least.

"Archers, ready your bows!"

Saewara did even better in the second round: two in the yellow, three in the red and one in the blue.

There was a tense wait while the Range Master had the remaining five contestants' scores counted. Saewara continued to stare at her hands, blocking out the world. Her heart started to race when the Range Master finally took his place with the names of the top two archers to go forward. She looked up then and studied his expression. The man wore a sour look, as if he had just taken a sip of vinegar.

Saewara knew then, the names he was about to call.

"Annan of the Wuffingas and Saewara of Tamworth—you are both through to the final round."

The crowd hooted and cheered. For the first time, Saewara allowed her gaze to travel over to where Annan stood at the end of the row. His face was carved of stone, his blue eyes glittering slits. It was the ultimate insult. To face-off with a woman in the final round, under the jeers of the crowd, was one of the biggest slights a man of noble birth could suffer.

Good, Saewara thought bitterly. *May you choke on this, Annan of the East Angles.*

Saewara caught her brother's eye on the edge of the crowd, and Penda winked at her. Ignoring him, she turned back to the target and notched an arrow into her longbow.

"Range Master," Penda called out, "let's raise the game a little—these two have had it easy till now. Move the targets back!"

The warrior nodded and shouted orders at two lads who rushed to obey. They moved the targets back to a ridiculous distance; farther than Saewara had ever shot.

Dog, she threw a venomous look at her brother. *You wish to humiliate us both.*

"Archers, you each have six arrows. Ready your bows!" the Range Master ordered. "On the count of three—loose your arrows! One, two, three!"

The twang of the bow-strings releasing echoed through the still crowd.

Saewara lowered her bow, and peered at the target.

"Red and red," the Range Master boomed. "Ready your bows!"

Saewara slotted an arrow, lifted her bow and aimed. She felt sweat bead on her forehead as she took a deep breath and held it. A moment later, she released the arrow and heard it sing as it flew.

"Red and red," the Range Master called out.

And so it continued. Saewara and Annan matched each other, shot for shot; twice on the red, twice on the blue—and one more on the red. Only one shot remained. Saewara's hands were clammy and her heart raced as she stole a glance in Annan's direction. He stood, at the end of the row, as tall and intimidating as Thor himself. He was slotting his last arrow into his bow when Saewara glanced his way; and feeling her gaze upon him, he finally looked up—acknowledging her for the first time.

Their gazes held for a moment, and Saewara felt the shock of it ripple down from the base of her ribs into her belly. Then, she tore her gaze away from his, took the sixth arrow from its quiver and slotted it.

"Ready your bows!" the Range Master barked. "One, two, three!"

The bow strings sang for the last time. The arrows flew and hit the targets with a dull thud; first Saewara's, and then Annan's.

The lads rushed to the targets to inspect them.

"Red!" One of them shouted upon reaching Saewara's target. "Just inside the line between the red and the yellow—but it's red!"

"Yellow!" shouted the second lad who stood before Annan's target. "On the line!"

"Annan of the East Angles wins!" the Range Master snarled the words as if they were poison. Although he would have disliked seeing Saewara best a man at archery, he had wanted to see Annan thoroughly humiliated even more.

Bitter defeat made tears well in Saewara's eyes. She hurriedly blinked them away and clenched her jaw in an effort to compose herself. It had been so close; she had only lost by a whisker. Yet, it was defeat all the same.

The crowd hooted and wolf-whistled.

"Congratulations, Annan," Penda called from the sidelines. "You bested my champion—well done."

Managing to regain control of herself, Saewara swiveled round to watch Annan walk down the row of targets toward the edge of the games area. His face was livid. He did not look like a man who had just won a competition.

Saewara did not blame him. Winner or not, he was still humiliated by having to compete against his betrothed in a low-born sport. The jeering crowd did not help matters. Annan stormed off the archery range, and Saewara stepped back hurriedly to let him pass. Reaching the edge, he threw down his bow and quiver with a look of pure disgust and walked away.

The crowd drew back to let him pass. Up close, none were brave enough to insult the wrathful East Angle.

Saewara watched him go, her belly twisting in dread. Glancing at her brother's cruel smile as he watched Annan stalk away from the games, Saewara realized that Penda had gotten his wish. He had humiliated Annan and taken revenge on his willful sister in one clever move.

A warrior's pride was not easily soothed. Far from merely resenting his betrothed, Saewara realized, with a sense of impending doom, that he would now hate her.

Chapter Six

The Lovers' Dance

THE MELANCHOLY STRAINS of a lyre drifted through the Great Tower of Tamworth, mingling with the rumble of voices. Long tables piled high with food and drink ringed the cavernous space, illuminated by the glow of the fire pits. It was a great feast of roast duck, boar and venison, tureens of leek soup, massive wheels of cheese and platters of griddle bread, roast carrots and mashed turnip. Dogs slunk under the tables, waiting for the morsels that would soon fall onto the rush-strewn floor, and slaves circled the space with jugs of mead and ale for the diners.

The mood was jovial and festive. It was the beginning of summer; the end of a long, warm day filled with entertainment and laughter. There was a betrothal to celebrate and delicious food to be enjoyed.

Yet there were some at the feast who did not share in the merriment.

Saewara sat near the head of the table, flanked by her brother to the right and her betrothed to her left. She sat on the bench, hands folded on her lap, staring down at the wooden plate before her, listening to the happy chatter of her nieces further down the table. Male laughter boomed across the hall as one of Penda's ealdormen made a ribald comment about one of the serving wenches.

Penda laughed along with them. He was in a merry mood this eve; Saewara had rarely seen him so relaxed. Cyneswide sat to his right, smiling demurely and content to let the men dominate the conversation.

Saewara did not glance Annan's way.

She knew he would also be ignoring her; after today's debacle, she did not blame him.

The guests fell upon the feast and Saewara woodenly helped herself to some duck, bread and roasted carrots. Misery had robbed her of an appetite but she knew she had to make a show of eating or she would anger her brother. A slave appeared at her elbow and poured her a cup full of strong mead. Saewara took one gulp, and then another. She usually disliked the taste of mead, preferring milk or water at meals, but this evening she craved oblivion; anything to take the edge off her unhappiness.

As she picked at her meal, Saewara chanced a furtive glance to her left, where her betrothed sat in silence. Annan looked handsome this eve, dressed in a royal blue tunic that matched his eyes, with his long blond hair loose about his shoulders. Yet his face was hard, and Saewara could see a nerve twitching in his jaw. He ate slowly, but without joy, speaking to no one. To his right sat Aldfrid, Penda's most trusted ealdorman. Aldfrid did not exchange a word with Annan, and the King of the East Angles likewise ignored him.

Saewara looked back at her meal and forced herself to continue eating. She wanted this evening to be over.

Annan chewed a piece of duck and nursed the slowly kindling rage that had been smoldering since he had arrived in Tamworth. The gods were testing him, it seemed. Ever since he had agreed to Penda's terms, that fateful evening on the edge of the battlefield, his life had taken a downward spiral.

Humiliation after humiliation. He was not sure how much more he could take. If Penda took one more liberty, Annan knew he would not be responsible for his actions.

Today had been torture.

Annan had been surprised to discover his betrothed was so skilled in archery, and under other circumstances, he would have enjoyed seeing a woman handle a bow and arrow with such mastery. Yet pitting him against his betrothed in front of a jeering crowd was inexcusable, and although she had done him no harm directly, Annan now loathed his wife-to-be, almost as much as he did Penda himself.

He took a deep draught of mead, feeling its warmth burn into the pit of his belly, and was suddenly aware of Saewara's gaze upon him. Like earlier, when he had sensed her gaze flick toward him, Annan ignored her. He could not look at any of them this evening. They all made him sick to his stomach.

Eventually, the mead relaxed Annan, especially as he ate lightly. When servants started to serve honey-seed cakes—signaling the meal was coming to an end—he lifted his head for the first time and glanced about him. His gaze drifted to his right and settled for a moment on his betrothed.

He hated to admit, in fact it galled him terribly, but Saewara was an extremely attractive woman. She wore a becoming white, sleeveless tunic, cinched at the waist with an amber-studded belt. The only other jewelry she wore was two bronze arm rings on her left bicep. The arm rings highlighted her beautifully shaped arms, whereas the dress accentuated her small but curvaceous figure; a tiny waist and swelling bosom. Her long, dark hair spilled over her shoulders and down her slender back.

In his inebriated state, Annan allowed himself a brief moment to appreciate his betrothed; yes, she was lovely, although too exotic for his tastes. In that tunic, she looked like one of the Roman noble women his grandfather had described to him as a boy. Her gaze was downcast and her cheeks flushed from mead; her eye-lashes were long and dark against her milky skin.

Realizing that he was, indeed, staring, Annan tore his gaze away and resolved not to look in Saewara's direction again. The mead had lowered his defenses, and softened his resentment. Yet, the rage was still lurking beneath his calm façade.

The sound of a woman's voice, accompanied by the lilting strains of a lyre, intruded upon Annan's mulling. He looked up to see Queen Cyneswide standing near the head of the table. She sung a rousing epic about love, loss, betrayal and hope. Her voice was hauntingly beautiful, and for a short while, Annan felt himself pulled into her story. He sipped his mead and listened broodingly to her words. When she sung about the vengeance of a wronged man, he felt his anger surge.

Yes, one day, he too would settle some scores. Penda might be victorious now, but there would come a day when Annan would wipe that smirk off his face.

Once Cyneswide finished her epic, the feasters burst into raucous applause. Their voices echoed off the damp stone walls and lifted high into the roof of the great tower. Then, another musician stepped up next to the lyrist and began to play a rousing tune.

Men and women rose from their seats at the long tables and made their way out into a wide rectangle of open floor that had been cleared for the dancing. The dance began; one that Annan had witnessed many times, where the men formed one line, and the women another. The two lines then moved in unison. The men twirled their partners one way, and then the other, as they moved down the line and brought their hands together to mimic an archway at the far end. At this point, the couple at the far end would run down the column of raised arms, hand in hand. It was a dance for lovers. Annan turned his back on it and refilled his cup of mead from the jug in front of him.

He had no wish to watch lovers dance this eve.

"The betrothed!" Penda rose to his feet, his eyes gleaming. He then raised his cup and stared straight at Annan. "This dance is for my lovely sister and her husband-to-be. Applaud them, as they lead this dance together!"

Annan slammed his cup down on the table and glowered at Penda. He should have known this would happen. The Mercian King would not let him be till he left Tamworth—and since the East Angles were due to leave at first light tomorrow, that left him little time for sport.

"Maggot-spawn," Annan muttered under his breath. "Let me be!"

"A dance!" Penda bellowed. "I shall have a dance from King Annan of the East Angles and his betrothed!"

"A dance!" those at the table chorused, their faces bright with mead and vindictive joy. "A dance!"

Annan glanced at Saewara. She had gone pink and was sitting with her hands cupped in her lap, her face tense. She looked as miserable as he felt. Yet, they were both backed into a corner. With a snarl, Annan rose to his feet and bent toward Saewara.

"Come on," he growled. "Let's give them what they want."

He took hold of her hand and pulled her, not ungently, to her feet. Despite her flushed cheeks, Saewara's hand was ice-cold.

It struck Annan, as he led her toward the cheering dancers, that those brusque words were the first he had spoken directly to his betrothed.

Saewara blinked back tears and forced herself to raise her chin and walk with what little dignity she still possessed onto the dance floor. Fortunately, Annan did not look her way. His hand was warm and strong in hers. She did not want to admit it, but his warmth suffused her hand and forearm, and gave her strength. Her fingers tingled from contact with him; a sensation she had never felt when taking her late husband's hand.

He had spoken to her harshly but there had been no roughness in the way he had pulled her to her feet. Despite all that had happened, Saewara felt a strange kinship with her betrothed. They were both humiliated by her brother's continuing delight in making sport of them in front of his ealdormen and thegns.

There would be no respite until they left the Great Tower of Tamworth.

Saewara took her place, opposite Annan at the end of the row of dancers and fixed her gaze upon the center of his chest—easier than raising her chin to look him in the eye as he towered above her.

The bone whistle and lyre, which had halted while Penda pressured them to dance, resumed their tune with renewed vigor. The watching feasters cheered and whistled. Ribald comments rose above the cheering and Saewara's cheeks burned even hotter at some of the filth her brother's men shouted out at them.

How I loathe this place, she thought, grinding her teeth in fury. She might have been going to a new home, one where she would be reviled, but the knowledge that she would only have to spend one more night under her brother's roof gave her a grim satisfaction.

The dancers exploded into movement, and Saewara had no more time to think on her humiliation, for suddenly, Annan had taken both her hands and was pulling her toward him.

Saewara's stomach dipped; an odd, dizzying sensation.

I should not have drunk so much mead.

It had been years since she had danced. Egfrid had hated dancing, and once the obligatory courtship rituals had been taken care of, he had never taken part in dancing on feast days, or even at Eōstre or Yule. It had been just as well, since he had been a poor dancer, and his brutality that started soon after they were wed, made her loath to touch him.

A strange thrill went through Saewara when Annan's hand rested on her waist for an instant. Then, he twirled her away from him. Saewara's heart pounded against her ribs. The heat of his hand had reached her skin, even through the thick fabric of her tunic.

Remembering the steps she had been taught as a girl, she dipped and curtsied before her partner, before circling coquettishly around him.

The hall roared around her, but Saewara ignored them all, concentrating on the dance. She stepped back toward Annan, and he took hold of both her hands. Together, they ran down the archway of raised arms to the end, before raising their own arms together, while the next couple began their dance.

Breathing heavily, Saewara finally raised her gaze to her betrothed's face. His gaze snared hers and for a few moments, under the privacy of their raised arms, they stared at each other.

Saewara stood, transfixed. A wave of need consumed her; a hunger that took her breath away. She had never experienced a sensation like it before in her twenty-five winters—the intensity of it frightened her.

Moments later, Annan ripped his gaze from hers, breaking the connection.

Saewara dropped her own gaze down to her feet and struggled to compose herself. What was that? Was that what lust felt like?

She wasn't sure she liked the sensation; it felt like stepping off a precipice, and losing control. The way he had looked at her had made her body melt like candle-wax.

They remained there a while, until the column of dancers broke apart and each couple twirled in a circle around the floor. Saewara kept her gaze planted on Annan's chest, and on the open neck of his tunic, where she could see the blond curls of his chest hair peeking up through the laced collar that had loosened with the dancing. The hunger returned but this time, Saewara shoved it aside. The mead had lowered both their defenses. Once the dancing finished, they would both return to their senses. She would not make the mistake of looking at his face again.

The dancing lasted an eternity for Saewara. When it finally ended, she broke free from Annan, without glancing in his direction, and fled back to the table. Returning to her seat, she poured herself a large cup of water and resolved never to touch mead again.

Annan took his seat next to his blushing bride-to-be and refused the offer of more mead from a passing serving wench. After what had just occurred on the dance-floor, it was best to keep a clear head. He stole a glance at Saewara and felt a shadow of the naked lust he had experienced during the dance, return.

Woden, she had stirred him.

Even now, he was not sure what had come over him. Yet as exciting as the sensation had been, it did not please Annan. If his bride had been another, he would welcome such a rush of desire. Yet, this woman was the sister of a man he deeply despised. Penda sought to crush both Annan and his people—and was using this marriage to do so.

I will not bed her, Annan resolved, staring down at the remains of his barely touched meal before him. *I will not have Penda make an even bigger fool of me than he has already.*

Chapter Seven

In the Darkness

"ARE YOU READY?"

"Almost, just give me a moment."

Saewara rolled up the last of her long woolen over-dresses and stuffed it into the sheepskin bag that stood on the rushes at her feet. She owned little, so packing for the trip to Rendlaesham had taken moments. Next to her stood Cyneswide, who had done her best to help Saewara make preparations for her departure from Tamworth.

Around them, the Great Tower of Tamworth was alive with the morning's activity. Women were baking griddle bread at the far end of the hall, while a group of ealdormen's wives sat gossiping at looms nearby. Children played with dogs in the center of the hall while a group of slaves stood gutting rabbits at one of the long tables.

Annan of the East Angles was nowhere in sight. Saewara guessed that he was already outside, impatient to depart for home.

"Do you have everything?" Cyneswide asked, still fussing over her sister-in-law. Despite that her face was serene, Saewara noted the anxiety in her sister-in-law's voice. The two women were friends, and even though Saewara was relieved to be leaving her brother's malevolent presence, she knew she would miss Cyneswide.

"I think so," Saewara replied, pulling the drawstring at the top of the bag closed. "Although I'm sure even if I've forgotten something it won't matter. I shall be a queen too soon, remember?"

Her bitterness was palpable and Saewara saw Cyneswide wince.

"It will not be so terrible," she replied in a low voice, aware that Penda was now waiting near the doors, ready to escort his sister out to her betrothed. "Annan does not seem unkind—and he is handsome ..." Cyneswide's voice trailed off when she saw Saewara's look of disdain. The Queen's eyes filled with tears and she stepped forward, clasping Saewara to her in a hug.

"I'm sorry, Saewara," she whispered in her ear. "Words will not put this right. Yet, I wish you well. I wish that happiness will find you."

Saewara nodded, softening toward her sister by marriage. This was not Cyneswide's fault. It was unfair to take out her bitterness on the one woman here who had befriended her.

"Saewara!" Penda's voice echoed across the hall, quietening the rumble of voices. "I am waiting—come!"

Saewara picked up her bag and made her way across the crowded floor to where Penda stood before the oaken doors.

"My wife has kindly gifted you one of her slaves." He motioned to a brown-haired girl dressed in a shapeless, homespun tunic and a woolen traveling cloak, who stood next to him. "She will serve you on the journey to your new home, and at Rendlaesham. Give her your bag."

The girl took the bag and met Saewara's gaze blankly. Saewara recognized her; the girl's name was Oswyn and she had been taken as a slave three winters earlier after Penda razed her village on the Welsh border and slew all her kin. The girl had been a ghostly presence within Penda's hall; a slave who bore her master a quiet, simmering hate. She masked it with a blank stare but Saewara could see the loathing in her eyes.

Saewara stared back at Oswyn for a few moments, reflecting on the fact that there were those far worse off than her, before turning her attention back to her brother.

"Very well," she said coldly, meeting his hard stare. "Let us be on our way."

Saewara stepped out into a mild morning, although the air was heavy and the sky a little cloudy. The East Angles awaited her; a grim mob on horseback in the yard before the Great Tower. Amongst them rode one of Penda's warriors, a surly young man who would bring word of the couple's handfasting back to Tamworth.

Annan sat at the head of the group, his expression shielded by the intimidating iron helmet he wore. Sitting there, towering over her as she made her way over to the shaggy bay pony that awaited her, he appeared incredibly intimidating.

Wordlessly, Saewara mounted the pony, while Oswyn clambered up on the back of the wagon that carried supplies.

"Goodbye, Annan of the East Angles." Penda stepped forward and looked up at Annan's iron-shielded face. "And remember. You are bound to me now. You will do as I tell you."

Annan sat motionless and did not respond to the Mercian King. Yet Saewara could see the tension in his shoulders. She could feel the rage emanating from him. Penda treated him like his dog. The smirks on the Mercian warriors' faces, as they looked on from behind their king, only added to the humiliation. The faces of the others in the East Angle party were thunderous.

You go too far brother, Saewara thought with a shiver. *One day you will bring hate down upon our people.*

Annan turned from Penda then and urged his stallion into a brisk trot. He sat deep in the saddle, the iron rings on his vest jingling as he led the way out of the yard and into the streets below.

Saewara did not farewell her brother. Instead, she turned her own mount and followed Annan, urging her pony into a jolting canter in order to keep up with him. They navigated the streets of Tamworth, ignoring the hostile looks and jeers of the townsfolk. Saewara closed her eyes as she felt something wet splatter against her skirts. Folk could be so cruel, she reflected. The people of Tamworth cared not that she was marrying to forge a political alliance—to them she was simply marrying the 'enemy'. To them, she was betraying her people.

I'd better get used to this, she told herself grimly, *for I will be treated far worse in Rendlaesham.*

They travelled east across green, rolling hills and through the dark woodlands of Mercia. The East Angles set a fast pace, eager to return to their own realm. They spoke little amongst themselves as they rode, and, judging from their scowling faces, were not in the mood for celebration or joviality. Penda's emissary rode at the back, ignored by all. Annan rode at the head of the column, his back ramrod straight.

He spoke to no one all morning.

Saewara soon tired of attempting to keep up with her betrothed. Her pony would be exhausted by the day's end if she tried to match the pace of Annan's stallion. Instead, she dropped back so that she rode alongside the wagon. However, Oswyn's surly face and cold gaze did not make for pleasant company.

They spent the rest of the day riding through bucolic landscape; wooded valleys and meadows strewn with spring flowers. It was lovely countryside but the East Angles did not appear to appreciate its beauty. They would not relax until they were no longer riding on Mercian soil.

That evening, they camped in the middle of a wide meadow, not far from a gently babbling brook. It was a mild night, but the men lit fires nonetheless. Annan and his warriors sat around the fire, deep in conversation. Their voices were hushed, as if they were taking care not to be overheard. Realizing she was not welcome at the fire side, Saewara retired to her tent, which she shared with Oswyn. The tent was made of tanned goat-hide and had a slit in the roof to allow the smoke out. Inside, the slave girl resolutely ignored her mistress, except to do her bidding when ordered. She was little company and Saewara wished she could have the tent to herself. Oswyn's surly face did little to lift her spirits.

The fresh air and a day in the saddle had exhausted Saewara. She sat, watching the glowing embers of the small fire pit in the center of her tent as she finished a light supper of bread and cheese; feeling her eyelids grow heavier by the moment. She had not thought that she would sleep well that night, but she was wrong. Saewara fell asleep next to the fire and did not awake until first light, when the noises of the men packing up camp roused her.

They continued east with the dawn. Unlike the day before, the sun did not show its face. The morning passed swiftly, and as they rode east, the weather gradually worsened. By the time they stopped at noon, the sky was completely overcast and the air had turned chill. Saewara took a bite of bread and cheese and glanced up at the sky. It looked to her as if their journey was about to turn damp.

The men ignored her while they ate a brief meal and took swigs of water from their water bladders. They discussed the journey ahead in low voices, although Saewara heard them mention that they would not likely cross the border into the Kingdom of the East Angles until the following morning. They would remain on Mercian soil for a while longer, it seemed. Saewara could see that this chafed them; every moment they remained in Penda's kingdom was a reminder of their subjugation. None of them looked her way, preferring to pretend she did not exist. Strangely, Saewara found the anonymity a relief. She had been the center of attention over the last few days, and had hated every moment.

It was starting to spit with rain when they resumed their journey. Shortly after, they left the hills behind and entered thick woodland. Saewara had heard of these woods and knew that they stretched for leagues in every direction. Once they emerged from them, the East Angles would be in their own kingdom once more.

Despite the worsening weather, the mood of Saewara's companions gradually improved as the day wore on. She hung back with the wagon, while ahead the rumble of men's voices drifted through the trees. Around them, the rain fell gently in a fine veil; coating the woodland without stirring so much as a leaf or a blade of grass. A narrow road, barely more than a faint track in places, led through the woods. Saewara noticed that the warriors kept a close eye on their surroundings as they rode. Woodland was a favorite spot for outlaws to pounce on unwary travelers. A king and his entourage, heavily armed and prepared, were an unlikely target but, despite this, the warriors were alert and watchful.

At dusk, they made camp in a small clearing not far from the road. A misty rain continued to fall as the warriors erected three tents; one for Annan, one for his betrothed, and one for Saba and a few of the other warriors who were not taking their turn to watch over the camp.

They lit a fire pit in Saewara's tent and carried in furs for her to sleep on, while Oswyn busied herself with making a pot of soup over the fire. Outside, Saewara could hear the men conversing in low voices as they cooked their evening meal over a large fire pit. Once again, she had the feeling they were deliberately keeping their voices quiet.

Saewara cared not for their conversation; instead, she was glad to be able to spend the evening in private. She hung up her and Oswyn's sodden cloaks to dry near the fire. She then sat down on the furs and watched the slave girl add a sprig of thyme to the onion soup she was preparing. Observing the girl's taut face and dead eyes, Saewara felt a pang of sadness. The iron slave collar about her neck was a constant reminder of her status, of her servitude.

Is there a woman alive who is not a slave? Saewara wondered sadly. *If we're not bound to our fathers, brothers or husbands, we are shackled to our masters. A woman has no will of her own.*

Saewara did not share her thoughts with Oswyn. The girl had made it clear that she had no interest in conversing with her mistress. She was polite and respectful when spoken to, but her eyes told another story.

Outside, just yards from the East Angles' camp, five hostile gazes watched the travelers make camp for the night. Hidden in the undergrowth, and lying as still as possible, the five men breathed slowly and bided their time.

The one who led this group, shifted his weight slightly to ease a cramp in his leg. He did not see why Coenwal could not have joined them.

After all, it was he who wanted the woman.

The others could not have cared less about her. Instead, Coenwal was sitting in front of a warm fire, waiting for them to deliver his prize, while the rest of them suffered on his behalf.

The outlaw's gaze rested on the tent nearest their hiding place. He had seen Saewara and her slave girl enter it a short while earlier. His gaze shifted then, to the two other tents nearby. It was a cramped clearing and when they moved from their hiding place, they would need to work quickly and quietly.

It was a long, cold miserable wait, but in many ways the perfect weather for an abduction. Only those watching the camp would bother to linger outside once the night drew out. It was then that they would make their move.

The outlaw's chilled fingers flexed around the bone hilt of the knife he clasped. Although he and his companions had hidden themselves well, he was cautious. He blinked rain out of his eyes and continued his vigil on the camp before him, watching as a tall, blond man of regal bearing strode toward one of the tents, after helping the others see to the horses.

King Annan of the East Angles.

After tonight, he would have to find himself another bride.

The soup was good and Saewara sat with her fingers clasped around her clay bowl, enjoying the warmth. For the first time in a long while, she felt a sense of well-being seep over her. She knew it would not last, this precious solitude. This was what she had been seeking at Bonehill—a quiet refuge to spend the rest of her days in. Yet, the chaos of a king's hall would not have this peace.

Saewara let go of her bowl with one hand and placed it over the wooden crucifix she wore under her thick tunic and over-dress. More than ever, she needed her faith, her strength. Not for the first time, she wondered what the famed 'Golden Hall' would be like, and just how unwelcoming the folk there would be.

"Oswyn," Saewara said gently upon noticing that the slave was now standing woodenly next to the fire pit, awaiting orders from her mistress. "Take some soup for yourself and sit down."

Oswyn nodded and did as she was bid. There was no gratitude on her face, just relief at being able to rest and eat. Saewara sipped meditatively at her soup before fishing out chunks of onion with pieces of griddle bread, and popping them into her mouth. It was the first time she had enjoyed food in days. Outside, she could not hear the rain, for it fell in a silent curtain; only the rise and fall of men's voices punctured the stillness.

The fire warmed the small tent quickly and, despite the smoke that hung in a pall over them, the women soon relaxed.

"The soup is delicious," Saewara said as she helped herself to another ladle. "My onion soup never ends up like this. They are always too watery."

"You need to cook the onions until they're soft before adding the water," Oswyn replied quietly. "That's the trick to a good onion soup."

Surprised that the girl had actually responded, Saewara gave her a smile. "Thank you, I will try that next time."

Oswyn nodded and looked down at her bowl.

Not wanting to press the girl further, Saewara lapsed back into silence. She was comfortable with remaining quiet, having never been a woman given to prattle. Yet, their brief exchange had warmed the atmosphere between Saewara and her servant a little.

Perhaps she will grow to trust me, Saewara thought, stretching out her chilled feet toward the fire and wiggling her bare toes in the warmth. *I will need someone on my side in Rendlaesham.*

The evening drew out and Saewara did not bother to emerge from her tent. She knew her presence was not welcomed. The men, Annan especially, would not want to see her face till morning.

After a long day of travel, Saewara felt fatigue pulling down at her. While Oswyn cleared away the dinner and took the pot and bowls outside to wash, Saewara readied herself for bed. Noticing that no bed had been made up for Oswyn, who would be expected to sleep on the ground next to the fire, Saewara took one of her furs and laid it down on the ground next to Oswyn's side of the fire pit. When the slave girl returned from washing up, her gaze widened to see a soft fur bed waiting for her.

"M'lady," she began, looking discomforted. "You can't give me a fur to sleep on, it's not ..."

"Of course I can," Saewara interrupted briskly. "I have plenty of furs—I can afford to share one."

"But, I'm your slave."

"No, you were my brother's slave," Saewara corrected her, "but he's not here. God willing, we'll never set eyes on him again."

Oswyn looked shocked at that but Saewara merely shook her head and motioned to Oswyn's new bed. "No one's going to bother us here. I suggest you take what comfort you can before we arrive in Rendlaesham."

The girl nodded reluctantly before making her way over to the bed Saewara had made up and sitting down on it. She gave her mistress a nonplussed look before stretching out. The expression on her face was almost comical but Saewara was careful not to show any sign of amusement. Trust was a fragile thing; hard won and easily shattered.

The women did not speak again. Instead, they lay on their fur beds, listening to the sounds of the surrounding camp and the crack and pop of the dying fire. Despite that she was exhausted, and that her bed was comfortable and warm, Saewara found herself staring up at the tent's weather-stained ceiling for a long while. Eventually, when she did sleep, her slumber was fitful and filled with dark dreams.

The sound of ripping leather tore Saewara from a frightening dream, in which she had been running from her brother through the empty streets of Tamworth. Penda had almost reached her; his cruel threats ringing in her ears, his hands reaching out to grasp her around the neck, when the noise woke her.

Saewara sat up in bed, disoriented and still half asleep, and tried to make sense of what was happening around her.

The fire pit gave out a faint glow from its embers; just enough for her to see a man's dark outline push his way into the tent through the rip he had just slashed in its side.

Terror stilled Saewara's breathing for a moment.

An intruder was in her tent.

She drew air into her lungs to scream a warning but the man was suddenly hurtling toward her. He landed on top of her on the furs, a huge hand clamping down on her mouth. She saw then, the outline of another man lurching through the gap in the tent, and the glint of a knife blade. She struggled viciously, trying to get free so she could warn the girl, but the man grabbed Oswyn, who had just awoken and was struggling to her feet. The slave let out a strangled cry that was cut off as the knife slashed down.

Oswyn crumpled to the ground.

The man dragged Saewara toward the opening. She writhed and twisted in his grip. When his hand shifted slightly across her mouth, she bit down hard on one of his fingers.

The man grunted and backhanded her across the face. Then, he slammed his hand back down over her mouth, so hard her lips crushed against her teeth. Tears of pain streamed down Saewara's face but she continued to struggle. Paying her no heed, for the man was easily twice her size, her assailant pulled her toward the rip in the tent, and out into the night.

Chapter Eight

The Reckoning

"ANNAN, WAKE UP!"

Saba's voice roused Annan from a deep sleep. He struggled upright in bed and met his friend's gaze. Saba stood at the tent's entrance, dripping water on to the ground.

"What is it?" Annan demanded, the remnants of sleep fading as he saw the alarm on Saba's face.

"Outlaws," Saba replied grimly. "They've killed all three men guarding Saewara's tent, slain her servant and taken your betrothed."

Annan leaped to his feet with a curse. Fortunately, he had slept with his breeches and boots on. He hurriedly pulled on a tunic and followed Saba out into the rain. On the other side of the small clearing he found his betrothed's tent empty, save for the corpse of the slave. They had slit her throat and left her there to drown in her own blood.

Annan cursed once more, viciously, fury turning him cold.

Relations between the East Angles and the Mercians were tenuous enough without his wife-to-be being kidnapped just two days out from Tamworth. Penda would blame him if Saewara perished tonight, before setting his fyrd on the Kingdom of the East Angles without mercy.

As if reading Annan's thoughts, Penda's servant, owl-eyed with sleep, stepped into the tent. Wordlessly, his gaze took in the scene before him, before he turned to Annan with a snarl.

"The King will hear of this!"

Annan ignored the young man. Instead, he turned to Saba, who stood at the tent's entrance awaiting orders.

"They won't be travelling fast in this weather—we'll track them. Leave five men behind to guard the camp, the rest of you are coming with me."

Saewara stared down at the darkness and blinked rain-water out of her eyes. Her captor carried her like a sack of grain, slung over one shoulder. Wet branches clawed at her and the man's shoulder dug into her ribs with each stride. Yet, despite his ragged breathing, the man did not slow his pace. Instead, he crashed through the woods, intent on his destination.

Terror chilled Saewara to the bone. An overwhelming, paralyzing fear had turned her mind blank.

The man ran on for a long while, into the heart of the woodland, where the trees grew dense and dark, before finally reaching a small campsite. Saewara lifted her head, staring at a collection of tattered, weather-stained tents huddled under the boughs of ancient oaks. Pale firelight seeped from the tents, illuminating them like lanterns in the night.

Moments later, her captor had carried her to the entrance of the largest of the tents and pushed his way inside. With a grunt, he off-loaded his captive onto the dirt floor. Saewara crumpled to the ground, her legs giving out from under her. Hands trembling, she pushed her wet hair out of her eyes, climbed to her feet and gazed around the tent.

The air smelled damp, despite the fire pit that flickered in the center. There was a sour smell of men's sweat, as if the tent had stood here for a while and never been aired. The stench caused her nose to wrinkle. The interior was sparsely furnished, except for a pile of furs at one end. Apart from her assailant—a huge man with a shaggy brown beard and hair, and hard, dark eyes—there was only one other occupant inside the tent.

Looking upon the man, who was staring at her intently, Saewara gaped in shock.

She recognized the man before her, and knew she was in deep trouble.

"You have done well," the man spoke to his companion, not taking his eyes off Saewara. "Were you followed?"

The huge man who had brought Saewara shook his head, scattering droplets of water everywhere. "We had to kill of a few of them to get into her tent but we managed to get away before the alarm was raised. They'll never manage to follow us in this weather."

The other man frowned. "Are you sure?"

"East Anglian dogs," the warrior replied before spitting on the ground to make his point. "We had to wait for hours in the rain till the moment was right—till most of the camp were sleeping like babes. The guards never suspected a thing. They never heard us coming; slitting their throats was easy. The king and his rabble don't know these woods like we do. I left a confusing trail behind us. They'll never find our camp."

"I hope you're right," his leader nodded. "Set up watch on the camp edge all the same. You can leave us now."

The huge man grunted, threw Saewara a lingering, lecherous look, and pushed his way back outside.

Saewara and the leader of the outlaws were now alone.

"Coenwal," Saewara said finally, her voice barely above a whisper. "So this is where you have been hiding?"

The man, of average height with a stocky build, stared back at her, unsmiling. Coenwal had changed much since she had last seen him in Tamworth over a year earlier. His lank brown hair was much longer and tied back with a leather thong at his nape. His grey eyes had dark circles under them, and bitterness and resentment had etched deep lines on a face that had once been handsome.

"Saewara," Coenwal replied, savoring her name in such an intimate manner that the fine hairs on the back of Saewara's neck prickled in warning. "You are even lovelier than I remember."

His gaze, hot and hungry, slid from her face, down the length of her body. Horrified, Saewara glanced down to see that the sleeveless linen tunic she had worn to bed, was sodden wet and clung to her body like a second skin. She may as well have been naked.

"Egfrid was wasted on you," Coenwal continued, not bothering to hide his appreciation. "The man was a weasel. You know I wanted you but your brother didn't think I was good enough. Now that whoreson is marrying you to an East Angle. I've saved you from a fate worse than death—you should thank me."

Saewara stared back at him, stone-faced. Truthfully, there was little difference between Egfrid and Coenwal—they were both arrogant, cruel men who thought little of women. Egfrid had been an ealdorman, whereas Coenwal was a thegn; too low in status to be considered a suitable match for the king's sister. Saewara had been relieved when Penda had flatly refused Coenwal's marriage proposal.

"Penda never realized your worth." Coenwal took a step toward her, causing Saewara to back away from him. "He would even wed you to the enemy."

"It's a political alliance," Saewara replied warily, hoping that by keeping Coenwal talking he would keep his distance from her. "You know the king plans to extend our borders east."

Coenwal snarled at that. "Penda's ambitions blind him to the needs of his own folk. He treads over all, including those who have served him loyally, to further his own glory."

Saewara frowned. Coenwal had a blinkered view of the past. As she remembered it, Penda had discovered that Coenwal's brother, Aedbald, had been plotting against him. He had killed Aedbald and banished Coenwal, who he suspected of aiding his brother, from the kingdom. Many believed that Penda, in letting Coenwal live, had shown uncharacteristic mercy.

Yet Coenwal did not appear to share the sentiment. He had not left Mercia. Instead, he was here, hidden deep in the woods near the East Anglian border, nursing his hatred and biding his time.

"I've been waiting for this day." Coenwal advanced toward her, around the edge of the fire pit. "The luscious Saewara, my captive. I will have you ... keep you for my own. Tomorrow, we shall break camp and travel south. Once we leave Mercia, Penda will never be able to retrieve you—and I will have my vengeance."

"You are mistaken," Saewara replied, backing further away from him. "My brother cares not of what becomes of me. If you get in the way of his ambitions however, it won't matter where you flee, he will find you. You've seen what he's capable of."

Coenwal's lip curled at that but he nevertheless continued his advance.

"Better to let me go," Saewara added, her voice quavering slightly in rising panic. "Return me to my betrothed and leave Mercia while Penda has no reason to bring his wrath down upon you."

"Silence," Coenwal spat. "I don't need a woman telling me what to do. Still your tongue."

A moment later, he had her backed up against the tent wall. Despite that Coenwal was not overly tall, he loomed over Saewara. He stank of stale sweat and onions. Up close his eyes were blood-shot, his skin florid from years of drinking an excess of mead.

"Look at you," his voice lowered to a lust-filled growl. "All innocent-looking. Yet, with a body like that you are anything but a blushing virgin."

His gaze dropped then, to the wooden crucifix that hung against her breast. His eyes hardened and, reaching out, he yanked it from about her neck.

"Christ-worshipping bitch." He tossed the crucifix on the fire and turned back to her. "At least your brother still worships the true gods, not this imposter that would have you keep your legs closed. A woman has no right to refuse a man."

Saewara acted without thinking. Rage surged inside her and turned her world blood red. She lashed out at Coenwal, slapping him hard across the face. He reeled back, in shock more than pain. For a moment, he went very still and the interior of the tent grew deathly quiet, save for the gentle crackling of burning wood in the hearth behind them.

"You hit me," he said, his voice incredulous, raising his hand to the red welt that had formed across one cheek. "Oh how I will enjoy making you pay for that."

"Get away from me," Saewara snarled, terror turning her savage.

"I think not." Coenwal grabbed her by the hair and yanked her against him, his free hand sliding up her body, squeezing and probing. "You're mine now, and this night you will pleasure me."

Saewara punched him in the stomach and had a moment's satisfaction in hearing him gasp for breath, before he roared in rage and flung her across the tent. "Whore!"

Saewara rolled to the ground and was scrambling to her feet when Coenwal reached her. He moved quickly for such a stocky man. This time, he pulled her up by her hair with one hand and slapped her hard across the face with the other.

"Dog!" Saewara screamed, kicking at him with her bare feet. Now that he had turned violent, she became even more enraged. She had endured years of brutality at Egfrid's hands. Years of torment and cruelty; days of dread between beatings. She would not go back to that life. She would die rather than return to it.

Coenwal, however, appeared to be enjoying himself.

"Fight all you like," he crowed, grabbing hold of the neck of her tunic. "It will make this all the more a night to remember."

With that he pulled downwards. Saewara heard the sound of linen ripping and felt her tunic give way. Cold air feathered her naked breast. Coenwal's mouth gaped in lust. He grabbed her breast and squeezed hard.

Saewara screamed and lashed out at Coenwal with her fist, smashing him hard in the eye. She fought him in a frenzy until he head-butted her, and threw her down on the furs. Dazed, her forehead throbbing, Saewara gazed up at him.

"Bitch," Coenwal growled, glaring down at her. His right eye was already starting to purple. "I'll have you now." With that, he began to unlace his breeches.

Saewara lay there, frozen in terror, watching him undress.

At that moment, the tent flap opened and a man stepped inside.

Saewara gasped.

It was Annan. Soaked through, his blond hair slicked back against his scalp and his sword raised, the East Angle looked dangerous, and enraged. He took one look at the scene before him and charged at Coenwal.

In one sharp movement, he plunged his sword into the base of the outlaw's neck. Coenwal never had a chance to reach for a weapon, or dodge the blow. Instead, he fell gurgling to the ground, grasping at the blade now lodged in his windpipe. Annan's face was terrifying as he kicked the outlaw to the ground until he lay still. Then, he pulled the blade free.

Then, and only then, did he turn to look at his betrothed. Saewara had sat up, and was doing her best to cover herself.

"Are you hurt?" he asked, his voice rough from the fury that still pulsed through him.

She shook her head. "I fought him, but he was too strong." She paused then, struggling to maintain her composure. "They killed Oswyn."

"I know—poor lass," Annan shook his head and looked down at Coenwal's contorted face, at the eye which had swollen shut, "and I'm sorry it took us this long to find you. He won't be touching you again."

With that, Annan removed the sodden cloak from around his shoulders and handed it to Saewara. She noticed he was deliberately avoiding looking at her.

"Cover yourself up," he said gruffly. "Let's get you back to camp."

Chapter Nine

A Gentle Moment

ANNAN AND SAEWARA emerged from the tent to find Saba waiting for them.

"Did you find them all?" Annan asked.

Saba nodded curtly in response. "We killed all the outlaws we found. If any survived they've run off into the woods."

Saba glanced at Saewara then; even in the misty shadows the concern was evident on his face.

"Are you well, Milady?"

"Yes, thank you," Saewara replied, her voice subdued, "although a few minutes more and I wouldn't have been."

Annan sheathed his sword, *Night Bringer,* and turned to Saewara. He looked down at her feet, which were bare. In his voluminous cloak she looked small and vulnerable. Her eyes were huge and dark on her pale face. "We have a long walk ahead of us," he told her. "Climb on my back and I'll carry you."

Her eyes widened. "Are you sure?" Her voice was husky from strain. "I can walk."

"I know you can," he replied, irritated, "but there's no need. Climb on my back."

Annan turned around and knelt so that she could wrap her arms around his neck. When he straightened up, she clamped her legs around his chest. He could feel the warmth of her body against his back, despite that they were both soaked. Annan did his best to clamp off his mind to it; frankly the events of this night had put him in a foul mood.

They set off, following the others through the rain shrouded woods.

"How did you find us so easily?" Saewara asked, her breath feathering his ear as she spoke. "They were sure you wouldn't."

"That was their mistake then. Both Saba and I can track anything," Annan replied, his tone matter-of-fact. "We learnt as soon as we could walk. They tried to mask their trail but they were in too much of a hurry to do a good job of it. It was like tracking a pack of stampeding boar through the woods—easy."

"The man you killed—he was one of my brother's thegns, banished just over a year ago."

Annan stiffened at this news. "Really?"

"He heard of my impending marriage and thought to wreak vengeance on Penda by ruining his sister."

Annan remained silent at this admission. The no-nonsense manner in which Saewara proclaimed this news shocked him. The lack of emotion in his betrothed's voice when she spoke of her brother spoke volumes about her rapport with him. She had been ill-treated; it was clear in the way she interacted with men. And after what he had witnessed in that outlaw's tent, Annan was not surprised.

Yet the image that had burnt into his memory like a brand, was not that of the outlaw, readying himself to rape his captive, or of the abject terror on Saewara's face, but of her loveliness. Even now he could visualize the lush globe of her milk-white breast and the dusky nipple.

Annan shook his head to clear it. The woman had been cringing in terror and all he could think about was her naked breast. Frankly, he sickened himself.

Although Saewara was a small woman, and easy to carry, it was a long, tiring journey through the woods back to camp. If anything, the rain had grown heavier, and by the time they spotted the glow of the tents through the trees, Annan felt as if there was not a part of him that was not soaked through.

Ignoring Penda's servant, who strode out to meet them, Annan carried Saewara to his own tent. He felt the man's gaze track him across the clearing but left Saba to explain what had happened.

Inside Annan's tent, a fire still burned. The air was warm and dry.

"Bring us some ale to warm," Annan instructed one of the warriors, "and some more wood for the fire."

He sighed in relief when Saewara slid off his shoulders onto the ground before he straightened his aching back.

"I'm sorry if I was heavy, Milord," Saewara murmured from behind him, her voice abashed. "You should have let me walk."

"You weren't heavy." Annan shook his head and gave a rueful smile. "I'm just getting old, it seems."

A warrior brought a jug of ale, which Annan put to warm over the fire. Annan then sent him out to retrieve Saewara's clothes from her tent. Almost immediately, their wet clothes started to steam. They would both need to change into dry clothes but, for the moment, they needed to warm themselves, from the inside out.

"Here." Annan passed Saewara a mug of hot ale. "This will warm you."

Saewara nodded and took the mug wordlessly, wrapping her fingers around it. She sat on a stool in front of the fire pit, still swathed in Annan's cloak; although it had slipped down on one shoulder, revealing the thin linen tunic beneath. Annan took a deep draught of warm ale, feeling it burn into his belly. A moment later, his gaze returned to Saewara.

"Are you sure he didn't hurt you?" he asked.

Saewara gave him a tight smile in return. "Nothing that can't be fixed."

Annan took another gulp of ale before stepping up to Saewara. He then hunkered down so that their gazes were eye level.

"You have a huge welt on your forehead. How did you get it? Let me have a look."

"Coenwal head-butted me," Saewara replied, wincing as Annan gently probed the inflamed skin with his fingertips.

"Coenwal, is that the bastard's name?"

Saewara nodded.

"You're right, no lasting damage," he finished checking her forehead.

"It all happened so quickly," Saewara replied, the words rushing out as if a dam had just burst inside her. "I woke up and they were inside the tent. Oswyn tried to raise the alarm but they cut her down."

Tears filled her eyes then, and she hurriedly brushed them away. "I tried to shout but they were too fast. I was sure they were going to kill me."

"You're a brave woman, Saewara," Annan replied gently. "I saw how you fought that outlaw."

Suddenly, Annan was aware of how close they were. His face was just inches from hers, and the warmth of the fire enveloped them. Saewara had closed her eyes; her lashes were long and dark against her pale skin. Her cheeks were flushed from the ale, and Annan could also feel his senses heightened. His gaze then travelled down Saewara's face, observing her delicate features and her full, sensual lips. Then, suddenly, his breath stilled in his chest.

The cloak shrouding her, had slipped open.

Her breast, in its soft glory, was visible. Annan closed his eyes. A strange ache took up residence in his chest. He longed to reach out and touch her. It would be easy to lower his lips to hers and kiss that full mouth.

What is wrong with you?

Annan swiftly rose to his feet and took a rapid step back. "Saewara, cover yourself up," he said, his voice strangely hoarse, turning so that she would have a moment of privacy; so she would not see his face.

Saewara made a soft sound of mortification as she realized that the cloak had slipped, and when Annan turned back toward her, she was covered up once more. A moment later, the warrior that Annan had sent to retrieve Saewara's possessions entered the tent.

"I will leave you to change," Annan told her brusquely, before draining the remnants of his ale and ducking outside into the rainy night.

Saewara watched Annan go; her forehead still tingling from where his fingertips had touched. She felt oddly light-headed but imagined it was a combination of the warm ale and shock from her ordeal.

Putting aside her empty cup, she rose to her feet and quickly stripped off her ruined tunic. She pulled a clean tunic from her bag and a woolen wealca to go over it and dressed as rapidly as she was able. Her hands trembled slightly as she fastened the over-dress's straps with two simple brooches.

When Annan returned to the tent a short while later, she was dressed and warming her feet in front of the fire.

He nodded at her and, without warning stripped off his sodden tunic before reaching for a dry one. Saewara hurriedly averted her gaze, staring into the dancing flames. However, one glance had been enough for her to appreciate his broad shoulders, finely muscled chest and back, and the masculine spray of crisp blond hair across his chest. Unaware of his betrothed's flushing cheeks, Annan shrugged the dry tunic over his head and began to unlace the garters around his calves. He then kicked off his sodden boots and stripped off his breeches. Annan moved with a complete lack of self-consciousness; a man who was completely comfortable with nakedness.

Saewara kept her eyes firmly downcast until he was clothed once more.

"It is only a short while till daybreak," he told her curtly. "I suggest you try and get some sleep or the next day of travel will exhaust you."

Saewara nodded, noticing that the coldness he had exhibited toward her before her abduction had returned. She had caught a glimpse of a different man for a short while after he had saved her—for the ordeal had momentarily bonded them—but now, it was as if that man had never existed. Instead, a cold stranger; the man who looked at her with resentment in his eyes, stood before her once more.

Bone-weary, Saewara climbed into the furs without a word. She snuggled into their warmth and closed her eyes, hearing Annan leave the tent.

I won't sleep, she told herself. *After tonight I shall never sleep again.* Yet moments after curling up in the furs, she fell into a deep, dreamless slumber.

They buried Oswyn in the clearing, as a wet dawn crept across the world.

Saewara stood at the edge of the grave, watching as Annan's warriors shoveled dirt over the girl's body.

"Her name was Oswyn and she might have found hope in her new life," Saewara murmured, catching the attention of both Annan and Saba who watched the burial beside her. "For there was no hope in her old one. We murdered her kin and stripped away her identity. She had every right to hate us, but I sense that she and I might have been friends. In a different life we would have been friends."

"Milady?" Saba spoke up, frowning. "Her death was not your fault."

Saewara looked up and met the warrior's gaze. She saw that he had kind eyes. Smiling sadly, Saewara shook her head.

"Death is the easy part," she looked back at the small, lonely grave. "In many ways I envy her."

"So you would trade places with her then?" Annan asked. Saewara met his dark blue-eyed gaze and held it. "You wish it was your throat they had cut last night?"

The words were brutal—he had meant them to be. Yet Saewara merely smiled.

"Yes, I would trade places with her," she replied simply. "At least she is now in peace."

With that, Saewara turned her back on the men and walked away from the grave, toward where a knot of warriors were readying the horses and finishing packing away the last of the camp. She had left Annan and Saba before she said more; before she said too much. Words, sharp, angry and bitter, made her throat ache from the effort it was taking not to shout them. However, she knew what men were like. Penda would have knocked her to the ground for even saying what she had. Although Annan did not appear to be brutal, she knew he would not appreciate her telling him that she would rather be in that grave than travelling to Rendlaesham to become his bride.

Annan watched her now with a slightly perplexed expression, as if he was trying to decide what to make of her. Saewara ignored him, busying herself with making sure her pony's saddle and bridle were adjusted properly, before tightening its saddle's girth.

Keep your mouth closed from now on, she warned herself. Men hated women with opinions. *Shrew, harpy, and fishwife*—she had been called all these things, and worse, by Penda and her late husband. Annan already resented her deeply; she did not want to give him even more reasons to do so.

Chapter Ten

The River Crossing

THE MOMENT THEY crossed the border from Mercia to the Kingdom of the East Angles, Saewara felt a sense of finality; a certainty she would never return to her homeland. It was an odd sensation—a mix of melancholy and longing for a place she had wanted to love but had never been accepted in, blended with a very real dread of what lay before her.

Mingled with all of this was relief; with each passing league they were drawing ever farther away from her brother.

Stepping from one world to another was easy. One moment they were riding through woodland with the rain beating down on their heads, the next the trees gave way and they rode out onto flat heathland under leaden skies.

The weather worsened as the day wore on. The ground squelched underfoot and the going became ever slower. Often, they would have to stop to dig the wagon out of the mud, or detour around areas that had become flooded.

Soon, Saewara forgot what it felt like to be dry. The only saving grace was that it was not overly cold, although the damp seemed to penetrate to the bone. The company rode in silence; after the events of the night before they were all exhausted and irritable from lack of sleep. Like the day before, Saewara fell back to the end of the group, riding alongside the wagon while Annan led the column.

The farther east they rode, the flatter the landscape became and the bigger the sky loomed overhead. Despite the foul weather, Saewara found herself looking about with interest. She had thought the whole world resembled the rolling, lush-green hills and wooded thickets of Mercia. She had not expected her new home to be so different – so flat.

That night they made camp on the only higher ground they could find. Saewara now shared a tent with Annan. The rain drummed on the roof of the tent while Saewara sat eating a light supper of stale bread, cheese and small, sweet onions.

She was alone. Annan ate with his men, which was a relief for Saewara. After the events of the last few days, relations were strained between them. For herself, Saewara was keenly aware of Annan's presence whenever he was near her. The night before, when he had touched the welt on her forehead, she experienced the same hunger she had felt during that fateful dance in Tamworth. She was not sure if he had also felt it, although judging from his swift departure from the tent and his refusal to come anywhere near her ever since, Annan was aware of the pull between them and did not want to encourage it.

She hardly blamed him—she was Penda of Mercia's sister, after all.

That night, Saewara slept on a pile of furs on one side of the fire pit, while Annan slept on the other. Saewara fell into an exhausted sleep as soon as she stretched out on the furs, and awoke to the dripping of water on her face from the slit at the top of the tent.

It was still raining.

Huddled under a heavy fur cloak, Saewara emerged from the tent to find Annan and his warriors breaking their fast with stale bread and broth. Annan wordlessly handed Saewara a cup of hot broth and a heel of bread before going to help the others ready themselves to move on.

The broth, although a bit insipid, revived Saewara somewhat and she helped the warriors load the provisions into the wagon.

"You don't have to help us, Milady," Saba told her with a grin as Saewara struggled over to the wagon with armloads of furs. "The king's betrothed should enjoy being waited upon."

Saewara shook her head and found herself returning Saba's grin. Smiling felt odd, and she realized that it was the first time she had done so in a long while. "The king's betrothed will get fat and lazy if she doesn't do anything for herself."

Saba laughed at that before going to dismantle the tents. Meanwhile, Saewara busied herself with packing away the food provisions and covering them with oiled cloth; packing the ends in tightly so that they did not get wet.

A short while later, the company set off for another long, wet day of travel. According to Saba, they still had another three days journey east before arriving in Rendlaesham. As in previous days, Saewara and her shaggy, bad-tempered pony brought up the rear of the group. She rode alongside the emissary that Penda had sent to ensure the handfasting actually took place. The young man was ill-tempered and did not invite conversation. She only learned that his name was Yffi, and that he bridled at being given this task; something none of the warriors had volunteered for. Eventually, Saewara tired of trying to draw Yffi into conversation, and they both rode in silence.

Despite the rain, Saewara found herself enjoying the monotony of the journey. It left her alone with her own thoughts. Unlike her brother's hall in Tamworth, where she had constantly felt observed and judged, no one paid her any mind here. Even Yffi was content to ignore her. She reveled in the peace and wished that it would never end.

Mid-morning the journey came to an abrupt end.

A river, swollen and muddy from the rains boiled before them. The bridge, which the East Angles had used to cross the river on their way west, had been washed out, making crossing the divide a risky and laborious process.

"Is there no way we can go around it? Another bridge up river maybe?" Saewara heard Saba ask Annan. Both men had dismounted near the riverbank and were looking despondently upon the obstacle in their path.

Annan shook his head. "The nearest bridges, both up and downriver, are at least three days' ride from here—and what's to say they haven't been washed out as well?"

Saba grunted, his brow furrowing as he gazed upon the swollen river.

"We could cross it, if we tie the horses together with rope and cross in a line. It will be difficult, and we'll have to leave the wagon behind, but if we're careful we'll manage it."

"We could be swept away," one of the other warriors piped up. "And I can't swim."

"Why don't we just wait out the rain?" another warrior, an older man, asked. "It can't continue like this for much longer. As soon as the rain stops the river will go down quick enough."

"That could be days," Saba replied before his gaze returned to the king. "What say you, Annan?"

"I don't like your plan much," Annan admitted with a scowl, "but since no one has a better solution, we should try to cross."

There were a few grumbles and dark looks, for it seemed that few of the warriors could swim. Only Annan, Saba and Saewara had ever learnt, and even they were nervous about crossing.

"In good weather children could cross this river," Saba said with a shake of his head as he dug out a long coil of rope from one of their packs. "Now it rages like a beast."

It took them a while to prepare themselves for the crossing. As much as possible was removed from the wagon and strapped to the horses' backs. Tying all the rope they carried into one length, they were able to link it through the horses' girths to form one chain. Saba complained that he would have preferred to have been able to wrap the rope around the waist of each person, but they did not have enough rope to do so – as such, each warrior would have to grab on to his horse's saddle as he waded beside it.

"I'll put you up on my stallion." Annan turned to Saewara, addressing her for the first time all day. "You should be safe there."

Saewara nodded, before casting an eye over the river. If anything it was flowing even more swiftly than when they had arrived at its banks. Although she had not said so to Annan, she was relieved to be carried across on horseback, unlike everyone else who would have to wade. That water looked freezing.

They began the crossing carefully. Annan helped Saewara up onto his horse's back before taking his place at the stallion's shoulder. Saewara's pony was tied up behind. They were in the middle of the chain; which gave Saewara some comfort. However, the stallion, sensing her nervousness sidestepped and bucked as they approached the water.

"Relax, Saewara," Annan said while he soothed the horse by stroking its quivering neck. "He can feel your fear."

Saewara tried to take Annan's advice, relaxing the grip her thighs had on the saddle and talking to the stallion in a gentle voice. The horse's ears flicked back and forth and Saewara felt the animal calm under her.

"That's right." Annan nodded in approval, his gaze meeting Saewara's briefly. "Hold on, here we go."

The first horses and warriors entered the raging river. Saba took the lead, with his huge, heavy-set bay stallion; a fierce creature that Saba had difficulty controlling as it surged into the water. The river was deep, reaching Saba's breastbone and halfway up his horse's chest. As her horse entered the river, Saewara glanced over her shoulder at her pony. Once they entered the river, the water rose up over the pony's back so only its head, neck and withers were above the water. She could see the whites of the pony's eyes and heard its shrill neigh of fear. Poor creature.

At first, they made good progress across the river. Saba had nearly reached the far bank and although the chill water lapped at Saewara's feet, she felt hopeful that she would get to the other side without getting drenched.

Then, disaster struck.

Annan's horse stumbled, suddenly floundering in the swirling water. For one moment, Saewara held on, believing that the stallion would find its footing once more. However, one misstep was all it took. The horse went under and Saewara pitched forward and fell into the river.

Cold water embraced her and Saewara came up gasping. She was already a few feet down river and struggled to stand up in the water. However, the current yanked her feet from under her, and she went under once more.

"Saewara!" Annan shouted, reaching for her. "Grab my hand!"

He was stretching toward her, struggling with his other hand to control the stallion. The horse was now squealing in terror and trying to lurch forward out of the line.

Annan's fingers brushed hers.

Saewara resurfaced, coughing. Then, she saw Annan let go of the rope as he threw himself forward and grabbed her hand.

A moment later, the river swept them both away.

"Annan!" The last thing Saewara heard, before the current sucked her beneath the river's surface, was Saba's shout. After that, the water blocked her ears.

Annan's hand was the only thing she had to cling on to.

When she resurfaced once more, lungs burning, it was Annan who had pulled her up. Gasping and spluttering, Saewara clung to him. He pulled her against him, while he lay on his back and lifted his head up in an attempt to get his bearings. Together they hurtled through the foaming water.

Their salvation came a short while later, when the river narrowed.

Willows draped over the river here. They both managed to grab hold of an overhanging branch, as they passed under it, and hoist themselves up. After catching their breath, Annan and Saewara inched their way along the branch's length, to safety.

Saewara dropped from the branch, on to the mossy bank, before collapsing onto her back. The grey sky wheeled above through the bright green growth of the willow trees and her pulse beat in her ears. Annan lay beside her, his breathing coming in ragged gasps.

"That," he gasped when he finally regained his breath "was Saba's stupidest idea yet. Remind me to punch him in the mouth when he catches up with us."

His unexpected attempt at humor caught Saewara off guard; especially so soon after they had avoided a watery death. She tried to laugh but hiccupped instead, before being seized by a coughing fit.

Eventually, she sat up and, pushing her wet hair off her face, turned to meet the gaze of her savior. Annan had pushed himself up into a sitting position. Their gazes met and held.

"You saved me—again," she croaked. "Twice in two days."

"A woman like you certainly keeps a man on his toes," he admitted. "Woden, I thought the river had swallowed you."

Saewara looked away from him, the laughter of moments ago draining from her; a chill that went right to her core replaced it.

"You should have let it," she said quietly, meaning every word. "It would have made both our lives easier."

"Enough, Saewara." Annan gently but firmly took hold of her chin and turned her face to him, forcing her to meet his gaze once more. She could see that her words had angered him. "Do you think me a monster, capable of letting a woman drown?"

"A woman you are being forced to marry," Saewara countered, her own anger rising. "You risked your life for someone you despise, I don't understand it."

"I don't despise you," Annan replied, his voice gentling. "None of this is your fault."

Their gazes held again, and once more Saewara was aware of her rising hunger. Being close to this man had a disturbing effect upon her. The sensation clawed its way up from her belly and nearly made her gasp with its intensity.

In Annan's eyes, she saw her own hunger reflected back at her. They sat so close that all it took was for Annan to bend his head over hers, a groan escaping him as he did so. Instinctively, Saewara tilted her head back, her lips parting slightly. Their mouths came together.

He was not gentle, and neither was she.

The moment their lips met, a surge of need—a sensation Saewara did not even realize her body had been capable of—exploded within her. She let out a soft cry and reached for him.

Annan pulled her roughly to him. One moment, they had been sitting side by side, the next she was on his lap, her mouth open under his, her hands tangling in his wet hair. They bit at each other's lips, as their tongues warred for dominance. Annan's hands slid down her wet back to the curve of her bottom before he pulled her hard against him.

Her need for him was so intense that Saewara's head swam. She groaned into Annan's mouth. He kissed her as if she was air and he was a drowning man. She had never known that a man and woman could kiss like this. She had never known that she could want a man so badly that it could push all other thoughts from her head; that it could literally make her feel ill with need.

He would have taken her there on the mossy bank, she was sure of it, and she would have begged him to, if a man's call had not reached them. Neither heard his shout at first, although the voice eventually reached them through their haze of passion.

"Annan! Saewara!"

Saba was searching for them.

Annan and Saewara broke apart as if they had just been doused with a pail of icy water. Annan stared at her, breathing heavily while he struggled to regain control of himself. Saewara watched him, and saw the haze of lust fade from his eyes. Her heart started to hammer against her ribs when she saw his gaze harden.

"I'm sorry, Saewara." His voice was cold and flat. "That was a mistake. It won't happen again—ever."

Saewara gaped at him. What did he mean? They were about to be handfasted. Was he not intending to bed her once they were married?

"Annan," Saewara began, reaching a tentative hand toward him.

"No," he backed away from her and rose to his feet. "You are part of the bargain I made to save my people. I didn't want this; I was to marry someone else when Penda forced you upon me. He sent you to bewitch me, to take his humiliation one step further, and he almost succeeded."

"No, that's not true. I've never bewitched anyone." Saewara felt hysteria rise inside her at the ridiculousness of the situation. Yet, the look on Annan's face was anything but comical. "Not even my own husband. I don't understand what you mean."

However, Annan was no longer listening to her. She watched, tears blurring her vision, as he strode away to find Saba.

Chapter Eleven

Homecoming

THEY REACHED RENDLAESHAM on a warm, sunny morning that basked the town in golden light. Saewara rode at Annan's side, her pony trotting to keep up with his stallion's brisk walk. Together, they rode down the last incline toward the gates.

Despite Saewara's apprehension and low spirits, she still found herself taking in her surroundings with interest. They rode through fields full of cabbages, onions, carrots, turnips and spring greens; it was a verdant, lush landscape. Rendlaesham lay in the fold between two low hills, and high above the thatched roofs of the town itself, she spied the magnificent 'Golden Hall' itself. Saewara could see it was an idyllic spot. Arable fields, a spreading apple orchard and straw thatch lay under a wide cerulean sky. The horizon seemed wider here. In other circumstances, Saewara would have been pleased to arrive in Rendlaesham; it was a pity she would not be welcomed.

The folk working the fields all stopped what they were doing and hailed the king and his entourage. Ahead, townsfolk poured out of the gates and lined the way in. All of them waiting to see the king and lay eyes on his Mercian betrothed. Rendlaesham was bustling, as folk from nearby villages had flooded the town to see the royal couple. Some children pushed their way to the front of the crowd, while others perched on their fathers' shoulders. Street vendors selling hot pies and bread wove through the throng, taking advantage of the occasion to hawk their wares.

Saewara kept her gaze fixed ahead, not daring to make eye contact with any of them. She remembered her own people's heckling when she had ridden out of Tamworth. Although none of this was any of her fault, a discontented people would find it easy to lay the blame on her.

She could feel their gazes, raking her from head to toe—some hostile, others merely curious. Many folk shouted out to the king, welcoming him home, although muttered insults about his choice of bride reached Saewara's ears once they entered the town itself. However, none were bold enough to shout abuse—not with the king riding at her side.

They rode through the town, up a wide dirt street to the high fence surrounding the Great Hall of the Wuffingas. Up close, the 'Golden Hall' appeared even more imposing than from a distance. Saewara could also see that a number of outbuildings spread around the base of the hall itself. Helmed warriors flanked the entrance, pulling the heavy gates apart to allow the king, his betrothed and warriors to enter a wide stable yard.

Saewara brought her pony to a halt and let her gaze travel up the wooden steps to the terrace at the top. There, before the great oaken doors, stood a small group. Among them was a tall blond man, who bore a striking resemblance to Annan, and a tall slender woman with hair the color of creamed honey. Saewara saw both their gazes fix upon her and she looked away under the intensity of their stares.

The trip here, despite its dangers and trials, had given Saewara respite from life in a king's hall. Now, she would no longer be ignored. There would be no anonymity; nowhere to hide from hostile stares and whispered insults.

Annan helped her down from her pony. It was a polite act, and Saewara was grateful for his steadying hand as she slid down to the ground. However, there was no warmth in his face when he looked at her.

"Come," he said, taking her arm as tradition dictated, and linking it through his. "Let me lead you into your new home."

To onlookers they must have appeared a genteel couple, Saewara thought, with Annan solicitously leading her up the steps to his hall. Yet ever since their kiss on the banks of the river, under the canopy of willow branches, Annan had turned into a cold stranger.

Part of her, the rational part, completely understood his behavior. They were enemies, after all. His revelation that he had been about to marry another made his anger toward her even more understandable. If she had not been enchanted by Annan, if even the sight of him had not made her pulse race, she too would have behaved coldly toward him. Because of him, she had not been able to retreat to a life of solitude in Bonehill. She had been forced to marry back into a world she despised; a world where women were bargained and traded like pieces of gold for power, land and titles.

Yet his rejection felt like a knife to the heart, and Saewara hated herself for caring. Yearning for something that was beyond her reach would only add to her unhappiness here. She needed to be strong. The vulnerability she had shown Annan needed to be forgotten; she had to build a wall around herself, re-immerse herself in her faith and put aside the desires of the flesh. Her body had betrayed her on the journey here; she had not been prepared for her reaction to the King of the East Angles. It had been an enchantment; one that stripped her of a lifetime's defenses.

Now that the surprise had passed, and Annan had made it clear how the land lay, Saewara had to focus on protecting herself. The 'Golden Hall' would be full of wolves in sheep's clothing and soon she would be surrounded by those who wished to see her ruin.

Courage Saewara. You've fought against worse than this. Penda is in Tamworth. Egfrid is dead. Neither of them can touch you here.

Annan mounted the last set of steps to his hall and steeled himself for the meeting he had been dreading.

Aethelhere and Hereswith. He had seen them waiting for him, the moment he had ridden into the stable yard. They would be married now. The thought made him feel ill.

Saba was right, he thought bitterly. *I should never have agreed to their marriage. I've now made myself a martyr.*

Saewara's hand lay lightly on his arm; a constant reminder of the mess he was now in. He did not glance her way as they stepped up onto the terrace before the oaken doors.

My life used to be so simple.

The woman he wanted to marry stood before him, while the woman he would be forced to marry walked at his side. The situation was further complicated by the fact that, although his attention was focused on the slender blonde at his brother's side, the sultry, dark haired woman beside him had succeeded in completely disarming him. Her touch was a brand on his naked skin. Even now, the memory of her lush body against his, and the hunger of their embrace, was enough to make his step falter.

She is Mercian. You will not touch her again.

With an effort, Annan banished the lingering memories and focused on the couple before him.

"Brother!" Aethelhere greeted him with a warm smile. "We were starting to worry that you would never come back to us!"

"The journey home took longer than expected," Annan replied, his gaze resting on his brother's face for a moment. "Outlaws and near drowning delayed us somewhat."

Aethelhere's eyes widened at that.

"I expect a full account over a cup of mead," he announced, before his gaze swiveled down to the woman who stood silently at Annan's side.

"So this is your new bride?"

"My betrothed," Annan corrected him. "We are not yet wed. Saewara, meet my brother Aethelhere and his wife Hereswith."

"Greetings," Saewara spoke for the first time since her arrival.

Annan forced himself to look at Hereswith then; the woman who was now wedded to his brother.

She was as lovely as he remembered; as pale and radiant as a new dawn, her eyes the color of a summer's sky. She returned his gaze boldly, unsmiling before nodding curtly.

"Milord."

"Hereswith."

"So when is your handfasting?" Aethelhere continued, a little of the friendliness and humor gone from his voice. Hereswith was his now, and it was evident he did not like his brother greeting her personally.

"Tomorrow," Annan replied, aware of how flat his voice sounded. It was as if he was announcing his own execution. "At noon."

The roar of voices inside the hall was deafening. Smoke from the cooking created a haze over the interior, although it could not dim the majesty of the cavernous space. The 'Golden Hall' of Rendlaesham may have been made of timber but Saewara decided it was no less impressive than the Great Tower of Tamworth for all that. The sheer height of the beamed ceiling above her made Saewara feel very small in comparison.

Turning her attention back to the feast before her, Saewara helped herself to a piece of roast pork and some braised onions. The clamor around her was strangely soothing. For the moment, at least, everyone was too focused on the feast to pay attention to the imposter in their midst.

Saewara sat at Annan's side, so close that their elbows often brushed as they reached for their cups or helped themselves to food. However, the two of them could not have been farther apart.

They did not look at each other during the feast.

To Saewara's left sat Aethelhere and his blonde wife. Next to the lovely Hereswith sat a brown-haired woman who would have been attractive if her face had not been creased in a permanent expression of disapproval.

Saba sat to Annan's right. The warrior was in good spirits this evening, and downed more than his fair share of mead. He flirted outrageously with the female slave who served them; a timid girl with long brown hair braided in a long plait down her slender back. In Saewara's opinion, Saba appeared to be frightening the girl, rather than impressing her, and the slave fled to serve the other end of the table as soon as she was able.

As the feast progressed, Saewara caught a snippet of conversation from Aethelhere and his wife.

"I have instructed the servants to prepare a suitable feast for tomorrow afternoon, after the handfast ceremony," the young woman told her husband.

"Make sure they bake the honey-seed cakes," he told her. "You can't have a handfasting without them."

Hereswith nodded demurely before, seeing that Saewara was observing them, allowing herself a sly smile.

"Of course, Aethelhere. They encourage fertility and I'd say that your brother's betrothed will need all the help she can get."

"Really?" Aethelhere raised an eyebrow at his wife. "Why do you say that?"

"Well, she was married for years, was she not, and never produced an heir? I'd wager the poor creature is barren."

Saewara looked down at her plate, her cheeks burning.

Poor creature.

However, there had been no pity in Hereswith's voice when she spoke those words, only a vindictive cruelty; the kind only a bitter, vengeful woman could manage.

Saewara had seen the look that passed between Annan and Hereswith earlier outside the hall. She had witnessed Aethelhere's jealousy and the sudden coolness between the two brothers. It appeared the situation was even more complicated than she had anticipated. If her instincts served her right, and they often did, Hereswith was the woman Annan was to marry before Penda's summons.

Instead of Annan, she had married his brother.

God help me, I've walked into a hornets' nest.

Saewara was digesting this realization when the slave-girl appeared once more with a platter of piping hot mutton pies. After days of travel and simple food, Saewara had a ravenous appetite. Even her lack of welcome here could not take the edge of it. She took one of the pies and flashed the girl a grateful smile.

The slave smiled back at her, her cheeks flushing in pleasure.

"Lovely Hilda." Saba leaned back and looked up at the slave as she made her way round to his side of the table. "How I missed your pretty face. Tell me, how fared you in my absence?"

"Well, M'lord," Hilda replied, refusing to meet his gaze.

"Ah now, no need to be coy," he grinned at her. "I know you missed me."

Saba was rewarded with a sharp, irritated look before the girl slapped a pie down in front of him and continued on her way down the table.

The warrior watched her go with a shake of the head.

"Well, at least Hilda doesn't still cower in terror every time you speak to her," Annan observed over the rim of his cup. "She must be warming to you."

"You should not encourage him, Milord," the brown-haired woman who sat next to Hereswith exploded, obviously unable to hold her tongue any longer. "The girl is a slave and should be treated as such."

Annan gave the woman a slow, measured look.

"Remind me of your name?" he asked her, his voice barely audible over the roar of drunken voices around them.

"Eldwyn," the woman replied, holding his gaze boldly.

"Eldwyn," Annan said her name slowly, as if considering his next words. "You are a newcomer to my hall, and welcome here, for you serve my brother and his wife. However, you will never tell me how I should or should not behave again. If you do so, I will have you packed off back to Bebbanburg before you have time to take your next breath. Do you understand me?"

The woman stared back at him sullenly, although her pale blue eyes held a look of uncertainty.

"Do you understand me?" Annan repeated, his voice still calm although, glancing at his face, Saewara could see the anger kindling in his eyes. "If you don't, you shall be leaving this evening."

"Yes, Milord," Eldwyn finally acquiesced, before staring down at her plate. "I am sorry."

Annan nodded before reaching for the jug of mead and refilling his cup. "While we're on the subject, you should all know that Sabert has asked me if he may pursue Hilda, and even wed her if she is willing. I have said that he may."

This statement drew looks of surprise, shock and disapproval from those seated around the king, but after Annan's reaction to Eldwyn, those who disagreed with Annan's decision wisely held their tongues.

Observing the scene, and seeing Saba's obvious delight that Annan had publicly given his blessing, Saewara momentarily forgot her own troubles.

Saba was an ealdorman. He could have had any woman and yet he was obviously smitten by that timid, waifish girl.

Annan had done something that Penda would never have. At the far end of the table, Saewara spied her countryman, Yffi. He watched the scene incredulously; like Saewara, he was nonplussed by Annan's behavior. Some kings and ealdormen gave slaves their freedom but to her brother they were just dogs; there to serve and to be whipped into submission when they defied him. Annan obviously saw the world differently.

Saewara turned and regarded her betrothed frankly for the first time that evening. He would know she was looking at him but she did not care. The conversation resumed around them and the moment passed.

Annan resisted her stare for a while longer before his gaze reluctantly met hers. As usual, the shock of it was like a punch to the belly, but this time she was ready for it. She pushed her body's response to him aside and met his gaze squarely.

"I suppose you want to upbraid me as well?" Annan said with a raised eyebrow. "Go ahead. I've dealt with one sharp tongue this evening, I can deal with another."

Saewara's mouth curved into a smile at that.

"Men rarely impress me," she replied, holding his gaze. "But you just did."

He drew back, surprised, before breaking eye contact and raising his cup of mead to his lips to hide his expression.

Saewara felt a surge of satisfaction, knowing that she had succeeded in rendering him speechless. Annan had not expected her to praise him; yet, her words had been spoken in truth. She had seen far too much of the worst of men in her life. It was a relief to know that men with humanity ruled in other corners of Britannia.

Saewara returned to her meal and took a bite of the suet crust pie.

Suddenly, she was aware of someone's gaze fixed upon her. Curious, she looked down the table and met Hereswith's cold stare. Looking upon the hatred on the young woman's face, Saewara realized that her own upcoming marriage to a man who did not want her was the least of her worries.

Her problems at Rendlaesham were only just beginning.

Chapter Twelve

The Handfasting

ON THE MORNING of her handfast ceremony, Saewara awoke in her bower with the dawn. She lay back on her furs, staring up at the beams high above, with a feeling of dread upon her.

The sounds of the hall beyond the thick tapestries that shielded her from view had roused her from a fitful sleep. She lingered in bed, in no hurry to leave the privacy of her bower. She had been grateful to be able to spend the night alone, away from the stares and whispers that had followed Saewara since her arrival at Rendlaesham. Her bower was tiny; nothing more than a cramped, yet private, space next to the king's quarters at the back of the hall. Apparently, this had been Raedwyn's bower—the fiery Wuffinga princess who had sent shock-waves through her family when she married the son of her father's arch-enemy; a man he had enslaved.

Saewara thought on that story, which had now become folklore—and often told at fire sides throughout Britannia. She would have liked to have met Raedwyn; a woman who, like her, had been born into a role of subservience and duty—but unlike Saewara had managed to create a life of her own choosing. Such women were a rarity in their world.

Saewara reluctantly climbed from the furs, her bare feet crunching on the rushes, and opened the small window above her bed. Pushing the wooden shutters open, she breathed in deeply. The air was cool and laced with the smell of grass and earth. She could hear the rise and fall of voices in the town below, punctuated by the bleating of goats and the honking of geese in the distance. She could see for leagues from here. Her window did not look over the town but over the vast apple orchards behind Rendlaesham and the meandering, willow-lined stream that ran through the heart of it. It was a picturesque setting, and in other circumstances, Saewara would have enjoyed it.

"Milady," a soft voice called from behind the tapestry. "May I come in?"

"Yes," Saewara called back, turning from the window. A moment later, the slave-girl, Hilda, entered her bower. This morning, she looked even more cowed than usual; her cheeks were flushed and she looked on the edge of tears.

"I have been sent to help you dress for your handfasting," she said timidly, her voice trailing off at the end.

Saewara stared back at her, surprised. They both knew it was not the way things were usually done.

A woman who was about to become queen was not dressed by a slave for her wedding ceremony. Preparing the bride for her wedding should be a grand occasion, and usually the woman would be surrounded by a flock of gushing and fussing ealdormen's wives.

That was not to be the case here on this occasion.

Even on her wedding day, they shunned her. That was how it could be with women; their weapons were subtler than men's, but when they put their mind to it they could be far crueler. Even without asking, Saewara knew that Hereswith was probably behind this. She had seen how Aethelhere's new bride glared at her yesterday. Even after only a day in Rendlaesham, she had also noted how Hereswith held court here, almost as if she were queen. The wives of Annan's ealdormen and thegns clustered around her, making it all the easier for Saewara to be excluded.

Saewara sighed and gave Hilda a brittle smile.

"Well, I am ready so let's begin. I have two dresses that might be suitable. Can you help me choose?"

Hilda nodded, her eyes wide on her thin face.

"'Tis not right," she whispered. "A woman should feel special on her wedding day."

Saewara shook her head and waved a hand in dismissal. "Truthfully, I prefer your company to theirs." She made her way over to where a collection of tunics and dresses hung against one of the tapestries. There, she took down two gowns—one a delicate cream color with a bell-neck and long sleeves; and the other dark green and sleeveless, with a low neckline and heavy gold belt that sat around her hips. "Which one?"

Hilda studied the dresses for a moment before shaking her head. "I'm not sure – they are both beautiful. You'll need to try them both."

After Saewara had tried on each gown, it was decided that, although the cream gown was, perhaps more suited to a handfast ceremony, the green dress suited Saewara best. It was made from fine wool, lined with linen and embroidered with gold around the neckline and hem. Unlike most of Saewara's dresses, this one had a deep neckline, which showed off the swell of her breasts. The dress left her arms bare and so Hilda pushed gold arm rings onto Saewara's arms, to match the gold thread and the heavy gold belt around her hips. Once they were satisfied with the dress, Saewara sat down on a low stool and let Hilda start on her hair.

They talked little, for Hilda was very shy and obviously cowed by those of a higher rank. However, the silence made Saewara brood and after a while, she attempted to draw the slave girl out of her timidity.

"Have you been here in service long?"

"Two winters," Hilda replied. "My father sold me to King Ricberht, hoping to find favor with the Usurper. The new king was pleased by the gift but killed my father all the same."

Saewara stared at Hilda in shock. Once again, the cruelty of the world they inhabited sickened her.

"I'm sorry, Hilda."

The slave shrugged. "It all seems a long while ago now. Fortunately Ricberht remained in power only a short time before Sigeberht returned from exile in Gaul and took back the throne for the Wuffingas." Hilda paused there, her eyes clouding in sadness. "I liked Sigeberht. He was a stern man, but kind. He did not deserve to die the way he did."

Saewara listened in silence. Of course, she knew of the battle that had claimed Sigeberht's life. It was said that Penda himself cut the King of the East Angles down; an easy enough task as Sigeberht had refused to bear arms and had gone into battle carrying only his staff.

"This hall was a lonely place after Sigeberht left," Hilda continued. Now that she had started speaking she could not stop. "He spent the last few months establishing a monastery. I wonder if it still stands, or whether the Mercians burned it to the ground."

Saewara looked away in shame. Knowing Penda's dislike for the god that his sister worshipped, she imagined it was the latter.

"When Sigeberht left he took Freya with him; she was my only friend here, and life here has not been the same since," Hilda concluded, her voice trailing off.

"Freya? Who was she?"

"Another slave that Ricberht had taken, just before Sigeberht and his men attacked Rendlaesham. She was not like the others here; she was free and strong despite all that had happened to her. One of Sigeberht's men fell in love with her, but they could not be together. They both followed the king to his new home. I wonder what happened to them. I hope they survived that battle—I hope they're together now."

Listening to Hilda's tale, Saewara was overcome with melancholy. There was something heart-rending in the matter-of-fact way that Hilda spoke about tragedy.

"Perhaps they are," she replied in a falsely bright voice, attempting to mask the despair that dragged at her. "Let us believe that they are."

The women lapsed into silence then while Hilda brushed out Saewara's hair in long waves. Then, she piled the hair up onto Saewara's head and secured the coils with amber pins. It was a long, laborious process. Once it was finished, Hilda stepped back to admire her handiwork.

"Milady, you look truly like a queen."

Despite herself, Saewara smiled back at her. "Thank you, Hilda— although I don't feel like one."

Finally, Saewara slipped on a pair of gold-threaded slippers and dabbed some rosewater behind her ears. Hilda was now beaming at her like a proud mother; not that Saewara knew what that felt like for her own mother had died birthing her, and she had grown up without being fussed over by anyone.

"I suppose it's time?" she sighed. "I might as well get this over with."

"It won't be so terrible," Hilda ventured, seeing Saewara's despair. "Annan is a good man."

Saewara glanced back at the slave, wondering if she knew that Annan had been planning to marry Hereswith. She must have done. She would have liked to mention Saba, to tell Hilda that the ealdorman was so infatuated with her that he had attained permission from the king to pursue her, yet she did not want to embarrass the girl. At this stage, she was not even sure if Saba's advances were welcome. Hilda had become so used to her life as a king's slave, she might not be able to accept another. Saba would have to be patient if he wished to win her over.

"Yes, he is a good man," Saewara admitted. "I don't dispute that. However, if only the world were that simple."

With those words Saewara turned, and leaving Hilda with a confused look on her face, pushed aside the tapestry.

Her betrothed awaited.

Saewara looked down at the ribbon that the elderly woman gently wrapped around her and Annan's joined left hands.

She and Annan stood facing each other, although neither of them had made eye contact since they took their places on the dais at the far end of the hall. As before, the touch of his hand on hers made her pulse race; yet the discomfort of having every gaze in the crowded hall piercing her through was even more distracting.

The woman before them was Greta, Annan's only surviving elderly blood relative. She was his father's older sister. A quiet woman with kind eyes, Greta finished tying the ribbon and stepped back from the couple.

"Do you both enter this union with a free will?" she asked.

Saewara was hit by a wave of hysteria at this question.

Now is your last chance, Annan, she thought grimly, resisting the urge to glance in the direction of her brother's emissary. Yffi stood near the front of the crowd beneath the dais, his gaze riveted on the couple. *I would refuse but my brother would tear me limb from limb if I did so.*

"Yes," Saewara responded, her voice barely above a whisper.

Annan's response was even quieter, yet audible in the still hall. "Yes."

"Annan, look into your betrothed's eyes," Greta instructed, a slight note of reprimand in her voice, "and say the words that will bind you."

Annan and Saewara's gazes met then, although unlike other times when she had looked into his eyes, Saewara saw nothing but bleak resignation there.

It is as if this is his hanging, not his wedding.

"I, Annan of the Wuffingas, King of the East Angles, take you Saewara, daughter of Pybba of Mercia, for my wife. I will defend your body with my life."

A watchful silence settled upon the hall before Saewara responded in kind.

"I, Saewara, daughter of Pybba of Mercia, take you, Annan of the Wuffingas, King of the East Angles, for my husband. I swear to never bring you harm or dishonor."

Then, together, Annan and Saewara said the words that would bind them.

"May we be made one."

Saewara held Annan's gaze, even though it took all her will not to look away.

Greta then passed Annan a small cup of mead; it was an ornamental cup painted gold and encrusted with precious stones. This was the next part of the ceremony; and much easier than making promises that held no feeling.

Saewara watched as Annan lifted the cup to his lips and took a sip. Wordlessly, he then passed the goblet to Saewara. She took a delicate sip before passing the cup back to him. As tradition dictated, Annan drained the rest in a one draught.

Once the cup was empty, Greta handed Saewara a delicately carved wooden plate with a single honey-seed cake sitting in its center. Although seed cakes would be served at the feast afterwards, this cake was different. Greta had prepared it herself and made just one cake, throwing away the rest of the batter. Only the newly-weds were allowed to taste this cake—it was for no one else.

Saewara broke off a piece of cake and gently fed it to Annan. It was an oddly intimate act, especially to share with a man who did not love her, in front of a hall of people who saw her as the enemy. Annan did the same, his fingers accidently brushing her lips as he did so.

They stood there, their faces solemn, while Greta unwound the ribbon that bound them.

"You are now man and wife," she announced. "Annan, kiss your bride."

The King of the East Angles stepped forward and, stooping, kissed Saewara lightly on the lips. It was light, the mere brushing of lips, yet Saewara's mouth tingled as he stepped away. The hall erupted into applause. The sound was muted, however, as those watching clapped more out of tradition and respect for the king than with any joy.

Saewara tore her gaze away from Annan and looked down at her feet. Her eyes filled with tears, blurring her vision.

It was done. Another loveless union. Another sacrifice for her people.

Chapter Thirteen

The Way of Things

THE SECOND FEAST in two days was in full swing inside the Great Hall of the Wuffingas. Such feasts were rare outside of festivities and that fact, coupled with the balmy warmth of early summer outside, created a celebratory atmosphere amongst the feasters.

Annan, however, was in no mood for celebration. He sat back in the carved wooden chair that his predecessors had all sat upon at the feasting table, and let his gaze travel along the long table that groaned under the weight of all the food. Hilda passed by with a jug of frothy mead and moved to refill the king's cup, but Annan shook his head and placed his hand over it, making it clear that he wanted no more to drink.

He would be relieved when this day was over.

Watching his ealdormen, thegns and kin eat, drink and make merry, Annan was struck by how fickle folk could be. One moment they were chafing under the Mercian yoke, enraged that their king had been forced to 'bend the knee' to the reviled Penda, the next they were celebrating at his handfasting as if they had not a care in the world. Further down the table, the callow youth that Penda had sent to witness the wedding was feeding his face, considerably more relaxed now that the handfasting was done. Tomorrow, the warrior would begin the journey back to Tamworth to inform the Mercian King that Annan had indeed wed Saewara.

The handfast ceremony itself had been more of an ordeal than he had expected. Saying words that meant nothing before a crowd of disappointed faces had weighed upon him.

The bride, despite the sadness in her eyes, had looked radiant. The green dress with its deep neckline, gold embroidered edging and heavy gold belt across the hips had accentuated her dark beauty and the lush curves of her petite frame. She had endured the ceremony with poise, although it had been evident that she had suffered through every moment.

Saewara sat now, at his left, picking at a plate of roast duck and sipping at a cup of mead. From this angle, he had an uninterrupted view of her creamy cleavage; a sight which he found distracting. Turning his attention from his new bride, Annan felt his gaze returning, not for the first time, to where his brother and Hereswith dined, further down the long table.

Aethelhere looked unbearably smug these days; although Annan did not blame him.

Hereswith appeared a goddess today—her tall, lithe frame was sheathed in a silky white gown, and she wore an amber necklace around her slender throat. His brother did not take his gaze of his lovely wife as he ate and drank, and fed her morsels off his plate. What galled Annan was that she appeared to be enjoying the attention. She giggled when he made jokes and blushed prettily when he whispered comments into her ear.

Realizing that the king was watching her, Hereswith glanced in his direction. Aethelhere was unaware of their connection, as he called to Hilda to refill his cup with mead.

For an instant, Annan and Hereswith's gazes fused—and in that moment Annan realized that her apparent enjoyment of his brother's company was all a ruse. In her eyes he saw her hurt, anger and bitterness. The intensity of her gaze told him all. She still wanted him.

Is it you she wanted? A voice taunted him. *Or was it your title? Hereswith wanted to be queen.*

They broke eye contact, just as Aethelhere turned back to his wife to ask her something, and the moment was lost.

Annan picked up a piece of roast duck, before placing it back on his plate. Suddenly, he had no appetite. Then, aware that someone was studying him intently, his gaze swiveled to his left.

Saewara was watching him.

With a sickening jolt he realized that she had seen his and Hereswith's gazes meet, and had witnessed the look that passed between them. Her face was impassive, impossible to read, but her gaze was speculative, assessing.

She was a clever woman, his new bride. She missed nothing. He had told her that he had intended to marry another, and it had not taken her long to realize who the woman was. Saewara held his gaze for a moment more before looking away. Just before she did so, he saw the disdain in her eyes.

The feasting had ended. Slaves cleared away the food scraps and wiped down the tables. The feasters, full of rich food and drink, lounged about the hall – some still at the long tables, others seated around the crackling fire, conversing in low voices. A lyrist sat in one corner of the great hall, playing a gentle, soothing tune.

Saewara drifted around the hall, pretending to be observing the wall hangings, tapestries and array of weaponry that hung there. In reality, she was not sure what she was supposed to do now. Once the feast ended, many folk had left the hall, returning to their own homes in the town below. It made her conspicuous, wandering around the huge space talking to no one, ignored by all, and she longed to step outside into the night and slip away forever.

Annan sat at the far end of the hall, chatting with Saba. Deep in conversation, both men ignored their surroundings. The women had shunned her. She had tried sitting near one group, who had appeared friendlier than Hereswith and her friends. Yet, they had all turned their back on her the moment she pulled up a stool near them; making it clear she was not welcome.

Thirsty after a huge meal and more mead than she was used to, Saewara walked over to the water barrel at the end of the hall, not far from the oaken doors that had been left ajar to let in the soft night air. On the way there she passed Hereswith and her hangers-on.

Unfortunately, she also overheard their conversation.

They spoke in high, excited voices with no regard to who heard them. If they noticed Saewara passing quietly behind them, they did not show it; for it was as if she were a ghost here.

"Wed or not, I think it won't be long before he rids himself of her." Eldwyn, the sharp-tongued woman who Annan had chastised yesterday was holding court as she stabbed her embroidery needle into the coverlet she was decorating. "He will not long suffer an enemy under his roof."

"He can't stand her," another woman, one of the ealdormen's wives, agreed with a vigorous nod. "It's plain to see."

"Can you blame him?" Hereswith spoke up now, her voice bordering on shrill. She had consumed a goodly amount of mead during the feast and her cheeks were now flushed, her eyes overly bright. "The woman is a drab."

The others fell silent at this, even Eldwyn. Oblivious to the awkwardness her comment had caused—for exotic as Saewara was, all could see that Annan's new bride was attractive—Hereswith pressed on. "She's too short and will soon run to fat. Did you see how she ate yesterday? She was practically bursting out of that hideous gown she wore for the handfasting."

Recovering from their ringleader's viciousness, Hereswith's companions all nodded with murmurs of agreement.

"And, I've heard she's barren," Eldwyn added triumphantly. "A plump wife who can't bear children—what has Annan landed himself with?"

They all laughed at that.

Saewara slipped from the hall, her stop at the water barrel forgotten.

Outside on the terrace, under the curious stares of the two helmeted warriors guarding the entrance, Saewara walked to the edge and took a few slow, deep breaths to calm herself. She knew they were merely being vindictive and cruel – those women were her enemy and would say anything to wound her—yet their words still cut deeply.

Drab, short, fat and barren.

It was difficult not to feel the sting of their poison. Saewara realized with a sinking heart, that Hereswith was only just beginning her campaign against the woman she considered her usurper. She knew enough of how the world worked to recognize a spoiled young woman enraged that her life had not worked out as planned. Saewara could see that Hereswith had ambitions; her anger went deeper than merely wanting Annan for her own. His brother was handsome and charming but he was not king. Hereswith wanted to be queen. It galled her to see another take what she perceived to be her rightful place.

Saewara had been dreading this. The politics of life inside a great hall had always repulsed her; she had seen enough backstabbing under her brother's roof at Tamworth to know what ambition did to some.

I never wanted this, she thought bleakly as she stared out at the night. It was overcast so she could not see the stars. *I wanted a quiet life, a simple life—but instead I was born into this one.* Saewara blinked back tears then, before brushing at her eyes angrily with the back of her hands.

They won't make me cry, she promised herself stubbornly. *I've faced worse than Hereswith and her coven. I won't let them win.*

However, Saewara was still not ready to return to the hall. She turned to one of the warriors, who had been watching her steadily since she stepped outside, her gaze meeting his squarely.

"Is there a Christian chapel here?" she asked.

The warrior nodded, his mouth pursing in disapproval. "It's on this side of the barracks—although you'll never find it in the dark."

"Take me to it," Saewara ordered, making her tone as authoritative and regal as possible.

The warrior hesitated.

"I'm waiting," Saewara said archly.

"This way then," the man muttered. He led her down the steep steps to the stable yard before turning right. They walked past the stable complex and up another set of steps that led to the barracks. Just before the sprawling, low-slung wattle and daub building that housed a large number of the king's warriors, Saewara spied the outline of a squat, timber building standing in the shadow of the barracks.

"I'll need your torch." Saewara turned to the warrior, who wordlessly handed it to her. "Wait here," she commanded him. "I won't be long."

Saewara pushed open the chapel door and stepped inside. It was an austere space, covered in a thin layer of dust; revealing that few who worshipped the same god as Saewara resided here in Rendlaesham. She had heard that King Raedwald had been baptized, although his wife had resolutely stayed faithful to the old gods. Of course, Sigeberht had been a devout Christian. Saewara suspected this chapel had not been touched since Sigeberht's departure from Rendlaesham nearly a year earlier.

Hanging the torch from a wall bracket, Saewara knelt on the dirt floor, before a plinth with a wooden cross perched on top of it. She clasped her hands before her and bowed her head, squeezing her eyes shut in an attempt to blot out her environment.

Please Lord, give me peace …

Yet even her prayers did not bring her solace this evening. Saewara's faith was not enough to bring her the peace she craved; it could not keep the world at bay.

The warrior did not have to wait long for his queen to re-emerge from the chapel. Wordlessly, she handed him back his torch and followed him back to the hall. Inside, Saewara kept her gaze fixed ahead as she strode past Hereswith and her friends. The women fell silent as she passed by; their gazes tracking her, daring her to look their way.

She ignored them.

It was getting late now, and Saewara decided it was time for her to retire. Usually, a bride would never go to bed before her husband on the night of her handfasting. Often, a fuss was made about sending the newly-weds off to their bower together. But this wedding was not like most. Ignoring her husband, Saewara mounted the dais and pushed past the heavy tapestry that separated the king and queen's bower from the rest of the hall.

Out of sight of all, Saewara struggled to undress without assistance. She knew she could have called upon Hilda for help but the slave was busy kneading dough for tomorrow morning's bread.

Saewara knew no one else would assist her.

Finally, she managed to loosen the laces at the back of her gown and squeezed out of it. Then, quickly, lest her husband step inside his bower and find his bride naked, she pulled a long linen tunic over her head and let it drop to her ankles, shrouding her body completely.

Plump. Barren. Drab.

Those words still echoed in Saewara's ears, making her want to hide away from the world for the rest of her days.

Standing on the fresh rushes in her bare feet, in the center of the bower she was to share with her husband, Saewara let her gaze travel around the space. It was a warm, inviting space and, in other circumstances, she would have been pleased to have it as her bower. An enormous pile of furs sat at one end with a small fire pit at the other. Embers glowed in the hearth, casting the bower in a warm light. A tapestry hung behind her and rabbit pelts had been sewn together to create wall hangings. A low table, with a clay washbasin upon it, sat against one wall. The privy was hidden behind a screen in the far corner of the bower.

Saewara hesitated a moment longer before crossing the bower to the pile of furs and climbing in.

She lay there for a while, staring up at the rafters, as the embers in the fire pit slowly dimmed. She wished only for sleep to take her, but knew she would not be able to relax until Annan came to bed.

Her husband finally made an appearance. Feigning sleep, Saewara listened to him moving quietly about the bower, undressing for bed. Unlike her choice to sleep wearing a tunic, she imagined Annan, like most folk, would sleep naked. The thought made her stomach twist nervously.

Moments later, she felt the furs shift beside her and thought Annan was climbing into bed beside her. However, when she opened her eyes a crack, she saw that he had, instead, taken two furs off his side and carried them a few feet away.

Saewara watched her husband, naked to the waist and barefoot, although still wearing breeches, make a bed up for himself. Without glancing in her direction, Annan lay down and turned to face the wall, pulling a fur up over his shoulders.

Annan had meant every word, it seemed, that he had spat at her on the riverbank. Not only would he not bed his Mercian wife, but he would not even share his bed with her. Despite the relief that she would be left alone—

for Saewara had no desire to share a bed with anyone at that moment—she felt the sting of rejection nonetheless.

The worst is over with now, she consoled herself, staring at her husband's back as she listened to his breathing deepening. *I'm here, wedded, and the way of things has been made clear, at least. I need now only be strong for what is to come.*

Chapter Fourteen

The Devil's Work

One month later ...

ANNAN STOOD ON top of the earthwork and watched the wagons, filled with river stone and earth, rumble in from the northeast. From this height—over thirty feet above the grasslands—he had a magnificent view in every direction; especially on a day such as this. The sky was a clear, cloudless blue from one horizon to the other, and the sun warmed the exposed skin of Annan's arms, shoulders and face.

'Devil's Dyke,' as it had been named by locals, was just over two leagues from end-to-end. Annan's forefathers had started work on it, nearly a hundred years earlier, but had then left it to deteriorate as other, more pressing, threats to the kingdom drew their attention. Even a century ago, the Wuffinga kings had sought to protect their land from the Mercians— even then they had known the danger their western neighbors presented.

Annan turned away from the approaching wagons, his gaze sweeping across the deep ditch that had been dug out of the western side. Black thorn and brambles filled the ditch in either direction, for as far as the eye could see, acting as a further defense.

Penda thinks he has beaten us, Annan thought, rebellious pride swelling within him. *He can force me to 'bend the knee', and can even make me marry his sister but he can't stop me from defending my borders.*

Of course, Penda would not welcome news that Devil's Dyke had been strengthened, and now extended from the impassable fens to the north, to the thickly wooded land to the south. Although he knew the news would reach Penda eventually, Annan had been careful not to mention his plans during his visit to Tamworth, and to keep all talk about the earthwork quiet while the Mercian emissary was in Rendlaesham. Yet now that the man had returned to Tamworth, Annan had focused on the dyke in earnest. He wanted it finished before the autumn.

With the speed of the current work, it would be finished well before then. To ensure the work was completed in good time, Annan had imposed a corvée; bringing in peasants from every corner of the kingdom to work on the dyke. It was not forced labor, for the men could return to their homes once they had completed their allotted period, but it was obligatory all the

419

same. The king called them, and they came, bringing whatever tools and materials they could spare. Annan had expected to see some resentment, for many of these peasants had left behind fields and crops that needed tending, yet it did not appear the case. After the East Angles' defeat at Barrow Fields, the folk knew that the kingdom sat on a knife-edge; they all had to play a role in defending it.

Annan watched a group of men now, hoisting earth and stones onto the top of the bank on great hauling ramps. Despite that it was back-breaking work, they did it with good cheer; the sound of their singing mingling with the creak of wood and the dull thud of shovels. A few of them saw Annan walking along the top of the dyke and waved to him. It pleased them to see their king overseeing the work—and Annan wished he could stay longer. However, he was due to leave the dyke this afternoon, and return to Rendlaesham.

"Good morning, M'lord," one of the men he had charged with managing the work in his absence, greeted Annan as he climbed down one of the tall ladders on the eastern side of the dyke. "She's magnificent, is she not?"

"The dyke's a credit to you all," Annan replied with a grin. "Once we're done here—it will be the finest in Britannia."

"Those Mercian dogs won't be crossing our border this way," the man continued, his face turning grim. "Although, they can die trying."

Annan's grin faded. "They will come," he assured the man, glancing up at the earthwork rearing above him; it was so tall that it blocked out the sun. "Let's hope that Devil's Dyke is enough to stop them."

A warm breeze ruffled Saewara's hair and feathered against the bare skin of her face and arms. A wet spring had developed into a balmy summer and Saewara raised her face to the friendly sun as she walked through Rendlaesham's gates.

It was a relief to be away from the 'Golden Hall' and to stretch her legs. For her first days here she had been too nervous to venture far from the hall. She had been terrified that townsfolk would stone her. Yet, the hostility within the hall had worn her down and even the prospect of being spat at, or hounded in the streets beyond, was not enough to keep her indoors. To make matters worse, Annan had been away, dealing with matters on his southern borders. He was due back this afternoon. His presence here seemed to keep the women's vindictiveness in check; without him their forked tongues had almost been intolerable.

Saewara left Rendlaesham by the back gates, which meant she avoided traversing the center of town. The view from this entrance was Saewara's favorite in Rendlaesham. From here she could see the narrow dirt road winding its way down the shallow valley amongst the swathe of apple trees. At the bottom, she caught a glimpse of the stream glittering in the sunlight and the bright green profusion of willows.

Carrying a wicker basket over one arm, Saewara made her way down the hill, in search of wild berries. She had heard that raspberries grew thick near the banks of the stream, and she wished to make a cake with them. The life of a noble woman, cooped up inside the stuffy, smoky, dark hall was a monotonous one. She had spent days at her spindle, loom or distaff but found more joy in helping the servants prepare food for the hall. The other women sneered at the sight of the queen pummeling dough, dusted up to the elbows in flour; or chatting with Hilda as they peeled vegetables for pottage together. However, the alternative was to sit on her own in a corner at her distaff and go quietly mad.

The men, Annan included, did not appear to care how Saewara spent her time, provided she contributed to the life inside the hall and did not make a nuisance of herself. Strangely, Saewara had found freedom in her new role, and enjoyed improving her skills as a cook. She had even tried Oswyn's onion soup one evening and had been pleased to see that most of the men asked for second helpings.

Halfway down the hill, Saewara left the road and wove her way through the rows of apple trees. They were fully in leaf, although would not show fruit for months yet. Saewara continued toward the stream. It was a peaceful spot and she would have preferred to sit down on the grass and spend the afternoon here. Yet, she could never absent herself from the hall for too long before Hereswith complained loudly that the new queen was shirking her duties.

Reaching the banks of the stream, Saewara started her search for raspberries. It did not take her long to find the fruit bushes. Bright red, plump and juicy, it was an effort not to eat as many berries as she picked. While she bent over the raspberry bushes, Saewara's gaze drifted across the babbling water of the stream to where willow trees draped across the water. The sight of the trees brought her sharply back to that afternoon, just over a moon's cycle earlier, on the banks of the flooded river.

Annan, his wet tunic and breeches clinging to his tall, hard body, staring into her eyes as if nothing in the world existed but her. The feel and taste of him as they kissed.

Saewara let out a quiet sigh and tore her gaze from the willows. It was strange what could trigger memories. For the last month, she had done her best to forget that incident. In the hall, it was easier than she had thought. Annan kept a polite, cold distance from her; only speaking to her when absolutely necessary. Every night, he dumped his furs a few yards away from hers and slept separately. They were two strangers sleeping in the same bower, and although the arrangement had discomforted Saewara initially, she had gradually grown used to it. At least he was not a cruel man who took pleasure in tormenting her, as Egfrid had. She too, had become used to treating him coolly, and days would pass without them even looking at each other.

Yet the memories that looking upon the banks of the willow-draped stream had triggered, reminded her of another man; a passionate man who had roused a response from Saewara, of which she never thought she was capable.

Brushing aside the lingering memories, Saewara turned her attention back to the task at hand. Her basket was filling up nicely and she was looking forward to baking a delicious sweet with them.

She had almost filled her basket, and was about to turn to leave, when the sound of voices—a man and woman, nearby—reached her. Saewara straightened up and looked across at the opposite bank, past the willows.

Her mouth curved into a sudden, and unexpected smile, when she saw who the man and woman were.

Saba and Hilda.

They were sitting further along the bank, almost out of Saewara's line of sight. Saba was leaning back on his hands while Hilda sat next to him, her legs curled under her. The ealdorman said something and Hilda burst into laughter.

It was a musical sound, full of joy and fragile hope, and Saewara stilled upon hearing it. She had never heard Hilda laugh before.

Watching them, their gazes meeting frequently as they talked, Saewara felt a pull of longing from deep inside her—if only a man would look at *her* like that.

Saba had trodden carefully since arriving back in Rendlaesham, and wooed Hilda gradually. Just days earlier, the girl had been avoiding him but, somehow, he had now convinced her to take a walk with him.

Eōstre had just passed, although Saba had not been able to convince Hilda to leave the hall and join the folk around the bonfire outside the town. Even mention of joining the revelers had made Hilda cringe. She knew only too well that if a man invited you to dance with him around the Eōstre fire, he would end up dragging you into the bushes to make love afterwards. Hilda, who had only known rape and brutality at the hands of men, had no intention of letting that happen. Saba had understood; he had not pressured her.

Saewara had watched the unfolding story between Saba and Hilda with a quiet joy. Even now the ealdorman, a formidable warrior, and intimidating to those who did not know him, sat a respectful distance from Hilda. However, it was clear from the way Hilda's cheeks flushed, and the frequency with which she made eye contact with Saba, that he was close to winning her trust.

As Saewara looked on, the girl timidly reached out and put her hand on Saba's arm. In response, he placed a hand over hers and smiled down at her.

Saewara turned then, and left the lovers alone. Her chest ached strangely. As happy as she was for the pair, the sight of their burgeoning love made her feel empty and alone. She walked briskly away, glad they had not seen her, and climbed the hill back to the gates. A short while later she made her way through the stable yard.

Horses and men filled the yard and Saewara had to weave her way through them, in order to reach the steps up to the hall. Annan had returned and was unsaddling his stallion. He glanced Saewara's way as she walked by and acknowledged her with a curt nod. Saewara nodded back before mounting the steps to the hall.

Inside the Great Hall, preparations for the evening meal were underway. With Hilda absent, the other slaves were panicking that they would not finish in time. Saewara set her basket aside for a moment and took charge. She started chopping carrots for the rabbit stew, before carrying them on a wooden board over to the bubbling cast-iron pot that hung over one of the fire pits.

Ignoring Hereswith and Eldwyn, who were sitting back from the fire, winding wool onto distaffs, Saewara poured the carrots into the stew and proceeded to add some sprigs of thyme and rosemary.

"Where's that girl—Hilda?" Eldwyn addressed Saewara sharply. "She should be here preparing the evening meal. The king shall have her whipped for idleness on her return."

"He won't do anything of the sort," Saewara replied, her voice icy. "Hilda has gone for a walk with Sabert. She will be back shortly, I'm sure."

Eldwyn's face screwed up at this news. "It's disgraceful," she sniffed before turning to Hereswith. "This would never happen in the Great Hall of the Northumbrian King. He would not allow one of his ealdormen to fraternize with a slave."

Hereswith nodded. "He would not allow many things that are permitted here," she said, her gaze spearing Saewara as she spoke.

Saewara ignored them both. Hereswith's meanness was growing ever bolder, as the young woman's bitterness grew like a canker. Saewara had become used to it.

Leaving the pair of ladies to their sniping, Saewara returned to the table at the back of the hall and began work on her cake. She mixed freshly churned butter and honey with ground spelt and eggs to make a batter, before pouring in the ripe raspberries. She then poured the batter into an iron pot before carrying the cake outside to bake in a clay oven, which had been built to one side of the stable complex.

Saewara was nervous to leave her cake unattended while it baked – lest one of the hungry warriors should help himself to it. As she waited, she sat down on a stool next to the ovens and watched the activity in the stable yard beyond.

Annan was talking to two of his thegns in the center of the yard, and Saewara, without even meaning to, found herself studying the tall, blond stranger who was her husband. He carried himself like a king, she thought, straight and proud. Due to the warmth of the afternoon, he had stripped off his cloak and was wearing a sleeveless tunic. Despite herself, Saewara found herself taking in the light gold of his skin, and the finely defined muscles of his arms.

Fortunately, Annan was too deep in conversation to notice that she was observing him. He had not yet seen her, sitting next to the clay oven.

Presently, Saba and Hilda entered the stable yard. At the sight of the king, Hilda became flustered and sprinted off up the steps to the hall to assist the other slaves with the evening meal. Saba watched her go with a wry shake of the head and turned to Annan. Even though their voices were faint at this distance, Saewara heard their conversation.

"Look, you've scared her off."

"Hardly. If I'd spent the afternoon looking at your ugly mug, I too would be looking for an excuse to get away."

Saba punched Annan playfully on the arm. "She finds my face interesting."

Annan grinned at that, and watching her husband, Saewara was struck at how handsome he was when he smiled.

"So, how goes things at Exning?" Saba asked, turning his attention to the reason for Annan's journey south. "How's the building progressing?"

"Faster than I expected," Annan replied with a note of pride in his voice. "The men are working from dawn to dusk. The local monks are calling it the 'devil's work' – as such the folk of the area have named it 'Devil's Dyke'."

Saba raised his eyebrows at this. "Penda's going to have a fit."

Annan gave him a slow look, as if he had already considered that prospect and cared not what the Mercian king thought.

"Of course. I don't expect our neighbors to like it."

A huge grin spread over Saba's face as he listened to Annan.

"What about 'bending the knee' to Penda?" he asked, deliberately baiting his friend.

However, Annan was in good spirits—the best Saewara had seen since their arrival back in Rendlaesham—and he refused to be baited. He merely shook his head, his expression hardening.

"I'm through doing that bastard's bidding. He can demand terms at the end of battle, and make me marry his sister to ensure peace, but he can't stop me from defending my own borders. You should see the fortifications, Saba – I wish Raedwald and my father were alive to witness them. I am having a hall built at Exning so I can spend more time there and oversee the work. Next time I visit, you're coming with me."

Saewara watched, still unobserved by Annan and Saba, as the men turned and made their way up the steps to the hall. Moments later, she could no longer hear their conversation.

Turning her attention back to the reason she was out here, Saewara used a thick jute cloth to pull her cake out of the oven to see if it was done. The top was golden and a delicious aroma filled her nostrils. She gingerly picked up the cake and turned to follow the men up to the hall.

I don't believe it. He's deliberately defying my brother.

The news both thrilled and terrified Saewara. On one hand, she loathed her brother enough that seeing others stand up to his bullying ways brought her enormous pleasure. Yet, on the other she knew what Penda did to those who crossed him.

She just hoped Annan was ready for the consequences.

Chapter Fifteen

Hare Pie

SAEWARA SLICED THE last leek into rings, before straightening up to ease her aching back. She had been preparing vegetables all morning and was starting to tire of it. The interior of the hall was quiet this afternoon. It was a cool, grey day outside and the mood inside was subdued. A few older men sat chatting by the fire while a group of woman—Hereswith and her friends—worked at looms in one corner. The king was nowhere to be seen, as he and a group of warriors, Saba and his brother Aethelhere among them, had gone hunting at dawn.

In contrast to the sedate mood of the hall's higher ranking occupants, slaves scurried above the vast space like worker ants. Two boys were refilling the water barrels in both corners of the hall, while another carried in stacks of firewood. Next to Saewara at the work table, its surface pitted and grooved from years of food preparation, Hilda kneaded yet another batch of griddle bread for the evening meal.

Transferring the leeks to a huge cast-iron pot for soup, Saewara glanced over at Hereswith and the other noble women. Even after a month, they had still not accepted her into their ranks—not that Saewara had tried to befriend any of them either. Their hostility made her keep her distance from 'the adders', as she and Hilda called them. The few times she sat down with embroidery, or her distaff, she did so as far as possible from them. Even now, they stared at her before whispering amongst themselves and bursting into peels of derisive giggles.

Saewara knew she should not let their disdain bother her, but after weeks of being treated like a *nithing*, when in fact she was now Queen of the East Angles, it had begun to wear her down.

She realized that by helping Hilda and the other slaves with the cooking, she just made it easier for them to single her out for ridicule. They did so now, pointing at her before dissolving into paroxysms of laughter.

"She dresses like a slave-girl," one of the women's shrill voices carried across the hall. "She can't be a highborn Mercian princess—I'd say Penda palmed off one of his Celtic slaves to the king. Annan was duped!"

Saewara's face burned and she stared down at the cauldron she had just emptied the chopped leeks into, pretending she had not heard the woman.

"Milady," Hilda murmured. "It's not right. You should not allow them to speak of you so. You are the queen, they should treat you with more respect."

"What would you have me do?" Saewara countered, her voice sharper than she intended. "Go over to that woman and slap her face? I will become even more hated than before."

"They are bullies," Hilda replied, showing a rare burst of spirit. "My rank dictates that I may say nothing to them, but you can."

Saewara listened without responding this time. She knew that Hilda spoke the truth; it was just that she felt so alone here. If she had the support of her husband it might have been different, but she could not imagine Annan caring. It was true that 'the adders' never spoke against their new queen with the king present, for they were wary of him, but all it took was for him to absent himself from the hall for a short while before the taunts began.

"You are strong, all can see it," Hilda continued, fixing Saewara with a pleading gaze, "but those women will break you if you let them."

Saewara nodded and gave her friend a brittle smile. "You are wise, Hilda. Saba is a fortunate man."

Hilda blushed at that. "We are not a couple," she murmured before giving Saewara a shy smile. "Yet."

Saewara smiled at that. "He can't take his eyes off you whenever you are near. We've all seen the way he looks at you. You know the king has given his permission for you to wed. Saba will ask you soon, I am sure of it."

Hilda looked flustered at that. She pummeled the dough she had been shaping with the back of her hand, flattening it into a wide disk.

"I never thought I'd marry anyone," she admitted quietly. "I thought this was to be my life—forever. I still can't bring myself to believe it. Saba is kind, strong and handsome. He could have any woman he wanted. Why me?"

"Because he sees your beauty, your gentle heart and your strength," Saewara replied before she cast a scowl in the direction of Hereswith and her coven. "A man like Saba would never be happy with one of those empty-headed women who clamor for his attention. It's you he wants."

"I don't understand it," Hilda repeated, before giving another shy smile, "although I would not stop him for the world."

Their conversation was interrupted then, by the arrival of the king and his men, back from a day's hunting.

Annan strode into the hall, and as usual, the sight of him stilled the breath in Saewara's chest. The man had an incredible presence. Whenever he entered a space, he drew the attention of those around him. Even though they lived under the same roof as virtual strangers, Saewara could not help but admire her husband's masculinity, his charisma. She noticed that she was not the only woman in the hall who noticed his attractiveness; the gazes of 'the adders' tracked Annan as he crossed the floor.

The king carried with him two large hares, holding each animal by its back legs. They were magnificent creatures with soft, tawny coats and dark, bright eyes.

Annan made his way over to the table where Saewara and Hilda stood. Saewara felt a jolt as the king approached her. She was used to being ignored. Annan placed the hares on the end of the table, his gaze meeting Saewara's.

"Hare pie this evening?" he asked hopefully.

Saewara gave her husband an arch look. "Do you enjoy my cooking, Milord?"

Annan raised his eyebrows, a smile tugging at the corners of his mouth. "I do. Although Saba's been nagging me for another one of your pies for weeks now. I promised him I'd ask you for a pie this evening."

"Very well," Saewara cast a glance at the hares. "I'd better get started, if you want to eat before midnight."

He left her to it, and Saewara got to work. She employed Hilda's help to skin and gut the hares. As she worked, Saewara was aware of the venomous looks she was getting from the women. They had seen the king stop and converse briefly with his wife—something he rarely did—and they did not like it. Saewara was sure they knew that the king and queen slept on separate beds every night. Hereswith especially, often gazed at the queen with victory in her eyes. She might not be able to have Annan but neither could his wife.

Saewara made the suet crust for the pie while Annan settled down with Saba and Aethelhere near one of the fire pits with a cup of ale. A feeling of contentment stole over Saewara as she worked. She had seen Annan enjoy her cooking, although he had never before complimented her. She wondered why it pleased her so, since they were husband and wife in name only. Yet, in a life where she was a ghost in her own hall, validation of her existence and of the contribution she made to life there, filled her with a sense of satisfaction.

The hare pie was an enormous success amongst the men. Saba rolled his eyes in ecstasy and asked for a third piece while Annan savored each bite of his. Aethelhere lavished praise on the cook as he held out his plate for a second helping, and received a vicious look from his wife. Oblivious to Hereswith's displeasure, Aethelhere blundered on.

"You are truly a cook of great talent, Saewara."

"Thank you." Saewara bowed her head graciously, a little overwhelmed by the praise. She noticed that Hereswith, Eldwyn and the other ealdormen's wives picked at their meals listlessly.

"Truly, I've never eaten a pie like it."

"It pleases me that you like it." Saewara felt her cheeks burn at the sudden attention she was receiving. After weeks of being ignored, it was difficult to adjust. Only Annan remained silent, although Saewara could feel his gaze rest upon her face as she answered his brother. She resisted the impulse to meet his gaze and glanced back down at her plate, instead.

"She used too many herbs," Hereswith spoke up, her voice clipped. "I prefer my food plainer."

"The rosemary and thyme are the perfect accompaniment to hare," Saba countered. "Can you do better, Hereswith?"

The young woman glowered at Saba in response but did not reply. Aethelhere chuckled at Saba's comment, only to receive a dig in the ribs from his wife. He turned and gave Hereswith a reproachful look.

"What's the matter with you tonight?" he hissed, slightly drunk after consuming three cups of mead in quick succession. "You look as if you've got a mouthful of horse piss."

Most of the men roared at that, although Saewara noticed that Annan did not.

Hereswith gave her husband a look that could have curdled milk and turned her shoulder to him. Aethelhere shrugged and turned back to his meal; his wife's anger already forgotten.

Conversation resumed at the table then, and Saewara was relieved to be ignored once more. She listened to Annan, Aethelhere and Saba's conversation, which had been interrupted in order to comment on the food.

"So do you think the hall is ready?" Saba asked with interest, before he took another bite of pie.

Annan nodded. "I received word yesterday that the last of the roof thatch has been finished. Truthfully, I would like to spend the rest of the summer at Exning to oversee the work on the dyke."

"Why don't we go there for a spell then?" Aethelhere suggested. "Leave a few of your ealdormen here to look after Rendlaesham and return here in the autumn once the work has been completed."

Annan nodded reluctantly, before he met his brother's gaze. "Wouldn't you rather stay here and look after Rendlaesham in my stead?"

Aethelhere shrugged. "I'd rather help you at Exning, if I may?"

"Very well," Annan nodded, his expression shuttered. He then turned to Saba. "Will you join me as well?"

"Of course," Saba replied without hesitation. "As long as Hilda accompanies your wife as her maid. I would prefer not to leave her for the summer."

"So be it," Annan nodded. "We need to make preparations but if we start tomorrow, we should be ready to depart within three days."

Saewara listened with interest.

I wonder when he will speak to me of his plans, she thought.

Judging from the conversation, she was also to join Annan in Exning. She was curious to see this Devil's Dyke – the border fortifications that would keep her brother's army at bay. Saewara had initially been pleased with these plans to leave Rendlaesham behind, until Aethelhere had asked to join his brother. For, if Aethelhere travelled to Exning, so would his wife.

Saewara's gaze swiveled to where Hereswith sat, her pretty face creased in annoyance. Even at Exning, Saewara would not be free of her tormenter.

The meal ended and the diners rose to take their places by the fire. Saewara got to her feet and glanced over at where her loom sat in a quiet corner of the hall. She did not enjoy weaving but she suddenly craved a moment of solitude and peace. She skirted the edge of the table, passing Hereswith and Eldwyn.

Suddenly, she felt hands shove her viciously between her shoulder blades. Saewara stumbled forward and fell flat on her face, skinning her knees on the rushes. She had been just inches from cracking her skull on the edge of the fire pit.

"Milord, it looks like your wife consumed a little too much mead this eve," one of Annan's thegn's bellowed.

Saewara scrambled to her feet, face flaming, and turned to face the individual who had shoved her—only to see Hereswith glide away to follow her husband, as if she had been at his heels the whole time.

It appeared that no one had seen Hereswith move; either that or they did not care.

Saewara watched as Annan turned and raised an eyebrow at his thegn. "No more than you, Bercthun." The king's gaze then shifted to his wife.

For the first time all evening, Saewara met Annan's gaze.

"Are you well, Milady?" he asked.

Saewara nodded, her cheeks burning. "Yes Milord. I just tripped."

She turned her back on them all then and retreated to her corner, taking a seat at her loom. Saewara watched Hereswith perch on a stool at Annan's side. Then, Hereswith leaned forward and whispered something to the king that made him laugh.

Bitch. A sudden, bitter rage surged within Saewara. *One day, you shall pay for that.*

Chapter Sixteen

Hereswith

THEY LEFT FOR Exning three days later.

The king and his entourage rode out of Rendlaesham on a bright, breezy morning. Clouds scudded across a robin's egg blue sky and the trill of a skylark accompanied Annan's departure from his hall. The folk of Rendlaesham crowded at the roadside to watch Annan leave—and now that Saewara was wedded to their king, they dared not spit insults at her as she rode past. Nonetheless, many of their gazes were unfriendly, and Saewara kept her own gaze fixed firmly on her horse's ears as they made their way down the main thoroughfare to Rendlaesham's main gates.

She only began to relax with they were riding through the fields south of Rendlaesham, with the town at their backs.

Saewara rode near the head of the column, on a spirited filly that kept pace with Annan's stallion, unlike the stubborn pony she had ridden here from Tamworth. Behind her rode a column of warriors, and behind them trailed Hereswith and Eldwyn. Another group of warriors and three wagons laden with goods brought up the rear of the company. Hilda, and two other slaves who had also been brought to serve the king at Exning, travelled with the wagons.

It was a relief to leave the 'Golden Hall' of the Wuffingas behind. Saewara knew that she would have to contend with Hereswith and Eldwyn at Exning, but at least the group of hangers-on—the ealdormen's wives who had followed Hereswith around in adoration—would be absent at their new hall.

The journey east would take them two full days and one night, if the good weather held. Remembering the deluge on their way to Rendlaesham, Saewara hoped it would. The sun on her face and the wind on her skin cheered her up no end. There was a freedom in riding a horse, and to be away from the daily domestic duties that slowly ground one down. She had discovered a certain joy in cooking, but even that, under the sour gazes of the other noble women, did not give her the lightness of spirit that riding out under an endless sky and wide horizon provided.

Annan gradually drew ahead of Saewara as the morning passed, and she found herself riding alone. She did not mind this in the least; despite his slight thawing toward her over the last few days, relations between them

431

were still strained. They continued to keep their distance, both emotionally and physically.

If only Egfrid had done the same during their marriage, she reflected. Saewara had been married to him, just after her sixteenth winter, on a warm spring day. She had spent little time with her betrothed before their handfasting and had been unprepared for the trauma of their wedding night. Her young husband had been drunk, and rough with her. Just four days after their handfast ceremony, Egfrid hit Saewara for the first time. She had dared disagree with him on a minor point and his fist had lashed out, nearly breaking her jaw. Unlike *some* violent men, who were overcome with remorse after striking their wives, the act had unleashed something brutal within Egfrid. He was not remotely sorry, and after that looked for excuses to lash out at his young wife.

Nine years of torture. Saewara preferred not to dwell on the worst moments of the last decade; instead, she had blacked them out, taking refuge in her faith and biding her time. When Egfrid died she had not been able to believe her good fortune – finally *wyrd* had looked upon her favorably, only to play a cruel trick on her once again.

Yet, with the sun beating down on her face and the smell of grass and warm earth around her, Saewara reflected that she had fared better than expected. She could not imagine the Kingdom of the East Angles ever feeling like home, or of the people here ever accepting her, but she was far from Tamworth and her brother's cruelty.

Moments of happiness, even in the smallest of measures, had to be savored when discovered. Even if they were fleeting.

At dusk, the king and his entourage camped by the banks of a stream, near a copse of coppicing lime trees. The warm weather had put most of the travelers in good humor, and Annan's warriors ribbed each other and laughed as they put up tents and started fires for cooking.

Tired after a day in the saddle, and knowing her muscles would be screaming the next day, Saewara watered and rubbed down her horse before walking stiffly toward the cluster of tents that now sat on the trampled grass. The men were already spit roasting a brace of rabbits over the fire and the smell of wood-smoke filled the balmy air.

The king's tent, the biggest of the group, had been erected in the center of the cluster, and Saewara made her way toward it. There would be time to rest before the rabbits were ready. She longed to stretch out her aching limbs on a bed of soft furs. However, Saewara was passing the first tent— the one where Aethelhere and Hereswith would sleep—when the cracking sound of a palm hitting flesh caught her by surprise.

The noise was followed by a whimper of pain.

"Stupid bitch!" Hereswith's voice cut through the warm air, causing all nearby who heard it to turn in surprise. "I told you to pack that gown. Why did you not obey me?"

"I'm sorry, Milady," Hilda's voice, low and shaking slightly, responded. "I packed all the gowns that you laid out. You did not tell me to pack the green one."

"Liar!"

The sound of Hereswith slapping Hilda across the face rang out once more. Saewara stood, breathless. Anger rose in a hot wave up through her body. Hilda had already endured much in her life. Hereswith had no right to raise a hand to her.

It was strange how she could endure ill-treatment herself but the thought of others being bullied or tormented made her blood boil.

Without thinking upon the consequences, and indeed not caring, Saewara pushed aside the tent flap and strode inside.

Hereswith stood in the center of the tent with Hilda standing before her. Tears streamed down the slave girl's lean face and she was clutching her cheek. Eldwyn stood nearby, where she was unpacking the items her mistress would need for the evening. The smug look on Eldwyn's face and the vicious look on Hereswith's both vanished as Saewara strode across to Hilda and took her by the arm.

"You will not touch Hilda again," she told Hereswith flatly before pushing Hilda gently toward the tent's exit.

"I will do as I please." Hereswith recovered swiftly, her face flushing. "Get out of my tent!"

"With pleasure," Saewara countered. "However, you will not command Hilda to do your bidding again. She serves me now. You will not speak to, nor touch her, ever again."

With that, Saewara turned and followed Hilda.

"How dare you!" Hereswith shrieked, rage turning her beautiful face ugly. "You cannot command me."

"I am the Queen of the East Angles." Saewara turned in the doorway, fixing Hereswith with an icy stare. "If you do not wish to obey me, I suggest you take up the matter with my husband."

That settled it. Hereswith stood, shaking with anger as Saewara calmly turned and stepped out of the tent. Unspeaking, she gently took hold of Hilda's arm and led her toward the king's tent.

Both Saba and Annan were still seeing to the horses, and had not witnessed the altercation. Saewara knew that Saba would be enraged to discover that Hereswith had been bullying Hilda. She wondered if Hereswith would have the gumption to complain to Annan.

"Are you well?" she asked Hilda when they were out of earshot. "Has she done that before?"

Hilda nodded, her pale blue eyes shining with tears. There was an angry, red welt on her left cheek. "I am well, thanks to you. She's slapped me, and other servants, ever since she arrived at the king's hall. However, her temper has gotten nastier of late. I swear to you she didn't ask me to pack that dress. She hit me because she was in ill humor and for no other reason."

"You don't have defend yourself to me." Saewara shook her head. "Whatever the reason, she had no cause to hit you."

"I thank you, Milady," Hilda repeated, brushing away tears, "but I take back what I said about you not standing up to her. Was that wise? You have just made an enemy."

Saewara smiled then. "I already had an enemy where Hereswith is concerned. If it is war she wants then it is war she shall have."

The flames from the fire pit danced against the inky depths of the night, and devoured a moth that fluttered too close. Annan watched the hapless insect dissolve in a shower of sparks before turning his attention back to the conversation of the other men around the fire. After a simple but delicious meal of roast rabbit, they were now sharing a cup of ale each before taking to their beds.

A pleasurable weariness seeped over Annan's body. He was looking forward to sinking into a mound of furs in his own tent. Another long day of travel lay before them tomorrow and apart from those assigned to keep watch, most of the travelers would be in for an early night.

All the women, save Hereswith, had already retired for the night.

She sat, a fur cloak around her shoulders, at Aethelhere's side, looking lovelier than Annan had ever seen her. The firelight accentuated her flawless skin and the gold in her hair. To make things worse, she kept glancing in Annan's direction, and he had to force himself not to meet her gaze. It was too risky to do so—what with Aethelhere sitting beside her.

The men were discussing the fortifications at Exning, and Annan's plans for the next stage of building. It was a subject that obviously was of interest to him, but fatigue and Hereswith's gaze kept distracting him. He wished she would go to bed.

As if reading his brother's mind, Aethelhere interrupted the discussion he was having with Saba to turn to his wife.

"Hereswith, it's late. Go to bed—I will join you soon enough."

She pouted in response before giving his arm a lingering squeeze, her gaze brazenly fixed upon Annan as she did so. "I will wait for you there then."

Not seeing the direction of his wife's gaze, Aethelhere puffed himself up as Hereswith walked away toward their tent.

"See," he grinned, throwing Annan a look of victory. "My wife cannot have enough of me."

Later, when the others had gone to bed and Aethelhere went off to join his wife, Saba turned to Annan with a shake of his head.

"Your brother is a fool."

"Why do you say that?" Annan replied, pretending he did not know what his friend was speaking about.

"I saw the way she was looking at you—and I can't believe Aethelhere didn't see it as well. He must be blind. It's a dangerous game you're playing. Be careful."

Annan frowned back at Saba and tipped the dregs of his ale onto the ground.

"There's no game," he replied firmly. "More's the pity."

Saba regarded Annan quietly for a moment or two, considering his next words, before he spoke; keeping his voice low so that they would not be overheard.

"She may be beautiful but she is vain and selfish. Why can't you see it? Your pompous brother is welcome to her. You have a wife, a lovely one. Why can't you be satisfied with her? Most men would welcome a woman such as Saewara."

Their gazes locked and held, before a sudden understanding crept across Saba's face. Being a man, he had not realized what all the women in the 'Golden Hall' had known within a day or two.

"Woden—you haven't bedded her, have you?"

Annan glared back at Saba. "Why don't you shut your mouth? This is none of your business."

"I don't believe it." Saba gave a low whistle and shook his head. "Why ever not?"

"She is Penda's sister—remember?" Annan ground out, struggling to keep his voice low. "I will not touch that Mercian dog's blood."

Saba's gaze did not leave Annan's face as the ealdorman absorbed his king's words.

"Whether you would have it or not, you are married to her," he said finally. "Making a martyr out of you both will not change the way of things. You seem intent on making yourself miserable. I do not understand it."

With that, Saba turned and walked away in search of his bed.

Annan watched him go, feeling as if he had been drenched with a bucket of icy water. For once, his friend's frank approach to life had grated on him.

Saba doesn't understand, he thought bitterly, leaving the warmth of the fire behind and heading toward his tent. *How can he?*

Inside his tent, he found his wife in a deep sleep, curled up like a kitten on her furs next to the glowing embers of a small fire. On the other side of the hearth, Saewara had made up a bed for him, as she had taken to doing ever since he had made it clear she would not be sharing his.

Annan sat down on his furs and took off his boots. His gaze rested then on Saewara's face; peaceful in sleep, her skin burnished by the fire's soft light.

Saba was wrong; it was not that he did not *want* Saewara. In one, very real, sense he did. If he'd had no desire for her physically, it would have been easy to share a bed with her. Yet after their tryst at the river, he did not trust himself with her.

I won't give in to this, he told himself before he lay down and turned his back on his wife's sleeping form. *If I do then Penda has won.*

Chapter Seventeen

New Beginnings

SABA WAS ENRAGED when he saw the welt on Hilda's face the next morning. She had been helping Saewara saddle her horse when the ealdorman strode across to greet them both.

Saba stopped short when he saw her cheek, his gaze meeting Hilda's.

"Who did this?" he demanded, his face turning hard.

Saewara and Hilda exchanged nervous glances. They had both been dreading this moment.

"Tell me!" Saba ordered, his tone brooking no refusal.

"Hereswith," Hilda eventually admitted, "but Saewara dealt with it, don't worry. She has forbidden Hereswith from having any contact with me. She won't touch me again."

Saba's gaze swiveled to Saewara.

"I thank you for that, Milady—however, the matter does not end there." With that, Saba marched off to find Aethelhere.

A short while later, angry voices echoed across the campsite.

Aethelhere, it seemed, did not know that his wife had a habit of lashing out at those who displeased her. He defended Hereswith blindly, as only a thoroughly infatuated man is able.

"Keep your wife in hand!" Saba roared.

"Calm down," Aethelhere shouted back. "Woden, she only hit a slave!"

That was the wrong thing to say.

It took Annan, and three other men, to pry Saba off Aethelhere and haul him away before the situation deteriorated further.

It was under a cloud of simmering resentment between Saba and Aethelhere that the journey east continued. The day was as bright and breezy as the day before had been and Saewara managed to keep abreast with Annan for most of the journey. Although the silence was companionable, Saewara felt the increasing urge to speak with her husband; to know of his plans for the future.

"I think you show valor in your decision to fortify your borders," she said finally, after gathering her courage to speak for most of the morning.

Annan gave her a sidewise look, surprise showing on his face.

"Really? I thought you would see it as an open act of defiance against your kingdom."

"Mercia is no longer my kingdom," Saewara reminded him gently. "Penda is no longer my king."

Annan glanced at her again, his expression unsure, before he spoke. "It's not valor that made me do it, but rebellion. I can't stay under your brother's yoke any more. If I don't do something now, I will become his puppet."

Annan fell silent then, and Saewara could see from his face that he was angry with himself. He had been much franker with her than either of them had expected. Such openness could get a man killed.

"Your people don't think less of you," she replied gently, pretending not to notice his discomfort.

"Yes, some do. They might not show it to my face, but ever since I took the throne there has been growing discontent. The only thing that keeps many from showing open resentment toward me is my bloodline. With Raedwald, Eorpwald and Sigeberht all dead, my brothers and I are all that remains of the Wuffinga dynasty. Many follow me for that reason alone."

"So by building these fortifications you hope to earn back their respect?"

Annan gave her a pained look before replying. "I would not put it in such blunt words—but yes, I suppose that's why I'm doing it."

His face grew serious then and he looked away, his gaze focusing far into the distance.

"You never met King Raedwald, or my father. They were the type of men that folk sing of around the fire; men that have stories told about them that will last for generations. They proved their valor again and again. Men would fight for them, die for them. Will I ever inspire the same loyalty in my fyrd?"

Saewara stared at Annan in disbelief. He carried himself in such a confident manner that she would never have guessed at the insecurity that plagued him. That he had even revealed it to her impressed her even more. She did not think less of him for it; in fact she found herself liking him for his honesty.

"I think you would be surprised at how readily your men would follow you into battle," she told him with a wry smile. "I've observed them with you for a while now. They think more of you than you realize."

Annan raised an eyebrow and glanced back in her direction.

"Perhaps ... yet, I think it's now time I acted like their king. It's time I earned their respect."

The sun hung low in the sky, sinking toward the western horizon, when the company approached Exning. Compared to Rendlaesham—a bustling town that spread out around the base of the king's hall—Exning appeared little more than a hamlet. A tall paling fence surrounded the village, enclosing a scattering of low-slung wattle and daub houses with thatched roofs. The settlement sat a short distance from the shadowy boughs of the dense Exning Woods that stretched southeast, guarding the narrow stretch of land between the woodland and the treacherous marshes to the north-west. Like the landscape farther north, the sky was enormous here, fringed by the strips of brown, gold and green of a flat countryside.

Riding alongside Annan, through the waving grass that had turned golden with the setting sun, Saewara let her gaze do a wide sweep. South of the settlement, she saw a patchwork of arable fields, sandwiched between Exning and the woodland. It was indeed a strategic spot. Like the others following behind, her gaze travelled to the high ridge of fresh earth in the distance; the back of the enormous dyke and ditch defense. Her eyes followed it north; in fact, Annan had told her that the earthwork ended only at the fens. The tiny figures of men, finishing work on Devil's Dyke for the day, were visible on the top of the fortification; their silhouettes outlined by the last rays of sun.

They rode into Exning to a crowd of excited villagers, who clustered around the gates, eager to catch a glimpse of the king and his party. Saewara felt inquisitive gazes upon her. Yet, they held none of the animosity she had felt in Rendlaesham. Life was different here, on the fringes of the kingdom. Politics did not play such a part in the lives of the folk of Exning—and for that, Saewara was enormously grateful.

Although it was considerably smaller than Rendlaesham, Exning had a prosperous, 'cared for' appearance. The houses, although small, were well maintained and tidy. In addition to the fields of produce outside, the folk also had small gardens inside the fence. Flowers bloomed, and the smell of baking bread and roasting rabbit wafted from open doorways.

Annan seemed to know exactly where he was going, and led the group of riders, with the laden carts bringing up the rear, to the far end of Exning. There, a handsome, timbered hall sat near where the palings of the perimeter fence stood highest. A collection of low buildings surrounded the hall; stables and lodgings for those who served the king but who would not reside inside the hall.

Saewara liked her new home on sight. It was much smaller than the 'Golden Hall' and far less intimidating. Life here would be simpler. The only shadow over it all was Hereswith and her sour-faced maid. Not for the first time, Saewara wished that Annan had left his brother behind at Rendlaesham. She watched Hereswith dismount, with her husband's assistance, and saw her face crease in displeasure as her gaze swept over the new hall.

"It's tiny," she hissed at Aethelhere, loud enough so that everyone – including Annan—heard. "This is no 'kingly hall'."

"No, Hereswith," Aethelhere replied, not bothering to hide the irritation in his voice, "but it will be our home till the autumn at least. You must get used to it."

Saewara stepped inside the hall and let a smile creep across her face.

It was simple, beautifully so, with just one enormous fire pit in the center of a rush-matting floor, and walls covered with rabbit pelt screens. Two long tables stretched from one end of the hall to the other, either side of the fire pit. At one, three local women were kneading the last of the griddle bread. A huge cauldron of venison stew bubbled over the hearth, its scent permeating the whole hall.

Warriors carried in the supplies, while Saewara made her way up the narrow wooden stairs of the low dais at the far end of the hall. At the back of the platform, screened from view by a heavy fur hanging, she found her lodgings. It was the only private space in the hall. All the other residents would sleep on furs in the main area; the highest ranking nearest the fire, and the slaves near the doors. Even Hereswith and Aethelhere would have to sleep in the common space, shielded only by a makeshift stretched leather screen from the others.

Saewara heard Hereswith complaining loudly as she stepped into her bower and let the hanging fall closed behind her. The hanging muted the sound beyond but, upon hearing Aethelhere tell his wife to stop carping, Saewara's smile widened. Perhaps Aethelhere's irritation was a sign of things to come – and she dared to hope that things would be different here at Exning. Maybe she would no longer be an imposter in her own home.

Night had fallen and it was getting late by the time everyone took their places at the two long tables either side of the fire pit. Saewara felt at her most relaxed since leaving Tamworth. She took a seat next to her husband, who was deep in a conversation about ditches with Saba, and favored Hilda with a wide smile as the girl filled up her wooden bowl with thick venison stew.

Saba broke off his conversation with the king a moment, to look up at Hilda as she bent over him with the tureen and ladle. He murmured something to her and Hilda's eyes shone, her cheeks growing delightfully pink, before she nodded.

Saewara watched them with an ache in her breast; the same she had felt when she had seen them on the banks of the stream outside Rendlaesham. It was heart-warming to see a couple so obviously smitten, gradually drawing closer with each passing day in a slow and timeless dance.

She had never known what that felt like.

Watching Saba and Hilda, she felt a stab of jealousy. It was unbidden and she denied it the moment the emotion surfaced. Yet, as Hilda moved on, to serve the warrior next to Saba, the joy on her friend's face made Saewara feel hollow and sad.

I will never have a man look at me like that.

After a long day of travel, and the flurry of unpacking that had followed, the king and his warriors did not stay up late. Once her meal had started to digest, Saewara left Annan chatting with his brother and Saba by the fire, and gratefully went to bed.

Her new bower reminded Saewara of a giant nest. The feel of soft fur under her bare feet made her sigh with pleasure as she quickly undressed and put on a light shift for bed. Clay cressets that burned oil, lined one wall of the bower, casting a soft glow over the space. As always, Saewara removed some of the furs from the huge bed in the corner and made up a bed for Annan a short distance away from hers. It had become an evening ritual for her now, and she thought nothing of it.

Saewara's muscles ached from two days in the saddle and she snuggled into the furs with another sigh of pleasure. She was still awake, staring up at the rafters and reflecting over the day's events, when Annan made an appearance.

As was her habit, Saewara turned from him while he undressed, smothered the guttering flames in the cressets and climbed into bed. She could hear him tossing and turning for a bit, trying to get comfortable, before he eventually spoke.

"Does your new hall please you, Saewara?"

His question, and the fact that he had actually spoken to her, momentarily stunned Saewara into silence. Conversation was not part of their nightly routine. They usually shared a bower as two strangers.

"Very much," she replied when she had recovered. "It suits me well."

"I prefer it to my hall in Rendlaesham," Annan said after a few moments. "I know it is not 'kingly' but I feel more myself here. It reminds me of my father's hall in Snape, where I grew up."

"I know what you mean—the 'Golden Hall' and the Great Tower of Tamworth are both impressive but not a 'home' in the way a hall like this is."

"We won't be able to stay here forever," Annan replied, regret lacing his voice, "as I will need to return to Rendlaesham at some point, but I would like to spend summers here in the future. What do you think?"

Warmth seeped through Saewara at Annan's words. He was speaking of the future, and he was including her in it. She would never have thought such an act could bring her such pleasure.

"I think that's an excellent idea," she answered him gently. "I would be happy to spend summers here."

Silence fell between them once more, although Saewara sensed that Annan had more to say. He was in a strange mood this evening; for the first time losing that aloof mask he had worn ever since their handfasting.

"Thank you for your support earlier today," he said, his voice faltering with sudden embarrassment. "I did not expect you to be in favor of my decision to no longer do Penda's bidding. I thought you would be angered by it. I felt that I had said too much."

Saewara gave a soft laugh at that. "I have no love for my brother," she admitted. "He treats his family much like he treats his enemies—with contempt. I was of no interest to him until he could use me to further his ambitions. He would have had me beheaded at the town gates if it had suited his purpose. For that reason, although I know the danger, your decision pleases me."

Annan fell silent at that and Saewara wondered if, this time, it was her who had said too much. His sudden warmth had encouraged her to be frank with him. She knew that some men disliked her straightforward manner. They wanted a woman who simpered and flattered—a woman like Hereswith. Egfrid had hated it when she addressed him as her equal.

However, it appeared that Annan had not been put off by her frankness.

"Whatever happens," he told her, in a tone that made Saewara believe every word, "I promise you that neither of us will be under Penda's thumb. Ever again."

Chapter Eighteen

The Gathering Storm

ALDFRID OF TAMWORTH was in a foul mood.

His ill-humor had begun two days earlier, and increased with every league east. Now, as the sun rode high in a windy sky, he was seething inside. He kicked his shaggy mare into a gallop, causing the beast to wheeze with the strain. He had pushed his horse hard since leaving Rendlaesham and cared not if the animal collapsed at the end of his journey. All that mattered to him was reaching Exning. He was the hand of the Mercian king – and he would demand answers.

Even now, the shock of arriving at Rendlaesham to discover that Annan had left nearly a moon's cycle earlier for Exning, left a bitter taste in his mouth.

What was the King of the East Angles doing on his south-western border?

Aldfrid, a shrewd, calculating man, had his suspicions, and those suspicions enraged him.

His horse was stumbling with exhaustion by the time Aldfrid spied the high paling fence that surrounded Exning in the distance. He rode across wide, flat grassland, and as he neared the sprawling hamlet, his gaze swiveled to the line of earth to the south; a massive earthwork that stretched right and left for as far as the eye could see. Even from this distance, the Mercian ealdorman saw that the earthwork was enormous; as high as five men standing on each other's shoulders. Of course, he had known that the East Angles had a ditch and dyke defense on their south-western border—but like many he believed it had fallen into ruin.

However, this was plainly not the case.

Aldfrid tore his gaze from the fortifications and urged his tired horse toward the gates of Exning.

Annan was standing outside his hall, examining a horse's swollen fetlock, when he heard the tattoo of hoof-beats approaching. He straightened up and shielded his eyes against the noon sun. A heavy-set, middle-aged man with a thick grey-streaked beard and hair thundered toward him on a lathered bay horse that looked fit to collapse. Annan continued to watch the rider as he drew nearer. His body tensed when he recognized the man's face.

Aldfrid of Tamworth. So Penda has sent his minion to make sure I have been beaten.

Annan had been waiting for this moment; ever since he had made his decision to finish Devil's Dyke it had shadowed him. In truth, he was relieved that this meeting had finally come. Watching Penda's emissary approach, he remembered his father's advice, spoken many years earlier when Annan had just reached manhood.

Whatever may come my boy, remember this—it's better to die a free man, on your feet with a sword in your hand, than live on your knees.

Annan had often forgotten Eni's words, especially of late when he preferred not to think about what his father would have to say about recent events. Yet upon seeing Aldfrid's enraged face, he was suddenly glad of his father's advice. He stepped forward, aware that behind him his men had stopped work and were gathering in a protective semi-circle around their king. Saba stepped in front of Annan, carrying a heavy axe. He barred Aldfrid's way as the heavy-set warrior swung down from his horse and strode toward the king.

"Halt," Saba growled, flexing his fingers on the axe's ash shaft, "or for the love of Woden, I'll swing."

Aldfrid grudgingly stopped, his iron-grey gaze fastening on Annan.

"Wes hāl!" Annan greeted the ealdorman, pretending not to notice the rancor on Aldfrid's face. "To what do I owe this unexpected visit?"

"You knew that Penda wishes to be kept updated," Aldfrid growled. "You should have sent word before leaving Rendlaesham."

"I am not a prisoner," Annan replied, keeping his voice amiable. "I am at liberty to move within my kingdom without informing Penda. Next he'll be wanting to know when I visit the privy."

This drew laughter from Annan's men. Aldfrid's face flushed purple before he responded. Annan could see it was taking all the warrior's self-control not to lose his temper completely.

"Travelling to your border—the border you share with Mercia—and fortifying a massive defense along it, is a blatant act of rebellion," he ground out.

"Rebellion?" Annan raised an eyebrow. "I think you're exaggerating. I am ruler of this land, and as such entitled to protect my border."

"You are bound to the King of Mercia." Aldfrid's voice was hoarse from the effort he was making not to shout. "He did not give you permission to build that wall."

Annan did not reply. Letting the ealdorman's last comment hang in the air between them, he looked steadily at Aldfrid, waiting.

"Where's Saewara?" Aldfrid's hard gaze swept the area. "What have you done with her? I demand to see her, now!"

"You will demand nothing here," Annan replied, coldness seeping into his voice. "However, if you *wish* to see my wife, you may."

With that, Annan glanced over his shoulder and instructed one of his men to fetch Saewara.

She arrived presently, wiping flour off her hands. Her face hardened when she saw Aldfrid.

"Come, my love," Annan said with a smile. "Your father's hand wishes to make sure you are alive and well. He was worried I might have done away with you."

Saewara gave Annan a hesitant smile and stopped at his side. Annan put a protective arm about her shoulders and drew her against him; relieved that she relaxed in response.

"Why would you think that, Aldfrid?" she asked in that low, musical voice of hers. A voice that made others take notice whenever she spoke. "Surely, you don't think my brother gave me to a man who would do me harm?"

Aldfrid glowered at her in response.

"Enough, woman," he growled. "Penda told me to make sure you were alive and well; I am merely carrying out his orders. I did not come here to exchange pleasantries with an East Angle's whore. Why don't you shut your mouth!"

"And why don't you keep a leash on your own tongue!" Annan cut in. He was trying to keep his temper under control, but Aldfrid of Tamworth was making it nearly impossible. "You will not speak to my wife so. Apologize now, or you will not be returning to Tamworth to report back to your master."

Aldfrid's eyes bulged, as he struggled to contain his rage. Yet, he remained stubbornly silent.

"Don't think I won't let Saba part your neck from your shoulders with that axe of his," Annan replied easily. "Be grateful that it's not me holding the axe – for I would do it without hesitation."

The silence stretched between them, and eventually Annan raised his arm to give Saba the order.

Realizing he had better speak now, or lose his head, Aldfrid spat out two words.

"I apologize."

"It's not me you need to address," Annan replied coldly. "Look at my wife and tell her you are sorry for insulting her."

Aldfrid's stocky body quivered with outrage but his gaze shifted to Saewara and stayed there.

"I am sorry, Milady, for insulting you."

Saewara stared back at him, not responding to the words that so obviously meant nothing. Glancing at her face, Annan realized that she had indeed spoken true when she had told him that life in her brother's hall had been difficult and cruel. Seeing the look on Aldfrid's face, Annan understood that she was nothing to them. They had forced Saewara into a marriage she did not want and then had the gall to insult her for it.

Annan almost wished that Saba would sink his axe blade into Aldfrid's bull neck all the same. He had not lied to Aldfrid; if he had been the one holding the axe, the temptation would have been too great.

"You have seen that Saewara is alive and well." Annan was the first to break the weighty silence. "You have seen that I am living here at Exning for the summer. What else would you know?"

"This fortification—what is your reason for it?"

"It defends my south-western border," Annan replied without hesitation. "Roman roads intersect here; many traders use this route to travel between kingdoms. After all that has happened over the last few decades, I would know who is coming and going – as any king would."

"You break the pledge you made to Penda," Aldfrid shouted, losing the battle to control his temper. "This will bring his wrath down upon you all!"

"So be it," Annan replied calmly. "If a king can't defend his own border then let Penda's wrath come."

"Are you a fool?" Aldfrid snarled. "He will destroy you. He will pummel you into the ground. He will make you crawl before he kills you."

Annan shrugged, concealing the anger that was twisting his gut. "I repeat. A king has the right to defend his borders. Penda should have made his terms clearer."

Pushed beyond endurance by Annan's calm refusal to be baited, or to make an outright admission of defiance, Aldfrid turned on his heel and strode back to his horse.

"You will regret this day," he told the king, swinging up into the saddle. "When Penda hears of this he will bring the might of his army down upon you."

"Thank you for the warning," Annan replied, "although I'd go easy on that horse on the way home, if I were you. The poor beast looks fit to collapse."

Aldfrid bared his teeth at Annan in response and spat on the ground. Then, without another word, he turned his horse around and kicked it into a sluggish canter. Geese scattered, hissing in rage, as Penda's emissary rode away.

Annan watched him go, keeping his arm loosely around Saewara's shoulders all the while. They remained there, even after Aldfrid disappeared from view and the sound of his horse's hooves faded.

Saewara spoke finally, glancing up at Annan's face. "That went well."

Annan laughed. It felt good; a release of tension after the confrontation with Aldfrid.

"It certainly did." Annan removed his arm from around Saewara's shoulders and stepped back from her, holding her gaze. His face grew serious. "I knew the moment would arrive sooner or later. I'm sorry though, that you had to be involved."

Saewara shook her head. She smiled then, although her eyes were sad. It was an expression he had often witnessed since her arrival in his kingdom. She was strong, his Mercian wife, and proud. Yet, she was unhappy. Annan felt a stab of self-reproach as he realized that he had only added to her melancholy.

"Aldfrid's words did not bother me," she replied, holding his gaze for a moment longer. "Truly, I've heard worse. What alarms me, is what will happen now." Her gaze flicked to where Aldfrid had disappeared. "It will take him a while to reach Tamworth, especially since you have blocked this border. He will have to tackle the marshes to the north or ride for days south to skirt the woods. It will give you time, but once he reaches Tamworth, Penda's reaction will be swift."

"We should have killed the bastard," Saba spoke up. The warrior's face was hard as he stared after Aldfrid. "That would have stopped him from running back to his master."

Annan shook his head. "It would have only delayed the inevitable. Penda will find out soon enough. I will send out riders today. I need to start gathering my *fyrd* to me."

"I will organize it," Saba replied, his eyes gleaming. He had been waiting for this moment.

Annan's gaze travelled around the faces of his men who stood nearby. He realized then, that they had all been waiting for this day. The day he defied the Mercians. Live or die, Penda was not their master, and never would be.

Chapter Nineteen

Lovers and Longing

SABERT AND HILDA were handfasted on a hot, mid-summer's day. The ceremony took place outdoors, under a wide blue sky, on the grassy meadows outside Exning.

The couple stood before an arch that had been festooned with wildflowers. Hilda was dressed in a creamy white tunic made of fine wool that accentuated her slender frame. She had daisies threaded through her long brown hair and her face was radiant. Saba stood before her, beaming down at his bride. He was dressed in a black tunic and leather breaches. Numerous gold arm rings decorated his muscular arms and he had tied his dark hair back at the nape with a leather thong.

Watching Saba and Hilda's faces, Saewara felt her eyes sting with tears. She discreetly brushed at her eyes, not bothered if anyone saw them. After all, many people cried at weddings. Besides, she was not weeping for herself, but for joy that Hilda was finally free and about to start a new life with the man she loved.

The king stood before the couple. Saba had asked Annan to act as celebrant, and although he had been a bit hesitant initially, Annan appeared at ease in this unfamiliar role. Saewara watched him wrap the ribbon about the lovers' hands, before he stepped back and let them pledge their vows to each other.

A huge crowd had gathered around Saba and Hilda. It was nearly ten days since Aldfrid's visit, and since then the fyrd—a king's army of hundreds of spears and axe-men, had been amassing on the grasslands outside Exning. More would come, Saba had promised. He had sent out riders, far and wide over the kingdom to call men to arms – and the men came, quicker than even Annan had expected.

The East Angles readied themselves for war.

Before the kingdom's defeat to the Mercians just over a year earlier, the East Angles had grown complacent. The Wuffinga kings had kept them safe; it had seemed unthinkable that another king would take their land for his own. Now their complacency was gone, they feared the Mercians and knew that they could no longer pretend the threat was not real. This fear galvanized them, and spurred them to Exning. The huge increase in man-power also meant that Devil's Dyke was nearing completion months ahead of schedule. Exning was no longer a sleepy village on the fringe of the kingdom but a bustling hive of industry. Forges burned night and day as smiths fashioned a mountain of spear-heads, arrow-heads, axe-heads and swords. Annan spent his evenings in discussion with Saba, Aethelhere, and his most trusted warriors, discussing battle tactics and the best method of defense against the Mercians.

Despite the shadow of approaching war, there was still time for a handfasting. In fact, such an event was celebrated with even more joy than usual. Marriage, like birth, was a life-affirming act. It reminded all present what they were fighting for, and what they stood to lose.

The ceremony concluded with Saba pulling the blushing Hilda into his arms for a passionate kiss. The crowd roared its approval and a thunderous applause followed. Saewara clapped enthusiastically along with the others, but could not help but note that Hereswith and Eldwyn, her constant companion, stood with pinched faces, nearby.

Since their arrival here in Exning, Saewara had rarely seen Hereswith smile. Relations between the Northumbrian beauty and Aethelhere had also deteriorated. They often argued, and days would pass in frosty silence. Aethelhere had stopped looking at his bride in adoration, and she ignored him. All had noticed the change in them both—and Saewara wondered what Annan thought of it. He too, had changed since arriving in Exning. His manner toward Saewara had thawed considerably. They would often chat companionably before bed in the evenings and, although they still slept separately, Saewara found herself looking forward to her nightly conversations with Annan. Unlike in Rendlaesham, where it was obvious that Hereswith's presence had disturbed him, he seemed not to notice her here—either that or he made a convincing show of ignoring her.

Despite that her marriage had never been consummated, Annan's apparent disinterest in the woman who he had once pined for, gave Saewara a ridiculous amount of pleasure. True, Hereswith's mood had become even nastier of late – her barbs even more cutting—but it was worth it to see that Annan had decided to move forward with his life.

Warriors carried out long tables into the meadow for the handfast feasting. It was a rare, and pleasant occasion to sit out for a feast under the warm sun. The chirp of crickets chorused with the rumble of conversation and bursts of laughter.

Saewara helped herself to a plate of strawberries drizzled with honey and cream, and enjoyed the feeling of the sun on her shoulders. She watched Saba feed Hilda a strawberry and smiled. It was wonderful to see Hilda so happy; she looked a different woman in her beautiful gown and without the iron slave-collar about her neck. She sat straighter; her eyes bright, and her cheeks flushed.

The love of a good man—and freedom—had made Hilda radiant.

The mead flowed and the platters of roast meat and vegetables slowly emptied. A musician started playing a jaunty tune on his bone whistle and couples began to rise from the table to dance. Saba, unsteady on his feet after copious amounts of mead, escorted his new bride into the middle of the swirling dancers.

Saewara watched them with wistful longing. It was the same dance she and Annan had been forced to participate in at Tamworth; only this one had a completely different feel. There were no hostile glares, unless you counted Hereswith and her maid, and everyone was in the mood to celebrate. It did not matter that war approached, for at least they were free. Watching them, Saewara decided that she liked the East Angles very much; and felt a far greater kinship to these people than she had ever felt to her own.

The dancing had been going on a short while when Hereswith rose from her seat and made her way around the table to where Annan sat lingering over a cup of mead.

"Milord," she greeted him, boldly meeting his gaze. "Will you dance with me?"

Annan stared back at her, surprised. Aethelhere was sitting at the other end of the table, deep in conversation and had not noticed that his wife had approached the king.

"I'm not much of a dancer," Annan protested half-heartedly. "Are you sure you want your feet trodden on?"

"I will take my chances, Milord," Hereswith replied with a demure smile before she held out a hand to him. "Shall we?"

Saewara watched as Annan got to his feet and took Hereswith's elbow, leading her into the dance.

She knew she had no right to feel jealous – but the sight of them, golden haired and fair, dancing together, was like a punch to the stomach.

No wonder he wanted her, Saewara thought bitterly. *They make a beautiful couple.*

The joy of the day suddenly disappeared.

How was it possible to go from contentment to desolation in just a few moments?

Why do I care so much?

A lyrist joined the whistle player and the music stepped up a pace. Annan was, in fact, a good dancer. He moved with grace and ease. Saewara's gaze tracked him and jealousy twisted her stomach. If she could, she would have clawed Hereswith's eyes out.

The blonde stared into Annan's eyes as they danced; her gaze not leaving his for a moment. It was a challenging gaze, a hungry gaze. The look of a desperate woman who knew the effect she had on men.

Disgusted, Saewara looked away. She could not bear to see them together.

Annan's head spun slightly as he whirled Hereswith around once more. He had eaten and drunk too much; and the dancing was starting to make him feel queasy. It did not help that Hereswith had fastened onto him like lichen – and seemed to have no intention of letting go.

She was still as beautiful as ever. Up close her skin was perfect, and her eyes a luminous blue. Yet, these days he was able to admit this to himself without feeling an aching sense of longing for a woman he could never have. Instead, he had observed Hereswith interact with his brother, and had found himself feeling relieved that he was not married to a woman who seemed constantly displeased with everything and everyone.

"Milord," Hereswith gasped, pressing close to him, her gaze fusing with his. "I am miserable."

"You are?" Annan replied, feigning ignorance. "I am sorry to hear that."

"Your brother is not half the man you are," she continued. "I wish I had never agreed to marry him."

Annan's body stiffened at that and his gaze narrowed. "Aethelhere is a good man; you could do far worse."

"I know," Hereswith's gaze dipped submissively before returning with an intensity that made Annan draw back slightly. "But he is not you. He will never be you. It is you I want."

"Hereswith," Annan replied gently. "I too wished for events to unfold differently than they have—but fate had another will. We are both married to others. I have made peace with my new life, maybe you should too. You would be happier."

"I don't wish to make peace with it!" Hereswith snapped, the demure façade evaporating as her anger surfaced. "I don't want to remain married to that oaf! You are the king, you can annul both our marriages and take me for your own. You have decided to defy Penda anyway. There's no need to remain married to that Mercian drab!"

"Enough!" Annan stopped dancing, nearly causing them to collide with another couple. "You will not speak of Saewara, or my brother, so." He wrenched himself out of her grip and took a step back, glaring at her. "One is my wife, the other my kin—you would do well to remember that."

Hereswith's blue eyes filled with tears—but it was too late. He had heard enough to know that his brother had been saddled with a shrew.

For the first time, it dawned upon Annan that he'd had a very narrow escape. The realization was akin to a bright dawn shedding light over a bleak landscape. He now pitied, rather than envied, his brother.

He could see Aethelhere now, elbowing his way through the dancers toward him with a face like thunder. Taking hold of Hereswith's elbow, Annan gently pushed her toward her husband.

"Your wife complains of my two left feet," he said affably when Aethelhere reached them. "She tells me I dance like a troll compared to you."

"Really?" Confusion warred with jealousy on Aethelhere's face. He was drunk and spoiling for a fight. Annan had no intention of giving him one. Whatever it took, Aethelhere needed to know that Annan no longer coveted his wife.

"I'm afraid so—just take a look at her face. It seems I've put her in ill-humor."

Aethelhere glanced at Hereswith's face and frowned. "Are you well?"

Hereswith nodded before favoring her husband with a brittle smile. "I am now that you've rescued me from this oaf."

A wary smile spread over Aethelhere's face. "An oaf, eh? You really know how to charm women, Annan."

"My apologies." Annan backed away with a shrug. "Now, if you'll excuse me, I really should get back to my wife. Saewara will be feeling neglected."

Aethelhere, satisfied that Annan had not been trying to seduce Hereswith, pulled his wife into the mêlée of dancers, while the king turned to return to his table. He had not lied about being keen to return to Saewara's side. After his encounter with Hereswith, it was if a fog had lifted.

Saba had been right—he had been a blind, stubborn fool. Despite that he had fought his attraction to her from the beginning, it had taken him a while to recognize Saewara's worth.

Too long.

However, upon emerging from the dancing, Annan stopped abruptly in his tracks. His gaze rested on the spot where he had left Saewara a short while earlier.

His wife's seat was empty.

Annan's gaze swept over the surrounding crowd, searching for the sensual features of his dark-haired wife. She had worn a becoming forest-green shift today, and was looking even lovelier than usual. He had wanted to tell her so.

Yet there was no sign of his wife among the revelers. Saewara had disappeared.

Chapter Twenty

A Meeting in the Woods

EXNING WOODS WERE dark and unwelcoming. Unlike the meadows beyond, where the sun warmed the earth and a soft breeze ruffled the grass, the air here was damp and cool. Saewara shivered as she stepped over a moss-covered, rotting log and rubbed her bare arms. It was like stepping from one world to another. She did not like these woods, for they were melancholy and sunless, but she sought refuge here all the same.

After watching Annan dance with Hereswith, all the joy of the day had seeped from Saewara, making her feel lost and very alone. The folk of Exning had continued their revelry but, whereas she had found it entertaining earlier, it merely grated upon her now.

Annan and Hereswith had looked so perfect together that it had made her feel ill to look upon them.

She needed to breathe. She needed peace and quiet—and the woods gave her the solitude she craved.

She did not venture far inside the woods, for she was afraid of getting lost; walking just far enough inside so that she could no longer hear the music and ringing voices. When only the chime of bird song and the rustle of forest creatures in the undergrowth surrounded her, Saewara sat down on a tree stump.

She felt so conflicted; a sickening jealousy that she did not understand, an ache of longing that she did not want to accept. She was also consumed by a bitter disappointment at how *wyrd* had treated her—and an anger that she cared at all.

This was a political alliance, she told herself as she brushed at the tears that blurred her vision. *I should not care.*

But she did.

She had been ready to give up on men; eager to embrace a nun's life at Bonehill without regrets. Even after her marriage to Annan, she had managed to keep the wall up for a time. Yet little by little, her defenses had come down. She had found that she enjoyed being Annan's wife; that although they kept their distance physically, he was a good, kind man who made her feel safe and protected.

Yet, seeing him with Hereswith had brought her fragile happiness crashing down.

The tears flowed faster now, and eventually Saewara gave up trying to stem them. She sat there, with her head in her hands and let herself cry—for what had been, what was, and what, she was sure, would be.

"I saw the queen, M'lord," a boy who was playing with a group of children on the outskirts of the revelers, answered the king's question. "A short while ago. She walked into the woods."

Annan smiled at the lad, and ruffled his hair in thanks, before leaving the boy to return to his friends. The king then crossed the wide stretch of grass and stepped under the dark eaves of Exning Woods.

He knew why Saewara had sought refuge here, and he did not blame her. Most likely, he sickened her. Saewara deserved so much better than the treatment she had received. It was bad enough that her own kin had treated her cruelly, but she had fared little better under his roof. It seemed that no one cared for her feelings; and he was no better than the rest.

He found her easily, for she had not ventured far from the forest edge. She sat with her head in her hands, gently sobbing.

Annan stopped in his tracks. He knew that he was intruding, and was not welcome. She had come here to be alone.

Shame washed over him.

I should not have followed her.

Annan stood there for a moment, before deciding to quietly retrace his steps. However, he had only taken one step back when Saewara realized that someone was watching her.

She bolted upright, dashing away the tears with the back of hands, her gaze fastening upon him.

"What are you doing here?" The first words out of her mouth were not welcoming. Annan inwardly cursed himself for following. Yet it was too late to slip away—and as such, he decided to be honest.

"Looking for you," he replied.

"Well, now you've found me."

"Yes, I have."

They stared at each other. Annan stared into her anger-filled eyes; the color of a stormy sky. Annan knew he should leave, but instead he stayed.

"Why are you angry?" he asked.

She looked away, staring down at her hands. "I am not."

"You are."

"Why don't you leave me be?" she shot back, refusing to meet his gaze once more. "What does it matter to you how I feel?"

"I'm sorry I danced with Hereswith," Annan said the words that had been rising within him, ever since he had noticed her absence from the feasting table. "But you need not worry. There was nothing it in. I care not for her."

Saewara looked at him then; her eyes flat with rage.

"Why are you telling me this?" she bit off every word. "What does it matter to me if you wish to bed half the village?"

"But I don't."

"I care not!" Saewara jumped to her feet and faced him.

They still stood at least ten feet apart but he could feel the anger emanating off her in waves. "You made it clear from the beginning how things were between us—and I accepted it. If you want to dance with Hereswith, that's your business."

"I don't want her, Saewara," Annan replied, taking a few steps forward to close the gap between them, "and I pity my brother."

"You pity him?" Saewara's eyebrows arched. "You've changed your tune."

"Men can be fools," Annan held her gaze steadily. "I am the first to admit it—in fact, I'm the biggest fool of the lot. When Penda ordered me to marry you, Hereswith signified the life I was giving up. I didn't know her then. I didn't know you either. She represented freedom, whereas you represented slavery."

Saewara did not respond. She continued to look at him in that direct, honest manner of hers. That look that had always disarmed him.

"I wanted you from the first moment I saw you," Annan blurted out the words before nearly choking on them.

Where did that come from?

Her eyes widened.

"What?"

"I know you will find that hard to believe," Annan replied, recovering from the admission that had cut him open and made him far more vulnerable than he ever wanted to be. "Even under Penda's stare, with the folk of Tamworth jeering in my face, you enchanted me—and I hated you even more for that."

"Annan," Saewara's voice had dropped to a whisper. "You don't have to say this."

"I do." Annan took another two steps forward, bridging the gap between them even further. "You think I am repulsed by you; I can see it in your eyes. Nothing could be further from the truth. I have kept my distance from you because I knew that once I bedded you I would be lost."

They continued to stare at each other. Annan saw the blush creep up Saewara's neck, and knew his words had touched her.

"And my brother would have won," she finished Annan's sentence for him.

Annan nodded. His heart started to hammer against his ribs and he felt as he had that day on the river bank. He was losing control, and was powerless to stop it.

"You are lovely." He stepped close to her—so close they were almost touching—and gazed down into her tear-filled eyes. "So lovely that sometimes it hurts me to look at you."

Saewara opened her mouth to reply but Annan smothered her words with his lips. One moment they were standing close, staring at each other. The next, he had pulled her hard against him, and his mouth covered hers.

Like that day on the riverbank, with the flooded river raging beside them, the kiss was not gentle. It was hungry and desperate; filled with much that was still unsaid. Saewara clung to him as if her life depended on it; her tongue warring with his, her sharp fingernails clawing into his back. The taste and feel of her unleashed something within Annan that no woman ever had; blotting out all thought, all reason. At that moment, he would have given all for the woman in his arms. The world could burn and he would not care—just as long as he had her.

They broke apart, breathless. Annan gazed into her eyes, and saw that they were glazed with lust. She stared at him, her lips swollen from the violence of his kisses. He had never wanted anything more in his life than to take her.

Yet once he did, he knew there would be no turning back.

"Come." He took hold of her hand and led her back toward the edge of the woods. The hall would be empty as the feasters continued to celebrate the handfasting. There would be no one to interrupt them. "Our bower awaits. From now on, we will be sharing the same bed. In fact, I'm never going to let you leave it."

Chapter Twenty-One

The Undoing

THE MOMENT THEY were hidden behind the fur hanging, that shielded their bower from the rest of the hall, Annan and Saewara lunged at each other.

Saewara groaned as she felt the hardness of his arousal pressed against her. Boldly, she reached down and stroked the length of it through his breeches. Annan gasped, growling low in his throat. Then, he gently took hold of her wrists and pulled her hands away from his body. His mouth came down over hers, and Saewara felt the world spin. He kissed her deeply, thoroughly—their fused mouths were the only parts of their bodies touching. Saewara kissed him back with abandon, struggling to free her wrists so that she could caress him again.

The same sensation that had carried her away on the riverbank entangled itself around her once more. She lost any sense of inhibition. A hunger raged within her; desperate to be fed.

Enjoying her frustration, Annan gave a low laugh and pushed her backwards toward the furs, before throwing her down on them. Saewara sat on the bed, gasping to catch her breath; her gaze never leaving his.

As she watched, he stepped back and began to undo his breeches. Seeing the direction of her gaze, his mouth curved into a wicked smile. Her heart began to hammer against her ribs and her mouth went dry. If he stood there staring at her like that for much longer she would not be responsible for her actions.

"Take your clothes off, Saewara."

It was not a request, but an order.

Saewara's hands trembled when she unbuckled the belt around her waist. Then, in one movement, she pulled the woolen dress and under-tunic over her head. Naked, she sat on top of the furs watching him strip his clothes off. His eyes never left her all the while; his hot gaze raking her body from head to toe.

She did the same, her gaze hungrily taking in every inch of him. Tall, strong and masculine; his arousal was magnificent. Her fingers ached to touch him.

"Please." She stretched out her arms to him. "Come here, Annan."

She did not need to ask twice.

Suddenly, he was on top of her, and kissing her as if he would never have another chance to do so. Once again, their passion was not gentle, not at all. Saewara twisted under Annan, arching her body against his, her nails raking at his back. They kissed, licked and bit at each other in a frenzy.

Annan's hands tangled in Saewara's hair, and he pulled her neck back so that he could bite her neck. Forcing her head back further, so that her body arched like a bow toward him, Annan bent over her breasts. When his hot mouth began to suckle her left breast, Saewara cried out, pressing against him as he drew the nipple deep into his mouth; and when he slid a hand between her thighs and stroked her gently there, she shuddered and groaned.

Eventually, Annan let go of Saewara and lay down on the furs, on his back. He then pulled her astride him. Surprised, for she had never made love to a man in this position, Saewara stared down at her husband's face—at his eyes that had turned a midnight blue. She ran her hands over the mature lines of his chest, over the ridges of old scars that had turned silver with time.

"Saewara," Annan whispered hoarsely, as her hands stroked over his belly to his hard shaft. "I swear you will be my undoing."

Saewara chuckled at that, enjoying the power she had over him. "I hope to be far more than that, Milord."

Gently now, he lifted her over him. His gaze fused with hers as she lowered herself onto him. The sensation of Annan inside her, filling her, made Saewara arch her back and groan.

It had never felt like this with Egfrid—never.

They began to move, in a timeless rhythm that had them both gasping within moments. Annan's hands gripped her hips and he pulled her down against him, harder and harder with each thrust of his hips. Then, he cupped her breasts, stroking them and gazing at them as she continued to ride him.

Eventually, not able to contain himself any longer, Annan took hold of her buttocks and arched toward her. He called her name, his body shaking.

Saewara's body hummed like a lyre played by a master musician. Pleasure crested in a hot wave through her body, and a moment later, she felt Annan explode within her.

They collapsed together on the furs; sweat-slicked and trembling, their limbs tangled. Saewara lay against Annan's chest, listening to his heart thundering. The bower spun around them and she suddenly realized why her sister by marriage held such power over her brother. For years, the bond between Penda and Cyneswide had mystified Saewara—but no more. Passion this powerful altered your mind; sapped your will. No wonder Annan had been wary of giving in to it.

Saewara knew that she would never see the world in the same way again.

They spent the rest of the day hidden away together in the privacy of their bower.

Annan and Saewara spoke little, dozing in-between explosive lovemaking that left them both unable to move—let alone speak—in the aftermath. Saewara found her hunger for her husband increased with each time he took her. Annan had ignited a bonfire within her that his kisses and touch just made burn all the brighter.

As the light faded outside, and the revelers returned from the meadows outside Exning, the lovers heard voices inside the hall. Fortunately, no one interrupted them, and they lay, cocooned together in the furs, enjoying the feel of skin against skin.

Eventually, hunger of a different kind drove Annan from their bed. Leaving Saewara waiting for him, naked, wrapped in the furs, he dressed silently and slipped out into the hall. A short while later, he returned with a platter of cold meat, cheese, griddle bread, slices of moist honey-seed cake and two large cups of ale.

They fell on the meal as if neither of them had eaten for days, before feeding each other pieces of cake at the end. The eating then turned to kissing, and the remains of their meal were pushed aside. The food was forgotten, as the hunger for each other's bodies returned.

Annan awoke in the depths of the night and stared up into the darkness.

Saewara was curled up next to him. The soft sound of her breathing was the only noise in the bower. It had been a life-changing day—one that he could hardly believe had occurred.

Annan lay there for a while, his thoughts wheeling, before he slid out of bed and quietly dressed. The intensity of what he felt for Saewara had turned his world upside down. He had not been ready for it, and indeed had not even realized the depths of his feelings until he followed her into the woods. He needed some time on his own to sort his thoughts out.

A night stroll was in order.

Throwing a cloak over his shoulders to ward off the cool night air, Annan picked his way over the sleeping figures in his hall and made his way across to the doors. Outside, the air was silky with only a slight crispness to it. The night was clear and a full moon lit his way as he walked through the deserted streets of Exning to the village gates. The sleepy guards opened the gates so that their king could make his way to Devil's Dyke.

Torches lit the length of the fortification, outlining its tall shadow against the night. Annan climbed a ladder up to the top, and greeted one of his warriors who was taking his turn at the nightly watch.

"How goes it?"

"Quiet, Milord."

"Very good—let's enjoy the peace while it lasts."

Annan made his way along the earthwork, casting the odd glance down at where torches burned along the eastern side of the the fortification. Devil's Dyke has been a massive undertaking and Annan knew that Penda would not be foolish enough to pit his fyrd against it. No, he would try another way in.

That suited Annan, for another way in meant that the two armies would not meet shield-wall to shield-wall. Instead, it would be on the marshes to the north, or the woods to the south. Which Penda would choose was anyone's guess.

The clean air sharpened Annan's senses and he drew deep breaths of it. Tonight, his thoughts could not remain on Penda and the approaching conflict between them for long. Instead, it moved to the Mercian King's winsome sister.

Saewara.

She had ruined him for any other woman—that was for certain. Even now, his feelings for Hereswith seemed trivial in comparison. It was no wonder he had spent so many years unmarried, for before Saewara he had never seen women as companions. They were either to be bedded and forgotten about or longed for from afar. Saewara had taught him that a woman, the right woman, could transform his world. He had often made fun of Saba for the way his friend had pursued Hilda, with no thought to how others might judge him. The ealdorman cared not what others thought of his love for Hilda; he knew her worth and had made sure everyone else knew it too.

Saba made him feel shallow and arrogant by comparison.

Yet despite that he could not imagine life without Saewara at his side, there was something that worried Annan; a worry that needled him even when he tried to push it from his thoughts.

Although she had married him, Saewara was still Mercian. He knew that blood flowed thicker than water—and even if she had been treated cruelly by her own kin, Annan wondered where her loyalties ultimately lay.

You're sleeping with the enemy, a cruel voice whispered. *Who is to say she will not betray you. If her brother triumphs, who is to say she will remain at your side.*

Stop it. Annan shook his head, cursing the part of him that trusted no one; the part of him that ensured his survival in a world where only strong men lived past boyhood. He did not want to think about this now; not after the most miraculous day of his life.

Let me enjoy this, he told the voice, drawing his cloak tightly around him despite that it was not cold. *I have never before truly loved a woman—just let me have this one.*

So be it, the voice sneered back, *but you have been warned. Remember, she is Mercian. Her brother married you to her for a reason. She is his pawn—placed in the enemy camp deliberately. When the time comes, he will expect her to do his bidding.*

Chapter Twenty-Two

The Shadow Approaches

SAEWARA STIRRED FROM a deep sleep and rolled over onto her back, stretching her limbs like a cat. Now that she and Annan shared a bed, she slept more soundly than she ever had before.

Beyond the hanging, she could hear the sounds of industry, as the servants prepared the first meal of the day. The smell of baking bread made Saewara's stomach rumble and she sat up. She glanced to her right and felt a stab of disappointment when she saw that Annan had already risen.

These days Annan rarely stayed in bed after dawn.

The preparations for the arrival of the Mercian army were gaining momentum. A tense, watchful atmosphere had settled upon Exning. A huge fyrd now camped outside the walls; a sea of goat-hide tents that stretched away into the distance. Annan spent his days overseeing the fabrication of weaponry and the training of his warriors. Whenever, she saw him during daylight hours, Annan was distracted, and often distant. Saewara did not blame him—he had a lot on his mind, after-all. Still, his aloofness stung slightly. It was like dealing with a stranger; a world away from the man she thought she knew.

And yet when he joined her in their bower late, after spending the evening discussing battle tactics with his men, Annan was hers. He came to her with the same fiery passion and need that he had the first time. After making love, they lay entangled on the furs and talked at length.

They spoke of the future—of the things they would do and the plans they would make when this was all over. They spoke of their hopes and their dreams. Annan revealed that he had remained unmarried by choice, having never trusted women. Saewara revealed the grief she had felt when the healer at Tamworth pronounced her barren. Would Annan grow to resent her if she never provided him with an heir? He had shaken his head vehemently at that, assuring her that she was enough.

In daylight, it was the memory of those conversations that stopped Saewara from doubting Annan. In the hall, he kept his distance from her— and few who lived within the hall would have guessed that the king and queen now shared a bed.

Saewara dressed in a thick wealca, suitable for the day's work, as she would be helping the other village women string bows. Although longbows and arrows were not traditionally used during battle, Annan wanted his army fully prepared. This was not to be a battle like the others, he warned his warriors as they stood one afternoon over the dirt and wooden scale model of Exning and the surrounding landscape that they had constructed in the yard outside his hall.

"If we meet them in the woods, longbows and arrows will be our best allies."

Saewara agreed with Annan; her brother was a brilliant tactician. He would not try to take on Devil's Dyke. Although she would never have dared voice the desire, Saewara wished that one of the longbows she was helping to make would be hers – and that she would be able to wield it in battle. However, such wishes were dreams. Annan would never let her join his fyrd; it was unthinkable. Even so, Saewara bridled at the frustration of not being able to join the bowmen in battle; few men had her aim.

The king was nowhere in sight when Saewara emerged from the bower. That did not surprise her.

She took a slice of griddle bread and a cup of hot broth from Hilda, to break her fast. Although no longer a slave, Hilda had stayed on to cook in the king's hall for the moment. She and Saba hoped to build a hall of their own once the Mercian threat passed.

I hope it passes, Saewara thought. A chill seeped through her as she gave Hilda a brittle smile. The thought of Annan facing Penda in battle made her break out in a cold sweat. She knew that Annan was a formidable warrior; she had heard many a tale of his valor in battle. Yet her brother was not like other men. He fought like a wrathful god—and he had never been bested.

The hall was a hive of activity, although Hereswith and her maid were ensconced in one corner, embroidering dresses as if the shadow of approaching war mattered not. Saewara felt a stab of irritation when her gaze rested on Hereswith. Her sister-in-law had flatly refused to help the other women with their preparations.

Aethelhere should take a firmer hand with you, Saewara thought before brushing crumbs off her skirts and handing Hilda back her empty cup. *If the battle goes ill, you will not be so full of yourself.*

The women exchanged venomous glances as Saewara made her way toward the door, before Hereswith turned back to Eldwyn and whispered something. The women burst into laughter.

Saewara ignored them and stepped outside.

Exning's streets were thronged with men and horses. A cacophony of noise – the shouts of men and battle practice, and the clang and hiss of weaponry being forged – assaulted Saewara's ears. Her skin prickled at the sound of it; war was close, she could sense it.

Weaving her way through the busy streets, being careful not to step on the horse dung which littered the ground, Saewara made her way to the clearing where the village women were stringing bows and attaching heads to arrow-shafts. Small mountains of arrows, fashioned out of Yew, rose around the industrious women. Saewara greeted some of the women and they called back to her warmly. She reached the group stringing hemp bowstrings to robust ash longbows and took her place among them.

Saewara picked up one of the longbows and, once again, felt a pang of frustration that she could not be of more use.

I'm lethal with a longbow—they should let me fight.

They worked hard all day, only stopping for a brief meal at noon, before continuing their labor. As they strung the longbows, the women shared stories, and one or two told epics of love and loss that had some of the listeners in tears by the end. Saewara listened in silence, enjoying her companionship with the women. Having grown up among noblewomen, who would stab another woman in the back if it suited them, it was a pleasure to be among women who enjoyed each other's company.

As they worked, Saewara noticed that the weather was taking a turn for the worse. It had been a hot spell of weather. Yet over the last day, the air had changed. It was now humid, with that charged feel that warns of a coming thunderstorm. Mid-afternoon, the thunder-clouds rolled in, and by the time the women were packing up their supplies and carrying them to the armory, ready for use, the first spots of rain stained the dusty streets.

Saewara was walking back to the hall when the first rumble of thunder echoed in the distance. She had just entered the hall when it boomed overhead and the storm unleashed its fury. Soon the damp, smoky air inside the hall steamed as men hung up their wet cloaks to dry near the fire pit. The sound of their voices, as they discussed their work and the preparations for battle, almost drowned out the booming thunder.

Saewara had taken Hilda's side, helping her prepare a pottage for the evening meal, when Annan entered. He was drenched to the skin and wringing water out of his hair. It was the first time she had seen him all day. She could not help it; her gaze travelled over him, taking in the strong, muscular planes of his body, evidenced by his sodden clothes. Feeling her gaze upon him, Annan looked across the hall and their gazes fused.

Embarrassed at being caught staring in front of everyone, Saewara felt her face heat up.

To her surprise, Annan winked at her and gave her a slow smile.

Saewara felt her embarrassment turn to desire. She knew that look only too well. Breaking eye contact, Annan then crossed the hall, and disappeared behind the wall hangings, in search of dry clothes. Saewara watched him go, and resisted the impulse to go after him. They both knew what would happen if she did.

What did it matter? True, the hall would bear witness to the queen disappearing into her bower and would notice that the king and queen were absent from the hall for the rest of the night—but why keep it secret? Annan did not seem to care, why should she?

Saewara wiped her hands on a cloth and excused herself.

She was half-way across the hall when the doors blew open, bringing with it a gust of rain that made the fire gutter in its hearth. Two rain-soaked warriors rushed inside. The look on their faces made Saewara stop in her tracks.

"Where's the king?" one of the men demanded, his gaze sweeping the hall.

"Annan!" Saewara called, trying to quell the rising panic in her breast.

Moments later, barefoot and naked to the waist, Annan emerged from his bower.

"Milord," the warrior who had demanded the king's presence, bowed. "The Mercians approach. Your scouts have spotted them a league southeast. They are coming through the woods as you predicted."

Saewara watched Annan's face harden and his eyes narrow. The fact that he had been right about Penda's decision to tackle them through the woods rather than the marshes, obviously gave him a little satisfaction.

Saewara's stomach pitched toward her feet; she had sensed that war was close but had hoped to have this night with her husband, at least.

That was not to be.

The hall erupted into controlled chaos. Annan sent men out to recall the scouts patrolling the edge of the marshland to the north, before he went to dress for battle. The evening meal was forgotten. The army of the East Angles had to be mobilized, and quickly.

Saewara joined her husband in their bower—however, not for the purpose they had both hoped for earlier. They did not speak as she helped him dress. She helped him with his heavy chain mail vest before lacing leather arm guards about his forearms and upper arms. Lastly, he buckled *Night Bringer* around his hips. Coated in armor, his hair tied back at his nape, he looked like a different man; hard and pitiless. Saewara was glad of it. The warrior before her would bring the man she loved home, safe.

With a jolt, Saewara realized that she, indeed, did love him.

Neither of them had voiced those words but now was not the right time. He did not need to see a woman's tears, nor to have her cling to him like a limpet. He needed her strength and, if it would bring him home, then she would give it.

Once Annan was dressed for battle, his helmet tucked under one arm, Saewara followed him out into the hall. Saba was there waiting, while Hilda finished helping him with his armor. Unlike Saewara, Hilda was not so stoic. She was in floods of tears as she handed him his lime-wood shield.

"Hush, Love." Saba pulled Hilda against him and kissed her. "I must go now. Wait for me."

"The fyrd is ready," Aethelhere, his usually good-humored, boyish face tense with purpose, announced. "Your men await your command, Annan."

A few steps behind Aethelhere stood Hereswith. She looked pale and frightened. She plucked at her husband's sleeve but he ignored her; his gaze was riveted on his brother's face, as was every other man's in the hall. This was the moment they had all been waiting for. They needed their king. They needed his strength. They needed to believe that, this time, the East Angles would best the Mercians.

"And I'm ready to join them," Annan replied, swinging his own shield onto his back. "Let's send those curs back where they belong."

Saewara thought he would stride from the hall then, intent on nothing but the battle ahead, but instead, he turned to her.

They stood close to one another. He was so much taller than her that Saewara had to crane her neck to meet his gaze—but meet their gazes did.

"Will you wait for me, Saewara?" he asked, unexpectedly.

She heard the sudden doubt in his voice and it stabbed her straight in the heart.

"Till the end of the world," she whispered, "and beyond—I will wait for you Annan of the East Angles. Come back to me safe."

Annan did not reply. Instead, he bent and kissed her, cupping her face with his hands. It was a hard, passionate kiss; the first any of the hall's inhabitants had seen them share. Saewara's lips stung as he pulled back. Suddenly, it was if they were alone in the hall. Saewara's chest ached with unshed tears. There was so much she wanted to say to him, but there was no time.

Then, the moment ended.

Annan turned, his cloak billowing, and the hall erupted into movement once more.

Saewara watched, feeling as if her heart had just been ripped from her chest, as the man she loved walked from the hall and out into the stormy night.

Chapter Twenty-Three

On the Eve of Battle

"HALT!"

PENDA, KING of the Mercians, stopped ankle deep in muddy water, and cast his gaze around Exning Woods. The light was fading; they had travelled as far as they had dared, as thunder boomed overhead and lightening forked dangerously in between the trees.

"We make camp here," he announced.

It was not an ideal spot, although in these woods it was difficult to find one that was. The trees clung, close to one another, as if protecting their brothers and sisters from intruders. Roots covered the ground in the higher spots and the ground turned to peaty bog whenever the forest floor sloped.

Penda stood, his hard gaze sweeping over his surroundings with calculating intensity. They were nearing Exning and he was sure that, despite his army's best efforts to move unnoticed, a scout would have spotted them by now.

"Milord." Aldfrid stepped up next to his king. "Should we not press on?"

Penda glanced at the ealdorman. Water streamed down Aldfrid's broad face and dripped off his beard. This was the second time today that Aldfrid had questioned his decisions.

There better not be a third.

"We stop here," Penda replied, his voice barely audible over the crash of thunder directly overhead. "The East Angles will meet us at dawn."

With that, Penda turned and shoved his way past the ealdorman. Aldfrid staggered back, nearly slipping over in the mud, but wisely held his tongue. Even so, Penda could feel the warrior's gaze upon him as he walked away.

Aldfrid had arrived back in Tamworth on foot, after his horse collapsed from exhaustion two days away from home and died, despite its rider's best efforts to drag it to its feet. The ealdorman had brought ill tidings with him—and a boiling hatred for Annan of the East Angles that turned him foul tempered and unpredictable. Aldfrid wanted Annan's head on a pike. He wanted the Kingdom of the East Angles to burn. He wanted vengeance at all costs.

Penda knew better than to hate his enemy.

Hate colored your judgment. It made you act from the belly, not the head. Hate made a man rush in to battle imprudently. Aldfrid would have had them floundering blind through woods they did not know, in foul weather, toward an enemy that would be lying in wait for them.

Hate turned wise men into fools.

Aldfrid had become an encumbrance of late, Penda reflected. If he survived the coming battle, the warrior would find himself out of favor once they returned to Tamworth.

Penda walked through his army, his gimlet gaze missing nothing, while his warriors made camp for the night. There was little space, or dry ground, for tents, so they merely strung up animal hide awnings between trees, to keep out the worst of the weather. They attempted to light fires with what little wood they could find that was not completely sodden.

The warriors greeted their king respectfully as he passed, but none attempted to converse with him. Their diffidence suited Penda. He did not wish to talk to anyone this evening; his thoughts were already moving forward, focusing on what would come tomorrow morning. Later, he would call his ealdormen to him and they would discuss their tactics for the coming battle. It would not be like the last confrontation with the East Angles. Then, they had met, shield-wall to shield-wall, on the wide expanse of Barrow Fields. That was the kind of warfare Penda liked; the kind he excelled in.

Taking on the enemy in the woods called for another approach.

It took Penda a long while to skirt the length and breadth of his *fyrd*, and it was dark when he returned to the front. Yet, the inspection had allowed him to focus his thoughts.

Annan's blatant defiance had caught Penda by surprise; something that rarely happened.

After all Penda's effort to break the East Angle's spirit—to turn him into a spineless puppet who would do his bidding—Annan had shown that he was, indeed, a Wuffinga king. Penda had not been angered, by this; yet, he could not let it continue unchallenged or unpunished. Annan would know that this time there would be no mercy when the battle turned against him. The time for pledges and pacts was over; if the East Angles would not bow before the Mercians then they would have to die.

Saewara should have sent word, Penda thought—a knife blade of anger slicing through his cool façade. *I told her to keep me informed. Why else does she think I married her to that Wuffinga whoreson?*

Saewara had always disappointed him. Even as a child, she had never done as she was told. Her husband had tried to beat it out of her but she was still as willful as ever.

This should have taught Saewara her place. Yet according to Aldfrid, the woman was as forthright as ever, and worse still, Annan appeared to have warmed to her.

Slut, Penda gritted his teeth before forcing Saewara from his thoughts. *I will take Annan alive and make you watch when I kill him.*

"The Mercians have made camp, M'lord." One of the scouts, a young man, barely out of boyhood, had returned to the front. His face was slick with rain, his fair hair plastered to his skull.

Behind him, lightening forked between the trees; illuminating the woodland for a moment, before it plunged once more back into darkness. It was a foul night to be out in, and at this rate they risked being hit by lightning. Still, they had little choice in the matter.

Annan nodded at the scout before glancing at where Saba stood behind him. "We shall make camp here then."

Indeed, the Mercians were so close, he could smell the faint whiff of wood smoke from their fires. They were confident, it seemed. It did not matter to them that lighting fires would alert the East Angles to their presence.

Penda knew that Annan would not attempt an attack until dawn.

He knows his enemy, Annan thought dryly, *or he thinks he does. That could be his first mistake.*

Behind him, Annan heard the sounds of his *fyrd* setting up camp; the snap of leather awnings going up, and the rustling and clanking of weapons being set down. It would be a long, uncomfortable night, and a tense one. Yet, Annan could feel a fire kindling in his belly, mixed with the thrill of fear that every wise man feels before going into battle. He did not love war the way Penda did, but he knew that on the battlefield, only a man who gave himself entirely to the madness of war had a chance of survival. Time took on a different pace during battle. Every moment drew out, while at the same time rushing forward with violent clarity. Annan's senses heightened in anticipation of what was to come; throwing every detail around him— every sight, smell and sound, into sharp clarity.

Less than a year ago, Annan had met Penda in battle, and the Mercian had humiliated him. Penda had bested him in sword combat but, instead of killing Annan there and then, he had taken him prisoner. They both knew it was a blow to any warrior's honor. Better to die with a sword in your belly, than to limp home defeated.

And here we are again.

Annan walked amongst his men, checking that they were all in good spirits and readying themselves mentally for battle. He need not have worried. He saw determination on his warriors' faces, and fierceness in their eyes. Many had waited long for this moment.

They would have their reckoning against the Mercians, or die trying.

Annan returned to the front, and dared to hope that the coming battle would go their way. This was a different army to the one Penda had encountered last time. Last autumn, the East Angles had been scattered and leaderless. Sigeberht had refused to lead them and instead, an unknown—a man called Ecgric, who few liked or trusted—had led the East

Anglian fyrd into battle. It had been a disaster from the outset. This time, the East Angles had their king. This time they had hope.

Taking refuge from the driving rain, under a wide awning between two young oaks, Annan sat down on a stump that someone had thoughtfully covered with sacking and attempted to dry himself off next to a hissing fire. His clothing and armor stuck to him like a second skin and weighed down on his limbs. It would have to stay that way though; he would not be taking it off until the battle was over.

Annan was eating a piece of bread and cheese, and staring into the guttering flames, when Saba joined him.

"Morale is good," the ealdorman grunted as he took a seat opposite Annan and helped himself to some bread and cheese.

"I noticed the same," Annan replied with a smile. "Better than I thought."

"It will take more than a bit of rain to douse these men's spirits," Saba countered. "They would go anywhere if you asked."

Annan's smile widened. "I knew there was a reason I kept you at my side, Saba."

Saba shrugged at that. "It's true—I wouldn't say it otherwise."

"I know—but after all that's happened, it surprises me that they follow me."

"They don't blame you for Barrow Fields." Saba frowned at the memory of that battle; for he too had been taken prisoner. "That was another king."

"Still, they know I was made to 'bend the knee', and that I agreed to marry Penda's sister. No other Wuffinga king has sunk so low."

"Certainly, you don't still regret Saewara do you?" Saba's eyebrows shot up. "You didn't seem sorry to have wedded her this afternoon."

Annan looked away, suddenly embarrassed by the turn their conversation had taken.

"Saewara is the best thing that has ever happened to me," he said finally, his voice quiet, "and I'd be a fool to deny it."

Saba grinned at him wolfishly. "Hilda said something had changed between you—but I didn't believe her until today. I am glad."

Annan met his friend's gaze once more, his smile returning. "You were always a bit on the slow side."

Saba snorted at that before taking a bite of bread and cheese. "You took your time," he said with his mouth full.

"Time I can never get back," Annan agreed. "I need to survive this, Saba. I need to return to her."

"You will," Saba's voice held so much force that Annan could not help but believe him. "We both will."

"I hope you two left some food for me?"

Annan and Saba's conversation halted as Aethelhere stepped under the awning and shook himself like a dog.

"Thunor's hammer, it's foul out there."

"As long as it drowns the Mercians in the night, I care not," Annan replied, handing his brother a hunk of bread and cheese. "Here."

Annan made room for Aethelhere on the tree stump and threw a few more damp twigs on the fire.

"So it starts at dawn?" Aethelhere's gaze met his brother's.

Annan nodded. "If we want to use the bowmen, we will need light."

Aethelhere nodded, his youthful face creased in thought. "I wonder if Penda has thought to employ the same tactic. After all, we all know how much Penda loves his shield-wall."

"That's what I'm counting on," Annan replied. "There will be no shield-wall in woods this thick. "If our bowmen can take down a few Mercians before our axes and spears reach them, it will help us no end."

Both Saba and Aethelhere nodded at that. Using bowmen in warfare had been a tactic used by the Romans, although ever since their departure, those of Britannia preferred to use their longbows for sport rather than war. Annan, who was a skilled archer, had always thought it a waste. Traditions sometimes turned men blind.

The three men fell silent then, each sinking into his own private thoughts. There was plenty to think on this night—on who they had left behind, on regret for those things left unsaid, and on what lay in wait for them all at dawn.

Chapter Twenty-Four

Saewara's Decision

AN ENTIRE DAY passed before someone brought word of the battle to Exning. In the interim, a tense silence had descended over the settlement. It seemed desolate, now that the fyrd had emptied out. Only the women, children and elderly remained. The village appeared abandoned, forsaken.

The storm had continued all through the night and for most of the next morning. When it finally spent itself, heavy skies, leaden with the promise of more rain, hung overhead. The weather cast a gloomy shadow over Exning and the atmosphere inside the hall was little better. The servants moved silently about the strangely empty space while the few noblewomen residing here, sat at their looms or distaffs near the fire.

Saewara could not stay seated for long, especially since to do so meant keeping company with Hereswith and Eldwyn. She was full of nervous energy and frustration at not being able to be of any real assistance to her husband. She helped Hilda clean the hall. They took advantage of the men's absence to replace the soiled rushes on the floor and carry furs outside to air. When she was not keeping busy, Saewara spent a great deal of time skirting Exning's perimeter; often straying beyond the fence to watch the path that led into the woods.

Saewara was outside, feeding the geese, when the messenger arrived.

"M'lady!" A thin figure limped out of the grey dusk and staggered toward her.

He was a young man, barely out of boyhood. His left arm had been hurriedly strapped to his body and dark blood seeped through the bandages. His face was pale with pain and loss of blood.

Saewara rushed to his side and led him into the hall. He leaned heavily against her, his breath coming in shallow gasps. Inside, Hereswith and Eldwyn hurriedly moved aside so that the young man could sit down in front of the fire.

"What news?" Saewara asked him. "Is the battle over?"

The young man shook his head. "We have fought them since dawn—with heavy losses on both sides. The battle is not yet done. The Mercians have pulled back for the night, and we have done the same. The fighting will resume at daybreak."

"And the king?"

"He lives," the warrior assured her with a brave smile, before his gaze shifted to Hilda and then to Hereswith, "as do your husbands."

Saewara ceased her questioning then and set about tending to the young man's wounds. His arm had been sliced deeply, presumably by an axe. Fortunately, the bone had not been shattered. However, it would take a while to heal and the resulting scar would coil around his bicep.

"Can you bind it up?" the boy asked anxiously. "I need to return to the battle."

"You won't be fighting with an arm in this state," Saewara told him crisply, "so let's have no more talk of you rejoining the army."

"But my king needs me," the warrior protested weakly. "I was proud to be an East Angle today, M'lady. The King fought like Woden himself. I want to return to his side."

"You can't use your fighting arm," Saewara responded with a shake of her head. "You have fought bravely, but how long do you think you'd survive, fighting crippled?"

The young man glared at her sullenly, but did not answer. They both knew she spoke the truth.

"The king sent you to bring word, and you have done so, despite your injuries," Saewara continued. "Let us take care of you."

The warrior hung his head, the fight going out of him. Saewara glanced across at Hilda, who had put water on to boil over the fire pit, in order to clean the wound. Her friend's face had gone the color of milk, yet she gave Saewara a tremulous, brave smile.

Saba was alive, and so was Annan.

The battle had not yet ended. There was still hope.

A still, watchful night settled over Exning.

Saewara stepped outside of the hall and breathed in the damp air, stained with the tang of wood-smoke. She pulled her fur cloak around her shoulders and attempted to gather her chaotic thoughts.

An idea—one that had germinated the night before, as she lay awake, alone in bed—returned once more.

She hated feeling so useless; hated having to wait while wyrd decided Annan's fate. She wanted to see him. She wanted to fight at his side.

I am not weak and useless, she thought, clamping her teeth together in frustration. *I have more skill with a longbow than most men. I am no longer Mercian. I want to be part of the army that opposes them—the army that bests them. Only then will I truly leave my past behind.*

Such thoughts were treacherous. Women did not join men on the battlefield. Women stayed behind and tended the home until their menfolk returned. Annan would be enraged; he would send her away.

Yet what if Mercia triumphed?

That hurried farewell would be the last she ever saw of Annan. She could not bear the thought. She had to see him, even from afar.

It would be best if he did not know that she had joined his fyrd. If he was unaware that she had slipped into the ranks of his bowmen, he would not be able to send her away—and she would be able to help without causing a distraction.

That is what I shall do, she decided, excitement making her stomach pitch wildly, *I shall dress as a man, shroud myself in a hooded cloak and take my place alongside the bowmen. Annan will not know I am there.*

She would not be able to tell anyone. They would all think her mad and would try to stop her. None of them—even Hilda—would understand.

Yet her mind was made up. Whatever the outcome, she would do it.

Annan's hall slept when Saewara slipped from her bower.

For the first time in her life, she was dressed in men's clothing. It felt odd to wear breeches and leather boots cross-gartered to the knee, instead of long skirts. She had stolen the clothing from one of the women in the hall, who had just finished mending the items for her twelve-year old son. On her top-half, Saewara wore a heavy tunic and a chain-mail vest that was too big for her. It was the smallest she could find in the armory, but it nearly reached her knees. Around her shoulders, she wore a thick cloak with a deep cowl. Saewara wrapped it tight about her, lest anyone see her leave, hiding her clothing from view.

She padded down the stairs into the open space beyond. The fire pit had died down to embers, casting the interior of the hall in a faint light; just enough for Saewara to make out the forms of those sleeping on the ground around it. Prudently, she skirted them, keeping close to the walls.

Holding her breath, Saewara gently pulled one of the heavy doors toward her, opening it just wide enough for her to be able to slip outside. She had just stepped away from the door, her thoughts focused on the next step of her plan—retrieving her longbow and quiver from the storehouse— when a hostile voice made her freeze mid-step.

"Where do you think you're going?"

A figure had slipped through the door behind her, and although it was too dark to make out the woman's features, Saewara recognized the voice instantly.

Hereswith.

"None of your business." Saewara swallowed the knot of panic in her throat and backed away from the door. "Go back to bed."

"Sneaking off, are you?" Hereswith's voice was wintry. "Hoping to find your brother and betray us all?"

"I'm going to fight," Saewara replied flatly, "alongside my husband."

Hereswith made a rude, unladylike noise, halfway between a laugh and a snarl. "Fight? You?"

"Yes, unlike you, I can do more than sew and gossip," Saewara shot back, momentarily losing her calm. "I learnt to use a longbow as soon as I could walk."

"What a strange woman you are," Hereswith replied. "Not feminine at all."

"Annan might disagree with you there."

"Really? It is me he wants—surely you know that."

"Maybe he did want you," Saewara admitted, "once … but then he realized, as most men do when given time, that you are a nasty bitch."

She heard Hereswith's hiss of outrage. She thought that the woman might lunge at her; but moments passed and Hereswith did not move.

"I'm going now," Saewara said coldly, "and while your husband—who you don't even pretend to love—is fighting for his people, why don't you give some thought to what will happen if the East Angles lose this battle?" Saewara let her words sink in before continuing. "I grew up among the Mercians, I know their ways. If you think my brother will be merciful with the widows of his enemies, think again. When Penda whores you to his men and you learn what they are truly capable of, you will wish you had treated Aethelhere better."

A shocked silence followed, and Saewara backed away into the shadows. She did not have time for this. Hereswith was close to ruining everything.

"I do care for Aethelhere." Hereswith spoke once more, her voice oddly subdued. "I don't want him to die in battle."

"Then it's a pity you never told him," Saewara replied. With that, she turned and moved away toward the storehouse.

"I'll raise the alarm." Hereswith's voice followed her, although it now lost its earlier conviction. "You won't get far."

Saewara did not respond. She had no control over what Hereswith chose to do next. All she could do was walk away and pray that her sister by marriage held her tongue.

Chapter Twenty-Five

The Captive

SAEWARA SLIPPED OUT of Exning and hugged the shadows around the high paling fence, avoiding the elderly men who were standing guard around the perimeter. Annan had left a garrison to watch over Devil's Dyke but, fortunately, Saewara was not travelling in that direction. Instead, she followed the narrow path into Exning Woods.

Once inside the woodland, it was as black as pitch. Stumbling over tree roots, Saewara waited until she was far enough away from the edge of the trees before taking the cover off the oil lamp she had removed from the storehouse. She let out a long breath in relief as pale golden light illuminated her surroundings. Gloomy even in daylight, the woods had a vaguely sinister air at night. A tangle of branches surrounded her, with the darkness impenetrable beyond.

Directly southeast—that was what the lad had told her. She had managed to extract the information from him after the injured messenger had downed a few cups of hot, spiced mead to take the edge off his throbbing arm. She had phrased the question so it sounded innocent enough, and the lad had answered her without hesitation. According to his reckoning, the East Angle army was camped quarter of a night's travel from Exning.

If she kept straight in her current direction, she would run into the back of Annan's fyrd soon enough.

It was hard going, and slower than she had anticipated. The ground was boggy from the storm and although this area was relatively low-lying, the land was anything but flat. Soon, Saewara found herself scrambling up banks, down gullies and across streams. All the while, she kept a death-grip on her little flickering lamp. Without it, she knew she would easily lose her way.

On and on she journeyed, deep into the dark woods. The farther she travelled, the more nervous Saewara became. What if she was going the wrong way altogether? What if she had accidently skirted the edge of the fyrd, and was unwittingly blundering straight toward her brother?

The last thought was enough to make her break out into a cold sweat.

Don't be a fool, Saewara—you're going the right way. Just keep walking.

479

Eventually, dripping with sweat now, her quiver heavy on her back, Saewara caught the whiff of wood smoke. She slowed her step, quickly covered her lamp, and followed the smell. The most difficult part was ahead; she would need to become a ghost. Presently, she spied the glow of firelight through the trees. Her heart started to pound and her palms grew clammy.

Suddenly, her plan seemed all too real.

Annan's fyrd lay before her and once she entered the camp, there would be no turning back. However, here cloaked in darkness, it was not too late—she could turn back and slip away without anyone knowing.

Saewara felt the strength go out of her legs. She crouched and breathed deeply, calming the fear that threatened to release her bladder. All the while, she kept her gaze upon the fires ahead.

What will it be—forward or back? You can't stay here all night?

Recovering from her paralysis, Saewara slowly rose to her feet. Then, squaring her shoulders and whispering a prayer, she moved toward the sleeping encampment.

"M'lord."

A voice roused Annan from where he dozed by the fire. He stirred on the damp furs and sat up, rubbing the sleep from his eyes.

"What is it?"

A warrior stepped into the tent, dipping his head under the low roof. It was a cramped space that had only enough room for the tiny fire pit, and a bed for the king. Still, it was luxury after the day he had spent fighting knee-deep in mud, blood and gore.

"Apologies for waking you, M'lord," the warrior rumbled, his own eyes hollowed with fatigue, "but we caught someone lurking around the fringes of the encampment. I thought I'd better bring him to you."

"A spy?"

The last remnants of sleep faded and Annan rose smoothly to his feet.

"Most likely—a lad. Tried to run like a hare when we spotted him."

With that, another warrior bundled a struggling figure into the tent. They had thrown a jute sack over their captive to stop him from escaping, but he still writhed desperately like a trout on a hook.

"Enough!" Annan ordered, stepping toward the captive. "Let's see you then."

The figure stopped struggling at Annan's command. In fact, he went deathly still, and stayed that way as Annan reached forward and yanked the jute sacking away.

The captive's hood fell back.

Annan stared at the individual before him, his breath stilling. The warriors flanking the prisoner gaped openly.

"What," Annan managed finally, his voice barely above a whisper, "are you doing here?"

Saewara stared back at her husband. Her heart-shaped face was pale; her dark eyes huge and frightened.

"Saewara." Annan spoke once more, his voice sharpening as the shock of seeing his wife, dressed as a man, with a longbow over one shoulder and a quiver of arrows on her back, before him, faded. In its place, he felt anger kindling. "You could have been killed on sight. Answer me. What, are you doing here?"

He watched her struggle to compose herself under his gaze. A blush crept up her slender neck and her eyes glittered. For a moment he thought she would start crying—but instead, her jaw hardened and she lifted her chin defiantly.

"I was attempting to join the ranks of your bowmen," she told him calmly, "without your knowledge—when these two stopped me."

"What?" Annan did not know whether to laugh or fly into a rage. "You intended to join my fyrd, without asking me?"

Saewara's sensuous mouth thinned. "You would never have given me permission."

"You're right, I wouldn't!" Annan roared. "Are you mad?"

To her credit, she did not cower before him.

"Leave us!" Annan ordered his men, his gaze not leaving Saewara's face. They went—but not without one last, awed look at their queen, dressed ready for battle. She stared at her husband without a trace of fear.

"I'm not mad," Saewara said quietly when they were alone. "I was tired of sitting at home, useless. You've seen me handle a longbow. I am of more use to you here than back in Exning waiting with the other women."

"Saewara." Annan took a deep breath, seeking to control his temper. "War is for men, not women. You had no right to come here. This is not your place."

"No!" It was Saewara's turn to shout. "I tire of men telling me where my place is. My place is where I choose it to be!"

Annan had never seen her lose her temper before—and even through his own rage, he had to admit she had never looked lovelier. She had curled her hands into fists, as if she would strike him, her eyes narrowing dangerously.

"This is my war as much as yours," she continued, breathless with fury. "I have more cause to hate Penda of Mercia than anyone. I want to be part of the army that sends his army running home with their tails between their legs. And if the battle goes ill—if you fall—I don't want my brother to ride into Exning with your head on a pike. I'd rather die here, by your side, than to wait for my brother's mercy. You know as well as I do that I'd be better off dead."

Saewara stopped then, breathing hard, her hands still clenched by her sides. She stood, staring at him. Her body was as taut as a bowstring, and her cheeks were flushed. Annan realized then, with a jolt, that she was bracing herself for him to lash out.

She expected him to strike her.

Anger suddenly drained from Annan.

"Saewara," he said, his voice growing husky. "I would never—never—raise a hand to you. You do realize that?"

She tore her gaze from his, staring down at her feet.

"I've been beaten for less," she replied.

"I repeat—I will never raise a hand to you." Annan stepped forward and gently took hold of her chin, raising her face so that her gaze met his once more. "I swear it."

Saewara's eyes glistened. She nodded but Annan saw that she was struggling to keep her composure.

"Don't send me away," she whispered. "I won't get in your way. I will stay with your bowmen—I won't encumber anyone. I swear."

"And how am I supposed to fight knowing that your life could be in danger?" Annan asked. "I don't think you realize what it's like out there. The violence, the blood, the screams of men as they die. There's a reason we keep women from battle—and it's not because we want all the glory for ourselves."

"I haven't romanticized it," Saewara whispered. "I've known terror. I've looked into a man's eyes and seen death there. There were times when I thought Egfrid would kill me. Once he beat me so badly I nearly died. Yet despite his best efforts, Egfrid did not break me, and neither did my brother. I'm not some sheltered high-born lady. I can fight."

Annan gave a bitter smile then—one that masked the stabbing pain in the center of his chest.

"Why, Saewara?" he whispered.

She stepped close to him then, staring up at him in that way that made his body melt. "Because this is my battle too," she whispered back. "Let me fight it."

He pulled her against him; his arms locking around her, his face burying in her hair.

"Damn you," he murmured, squeezing his eyes shut to stem the tears that suddenly scalded his eyelids. "My life was so much simpler before you entered it—empty—but so much easier."

He felt her laugh against him; a sudden release of tension after all that had been said between them. "I was sent to torment you, Annan of the East Angles—but I am not sorry for it. For once, my brother did us both a favor."

The feel of her against him, her warmth even through the layers of clothing between them, burned into his flesh. His hands slid down her back and over the firm curves of her buttocks. The breeches she wore molded to her flesh.

Annan groaned and pulled away from Saewara, his heart pounding. She looked up at him, her eyes dark with longing, and he was lost. Hunger consumed him and he bent over her, his mouth slanting over hers.

Saewara responded by linking her arms around his neck and opening her mouth, her tongue tangling with his. Her hands travelled over his torso but were denied contact with his skin by the layers of chain mail and leather. She made a low noise of frustration deep in her throat, before her hands travelled lower to his leather breeches.

Annan took charge then. He reached under the long chain-mail tunic she wore and undid the laces of her breeches. Then, he leant forward and kissed her deeply as he unlaced his own breeches. After that, he pushed her gently down onto the furs—on to her hands and knees. The sight of her naked rear, round, perfect and gleaming pale in the firelight, excited him beyond measure. Not lingering further, Annan knelt behind Saewara and entered her in one smooth movement.

They both gasped. She whimpered his name and he was lost.

Gripping her hips, Annan moved inside her. He tried to be slow—he had wanted to be gentle—yet, he was overwhelmed by an animalistic desire to take her hard. The impulse was so strong that he resisted only moments before giving in.

Saewara arched her back and pushed her hips back to meet each thrust, encouraging him. She groaned and gasped, her body shuddering. Then, her knees gave way and she collapsed onto the furs. Annan held her hips up, thrusting into her again and again until he found his release.

Afterwards, they lay together, panting, on the furs. When he had sufficiently recovered, Annan rolled off Saewara and pulled her gently against his chest. He stroked her hair and held her close as their breathing slowed and reality seeped back into their world.

"Annan." Saewara propped herself up on one elbow and stared down at him. The softness in her eyes made him want to weep; something he had not done since his father's death. "Whatever happens from this moment forward," she whispered, "you need to know that I love you."

Annan stared back at her, his breathing growing shallow as he tried to keep his composure. "Lovely Saewara," he murmured back, feeling as if his heart was being torn in two. "You brought joy into my life when I least expected it. I can't imagine life without you."

He paused then, struggling to keep his composure. "I love you so much that it scares me."

She gave a gentle smile, and reaching out wiped away a tear from his cheek. "My brave wolf, my kind-hearted lover. If only the world had more men like you in it."

Chapter Twenty-Six

The Battle of Exning Woods

A MISTY DAWN broke over the woodland. A thin fog wreathed between the trees as the two armies packed up with the rising sun and readied themselves to do battle.

After sleeping in each other's arms for the remainder of the waning night, Annan and Saewara had awoken strangely rested, despite that they could have slept longer. They spoke little as they dressed, both calm despite the coming fight.

The king and queen emerged from the tent to find Saba and Aethelhere waiting for them. The two men had heard that the queen had joined them— the entire fyrd had by now. Saba and Aethelhere's gazes settled upon Saewara, taking in her battle dress and weaponry. Their expressions were stony. She returned their gazes evenly; she did not blame them for their reaction. She had not planned on making her presence known, although in retrospect, her plan had been flawed from the beginning.

She had only ventured a few yards inside the encampment when she had realized that it would be impossible to slip through it without being noticed.

"Saewara will join the bowmen," Annan told them coolly. "Aethelhere, take her to them."

"What?" Aethelhere did not try to hide his displeasure. "She's staying?"

"She is," Annan replied in a tone that brooked no argument. "Go on—we don't have much time."

Saewara glanced quickly at her husband. "Till after the battle, Milord," she said quietly. "Fight well."

Annan smiled at her. "You too, my love— keep your aim steady—and keep back from the front. Follow the lead from the other archers."

Saewara nodded. She was glad for the formality this morning. Enough had been said last night. No further words were needed, especially now in front of Annan's warriors. If she was to stay on and fight then she needed to prove that she had the nerve for it.

Aethelhere led her away, and Saewara followed without a backwards glance. Male gazes followed her steps but Saewara ignored them. She had pulled her hair back into a tight braid and wore her cloak about her shoulders. Her longbow was slung across one shoulder, her quiver of arrows across the other.

They reached the bowmen, who watched Saewara curiously as she stopped before them.

"Queen Saewara will join you," Aethelhere told them. His voice was dispassionate. Saewara could feel the disapproval radiating off him. He then turned and met her gaze.

"They won't be able to look out for you once the battle starts," he told her curtly. "You will be on your own."

"I know that," Saewara responded with a half-smile. "Thank you, Aethelhere."

Aethelhere regarded her for a moment before shaking his head slowly. "Are you really as good with that longbow as Annan says?"

"Better," Saewara replied without a trace of a smile. "I should have beaten him in that tournament at Tamworth."

A smile tugged at Aethelhere's mouth. "Very well—we'll see, shall we?"

With that, he turned on his heel and strode away, his fur cloak billowing behind him.

Saewara watched Aethelhere go and wondered if she would see him again. Today would decide it for them—Mercians or East Angles, one side had to win.

Annan moved toward the front with Saba at his side. Their shields were slung over their backs, their swords still in their scabbards. The two men did not speak, sharing the easy silence that only good friends have. Annan knew he did not need to explain himself to Saba; even if the ealdorman might not agree with his decision to let Saewara stay and fight, he would never challenge Annan on it. He knew it was not a decision the king would have taken lightly.

Still, it was a shocking decision, and Annan had felt the effect ripple through his army. This was yet another reason men preferred to keep women away from battle he thought dryly—they were a distraction. Saewara was quite a sight in her battle gear; if anything it heightened her fierce beauty rather than hid it.

Annan allowed himself one more thought of his wife, as he had seen her last – strong and proud with a calm that awed him—before he snapped that part of his mind closed and focused on the coming battle.

"The Mercians are forming their lines, M'lord," one his warriors informed Annan as he reached the front. "As soon as the mist clears they will make their move."

"They will make their move before then," Annan replied quietly, drawing looks of surprise from the warriors surrounding him, Saba included. "Penda got a nasty surprise yesterday when we set our bowmen on them. Today, we do not have the element of surprise. Penda will attack before the bowmen can get a clear view."

"Are you sure?" Saba asked, frowning as his gaze swept the misty forest. "Sounds like a risky move on Penda's part."

"No," Annan admitted, "however, I put myself in his place and thought what I'd do if I hadn't brought bowmen with me. I wouldn't give the enemy a chance to fell my men with their arrows. I'd move before they had me in their sights."

Saba's face had grown grim, although he eventually nodded in agreement. "Have you warned the bowmen?"

"Last night," Annan replied. "I've told them to move back and wait for my command. They will not be able to fire into the front lines, as we would have already engaged them. Instead, I want them to aim for the second group who will be rushing up to join their comrades."

At that moment, Aethelhere joined them. The brothers' gazes met for a moment, and a silent message passed between them before Annan nodded.

Saba quickly filled Aethelhere in on Annan's concerns while the king made his way down the lines, speaking quietly with his men, and alerting them to the imminent attack. When the king returned, the swirling mist was starting to clear.

Annan unsheathed *Night Bringer* and took his place next to his brother.

Patches of the shadowy woodland beyond became visible. Quiet and watchful, Annan's fyrd grew still, weapons held at the ready, and waited for the enemy to come.

Penda unsheathed his sword and inspected the blade. It had taken a battering yesterday, but the magnificent blade was still unscarred. *Æthelfrith's Bane.* A sword fit for a king—pried out of Ecgric the Eager's dead hands after the Battle of Barrow Fields. Such a sword should never have belonged to such a craven.

Penda loved to fight with this sword; it felt made for him. It was the perfect weight and balance – and the pommel fitted his hand as if it was merely an extension of his arm. It had dealt death with joy yesterday, and would do so again today.

"Are we ready?" Penda turned to Aldfrid, who stood to his right. The ealdorman returned his gaze with a surly expression. Having taken a few wounds the day before—gashes to his left arm and leg from a crazed East Angle axe-man—Aldfrid was in ill humor today.

"Yes," he finally acknowledged with a frown, "although I think we should wait till the mist clears. We're stumbling forward blind this way."

"I have already explained to you why we need to move now," Penda replied, his voice quiet with feigned patience. "Unless you want an arrow in your chest, it's the best chance we have of breaking through their front lines."

"Well, you lead the men in then," Aldfrid snarled. "I'm not going first— we might as well rush in blind-folded."

Aldfrid's last comment was a mistake, a costly one.

Penda had put up with the ealdorman's incessant grumbling ever since they had left Tamworth. Yet at Aldfrid's latest insolence, his patience snapped. Moving with the deathly speed that had made him so formidable in battle, the Mercian king turned on Aldfrid and plunged his blade into the base of his neck.

The ealdorman fell without a sound, his eyes bulging as he clutched at the blade. Penda did not utter a word. He kicked the man to the ground and placed a heavy boot on his chest, watching with cold eyes while Aldfrid died. Around him, his warriors stirred uneasily; not one of them daring intervene.

When he was sure Aldfrid was dead, Penda stepped back from his corpse and turned to the watching gazes of his fyrd.

"Does anyone else have something to say?" he asked.

Their silence was the only answer he needed.

"Very well. On my command, we move!"

Saewara had taken her place in the ranks of bowmen and had just notched her first arrow, when the battle started.

She had expected shouts and the crunch of metal colliding with flesh. Yet instead, there was a sudden release of tension in the air around her and a whisper of movement down below.

The bowmen stood on a slight rise, fanned out in a horseshoe at the point where they would get the clearest view of the enemy. Unfortunately, as the first cries of men dying and the clang of spears against shields reached them, they could see nothing because of the swirling mist. It was starting to clear, but it was not safe to start loosing arrows.

Wulfhere, the leader of the bowmen, had dourly informed Saewara that Annan suspected the Mercians would attack before the mist cleared; and it appeared the king had been right. As such, they stood much further back than the day before. This morning, they would have to bide their time before engaging the Mercians.

"Loose your arrows on my command." Wulfhere's voice cut through the rapidly increasing din of battle. "Remember to keep the rhythm once you start – notch, draw, loose. When I say so—move back—and if I tell you to run, do it!"

Saewara felt her heart start to hammer against her ribs at these words. Everything was suddenly becoming very real. She had steeled herself for this moment; but no amount of preparation could ready her for the screams of men dying and the brutal sound of physical combat.

Somewhere, in the heart of that clash, Annan was fighting for his life.

The mist started to clear and Saewara took a few deep, slow breaths to calm her nerves. She needed to keep her hands steady or she would be no use to anyone.

Suddenly, the mist cleared and Saewara received her first, horrifyingly clear, view of the fighting. Men writhed in spaces between trees, floundering on the uneven ground. They thrust spears, heaved axes and, those who were high ranking enough to wield swords, sliced their way through the fray.

Saewara did not look for Annan. That was not why she was here—she had to concentrate, and that meant putting her husband out of her thoughts.

"Notch!" Wulfhere commanded, the hard edge to his voice, galvanizing Saewara's resolve. "Draw!"

The row of bowmen obeyed. Saewara held her breath and aimed, as she had been instructed, at the second group of Mercian warriors, who were now moving forward to join those at the front ranks.

"Loose!"

Once the first arrow was loosed, the battle became a blur.

Saewara did as Wulfhere bid.

Notch, draw, loose. Notch, draw, loose.

She developed a steady rhythm—and men fell.

Even at this distance, she recognized some of the men she killed. Among them was Thyrdwulf—the cold warrior, one of her brother's best, who had dragged her back from Bonehill. She felt no pleasure at killing him, only a chilling relief that a man who was almost as cruel as her brother, no longer walked the earth. He fell, with an arrow lodged deep in his windpipe and was trampled by his comrades.

After a time, Saewara's fingers grew raw from the bowstring and her arms burned with fatigue, yet she did not halt. Her aim was lethal. She only lowered her bow when her quiver was empty, and only then was it to take another.

She had just started on her second quiver when Wulfhere's shout brought the firing to a halt. Saewara could see why. The numbers were swelling down below. Men now fought elbow-to-elbow; the ranks of Mercians and East Angles had suddenly merged so it was impossible to determine where one started and the other ended. Even more worryingly, the tide of men had started to surge toward the higher ground where the bowmen stood.

"Fall back!" Wulfhere shouted.

Saewara moved back, shoulder to shoulder with the other bowmen. However, the trees grew thick behind them and they were forced to shift apart. Sheltered from view by the trees, each archer took up position.

"Be sure of your marks before loosing your arrows!" Wulfhere bellowed.

A moment later, a hand axe came hurtling through the misty air.

Wulfhere slumped to the ground, the axe embedded in this forehead. He lay there twitching, just yards from where Saewara stood.

The horror of it made Saewara reel back and cling to a tree trunk for support. One moment Wulfhere had been alive, shouting orders at his bowmen—and the next he was gone. The reality of how close danger was, and the fact that the battle had now reached the point where it could turn either way, made her want to turn tail and flee.

Instead, she heaved Wulfhere's quiver of arrows onto her back, next to the one she had already. Then, whispering a prayer for the dead man, she looked for a tree to climb.

Saewara chose a sturdy beech tree; old with spreading branches close to the ground and a thick foliage to hide herself in. Her hands, wet with sweat, slipped on the rough bark as she climbed. Her pulse pounded in her ears; so loud that it even drowned out the roar of battle close by.

Perhaps it was not wise to climb a tree so close to where the battle raged—the other archers had fallen back to where it was safer. Yet Saewara had a plan. She knew her aim was good, and settling in the fork between two branches, she pulled the foliage aside and saw that she had a remarkably clear view of both armies, breaking upon each other like waves against a shingle shore.

The sight made her hands shake. Once again, she was reminded that somewhere in the middle of that nightmare, Annan fought.

Please Lord, keep him safe.

Regaining control of her nerves, Saewara notched an arrow and drew, her eyes scanning the mêlée. Whenever her gaze seized upon one of the East Angles that she recognized, especially if he was in trouble with an opponent, and if she had a clear shot, she loosed an arrow. More often than not, her shot saved that man's life. She was careful and deliberate, her arms trembling with the strain of keeping the bowstring drawn—but one by one, she picked the Mercians off.

The battle raged on, and for a while it seemed as if no side was gaining the advantage. Men fell, only to be trampled by the living, and for every man that died there was another to replace him.

However, such savagery could not continue forever.

The fighting slowly inched closer to Saewara's hiding place and she began to run low on arrows. She would need to replenish her supplies soon, but had no wish to do so in the middle of slashing blades and axes.

She was down to her last five arrows when she spotted Annan amongst the fray.

He was fighting her brother.

Saewara's breathing stilled and her heart missed a beat. For a moment, she just watched, horrified, as the two kings slashed at each other. The blades of their swords were dark with blood. Both men were injured— Penda was bleeding profusely from a gash to his right cheek and Annan's left shoulder was slick with blood— yet they fought with savage determination as if the battle had just started and they had all the energy in the world.

Transfixed, Saewara stared down at Annan and Penda as they drew closer still to her hiding place.

They were both formidable swordsmen, but even to her untrained eye, Saewara could see her brother was better. No wonder Penda still worshipped the old gods; he wielded a sword like Thunor himself bent on destruction. He was a frightening and terrible sight—and yet Annan did not appear remotely cowed by him. Her husband's face was a black mask of determination and something Saewara had never seen in him before— hatred. Penda had given Annan reason to loathe him, and it was that which fueled Annan; forced him on even though Penda was slowly gaining the upper hand.

I have to stop this.

Saewara notched an arrow and raised her longbow.

I can't let Penda kill Annan. I won't let him.

But it will mean killing your own brother, her conscience needled her. *Can you live with yourself if you do?*

A moment later, the decision was made for her. Annan slipped on a patch of gore, and went down. Penda was on him in an instant, raising his sword to skewer his opponent.

Draw and loose.

The arrow flew through the air and landed with a meaty thud in Penda's flank.

The Mercian king roared, rearing back.

Saewara did not hesitate. She loosed another arrow, this one hitting her brother in the right shoulder. Penda staggered. He was right handed and the arrow had hit deep, for his sword fell from limp fingers on to the ground. His free hand clutched, uselessly, at the arrow embedded in his shoulder while his gimlet gaze frantically searched his surroundings, seeking the bowman who had wounded him.

Annan was scrambling to his feet when Penda's warriors surged forward and seized their king, heaving him back into the fold.

Giving a shout, Annan went to follow his enemy. However, four of his men threw themselves upon their king and hauled him away. Penda was badly injured—he would trouble them no longer. If Annan followed him, he would not emerge alive.

Saewara sunk back against the beech's trunk, her ash longbow slipping from her numb fingers. The energy that had fueled her till now suddenly seeped away and she felt barely able to move, let alone pay attention to what was happening on the forest floor below. She was trembling, violently; whether from relief or horror, she could not be certain.

The battle drew out for a while longer before the harsh sounds of iron against iron, and the cries and shouts of men, died away.

Eventually, Saewara forced herself to slide along the branch and part the foliage once more. She had to see who had gained the upper hand, even if she dreaded knowing.

Warily, she peeked out, steeling herself for what she would see. Her gaze settled upon the ravaged woodland below. Once a virgin, untouched spot, it was now gouged and ravaged by man. Bodies, twisted and maimed, littered the peaty ground. Survivors staggered amongst the dead, some injured and leaning against the trees for support. The only sound was the whimpers of the injured and dying.

Saewara craned forward, her eyes straining to recognize any of the faces. She only prayed that when she did, they were not Mercian.

Eventually, a man, tall and blond, wearing chainmail and covered in blood and dirt, limped into the clearing directly under Saewara's hiding place. There, he stopped and looked up into the trees.

She saw his face and her heart expanded with joy.

"Saewara," Annan called, his voice hoarse with exhaustion and pain.

"You can come out now, Love—it's safe, it's over. We've won."

Chapter Twenty-Seven

Things Unsaid

"IT WAS YOU, wasn't it?"

Saewara felt Annan's gaze upon her as she dropped from the beech's lowest branch onto the ground. "You loosed the arrows that brought Penda down."

Saewara turned to her husband, unsure whether to tell the truth. She wondered if doing so would anger him. After all, she had intervened in a fight to the death. She may have caused Annan to feel he had lost honor.

Yet, when her gaze met his, her trepidation vanished. He was looking at her with such a soft expression that it was all she could do not to burst into tears.

"Yes," she admitted. "I'm only sorry I did not kill him."

"Come here."

She stumbled forward into his arms, the stench of blood and death filling her nostrils. Only then did she let the tears come. His arms closed tightly around her and Saewara felt safe for the first time since the battle had begun. The floodgates opened and she sobbed against his chest as if her heart would break. She had seen so much violence and death today— enough to last many lifetimes.

"You were right," she sobbed, barely able to get the words out. "War is the province of men—women have no place on a battlefield."

"My wife," Annan murmured, his voice husky. "We won because of you."

Saewara pulled back, blinking at him through her tears. "What?" She hiccoughed. "How is that possible?"

Annan gave a lopsided smile and, reaching out, wiped the tears from her cheeks.

"Penda is the greatest warrior his people have ever known," he explained. "The Mercians have never lost a battle with him at the helm. You've seen him fight—you *know* why."

Saewara nodded, still not truly understanding.

"When you injured your brother and his men carted him off, the rest of his *fyrd* folded. The problem with having such a strong leader is that Penda carried his army. He was its backbone—its strength. With him no longer in charge, the Mercians scattered. It was not long before we beat them back, and those still wishing to live retreated."

Saewara shook her head, scarcely able to believe it. "You won because your army was strong, not because of me."

Annan's smile widened. "Believe what you will—but I and the others know the truth of it."

At that moment, Saewara realized that a huge crowd of bloodied, battered men now surrounded them.

Saewara's face broke into a wide smile when she saw that Aethelhere and Saba were among them. Unlike before the battle, the two warriors now gazed at Saewara with awestruck expressions.

"What a woman," Saba grinned before stepping forward and pulling Saewara into a bear hug. When Saba finally released her, after nearly cracking her ribs, Aethelhere stepped up to speak to the queen.

"I should never have doubted you," he told her, his blood-streaked face beaming. "You saved my brother's life and turned the battle in our favor. We owe you so much more than our lives, Saewara. We owe you our freedom."

Saewara stared back at him and felt fresh tears stream down her face. She then glanced at Annan who gave her another smile, although this one was tender, private. He put a protective arm around her shoulders and gently drew her against him. The warmth of his body against hers soaked into Saewara's body and gave her strength.

Holding his wife close, Annan turned to the amassing crowd of warriors—spearmen, axe-men, bowmen and swordsmen.

"Remember this day!" he called to them, raising his blood-stained sword aloft. "For this was the day we sent the Mercians home, whipped and beaten. This is the day a woman fought alongside her menfolk and triumphed. Now, we go home to our families and rejoice!"

It was late afternoon before the East Angles left the battleground. They left the Mercian dead behind—there were too many to bury or burn—and carried as many of their own dead as they could with them. It was a slow march back to Exning and they were forced to spend the night in the woodland before resuming their journey at first light.

Annan's fyrd reached Exning, just as the first rays of sun were peeking over the high paling fence. The village folk had been awaiting their return, and as soon as they were recognized as friend rather than foe, shouts rang through the air and a stream of villagers rushed out to greet the army.

Saewara watched the human tide approach and found herself smiling so wide that her face hurt. The joy in their faces, the tears running down their cheeks, reminded her that it had been all worth it. The thought of the Mercians taking this place was unthinkable. Yet she knew that if her brother had been victorious he would have burned Exning to the ground and have done unthinkable things to its inhabitants.

"Saba!" Hilda's cry reached Saewara's ears. She watched as her friend hurtled through the crowd, skirts flying, toward them. Hilda barreled into her husband's arms, nearly knocking Saba off his feet.

"Watch out little bird," he laughed as she threw her arms around his neck and showered his face with kisses. "I'm getting on in years—you'll stop my heart!"

In response Hilda—timid, reticent Hilda who had wilted under Saba's attention just a couple of months earlier—silenced her husband with a passionate kiss.

The crowd roared its approval. There was no more joyous sight than to see lovers reunited.

As they neared the gates of Exning, a tall, willowy blonde wove her way through the pressing crowd to the front. Dressed in a plain, beige, woolen tunic, Hereswith's beauty still shone like a single ear of golden barley in a ploughed field. For once, she was alone. Eldwyn, her forked-tongued maid, was nowhere in sight.

Hereswith's face was serious, her eyes huge and frightened as she scanned the approaching fyrd. She was searching for someone.

However, it was not Annan she was looking for. Her gaze slid over him without hesitation and fixed on the man who walked a few paces behind him: Aethelhere.

Saewara watched, intrigued, as Hereswith's blue eyes filled with tears. The knuckles of her hands that clutched her skirts were white. She was clearly afraid of approaching her husband, for they had not parted well.

Hereswith and Aethelhere stopped a couple of yards from each other and the crowd stilled, parting to give them room.

"Husband," Hereswith murmured; her voice for once was free of artifice.

"Wife," Aethelhere replied, his gaze coolly meeting hers.

Seeing that his response was less than warm, Hereswith swallowed and took another, tentative, step toward him. "I am glad to have you home," she said, her voice quavering with anxiety. "Are you hurt?"

Aethelhere looked at her quizzically, clearly trying to reconcile the woman who stood before him with the shrew he had left behind. "Nothing that will not heal," he replied, his tone more neutral than before.

Hereswith took another step toward him, her gaze never leaving his face. Even though hundreds of eyes were upon them, she did not seem to notice, or care.

"Aethelhere," she said, her voice low and urgent. "I know things were said before you left—things we can never take back—but after you had gone, I thought of you never returning. It felt as if my heart had been torn from my breast. I'm so glad you came back to me—please don't ever leave again."

Aethelhere stared at her, his eyes widening. Yet, when he did not respond to her plea, Hereswith's gaze dropped to her feet and she covered her face with her hands. Her body trembled with the effort she was making not to cry.

The crowd watched, entranced, as Aethelhere stepped toward his wife, closing the gap between them.

"Hereswith," he said, gently taking hold of her wrists and pulling them away from her face. "Look at me."

She did, and for a moment the pair of them just stared at each other—as if they were truly seeing the person before them for the first time.

"I wanted you from the moment you arrived at Rendlaesham," he murmured, his expression suddenly vulnerable, "but do you really want me?"

"Yes," Hereswith whispered.

That was enough. His eyes shining with tears, Aethelhere pulled her into his arms and kissed her deeply for all the world to see.

Blessed with yet another happy reunion, the folk of Exning roared their approval once more.

Saewara brushed away a tear that had escaped, and turned to Annan, only to find her husband watching her closely.

"You would cry over Hereswith?" he asked, amused. "She would have had you strung up outside the gates without hesitation upon your arrival in Rendlaesham."

"I know she would have," Saewara replied with a wry smile, blinking away more tears. "And I would have cheerfully drowned her in a water barrel—but times change. People change."

"Yes they do, wise Saewara." He smiled down at her without a trace of mockery before reaching out to caress her cheek. "You and I are proof of that, are we not?"

Epilogue

The Baptism

One year later ...

A HOT, LATE summer's day drew to a close, casting long shadows across the grasslands outside Exning. The sun slid toward the western horizon, the last rays glinting on the glistening surface of a large pool, surrounded by draping willows.

A man, a woman and a monk stood at the edge of the pool.

The man was tall and blond, and appeared regal in a black tunic and breeches with a fine fur cloak hanging from his broad shoulders; and the woman was small and curvaceous with a mane of dark hair and eyes the color of a thundercloud. In her arms, the woman carried a babe. The infant was barely older than a moon's cycle but with a shock of dark hair like her mother's. Tiny fingers clasped at the warm air, and eyes that were already showing signs of being deep-blue, like her father's, stared up at the sky.

A monk dressed in a rough, homespun tunic, stepped close to the couple. He was a middle-aged man with a kind face and work-worn hands. Not far from the edge of the pool, hidden behind the bright green of the willows, was a low-slung thatched hall where this monk and his companions lived and worked the small gardens around it.

This pool was known by those who lived locally as St Mindred's Well—and it was here that the King and Queen of the East Angles had brought their daughter to be baptized.

Saewara smiled at the monk—Swidhelm was his name—and gently handed her daughter to him. Aethelthryth made a faint mewling sound in protest at being parted from her mother but soon quietened in the monk's gentle embrace. Under the king and queen's watchful gazes, Swidhelm brought the infant girl to the edge of the pool, where he knelt and dipped his hand into the water. The waters of St Mindred's Well were warm this evening, after a sweltering day that had kept most folk inside. As such, the baby did not squall when the monk dripped water onto her forehead.

Saewara looked on as Swidhelm murmured the words of the baptism in Latin over her daughter. When the monk had finished, he handed Aethelthryth back to her mother with a smile.

"It is done—may the Lord bless you all."

Saewara looked at her husband, and he met her gaze steadily.

"Is that it?" Annan asked, incredulous. "If I'd known a baptism took such little time and fuss, I'd have agreed to it earlier."

Saewara gave Annan a quelling look and fell into step with him as they walked away from the pool.

"Come—a feast awaits back in Exning." Annan put an arm around his wife's shoulder. "The folk have got a boar roasting on a spit. Let's join them."

They walked across the golden fields, through the softly whispering grass, enjoying the balmy evening and the rare moment alone. Saewara took a deep breath of the warm air, laced with the scent of dry grass and warm earth, and felt a sense of well-being steal over her. Above her, the wide East Anglian sky, now decorated with lilac and pink ribbons, stretched for eternity. It was a beautiful, peaceful country. She had grown to love living in Exning. Life was gentle here; the folk welcoming and kind.

Still walking at Annan's side, she voiced her thoughts to him.

"Can't we stay on here? Do we really have to go back to Rendlaesham?"

Annan smiled at her questions—it was not the first time he had heard them over the past days. Ever since he had announced that they would have to return to Rendlaesham at Winterfylleth—the period of the year when autumn slipped into winter—she had tried to convince him otherwise.

"I know you don't have fond memories of Rendlaesham," Annan told her, "but you'll see that this time it will be different. The people will accept you now. I am king, and my place is there. Our victory against the Mercians has bought us additional time at Exning, but if I stay away any longer, the people will start to feel their king is not doing his duty. To rule a kingdom requires sacrifice, Saewara—but it's a small price to pay. There are worse places than Rendlaesham. Don't worry, we shall return to Exning next summer."

"I know," Saewara replied, meeting his gaze. "It's just that we have been so happy here. I know it is my past speaking, but I worry that our happiness is fragile, and that the moment we leave, things will change."

Saewaera watched Annan frown. Her words had cast a shadow over the balmy evening. She had not wished them to; but these worries had plagued her for days and she had not shared them. She wondered if she had done the right thing in doing so now.

"Saewara." Annan halted, forcing her to do the same. "Do you really think what we have will not last?"

Saewara flushed at his implication. "I don't doubt our love, of course not. We have gone through too much to reach this point for me ever to doubt that. No, I doubt forces beyond our control. My brother still lives, and while he draws breath you and I will never be truly safe."

Annan returned her gaze, although the fact that he had not instantly denied her fears only made anxiety curl in the pit of Saewara's belly.

"We can't let Penda cast a shadow over what we have," Annan said quietly. "If we do that then he has won. There may come a day when I meet him again in battle—but we can't live in dread of that day. He has gone quiet for the moment, licking his wounds and rebuilding his strength. For now, the Kingdom of the East Angles is safe, and will prosper. We have many things to look forward to, Saewara. Let's not let Penda ruin our happiness."

Tears stung Saewara's eyes as she listened to her husband. "I know you speak the truth," she replied quietly. She was sorry now that she had brought this subject up, for although Annan had done his best to assuage her fears, he had not denied them. It had been foolish to expect him to—the threat was still there. It always would be.

They walked on, and soon Exning's paling fence bristled against the sunset.

"Battle, death, honor and vengeance," Annan spoke once more, his tone subdued. "They are a part of our world. I'm a king and I cannot escape the fact that they affect me more than most. I knew this when I was crowned. I never wanted the responsibility, especially given the pledge I made to your brother. I wanted it even less when he forced me to marry you."

His words hung between them for a moment before he continued. "Yet all that has changed. Penda unwittingly gave me one of life's greatest gifts. He meant to break me, but instead he made me stronger. Now that I am happy—now that I have you by my side—I need not fear what comes. This peace may not last, but while it does I intend to enjoy it."

His gaze met Saewara's then and he smiled—a warm, carefree smile—as if sharing these thoughts with her had freed him of any nagging worry and doubt. He was strong; she had seen that in him from the first. It was more than just a warrior's strength—the courage to meet your enemy in battle and stare him in the eye—but a quieter, deeper strength that comes from making peace with who you are. Annan knew exactly who he was—the good and the bad.

"You speak true again," she smiled back, a little of her own tension easing. "You always do."

"Music to mine ears," he laughed. "Let me remind you of that next time I enrage you."

"You make me sound like a harpy!" She playfully punched him on the arm, causing Aethelthryth to squawk in protest.

Their gazes met then, and held. Saewara felt her breathing still when she saw her own hunger reflected in his gaze. Since Aethelthryth's birth, Annan had stayed from her bed; the birth had been difficult and he had been afraid of hurting her. However, the time apart was weighing upon them both.

I am fortunate, she thought. *I have a husband and a child; I love and am loved in return. I am no longer alone in the world—I no longer rail against my lot.*

Things could have turned out very differently. It had been a surprise to find herself pregnant with Aethelthryth—for she had thought herself barren. Her pregnancy had been an unexpected joy; she hoped there would be others.

"Tonight, you will come to my bed?" she asked, blushing at her own directness.

"Is it not still too early?" he asked, hope flaring in his eyes.

Saewara shook her head. "I have missed you."

A grin spread across Annan's face then and he put an arm around her shoulders, once more, as they crossed last stretch of grass to Exning's gates. "Then tonight I will have to give you the attention you deserve," he replied, injecting a sultry undertone into every word. His smile was private and wicked, making promises for later.

Saewara smiled back, excitement fluttering at the base of her stomach.

Annan is right. Saewara's fears melted away into the recesses of her mind. Worrying about the future was as pointless as trying to hold back the tide. Who knew how much time any of them had? All she knew was that at this moment, there was no happier, or luckier, woman alive.

The End

Historical Note

As with the previous two books of the Kingdom of the East Angles Saga, *The Deepening Night* is based on actual historical figures and events.

Annan of the East Angles did rule from around 636—653 AD (although his real name was Anna – which I had to alter slightly for my readers' benefit). I have taken some 'author's license' with the dates. Since this story takes place in 630 AD, I have shifted Annan's time line slightly.

The conflict between the Kingdoms of the East Angles and Mercia was very real in this period. I have used some historical events, and shifted others to suit the story. It was Annan's brother, Aethelhere, who actually 'bent the knee' to the warmongering Mercian king, Penda—and, in fact, Aethelhere died at the Mercian King's side in the Battle of the Winwæd, in circa 655 AD.

Regarding this story's heroine, there is some historical reference to Annan having a 'consort' named Saewara—although some references mention a woman named Hereswith as his possible wife. On further inspection, it appears that Hereswith was, in fact, married to one of Annan's brothers. For the purposes of this tale, I decided that Aethelhere would be the lucky man! My initial research into Annan's family tree was what gave me the idea for this novel's 'love triangle'.

The last half of the novel is centered on Devil's Dyke; a ditch and bank defense, which the East Angles built to defend their kingdom from the Mercians. Set in the heart of rural Cambridgeshire, Devil's Dyke is often described as Britain's finest Anglo-Saxon earthwork of its kind—and it's certainly one of the best surviving. There are historical records of King Anna of the East Angles, spending time in Exning, possibly overseeing work on the dyke.

The ancient monument stretches for seven and a half miles, and reaches 10m (33ft) in height. The dyke is made up of a defensive earth bank and ditch, originally built to control access from the nearby Roman roads, including the Icknield Way.

A number of excavation projects have been carried out, but still little is known about its creators. Archaeologists place its construction in the fifth or sixth century AD—although for the purposes of this story, I set the completion a little later. Another change, on my part, was the use of the name 'Devil's Dyke'. This name is believed to be a post-medieval one, with references to 'Reach Dyke' documented during William the Conqueror's siege of Ely in the 11th century.

And, just in case you're wondering—historical records state that Annan and Saewara had four children: Jurmin, Seaxburh, Aethelthryth and Aethelburh. It's not known when Saewara died, but Annan, and his son Jurmin, both met their ends in 653 AD at the Battle of Bulcamp, on the Blythburgh marshland in Suffolk. Here, the East Angles fought, and lost against Penda and the Mercians—their old foes. Annan would have been nearing sixty years of age by the time he died in battle, whereas his son would, tragically, have just reached warrior age. Annan's death marked the end of the golden age of the Kingdom of the East Angles; from this point on it would be overshadowed by its powerful neighbor, Mercia.

Night Shadows

A Novella

JAYNE CASTEL

***

For all the romantics in the world – for those who believe in second chances.

***

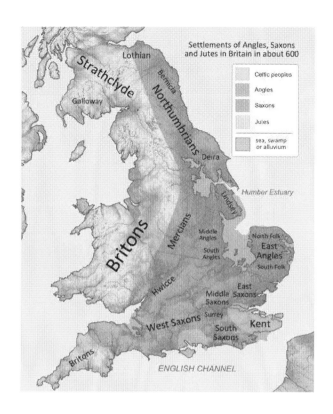

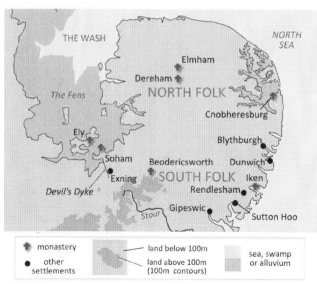

Here is my secret. It is very simple:
It is only with the heart that one can see rightly;
what is essential is invisible to the eye.
—Antoine de Saint Exupéry

Prologue

The Proposal

The village of Went, the Kingdom of the East Angles – Britannia

Spring 609 AD

THE SQUEALS OF children playing in the dirt in front of the hall echoed through the warm air. A glorious spring day was coming to a close. The sun cast a honeyed light across the village of Went, staining the timber and thatch of the surrounding houses a deep gold. The children—three boys and a girl—raced each other excitedly around the wide space in the center of the village, shouting with delight.

Cynewyn paused from scattering grain for the geese that clustered at her feet and watched the children with a smile, enjoying their enthusiasm and joy. Not so long ago, she had been one of those children; now she had left that carefree life behind.

Cynewyn stood before her father's hall, lingering at her task. She glanced up at the wide amber-streaked sky. The sun was a balm on her skin after weeks of rain and cold. Emptying her pot of grain, Cynewyn was about to retreat inside, when she spied a well-built young man with short, light-brown hair striding across the yard toward her. His face was set with purpose.

Wilfrid was of the same age as her—eighteen winters—and he was staring at Cynewyn with unnerving intensity. Other men laughed and flirted, but not Wilfrid. He took everything, including himself, seriously. He appeared to be making directly for her, and Cynewyn had little choice but to await his arrival.

Judging from the intensity of his gaze, the tense set of his shoulders, and the resolute determination of his stride—Wilfrid of Went was preparing himself for a confrontation.

"Good evening, Cynewyn," he greeted her. His voice, a low rumble for a man of his age, always took Cynewyn by surprise. She had never heard him raise his voice, and when he spoke, it was always with unwavering purpose. Unlike the men in her family, who were garrulous and loud, Wilfrid used words sparingly.

"Evening, Wil," she replied pleasantly, meeting his stare. She noticed that his hazel eyes looked almost green in this light. "It's a while since I saw you last."

"I've been away," Wilfrid answered, his gaze becoming even more penetrating.

Cynewyn felt her body grow hot and uncomfortable under his stare. He looked at her like he was about to devour her; the hunger in his eyes made Cynewyn flush. She stepped back from him and gave a flirtatious smile in an attempt to lighten the mood between them.

"Away? Where?"

"On the border—our neighbors are making trouble again," he replied, before glancing down at the ground, his face awkward. "I missed you."

Cynewyn hid her embarrassment with another smile. She was not sure how she expected her to respond. She had not missed him at all. Why would she? Still, his infatuation made her feel beautiful and desirable, and she found herself enjoying the attention.

"How gallant of you." She returned his gaze through her lashes, noticing the way his eyes travelled from her eyes down to her mouth. "Why did you miss me?"

Wilfrid reddened slightly at the question. He was obviously not used to flirting, and was unsure how to respond.

"I missed seeing you," he eventually managed. Then, he blurted. "I want to ask your father's permission for us to wed. If he says 'yes', will you marry me, Cynewyn?"

She stared back at him, taken aback by the proposal. He really was no fun at all. She had been enjoying the attention until he ruined things.

In truth, she had no interest in Wilfrid. Not only was he of a low rank, but he was too quiet, intense and humorless for her tastes. He always wore an expression as if he bore the weight of the world upon his shoulders. Besides, Cynewyn had already been promised to Aldwulf, the charismatic son of an ealdorman who lived in the neighboring village. Blond, handsome and charming, Aldwulf never failed to make her laugh. She had been delighted when her father suggested the match.

Silence stretched between Cynewyn and Wil, before he stepped closer still and gently took her hand. It was the first time he had ever touched her. His hand was warm, dry and strong. The sensation of their skin touching gave Cynewyn a jolt in the pit of her belly—it was an oddly stirring sensation. Nonetheless, Cynewyn had to resist the urge to jerk her hand from his.

"Will you?" he repeated.

Cynewyn gave Wil a sweet smile and extracted her hand from his. She took two steps back, almost treading on a goose in her haste. The bird gave an enraged hiss and flapped at her.

"You will have to ask my father," she replied, lowering her eyes demurely, for she knew exactly what her father's response would be. "If he agrees, I will marry you."

Wilfrid smiled. The expression transformed his face, making him look handsome.

"I will ask him then," he told her, his discomfort dissolving. "I will do it now."

Without another word, Wilfrid turned and strode into her father's hall.

Cynewyn watched him go, incredulous. The man's presumption stunned her. He was low-born. Did he really think he could wed an ealdorman's daughter? How could he have mistaken her light-hearted flirting for real interest?

Picking up her skirts, for she did not wish to miss a moment of what was about to unfold under her father's roof, Cynewyn followed her suitor inside.

Eomer of Went was sitting at a long table with his men. He was playing *Hnefatafl*, 'King's Table'; a game where two players moved wooden pieces across a board with twenty-six squares in an attempt to capture the king of the opposing player. He was exchanging good-natured threats with the warrior playing him, when Cynewyn entered the hall at Wilfrid's heels.

Skirting the shadows, Cynewyn made her way over to where her mother was sitting near the fire pit, weaving a tapestry at a huge loom. Silently, Cynewyn took a seat beside her and picked up her distaff. She then resumed the task she had spent the afternoon at before escaping outside to feed the geese and enjoy the sunset—winding wool onto the wooden spindle.

"Wilfrid!" Eomer boomed, his gaze resting on the young man who had stopped before the table. "Fancy a game, eh?"

"M'lord," Wilfrid began. His voice cracked slightly, betraying his nerves. "No, this evening. I have come to ask your permission."

Eomer of Went inclined his head, his blond eyebrows raising. "For what, lad?"

The hall went still; all gazes fastening on Wilfrid. Suddenly, Cynewyn felt an unexpected pang of pity for the youth. He might be arrogant, but she did not envy him his impending humiliation.

"I wish to wed your daughter."

Wilfrid's voice, although quiet, echoed in the shocked silence. Cynewyn stared at her father and felt a brief surge of panic at the blank expression she saw there.

What if he agreed? She had not paused to consider that possibility.

A moment passed and then Eomer's face creased into a smile, a pitying one. Relief flooded through Cynewyn and she breathed once more.

"You would not be the first lad who has taken a shine to my comely daughter," he said, shaking his head. "Yet she is promised to another. Did she not tell you?"

The look on Wilfrid's face caused some of the other warriors present to snigger.

"Who?" Wilfrid finally managed when he had recovered from the shock.

"Aldwulf of Blackhill," Eomer replied, giving Wilfrid a patronizing smile. "He's an ealdorman's son—you're a free man with a spear like your father before you. I can't wed my only daughter to a man of such a low rank. You understand?"

"No," Wilfrid answered, his voice flat and harsh, "I don't." His gaze shifted to Cynewyn. Their gazes met and for an instant, Cynewyn saw his naked anger and humiliation.

You knew, that gaze accused her. *You knew and didn't warn me.*

"I may not be high-born." Wilfrid turned his attention back to the ealdorman. "But I am one of your warriors. I have served you loyally and will continue to do so. I would protect your daughter with my life."

Eomer roared with laughter at that. His warriors joined him, and the sound echoed mockingly through the hall.

"I'm sure you would." Eomer straightened up, still holding his belly, although his tone held a warning that he was tiring of this conversation. "But the answer still is no. You are not worthy of her."

Wilfrid's breath hissed between his clenched teeth. His face was flushed and his eyes glittered with rage.

"I'm as worthy of her as any man!" he snarled.

"Careful, lad," the ealdorman warned, the amusement draining from his face. "You're over-stepping the mark. Now, off you go. Let me get back to my game."

"If I'm not worthy of Cynewyn, then I'm not worthy to serve you!" Wilfrid replied, not moving.

A deathly hush settled over the hall. All gazes were upon Wilfrid as the young man removed the two bronze arm rings he wore on his right bicep and hurled them to the rush-matting at his feet. They were rings that the ealdorman had gifted him for his loyalty and valor.

"As you reminded me—I am a free man," Wilfrid ground out. Eomer stared back at him, momentarily struck speechless. "I serve whom I choose. From this moment on, I no longer follow you."

With that, Wilfrid turned and, not sparing another glance in Cynewyn's direction, stalked from the hall and out of their lives.

Chapter One

The Thaw

The Village of Went, the Kingdom of the East Angles

Ten years later . . .

WILFRED RODE INTO the ruins of Went and felt his stomach twist. Shock and unexpected grief hit him like a falling axe.

What in the name of Woden has happened here?

He rode in the midst of a group of forty warriors. After three days travel through biting cold and melting snow, they had emerged from the thick woodland that created a natural border between the kingdom of the East Angles and that of the East Saxons. Until now, a long, bitter winter had made travel impossible. As soon as the thaw came, the king had sent them to patrol the southern borders, where there had been rumors of problems with the East Saxons before Yule. The company approached the village, expecting to see its high paling fence bristling against the sky, with spear-wielding warriors before the gate.

Instead, Went no longer existed.

They passed, single-file, through the remains of the charred gates and what had once been a tall fence. Only fragments remained, the rest was little more than a dark line in the cold earth.

Bracing himself for what was to come, Wil bent his head against the chill wind that whistled through Went. Even if he had been unhappy here, and never felt the urge to return, he could not bear to see the village where he had been born reduced to ruins.

Wil heard some of the men around him utter curses as they gazed around at the village. It looked as if *Nithhogg* himself—the great beast of the underworld—had laid waste to it. Scorched palings stood out against a pale sky and the rest of it was little more than a collection of blackened, twisted remnants.

The warriors rode through Went, their gazes scouring the devastation. At the center of the village stood the skeleton of the ealdorman's hall, and next to it was the remains of a huge funeral pyre. A few of the warriors dismounted here, and started searching the ruins. One of them was Heolstor, their leader. A tall, balding man, his face was thunderous as he circuited the pyre. Like his companions, he was at a loss for words.

"Look who I found skulking in the shadows." One of the warriors emerged from behind the ruins of the ealdorman's hall. He hauled two emaciated figures after him—both lads barely ten winters old. The boys were plainly petrified, their eyes huge on thin faces. They struggled weakly as the man dragged them before Heolstor.

"Scavengers, eh?" Heolstor fixed the lads in a hard gaze.

"Please, M'lord," one of the boys gasped. "We weren't scavenging—I promise. We're from Blackhill."

The boy who had not yet spoken started to snivel, only to receive a quelling look from his companion.

Heolstor continued to stare at them. "Blackhill? You're far from home, boy," he replied. "Tell me what happened here."

"It was the East Saxons," the first boy spoke up once more. "They came just after Yule, not long before the snows. They slaughtered everyone."

The lad's voice died away as the warriors surrounding him burst into mutters of outrage. His courage bolstered, the boy continued.

"Folk from our village discovered them, days later. There were signs of a great battle. We built a pyre and burned the dead."

Heolstor's face was a hard mask as he listened to the end of the lad's tale. His gaze swept around the charred remnants of Went. "Those dogs will pay for this."

Rumbles of assent echoed around him, although Wil remained silent. His mind and senses were still reeling at what he had just heard.

"And your village?" Heolstor turned back to the lads. "Was Blackhill attacked?"

Both boys shook their heads, although the grief that flared in their gazes was impossible to miss.

"Blackhill still stands," the first lad replied. "But it is full of women, the sick, and those who are too old, or young, to fight—there are few men left. The ealdorman and his warriors are all dead."

"Dead?"

"After the East Saxons slaughtered the folk of Went, Aldwulf, the ealdorman of our village, vowed vengeance. He took his men and went out hunting for them. The snow was falling thick, yet they went anyway. They met an East Saxon war band, but they were outnumbered . . ." the boy broke off here, visibly struggling to control the grief that welled within him. Beside him, his companion was weeping openly. "Our father was among them."

Watching the boys, who were obviously brothers, Wil felt his earlier grief resurface. Once more, the intensity of it surprised him. He had often thought of Went, and all its memories, as another life.

"Wil." The warrior next to him, a man of Wil's age with long, dark hair and a thick beard to match, roused him from his thoughts. "You didn't have kin still here, did you?"

Wil looked up and met his friend's concerned gaze. Aelin was one of the few in the king's hall that Wil had truly befriended, for he trusted few.

"My parents both died a few years before I left," he replied with a shake of his head. "There was no one left I'd grieve for."

The king's men took the lads with them and left the ashes of Went behind. The subdued company of warriors rode out onto a wide meadow. Clumps of dirty snow covered the ground in parts, although it was melting fast.

Wil glanced up at the pale sun; it was still high in the sky. However, they had a good distance to cover before reaching Blackhill. The boys had, indeed, traveled far from home—unwise with East Saxon war bands on the move.

The light was beginning to dim—the shadows lengthening—when the horsemen eventually clattered over the bridge leading to Blackhill. The cruel wind had dropped, although the cold was still biting. Grateful for his thick fur cloak that he had pulled up around his ears, Wil gazed up at the wooded hill before them and the outline of a tall paling fence at its summit.

Blackhill.

Wil felt his stomach twist once more—not in grief—but in dread for who he might see in the village of Blackhill.

A woman he had spent a decade trying to forget.

She might never have married Aldwulf of Blackhill.

She might be dead.

They might have left this place.

Many thoughts tumbled through Wil's mind as he followed the column of riders up the narrow road leading to the village gates. The shock at seeing Went destroyed had distracted him from his memories.

Ten years is too long, Wil told himself, angered that after all this time thoughts of her still affected him. *You need to let this go.* And yet, he had never been able to. He had wanted Cynewyn since the beginning of his thirteenth winter—he had ached for her. She had never returned the sentiment, not even minimally. Her rejection, and his humiliation before her father, still stung. He had never been able to heal that scar. Some wounds cut too deep.

Pushing his thoughts aside, Wil focused his attention on the huge wooden gates looming before them.

It's time, he thought grimly, *to face your past.*

"Cynewyn." A woman's voice echoed across the hall. "There are men here— the king's men."

Cynewyn looked up from her sewing to see Mildthryth, her mother-in-law, walking toward her. Mildthryth was a small woman, like Cynewyn, with thick blonde hair, threaded with grey. The events of the last few months might have broken a weaker woman—but not Mildthryth. Her blue eyes, although hollow with grief, were resolute.

Cynewyn had always liked her mother-in-law. She wished her husband could have inherited some of his mother's strength. Instead, Aldwulf had taken after his father; a pleasure-seeking man with a lazy streak.

"Really?" Cynewyn gave her mother-in-law a quizzical look before laying aside her sewing and rising to her feet. "Did someone send word?"

Mildthryth shook her head. "Not that I know of."

"Well, let us see what brings them to Blackhill."

Together, the two women walked across the rush-matting floor to the doors. This hall had once been dominated by men; the low timbre of male voices echoing amongst the rafters. Now, only women filled the space—frightened women with pinched faces and haunted eyes.

It had been a bitter winter, in more ways than one. The weather had been the coldest in years; a vicious wind had howled in from the north, bringing hail and snow storms that covered the world in a thick, white blanket. Even now, with the first signs of spring appearing —bright green shoots pushing up through the damp earth—the warmth of summer was a distant memory. The heavy snow, which had made travel near to impossible, had been a blessing as well as a curse. It had prevented the East Saxons from destroying Blackhill, like they had Went.

Cynewyn stepped outside and pulled the fur cloak she wore close about her. Even though the blustery wind had died, the air had teeth to it. However, her attention was immediately distracted from the cold by the sight of over two dozen men filling the clearing in the center of the village.

Men. Their voices sounded loud and rough after long weeks of only women, children and elderly for company. Dressed in leather armor, with lime-wood shields hanging from their backs, and shields and axes at their sides, they were a forbidding sight. The warriors dismounted from their horses, many of them looking about with interest.

Two boys dismounted with the warriors. Cynewyn recognized them instantly. Beorn and Rodor had run off after an argument with their mother two days earlier and had not been seen since. Judging from their taut, white faces and frightened eyes, the lads had not enjoyed their time away from Blackhill. They ran to where their mother emerged from a low, wattle and daub dwelling. Ealhwyn's face, work-worn and haggard, sagged in relief as she pulled her sons into a fierce embrace.

Cynewyn walked forward to greet the newcomers. The other villagers fell in behind her, silently acknowledging Aldwulf's widow as their leader.

One of the warriors, a tall, balding man with a short blond beard, approached Cynewyn.

"Are you the mistress of Blackhill?"

"Yes—what's left of it," Cynewyn replied. "Aldwulf of Blackhill was my husband. Eomer of Went was my father."

"I am Heolstor," he told her. "I lead the king's men. We have just come from Went."

Cynewyn nodded; a chill went through her at the flatness of his tone. She knew what had greeted him at Went, for she had seen it herself. She would never forget the sight of the shell of her father's hall, or seeing his charred corpse lying over that of her mother. Eomer of Went had died trying to save his wife.

Blinking back tears, Cynewyn looked away from Heolstor. Instead, her gaze scanned the amassing crowd of men.

"You are very welcome," she said huskily. "The East Saxons could attack at any time."

Heolstor did not reply. When Cynewyn glanced back at him, she saw that he was frowning.

"It is not safe here, Milady," he told her flatly. "We cannot let you remain at Blackhill."

Cynewyn went still. "*Hwaet?*"

"You have lost nearly all your menfolk." Heolstor's frown deepened at her sharp tone. "We cannot remain here to protect you from the East Saxons."

Cynewyn felt her body grow cold. "This is our home—we can't leave it."

"You must," Heolstor replied flatly.

"*Nithhogg* take you!" Cynewyn snarled. "This land has been in our families for generations. The East Saxons have burned our villages and terrified our folk for too long—we cannot just walk away!"

"Watch your tongue, woman," Heolstor growled. "I did not travel here to argue with a fishwife. Insult me again and I will knock you down."

Cynewyn glared back at the warrior, her hands balling into fists.

This was the last straw. Bitterness threatened to overwhelm her, as years of unhappiness and frustration surged to the fore. It was only Mildthryth's hand on her arm, firm and cautioning, that made her keep her rage in check.

"We will stay here overnight," Heolstor informed her. "Tomorrow morning, the remaining villagers will pack up what they can carry and we will escort you back to Rendlaesham."

"But what shall we do there?" Mildthryth spoke up then. Her voice was calm, but Cynewyn could hear the core of iron just beneath. Like her, Mildthryth was furious. "We have no property, no land."

"You must take it up with the king," Heolstor replied, glancing around as if he could not wait to rid himself of these irksome women and their questions. "He may compensate you for your losses."

"Some losses cannot be compensated for," Mildthryth countered, her eyes narrowing into angry slits. "You cannot bring back our dead."

"Enough," the warrior growled, his patience snapping. "We have travelled long in cold weather, and are weary and in need of food and a warm fire. Your prattle can wait till later."

With that, Heolstor turned and shouted orders to his men. "Aelin, Wilfrid—start bringing in our supplies—the rest of you see to the horses."

Two men, who had just dismounted, nodded brusquely. One of them, with a shaggy beard obscuring his face, turned and started unstrapping saddlebags to bring inside. However, his companion paused a moment, his gaze riveted upon Cynewyn.

Cynewyn returned his stare, irritated by his unwavering attention, before freezing.

She knew that face.

It had been a decade; years that had turned Wilfrid of Went from a surly youth into an intimidating man. He was more muscular than she remembered, and his shoulders were broader. However, she recognized his face, clean shaven and serious; his light brown-hair still cut close to his scalp. His hazel-eyed stare was as intense as ever, although he did not look at her as he once had.

Ten years later, there was no youthful longing in his gaze.

"*Wes hāl,* Cynewyn," he greeted her brusquely, his voice as deep and low as she remembered. Then, as if suddenly aware that he had been staring, he tore his gaze from her face and moved to do as he had been bid.

Chapter Two

An Awkward Reunion

WIL TURNED AWAY and strode over to where Aelin was hoisting saddlebags over his shoulder, in preparation for carrying them inside.

Damn her. She was even more beautiful than he remembered. Enraged and facing Heolstor, she had been mesmerizing. The past decade had turned her from a pretty girl into a stunning woman. She was small with lush curves, creamy skin, and a mane of light-brown hair—the same color as his. Her eyes—he had never forgotten them—were a deep sea-blue. Even swathed in furs, her face pinched with cold and anger, Cynewyn made his pulse race.

Wil inwardly cursed her once more. He had hardened himself for this moment, and had found himself praying to Woden for the strength to hate her. Yet, one look into those eyes and he was lost.

That woman makes you weak, he told himself as he slung a sack over his shoulder. *Because of her you have never been able to love another. You were nothing to her. She knew she was promised to another and she let you humiliate yourself before her father. She thought you a fool—a low-born spearman who deserved nothing better. You should hate her.*

Wil carried the sack across to the hall, passing Cynewyn and the other folk remaining in Blackhill, who had come out to greet the king's men. Cynewyn refused to meet his eye as he passed her. She held her chin high, her gaze looking through him.

Bitterness filled Wil's mouth like gall. Even now, years later, she still thought she was better than him.

The fire pit glowed in the center of the hall, shedding its warmth over the men and women seated at the long tables either side of it. Yet, this was no celebratory feast, and the mood this eve was subdued. The meal was pottage, made from cabbage, onion, and turnip, served with griddle bread and some hard cheese that the king's men had brought with them.

At the end of one of the long tables, taking her late husband's place—for there was no male kin left to lead the village—Cynewyn took a sip of watered-down ale from her wooden cup. Her anger simmered, overriding the grief and desperation at losing her kin and husband in just one winter.

How dare this Heolstor drag them away from Blackhill, leaving her people's land to the East Saxons—those whoresons had turned the last few years into a nightmare. Went and Blackhill needed vengeance, not a retreat.

This will not end here, she vowed before taking a mouthful of pottage. *I will petition the king when we arrive at Rendlaesham. He will return us to our land.*

"This pottage is foul." Heolstor, sitting to Cynewyn's left, pushed away his bowl with a grimace of disgust. "Are you trying to poison us woman?"

Cynewyn's simmering anger began to boil. This man was almost as offensive as the decision he had made on their behalf.

She caught Mildthryth's gaze to her right, and the older woman rolled her eyes. Heolstor had the manners of a goat.

"Turnips and cabbages are all we have," Cynewyn told him coldly. "It has been a long winter. We have little food left."

Heolstor grunted at this and took a draught from his cup.

Further down the table, Cynewyn was aware of Wilfrid's stony presence. He said nothing and avoided looking in her direction. Still, she was aware of him all the same.

He hasn't changed. Still as taciturn and arrogant as ever.

Still, there was a part of Cynewyn that had wondered over the years— and wondered now—what her life would have been like if she had married Wilfrid instead of Aldwulf.

Aldwulf.

Her husband had died in agony, with a deep wound to the stomach; a terrible death. No man—not even a drunkard who preferred drowning himself in a barrel of mead every evening rather than making love to his wife—deserved that.

Poor Aldwulf. This was not the life you wanted.

He had become an ealdorman only a year after they had married, after his father broke his neck while out hunting. Soon after that, their problems with the East Saxons intensified. Both Went and Blackhill sat close to the border, on land that the East Saxons had long claimed as theirs. Eomer of Went and Aldwulf of Blackhill had done their best to protect the villages. They erected perimeter fences and had men watch the walls, day and night, yet it had not kept their enemy at bay. However, neither of the ealdormen had thought that East Saxons would attack the villages outright. How wrong they had both been.

Cynewyn looked down at her bowl of pottage and blinked back tears.

This was not the life she had wanted either. Her parents dead, two still-born babes and a mead-soaked husband who had ignored her. At twenty-eight winters, she felt old beyond her years.

Taking a deep breath, Cynewyn squared her shoulders and reached for a piece of griddle bread. Still, she mused, her gaze flicking across to Wilfrid once more—his face an inscrutable mask—marriage to a humorless oaf might have been even worse.

Once the evening meal had finished, the women cleared away the wooden cups and dishes, while the men made themselves comfortable by the fire.

Although she was used to men doing as they pleased, and clearing up after them, Cynewyn felt a stab of annoyance at tidying up after Heolstor and his men. They were not her kin and were unwelcome in Blackhill. She resented their presence under her roof.

Mildthryth washed the wooden plates, bowls, and clay cups in a great tub of hot water; while Cynewyn wiped down the tables with a damp cloth. Around them, the king's men made themselves comfortable. Some sat down on their fur cloaks before the fire pit while others remained at the tables. A group of them at one of the tables was playing a riddle game. Cynewyn caught the end of one of the riddles.

"The scars from sword wounds gape wider and wider," the man finished with a flourish. *"Death blows are dealt me by day and by night."*

The warriors scratched their heads and attempted to decipher it. Despite herself, Cynewyn gave a small smile. She knew that riddle; it had been one of her father's favorites. However, it appeared to have stumped these men.

The man who had recited the riddle folded his arms over his chest. "I knew you wouldn't find this one so easy." He grinned, victorious.

Eventually, one of warriors—a young man with a sharp-featured face— called out.

"It's a shield."

A roar went up at that, for the riddle had been a clever one, and had whet their appetites for more.

Half listening, as another warrior tried his luck, Cynewyn passed by where Wilfrid sat quietly conversing with his bearded friend; the one Heolstor had named Aelin. The men were deep in discussion and had not been paying attention to the riddle game. They broke off their conversation and glanced her way as she stopped before them.

"Thank you for your hospitality, Lady Cynewyn." Aelin smiled at her, genuine warmth in his eyes. "I know it matters not, but I am sorry for all of this. It's not right to be forced to abandon your home."

Cynewyn found herself smiling back, although the expression felt strange on her face. How long was it since she had smiled or laughed?

"I thank you," she murmured, deliberately keeping her gaze away from Wilfrid, who she could feel looking at her. "It has been a cruel year."

"Did none of your kin escape Went?" Wilfrid asked, his voice gentle.

Cynewyn shook her head, fighting sudden tears. She could not look at him. Just Wil's presence here reminded her of another world; another life. She had grown up protected by a loving family, believing that life was fair and good, and that she would marry a man who would cherish and love her, as her father had loved her mother. The reality of life, however, was injustice, neglect, loss, and disappointment. She was not the same girl that

Wilfrid had humiliated himself over—she felt hollowed out on the inside. If he looked into her eyes, he would see it.

Cynewyn hurriedly wiped the table and moved on then, leaving them to their conversation. The group of warriors nearby were still exchanging riddles, their laughter echoing through the hall.

The sound grated upon Cynewyn. She wanted nothing more than to retire early—to hide behind the wall-hangings that divided her bower from the rest of the hall. However, since they were due to leave tomorrow, there was much to be done; much to prepare before she could sink into the welcome softness of her bed of furs.

"She's comely, the ealdorman's widow." Aelin caught Wil's eye and winked. "You did not mention that."

Wil shrugged, feigning indifference. "It matters not. You saw for yourself that she has a forked tongue."

"I'd prefer to call her 'fiery'," Aelin replied with a grin. "Just how I like my women."

A hot, unexpected, blade of jealousy stabbed Wil in the guts. He snorted, unable to keep the mask in place any longer.

"Isn't Aeva enough for you?" he asked, referring to the young woman that Aelin had been spending time with back in Rendlaesham. "Some women are not worth the trouble, believe me."

Aelin watched Wil, his grin fading as a sudden realization dawned upon him.

"Thunor's hammer – you were in love with her, weren't you?"

"Shut your mouth," Wil snarled back.

Aelin gave a low whistle and shook his head. "Well, that explains a lot."

"What?" Wil snapped, suddenly hating his friend. Aelin's sharpness, a trait that he had always liked, now grated upon him. "What does it explain?"

"Your bitterness," Aelin replied without hesitation. "Your anger. There have been times I thought you hated women."

Wil stared back at Aelin, momentarily struck dumb by his observation. "Enough," he eventually ground out. "I tire of this game."

Aelin nodded, not pushing him further, although his expression remained thoughtful. Wil pushed aside his half-empty cup of ale and got to his feet. Suddenly, he wished to be anywhere in Britannia but in this village, and in this hall.

Sometimes the past was best left alone.

Chapter Three

Departure from Blackhill

THE NEXT MORNING dawned cloudy and cold. Cynewyn stepped out of her hall and pulled her fur cloak close, suppressing a shiver. It was hard to believe spring was approaching; for the air still held the raw chill of winter. Gritting her teeth against the sting of the morning air on her face, Cynewyn made her way down the wooden steps and across the muddy clearing. Usually, the center of Blackhill was filled only with a few geese, or children playing. However, this morning it was heaving with men, horses, and wagons; a hive of activity. Villagers were packing the wagons with as many of their possessions, and animals, as they could manage.

Cynewyn frowned when she saw some of the women were in tears. This was wrong—tearing folk from the only homes they had known, and leaving the village to those who had no right to it.

At the heart of the crowd, Cynewyn found Mildthryth standing, toe to toe, with Heolstor. Her mother-in-law's face was flushed with anger. In her arms, she carried a goose. A placid nanny-goat stood at her side.

"We're not leaving our animals behind," Mildthryth insisted, her voice strained from the effort she was making not to shout, "so that our enemies can have them!"

"Enough, woman!" Heolstor growled. "I tire of being argued with at every turn. If you want to bring your animals then they are *your* responsibility. However, I'm not towing a menagerie behind us to Rendlaesham. If you want to bring that goat, you can lead it!"

"These animals are the only wealth we have," Mildthryth countered, not remotely cowed by the huge warrior that stood over her. "Your men need to help us fashion crates for the ducks and geese. They will have to carry more supplies on their horses so that we can use the carts for the pigs, sheep, and goats."

"You don't give the orders here." Heolstor's patience snapped. "We bring what we can carry—and we leave the rest behind!"

With that, the warrior turned and strode off into the crowd, bellowing at his men. Cynewyn stepped up next to Mildthryth. She was taken aback to see the fury on her mother-in-law's face.

"That man is a pig," Mildthryth snarled.

Cynewyn shook her head, despair settling over her in a smothering blanket. "It's as if we are to blame for all of this."

"You're not." A male voice sounded behind them. The women turned to see Wilfrid standing close by; he had overheard the entire argument. His face, as usual, was unreadable, yet Cynewyn saw anger in his eyes. "We shall help you bring as much of your livestock as we can carry," he told them. "Aelin is making wattle crates for your ducks and geese. We will leave as little as possible behind."

Mildthryth nodded, her face softening. "I thank you. What's your name?"

"Wilfrid of Went," he replied, meeting her gaze with the barest hint of a smile on his lips.

The women watched Wilfrid walk off. He joined Aelin at the far side of the clearing, where the bearded warrior was hurriedly constructing crates.

"Wilfrid of Went. A good man that one," Mildthryth observed quietly, "and handsome too. If only I was still young and comely. He would be just the man to warm my bed."

"Mildthryth!" Cynewyn turned to her mother-in-law, not bothering to hide her surprise. "Surely, he's too dour for your tastes?"

Mildthryth smiled, enjoying her daughter-in-law's discomfort. "Once, perhaps. My husband and son were both charming." The smile faded then. "But in many ways useless . . ."

"Useless?" Cynewyn interrupted her, aghast at Mildthryth's bluntness. "How can you speak of your kin so?"

"You know it to be the truth," her mother-in-law replied, unchastised, although her voice was tinged with sadness. "We both made a similar mistake, dear Cynewyn, in choosing appearance over substance. These days I am a little wiser. I see beyond a man's looks and charm. There is a strength, a power in a man who says little but keeps his word. I am old now—it's likely I will never have a man want me again. However, you are young enough for a second chance. I hope that, one day, you find another husband; one that doesn't disappoint you as my son did."

Cynewyn stared back at her mother-in-law. She had not realized it had been so painfully obvious.

"I wanted to love him," she replied, her voice barely above a whisper, her eyes filling with tears.

"I know." Mildthryth smiled, her own eyes glittering. "Watching you together was like seeing my own life replaying before me."

She stepped forward and gave Cynewyn a quick, hard, hug. "Come," she said briskly, brushing away a tear that had escaped and was running down her cheek. "We have a life to pack away."

It was late morning before the folk of Blackhill finished readying themselves for departure. Standing alone inside the hall, Cynewyn could hear Heolstor berating an elderly woman who was slower than most. He had grown evermore impatient as the morning progressed, and as the sun rose toward its zenith, he started to vent his frustration.

"Stop dragging your heels, you dim-witted hag!" he roared.

Mannerless churl, Cynewyn thought, casting her gaze around the interior of what had been her home for the past decade. *If I was a man, I'd knock him down for that.*

It was an odd sensation, standing inside the ealdorman's hall for one last time. The hall was empty and still, in stark contrast with the frenetic activity outside. The quiet caused Cynewyn to momentarily retreat to her own world. She gazed around the interior, reflecting on the years she had spent here. The embers in the fire pit were cold, and they had stripped the space of anything valuable—yet it still looked lived in, as if the inhabitants had merely stepped out for a short while.

"Where is the ealdorman's wife?" Heolstor's irate voice reached Cynewyn from outside as she walked to the center of the hall and took one last, lingering look around. "I've had enough of being delayed. Where is that bitch?"

Cynewyn took a deep breath and ignored the warrior's shouting. She would leave when she was ready, and not a moment before. She had gotten used to being her own mistress of late—of no longer submitting to a man's will—and had discovered that she enjoyed it.

When I start again in Rendlaesham it will be on my own, she told herself, a thrill of power running through her at the thought. *I will not be another man's chattel.*

Suddenly, the doors to the hall opened and a silhouette—that of a man of average height, but muscular—was outlined against the pale morning light.

Wilfrid stepped inside and pulled the doors closed behind him, his gaze meeting Cynewyn's across the wide space.

"Heolstor is getting impatient," he said gently. Wilfrid crossed the floor toward her, his boots crunching on the rushes. He stopped a couple of yards from Cynewyn, their gazes still fused. "We should go."

Cynewyn nodded, her pulse quickening. They were alone, for the first time since that day, all those years ago, when he had asked her to marry him. His nearness had a disturbing effect upon her. She suddenly felt a little short of breath and lightheaded. He was looking at her with that same, hungry intensity as he had back then; only now she was in no mood to flirt, or to dismiss him. His gaze made the fine hair on her arms prickle.

Aldwulf had never looked at her like that.

Breaking eye-contact, Cynewyn gave the hall one last look before walking past Wilfrid, toward the doors.

"Very well," she sighed. "I am ready now."

A breeze whispered through the trees as the procession of warriors, women, children and elderly made its way out of Blackhill and down the slope leading away from the village. The ground was muddy from the thaw, and slushy piles of snow still lay on the banks either side of the road.

Many of the warriors walked, leading the less able-bodied of Blackhill on their horses. Heolstor, one of the few warriors who had not offered his horse to one of the elderly or infirm, led the group. Heavily laden carts brought up the rear, filled with crates of indignant fowl, bleating sheep, and squealing pigs. The carts trundled down the incline with a number of goats, tied to the back, trotting behind.

Cynewyn walked in the middle of the column; a heavy leather bag, filled with her few possessions, slung across her front. She wore her thickest fur cloak, pulled tight about her to ward off the cold. Mildthryth walked a few paces behind her, carrying her possessions in a basket on her back.

The folk of Blackhill were subdued, and followed the king's men silently. Many of the women wept, but Cynewyn was dry-eyed. She felt oddly numb. Although Blackhill had been her home, she had not been particularly happy there. There was little she would miss. It was only pride and the promise of an uncertain future in Rendlaesham that made her cling to the past.

It was late afternoon, the pale sun low in the sky, when the travelers reached the ruins of Went. Heolstor led them around the blackened stumps of the perimeter fence, rather than taking them through the heart of the village.

Cynewyn had wanted to keep her gaze averted from the ruins, but found she could not. She stared at the collection of charred remains, at the husk of her father's hall, and felt grief well within her. Over the years, Went had represented happiness and security, and contained the memories of a blessed childhood—but now even that was lost to her.

Blinking back scalding tears, Cynewyn glanced ahead at where Wilfrid was leading two children atop his horse. She saw him gaze across at the ruined village and wondered if he had any regrets about leaving Went. Her father had been furious after Wil had thrown his arm rings on the floor at his feet and stormed off. Eomer of Went had been a proud man, and he had liked Wil. Cynewyn had wondered if her father ultimately blamed her for the whole incident. In many ways it had been her fault; she should not have encouraged Wil to go before her father. She had known what the ealdorman's response would be. In truth, she had wanted to see Wil humiliated.

I was so different then, she thought with a touch of bitterness, *so sure of the world and my place in it.*

Cynewyn was aware then that someone was staring at her. She looked up and met Wil's gaze. She knew he could see her naked despair, and suddenly hated him for it. They stared at each other a moment, before Cynewyn dropped her gaze to the muddy ground. She did not look up until they had left Went, and all its memories, behind.

They had not traveled far from Went when the shadows grew deeper, and the light started to dim, warning that dusk was not far off. They now approached the thick swathe of woodland.

"Halt!"

The column had almost reached the shadowy boughs of the woods when Heolstor pulled up short, raising his hand for those following him to do the same.

Cynewyn peered ahead, frowning.

What was amiss ahead?

Her breath caught in her throat when she saw what had caused him to stop so abruptly.

A ragged company of men, all on foot and armed with axes and spears, emerged from the trees. There were at least sixty of them. Lean-faced and wild-eyed, they approached the travelers warily, weapons raised.

One of the men—a huge warrior with grizzled brown hair and a heavy-featured face—stepped forward from the group. He carried a massive war-axe, and his gaze was riveted on Heolstor's face.

"Finally," the stranger growled before giving a wide smile that showed his teeth. "We were beginning to think you weren't coming."

Heolstor stared back at him, his face hard, before finally responding. "Who are you? Name yourself."

"My name is not important," the warrior replied, his smile fading. "We are East Saxons—that is all you need to know."

"You're on East Angle soil." Heolstor's gaze narrowed.

"This is our land," the axe-wielding warrior replied, his own gaze narrowing.

"This land belongs to Raedwald of the East Angles," Heolstor growled. "Would you bring his wrath down upon you?"

In response to this, the East Saxon warrior spat on the ground. "I care not for the wrath of your king. For years, these East Angle dogs have settled and worked the land that should have been ours. Stand aside and let us have their animals, any possessions of worth, and their comeliest women." The man's face twisted into a leer. "You can have the rest."

Heolstor drew his sword. "East Saxon whoreson—you don't command here!"

Suddenly, there was a flutter of movement from the line of East Saxons. Heolstor grunted.

A hand axe had hurtled through the air, and was now embedded in his chest. He stared down at it in mute shock. When he looked up, blood seeped from between his lips and dribbled down his chin. Heolstor opened his mouth to speak but no words came.

A moment later, he slumped sideways and fell off his horse.

Chapter Four

Refuge in the Woods

CYNEWYN HAD NEVER seen a battle, let alone been in the midst of one before. One moment, they had all been standing still, as dusk crept across the land, watching as Heolstor slid from his horse—the next, the world exploded.

Weapons drawn, the warriors on both sides gave battle cries and sprinted for each other, while the women shrank back, dragging their children with them. Tearing her eyes from the mayhem just yards in front, Cynewyn rushed back to where the villagers cowered.

"Leave the carts," she cried. "Follow me!"

Cynewyn grabbed Mildthryth by the arm and dragged her mother-in-law after her. The older woman had frozen with fear the moment the fighting had started. She clung to Cynewyn now—taking her lead.

The villagers all did as they were told. Their prized possessions fell to the ground, the carts of livestock abandoned. The folk of Blackhill knew what capture meant; they knew what the East Saxons did to their enemies.

The roar of battle behind them spurred all of the villagers on—young and old. Cynewyn knew she needed to lead the folk in a wide circle around the fighting and into the woods. Once they reached the trees, if they could get past the fighting and escape into the woodland, the villagers might have a chance.

"Make for the woods!" Cynewyn pushed Mildthryth ahead. "Go left and skirt the edge of the fighting. I'll get the stragglers."

Mildthryth nodded, her face pale but resolute. "Come!" Her mother-in-law dropped her basket of belongings on to the ground, for it would only slow her down, and picked up her skirts. "Follow me!"

Cynewyn went back to where the elderly and young brought up the rear of the group. Those on horseback, she sent on ahead.

"Ride!" she shouted. "Don't look back!"

Around them, the sounds of battle—the clang of iron and the shouts, and cries, of men—were deafening. Cynewyn dared not glance back to see if one side was gaining the upper hand. However, when the thunder of battle did not dim, but grew even louder, she forced herself to look back over her shoulder.

Her breath stilled.

A flank of the East Saxon war band had split away from the others and were coming straight for the fleeing villagers. Some of the East Angle warriors were rushing to intercept them.

Cynewyn was at the rear of the group. The others had taken her advice and were running for the trees. The first of them—Mildthryth among them—had just reached the edge of the woodland.

A sob caught in Cynewyn's throat. The East Saxons had almost reached her; she would not make it.

Then, without warning, her skirts caught around her legs and she tripped.

She hit the ground hard, skinning her knees and the palms of her hands. Scrambling to her feet, she turned to find an East Saxon warrior running for her, his spear held above his head. Horrified, Cynewyn stared at him, knowing that she could not outrun him. He was about to skewer her.

Suddenly, the warrior crumpled, just a few feet from Cynewyn. His spear skimmed along the ground and came to rest at her feet. Wilfrid stepped up behind him, and withdrew his sword from between the man's shoulder blades.

For a brief instant, Cynewyn and Wil stared at each other. Then, Wil tore his gaze from hers and turned to face his pursuers.

"Cynewyn," Wil ordered roughly, "get behind me!"

Cynewyn scooped up the spear, and gripping the ash shaft tightly, did as she was told.

Another spearman came at them, yelling in fury. Wil fought him off, and felled his opponent with a blade to the throat. Slowly—foot by foot—Wil and Cynewyn inched back toward the edge of the woods. Yet, if Wil continued to stand and fight, the East Saxons would draw a net closed around them and there would be no escape.

Cynewyn realized that they would have to turn-tail and run soon, while they still had the chance. Wilfred obviously was thinking along the same lines, for he kept a steady progress backward, fighting off each man who charged him. However, after a while, his movements became choppy and sluggish, and Cynewyn realized that he was injured. His strength was starting to fail.

They had almost reached the trees when Wil staggered. An axe-man slashed at him, beating him back relentlessly. Moments more, and the axe's blade would slice into Wil.

Still gripping the ash spear, Cynewyn rushed at the man and slammed the spear into his belly, feeling the axe-blade whisper past her ear as she did so.

The man let out a terrible scream and slumped forward, his axe slipping from nerveless fingers.

Wilfrid grabbed Cynewyn by the arm and hauled her into the woods. They dove into the trees, crashing through the undergrowth of bracken, blackthorn, and brambles.

The East Saxons came after them.

A sob of despair welled in Cynewyn's breast. She had been a fool to think they would be safe once they reached the trees; the East Saxons had no intention of letting their quarry flee. She and Wilfrid fled through the woods like two deer pursued by wolves. Wil kept a tight hold of her hand, dragging Cynewyn through ever thicker undergrowth and avoiding the open spaces between trees where it would be easier to catch them. Cynewyn felt the brambles tear at her skirts and claw at her skin, but she ran on, her lungs burning from the effort.

If they stopped now it would be over for them both.

Still their hunters followed. They were gaining on them now; Cynewyn could hear their shouts and the crashing and snapping of the undergrowth giving way behind her.

They would never outrun them.

Cynewyn glanced down at where Wil's hand gripped hers. His hand was red with blood from a wound on his upper arm. She could see he was tiring. Neither of them could run like this for much longer.

Suddenly, Wil unexpectedly pivoted to the left, hauling Cynewyn after him. A few yards later, they skidded down a bank into a shallow hollow filled with ferns. Wil abruptly pulled Cynewyn against him and threw himself to the ground.

Together they rolled into a cramped space just under the lip of the bank, squeezing themselves in. Wil reached past Cynewyn and pulled the ferns over them. A moment later, she heard men crashing down the bank and into the hollow. They did not stop. Wil and Cynewyn lay, not even daring to breathe, listening as the sounds of their pursuers faded.

Cynewyn's heart thundered in her ears. She lay limply against Wil, feeling nauseous with exhaustion. Her head was pressed up against his chest. She could feel wetness—his blood—on her cheek and hear his heart pounding as if it was trying to pry its way out of his rib cage.

They lay there for a long while, daring not move from their hiding place lest their pursuers find them. Eventually, when they squeezed out of their cramped hiding place and emerged from the bed of ferns, the last light of dusk was settling across the woodland.

They gazed silently around the shadowed woods—for neither had spoken a word since taking flight—their eyes straining in the half-light. Eventually, satisfied that no one was stalking them, Wil turned to Cynewyn.

"Are you hurt?" he asked, his voice hoarse.

She shook her head. "But you are."

He nodded, his gaze flicking once more to the shadows. Cynewyn could see he was tense, and after what they had just endured she did not blame him.

"We'll see to that later," he replied gruffly. "For now, I suggest we get as far from here as we can before the light fades completely."

Without another word, he led the way, up the bank and out of the hollow.

Chapter Five

Night Shadows

THE MOON WAS rising over the treetops when they finally stopped their journey north. Night shrouded the woodland, turning it into a world of deep shadows and muted sounds. Cynewyn and Wilfrid made camp for the night in the heart of the woods, far from the southern fringes where they had lost their pursuers.

They found shelter for the night under a great fallen oak, next to a clear stream.

"Will we be safe here?" Cynewyn asked.

"I believe so," Wil replied. He paused from where he had been ripping bark off the fallen oak to use for a fire, and cast his gaze around the secluded spot. "They won't bother traveling this far north—it grows dangerous for them, the farther they travel into our kingdom. This campsite should keep us safe for the night."

Those were the first words they had exchanged in hours. There was a tension between them, which had grown, once the fear of capture had ebbed. Cynewyn had avoided glancing in Wil's direction, as she grew ever more aware of his presence.

It was a clear night, and the moon cast a silver light over the trees. The air had grown chill; something that had not bothered either of them while they were walking. However, now that they had stopped, Cynewyn found herself shivering—as much from the shock of what they had just lived through as from the cool night.

Wil lit a small fire, assuring her it was safe to do so, as they were now far north of where they had lost their pursuers. There was no meal; this eve, they would have to go hungry. Growling stomachs were a small price to pay for their lives. Nonetheless, Cynewyn would have welcomed a wheel of crusty griddle bread and a slab of sharp goat's cheese.

Seated by the fire, Wil shrugged off his fur cloak and, for the first time, examined the wound he had taken to his bicep. Dry blood encrusted his arm, but Cynewyn could see that it was a deep laceration. He saw her observing him and winced.

"A spear."

"I should wash and bind it."

"Bind it? With what?"

Cynewyn unlaced her fur-lined boots and placed them near the fire. She reached under the ankle-length woolen tunic she wore, to her linen under-tunic, and ripped a long swathe of fabric off from around the hem. She tore the strip into two pieces.

Looking up, she met Wil's gaze.

"There's enough moonlight for me to see well enough," she explained. "Follow me down to the stream, and I shall cleanse your arm."

Wil nodded, before unlacing his boots and following her, barefoot, down to the stream. Clear water, sparkling in the moonlight, trickled over smooth stones. Cynewyn stepped into the water, her breath hissing between her teeth.

Thunor's hammer it's cold.

Wetting one of the pieces of linen, she waited for Wil to step into the stream next to her. Then, she reached out and washed away the encrusted blood—working her way up from his hand to his shoulder. After that, she gently bathed the deep cut on his bicep.

"This will need stitching," she observed. "You will have an impressive scar."

Wil gave a pain-filled grunt in response.

As she finished bathing the wound, Cynewyn was aware of his proximity. She could feel his gaze upon her face, and she felt her pulse quicken in response. She wished he would stop staring at her—it was unnerving.

"Cynewyn," he said her name like a caress.

"Yes?" she replied, reaching for the second strip of linen to bind the wound.

"Did you love your husband?"

Cynewyn froze, and her face flamed at his boldness.

"You don't ask everyday, ordinary questions like other folk, do you?" she replied, covering her embarrassment with sharpness. Avoiding his gaze, she wrapped the linen around his bicep.

"Did you?" he persisted.

Cynewyn glanced up at him, annoyed, before instantly regretting it. His eyes, gleaming in the moonlight, fused with hers.

"What does it matter?" she replied, unable to keep the bitterness from her voice.

"It matters to me," he answered, his voice soft; his gaze never left hers for a moment.

"It shouldn't," Cynewyn snapped. She looked back down at the bandage, which she tied firmly about the wound. "Best to let the past stay in the past—where it belongs."

"For you perhaps," he replied, before asking once more. "Did you love him?"

"For the love of Woden—just leave it be!"

"I have to know, Cynewyn. All these years, I've never forgotten you. Were you happy?"

"No," Cynewyn snarled, still avoiding his gaze. "No—I didn't love Aldwulf. I never wished him ill but I never loved my husband. And no—I wasn't happy. You have your answer. Are you content now?"

Silence stretched between them then and Cynewyn felt his gaze, hot and searching on her face, willing her to look at him.

"*Nithhogg* take you!" she snarled once more, her patience snapping. "Stop staring at me!"

She stepped back abruptly, stumbling on the slippery stones. However, she cared not—she was desperate to put some space between them. He was too close; she could not breathe.

Wil put his hands out to steady her. A moment later he pulled her roughly against him and his mouth came down upon hers.

The kiss was passionate, and brief, for Cynewyn yanked herself away and slapped him hard across the face.

"How dare you!" she hissed. She turned and struggled toward the edge of the stream. "Churl!"

He came after her, dragged her back into his arms and smothered her curses and insults with his mouth.

Cynewyn fought him hard; as hard as she fought her own desire. Yet, his touch, the feel of his lips searing hers, his hard body against her belly and breasts, his hands pressing into the small of her back—were all her undoing.

With a gasp of surrender, she stopped fighting and her lips parted under his.

Desire knifed through the pit of her belly and made her legs weaken.

She heard him groan, deep in his throat. With one hand he pulled her hard against him, letting her feel his shaft—stiff against her belly—and with the other he tangled his fingers in her hair and sensually stroked the nape of her neck. His touch unleashed something within Cynewyn; a hunger she had never felt in a man's arms.

Gasping with the force of it, she slid her hands up his chest, feeling the sculpted muscles under the sleeveless leather tunic and linen under-tunic he wore. He kissed her thoroughly, with the same intensity as his stare, exploring her mouth with his tongue, and gently biting her lips. Cynewyn shuddered from the intense pleasure his kisses gave her.

You should not be doing this, her conscience needled her. *Your husband is only dead two moon cycles—and the last thing you need is to be beholden to another man.*

Still, she could not stop herself from kissing him back, from pressing her body urgently against his. The yearning for something she could not name, could not even describe, grew with each passing moment.

Wil slid his hands over the curve of her bottom and picked her up; his mouth never left hers as he waded out of the stream. In response, Cynewyn wrapped her legs around his waist, gasping with excitement at the feel of his manhood pressed against her. She lifted her hips and pressed herself harder still against him—and was rewarded by a groan.

"Cynewyn," he gasped, carrying her up the bank to the fire.

Under the shelter of the oak, Wil sank to his knees on the fur cloak he had discarded earlier, his hands trembling as he undid the girdle about her waist. Then, he reached down and took hold of the hem of her tunics, pulling both of them over her head.

Cynewyn sat naked on his cloak and watched Wil undress before her. As he did so, his gaze roamed over her nakedness. She did the same, drinking him in. Wil's naked body was as she had imagined it; strong and muscular. He was broad shouldered and narrow hipped. His arousal was impossible to miss, straining against his flat belly. Cynewyn's mouth went dry at the sight of it, ridding her of any inhibition. She reached out and stroked the hard column of his shaft, her excitement rising when he groaned once more.

Wil pulled her to him, and onto his lap, astride him. His hands stroked her breasts, and he pushed her up onto her knees so that he could suckle each nipple. Despite the fire flickering beside them, it was a cool night. Chill air feathered across their naked skin. However, Cynewyn hardly noticed, groaning at the pleasure of his hot mouth. She pressed herself against him, making him suckle her breast harder.

Her body trembled when he eventually took hold of her hips and lowered her gently onto him, impaling her deeply. Cynewyn threw back her head and gave a long moan of pleasure. Never in her wildest dreams had she imagined it could be like this. All those years of tepid lovemaking with Aldwulf, who more often than not came to her mead-soaked and uninterested, she had not realized what she was missing.

Who would have thought that Wilfrid of Went—the man she had dismissed without a second thought all those years ago—could provoke such passion in her. Her hunger for him was so powerful that she almost felt ill. Fiercely, she brought her mouth down upon his, kissing him wildly—and he responded in kind.

Moments later, she was under him, her legs pushed back and splayed wide; and he was moving inside her with exquisite slowness, his gaze never leaving hers all the while.

"Wil," she gasped, reaching for him, "please."

He gave a sensual smile—so different from the serious mask he presented to the world. His smile was filled with promise. "There's plenty of time," he whispered, his voice sliding over her like honey. "Why rush this?"

Cynewyn's body trembled in response; a deep, flooding, heat spreading from her loins up through the pit of her belly. She gazed at him through half closed lids as he moved within her, watching the way the firelight danced on his skin that was now slick with sweat. She could feel the tremors that ran through his body, every time he arched his hips against her; his hard won self-control was starting to slip.

Finally, her pleasure crested, and she thrust her hips up against him, wrapping her legs about him, her body shuddering. Cynewyn threw back her head and cried out, gasping his name and reaching for him.

She heard him cry out then, thrusting deep into her as he gave in to the desire that consumed him. The ache in her loins exploded into pulsing pleasure and she screamed again when he thrust deep into her once more.

A moment later, Wil reared back and gasped her name as he found his release.

Sweat soaked and panting, they lay, their limbs entangled, on the fur cloak. Cynewyn's mind was devoid of thought, of worry, for the first time in many years. Her body was a gently rippling pool of pleasure. The musky smell of Wil's skin, and the feel of his strong body entwined with hers, altered her senses, and made rational thought impossible.

They had only been lying there a short while, recovering from the lovemaking that had rocked them both to the core, when Wil propped himself up on an elbow and looked down at her. His hazel eyes were dark in the firelight. Their gazes met, and Cynewyn felt the same rising hunger that had consumed her earlier return. Wil did not speak; instead, his gaze slid down the length of her prone body, devouring her. Then, his mouth came down over hers. The kiss was soft and tender initially, before it deepened into something else entirely.

Wil was still inside Cynewyn, but she felt his shaft harden as their passion re-awoke. She gasped into his mouth and arched against him, hearing his sharp intake of breath in response.

This night, neither of them would sleep.

Chapter Six

Daylight

A MISTY DAWN crept across the woodland, chasing away the night. The embers of last night's fire smoldered next to the man and woman who stirred next to it.

Eventually, after exhaustion had claimed them both, Cynewyn had fallen into a deep and dreamless sleep under the shelter of the fallen oak; yet, the chill of the dawn and the sunlight filtering in through the gaps in the trees roused her. They had slept on Wil's cloak, and pulled Cynewyn's fur cloak over them to keep warm. However, now that the night's enchantment had ended, Cynewyn had started to shiver in the cold.

Wil rolled away from her with a soft groan of protest, his eyes opening, as she slid from under him and rose to her feet.

"Cynewyn?"

"It's cold," she replied softly. "I need to get dressed."

She could feel his gaze upon her as she retrieved her tunics, from where Wil had flung them into the bushes. Now that night had gone, she suddenly felt self-conscious and had to force herself not to cover herself up under his gaze.

It's a bit late for modesty now, she thought wryly, pulling her long linen under-tunic over her head and letting it fall about her ankles, *you went too far last night to play the blushing maid now*. But blush Cynewyn did, when she remembered what he had done to her, and she to him, over the arc of the long night.

Keeping her gaze averted from Wil, she reached for the thicker, woolen tunic that would keep her warm. Her body trembled with cold as she tied her girdle about her waist.

Wil also rose to his feet. Not in the slightest self-conscious, he went to retrieve his clothing—and despite that she was no longer held thrall by the passion that consumed them both till exhaustion—Cynewyn found herself admiring his naked, masculine body. Wil pulled on his breeches and turned back to her, as Cynewyn hurriedly looked away lest he see her staring.

It was awkward this morning. After everything that they had shared, shrouded by darkness, Cynewyn now felt at a complete loss for words. She could not bring herself to regret what had passed between them; yet, at the same time, she was aware that she barely knew this man. Before they had fallen upon each other in a lust-filled frenzy, they had barely spoken. If she wished to remain unshackled, this was not the way to go about it.

He saved your life, and you were grateful, that's why you responded how you did, she told herself as she sat down and pulled on her fur-lined boots. However, she knew the truth of it. She had wanted him. Ever since she had locked gazes with Wil back in Blackhill, this had been building. Being alone together, in the middle of the woods, had just made it all the easier to give in.

Cynewyn slung her fur cloak about her shoulders. Her stomach growled, aching with sudden hunger. Last night had distracted her from her empty belly. She was ravenous now—but there was no food to be had.

"Let's go," she told Wil, glancing across their campsite for the last time. Last night already felt like a bewitching; one that could not withstand daylight. "We need to reach the others."

Wil nodded, his gaze searching her face.

"Are you well?" he asked, taking a step toward her.

She nodded, smiling more brightly than necessary and stepping back from him. "Just hungry—and thirsty."

He stepped closer still, reaching for her, but Cynewyn slipped away, avoiding his gaze.

"We need to go," she murmured.

Wil stood watching her a moment before he nodded, his expression shuttered. "Very well."

They left the campsite, quenching their thirsts at the stream before Wil led the way north. The mist began to clear, and the sun, containing more warmth than it had since autumn, burned the last of the fog away. The sky above the tree tops turned a bright robin's egg blue.

Wil and Cynewyn continued in silence for most of the morning. Cynewyn walked a few paces behind him, her gaze often straying—against her will— to the muscular breadth of his back and shoulders. She could tell her distance this morning had thrown him. He did not show hurt on this face but she had seen it flare in his eyes.

Part of her, the part that had delighted in every moment they had shared the night before, ached at the coldness she feigned this morning. Yet, they had spoken little during the night, making it easier this morning to create a gulf between them.

From her vantage point behind him, Cynewyn could see the tension in his shoulders. He was a man quite unlike any she had ever met; he presented a reserved mask to the world but last night had revealed a molten core. He was so much more than he appeared—frighteningly so.

And yet, with her husband just recently departed, their coupling had been as ill-timed as it was ill-advised. She was an ealdorman's widow—the king would not look kindly upon her if she arrived in Rendlaesham, arm-in-arm with one of his thegns. Worse still, he might insist that they marry. Cynewyn's stomach cramped at the thought. She could not allow that to happen. Her newfound freedom was too important to her to throw away over one night of passion.

Mid-morning, they came upon a patch of raspberries—the first of the spring. Famished, they fell upon the berries, picking the bushes clean. It was a light meal but it took the edge off their hunger nonetheless. Finishing her last mouthful, Cynewyn straightened up and gazed around the glade in which they stood. With the sun dappling the ground, and shafts of golden light filtering through the branches above them, it was an idyllic spot—far from the hardship and disappointment of everyday life. Had circumstances been different, she would have liked to remain here and enjoy the tranquility.

However, as she gazed around at her surroundings, Cynewyn was aware of Wil staring at her. Eventually, unable to ignore him any longer, she let her gaze meet his.

Wil stared at Cynewyn, drinking in the blueness of her eyes, her sensual features, and milky skin. At last, she had acknowledged his existence. Perhaps there was hope after all. Maybe she had just needed time to come to terms with what had happened between them.

It had changed his life.

He had never dared dream that he could ever have the lovely Cynewyn, daughter of Eomer of Went. Even now, he had to remind himself that last night had been real and not some erotic dream. In fact, her coldness this morning had made him wonder if last night had just been some forest enchantment—a spell broken by daylight.

Her detachment—the way she had shrank back from him when he tried to kiss her—had stung. But now she returned his gaze, and in her eyes he could see conflict.

"Cynewyn," he began, stepping close to her. He noted that her lips, still bee-stung from last night, were stained raspberry. "Do you regret what happened between us?"

He watched her swallow, her face tensing. That expression told him all, cutting him to the quick.

"We should not have done it," she murmured. "It can only bring trouble to us both?"

"Why?" he stepped closer, staring down at her face, aching to kiss her—even though her words wounded him. Her gaze told him a different story; her pupils were dilated as she held his gaze, reacting to his nearness. "Tell me why we can't be together?"

"It wouldn't work," she protested weakly, her cheeks flushing. "I'm an ealdorman's daughter and you're a . . ."

"So it still comes back to rank?" he ground the words out, cutting her off, his anger flaring. "You still think I'm not worthy? I'm no longer the spearman you rejected. I'm the king's thegn. Surely, after everything that's happened, you don't still think you're better than me?"

He saw her gaze narrow and knew that he had hit a nerve.

"I am still an ealdorman's daughter," she informed him imperiously, "not some farmer's daughter whose skirts you can lift whenever it pleases you."

Wil laughed at that, although there was no humor in it. He took a step closer so that they were almost touching. "You're not so different to other women, Cynewyn," he told her, his voice lowering. "You like to think you're better than the rest, but with a man between your legs you're all the same."

Cynewyn lashed out and struck him hard across the face. "Dog!" she snarled. "I won't be making the same mistake twice!"

With that she raised her hand to strike him again.

However, this time Wil was ready for her. He seized both her wrists and held her fast. His cheek burned but he tried to ignore it as he glared down at her.

"You are too free with your hands," he spoke calmly, although he boiled with rage inside. "It's not wise to lash out at someone twice your size."

"Churl!" She struggled to break free of his grip. "Let go of me!"

In response, Wil pushed her backward a few paces so her back was pressed against the rough bark of a beech tree. Even as angry as he was, Cynewyn's nearness affected him like strong mead. He had the overwhelming desire then to smother her curses with his lips, to smooth away their angry words with his hands.

It was all going wrong. He had said things, they both had—ugly things that they could not take back. He wanted to make it right again, yet he had no idea what he could do to breach the gulf between them.

He did then, the only thing he thought could bring them close again. He kissed her.

Cynewyn struggled against his embrace, her knee knifing upwards toward his groin. Anticipating her, he pressed his body hard against hers, pushing her knee aside. As soon as his mouth left hers, Cynewyn spat a curse at him, so Wil kissed her again. His hands pinned her wrists against the tree trunk. He kissed her hard, his lips bruising hers—letting her feel his rage and frustration—and she fought him in return.

Wil continued to kiss her, his mouth gradually softening. It took a while, but eventually he heard her groan in surrender. Without hesitation, he slid his tongue between her lips and released her wrists, pulling her body hard against his. Wil hitched up her skirts, his hands sliding up the smooth skin of her thighs before parting her legs.

Cynewyn arched against him, a soft whimper escaping her. Wil's breath caught in his throat as hunger consumed him.

This woman was his undoing.

He entered her with one smooth thrust, gasping at how hot and wet she was. Despite her anger, despite her words, her body could not deny the truth. Wil groaned her name and gave in to his instincts. Last night he had held back, he had drawn out their pleasure, enjoying the game between them. Today, he let himself be drawn into the whirlpool of want that claimed them both.

He drove hard into her, his hands grasping her smooth, firm buttocks, and angling her hips up against him so that he could penetrate deeper still. Moments later, Cynewyn shuddered against him, her sobs of ecstasy echoing across the glade—and Wil heard his own hoarse cries, joining hers. He thrust deep inside her one last time and found his release.

Sweat-soaked and panting, they slid to the ground.

Wil's heart was pounding, his mind a tangle of conflict. They clung together for a few moments more, waiting for the haze of passion to subside. However, Wil dreaded the moment she came to her senses. He did not want to look into her eyes, for he knew what he would see there. Her body had given in to him, but her will had not.

Neither spoke for a long while, as their breathing slowed and lucidity returned. Eventually, knowing he could put the moment off no longer, Wil propped himself up on one elbow and stared down at her. Something inside his chest twisted when he saw her face.

Cynewyn was crying.

"Get off me," she whispered before averting her face and refusing to look at him.

"I'm sorry, Cynewyn," he whispered back, his throat aching with sudden grief. He had lost whatever slim chance he'd had of winning Cynewyn over; she hated him now. "Did I hurt you?"

She shook her head, still refusing to look at him. "Please get off me," her voice had a pleading edge to it that cut him deeply.

Wil climbed to his feet and gently helped her up. Cynewyn turned her back on him, pulling her fur cloak close. Suddenly, the beauty faded from the glade, and the sun lost its heat. Despair clouded the fragile hope that Wil had been holding close since last night. He was not good with words; there was nothing he could of think of that would put this right.

Silently, he led the way out of the glade.

Chapter Seven

No Longer Alone

IT WAS EARLY afternoon when Wil and Cynewyn left the woodland behind. They had not spoken since the glade, and the silence weighed heavily between them. Cynewyn trailed at Wil's heels, relieved when they finally stepped out from under the shadowy boughs onto flat heathland. There was a light breeze out here on the heath, although the sun still shone, warming Cynewyn's face as she walked.

Cynewyn was glad the woods were behind them. Now that they were on the heath, they were likely to encounter a village, or other travelers. Anything to prevent them spending another night together—alone.

She did not trust herself with him, and did not trust him to keep his distance.

Even now, her cheeks flamed when she remembered how she had behaved in the glade. One moment she had been fighting him, the next gasping for his touch. One moment she had been telling him they could never be together—the next, her body had betrayed her.

Women who gave out conflicting messages, as she had, ended up in trouble; raped or worse. She sensed that Wil was not a violent, or cruel man, but he was a man nonetheless. She was playing a dangerous game, one she wanted to end.

I need to reach Rendlaesham, she told herself, her eyes scanning her surroundings for any sign of settlement. *I need to start a new life*. Marriage had brought her nothing but frustration and sadness. Perhaps, with the king's help, she could start again—alone. She had not been able to tell Wil the real reason it could not continue between them; telling a man that she would rather remain unwed was treasonous in the world they inhabited. Instead, it had been easier to use their differing rank as an excuse, even if it had earned his contempt.

What if our coupling has given me a child?

The thought turned Cynewyn to ice. She had already suffered through two pregnancies, only to give birth to stillborn babes. She could not bear the thought of facing that again. Tears stung her eyelids at the memory of her grief, as she had held the dead infants in her arms. Aldwulf had been no solace. He had merely gone off to drown himself in mead. Only Mildthryth had comforted her; only she seemed to realize how Cynewyn had grieved.

She could not change what had happened, and so Cynewyn forced thoughts that she might bear Wil's child from her mind. She needed to focus on reaching Rendlaesham. She needed to distract herself from the memories of that man, and what they had shared. Fresh tears stung her eyelids but she hurriedly brushed them away.

Why was life so hard? Her mother had never told her how it was between men and women. She wished someone had warned her.

The sun was sliding toward the western horizon, the sky laced in pink and gold, when they spotted the outlines of figures up ahead. There were a few horses, their shapes silhouetted against the sunset, and at least two dozen folk.

Cynewyn's heart started to pound and her spirits lifted.

The folk of Blackhill—we've found them!

Wil glanced back over his shoulder, and their gazes met briefly. For the first time ever, his gaze did not sear hers; there was no hunger in his eyes, no longing on his face. She was staring at a mask. Although the sight of his coldness gave Cynewyn an odd pang, which she hurriedly pushed aside, she was grateful for it.

At last, he now understands.

Whatever had ignited between them in the woods was now over.

"Your people," he told her, his voice flat. "We have found them."

"And the king's men?" Cynewyn reached his side, squinting against the sun as she tried to make out the figures. Had any of the warriors survived?

"We shall soon see," Wil replied. "Come, let's join them."

The group saw them approach, and Cynewyn spied Mildthryth among them. Letting out a whoop of joy, her mother-in-law rushed toward her, breaking away from the group of survivors. She raced across the stretch of grass between them and launched herself at Cynewyn, grasping her in a fierce hug.

"I thought you were lost!" Mildthryth's gaze glistened with tears as she stepped back, studying Cynewyn's face. "Are you well? Did they hurt you?"

Cynewyn shook her head, struggling to compose herself. "Wilfrid saved me," she motioned to the silent warrior beside her. "Thanks to him, we managed to hide from the East Saxons in the woods and slip away once they had moved on."

Mildthryth nodded, taking this news in, before her gaze shifted to Wil. "I thank you, Wilfrid of Went, for keeping Cynewyn safe."

He nodded and gave a small smile in reply.

Mildthryth smiled back, before looping her arm through Cynewyn's. Then, she steered her toward where the group were making camp for the night. "Come—the men killed a boar in the woods. They're roasting it now."

Cynewyn's stomach growled at the prospect; she felt weak with hunger and her mouth filled with saliva at the thought of roast boar. There were tears and laughter as the folk of Blackhill welcomed her back. By some miracle, they had not lost one villager during the ambush. Cynewyn's quick thinking and the valor of the king's men had given them the time to escape through the woods.

However, the warriors who had been escorting them had not been so fortunate.

There had been around forty of them—now there were less than ten men remaining. Cynewyn felt a surge of despair at the realization that so many of them had fallen; the life of a warrior was so brutal and short.

Among the survivors was the bearded warrior, Aelin. His friend's face lit up with joy at seeing Wil approach. He strode forward to meet him.

"I knew you'd make it out alive," Aelin slapped Wil on the back, before slinging an arm over his friend's shoulders and steering him toward the fire. "Thank Woden for it!"

Cynewyn heard the low rumble of Wil's voice as he responded, although their conversation was immediately swallowed up by the chatter of the villagers that now clustered around them.

Cynewyn ruffled the hair of a little boy who clung to her skirts, her gaze meeting Mildthryth's once more.

"Come." Mildthryth led her through the excited villagers to where a huge boar was spit-roasting over glowing embers. "You need food and rest."

Cynewyn nodded, grateful that the older woman was taking charge. She felt oddly numb and detached all of a sudden, as if she was watching this entire scene from afar.

It's just hunger and exhaustion, she told herself. *Once you've eaten and slept, the world will return to normal again.*

Cynewyn glanced over, at where Wil drank deeply from a water bladder on the other side of the fire. When he lowered it, his face was like stone.

That face, so different from the man who had gazed into her eyes while he moved inside her, made Cynewyn feel wretched.

I caused that.

Cynewyn turned away, her stomach suddenly twisting in guilt. She desperately needed to rest. She hoped that tomorrow would bring clarity and a fresh start, for right now she felt strangely adrift.

The night drew out; the crackling flames in the fire pit the only noise on the silent heath. The king's men were taking turns at watching the sleeping camp, allowing the folk of Blackhill to stretch out under the stars.

Wil sat on the edge of the fire, staring into the glowing embers. He was exhausted, and wanted nothing more than for sleep to claim him. Yet, it would not come. His eyes burned with fatigue, his limbs ached—but still, his mind would not let him slip over the abyss into oblivion.

"Can't sleep?" Aelin, returning from taking the first watch, sat down next to Wil.

Wil shook his head, avoiding his friend's gaze. He had rarely known happiness during his life, but the misery that now claimed him caused a deep ache in the center of his chest.

"Did Went bring back memories?" Aelin asked, mistaking the reason for his friend's melancholy.

Wil nodded. "My father was a brute who beat me, and my mother was a cold, bitter woman," he said quietly, deliberately failing to mention the real reason for his bleak mood. "They both died of a fever that raged through Went one winter. I barely grieved for either of them."

Silence fell between the friends then, as Aelin digested Wil's words. It was not an unusual tale, for childhood and innocence were short-lived for most folk. Still, it was the first time in all the years they had known each other that Wil had divulged details of his life in Went.

"It does not matter how much we distance ourselves, how far we run—the past always shadows us," Wil continued, his voice barely above a whisper.

"You've achieved much in the past decade," Aelin reminded him. "You're now one of the king's thegns. You fought at the king's side and proved your valor and loyalty."

Wil nodded, not disputing Aelin's words. It was true, he had spent most of the last decade at Raedwald's side. He and Aelin had fought alongside the king during the East Angles' campaign against the Northumbrians. They had seen the king's son, Raegenhere, fall under the Northumbrian king's blade—and had witnessed Raedwald cut down Aethelfrith of Northumbria in a blind rage. It had been a terrible battle; but despite the death of Raedwald's beloved son, the East Angles had bested their enemies.

Yes, he had achieved much, and travelled far from the loneliness of his life in Went—but it never filled the void inside.

Chapter Eight

Return to Rendlaesham

THE FIRST SIGN that Cynewyn had of Rendlaesham—the seat of the king—was the straw thatched roof of his great timbered hall gleaming in the noon sun.

She had never traveled this far north; until now she had never had reason to leave the area in which she had grown and married—few folk did. Rendlaesham had seemed another world away.

Nestled in the fold between two softly curving hills, the town dominated the landscape. A huge, spiked paling fence surrounded a mass of wattle and daub houses. The town climbed the side of one of the hills to where a massive timbered hall rose above the thatched roofs.

It was a crisp day, with blue sky and scudding clouds. As they approached Rendlaesham, Cynewyn caught the scent of wood-smoke. They made their way toward the main gates, along a road that bisected fields of cabbages, turnips, carrots, and onions. *Ceorls*, the lowest rank of free men and women under the king, worked the fields. Many straightened up at the sight of the group of travelers arriving from the south; their faces scrutinizing the newcomers with interest. One of the young women by the roadside—a pretty girl with dark-blonde hair— spied the warriors leading the group.

"Aelin!" she called out, her tired face brightening. "You're back!"

"*Wes hāl,* Aeva," Aelin called back with a wave, breaking free of the group to greet her. "How about a kiss to welcome me home?"

Her face split into a wide smile. "Come here then!"

Ignoring the wolf-whistles and ribald comments of the men behind him, Aelin did just that. He strode over to the girl and scooped her up into his arms, kissing her soundly for all to see.

Watching them, Cynewyn felt a sudden pang. That was how it was between some men women—easy and uncomplicated. Why had it never been like that for her?

"Young love," Mildthryth commented from beside Cynewyn, a trace of longing in her voice. "Such a beautiful thing."

Cynewyn did not reply. Instead, she tore her gaze away from where Aelin, seeming to have forgotten that he had an audience—or perhaps not caring—was continuing to kiss the winsome Aeva. Indeed, it was a beautiful thing.

That was why she could not look upon it.

Leaving the lovers to their reunion, the travelers approached Rendlaesham's walls and entered the town through the main gates. They followed the main thoroughfare up the hill, past the mead hall and to the high fence that encircled the base of the 'Golden Hall' as it was known throughout the land.

Helmeted, spear-wielding warriors blocked the way, stepping aside when they recognized the cluster of warriors leading the group of travelers.

"Wes hāl, Wilfrid." One of them nodded at Wil as he passed by. "You're back early. Where are the others?"

"Dead," Wil replied, his face grim. "An East Saxon war band attacked us near the southern border. Went has been destroyed and Blackhill has lost its warriors. The folk behind me are all who remain of the two villages."

The warrior shook his head in disgust. "Those honorless bastards!"

"Don't worry," Wil assured him. "The king will hear of this."

The warriors stepped aside and let the weary travelers through the gates. Cynewyn, who was walking close behind Wil, entered the stable yard and looked around her with interest. It was a hive of activity. Men were shoeing horses at one end, women were removing cakes from a huge clay oven at the other; and slaves were crossing the yard, weighed down with buckets of water that they had collected from the well next to the stables.

Upon spying the ragged group of king's men and villagers, stablehands emerged to help them with their horses. Cynewyn was helping a little girl down from a horse when a good looking young man with wavy blond hair appeared at her side.

"Here M'lady," he grinned. "I'll do that."

"I thank you." Cynewyn stepped back and let him set the girl on the ground. He then started unstrapping saddle bags. Cynewyn looked on, relieved to have this man's assistance. She was drained after the events of the last few days and wished for nothing more than to stretch out on a bed of soft furs, and sleep.

The stablehand removed the bags in quick, deft movements, before turning back to Cynewyn with another charming smile. "It's a pleasure to be of service."

Cynewyn favored him with a subdued smile in return. She remembered days, long past, when she would have responded eagerly to his flirting. Now, it just reminded her of how much the years had changed her; charming, silver-tongued men no longer held the appeal they once had.

She turned then, and followed the warriors and folk of Blackhill, up the steep wooden steps to the king's hall. When, she entered the 'Golden Hall', Cynewyn caught her breath. She had heard many a story of its magnificence, but nothing had prepared for her the reality. It was like standing inside the ribcage of some great beast. The blackened beams above their heads, stained from the huge fire pit in the center of the hall, were impossibly huge. Cynewyn's gaze travelled over the richly woven tapestries, weaponry, and furs that hung from the walls. It was all so sumptuous and grand.

Ealdormen, thegns, and their kin filled the Great Hall. The crowd parted to allow the group of warriors and villagers through. Cynewyn felt their gazes upon her but pretended not to notice. Instead, she focused her attention ahead, to the far end of the vast space. There, seated upon a carved wooden throne, on a raised dais, was King Raedwald himself.

Cynewyn could see the stories about the king were true. Even though he was nearing fifty winters, he was still a handsome, virile man. He was tall, broad-shouldered, and muscular with a mane of grey-streaked blond hair and deep-blue eyes. She imagined that in his prime, he would have had women spellbound.

Raedwald sat, relaxed in his throne, his handsome face expressionless. As she drew closer, Cynewyn noted the deep lines on his face, and recognized them as lines of grief. She had heard of how he had lost his beloved son, just three years earlier, in battle.

The loss had clearly left its mark upon him.

A striking woman with thick grey-streaked red hair and intelligent slate-grey eyes sat to his left, and beside her a girl of around fifteen winters—a beautiful maid, with a mane of golden curls, sea-blue eyes, and flawless skin. To the right of the king sat a young man with short brown hair, a sharp-featured face, and the same grey eyes of his mother.

These were the king's kin: his wife Seaxwyn, his daughter Raedwyn; and his surviving son, Eoprwald.

"Wilfrid," the king greeted his thegn. "What news do you bring from the south?"

"Treachery," Wil replied, his face grim. "Our neighbors have turned against us."

King Raedwald's blue eyes turned cold. "Tell me all," he commanded.

Wil spoke then of what had befallen them, his low voice echoing in the hushed hall. As he described the destruction of Went, the death of the warriors of Blackhill, and the attack on the edge of the woodland, Cynewyn kept her gaze riveted on the king's face, attempting to gauge his reaction. The king listened, his face growing dark. By the time Wil concluded his tale, King Raedwald's expression was murderous.

"There will be retribution for this," Raedwald said finally. "This death and destruction will be avenged. I will lead a company of men south tomorrow. We will find this war band and take their heads." The king turned then, his hard gaze meeting that of his son. "Eorpwald, you will join me."

The young man nodded, his face tensing slightly. "Yes, *fæder*."

Raedwald turned then, looking over the group of folk who stood behind Wil.

"Did any of the ealdormen's kin survive?"

"Yes, Milord," Wil replied, "Lady Cynewyn—Eomer of Went's daughter, and Aldwulf of Blackhill's widow—is here."

Wil turned, and his gaze met Cynewyn's. "Milady, come forward."

Cynewyn did as she was bid and curtsied before the king, feeling his eyes on her face. When she dared look up, she saw frank appreciation there.

"Greetings, Milord." She ducked her head, suddenly embarrassed by the intensity of his gaze.

"Lady Cynewyn," he said her name, causing her to look up and make eye contact once more. "I am sorry for your loss. The East Saxons will pay for what they have done."

"I thank you, Milord," she replied. She paused then, before the question that had been burning within her ever since they had entered Rendlaesham's gates, burst forth. "When can we return to our homes?"

The king held her gaze for a moment, before shaking his head. She could see the answer in his eyes before he spoke.

"I cannot allow you to return to Blackhill," he replied. "You have lost all your menfolk—you will not survive long on your own."

"But Milord," she exclaimed. "My people have worked that land for generations, we have poured our blood, sweat, and tears into it. We must return to it."

The king watched her for a moment, before his gaze shifted to the faces of those standing behind Cynewyn.

"This is your new home," he informed them, his tone hardening just enough to let them know that if they disputed his words, they did so at their own peril. "The folk of Blackhill will have homes built here in Rendlaesham and land to work."

The king's gaze shifted back to Cynewyn. "You are too young and lovely to remain a widow Lady Cynewyn. I shall have to find you a suitable husband to replace the one you lost."

Panic knifed through Cynewyn at these words.

A husband was the last thing she wanted—she had not rejected Wil so that the king could arrange a marriage with another.

"Milord," she spoke up, hearing the shrill edge to her voice but unable to stop herself. "I would prefer to remain unwed. I do not wish to marry again."

He raised his eyebrows at that. "I cannot build a hall for a woman."

This comment drew laughter from some of the men nearby, although Cynewyn noticed that Wil did not laugh.

"You will need to remarry, if you wish to live at the same rank as before," King Raedwald told her with a shake of his head, dismissing her protests. He then stood up, signaling that their conversation had come to an end. "For now, let me offer you and the folk of Blackhill my hall's hospitality. Let us drink and feast. I can't bring back those you have lost, but I can offer all of you a new life here in Rendlaesham."

Chapter Nine

The King's Will

A WARM BREEZE ruffled Cynewyn's hair and feathered across her face, bringing with it the scent of grass and blossom. She walked outside Rendlaesham's walls, to the scattering of timbered houses the men were building. Nearly a moon cycle had passed since their arrival in Rendlaesham. During that time, Raedwald had departed for the kingdom's southern border and had not returned.

In the meantime, work had started on the new homes for the folk of Blackhill. Raedwald's men were hard at work, digging in poles for the four corners of each dwelling and constructing woven wattle panels that would be smeared with mud to create the wattle and daub walls. Meanwhile, the children had been collecting water reed and rushes from the nearby stream to use for the thatched roofs.

If only one of those homes was to be hers.

Cynewyn approached the skeletons of the new dwellings, walking along the narrow dirt road that ran between them. Folk waved to her from where they had turned the land into vegetable plots. Their industry never ceased to amaze her; her people had lost everything but they still had hope.

She wished she shared their optimism.

Every night, she spread out her fur cloak on the rush-matting floor of the king's Great Hall and wondered when the axe would fall. She had been granted a reprieve while Raedwald was dealing with the East Saxons, but once the king returned he would not waste time announcing the name of her future husband. Just the thought made her want to turn tail and flee from Rendlaesham, never to return.

The reality of her situation here in Rendlaesham had been a slap to the face. She had gotten used to her freedom in Blackhill; she and her mother-in-law had ruled the village after Aldwulf died, and they had done it better than her husband ever had. She had forgotten that the rest the kingdom was not Blackhill. The king would not send her home, and nor would he just give her a new hall. She was a woman, and young enough to marry again and bear children. He would find a suitable husband for her.

Thoughts of her future made Cynewyn's chest ache. For the first time ever, she saw only bleakness and emptiness before her.

It was a good spot, on the eastern side of the town's walls. The land was verdant with fertile soil, excellent for growing crops—Raedwald had been generous. The king had promised to build a perimeter fence once the houses were finished, which would keep the wolves out in the winter and give the inhabitants a greater sense of security.

As she walked through the first dwellings, Cynewyn's gaze spied Wil up ahead. He was sawing a piece of wattle in half with an iron saw, his back to her.

Cynewyn's step faltered. It was the first time she had seen him in days, for of late he had avoided her. Even at meals in the Great Hall, he sat as far as possible from her, making it impossible for their gazes to meet, even by accident.

Could she blame him?

Seeing him now, naked to the waist as he worked, his skin glistening with sweat, Cynewyn felt an ache of longing consume her. Traitorous body—how she hated the effect this man had on her. And still, a part of her wanted to talk to him, to find out how he fared and what his plans were. He could be charmless and taciturn, but she had found herself missing his company once they rejoined the others. Once again, her thoughts and feelings contradicted her rational mind.

Feeling someone's gaze upon him, Wil straightened up from sawing the wattle and glanced over his shoulder. Cynewyn could see that the injury on his arm had healed well, although he would bear the scar for the rest of his life. His body stilled when their gazes met. However, there was no warmth in his eyes or face at seeing her.

"Greetings, Wil." She gave him a wan smile. "How goes it?"

He gave her a dismissive look, not even bothering to respond to her, before disappearing inside the hut he was constructing. Hurt lanced through Cynewyn at his rudeness. Without stopping to think about what she was doing, she stalked after him, entering the shadowy space where he had just erected a wattle panel.

"You could at least be civil when we meet," she told him. "I don't wish you ill."

He glanced over his shoulder at her as he wedged the wattle he had cut into place in the panel. "How generous of you," he replied coldly. "Do you expect me to be grateful for that?"

"I expect you to at least answer me when I greet you."

Wil turned then and advanced upon her. Cynewyn took a hasty step backward against the door frame. He stood over her, so close she could smell the musky scent of fresh sweat on his skin.

"You are not my mistress," he told her, his voice flat with anger, his hazel gaze burning into hers. "I don't answer to you—now or ever. If I wish not to greet you, then that is my choice."

They stood so close, he could have easily have bent his head and kissed her then. Yet, Cynewyn could see that she had hurt him too deeply for him to ever make such an attempt again. They had left that path behind in the shadowy woods. She had made that choice; it was too late to regret it now.

As if reading her thoughts, his lip curled and he stepped back from her.

"I made an ill choice all those years ago," he told her coldly. "Pining for a woman who thought me no better than a dog to run at her heels. Those days are now over. Leave me alone, Cynewyn—I have no wish to speak with you again."

With that, he left the dwelling, and moments later, she heard the sound of iron against wood as he resumed work.

Sick to her stomach, Cynewyn left the structure and walked away without a backward glance. She knew she should not care. After all, this was entirely her doing—it was her choice, her preference.

Why then, did her vision blur with tears?

She made her way along the dirt road, back to Rendlaesham's gates, before walking up the wide thoroughfare that led to the 'Golden Hall'. The spring weather had brought the folk of Rendlaesham outdoors. Children played on the streets, their cries echoing in the warm air, and women sat outside at their distaffs and looms, enjoying the sun on their faces as they worked. Once she reached the king's hall, Cynewyn would also return to 'woman's work'; an afternoon of winding wool onto a spindle, ready to be used on a loom, awaited her.

Not relishing the prospect, Cynewyn slowed her pace and inhaled the aroma of freshly baking bread as she passed the ovens. The door to the low-slung building was open and she caught sight of the baker removing a batch of honey cakes from the massive clay oven. Acknowledging his cheery wave with a strained smile, Cynewyn continued up the street, past the mead hall. The mead hall was empty—it was too early in the day, the weather too bright, for drinking.

In just one moon's cycle, Rendlaesham had come to feel like home. Cynewyn preferred it to Blackhill; this town was vibrant and prosperous compared to her dying village. Yet, today, nothing—not the sun on her face, nor the carefree sound of children's laughter—could lift her mood.

She entered the stable yard beneath the 'Golden Hall', and was half-way across it when a blond youth intercepted her.

"How goes it M'lady?"

Cynewyn, interrupted from bleak thoughts, recognized him as the stablehand who had helped her with her horse when she arrived at Rendlaesham. She had seen him a few times since then, and had caught him staring at her more than once.

"*Wes hāl*," she greeted him distractedly. She was vaguely irritated that he was effectively blocking her path, forcing her to halt and speak to him.

"It is a fair day, is it not?" he grinned, his gaze sweeping down from her face over her body, lingering on her curves. She was wearing a blue woolen *wealca*—a long tunic dress clasped at the shoulders by two brooches over a long linen tunic—that left her arms bare. It was a plain dress but the color matched her eyes. However, it was not the dress he was admiring.

She nodded, and was just about to step around him and continue on her way, when his gaze met hers once more.

"Are you well?" he asked, the grin fading slightly. "You're very pale."

Cynewyn shook her head, irritated that her misery was so evident. "I am just weary, that is all," she replied. She moved past him then, just as he was about to say something else, and hurried toward the steps. Cynewyn could not face men these days, especially not after what Wil had just said to her. She wanted only to be left alone.

She had almost reached the steps when a rumbling noise, like rolling thunder, reached her.

Horses.

Swiveling on her heel, Cynewyn watched a stream of men on horseback enter the stable yard. They were warriors dressed in battered and dirt-encrusted leather armor; shields on their backs and spears at their sides. Cynewyn's stomach twisted—she had not thought this day could get any worse.

The king had returned to Rendlaesham.

The roar of voices inside the king's hall was deafening.

Ealdormen, thegns, and their kin jostled for a place at one of the long tables, readying themselves for a great feast. Slaves were spit-roasting the carcasses of two deer over the great hearth at the center of the hall. The air was thick with smoke, despite the gaps in the ceiling above, which had been designed to let the smoke out. However, the aroma of roasting meat made up for the discomfort of stinging eyes and irritated lungs.

Slaves carried great wheels of griddle bread around the hall, depositing it next to the platters of roast carrots and onions that sat on the long tables lining the hall. Others carried jugs of mead around, filling up the feasters' cups.

Cynewyn held out her cup to be filled before taking a large gulp of the pungent drink. She had never enjoyed mead, especially after it became her husband's greatest solace; yet this eve she sought to numb herself. She was seated near the head of the table, at the king's insistence, and knew that it boded ill for her.

To make matters worse, Raedwald had insisted that Wil also sat at his end. To his credit, Wil looked as if he would rather be anywhere but here. Raedwald, who was already well into his cups this evening, did not appear to notice his thegn's grim expression. Wil sat facing Cynewyn, although a little further up the table. He did not look her way once as the meal begun.

Next to Cynewyn, Mildthryth helped herself to some griddle bread and smiled at the man seated to her right. His name was Coenred; he was another one of the king's thegns. A balding man with bright blue eyes and a booming laugh, Coenred had formed an attachment with the widow since their arrival at Rendlaesham. For the past few days both Coenred and Mildthryth had made sure that they sat near to each other at every meal.

Cynewyn, despite her misery, was delighted for her mother-in-law's burgeoning happiness. She knew that Mildthryth had despaired of ever finding love; she had been widowed a long while and had not dared to hope that she might marry once again. Coenred did not bother to hide his infatuation. Even now, he did not take his gaze off the small blonde beside him.

Cynewyn heard Mildthryth laugh at something her suitor had whispered in her ear, and noted the joy in that sound. She had never heard Mildthryth laugh like that before. She looked a decade younger this eve. Her cheeks were flushed, although not with mead; her eyes bright with laughter as she gazed into Coenred's eyes.

A wistful smile curled the edges of Cynewyn's mouth. No one deserved happiness more than Mildthryth.

Cynewyn looked away from the happy couple and took another deep draught of mead, feeling warmth seep through her body. For the first time she understood why Aldwulf had sought oblivion in drink.

"A toast," Raedwald's voice boomed across his hall, drawing the feasters' attention. He held out his cup to be refilled. "To victory!"

Opposite the king, his son—Eorpwald—raised his own cup. The lad was sporting a nasty gash on his left forearm after their skirmish with the East Saxon war band on the kingdom's southern border. However, his gaze was bright with triumph this evening. The prince looked older and surer of himself, compared to the last time Cynewyn had seen him.

"Was it the work of the East Saxon king?" Wil asked, his gaze meeting Raedwald's. "Did he send his men to attack us?"

Raedwald shook his head. "They were outlaws who believed that the land south of the woods belonged to the East Saxons, not the East Angles. Their king had already denied them but they decided to take the land anyway."

"We met them near Blackhill," Eorpwald spoke for the first time, his voice low but firm. "Their numbers had swollen to nearly a hundred, as word of their victory over the folk of Went and Blackhill spread."

"It was a bloody fight." Raedwald slapped his son across the back. "But in the end we had our vengeance."

"So King Sexred really had no idea?" Cynewyn blurted out, incredulous. She could not believe those warriors, who had destroyed Went and killed her husband, had not been sent by their king.

"No." Raedwald's gaze met hers. "To be sure, we rode south to Colenceaster, and I spoke to Sexred himself. I am content that the East Saxon King spoke the truth. They were outlaws; the matter has now been dealt with."

The matter has not been dealt with, Cynewyn thought, silently fuming. No amount of bloodshed would ever bring her parents back, or would ever right the wrongs that had been committed against her people.

"Can't we rebuild Went and resettle Blackhill?" she asked. "Surely, we can reclaim our land now that the outlaws have been dealt with?"

"No, there are too few of you left." The hard edge to the king's tone was unmistakable. "You will remain here at Rendlaesham."

Silence fell at the table and Cynewyn looked down at the wooden plate before her. She burned to argue the point and had to bite down on her tongue to stop herself. The king considered the matter closed; she would be a fool to anger him now.

"Wilfrid." Raedwald turned to his thegn. "Speaking of the folk of Blackhill, how goes the building?"

"Well, Milord," Wil replied with a tight smile. "Another moon's cycle and the villagers can move into their new homes."

The king nodded, pleased at the news, before turning his attention to the platters of roast venison that slaves were now bringing to the table. He helped himself to a huge plate. Further down the table, Cynewyn took a slice of roast venison. She was picking at her meal, her appetite dulled, when the king called her name.

"Lady Cynewyn." Raedwald fixed her in that disarming midnight blue gaze of his—and Cynewyn knew she would not like what was coming. "On my return journey from Colenceaster, I spoke with a man who will make you an excellent husband. He's one of my ealdormen, of course: Oxa of Soham. Like you, he is recently widowed."

"Oxa? Isn't he a bit old for Lady Cynewyn, *fæder*?" the king's daughter, Raedwyn, spoke up from where she had been sitting quietly beside her mother, listening to the conversation with interest.

The king cast an indulgent gaze over his golden haired daughter. "He's not that old, Raedwyn. You speak with the eyes of the very young. He's fifteen winters older than our Lady Cynewyn, no more."

Raedwald then turned his attention back to Cynewyn. "What say you Milady? Shall I send for Oxa, so you can meet him?"

Cynewyn felt like a hare trapped by wolves on all sides. She was painfully aware of Wil sitting there, his presence radiating out toward her like a furnace. However, she did not make the error of looking his way. He would not thank her for it.

"As you wish, Milord." She bowed her head so that none present could see the despair in her eyes.

"Very well." The king raised his cup once more for a passing slave to refill. "If I send for Oxa tomorrow, he should arrive here just after Ēostre. Let us make us another toast—for it will be an excellent match!"

Chapter Ten

Ēostre

OUTSIDE THE WALLS of Rendlaesham, the folk built two large bonfires from birch branches and twigs in preparation for the spring fertility festival—Ēostre. Meanwhile, inside the walls bustled with activity as a group of men erected a birch maypole in the market square, and women placed bouquets and garlands of bright yellow, sweet-smelling gorse flowers throughout the town. The gorse flower's bright yellow evoked the sun; Ēostre celebrated fertility and the rebirth of warmth and light of the coming summer.

The weather was warming, and a buzz of excitement regarding the approaching festival infused Rendlaesham.

Cynewyn was one of the few who did not view the steadily growing mounds of twigs on the edge of the apple orchards with anticipation. The maypole merely reminded her of her coming union with a man she had never met. The cloying scent of the gorse flowers reminded her of the garlands that would surround her during the handfasting. It was all she could do, in the days before Ēostre, not to bolt from Rendlaesham.

She would have, had there been somewhere to go.

The days slid by with terrifying swiftness. Cynewyn did her best to keep busy, helping the other women in the Great Hall with their endless chores of sewing, weaving, winding, and mending.

Often, she would bring her work outside and sit on the wide terrace before the great oaken doors of the 'Golden Hall'. Working in daylight was better for her eyes, and it was a relief to be free of the fetid, smoky air inside the hall. Up on the terrace, the air was warm and the sweet perfume of blossom laced the breeze. From this height, she had an unobstructed view of the surrounding landscape—the spray of pale pink blossom from the apple orchards, and the explosion of bright green from the willows lining the stream far below. Cynewyn could see why the Wuffinga kings had decided to build their Great Hall here. Rendlaesham sat in an idyllic spot; a place the locals were proud to call home.

Only, it would not be her home for much longer. Soon, Oxa of Soham would take her away from Rendlaesham, away from Mildthryth and the folk of Blackhill—the only people she cared for. The only folk who cared what happened to her.

A hard knot of dread formed in Cynewyn's belly at the thought.

Try as she might, Cynewyn could not stall the steady progress of time, and eventually the eve of Ēostre arrived.

A warm, breezy day drew to a close in a gentle, golden sunset. At dusk, the wind died and the air grew still and heavy with the smell of lush grass, gorse, and blossom. Owing to the mild weather, the townsfolk, including the king and his kin, feasted outdoors.

Cynewyn would have preferred to have hidden away, and let the folk of Rendlaesham enjoy their festival without her company, but it was impossible. She was part of the king's hall now, and the king's daughter, Raedwyn, had developed a particular fondness for her. The girl's excitement for the spring celebrations showed on her face as she walked through the milling crowds, arm in arm with Cynewyn.

"Haven't they done a wonderful job of the decorations?" Raedwyn gasped, her gaze sweeping over the garlands of yellow spring flowers that hung from the surrounding trees, looping in streamers between the apple trees.

Cynewyn nodded and gave the princess a smile. "It's magical," she admitted.

Together, they made their way over to the long feasting tables. Nearby, lamb and goat kid roasted over fire pits, while a spread of delicacies waited upon the tables: honey griddle cakes, rich breads studded with seeds, tureens of thick cream, baskets of strawberries and raspberries, massive wheels of cheese, and bowls of fresh spring greens. It was luscious, rich food—all laid out to represent, and encourage, fertility.

Raedwyn and Cynewyn sat down toward the end of one of the long tables, upon a low bench. Around them, some of the townsfolk were already beating the festival drums; a throbbing rhythm, designed to awaken revelers' passions as the eve progressed. Slaves poured frothy cups of mead, a necessity at Ēostre, and passed them around the table.

Cynewyn watched as Mildthryth took a seat next to Coenred further down the table. Neither of them bothered to hide their infatuation for each other, not on this eve. Coenred fed Mildthryth a strawberry before leaning down to give her kiss.

Tears stung Cynewyn's eyes and she looked away. She was happy for them both but their joy just made her misery cut deeper.

It had been a mistake to attend the spring festivities. She should have begged off, or feigned sickness—anything to avoid spending the night surrounded by lovers. Aelin and Aeva sat together at another table, unable to keep their hands and lips off each other. Later, many couples would go 'green gowning'. They would run off into the trees, find a secluded spot, and make love. It was the night of joining.

Cynewyn took a sip of mead and let her gaze travel around the tables. She was looking for a familiar face, searching for a man she had not seen in days.

Wil had made an even greater effort to avoid her of late; ever since Raedwald had announced the name of her husband-to-be. His actions did not surprise her, especially after their last conversation, and yet she found herself missing him. The sensation was a constant ache at the base of her ribs, with her day and night.

She eventually spied Wil at a table on the far side of the clearing. He was chatting to another warrior. The man said something and Wil laughed. Watching him, Cynewyn felt her chest constrict; she had not forgotten how handsome he was when he smiled, how it transformed his face. The sight of him enjoying himself only added fuel to her misery. It appeared that he had made the wise decision of moving on and forgetting her. Cynewyn stared down at her hands and bit the inside of her cheek to stop herself from crying.

No—she should never have let Raedwyn talk her into attending Ēostre.

"Cynewyn?" Raedwyn's sweet voice reached her, tinged with concern. "Are you well?"

Cynewyn looked up and schooled her features into a serene mask. "Of course," she said brightly. "Would you pass me the strawberries, Raedwyn?"

The Ēostre fires roared, illuminating the still night. The drums beat a primal rhythm and the folk of Rendlaesham celebrated. They danced with oblivion, fueled by strong mead and rich food. They danced to celebrate the end of a bitter winter and the joy of the coming summer—to rejoice in abundance and growth.

The king and queen sat upon a wooden dais, watching the dancing. Their daughter sat with them; Raedwyn was too young to take part in the revelry, and these days Raedwald and Seaxwyn preferred to watch the dancers rather than join them.

Cynewyn hung back as far as she was able from the revelry. She had no desire to take part. Even the mead she had drunk had not numbed the ache in her chest; if anything it had brought her regrets to the fore.

Her gaze moved over the crowd, once again looking for Wil. However, this time, she did not find him.

I was a fool, she thought bitterly. She had pushed him away for a hope, an illusion—one the king had shattered. *I could have been his*, she thought, letting the tears run silently down her face. *Instead, I told him he wasn't good enough for me. I got what I deserved in return; an arranged marriage to a stranger.*

There was no point in lamenting her choices now, not when Wil hated her and her new husband was on his way to Rendlaesham. However, there was an odd relief in admitting it to herself.

She remembered Mildthryth's words back in Blackhill, when she had shocked Cynewyn by telling her that men like her late husband and son never made good husbands.

I would have been happy with Wil, she thought wiping away the last of her tears. *Only it matters not now.*

"M'lady Cynewyn—you look ravishing this eve."

A male voice suddenly intruded upon her thoughts, and Cynewyn looked up to see the blond stablehand staring down at her. He was tall, even taller than Aldwulf had been, and she had to crane her neck to meet his gaze. His eyes were bright, his cheeks flushed with mead, and the firelight caught the angles of his handsome face.

"Good evening," Cynewyn greeted him with a bright smile, hoping that he did not see that she had been crying. "You know my name, but it seems I do not know yours."

"Tolan," he grinned, stepping closer to her. "I made it my business to learn your name the moment you arrived in Rendlaesham M'lady. Your beauty stole my heart."

Cynewyn shook her head, her smile turning rueful. "You flatter me. There are many women as pretty in Rendlaesham."

Tolan shook his head, his expression turning serious. "It is the truth. Your eyes are the color of a summer's sky, your skin is like milk, your lips are like rose petals, your hair is..."

Cynewyn's laughter cut him off. "Please," she said, not unkindly, before placing a hand on his arm. "I am a widow, not a blushing young maid you need to impress."

The young man looked momentarily crestfallen, although the fact that she had touched his arm, emboldened him.

"Dance with me!" He placed his hand over where hers gently rested on his forearm, and pulled her toward the nearest fire. "Let us celebrate Ēostre together, as man and woman—not stablehand and widow!"

Cynewyn shook her head and pulled back from him.

"No, Tolan." For the first time since he had approached her, she felt a twinge of discomfort. The mead had made him bold, far bolder than he had right to be. "I don't wish to dance."

"Come, Cynewyn," He took hold of her arm, his fingers digging into her flesh. "I will not take 'no' for an answer."

"Look at that." Aelin nudged Wil on the arm and pointed at the nearest fire. "Tolan's asked Cynewyn to dance."

Wil looked up from where he had been staring down at his boots, and followed his friend's gaze, across the jostling crowd to where a young man pulled Cynewyn toward the dancing. Jealousy slashed through him—the sensation so sharp it momentarily took his breath away. He knew Tolan. The youth was full of himself, but Wil could not believe he had managed to convince Cynewyn to dance with him.

Isn't a stablehand beneath you? He thought bitterly.

For his part, Wil had spent the evening trying to ignore Cynewyn, even when he had sensed her gaze upon him. He had been trying to fade into the shadows, and had found a quiet spot against an apple tree. But Aelin, having taken a break from the dancing, had sought him out.

"He doesn't have a chance with Cynewyn," Aelin observed, wiping sweat from his brow. "Isn't her betrothed due to arrive here at any moment?"

Wil nodded, his gaze still riveted on the fire, where Tolan pulled Cynewyn into his arms and twirled her around. Was it his imagination, or did she appear to be resisting him?

"Either tomorrow or the day after," he replied tonelessly.

Wil felt Aelin's gaze upon him, and wished his friend would leave him be, retrieve Aeva and rejoin the dancing. He was not in the mood for company this eve.

"Something happened between you after the ambush?" Aelin asked finally. "Didn't it?"

Wil tore his gaze away from the dancing, his gaze narrowing. "What?"

"You heard me. You've not been the same since."

"Leave it be," Wil growled. "You know nothing."

Aelin shook his head and gave Wil a rueful smile. "I'm no fool. I saw her staring at you tonight—and just then when you looked at her, I saw it in your eyes. Why are you letting her go?"

"To let someone go they need to have been yours to begin with," Wil replied, his voice bleak.

Aelin's smile widened. "I knew it."

"Go torment someone else," Wil replied, angry now. "So I've just proved you right—congratulations."

Aelin watched him silently a moment. Wil's gaze returned briefly to the dancing, where Tolan had his hands around Cynewyn's waist and was pulling her against him. The sight made him feel sick. His stomach knotted in rage.

"Your time is running out Wil," Aelin told him gently. "I'm going to find Aeva now. You get your wish; I'll leave you in peace. Remember this though—a man only has but a few chances in life to make things right. Don't waste this one."

With that, Aelin walked off, disappearing into the heaving crowd of revelers. Wil watched him go, conflict writhing within him. Aelin's self-righteous advice made him want to smash his fist into his friend's face. At the same time, he knew Aelin was right.

Wil looked back at the dancing, his gaze scanning the silhouettes of men and woman in front of the flames, as he looked for Cynewyn. Moments later, Wil's anger and frustration dissolved. His breath stilled, and alarm coursed through him.

Cynewyn and Tolan had disappeared.

Cynewyn stumbled through the undergrowth, panic clawing at her breast. Behind her, she heard a man's heavy tread and the rasp of his breathing.

"Cynewyn." Tolan's voice was rough with passion. "Don't run from me."

But run, she did. She had not wanted to dance with him; she had made that clear. Yet, he had dragged her into the revelry and forced her to, while he man-handled her like a piece of meat. His charm, easy manner, and flattery had made her trust him; however, the moment he dragged her toward the bonfire, she had known the truth.

This man wanted her, and intended to have her tonight, whatever the cost.

Round and round the fire they had danced, and then, suddenly, Tolan had pulled her away from the dancers and into the bushes behind. Cynewyn, seized with terror, had kicked him in the shins and made a run for it.

She had been glad of the cover that the undergrowth provided, but when she broke free of the bushes, Cynewyn realized that she was easy prey. She sprinted down the hill, in-between the lines of shadowed apple trees, her heart hammering in her ears. Behind her, the drums of Ēostre continued pounding, oblivious to her plight.

She had not run far when a man's hand clamped around her arm and pulled her up short. Cynewyn turned on him, fighting like a cat, but he was much stronger than her.

Tolan laughed at her defiance, his eyes gleaming in the glow from the fires. Her resistance only seemed to excite him. "Feisty wench," he gasped, out of breath from the chase. "Like to play games, don't you?"

He threw her to the ground and climbed on top of her, pushing up her skirts.

"Get off me!" Cynewyn screamed. On a quiet night, her voice would have carried, but this eve, with the drums and the roar of revelry, her scream was lost.

"Quiet now," he grinned down at her, reaching to unfasten his breeches. "You'll enjoy this, almost as much as I will."

A moment later, Tolan gave a strangled cry and fell backward. Another man's silhouette appeared, outlined in the glow of the fires further up the hill. The newcomer had pulled Tolan off her by his hair. Cynewyn struggled backward along the dew-laden ground and pushed her skirts down. Meanwhile, the stablehand staggered to his feet, fists raised. His assailant stepped forward to meet him, the man's face suddenly illuminated by the fires.

Cynewyn gasped.

It was Wil. His face was hard; she had never seen him so angry. He looked ready to kill the man before him. Tolan swung for his opponent, and Wil blocked the punch easily, before slamming Tolan in the jaw with his right fist.

Tolan slumped to the ground like a sack of barley. Wil stood over him, waiting for Tolan to rise, but he did not.

Cynewyn inched forward. "Is he dead?" she asked, her voice barely above a whisper.

Wil knelt down and felt for a pulse before shaking his head. "Just knocked out—shouldn't wake for a while though."

Wil got to his feet, and for a moment the pair of them just stared at each other. The Ēostre firelight flickering across their skin.

"I didn't want to go with him," Cynewyn said.

"I know," Wil replied, his face still hard and shuttered, not giving his thoughts away.

"Thank you, Wil." Cynewyn took another step toward him. "He would have raped me." Suddenly, she was breathless and tongue-tied. There was so much she wanted to say to him, but now they had a precious moment together, the words would not come.

"Are you hurt?" he asked.

Cynewyn shook her head. Their gazes fused, and she saw the hurt and longing in his eyes.

"Cynewyn," he said her name, and the sound of it was so intimate that she felt her face grow hot. It reminded her of that night they had spent together, alone in the woods with only the trees and starlight for company. "I know I am not an ealdorman," he continued, his voice steady. "I'm not of noble blood and have no hall or servants to offer you, but I would treat you like a queen. I love you, and will love you till I die. Is that not enough for you? Or would you prefer to marry a man you've never met, only because he is of noble birth and I am not."

Tears streamed down Cynewyn's cheeks at these words.

"Wil," she murmured, her voice trembling with the effort she was making not to break down and sob. "I am sorry for everything I said, for everything I made you think. I was foolish and vain. I thought the king would grant me the freedom to run my own hall—that I would be free of having to do a man's bidding. I ignored what I felt for you. I'm so sorry I hurt you."

Wil stepped forward so that were standing only inches apart. She could smell the warm, male musk of his skin; a scent that made her pulse quicken in memory. Gods, how she had missed him—his smell, his voice, and the feel of his gaze upon her.

"So my rank matters not to you?" he asked.

Cynewyn heard the hope in his voice and felt something inside her break. She buried her head in her hands as sobs wracked her.

"No," she finally managed through her tears. "Although, I understand if you hate me for what I've done."

He pulled her into his arms then. She could hear his heart racing against hers. "I could never hate you," he murmured into her hair. "It's me who should ask forgiveness. I took you roughly that morning in the woods. I should never have done that. I'm sorry."

Cynewyn raised her head and pressed her mouth fiercely against his. "I love you," she whispered against his lips.

They stood together, entwined in the darkness, while the revelry continued behind them. For a while, neither spoke, as they savored the truth that had passed between them; a rare and fragile moment that neither wanted to shatter.

Eventually, Cynewyn pulled back, her breathing steady after the solace of his embrace. She met his gaze and saw the naked vulnerability there. The mask was gone. The man who loved her stared back at her.

"Take me away from here," she whispered. "Let's go now, and never come back."

Wil's eyes widened in shock. "You would leave here?" he asked. "Leave everything behind?"

Cynewyn nodded. "If it means we can be together—yes."

Wil stared at her for a moment longer, before a smile crept across his face. "There will be no going back," he told her. "You'll be stuck with me. Are you ready for that?"

Cynewyn smiled back and, reaching out, took his hand in hers.

"I'm ready," she replied.

They turned away from the fires of Ēostre and stepped over Tolan's prone body. Hand in hand, the lovers walked down the hill, and through the apple orchard. Moments later, the night shadows swallowed them.

Epilogue

Merwenna

Nine months later . . .

WILFRID OF WENT stood before the closed door to the low wattle and daub dwelling, and resisted the urge to barge his way inside.

The mid-wife, a local woman named Cille, was good-hearted but bossy to the extreme. He had wanted to stay by his wife's side—keep hold of her hand during the ordeal—but once the birth drew out, Cille had ordered him outside.

It's like I'm a dog she doesn't want under her feet. Wil ground his jaw and started pacing, back and forth, across the threshold. *If she does not call me soon, I will break that door down.*

Around him, the late winter chill made its presence felt. Even though he wore a thick fur cloak about his shoulders and fur-lined boots, Wil's limbs felt numb with cold. His breath steamed in front of him. It was an achingly damp day, here on the outskirts of Gipeswic, near the banks of the River Orwell. The remnants of a snow-fall, one that had kept them house-bound for days, were now but all gone; there were just a few patches of melting snow remaining. The sky above was pale, and there was no sign of the sun.

Wil blew on his aching fingers and glanced around at the collection of thatched cottages that surrounded them. Gipeswic had provided a good home for them during Cynewyn's pregnancy; he had managed to find enough work to feed and clothe them, although they would soon need to move on from here—possibly to Mercia, where Wil would seek to find an ealdormen to serve.

There was no going back to Rendlaesham, both Wil and Cynewyn had been clear about that. Neither of them disliked Rendlaesham, or King Raedwald, who had treated them well. However, it would have been awkward to return there and explain themselves, after running away during Ēostre. Raedwald might have been angered that they had gone behind his back. Their future lay somewhere else.

The wail of a babe, split the freezing air, causing Wil to halt mid-stride. Had he imagined it?

As if in answer, another lusty wail erupted from the dwelling. Wil's face split into a wide smile. Not waiting for Cille to fetch him, he threw open the door to his home and strode inside.

The cottage that he and Cynewyn shared was small and simple. It was no king or ealdorman's hall, although neither of them cared. Cynewyn had made this small cottage a real home. Sweet-smelling rushes covered the dirt floor, and rabbit pelts covered the walls, keeping the cold out. A hearth glowed in the center of the space, illuminating the pale, exhausted face of a woman who lay upon a pile of furs.

"Wil!" Cynewyn greeted him with a tired smile. "You have a daughter."

Wil felt joy wash over him at this news. He stood there next to the fire pit, grinning like a fool at his wife. "A daughter."

Cille had just finished swaddling the babe in a fur, and Wil caught a glimpse of a red, angry little face, before the mid-wife passed the child to Cynewyn.

"She's a feisty little thing." Cille winked at Wil. "You'll soon have to deal with yet another strong-willed female!"

Wil laughed at that, and approached his wife, kneeling next to her. "I would not expect Cynewyn's daughter to be anything but a force to be reckoned with."

"I will accept that as a compliment," Cynewyn replied archly. Her gaze met Wil's then; he saw the exhaustion on her face, and the joy in her gaze. After two still-births, Cynewyn had been terrified that she would not bear a living child. Yet, right from the beginning this pregnancy had been different to the others. The growing babe had been active in her womb—and she had dared hope that it would be healthy.

"Is she well?" he asked.

Cynewyn nodded. They both looked down at the crumpled little face and the down-covered skull of the infant, and Wil was overcome by the urge to cry. He reached out and stroked the baby's cheek. "She's so tiny," he murmured. "What will you name her?"

"Do you like 'Merwenna'?" she asked, her face hopeful. "It was the name of my little sister, who died during her fourth winter. I would like to name our daughter after her."

"Merwenna," Wil said the name aloud before smiling. "I like it—a strong name."

"Then, Merwenna it is," Cynewyn's smiled widened. "I'm so relieved that she's healthy."

Wil reached out and stroked her cheek. "You did well, love."

Cynewyn gazed back at him and Wil felt the same pull her presence always provoked in him. Even after nearly a year together, he still felt a jolt of excitement when their gazes locked. Her presence injected the world with color and even took the sting out of winter's chill.

"I hope to give you more children," she told him, her smile fading and her gaze intensifying, "and a son."

Wil gazed back at her, aware that many women worried that their husbands preferred sons to daughters. He was not one of those men.

"If we have more children, so be it," he told her with a shake of his head, "but I am content with what I have—you, and Merwenna, are enough to fill my life with joy."

He saw her eyes fill with tears and knew that his words had touched her. She knew he did not say such things lightly; he had meant every word. Leaning forward, Wil kissed Cynewyn gently on the lips. He had known enough loneliness, desolation, and disappointment in his life to appreciate happiness once he had found it. He would never take any of this for granted.

Neither of them would.

The End

About the Author

Award-winning author Jayne Castel writes epic Historical and Fantasy Romance. Her vibrant characters, richly researched historical settings and action-packed adventure romance transport readers to forgotten times and imaginary worlds.

Jayne is the author of the Amazon bestselling BRIDES OF SKYE series—a Medieval Scottish Romance trilogy about three strong-willed sisters and the men who love them. An exciting new series about three lost Roman centurions and the brave-hearted Scottish women who love them, THE IMMORTAL HIGHLAND CENTURIONS is now available as well. In love with all things Scottish, Jayne also writes romances set in Dark Ages Scotland ... sexy Pict warriors anyone?

When she's not writing, Jayne is reading (and re-reading) her favorite authors, cooking Italian feasts, and taking her dog, Juno, for walks. She lives in New Zealand's beautiful South Island.

Connect with Jayne online:
www.jaynecastel.com
www.facebook.com/JayneCastelRomance/
Email: **contact@jaynecastel.com**

Printed in Great Britain
by Amazon

11280172R10326